THE EDGE
&
IN THE FRAME

DICK FRANCIS wrote more than forty international best-sellers and was widely acclaimed as one of the world's finest thriller writers. His awards included the Crime Writers' Association's Cartier Diamond Dagger for his outstanding contribution to the genre, and an honorary Doctorate of Humane Letters from Tufts University of Boston. In 1996 Dick Francis was made a Mystery Writers of America Grand Master for a lifetime's achievement and in 2000 he was awarded the CBE in the Queen's Birthday Honours list. Sadly he died in 2010.

D0889564

Also by Dick Francis and Felix Francis

Dead Heat   Silks

Also by Dick Francis

Dead Cert   Nerve   For Kicks

Odds Against   Flying Finish   Blood Sport

Forfeit   Enquiry   Rat Race

Bonecrack   Smokescreen   Slay-Ride

Knock Down   High Stakes   Longshot

Decider   Risk   Trial Run

Whip Hand   Reflex   Twice Shy

Banker   The Danger   Proof

Break In   Bolt   Hot Money

Straight   Comeback   Driving Force

Wild Horses   Come to Grief   To the Hilt

10lb Penalty   Field of 13   Second Wind

Shattered   Under Orders

Autobiography

The Sport of Queens

Biography

Lester: the Official Biography

Dick Francis

THE EDGE
&
IN THE FRAME

PAN BOOKS

The Edge first published 1988 by Michel Joseph
First published by Pan Books 1989
In the Frame first published 1976 by Michel Joseph
First published by Pan Books 1978

This omnibus first published 2011 by Pan Books
an imprint of Pan Macmillan, a division of Macmillan Publishers Limited
Pan Macmillan, 20 New Wharf Road, London N1 9RR
Basingstoke and Oxford
Associated companies throughout the world
www.panmacmillan.com

ISBN 978-0-330-54547-1

For *The Edge* the author is grateful to the estate of Dylan Thomas and
the publishers J.M. Dent & Sons for permission to quote lines from
'Do Not Go Gentle Into That Good Night' from *The Poems*.

1 3 5 7 9 8 6 4 2

A CIP catalogue record for this book is available from
the British Library.

Typeset by SetSystems Ltd, Saffron Walden, Essex
Printed in the UK by CPI Mackays, Chatham ME5 8TD

THE EDGE

The villains in this story are imaginary.
The good guys may recognize their own virtues!

Many thanks to

SHANNON WRAY
formerly of Penguin Books, Canada, who started the
train rolling

SHEILA BOWSLAUGH
and Sam Blyth of Blyth & Co, travel entrepreneurs

BILL COO
Manager of Travel Communications, VIA Rail,
and the staff of Union Station, Toronto

HOWARD SHRIER and TED BISAILLION
actor/writers

and
Col. Charles (Bud) Baker, Chairman of the Ontario
Jockey Club,

Krystina Schmidt, caterer; American Railtours Inc.,
operators of private rail cars,

and John Jennings, who travelled the trains with horses.

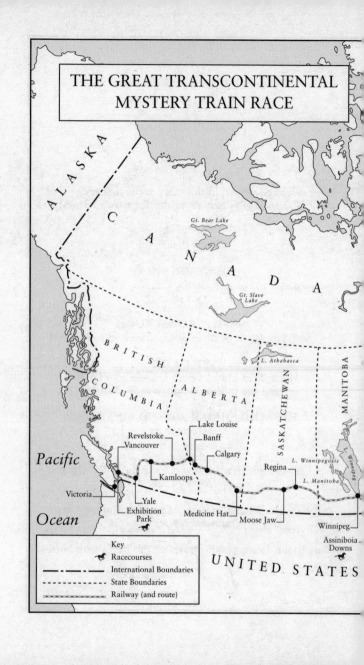

THE GREAT TRANSCONTINENTAL
MYSTERY TRAIN RACE

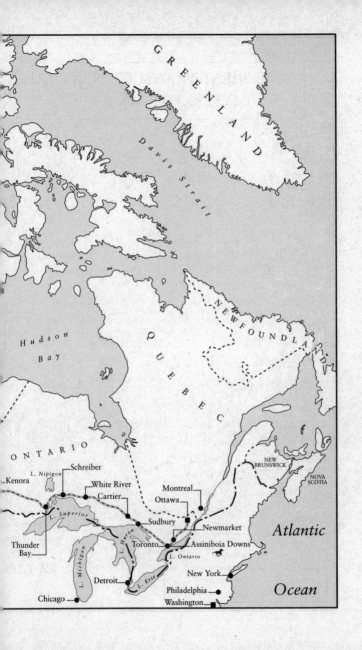

CHAPTER ONE

I was following Derry Welfram at a prudent fifty paces when he stumbled, fell face down on the wet tarmac and lay still. I stopped, watching, as nearer hands stretched to help him up, and saw the doubt, the apprehension, the shock flower in the opening mouths of the faces around him. The word that formed in consequence in my own brain was violent, of four letters and unexpressed.

Derry Welfram lay face down, unmoving, while the fourteen runners for the three-thirty race at York stalked closely past him, the damp jockeys looking down and back with muted curiosity, minds on the business ahead, bodies shivering in the cold near-drizzle of early October. The man was drunk. One could read their minds. Mid-afternoon falling-down drunks were hardly unknown on racecourses. It was a miserable, uncomfortable afternoon. Good luck to him, the drunk.

I retreated a few unobtrusive steps and went on watching. Some of the group who had been nearest to Welfram when he fell were edging away, looking at the

1

departing horses, wanting to leave, to see the race. A few shuffled from foot to foot, caught between a wish to desert and shame at doing so, and one, more civic-minded, scuttled off for help.

I drifted over to the open door of the paddock bar, from where several customers looked out on the scene. Inside, the place was full of dryish people watching life on closed-circuit television, life at second hand.

One of the group in the doorway said to me, 'What's the matter with him?'

'I've no idea.' I shrugged. 'Drunk, I dare say.'

I stood there quietly, part of the scenery, not pushing through into the bar but standing just outside the door under the eaves of the overhanging roof, trying not to let the occasional drips from above fall down my neck.

The civic-minded man came back soon, followed by a heavy man in a St John's Ambulance uniform. People had by now half-turned Welfram and loosened his tie, but seemed to step back gladly at the approach of officialdom. The St John's man rolled Welfram fully on to his back and spoke decisively into a walkie-talkie. Then he bent Welfram's head backwards and tried mouth-to-mouth resuscitation.

I couldn't think of any circumstance which would have persuaded me to put my mouth on Welfram's. Perhaps it was easier between absolute strangers. Not even to save his life, I thought, though I'd have preferred him alive.

Another man arrived in a hurry, a thin raincoated

man I knew by sight to be the racecourse doctor. He tapped the ambulance man on the shoulder, telling him to discontinue, and himself laid first his fingers against Welfram's neck, then his stethoscope against the chest inside the opened shirt. After a long listening pause, perhaps as much as half a minute, he straightened and spoke to the ambulance man, meanwhile stuffing the stethoscope into his raincoat pocket. Then he departed, again in a hurry, because the race was about to begin and the racecourse doctor, during each running, had to be out on the course to succour the jockeys.

The ambulance man held a further conversation with his walkie-talkie but tried no more to blow air into unresponsive lungs, and presently some colleagues of his arrived with a stretcher and covering blanket, and loaded up and carried away, decently hidden, the silver hair, the bulging navy-blue suit and the stilled heart of a heartless man.

The group that had stood near him broke up with relief, two or three of them heading straight for the bar.

The man who had earlier asked me, asked the new-comers the same question. 'What's the matter with him?'

'He's dead,' one of them said briefly and unnecessarily. 'God, I need a drink.' He pushed his way into the bar, with the doorway spectators, me among them, following him inside to listen. 'He just fell down and died.' He shook his head, 'Strewth, it makes you think.'

He tried to catch the barman's eye. 'You could hear his breath rattling . . . then it just stopped . . . he was dead before the St John's man got there . . . Barman, a double gin . . . make it a treble . . .'

'Was there any blood?' I asked.

'Blood?' He half looked in my direction. ''Course not. You don't get blood with heart attacks . . . Barman, a gin and tonic . . . not much tonic . . . get a shunt on, will you?'

'Who was he?' someone said.

'Search me. Just some poor mug.'

On the television the race began, and everyone, including myself, swivelled round to watch, though I couldn't have said afterwards what had won. With Derry Welfram dead my immediate job was going to be much more difficult, if not temporarily impossible. The three-thirty in those terms was irrelevant.

I left the bar in the general break-up after the race and wandered about inconclusively for a bit, looking for other things that were not as they should be and, as on many days, not seeing any. I particularly looked for anyone who might be looking for Derry Welfram, hanging around for that purpose outside the ambulance-room door, but no one arrived to enquire. An announcement came over the loudspeakers presently asking for anyone who had accompanied a Mr D. Welfram to the races to report to the clerk of the course's office, so I hung about outside there for a while also, but no one accepted the invitation.

Welfram the corpse left the racecourse in an ambulance en route to the morgue and after a while I drove away from York in my unremarkable Audi, and punctually at five o'clock telephoned on my car phone to John Millington, my immediate boss, as required.

'What do you mean, he's dead?' he demanded. 'He can't be.'

'His heart stopped,' I said.

'Did someone kill him?'

Neither of us would have been surprised if someone had, but I said, 'No, there wasn't any sign of it. I'd been following him for ages. I didn't see anyone bump into him, or anything like that. And there was apparently no blood. Nothing suspicious. He just died.'

'Shit.' His angry tone made it sound as if it were probably my fault. John Millington, retired policeman (Chief Inspector), currently Deputy Head of the Jockey Club Security Service, had never seemed to come to terms with my covert and indeterminate appointment to his department, even though in the three years I'd been working for him we'd seen a good few villains run off the racecourse.

'The boy's a blasted amateur,' he'd protested when I was presented to him as a fact, not a suggestion. 'The whole thing's ridiculous.'

He no longer said it was ridiculous but we had never become close friends.

'Did anyone make waves? Come asking for him?' he demanded.

'No, no one.'

'Are you sure?' He cast doubt as always on my ability.

'Yes, positive.' I told him of my vigils outside the various doors.

'Who did he meet, then? Before he snuffed it?'

'I don't think he met anybody, unless it was very early in the day, before I spotted him. He wasn't searching for anyone, anyway. He made a couple of bets on the Tote, drank a couple of beers, looked at the horses and watched the races. He wasn't busy today.'

Millington let loose the four-letter word I'd stifled. 'And we're back where we started,' he said furiously.

'Mm,' I agreed.

'Call me Monday morning,' Millington said, and I said, 'Right,' and put the phone down. Tonight was Saturday. Sunday was my regular day off, and Monday too, except in times of trouble. I could see my Monday vanishing fast.

Millington, in common with the whole Security Service and the Stewards of the Jockey Club, was still smarting from the collapse in court of their one great chance of seeing behind bars arguably the worst operator still lurking in the undergrowth of racing. Julius Apollo Filmer had been accused of conspiring to murder a stable lad who had been unwise enough to say loudly and drunkenly in a Newmarket pub that he knew things about Mr effing-blinding Filmer that would get the said arsehole chucked out of racing quicker than Shergar won the Derby.

The pathetic stable lad turned up in a ditch two days later with his neck broken, and the police (Millington assisting) put together a watertight-looking conspiracy case, establishing Julius Filmer as paymaster and planner of the crime. Then, on the day of his trial, odd things happened to the four prosecution witnesses. One had a nervous breakdown and was admitted in hysteria to a mental hospital, one disappeared altogether and was later seen in Spain, and two became mysteriously unclear about facts that had been razor-sharp in their memories earlier. The defence brought to the witness box a nice young man who swore on oath that Mr Filmer had been nowhere near the Newmarket hotel where the conspiracy was alleged to have been hatched but had instead been discussing business with him all night in a motel (bill produced) three hundred miles away. The jury was not allowed to know that the beautifully-mannered, well-dressed, blow-dried, quietly spoken youth was already serving time for confidence tricks and had arrived at court in a Black Maria.

Almost everyone else in the court – lawyers, police, the judge himself – knew that the nice young man had been out on bail on the night in question, and that even though the actual murderer was still unknown, Filmer had beyond doubt arranged the stable lad's killing.

Julius Apollo Filmer smirked with satisfaction at the

'Not Guilty' verdict and clasped his lawyer in a bear-hug. Justice had been mocked. The stable lad's parents wept bitter tears over his grave and the Jockey Club ground its collective teeth. Millington swore to get Filmer somehow, anyhow, in the future, and had made it into a personal vendetta, the pursuit of this one villain filling his mind to the exclusion of nearly everything else.

He had spent a great deal of time in the Newmarket pubs going over the ground the regular police had already covered, trying to find out exactly what Paul Shacklebury, the dead stable lad, had known to the detriment of Filmer. No one knew – or no one was saying. And who could blame anyone for not risking a quick trip to the ditch.

Millington had had more luck with the hysterical witness, now back home but still suffering fits of the shivers. She, the witness, was a chambermaid in the hotel where Filmer had plotted. She had heard, and had originally been prepared to swear she had heard Filmer say to an unidentified man, 'If he's dead, he's worth five grand to you and five to the hatchet, so go and fix it.'

She had been hanging fresh towels in the bathroom when the two men came in from the corridor, talking. Filmer had been abrupt with her and bundled her out and she hadn't looked at the other man. She remembered the words clearly but hadn't of course seen their significance until later. It was because of the word 'hatchet' that she remembered particularly.

A month after the trial Millington got from her a half-admission that she'd been threatened not to give evidence. Who had threatened her? A man she didn't know. But she would deny it. She would deny everything, she would have another collapse. The man had threatened to harm her sixteen-year-old daughter. Harm . . . he'd spelled out all the dreadful programme lying ahead.

Millington, who could lay on the syrup if it pleased him, had persuaded her with many a honeyed promise (that he wouldn't necessarily keep) to come for several days to the races, and there, from the safety of various strategically placed security offices, he'd invited her to look out of the window. She would be in shadow, seated, comfortable, invisible, and he would point out a few people to her. She was nervous and came in a wig and dark glasses. Millington got her to remove the glasses. She sat in an upright armchair and twisted her head to look over her shoulder at me, where I stood quietly behind her.

'Never mind about him,' Millington said. 'He's part of the scenery.'

All the world went past those windows on racing afternoons, which was why, of course, the windows were where they were. Over three long sessions during a single week on three different racecourses Millington pointed out to her almost every known associate and friend of Filmer's, but she shook her head to them all. At the fourth attempt, the following week, Filmer himself strolled past, and I thought we'd have a repeat of the hysterics: but though our chambermaid wobbled and wept and begged for repeated assurances he would never know she had seen him, she stayed at her post. And she astonished us, shortly after, by pointing towards a group of passing people we'd never before linked with Filmer.

'That's him,' she said, gasping. 'Oh my God . . . that's him . . . I'd know him anywhere.'

'Which one?' Millington said urgently.

'In the navy . . . with the grey sort of hair. Oh my God . . . don't let him know . . .' Her voice rose with panic.

I could hear the beginnings of Millington's reassurances as I fairly sprinted out of the office and through to the open air, slowing there at once to the much slower speed of the crowd making its way from paddock to stands for the next race. The navy suit with the silvery hair above it was in no hurry, going along with the press. I followed him discreetly for the rest of the afternoon, and only once did he touch base with Filmer, and then as if accidentally, as between strangers.

The exchange looked as if navy-suit asked Filmer the time. Filmer looked at his watch and spoke. Navy-suit nodded and walked on. Navy-suit was Filmer's man, all right, but was never to be seen to be that in public: just like me and Millington.

I followed navy-suit from the racecourse in the going-home traffic and telephoned from my car to Millington.

'He's driving a Jaguar,' I said, 'licence number A 576 FDD. He spoke to Filmer. He's our man.'

'Right.'

'How's the lady?' I asked.

'Who? Oh, her. I had to send Harrison all the way back to Newmarket with her. She was half off her rocker again. Have you still got our man in sight?'

'Yep.'

'I'll get back to you.'

Harrison was one of Millington's regular troops, an ex-policeman, heavy, avuncular, near to pensioned retirement. I'd never spoken to him, but I knew him well by sight, as I knew all the others. It had taken me quite a while to get used to belonging to a body of men who didn't know I was there; rather as if I were a ghost.

I was never noticeable. I was twenty-nine, six foot tall, brown-haired, brown-eyed, twelve stone in weight with, as they say, no distinguishing features. I was always part of the moving race crowd, looking at my racecard, wandering about, looking at horses, watching races, having a bet or two. It was easy because there were always a great many other people around doing exactly the same thing. I was a grazing sheep in a flock. I changed my clothes and general appearance from day to day and never made acquaintances, and it was lonely quite often, but also fascinating.

I knew by sight all the jockeys and trainers and very many owners, because all one needed for that was eyes and racecards, but also I knew a lot of their histories from long memory, as I'd spent much of my childhood and teens on racecourses, towed along by the elderly race-mad aunt who had brought me up. Through her knowledge and via her witty tongue I had become a veritable walking data bank; and then, at eighteen, after her death, I'd gone world-wandering for seven years. When I returned, I no longer looked like the unmatured youth I'd been, and the eyes of the people who had known me vaguely as a child slid over me without recognition.

I returned to England finally because at twenty-five I'd come into inheritances from both my aunt and my father, and my trustees were wanting instructions. I had been in touch with them from time to time, and they had despatched funds to far-flung outposts fairly often, but when I walked into the hushed book-lined law office of the senior partner of Cornborough, Cross and George, old Clement Cornborough greeted me with a frown and stayed sitting down behind his desk.

'You're not ... er ...?' he said, looking over my shoulder for the one he'd expected.

'Well ... yes, I am. Tor Kelsey.'

'Good Lord.' He stood up slowly, leaning forward to extend a hand. 'But you've changed. You ... er ...'

'Taller, heavier and older,' I said, nodding. Also sun-tanned, at that moment, from a spell in Mexico.

'I'd ... er ... pencilled in lunch,' he said doubtfully.

'That would be fine,' I said.

He took me to a similarly hushed restaurant full of other solicitors who nodded to him austerely. Over roast beef he told me that I would never have to work for a living (which I knew) and in the same breath asked what I was going to do with my life, a question I couldn't answer. I'd spent seven years learning how to live, which was different, but I'd had no formal training in anything. I felt claustrophobic in offices and I was not academic. I understood machines and was quick with my hands. I had no overpowering ambitions. I wasn't the entrepreneur my father had been, but nor would I squander the fortune he had left me.

'What have you been doing?' old Cornborough said, making conversation valiantly. 'You've been to some interesting places, haven't you?'

Travellers' tales were pretty boring, I thought. It was always better to live it. 'I mostly worked with horses,' I said politely. 'Australia, South America, United States, anywhere. Racehorses, polo ponies, a good deal in rodeos. Once in a circus.'

'Good heavens.'

'It's not easy now, though, and getting harder, to work one's passage. Too many countries won't allow it. And I won't go back to it. I've done enough. Grown out of it.'

'So what next?'

'Don't know.' I shrugged. 'Look around. I'm not getting in touch with my mother's people, so don't tell them I'm here.'

'If you say so.'

My mother had come from an impoverished hunting family who were scandalized when at twenty she married a sixty-five-year-old giant of a Yorkshireman with an empire in second-hand car auctions and no relatives in *Burke's Peerage*. They'd said it was because he showered her with horses, but it always sounded to me as if she'd been truly attracted. He at any rate was besotted with her, as his sister, my aunt, had often told me, and he'd seen no point in living after she was killed in a hunting accident, when I was two. He'd lasted three years and died of cancer, and because my mother's family hadn't wanted me, my aunt Viv Kelsey had taken me over and made my young life a delight.

To Aunt Viv, unmarried, I was the longed-for child she'd had no chance of bearing. She must have been sixty when she took me, though I never thought of her as old. She was always young inside; and I missed her dreadfully when she died.

Millington's voice said, 'The car you are following . . . are you still following it?'

'Still in sight.'

'It's registered to a Derry Welfram. Ever heard of him?'

'No.'

Millington still had connections in the police force and seemed to get useful computerized information effortlessly.

'His address is down as Parkway Mansions, Maida Vale, London,' he said. 'If you lose him, try there.'

'Right.'

Derry Welfram obligingly drove straight to Parkway Mansions and others of Millington's minions later made a positive identification. Millington tried a photograph of him on each of the witnesses with the unreliable memories and, as he described to me afterwards, 'They both shit themselves with fear and stuttered they'd never seen the man, never, never.' But they'd been so effectively frightened, both of them, that Millington could get nothing out of them at all.

Millington told me to follow Derry Welfram if I saw him again at the races, to see who else he talked to, which I'd been doing for about a month on the day the navy-suit fell on its buttons. Welfram had talked intensely to about ten people by then and proved he was comprehensively a bearer of bad news, leaving behind him a trail of shocked, shivering, hollow-eyed stares at unwelcome realities. And because I had an ingenious camera built into binoculars (and another that looked like a cigarette lighter) we had recognizable portraits of most of Welfram's shattered contacts, though so far identifications for less than half. Millington's men were working on it.

Millington had come to the conclusion that Welfram

was a frightener hired to shake out bad debts: a rent-a-thug in general, not solely Filmer's man. I had seen him speak to Filmer only once since the first occasion, which didn't mean he hadn't done so more often. There were usually race meetings at three or more different courses in England each day, and it was a toss-up, sometimes, to guess where either of the quarries would go. Filmer, moreover, went racing less often than Welfram, two or three times a week at most. Filmer had shares in a great many horses and usually went where they ran; and I checked their destinations every morning in the racing press.

The problem with Filmer was not what he did, but catching him doing it. At first sight, second sight, third sight he did nothing wrong. He bought racehorses, put them in training, went to watch them run, enjoyed all the pleasures of an owner. It was only gradually, over the ten years since Filmer had appeared on the scene, that there had been eyebrows raised, frowns of disbelief, mouths pursed in puzzlement.

Filmer bought horses occasionally at auction through an agent or a trainer but chiefly acquired them by deals struck in private, a perfectly proper procedure. Any owner was always at liberty to sell his horses to anyone else. The surprising thing about some of Filmer's acquisitions was that no one would have expected the former owner to sell the horse at all.

I had been briefed about him by Millington during my first few weeks in the Service, but then only as someone to be generally aware of, not as a number one priority.

'He leans on people,' Millington said. 'We're sure of it, but we don't know how. He's much too fly to do anything where we can see him. Don't think you'll catch him handing out bunches of money for information, nothing crude like that. Look for people who're nervous when he's near, right?'

'Right.'

I had spotted a few of those. Both of the trainers who trained his horses treated him with caution, and most of the jockeys who rode them shook his hand with their fingertips. The Press, who knew they wouldn't answer questions, hardly bothered to ask them. A deferential decorative girlfriend jumped when he said jump, and the male companion frequently in attendance fairly scuttled. Yet there was nothing visibly boorish about his general manner at the races. He smiled at appropriate moments, nodded congratulations to other owners in the winners' enclosures and patted his horses when they pleased him.

He was in person forty-eight, heavy, about five foot ten in height. Millington said the weight was mostly muscle, as Filmer spent time three days a week raising a sweat in a gym. Above the muscle there was a well-shaped head, large flat ears and thick black hair flecked with grey. I hadn't been near enough to see the colour of his eyes, but Millington had them down as greenish brown.

Rather to Millington's annoyance I refused to follow Filmer about much. For one thing, in the end he would have been certain to have spotted me, and for another it wasn't necessary. Filmer was a creature of habit, moving from car to lunch to bookmaker to grandstand to paddock at foreseeable intervals. At each track he had a favourite place to watch the races from, a favourite vantage point overlooking the parade ring and a favourite bar where he drank lager mostly and plied the girlfriend with vodka. He rented a private box at two racecourses and was on the waiting list at several more, where his aim seemed to be seclusion rather than the lavish entertainment of friends.

He had been born on the Isle of Man, that tax-haven rock out of sight of England in the stormy Irish Sea, and had been brought up in a community stuffed with millionaires fleeing the fleecing taxes of the mainland. His father had been a wily fixer admired for fleecing the fled. Young Julius Apollo Filmer (his real name) had learned well and outstripped his father in rich pickings until he'd left home for wider shores; and that was the point, Millington said gloomily, at which they had lost him. Filmer had turned up on racecourses sixteen or so years later giving his occupation as 'company director' and maintaining a total silence about his source of considerable income.

During the run-up to the conspiracy trial, the police had done their best to unravel his background further, but Julius Apollo knew a thing or two about offshore companies and had stayed comfortably ravelled. He still officially lived on the Isle of Man, though he was never there for long. During the flat season he mostly divided his time between hotels in Newmarket and Paris, and in the winter he dropped entirely out of sight, as far as the Security Service was concerned. Steeplechasing, the winter sport, never drew him.

During my first summer with the Service he had bought, to everyone's surprise, one of the most promising two-year-olds in the country. Surprise, because the former owner, Ezra Gideon, was one of the natural aristocrats of racing, a much respected elderly and extremely wealthy man who lived for his horses and delighted in their successes. No one had been able to persuade him to say why he had parted with the best of his crop or for what price: he bore its subsequent high-flying autumn, its brilliant three-year-old season and its eventual multi-million-pound syndication for stud with an unvaryingly stony expression.

After Filmer's acquittal, Ezra Gideon had again sold him a two-year-old of great promise. The Jockey Club mandarins begged Gideon practically on their knees to tell them why. He said merely that it was a private arrangement: and since then he had not been seen on a racecourse.

On the day Derry Welfram died I drove homewards to London wondering yet again, as so many people had wondered so often, just what leverage Filmer had used on Gideon. Blackmailers had gone largely out of business since adultery and homosexuality had been blown wide open, and one couldn't see old-fashioned upright Ezra Gideon as one of the newly fashionable brands of transgressor, an insider-trader or an abuser of children. Yet without some overwhelming reason he would never have sold Filmer two such horses, denying himself what he most enjoyed in life.

Poor old man, I thought. Derry Welfram or someone like that had got to him, as to the witnesses, as to Paul Shacklebury dead in his ditch. Poor old man, too afraid of the consequences to let anyone help.

Before I reached home the telephone again purred in my car and I picked up the receiver to hear Millington's voice.

'The boss wants to see you,' he said. 'This evening at eight, usual place. Any problem?'

'No,' I said. 'I'll be there. Do you know ... er ... why?'

'I should think,' Millington said, 'because Ezra Gideon has shot himself.'

CHAPTER TWO

The boss, Brigadier Valentine Catto, Director of Security to the Jockey Club, was short, spare, and a commanding officer from his polished toecaps to the thinning blond hair on his crown. He had all the organizational skills needed to rise high in the army, and he was intelligent and unhurried and listened attentively to what he was told.

I met him first on a day when old Clement Cornborough asked me again to lunch to discuss in detail, as he said, the winding up of the trust he'd administered on my behalf for twenty years. A small celebration, he said. At his club.

His club turned out to be the Hobbs Sandwich Club, near the Oval cricket ground, a Victorian mini-mansion with a darkly opulent bar and club rooms, their oak-panelled walls decorated with endless pictures of gentlemen in small cricket caps, large white flannels and (quite often) side-whiskers.

The Hobbs Sandwich, he said, leading the way through stained-glass panelled doors, was named for two great Surrey cricketers from between the wars, Sir Jack Hobbs, one of the few cricketers ever knighted, and Andrew Sandham, who had scored one hundred and seven centuries in first-class cricket. Long before I was born, he said.

I hadn't played cricket since distant days at school, nor liked it particularly even then: Clement Cornborough proved to be a lifelong fanatic.

He introduced me in the bar to an equal fanatic, his friend Val Catto, who then joined us for lunch. Not a word about my trust was spoken. The two of them talked cricket solidly for fifteen minutes and then the friend Catto began asking questions about my life. It dawned on me uneasily after a while that I was being interviewed, though I didn't know for what; and I learned afterwards that in conversation one day during the tea interval of a cricket match Catto had lamented to Cornborough that what he really needed was someone who knew the racing scene intimately, but whom the racing scene didn't know in return. An eyes-and-ears man. A silent, unknown investigator. A fly on racing's wall that no one would notice. Such a person, they had sighed together, was unlikely to be found. And that when a few weeks later I walked into Cornborough's office (or at least by the time I left it) the lawyer had suffered a brainwave which he passed on to his friend Val.

The Hobbs Sandwich lunch (of anything but sandwiches) had lasted through a good chunk of the afternoon, and by the end of it I had a job. I hadn't taken a lot of persuading, as it seemed interesting to me from the start. A month's trial on both sides, Brigadier Catto said, and mentioned a salary that had Cornborough smiling broadly.

'What's so funny?' the Brigadier asked. 'That's normal. We pay most of our men that at the start.'

'I forgot to mention it. Tor here is ... um ...' He paused, perhaps wondering whether finishing the sentence came under the heading of breaking a client's right to confidentiality, because after a short while he went on, 'He'd better tell you himself.'

'I accept the salary,' I said.

'What have you not told me?' Catto asked, suddenly very much the boss, his eyes not exactly suspicious but unsmiling: and I saw that I was not binding myself to some slightly eccentric friendly cricket nut, but to the purposeful, powerful man who had commanded a brigade and was currently keeping horse racing honest. I was not going to be playing a game, he was meaning, and if I thought so we would go no further.

I said wryly, 'I have a private income after tax of about twenty times the salary you're offering, but I'll take your money all the same, sir, and I'll work for it.'

He listened to the underlying declaration of commitment and good faith, and after a long pause he smiled briefly and nodded.

'Very well,' he said. 'When can you start?'

I had started the next day at Epsom races, relearning

the characters, reawakening sleeping memories, hearing Aunt Viv's bright voice in my ear about as clearly as if she were alive. 'There's Paddy Fredericks. Did I tell you he used to be married to Betsy who's now Mrs Glovebinder? Brad Glovebinder used to have horses with Paddy Fredericks but when he pinched Betsy, he took his horses away too . . . no justice in the world. Hello Paddy, how are things? This is my nephew Torquil, as I expect you remember, you've met him often enough. Well done with your winner, Paddy . . .' and Paddy had taken us off for a drink, buying me a Coke.

I came face to face unexpectedly with the trainer Paddy Fredericks that first day at Epsom and he hadn't known me. There hadn't been a pause or a flicker. Aunt Viv had been dead nearly eight years and I had changed too much; and I had been reassured from that early moment that my weird new non-identity was going to work.

On the grounds that racing villains made it their business to know the Security Service comprehensively by sight, Brigadier Catto said that if ever he wanted to speak to me himself, it would never be on a racecourse but always in the bar of the Hobbs Sandwich, and so it had been for the past three years. He and Clement Cornborough had sponsored me for full membership of the club and encouraged me to go there occasionally on other days on my own, and although I'd thought the Brigadier's passion for secrecy a shade obsessive I had fallen in with his wishes and come to enjoy it, even if I'd learned a lot more about cricket than I really wanted to.

On the night of Derry Welfram's death, I walked into the bar at ten to eight and ordered a glass of Burgundy and a couple of beef sandwiches which came promptly because of the post-cricket-season absence of a hundred devotees discussing leg-breaks and insider politics at the tops of their voices. There were still a good number of customers, but from late September to the middle of April one could talk all night without laryngitis the next day, and when the Brigadier arrived he greeted me audibly and cheerfully as a fellow member well met and began telling me his assessment of the Test team just assembled for the winter tour abroad.

'They've disregarded Withers,' he complained. 'How are they ever going to get Balping out if they leave our best in-swinger biting his knuckles at home?'

I hadn't the faintest idea, and he knew it. With a gleam of a smile he bought himself a double Scotch drowned in a large glass of water, and led the way to one of the small tables round the edge of the room, still chatting on about the whys and wherefores of the selected team.

'Now,' he said without change of speed or volume, 'Welfram's dead, Shacklebury's dead, Gideon's dead, and the problem is what do we do next?'

The question. I knew, had to be rhetorical. He never

called me to the Hobbs Sandwich to ask my advice but always to direct me towards some new course of action, though he would listen and change his requirements if I put forward any huge objections, which I didn't often. He waited for a while, though, as if for an answer, and took a slow contemplative mouthful of weak whisky.

'Did Mr Gideon leave any notes?' I asked eventually.

'Not as far as we know. Nothing as helpful as telling us why he sold his horses to Filmer, if that's what you mean. Not unless a letter comes in the post next week, which I very much doubt.'

Gideon had been frightened beyond death, I thought. The threat must have been to the living: an ongoing perpetual threat.

'Mr Gideon has daughters,' I said.

The Brigadier nodded. 'Three. And five grandchildren. His wife died years ago, I suppose you know. Am I reading you aright?'

'That the daughters and grandchildren were hostages? Yes. Do you think they could know it?'

'Positive they don't,' the Brigadier said. 'I talked with his eldest daughter today. Nice, sensible woman, about fifty. Gideon shot himself yesterday evening, around five they think, but no one found him for hours as he did it out in the woods. I went down to the house today. His daughter, Sarah, said he's been ultra-depressed lately, going deeper and deeper, but she didn't know what had caused it. He wouldn't discuss it. Sarah was in tears, of course, and also of course feeling guilty because she didn't prevent it; but she couldn't have prevented it, it's almost impossible to stop a determined suicide, you can't force people to go on living. Short of imprisonment, of course. Anyway, if she was any sort of a hostage, she didn't know it. It wasn't that sort of guilt.'

I offered him one of my so far uneaten sandwiches. He took one absent-mindedly and began to chew, and I ate one myself. The problem of what to do about Filmer lay in morose wrinkles across his brow and I'd heard he considered the collapse of the conspiracy trial a personal failure.

'I went to see Ezra Gideon myself after you and John Millington flushed out Welfram,' he said. 'I showed Ezra your photograph of Welfram. I thought he would faint, he went so white, but he still wouldn't speak. And now, God damn it, in one day we've lost both contacts. We don't know who Filmer will get to next, or if he's already active again, and we'll have the devil's own job spotting another frightener.'

'He won't have found one himself yet, I shouldn't think,' I said. 'Certainly not one as effective. They aren't that common, are they?'

'The police say they're getting younger.'

He looked unusually discouraged for someone whose success rate in all other fields was impressive. The lost battle rankled: the victories had been shrugged off. I drank some wine and waited for the commanding officer to emerge from the worried man, waited for him to unfold the plan of campaign.

He surprised me, however, by saying, 'I didn't think you'd stick this job this long.'

'Why not?'

'You know damn well why not. You're not dim. Clement told me the pile your father left you simply multiplied itself for twenty years, growing like a mushroom. And still does. Like a whole field of mushrooms. Why aren't you out there picking them?'

I sat back in my chair wondering what to say. I knew very well why I didn't pick them, but I wasn't sure it would sound sensible.

'Go on,' he said. 'I need to know.'

I glanced at his intent eyes and sensed his concentration, and realized suddenly that he might mean in some obscure way to base the future plan on my answer.

'It isn't so easy,' I said slowly, 'and don't laugh, it really isn't so easy to be able to afford anything you want. Short of the Crown Jewels and trifles like that. Well . . . I don't find it easy. I'm like a child loose in a sweetshop. I could eat and eat . . . and make myself sick . . . and greedy . . . and a jellyfish. So I keep my hands off the sweets and occupy my time following crooks. Is that any sort of answer?'

He grunted non-committally. 'How strong is the temptation?'

'On freezing cold days in sleet and wind at, say,

Doncaster races, very strong indeed. At Ascot in the sunshine I don't feel it.'

'Be serious,' he said. 'Put it another way. How strong is your commitment to the Security Service?'

'They're really two different things,' I said. 'I don't pick too many mushrooms because I want to retain order . . . to keep my feet well planted. Mushrooms can be hallucinogenic, after all. I work for you, for the Service, rather than in banking or farming and so on, because I like it and I'm not all that bad at what I do, really, and it's useful, and I'm not terribly good at twiddling my thumbs. I don't know that I'd die for you. Is that what you want?'

His lips twitched. He said, 'Fair enough. How do you feel about danger nowadays? I know you did risky enough things on your travels.'

After a brief pause, I said, 'What sort of danger?'

'Physical, I suppose.' He rubbed a thumb and fore-finger down his nose and looked at me with steady eyes. 'Perhaps.'

'What do you want me to do?'

We had come to the point of the meeting, but he backed away from it still.

I knew in a way that it was because of what he'd called the mushrooms that he'd grown into the way of speaking to me as he did, proposing but seldom giving straight orders. He would have been more forthright if I'd been a junior army officer in uniform. Millington, who didn't know about the mushrooms,

29

could uninhibitedly boss me around like a sergeant-major, and did so pretty sharply under pressure.

Millington mostly called me Kelsey and only occasionally, on good days, Tor. ('Tor? What sort of name is that?' he'd demanded at the beginning. 'Short for Torquil,' I said. '*Torquil?* Huh. I don't blame you.') He always referred to himself as Millington ('Millington here,' when he telephoned) and that was how I thought of him: he had never asked me to call him John. I supposed that a man who had served in a strongly hierarchical organization for a long time found surnames natural.

The Brigadier's attention still seemed to be focused on the glass he was slowly revolving in his hands, but finally he put it down precisely in the centre of a beer mat as if coming to a precise conclusion in his thoughts.

'I had a telephone call yesterday from my counterpart in the Canadian Jockey Club.' He paused again. 'Have you ever been to Canada?'

'Yes,' I said. 'Once, for a while, for maybe three months, mostly in the west. Calgary . . . Vancouver . . . I went up by boat from there to Alaska.'

'Did you go to the races in Canada?'

'Yes, a few times, but it must be about six years ago . . . and I don't know anyone—' I stopped, puzzled, not knowing what kind of response he wanted.

'Do you know about this train?' he said. 'The Transcontinental Mystery Race Train? Ever heard of it?'

'Um,' I said, reflecting. 'I read something about it the

other day. A lot of top Canadian owners are going on a jolly with their horses, stopping to race at tracks along the way. Is that the one you mean?'

'It is indeed. But the owners aren't all Canadian. Some of them are American, some are Australian and some are British. One of the British passengers is Julius Filmer.'

'Oh,' I said.

'Yes, oh. The Canadian Jockey Club has given its blessing to the whole affair because it's attracting worldwide publicity and they are hoping for bumper attendances, hoping to give all Canadian racing an extra boost. Yesterday, my counterpart, Bill Baudelaire, told me he'd been talking with the company who are arranging everything – they've had regular liaison meetings, it seems – and he found there was a late addition to the passenger list, Julius Filmer. Bill Baude-laire of course knows all about the conspiracy fiasco. He wanted to know if there wasn't some way we could keep the undesirable Mr Filmer off that prestigious train. Couldn't we possibly declare him *persona non grata* on all racetracks, including and especially Cana-dian. I told him if we'd had any grounds to warn Filmer off we'd have done it already, but the man was acquitted. We can't be seen to disgrace him when he's been declared not guilty, we'd be in all sorts of trouble. We can't warn him off for buying two horses from Gideon. These days, we can't just warn him off because we want to, he can only be warned off for transgressing against the rules of racing.'

All the frustrated fury of the Jockey Club vibrated in his voice. He wasn't a man to take impotence lightly.

'Bill Baudelaire knows all that, of course,' he went on. 'He said if we couldn't get Filmer off the train, would we please get one of our grandees *on*. Although the whole thing is sold out, he twisted the arms of the promoters to say they would let him have one extra ticket, and he wanted one of our stewards, or one of the Jockey Club department heads, or me myself, to go along conspicuously, so that Filmer would know he was being closely watched and would refrain from any sins he had in mind.'

'Are you going?' I asked, fascinated.

'No, I'm not. You are.'

'Um . . .' I said a shade breathlessly, 'I hardly fit the bill.'

'I told Bill Baudelaire,' the Brigadier said succinctly, 'that I would send him a passenger Filmer *didn't* know. One of my men. Then if Filmer does try anything, and after all it's a big if, we might have a real chance of finding out how and what, and catching him at it.'

My God, I thought. So simple, put like that. So absolutely impossible of performance.

I swallowed. 'What did Mr Baudelaire say?'

'I talked him into agreeing. He's expecting you.'

I blinked.

'Well,' the Brigadier said, 'not you by name.

Someone. Someone fairly young, I said, but experienced. Someone who wouldn't seem out of place ...' his teeth gleamed briefly ' ... on the millionaires' express.'

'But—' I said, and stopped dead, my mind full of urgent reservations and doubts that I was good enough for a job like that. Yet on the other hand, what a lark.

'Will you go?' he asked.

'Yes,' I said.

He smiled. 'I hoped you might.'

Brigadier Catto, who lived ninety miles from London in Newmarket, was staying overnight, as he often did, in a comfortable bedroom upstairs in the club. I left him in the bar after a while and drove the last half-mile home to where I lived in a quiet residential street in Kennington.

I had looked in that district for somewhere to put down a few roots on the grounds that I wouldn't be bothered to use the club much if I lived on the other side of London. Kennington, south of the Thames, rubbing shoulders with the grittiness of Lambeth and Brixton, was not where the racing crowd panted to be seen, and in fact I'd never spotted anyone locally that I knew by sight on the racecourse.

I'd come across an advertisement: 'House share available, for single presentable yuppy. Two rooms, bath, share kit, mortgage and upkeep. Call evenings', and although I'd been thinking in terms of a flat on my own, house sharing had suddenly seemed attractive, especially after the loneliness of work. I'd presented myself by appointment, been inspected by the four others in residence, and let in on trial, and it had all worked very well.

The four others were currently two sisters working in publishing (whose father had originally bought the house and set up the running-mortgage scheme), one junior barrister who tended to stutter, and an actor with a supporting role in a television series. The house rules were simple: pay on the dot, show good manners at all times, don't pry into the others' business, and don't let overnight girl/boy friends clog up any of the three bathrooms for hours in the morning.

There was a fair amount of laughter and camaraderie, but we tended to share coffee, beer, wine and saucepans more than confidences. I told them I was a dedicated racegoer and no one asked whether I won or lost.

The actor, Robbie, on the top floor, had been of enormous use to me, though I doubted he really knew it. He'd invited me up for a beer early one evening a few days after I went to live there, and I'd found him sitting before a brightly lit theatrical dressing table creating, as he said, a new make-up for a part he'd accepted in a play. I'd been startled to see how a different way of brushing his hair, how a large false moustache and heavier eyebrows had changed him.

'Tools of the trade,' he said, gesturing to the grease-paints and false hair lying in neat rows and boxes before him. 'Instant stubble, Fauntleroy curls – what would you like?'

'Curls,' I said slowly.

'Sit down, then,' he said cheerfully, getting up to give me his place, and he brought out a butane hair curler and wound my almost straight hair on to it bit by bit there and then, and within minutes I looked like a brown poodle, tousled, unbrushed, totally different.

'How's that?' he said, bending to look with me into the looking-glass.

'Amazing.' And easy, I thought. I could do it in the car, any time.

'It suits you,' Robbie said. He knelt down beside me, put his arm round my shoulders, gave me a little squeeze and smiled with unmistakable invitation into my eyes.

'No,' I said matter-of-factly. 'I like girls.'

He wasn't offended. 'Haven't you ever tried the other?'

'It's just not me, dear,' I said, 'as one might say.'

He laughed and took his arm away. 'Never mind, then. No harm in trying.'

We drank the beer and he showed me how to shape and stick on a bold macho moustache, holding out a pair of thick-framed glasses for good measure. I regarded the stranger looking back at me from the glass and said I'd never realized how easy it was to mislead.

'Sure thing. All it takes is a bit of nerve.'

And he was right about that. I bought a butane hair curler for myself, but I took it with me for a week in the car before I screwed myself up to stop in a lay-by on the way to Newbury races and actually use it. In the three years since then, I'd done it dozens of times without a thought, brushing and damping out the effects on the way home.

Sundays I usually spent lazily in my two big bright rooms on the first floor (the barrister directly above, the sisters below) sleeping, reading, pottering about. For about a year some time earlier I'd spent my Sundays with the daughter of one of the Hobbs Sandwich members, but it had been a mutual passing pleasure rather than a grand passion for both of us, and in the end she'd drifted away and married someone else. I supposed I too would marry one day: knew I would like to: felt there was no hurry this side of thirty.

On the Sunday morning after meeting the Brigadier in the club I began to think about what I should pack for Canada. He'd told me to be what I spent so much time not being, a rich young loafer with nothing to do but enjoy myself. 'All you need to do is talk about horses to the other passengers and keep your eyes open.'

'Yes,' I said.

'Look the part.'

'Yes, right.'

'I've caught sight of you sometimes at the races, you

36

know, looking like a stockbroker one day and a hillbilly the next. Millington says he often can't see you, even though he knows you're there.'

'I've got better with practice, I suppose, but I never really do much. Change my hair, change my clothes, slouch a bit.'

'It works,' he said. 'Be what Filmer would expect.'

It wasn't so much what Filmer would expect, I thought, looking at the row of widely assorted jackets in my wardrobe, but what I could sustain over the ten days the party was due to take before it broke up.

Curls, for instance, were out, as they disappeared in rain. Stuck-on moustaches were out in case they came off. Spectacles were out, as one could forget to put them on. I would have to look basically as nature had ordained and be as nondescript and unnoticeable as possible.

I sorted out the most expensive and least worn of my clothes, and decided I'd better buy new shirts, new shoes and a cashmere sweater before I went.

I telephoned Millington on Monday morning as instructed and found him in his usual state of disgruntlement. He had heard about the train. He was not in favour of my going on it. The Security Service (meaning the Brigadier) should have sent a properly trained operative, an ex-policeman preferably. Like himself, for instance. Someone who knew the techniques of investigation and could be trusted not to destroy vital evidence through ignorance and clumsiness. I listened without interruption for so long that, in the end, he said sharply, 'Are you still there?'

'Yes,' I said.

'I want to see you, preferably later this morning. I'll have your air ticket. I suppose you do have an up-to-date passport?'

We agreed to meet, as often before, in a reasonably good small snack bar next to Victoria Station, convenient for both Millington who lived a couple of miles south-west across Battersea Bridge, and for me a few stops down the line to the south.

I arrived ten minutes before the appointed time and found Millington already sitting at a table with a mug of brown liquid and several sausage rolls in progress. I took a tray, slid it along the rails in front of the glass-fronted serving display and picked a slice of cheesecake from behind one of the small hinged doors. I actually approved of the glass-door arrangement: it meant that with luck one's cheesecake wouldn't have been sneezed on by the general public, but only by a cook or two and the snack bar staff.

Millington eyed my partially hygienic wedge and said he preferred the lemon meringue pie himself.

'I like that too,' I said equably.

Millington was a big beer-and-any-kind-of-pie man who must have given up thankfully on weight control when he left the police. He looked as if he now weighed about seventeen stone, and while not gross was definitely a solid mass, but with an agility also that he put to good use in his job. Many petty racecourse crooks had made the mistake of believing Millington couldn't snake after them like an eel through the crowds, only to feel the hand of retribution falling weightily on their collar. I'd seen Millington catch a dipping pickpocket on the wing: an impressive sight.

The large convenience-food snack bar, bright and clean, was always infernally noisy, pop music thumping away to the accompaniment of chairs scraping the floor and the clatter of meals at a gallop. The clientele were mostly travellers, coming or going on trains lacking buffet cars, starving or prudent; travellers checking their watches, gulping too-hot coffee, uninterested in others, leaving in a hurry. No one ever gave Millington and me a second glance, and no one could ever have overheard what we said.

We never met there when there was racing at places like Plumpton, Brighton, Lingfield and Folkestone: on those days the whole racing circus could wash through Victoria Station. We never met, either, anywhere near the Security Service head office in the Jockey Club, in Portman Square. It was odd, I sometimes thought, that I'd never once been through my employer's door.

Millington said, 'I don't approve of you travelling with Filmer.'

'So I gathered,' I said. 'You said so earlier.'

'The man's a murderer.'

He wasn't concerned for my safety, of course, but thought me unequal to the contest.

'He may not actually murder anyone on the train,' I said flippantly.

'It's no joke,' he said severely. 'And after this he'll know you, and you'll be no use to us on the racecourse, as far as he's concerned.'

'There are about fifty people going on the trip, the Brigadier said. I won't push myself into Filmer's notice. He quite likely won't remember me afterwards.'

'You'll be too close to him,' Millington said obstinately.

'Well,' I said thoughtfully, 'it's the only chance we've ever had so far to get really close to him at all. Even if he's only going along for a harmless holiday, we'll know a good deal more about him this way.'

'I don't like wasting you,' Millington said, shaking his head.

I looked at him in real surprise. 'That's a change,' I said.

'I didn't want you working for us, to begin with,' he said, shrugging. 'Didn't see what good you could do, thought it was stupid. Now you're my eyes. The eyes in the back of my head that the villains have been complaining about ever since you started. I've got the sense to know it. And if you must know, I don't want to lose you. I told the Brigadier we were wasting our trump card, sending you on that train. He said we might be playing it, and if we could get rid of Filmer, it was worth it.'

I looked at Millington's worried face. I said slowly, 'Do you, and does the Brigadier, know something about Filmer's travel plans that you've not told me?'

'When he said that,' Millington said, looking down at his sausage rolls, 'I asked him that same question. He didn't answer. I don't know of anything myself. I'd tell you, if I did.'

Perhaps he would, I thought. Perhaps he wouldn't.

The next day, Tuesday, I drove north to Nottingham for a normal day's hard work hanging around doing nothing much at the races.

I'd bought the new clothes and a new suitcase and had more or less packed ready for my departure the next morning, and the old long-distance wanderlust that had in the past kept me travelling for seven years had woken from its recent slumber and given me a sharp nudge in the ribs. Millington shouldn't fear losing me to Filmer, I thought, so much as to the old seductive tug of moving on, moving on . . . seeing what lay round the next corner.

I could do it now, I supposed, in five-star fashion, not backpacking; in limousines, not on buses; eating haute cuisine, not hot dogs; staying in Palm Beach, not dusty backwoods. Probably I'd enjoy the lushness for a while, maybe even for a long while, but in the end, to stay real, I'd have to get myself out of the sweet-shop and do some sort of work, and not put it off and off until I no longer had a taste for plain bread.

I was wearing, perhaps as a salute to plain bread, a well-worn leather jacket and a flat cloth cap, the bin-oculars-camera slung round my neck, a racecard clutched in my hand. I stood around vaguely outside the weighing room, watching who came and who went, who talked to whom, who looked worried, who happy, who malicious.

A young apprentice with an ascendant reputation came out of the weighing room in street clothes, not riding gear, and stood looking around as if searching for someone. His eyes stopped moving and focused, and I looked to see what had caught his attention. He was looking at the Jockey Club's paid steward, who was acting at the meeting as the human shape of authority. The steward was standing in social conversation with a pair of people who had a horse running that day, and after a few minutes he raised his hat to the lady and walked out towards the parade ring.

The apprentice calmly watched his departing back, then made another sweep of the people around. Seeing nothing to worry about he set off towards the stand the jockeys watched the races from and joined a youngish man with whom he walked briefly, talking. They parted near the stands, and I, following, trans-

ferred my attention from the apprentice and followed
the other man instead; he went straight into the bookmakers' enclosure in front of the stands, and along the
rows of bookmakers to the domain of Collie Goodboy
who was shouting his offered odds from the height of
a small platform the size of a beer crate.

The apprentice's contact didn't place a bet. He
picked up a ledger and began to record the bets of
others. He spoke to Collie Goodboy (Les Morris to his
parents) who presently wiped off the offered odds from
his board, and chalked up new ones. The new odds
were generous. Collie Goodboy was rewarded by a rush
of eager punters keen to accept the invitation. Collie
Goodboy methodically took their money.

With a sigh I turned away and wandered off up to
the stands to watch the next race, scanning the crowds
as usual, watching the world revolve. I ended up
standing not far from the rails dividing the bookmakers'
section of the stands (called the Tattersalls enclosure)
from the club, the more expensive end. I often did
that, as from there one could see the people in both
enclosures easily. One could see also who came to the
dividing rails to put bets on with the row of bookmakers
doing business in that privileged position. The 'rails'
bookmakers were the princes of their trade; genial,
obliging, fair, flint-hearted, brilliant mathematicians.

I watched as always to see who was betting with
whom, and when I came to the bookmaker nearest to

the stands, nearest to me, I saw that the present customer was Filmer.

I was watching him bet, thinking of the rail journey ahead, when he tilted his head back and looked straight up into my eyes.

CHAPTER THREE

I looked away instantly but smoothly, and presently glanced back.

Filmer was still talking to the bookmaker. I edged upwards through the crowd behind me until I was about five steps higher and surrounded by other racegoers.

Filmer didn't look back to where I'd been standing. He didn't search up or down or sideways to see where I had gone.

My thumping heart quietened down a bit. The meeting of eyes had been accidental: had to have been. Dreadfully unwelcome, all the same, particularly at this point.

I hadn't expected him to have been at Nottingham, and hadn't looked for him. Two of his horses were certainly down to run, but Filmer himself almost never went to the Midland courses of Nottingham, Leicester or Wolverhampton. He had definite preferences in racecourses, as in so much else: always a creature of habit.

I made no attempt to shadow him closely, as it wasn't

necessary: before the following race he would be down in the parade ring to watch his horse walk round and I could catch him up there. I watched him conclude his bet and walk away to climb the stands for the race about to start, and as far as I could see he was alone, which also was unusual, as either the girlfriend or the male companion was normally in obsequious attendance.

The race began and I watched it with interest. The chatty apprentice wasn't riding in it himself, but the stable that employed him had a runner. The runner started third favourite and finished third last. I switched my gaze to Collie Goodboy, and found him smiling. A common, sad, fraudulent sequence that did racing no good.

Filmer stepped down from the stands and headed in the direction of the saddling boxes, to supervise, as he always did, the final preparation for his horse's race. I drifted along in his wake to make sure, but that was indeed where he went. From there to the parade ring, from there to place a bet with the same bookmaker as before, from there to the stands to watch his horse race. From there to the unsaddling enclosure allotted to the horse that finished second.

Filmer took his defeat graciously, making a point as always of congratulating the winning owner, in this case a large middle-aged lady who looked flushed and flattered.

Filmer left the unsaddling enclosure with a smirk of

self-satisfaction and was immediately confronted by a young man who tried to thrust a briefcase into his hand.

Julius Apollo's face turned from smug to fury quicker than Shergar won the Derby, as Paul Shacklebury would have said. Filmer wouldn't take the case and he practically spat at the offerer, his black head going forward like a striking cobra. The young man with the briefcase retreated ultra-nervously and in panic ran away, and Filmer, regaining control of himself, began looking around in the general direction of stewards and pressmen to see if any of them had noticed. He visibly sighed with relief that none of them showed any sign of it – and he hadn't looked my way at all.

I followed the demoralized young man, who still held on to the briefcase. He made straight for the men's cloakroom, stayed there for a fair time and came out looking pale. Filmer's effect on people's guts, I reflected, would put any laxative to shame.

The shaken youth with the briefcase then made his nervous way to a rendezvous with a thin, older man who was waiting just outside the exit gate, biting his nails. When the thin man saw the briefcase still in the nervous youth's possession he looked almost as furious as Filmer had done, and a strong argument developed in which one could read the dressing-down in the vigorous chopping gestures, even if one couldn't hear the words.

Thin man poked nervous man several times sharply

in the chest. Nervous man's shoulders drooped. Thin man turned away and walked off deep into the car park.

Nervous man brought the briefcase with him back through the gate and into the nearest bar, and I had to hang around for a long time in the small crowd there before anything else happened. The scattered clientele was watching the television: nervous man shuffled from foot to foot and sweated, and kept a sharp lookout at the people passing by outside in the open air. Then, some time after Filmer's second runner had tried and (according to the closed-circuit commentary) lost, Filmer himself came past, tearing up betting tickets and not looking pleased.

Nervous man shot out from his waiting position just inside the door of the sheltering bar and offered the briefcase again, and this time Filmer took it, but in fierce irritation and with another sharp set of glances around him. He saw nothing to disturb him. He was leaving after the fifth of the six races and all forms of authority were still engaged to his rear. He gripped the case's handle and strode purposefully out on his way to his car.

Nervous man shuffled a bit on the spot a bit more and then followed Filmer through the exit gate and into the car park. I tagged along again and saw both of them still making for their transport, though in different directions. I followed nervous man, not Filmer, and saw him get into the front passenger seat of a car already occupied by thin man, who still looked cross. They didn't set off immediately and I had time to walk at a steady pace past the rear of their car on the way to my own which was parked strategically, as ever, near the gate to the road, for making quick following getaways. I memorized their number plate in case I later lost them; and out on the road, comfortably falling into place behind them, I telephoned Millington.

I told him about the briefcase and read him the number plate still ahead in my sight.

'The car's going north, though,' I said. 'How far do you want me to go?'

'What time's your flight tomorrow?'

'Noon, from Heathrow. But I have to go home first to pick up my gear and passport.'

He thought for a few moments. 'You'd better decide for yourself. If he gets on the motorway to Scotland . . . well, don't go.'

'All right.'

'Very interesting,' Millington said, 'that he didn't want to be seen in public accepting that briefcase.'

'Very.'

'Anything special about it?'

'As far as I could see,' I said, 'it was black, polished, possibly crocodile, with gold clasps.'

'Well, well,' Millington said vaguely. 'I'll get back to you with that car number.'

The thin man's car aimed unerringly for the motorway in the direction of Scotland. I decided to keep on going at least until Millington called back, which he did with impressive speed, telling me that my quarry was registered to I. J. Horfitz, resident of Doncaster, address supplied.

'All right,' I said, 'I'll go to Doncaster.' An hour and a bit ahead, I thought, with plenty of time to return.

'Does that name Horfitz ring any bells with you?' Millington asked.

'None at all,' I said positively. 'And by the way, you know that promising young apprentice of Pete Shaw's? All that talent? The silly young fool passed some verbal info to a new character on the racecourse who turned out to be writing the book for Collie Goodboy. Collie Goodboy thought it good news.'

'What was it, do you know?'

'Pete Shaw had a runner in the second race, third favourite, finished nearly last. The apprentice knew the score, though he wasn't riding it.'

'Huh,' Millington said. 'I'll put the fear of God into the lot of them, Pete Shaw, the owner, the jockey, the apprentice and Collie Goodboy. Stir them up and warn them. I suppose,' he said as an afterthought, 'you didn't get any photos? We haven't any actual proof?'

'Not really. I took one shot of the apprentice talking to Collie's man, but they had their backs to me. One of Collie's man with Collie. One of Collie's board with the generous odds.'

'Better than nothing,' he said judiciously. 'It'll give them all an unholy fright. The innocent ones will be

livid and sack the guilty, like they usually do. Clean
their own house. Save us a job. And we'll keep a permanent eye on that stupid apprentice. Ring me when you
get to Doncaster.'

'OK. And I took some more photos. One of the
nervous young man with the briefcase, one of him with
the thin man . . . er . . . I. J. Horfitz possibly, I suppose,
and one of Filmer with the briefcase, though I'm not
sure if that one will be very clear, I had almost no time
and I was quite far away, and I was using the cigarette
lighter-camera, it's less conspicuous.'

'All right. We need that film before you go. Um . . .
er . . . you'd better give me a ring when you're on the
way back, and I'll have thought of somewhere we can
meet tonight. Right?'

'Yes,' I said. 'Right.'

'This Horfitz person, what did he look like?'

'Thin, elderly, wore a dark overcoat and a black trilby,
and glasses. Looked ready for a funeral, not the races.'

Millington grunted in what seemed to me to be recognition.

'Do you know him?' I asked.

'He was before your time. But yes, I know him. Ivor
Horfitz. It must be him. We got him warned off for life
five years ago.'

'What for?'

'It's a long story. I'll tell you later. And I don't
think after all you need to spend all that time going to
Doncaster. We can always find him, if we want to. Turn

51

round at the next exit and come back to London, and I'll meet you in that pub at Victoria. Not the snack bar; the pub.'

'Yes, right. See you in about ... um ... two and a half hours, with luck.'

Two and a half hours later, beer-and-pork-pie time in a dark far corner in a noisy bar, Millington's preferred sort of habitat.

I gave him the exposed but undeveloped film, which he put in his pocket saying, 'Eyes in the back of my head,' with conspicuous satisfaction.

'Who is Horfitz?' I said, quenching the long drive's thirst in a half-pint of draught. 'Did you know he knew Filmer?'

'No,' he said, answering the second question first. 'And Filmer wouldn't want to be seen with him, nor to be seen in any sort of contact.'

'What you're saying,' I said slowly, 'is that the messenger, the nervous young man, is also known by sight to the stewards ... to you yourself probably ... because if he were an unidentifiable stranger, why should Filmer react so violently to being seen with him; to being seen accepting something from him?'

Millington gave me a sideways look. 'You've learned a thing or two, haven't you, since you started?' He patted the pocket containing the film. 'This will tell us if we know him. What did he look like?'

'Fairly plump, fairly gormless. Sweaty. Unhappy. A worm between two hawks.'

Millington shook his head. 'Might be anyone,' he said.

'What did Horfitz do?' I asked.

Millington bit into pork pie and took his time, speaking eventually round escaping crumbs of pastry.

'He owned a small stableful of horses in Newmarket and employed his own trainer for them, who naturally did what he was told. Very successful little stable in a quiet way. Amazing results, but there you are, some owners are always lucky. Then the trainer got cold feet because he thought we were on to him, which we actually weren't, we'd never reckoned him for a villain. Anyway, he blew the whistle on the operation, saying the strain was getting too much for him. He said all the horses in the yard were as good as interchangeable. They ran in whatever races he and Horfitz thought they could win. Three-year-olds in two-year-old races, past winners in maidens-at-starting, any old thing. Horfitz bought and sold horses continually so the yard never looked the same from week to week, and the stable lads came and went like yo-yos, like they do pretty much anyway. They employed all sorts of different jockeys. No one cottoned on. Horfitz had some nice long-priced winners but no bookmakers hollered foul. It was a small unfashionable stable, see? Never in the newspapers. Because they didn't run in big races, just small ones at tracks the press don't go to, but you can win as much by betting on those as on any others. It was all pretty low-key, but we found out that Horfitz had made literally hundreds of thousands, not just by betting but by selling his winners. Only he always sold the real horses which fitted the names on the racecard, not the horses that had actually run. He kept those and ran them again, and sold the horses in whose names they'd run, and so on and so on. Audacious little fiddle, the whole thing.'

'Yes,' I agreed, and felt a certain amount of awe at the energy and organization put into the enterprise.

'So when the trainer ratted we set a few traps with his help and caught Horfitz with his pants down, so to speak. He got warned off for life and swore to kill his trainer, which he hasn't done so far. The trainer was warned off for three years with a severe caution, but he got his licence back two years ago. Part of the bargain. So he's in business again in a small way but we keep his runners under a microscope, checking their passports every time they run. We're a lot hotter at checking passports randomly all over the place now, as of course you know.'

I nodded.

Then Millington's jaw literally dropped. I looked at the classic sign of astonishment and said, 'What's the matter?'

'Gawd,' he said. 'What a turn-up. Can you believe it? Paul Shacklebury, that murdered stable lad, he was working for Horfitz's old trainer.'

I left Millington frowning with concentration over a replenished pint while he tried to work out the significance of Horfitz's old trainer employing a lad who was murdered for knowing too much about Filmer. What had Paul Shacklebury known, Millington demanded rhetorically for the hundredth time. And, more to the minute, what was in the briefcase, and why was Horfitz giving it to Filmer?

'Work on the sweating messenger,' I suggested, getting up to go. 'He might crack open like the trainer. You never know.'

'Maybe we will,' Millington said. 'And Tor . . . look out for yourself on the train.'

He could be quite human sometimes, I thought.

I flew to Ottawa the next day and gave in to temptation at Heathrow to the extent of changing my ticket from knees-against-chest economy to full-stretch-out first class. I also asked the Ottawa taxi driver who took me into the city from the airport to find me a decent hotel; he cast a rapid eye over my clothes and the new suitcase and said the Four Seasons should suit.

It suited. They gave me a small pleasant suite and I telephoned straight away to the number I'd been given for Bill Baudelaire. He answered himself at the first ring, rather to my surprise, and said yes, he'd had a telex to confirm I was on my way. He had a bass voice with a lot of timbre even over the wires and was softly Canadian in accent.

He asked where I would be in an hour and said he

would come around then to brief me on the matter in hand, and I gathered from his circumspect sentences that he wasn't alone and didn't want to be understood. Just like home, I thought comfortably, and unpacked a few things, and showered off the journey and awaited events.

Outside, the deepening orange of the autumn sunshine was turning the green copper roofs of the turreted stone government buildings to a transient shimmering gold, and I reflected, watching from the windows, that I'd much liked this graceful city when I'd been here before. I was filled with a serene sense of peace and contentment, which I remembered a few times in the days lying ahead.

Bill Baudelaire came when the sky had grown dark and I'd switched on the lights, and he looked round the suite with quizzical eyebrows.

'I'm glad to see old Val has staked you to rooms befitting a rich young owner.'

I smiled and didn't enlighten him. He'd shaken my hand when I opened the door to him and looked me quickly, piercingly up and down in the way of those used to assessing strangers instantly and with no inhibitions about letting them know it.

I saw a man of plain looks but positive charm, a solid man much younger than the Brigadier, maybe forty, with reddish hair, pale blue eyes and pale skin pitted by the scars of old acne. Once seen, I thought, difficult to forget.

He was wearing a dark grey business suit with a cream shirt and a red tie out of step with his hair, and I wondered if he were colour-blind or simply liked the effect.

He walked straight across the sitting room, sat in the armchair nearest to the telephone and picked up the receiver.

'Room service?' he said. 'Please send up as soon as possible a bottle of vodka and . . . er . . .' He raised his eyebrows in my direction, in invitation.

'Wine,' I said. 'Red. Bordeaux preferably.'

Bill Baudelaire repeated my request with a ceiling price and disconnected.

'You can put the drinks on your expense sheet and I'll initial it,' he said. 'You do have an expense sheet, I suppose?'

'I do in England.'

'Then start one here, of course. How are you paying the hotel bills?'

'By credit card. My own.'

'Is that usual? Never mind. You give all the bills to me when you've paid them, along with your expense sheet, and Val and I will deal with it.'

'Thank you,' I said. Val would have a fit, I thought, but then on second thoughts, no he probably wouldn't. He would pay me the agreed budget; fair was fair.

'Sit down,' Bill Baudelaire said, and I sat opposite him in another armchair, crossing one knee over the other. The room seemed hot to me with the central heating, and I wasn't wearing a jacket. He considered me for a while, his brow furrowing with seeming uncertainty.

'How old are you?' he said abruptly.

'Twenty-nine.'

'Val said you were experienced.' It wasn't exactly a question, nor a matter of disbelief.

'I've worked for him for three years.'

'He said you would look this part . . . and you do.' He sounded more puzzled than pleased, though. 'You seem so polished . . . I suppose it's not what I expected.'

I said, 'If you saw me in the cheaper sections of a racecourse, you would think I'd been born there, too.'

His face lightened into a smile. 'Right, then. I'll accept that. Well, I've brought you a whole lot of papers.' He glanced at the large envelope that he had put on the table beside the telephone. 'Details about the train and about some of the people who'll be on it, and details about the horses and the arrangements for those. This has all been an enormous undertaking. Everyone has worked very hard on it. It's essential that it retains a good, substantial, untarnished image from start to finish. We're hoping for increased worldwide awareness of Canadian racing. Although we do of course hit world headlines with the Queen's Plate in June or July, we want to draw more international horses here. We want to put our programmes more on the map. Canada's a great country. We want to maximize our impact on the international racing circuit.'

'Yes,' I said, 'I do understand.' I hesitated. 'Do you have a public relations firm working on it?'

'What? Why do you ask? Yes, we do, as a matter of fact. What difference does it make?'

'None, really. Will they have a representative on the train?'

'To minimize negative incidents? No, not unless . . .' he stopped and listened to what he'd said. 'I'm using their jargon, damn it. I'll watch that. So easy to repeat what they say.'

A knock on the door announced the drinks in the charge of an ultra-polite slow-moving waiter who knew where to find ice and mixers in the room's own refrigerator. The waiter took his deliberate time over uncorking the wine, and Bill Baudelaire, stifling impatience, said we would do the pouring ourselves. When the tortoise waiter had gone he gestured to me to help myself, and on his own account fixed a lengthy splash of vodka over a tumblerful of cubes.

He had suggested to the Brigadier that I should meet him first here in Ottawa, as he had business in that city which couldn't be postponed. It would also, they both thought, be more securely private, as everyone going on the train in the normal way would be collecting in Toronto.

'You and I,' Bill Baudelaire said over his vodka, 'will fly to Toronto tomorrow evening on separate planes, after you've spent the day absorbing all the material I've brought you and asking any questions that arise. I propose to drop by your sitting room here again at two o'clock for a final briefing.'

'Will I be able to get in touch with you fairly easily after tomorrow?' I asked. 'I'd like to be able to.'

'Yes, indeed. I'm not going on the train myself, as of course you know, but I'll be at Winnipeg for the races there, and at Vancouver. And at Toronto, of course. I've outlined everything. You'll find it in the package. We can't really discuss anything properly until you've read it.'

'All right.'

'There's one unwelcome piece of news, however, that isn't in there because I heard it too late to include. It seems Julius Filmer had bought a share in one of the horses travelling on the train. The partnership was registered today and I was told just now by telephone. The Ontario Racing Commission is deeply concerned, but we can't do anything about it. No regulations have been broken. They won't let people who've been convicted of felonies such as arson, fraud or illegal gambling own horses, but Filmer hasn't been convicted of anything.'

'Which horse?' I said.

'Which horse? Laurentide Ice. Quite useful. You can read about it in there.' He nodded to the package. 'The problem is that we made a rule that only owners could go along to the horse car to see the horses. We couldn't have everyone tramping about there, both for security reasons and for preventing the animals being upset. We thought the only comfort left to us about Filmer's being on the train was that he wouldn't have access to the horse car, and now he will.'

'Awkward.'

'Infuriating.' He refilled his glass, with the suppressed violence of his frustration. 'Why for God's sake couldn't that goddam crook have kept his snotty nose out? He's trouble. We all know it. He's planning something. He'll ruin the whole thing. He practically said as much.' He looked me over and shook his head. 'No offence to you, but how are you going to stop him?'

'It depends what needs to be stopped.'

His face lightened suddenly to a smile as before. 'Yes, all right, we'll wait and see. Val said you don't miss things. Let's hope he's right.'

He went away after a while and with a great deal of interest I opened the package and found it absolutely fascinating from start to finish.

'The Great Transcontinental Mystery Race Train', as emblazoned in red on the gold cover of the glossy prospectus, had indeed entailed an enormous amount of organization. Briefly, the enterprise offered to the racehorse owners of the world a chance to race a horse in Toronto, to go by train to Winnipeg, and race a horse there, to stop for two nights at a hotel high in the Rockies, and to continue by train to Vancouver, where they might again race a horse. There was accommodation for eleven horses on the train, and for forty-eight human VIP passengers.

At Toronto, Winnipeg and Vancouver there would be overnight stays in top-class hotels. Transport from train to hotels to races and back to the train was also included as required. The entire trip would last from lunch at Toronto races on the Saturday, to the end of the special race day at Vancouver ten days later.

On the train there would be special sleeping cars, a special dining car, two private chefs and a load of good wine. People who owned their own private rail cars could, as in the past, apply for them to be joined to the train.

Every possible extra luxury would be available if requested in advance, and in addition, for entertainment along the way, an intriguing mystery would be enacted on board and at the stopovers, which passengers would be invited to solve.

I winced a shade at that last piece of information: keeping eyes on Filmer would be hard enough anyhow without all sorts of imaginary mayhem going on around him. He himself was mystery enough.

Special races, I read, had been introduced into the regular programmes at Woodbine racecourse, Toronto, at Assiniboia Downs, Winnipeg, and at Exhibition Park, Vancouver. The races had been framed to be ultra-attractive to the paying public, with magnificent prize money to please the owners. The owners of the horses and indeed all the train passengers would be given VIP treatment at all the racecourses, including lunch with the presidents.

It wasn't to be expected that owners would want to run the horses on the train three times in so short a span.

Any owner was free to run a horse just once. Any owner (or any other passenger on the train) was free to bring any other of his horses to Toronto, Winnipeg or Vancouver by road or by air to run in the special races. The trip was to be a light-hearted junket for the visitors, a celebration of racing in Canada.

In smaller print after all that trumpeting came the information that accommodation was available also for one groom for each horse. If owners wanted space for extra attendants, would they please specify early. Grooms and other attendants would have their own dining and sleeping cars and their own separate entertainments.

Stabling had been reserved at Toronto, Winnipeg and Vancouver for the horses going by train, and they would be able to exercise normally at all three places. In addition, during the passengers' visit to the mountains, the horses would be stabled and exercised in Calgary. The good care of the horses was of prime importance, and a veterinarian would be at once helicoptered to the train if his services should become necessary between scheduled stops.

Next in the package was a pencilled note from Bill Baudelaire:

All eleven horse places were sold out within two weeks of the first major announcement.

All forty-eight VIP passenger places were sold within a month.
There are dozens of entries for the special races.
This is going to be a success!

After that came a list of the eleven horses, with past form, followed by a list of their owners, with nationalities. Three owners from England (including Filmer), one from Australia, three from the United States and five from Canada (including Filmer's partner).

The owners, with husbands, wives, families and friends, had taken up twenty-seven of the forty-eight passenger places. Four of the remaining twenty-one places had also been taken by well-known Canadian owners (identified by a star against their names), and Bill Baudelaire, in a note pencilled at the bottom of this passenger list had put, 'Splendid response from our appeal to our owners to support the project!'

There were no trainers mentioned on the passenger list, and in fact I later learned that the trainers were making their own way by air as usual to Winnipeg and Vancouver, presumably because the train trip was too time-consuming and expensive.

Next in the package came a bunch of handouts from the three racecourses, from the Canadian railway company and from the four hotels, all shiny pamphlets extolling their individual excellences. Finally, a fat brochure with good colour plates put together by the travel organizers in charge of getting the show on the railroad, a job which seemed well within their powers since they apparently also arranged safaris to outer deserts, treks to the Poles and tours to anywhere anyone cared to go.

They also staged mysteries as entertainment; evenings, weekends, moving or stationary. They were experts from much practice.

For the Great Transcontinental Mystery Race Train, they said, they had arranged something extra special. 'A mystery that will grab you by the throat. A stunning experience. All around you the story will unfold. Clues will appear. BE ON YOUR GUARD.'

Oh great, I thought wryly. But they hadn't finished. There was a parting shot.

'BEWARE! MANY PEOPLE ARE NOT WHAT THEY SEEM.'

CHAPTER FOUR

'How can they stage a play on a train?' I asked Bill Baudelaire the next day. 'I wouldn't have thought it would work.'

'Mysteries are very popular in Canada. Very fashionable,' he said, 'and they don't exactly stage a play. Some of the passengers will be actors and they will make the story evolve. I went to a dinner party... a mystery dinner party... not long ago and some of the guests were actors, and before we knew where we were, we were all caught up in a string of events, just as if it were real. Quite amazing. I went because my wife wanted to. I didn't think I would enjoy it in the least, but I did.'

'Some of the passengers...' I repeated slowly. 'Do you know which ones?'

'No, I don't,' he said, more cheerfully than I liked. 'That's part of the fun for everyone, trying to spot the actors.'

I liked it less and less.

'And of course the actors may be hiding among the other lot of passengers until their turn to appear comes.'

'What other lot of passengers?' I said blankly.

'The racegoers.' He looked at my face. 'Doesn't it say anything about them in the package?'

'No, it doesn't.'

'Ah.' He reflected briefly. 'Well, in order to make the trip economically viable, the rail company said we should add our own party to the regular train which sets off every day from Toronto to Vancouver, which is called the Canadian. We didn't want to do that because it would have meant we couldn't stop the train for two nights in Winnipeg and again for the mountains, and although the carriages could be unhitched and left in a siding, we'd be faced with security problems. But our own special train was proving extremely, almost impossibly, expensive. So we advertised a separate excursion . . . a racegoing trip . . . and now we have our own train. But it has been expanded, with three or four more sleeping cars, another dining car, and a dayniter or two according to how many tickets they sell in the end. We had an enormous response from people who didn't want to pay what the owners are paying but would like to go to the races across Canada on vacation. They are buying their tickets for the train at the normal fare and making their own arrangements at the stops . . . and we call these passengers the racegoers, for convenience.'

I sighed. I supposed it made sense. 'What's a day-niter?' I said.

'A car with reclining seats, not bedrooms.'

'And how many people altogether will be travelling?'

'Difficult to say. Start with forty-eight owners . . . we call them owners to distinguish them from the racegoers . . . and the grooms. Then the actors and the people from the travel company. Then the train crew and stewards, waiters, chefs and so on. With all the racegoers . . . well, perhaps about two hundred people altogether. We won't know until we start. Probably not then, unless we actually count.'

I could get lost among two hundred more easily than among forty-eight, I thought. Perhaps it might not be too bad. Yet the owners would be looking for actors . . . for people who weren't what they seemed.

'You asked about contact,' Bill Baudelaire said.

'Yes.'

'I've discussed it with some of our Jockey Club, and we think you'll simply have to telephone us from the stops.'

I said with some alarm, 'How many of your Jockey Club know I'm going on the train?'

He looked surprised. 'I suppose everyone in the executive office knows we'll have a man in place. They don't know exactly who. Not by name. Not yet. Not until I'd met you and approved. They don't and won't know what you look like.'

'Would you please not tell them my name,' I said.

He was half bewildered, half affronted. 'But our Jockey Club are sensible men. Discreet.'

'Information leaks,' I said.

He looked at me broodingly, vodka and ice cubes tinkling in a fresh glass. 'Are you serious?' he said.

'Yes, indeed.'

His brow wrinkled. 'I'm afraid I may have mentioned your name to one or two. But I will impress on them not to repeat it.'

It was too late, I supposed, for much else. Perhaps I was getting too obsessed with secrecy. Still . . .

'I'd rather not telephone direct to the Jockey Club,' I said. 'Couldn't I leave messages where only you will get them? Like your own home?'

His face melted into an almost boyish grin. 'I have three teenage daughters and a busy wife. The receiver is almost never in the cradle.' He thought briefly, then wrote a number on a sheet of a small notepad and gave it to me.

'Use this one,' he said. 'It's my mother's number. She's always there. She's not well and spends a good deal of time in bed. But her brains are intact. She's quick-witted. And because she's ill, if she calls me at the office she gets put straight through to me or else she gets told where to find me. If you give her a message, it will reach me personally with minimum delay. Will that do?'

'Yes, fine,' I said, and kept my doubts hidden. Carrier pigeons, I thought, might be better.

'Anything else?' he asked.

'Yes . . . do you think you could ask Laurentide Ice's owner why he sold a half-share to Filmer?'

'It's a she. I'll enquire.' He seemed to have hesitations in his mind but he didn't explain them. 'Is that all?' he said.

'My ticket?'

'Oh yes. The travel company, Merry & Co, they'll have it. They're still sorting out who's to sleep where, since we've added you in. We'll have to tell *them* your name, of course, but all we've said so far is that we absolutely have to have another ticket and even if it looked impossible it would have to be done. They'll bring your ticket to Union Station in Toronto on Sunday morning and you can pick it up there. All the owners are picking theirs up then.'

'All right.'

He stood up to go. 'Well . . . bon voyage,' he said, and after a short pause added, 'Perhaps he won't try anything.'

'Hope not.'

He nodded, shook my hand, finished the last of his vodka at a gulp and left me alone with my thoughts.

The first of those was that if I were going across a whole continent by train I might as well start out as I meant to go on. If there was a train from Ottawa to Toronto I would take it instead of flying.

There was indeed a train, the hotel confirmed.

70

Leaving at five-fifty, arriving four hours later. Dinner on board.

Ottawa had shovelled its centre-of-town railway station under a rug, so to speak, as if railways should be kept out of sight like the lower orders, and built a great new station several miles away from anywhere useful. The station itself, however, proved a delight, a vast airy tent of glass set among trees with the sun flooding in with afternoon light and throwing angular shadows on the shiny black floor.

People waiting for the train had put their luggage down in a line and gone to sit on the seats along the glass walls, and thinking it a most civilized arrangement I put my suitcase at the rear of the queue and found myself a seat also. Filmer or not, I thought, I was definitely enjoying myself.

Dinner on the train was arranged as in aeroplanes with several stewards in shirtsleeves and deep-yellow waistcoats rolling first a drinks trolley, then a food trolley down the centre aisle, serving to right and left as they went. I watched them idly for quite a long time, and when they'd gone past me I couldn't remember their faces. I drank French wine as the daylight faded across the flying landscape and ate a better-than-many-airlines dinner after dark, and thought about cha-meleons; and at Toronto I took a cab and booked into another in the chain of the Four Seasons Hotels, as I had told Bill Baudelaire I would.

In the morning, a few hundred thoughts later, I followed the hotel porter's directions and walked to the offices of the travel organizers, Merry & Co, as given in their brochure.

The street-level entrance was unimposing, the building deceptively small, but inside there seemed to be acres of space all brightly lit, with pale carpeting, blond woods and an air of absolute calm. There were some green plants, a sofa or two and a great many desks behind which quiet unhurried conversations seemed to be going on at a dozen telephones. All the telephonists faced the centre of the huge room, looking out and not at the walls.

I walked to one desk whose occupant wasn't actually speaking on the wire, a purposeful-looking man with a beard who was cleaning his nails.

'Help you?' he asked economically.

I said I was looking for the person organizing the race train.

'Oh yes. Over there. Third desk along.'

I thanked him. The third desk along over there was unoccupied.

'She'll be back in a minute,' comforted the second desk along. 'Sit down if you like.'

There were chairs, presumably for clients, on the near side of the desks. Comfortable chairs, clients for the pampering of, I thought vaguely, sitting in one.

The empty desk had a piece of engraved plastic on it announcing its absent owner's name: Nell. A quiet voice behind me said, 'Can I help you?' and I stood up politely and said, 'Yes, please.'

She had fair hair, grey eyes, a sort of clean look with a dust of freckles, but she was not as young, I thought, as her immediate impression, which was about eighteen.

'I came about the train,' I said.

'Yes. Could you possibly compress it into five minutes? There's such a lot still to arrange.' She walked round to the back of her desk and sat, looking down at an array of list upon list.

'My name is Tor Kelsey,' I began.

Her head lifted fast. 'Really? The Jockey Club told us your name this morning. Well, we've put you in because Bill Baudelaire said he'd cancel the whole production if we didn't.' The unemphatic grey eyes assessed me, not exactly showing that she didn't think the person she saw to be worth the fuss, but pretty near. 'It's the dining car that's the trouble,' she said. 'There are only forty-eight places. We have to have everyone seated at the same time because the mystery is acted before and after meals, and two or three of those places are taken by actors. Or are supposed to be, only now there isn't room for them either, as my boss sold too many tickets to late applicants, and you are actually number forty-nine.' She stopped briefly. 'I suppose that's our worry, not yours. We've given you a roomette for sleeping, and Bill Baudelaire says anything you ask for will we please let you have. We said what would you ask for and he didn't know. Maddeningly unhelpful. Do you yourself know what you want?'

'I'd like to know who the actors are, and the story they're going to enact.'

'No, we can't do that. It'll spoil it for you. We never tell the passengers anything.'

'Did Bill Baudelaire tell you,' I asked, 'why he so particularly wanted me on the train?'

'Not really.' She frowned slightly. 'I didn't give it much thought, I've so much else to see to. He simply insisted we take you, and since the Jockey Club are our clients, we do what the client asks.'

'Are you going on the train?' I asked.

'Yes, I am. There has to be someone from the company to sort out the crises.'

'And how good are you at secrets?'

'I keep half a dozen before breakfast every day.'

Her telephone rang quietly and she answered it in a quiet voice, adding her murmur to the hum of other murmurs all round the room. I realized that the quiet was a deliberate policy, as otherwise they would all have been shouting at the tops of their lungs and not hearing a word their callers said.

'Yes,' she was saying. 'Out at Mimico before ten. Four dozen, yes. Load them into the special dining car. Right. Good.' She put the phone down and without pause said to me, 'What secret do you want kept?'

'That I'm employed by the Jockey Club . . . to deal with crises.'

'Oh.' It was a long sound of understanding. 'All right, it's a secret.' She reflected briefly. 'The actors are holding a run-through right now, not far away. I've got to see them sometime today, so it may as well be at once. What do you want me to tell them?'

'I'd like you to say that your company are putting me on the train as a trouble-spotter, because a whole train of racing people is a volatile mass looking for an excuse to explode. Say it's a form of insurance.'

'Which it is,' she said.

'Well, yes. And I also want to solve your problem of the forty-ninth seat. I want to go on the train as a waiter.'

She didn't blink but nodded. 'Yes, OK. Good idea. Quite often we put one of the actors in as a waiter, but not actually on this trip, luckily. The rail company are very helpful when we ask. I'll fix it. Come on, then, there's such a lot still to do.'

She moved quickly without seeming to, and presently we were skimming round corners in her small blue car, pulling up with a jerk outside the garage of a large house.

The rehearsal, if you could call it that, was actually going on in the garage itself, which had no car but a large trestle table, a lot of folding chairs, a portable gas heater and about ten men and women standing in groups.

Nell introduced me without mentioning my name. 'We're taking him on the train as company eyes and ears. Anything you think might turn into trouble, tell him or me. He's going as a service attendant, which will mean he can move everywhere through the train without questions. OK? Don't tell the paying passengers he's one of us.'

They shook their heads. Keeping the true facts from the passengers was their daily occupation.

'OK,' Nell said to me. 'I'll leave you here. Phone me later.' She put a large envelope she was carrying on to the table, waved to the actors and vanished, and one of them, a man of about my own age with a mop-head of tight, light brown curls came forward, shook my hand and said, 'She's the best in the business. My name's David Flynn, by the way, but call me Zak. That's my name in the mystery. From now on, we call each other by the mystery names, so as not to make mistakes in front of the passengers. You'd better have an acting name, too. How about . . . um . . . Tommy?'

'It's all right by me.'

'Right, everybody, this is Tommy, a waiter.'

They nodded, smiling, and I was introduced to them one by one by the names they would use on the train.

'Mavis and Walter Bricknell, racehorse owners.' They were middle-aged, dressed like the others in jeans and casual sweaters. 'They're married in real life too.'

David/Zak went briskly along the row, an enormously positive person, wasting no time. 'Ricky . . . a groom in the mystery, though he'll be travelling with the racegoers, not the grooms. His part in the mystery finishes at Winnipeg, and he'll be getting off there. This is Raoul, racehorse trainer for the Bricknells, their guest on the train. Ben, he's an old groom who has ridden a few races.' Ben grinned from a small, deeply-lined face, looking the part. 'This is Giles: don't be taken in by his good looks, he's our murderer. This is Angelica, who you won't see much of as she's the first victim. And Pierre, he's a compulsive gambler in love with the Bricknells' daughter, Donna, and this is Donna. And last, this is James Winterbourne, he's a big noise in the Ontario Jockey Club.'

I don't think I jumped. The big name in the Ontario Jockey Club wore a three-day beard and a red trilby hat, which he lifted to me ceremoniously. 'Alas,' he said, 'I'm not travelling. My part ends with giving the train an official blessing. Too bad.'

David/Zak said to me, 'We're walking through the first scene now. Everyone knows what to do. This is Union Station. This is the gathering point for the passengers. They're all here. Right, guys, off we go.'

Mavis and Walter said, 'We're chatting to other passengers about the trip.'

Pierre and Donna said, 'We're having a quiet row.'

Giles said, 'I'm being nice to the passengers.'

Angelica: 'I am looking for someone called Steve. I ask the passengers if they've seen him. He is supposed to be travelling, but he hasn't turned up.'

Raoul said, 'I put my two cents' worth into Pierre and Donna's quarrel as I want to break them up so

I can marry her myself. For her father's money, of course.'

Pierre said, 'Which I furiously point out.'

Donna: 'Which I don't like, and am near to tears.'

Ben: 'I ask Raoul for a handout, which I don't get. I tell a lot of people he's stingy, after I worked for him all those years. The passengers are to find me a nuisance. I tell them I'm travelling on the racegoers' part of the train.'

James Winterbourne said, 'I ask for attention and tell everybody that we have horses, grooms, racegoers and all your owners and friends on the train. I hope everyone will have a great time on this historic re-enactment, etc., etc., for the glory of Canadian racing.'

Ricky said, 'I arrive. One of the station staff – who will be Jimmy (not here now) in staff uniform – tries to stop me, but I run in among the passengers, bleeding all over the place, shouting that some thugs tried to hijack one of the horses off the train, but I shouted and the maintenance men in the loading yard chased them away. I think the owners should know.'

Zak said, 'Jimmy runs off to fetch me and I stride in and tell everyone not to be worried, all the horses are safe and on the train, but to make sure things are all right in future I will go on the train myself. I am the top security agent for the railway.' He looked round the company. 'All right so far? Then James Winterbourne calms everyone down and tells them to board the train at Gate 6, Track 7. I'll check that that's still right, on Sunday morning, but that's what we've been told so far.'

The Bricknells said, 'We ask you which horse they were trying to hijack, but you don't know. We try to find Ricky, to ask him. He's not our groom, but we are always anxious sort of people.'

'Right,' Zak said. 'So we are all on board. It'll take a good half-hour. Ricky gets bandaged by Nell in plain view, beside the train. The train leaves at twelve. Then everyone gathers shortly afterwards in the dining room for champagne. We do scene two next, just before lunch.'

They 'walked through' scene two, which was shorter and chiefly established Zak as being in charge, and had Ricky coming to say that he didn't know which of the horses the horse-nappers had been making for . . . they had come into the horse car wearing masks, brandishing clubs. . . . Ricky had been alone out there in the loading yard as all the other grooms had gone back to the station's coffee shop.

The Bricknells were a-twitter. Angelica was distraught that Steve hadn't turned up. Who cared about a horse, where was Steve?

Who was Steve? Zak asked. Angelica said he was her business manager. What business? Zak asked. None of yours, Angelica tartly said.

'Right,' Zak said, 'about now it has dawned on the thickest passenger that this is all fiction. They'll be smiling. So lunch is next. Everyone gets the afternoon to relax. Our next scene is during drinks before dinner. That's the one we rehearsed before Nell came. Right. We may have to change things a bit as we go along, so we'll do the rest of the final walk-throughs in one of the bedrooms, a day at a time.'

The others thought this reasonable and began to put on their coats.

'Don't you have a script?' I asked Zak.

'No formal words to learn, if that's what you mean. No. We all know what we've got to establish in each scene, and we improvise. When we plan a mystery, the actors get a brief outline of what's going to happen and basically what sort of people they are, then they invent their own imaginary life stories, so that if any passenger asks questions in conversations, they have the answers ready. I'd advise you to do it, too. Invent a background, a childhood . . . as near as possible to the real thing is always easiest.'

'Thanks for the tip,' I said. 'Will you let me know your plans each day, and also tell me instantly if anything odd happens you don't expect? Even small things, really.'

'Yes, sure. Ask Nell, too. She knows the story. And there are some actors who weren't here today because they don't get activated until later on the trip. They're on the passenger list. Nell will point them out.'

He stifled a yawn and looked suddenly very tired, a complete contrast to two minutes earlier, and I suspected he was one of those people who could turn energy on and off like a tap. One of Aunt Viv's best friends had been an elderly actor who could walk down to the theatre like a tired old pensioner and go out on the stage and make the audience's hair stand on end with his power.

David Flynn, offering me a lift if I needed one, was beginning to move with a sort of lassitude that one would never have seen in Zak. He picked up Nell's large envelope, opened it and distributed its contents to the others: luggage labels saying 'Merry & Co', and photocopied sheets of 'Information and Advice to Passengers'.

Scene dressing, I supposed. I asked him if he would be going anywhere near the Merry & Co office and he said he would detour that way and was as good as his word.

'Do you do this all the time?' I asked on the way.

'Act, do you mean? Or mysteries?'

'Either.'

'Anything I'm offered,' he said frankly. 'Plays. Commercials. Bit parts in series. But I do mostly mysteries now that they're so popular, and nearly all for Merry & Co. I write the stories to suit the occasion. I was engaged for a doctors' convention last week, so we did a medical crime. Just now it's racing. Next month I've got to think up something for a fishing club weekend train trip to Halifax. It keeps me employed. It pays the bills. It's quite good fun. It's not Stratford-upon-Avon.'

'What about the other actors?' I asked. 'The ones in the garage.'

'Much the same. It's work. They like the train trips, even if it does mean shouting all the scenes against the wheel noise when we're going along, because the dining cars are so long. Not by any means the right shape for a stage. We don't always use the same actors, it depends on the characters, but they're all friendly, we never take anyone who can't get along. It's essential to be tolerant and generous, to make our sort of improvisation work.'

'I'd no idea mysteries were such an industry.'

He gave a small sideways smile. 'They have a lot in England too, these days.'

'Um . . .' I said, as he braked to a halt outside the Merry & Co offices. 'How English do I sound to you?'

'Very. An educated Englishman in an expensive suit.'

'Well, the original plan was for me to go on the train as a wealthy owner. What would you think of my accent if I were dressed as a waiter in a deep-yellow waistcoat?'

'Harvest gold, that's what they call that colour,' he said thoughtfully. 'I wouldn't notice your accent so much, perhaps. There are thousands of English immigrants in this country, after all. You'll get by all right, I should think.'

I thanked him for the lift and got out of the car. He yawned and turned that into a laugh, but I reckoned the tiredness was real. 'See you Sunday, Tommy,' he said, and I dryly said, 'Sure thing, Zak.' He drove away with a smile and I went into the Merry & Co office where the earlier calm had broken up into loud frenetic activity on several telephones.

'How *could* twenty-five of our bikers all burst their tyres at once?'

'They won't reach Nuits-St Georges tonight.'

'Any suggestions for alternative hotels?'

'Where do we *find* fifty new tyres, assorted, in France? They've cut them to ribbons, they say.'

'It was sabotage. It has to be.'

'They rode over a cattle grid which had spikes.'

Nell was sitting at her desk talking on her telephone, one hand pressed to her free ear to block out the clamour.

'Why didn't the fools pick up their bikes and walk across?'

'Nobody told them. It was a new grid. Where *is* Nuits-St Georges? Can't we get a bus to go and pick up the bikes? What bus company do we use in that part of France?'

'Why isn't our French office dealing with all this?'

I sat on Nell's client chair and waited. The hubbub subsided: the crisis was sorted. Somewhere in Burgundy, the bikers would be transported to their dinners on sturdier wheels, and new tyres would be found in the morning.

Nell put her receiver down.

'You arrange cycling tours?' I said.

'Sure. And trips up Everest. Not me personally, I do mysteries. Do you need something?'

'Instructions.'

'Oh, yes. I talked to VIA. No problems.'

VIA Rail, I had discovered, was the company that operated Canada's passenger trains, which didn't mean that it owned the rails or the stations. Nothing was simple on the railways.

'VIA,' Nell said, 'are expecting you to turn up at Union Station tomorrow morning at ten to get fitted for a uniform. Here's who you ask for.' She passed me a slip of paper. 'They've got hand-picked service people going on this trip, and they'll show you what to do when you meet them at the station on Sunday morning. You'll board the train with them.'

'What time?' I asked.

'The train comes into the station soon after eleven. The chefs and crew board soon after. Passengers board at eleven-thirty, after the reception in the station itself. The train leaves at twelve. That's thirty-five minutes earlier than the regular daily train, the Canadian, which will be on our heels as far as Winnipeg.'

'And the horses will have boarded, I gather, out in a loading area.'

'Yes, at Mimico, about six miles away. That's where they do maintenance and cleaning and put the trains together. Everything will be loaded there. Food, wine, flowers, everything for the owners.'

'And the grooms?'

'No, not them. They're being shipped back to the station by bus after they've settled the horses in. And you might like to know we've another addition to the train, a cousin of our boss, name of Leslie Brown, who's going as horsemaster, to oversee the horses and the grooms and keep everything up that end in good order.'

'Which end?'

'Behind the engine. Apparently horses travel better there. No swaying.'

While she was talking, she was sorting postcards into piles: postcards with names and numbers on.

'Do you have a plan of the train?' I asked.

She glanced up briefly and didn't exactly say I was a thundering nuisance, but looked as if she thought it. Still, she shuffled through a pile of papers, pulled out a single sheet and pushed it across the desk towards me.

'This is what we've asked for, and what they say we'll get, but the people at Mimico sometimes change things,' she said.

I picked up the paper and found it was written in a column.

Engine
Generator/boiler
Baggage car
Horse car
Grooms/sleeping

	Grooms/dining/dome	
(Racegoers)	Sleeping	
"	Sleeping	
"	Sleeping	
"	Dayniter	
"	Dining	
(Owners)	Sleeping (Green)	26
"	Sleeping (Manor)	24
"	Sleeping (Mount)	16
"	Special dining	
"	Dome car (Park)	8
"	Private car	4
		78 if full

(Owners includes actors, Company
and VIA executives, chefs and service
crew, most in Green.)

'Do you have a plan of who sleeps where?' I asked.
For answer she shuffled through the same pile as
before and gave me two sheets stapled together. I
looked first, as one does, for my own name; and
found it.

She had given me a room – a roomette – that was
right next door to Filmer.

CHAPTER FIVE

I walked back to the hotel and at two o'clock local time telephoned to England, reckoning that seven o'clock Friday evening was perhaps a good time to catch Brigadier Catto relaxing in his Newmarket house after a busy week in London. I was lucky to catch him, he said, and he had news for me.

'Remember Horfitz's messenger who gave the briefcase to Filmer at Nottingham?' he asked.

'I sure do.'

'John Millington has identified him from your photographs. He is Ivor Horfitz's son, Jason. He's not bright, so they say. Not up to much more than running errands. Delivering briefcases would be just about his mark.'

'And he got that wrong, too, according to his father.'

'Well, there you are. It doesn't get us anywhere much, but that's who he is. John Millington has issued photos to all the ring inspectors, so that if they see him they'll report it. If Horfitz plans on using his son as an on-course errand boy regularly, we'll make sure he knows we're watching.'

'He'd do better to find someone else.'

'A nasty thought.' He paused briefly. 'How are you doing, your end?'

'I haven't seen Filmer yet. He's staying tomorrow night at a hotel with most of the owners' group, according to the travel company's lists. Presumably he'll be at the official lunch with the Ontario Jockey Club at Woodbine tomorrow. I'll go to the races, but probably not to the lunch. I'll see what he's doing, as best I can.' I told him about Bill Baudelaire's mother, and said, 'After we've started off on the train, if you want to get hold of me direct, leave a message with her, and I'll telephone back to you or John Millington as soon as I'm able.'

'It's a bit hit or miss,' he grumbled, repeating the number after I'd dictated it.

'She's an invalid,' I added, and laughed to myself at his reaction.

When he'd stopped spluttering, he said, 'Tor, this is impossible.'

'Well, I don't know. It's an open line of communication, after all. Better to have one than not. And Bill Baudelaire suggested it himself. He must know she's capable.'

'All right then. Better than nothing.' He didn't sound too sure, though, and who could blame him. Brigade commanders weren't accustomed to bedridden grandmothers manning field telephones. 'I'll be here at home on Sunday,' he said. 'Get through to me, will you, for last-minute gen both ways, before you board?'

'Yes, certainly.'

'You sound altogether,' he said with a touch of disapproval, 'suspiciously happy.'

'Oh! Well . . . this train looks like being good fun.'

'That's not what you're there for.'

'I'll do my best not to enjoy it.'

'Insubordination will get you a firing squad,' he said firmly, and put down his receiver forthwith.

I put my own receiver down more slowly and the bell rang again immediately.

'This is Bill Baudelaire,' my caller said in his deep-down voice. 'So you arrived in Toronto all right?'

'Yes, thank you.'

'I've got the information you asked for about Laurentide Ice. About why his owner sold a half-share.'

'Oh, good.'

'I don't know that it is, very. In fact, not good at all. Apparently Filmer was over here in Canada at the end of last week enquiring of several owners who had horses booked on the train if they would sell. One of them mentioned it to me this morning and now I've talked to the others. He offered a fair price for a half-share, they all say. Or a third-share. Any toehold, it seems. I would say he methodically worked down the list until he came to Daffodil Quentin.'

'Who?'

'The owner of Laurentide Ice.'

'Why is it bad news?' I asked, taking the question from the disillusionment in his voice.

'You'll meet her. You'll see,' he said cryptically.

'Can't you tell me?'

He sighed audibly. 'Her husband, Hal Quentin, was a good friend of Canadian racing, but he died this time last year and left his string of horses to his wife. Three of them so far have died in accidents since then, with Mrs Quentin collecting the insurance.'

'Three!' I said. 'In a year?'

'Exactly. They've all been investigated but they all seem genuine. Mrs Quentin says it's a dreadful coincidence and she is most upset.'

'She would be,' I said drily.

'Anyway, that is who has sold a half-share to Julius Filmer. What a pair! I phoned just now and asked her about the sale. She said it suited her to sell, and there was no reason not to. She says she is going to have a ball on the train.' He sounded most gloomy, himself.

'Look on the bright side,' I said. 'If she's sold a half-share she can't be planning to push Laurentide Ice off the train at high speed for the insurance.'

'That's a scurrilous statement.' He was not shocked, however. 'Will you be at Woodbine tomorrow?'

'Yes, but not at the lunch.'

'All right. If we bump into each other, of course it will be as strangers.'

'Of course,' I agreed; and we said goodbyes and disconnected.

Daffodil Quentin, I reflected, settling the receiver in its cradle, had at least not been intimidated into selling. No one on the business end of Filmer's threats could be looking forward to having a ball in his company. It did appear that in order to get himself on to the train as an owner, he had been prepared to spend actual money. He had been prepared to fly to Canada to effect the sale, and do the return to England to collect the briefcase from Horfitz at Nottingham on Tuesday, and to fly back to Canada, presumably, in time for tomorrow's races.

I wondered where he was at that moment. I wondered what he was thinking, hatching, setting in motion. It was comforting to think that he didn't know I existed.

I spent the rest of the afternoon doing some shopping and walking and taxi-riding around, getting reacquainted with one of the most visually entertaining cities in the world. I'd found it architecturally exciting six years earlier, and it seemed to me now not less but more so, with glimpses of its slender tallest-in-the-world free-standing tower with the onion bulge near its top appearing tantalizingly between angular highrises covered with black glass and gold. And they had built a whole new complex, Harbourfront, since I'd been there before, a new face turned to Lake Ontario and the world.

At six, having left my purchases at the hotel, I went back to Merry & Co's warm pale office and found many of the gang still working. Nell, at her desk, naturally on the telephone, pointed mutely to her client chair, and I sat there and waited.

Some of the murmurers were putting on coats, yawning, switching off computers, taking cans of cold drinks out of the large refrigerator and opening them with the carbonation hissing. Someone put out a light or two. The green plants looked exhausted. Friday night; all commercial passion spent. Thank God for Fridays.

'I have to come in here tomorrow,' Nell said with resignation, catching my thought. 'And why I ever said I'd have dinner with you tonight I cannot imagine.'

'You promised.'

'I must have been mad.'

I'd asked her after she'd shown me the train's sleeping arrangements (which perhaps had been my subconscious making jumps unbeknown to me), and she'd said, 'Yes, all right, I have to eat,' and that had seemed a firm enough commitment.

'Are you ready?' I asked.

'No, there are two more people I positively must talk to. Can you ... er ... wait?'

'I'm quite good at it,' I said equably.

A few more lights went out. Some of those remaining shone on Nell's fair hair, made shadows of her eyes and put hollows in her cheeks. I wondered about her, as one does. An attractive stranger; an unread book; a beginning, perhaps. But there had been other beginnings, in other cities, and I'd long outgrown the need to hurry. I might never yet have come to the conventional ending, but the present was greatly OK, and as for the future . . . we could see.

I listened without concentration to her talking to someone called Lorrimore. 'Yes, Mr Lorrimore, your flowers and your bar bottles will already be on the train when it comes into the station. . . . And the fruit, yes, that too. . . . The passengers are gathering at ten-thirty for the reception at the station. . . . Yes, we board at eleven-thirty and leave at twelve. . . . We're looking forward to meeting you too . . . goodbye, Mr Lorrimore.' She glanced over at me as she began to dial her next number, and said, 'The Lorrimores have the private car, the last car on the train. Hello, is that Vancouver racecourse . . . ?'

I listened to her discussing entry arrangements for the owners. 'Yes, we're issuing them all with the special club passes . . . and yes, the other passengers from the train will be paying for themselves individually, but we're offering them group transport. . . .' She put down the receiver eventually and sighed. 'We've been asked to fix moderate-price hotels and bus transport for so many of the racegoers that it's like duplicating the whole tour. Could you wait for just one more call . . . or two?'

We left the darkened office almost an hour later and

even then she was still checking things off in her mind and muttering vaguely about not forgetting scissors and clips to go with the bandages for Ricky. We walked not very far to a restaurant called the Fluted Point People that she'd been to before and whose menu I had prospected earlier. Not very large, it had tables crammed into every cranny, each dimly lit by a candle lantern.

'Who are the Fluted Point People,' I asked, 'in general?'

'Heaven knows,' Nell said.

The waiter, who must have been asked a thousand times, said the fluted point people had lived on this land ten thousand years ago. Let's not worry about them, he said.

Nell laughed and I thought of ten thousand years and wondered who would be living on this land ten thousand years ahead. Fluted points, it transpired, described the stone tools in use over most of the continent: would our descendants call us the knife and fork people?

'I don't honestly care,' Nell said, to those questions. 'I'm hungry right now in Toronto today.'

We did something about that in the shape of devilled smoked salmon followed by roast quail. 'I hope this is all on your expense account,' she said without anxiety as I ordered some wine, and I said, 'Yes, of course,' untruthfully and thought there was no point in having money if one didn't enjoy it. 'Hamburgers tomorrow,' I said, 'to make up for it.'

Nell nodded as if that were a normal bargain she well understood and said with a galvanic jump that she had forgotten to order a special limousine to drive the Lorrimores around at Winnipeg.

'Do it tomorrow,' I said. 'They won't run away.'

She looked at me with a worried frown of indecision, and then round the comfortable little candlelit restaurant, and then at the shining glass and silver on the table and then back to me, and the frown dissolved into a smile of self-amusement.

'All right. Tomorrow. The Lorrimores may be the icing on this cake but they've meant a lot of extra work.'

'Who are the Lorrimores?' I asked.

She looked at me blankly and answered obliquely, 'Where do you live?'

'Ah,' I said. 'If I lived here, I would know the Lorrimores?'

'You certainly wouldn't ask who they are.'

'I live in London,' I said. 'So please tell me.'

She was wearing, as so many women in business tended to, a navy suit and white blouse of such stark simplicity as to raise questions about the warmth of the soul. Women who dressed more softly, I thought inconsequentially, must feel more secure in themselves, perhaps.

'The Lorrimores,' Nell said, showing no insecurity, 'are one of the very richest families of Toronto. Of Ontario. Of Canada, in fact. They are the society magazines' staple diet. They are into banking and good works. They own mansions, endow art museums, open charity balls and entertain heads of state. There are quite a few of them, brothers, sisters and so on, and I'm told that in certain circles, if Mercer Lorrimore accepts an invitation and comes to your house, you are made for life.' She paused, smiling. 'Also he owns great racehorses, is naturally a pillar of the Ontario Jockey Club and has this private railcar which used to be borrowed regularly by campaigning politicians.' She paused again for breath. 'That's who's honouring our train – Mercer Lorrimore, the big chief of the whole clan, also Bambi, his wife, and their son Sheridan and their daughter Xanthe. What have I left out?'

I laughed. 'Do you curtsy?'

'Pretty nearly. Well, to be honest, Mercer Lorrimore sounds quite nice on the telephone but I haven't met him yet or any of the others. And he phones me himself. No secretaries.'

'So,' I said, 'if Mercer Lorrimore is on the train, it will be even more in the news from coast to coast?'

She nodded. 'He's going For the Benefit of Canadian Racing in capital letters on the Jockey Club's PR hand-out.'

'And is he eating in the dining car?' I asked.

'Don't!' She rolled her eyes in mock horror. 'He is supposed to be. They all are. But we don't know if they'll retreat into privacy. If they stay in their own car, there might just be enough room for everyone else to sit down. It's a shambles in the making though, and it was made by my boss selling extra tickets himself when he knew we were full.' She shook her head over it, but with definite indulgence. The boss, it appeared, ranked high in her liking.

'Who did he sell them to?' I asked.

'Just people. Two friends of his. And a Mr Filmer, who offered to pay double when he found there was no room. No one turns down an extra profit of that sort.' She broke open a roll with the energy of frustration. 'If only there was more room in the dining car, we could have sold at least six more tickets.'

'David ... er ... Zak was saying the forty-eight-seater was already stretching the actors' vocal cords to the limit against the noise of the wheels on the rails.'

'It's always a problem.' She considered me over the candle flame. 'Are you married?' she said.

'No. Are you?'

'Actually, no.' Her voice was faintly defensive, but her mouth was smiling. 'I invested in a relationship which didn't work out.'

'And which was some time ago?'

'Long enough for me to be over it.'

The exchange cleared the ground, I thought, and maybe set the rules. She wasn't looking for another relationship that was going nowhere. But dalliance? Have to see ...

'What are you thinking?' she asked.

'About life in general.'

She gave me a dry look of disbelief but changed the subject back to the almost as compelling matter of trains, and after a while I asked her the question I'd had vaguely in mind all day.

'Besides the special passes for the races, and so on,' I said, 'is there anything else an owner of a horse is entitled to? An owner, that is to say, of one of the horses travelling on the train?'

She was puzzled. 'How do you mean?'

'Are they entitled to any privileges that the other people in the special dining car don't have?'

'I don't think so.' Her brow wrinkled briefly. 'Only that they can visit the horse car, if that's what you mean.'

'Yes, I know about that. So there's nothing else?'

'Well, the racecourse at Winnipeg is planning a group photograph of owners only, and there's television coverage of that.' She pondered. 'They're each getting a commemorative plaque from the Jockey Club when we get back on the train at Banff after the days in the mountains.' She paused again. 'And if a horse that's actually on the train wins one of the special races, the owner gets free life membership of the clubs at all three racecourses.'

The last was a sizeable carrot to a Canadian, perhaps, but not enough on its own, surely, to attract Filmer. I sighed briefly. Another good idea down the drain. So I was left with the two basic questions: why was Filmer on the train, and why had he worked so hard to be an owner? And the answers were still I don't know and I don't know. Highly helpful.

We drank coffee, dawdling, easy together, and she said she had wanted to be a writer and had found a job with a publisher ('which real writers never do, I found out') but was very much happier with Merry & Co, arranging mysteries.

She said, 'My parents always told me practically from birth that I'd be a writer, that it ran in the family, and I grew up expecting it, but they were wrong, though I tried for a long time, and then I was also living with this man who sort of bullied me to write. But, you know, it was such a *relief* the day I said to myself, some time after we'd parted and I'd dried my eyes, that I was not really a writer and never would be and I'd much rather do something else. And suddenly I was liberated and happier than I could remember. It seems so stupid, looking back, that it took me so long to know myself. I was in a way brainwashed into writing, and I thought I wanted it myself, but I wasn't good enough when it came to the point, and it was such hard work, and I was depressed so much of the time.' She half laughed. 'You must think I'm crazy.'

'Of course not. What did you write?'

'I was writing for a women's weekly magazine for a while, going to interview people and writing up their lives, and making up lives altogether sometimes if I couldn't find anyone interesting or lurid enough that week. Don't let's talk about it. It was awful.'

'I'm glad you escaped.'

'Yes, so am I,' she said with feeling. 'I look different, I feel different, and I'm much healthier. I was always getting colds and flu and feeling ill, and now I don't.' Her eyes sparkled in the light, proving her right. 'And you,' she said, 'you're the same. Light-hearted. It shows all over you.'

'Does it, indeed?'

'Am I right?'

'On the button, I suppose.'

And we were lucky, I thought soberly, paying the bill. Light-heartedness was a treasure in a world too full of sorrows, a treasure little regarded and widely forfeited to aggression, greed and horrendous tribal rituals. I wondered if the Fluted Point People had been light-hearted ten thousand years ago. But probably not.

Nell and I walked back to where she had parked her car near the office: she lived twenty minutes' drive away, she said, in a very small apartment by the lake.

To say good night we kissed cheeks and she thanked me for the evening, saying cheerfully that she would see me on Sunday if she didn't sink without trace under all the things she still had to do on the next day, Saturday. I watched her tail lights recede until she turned a corner, then I walked back to the hotel, slept an untroubled night, and presented myself next morning at ten sharp in the Public Affairs office, at Union Station.

The Public Affairs officer, a formidably efficient lady, had gathered from Nell that I was one of the actors, as they had helped with actors before, and I didn't change that understanding. She wheeled me back into the cavernous Great Hall of the station (which she briskly said was 250 feet long, 84 feet wide and had a tiled arched ceiling 88 feet above the floor) and led me through a heavy door into an undecorated downstairs duplication of the grandeur upstairs, a seemingly endless basic domain where the food and laundry and odd jobs of the trains got seen to. There was a mini power station also, and painting and carpentering going on all over the place.

'This way,' she said, clattering ahead on snapping heels. 'Here is the uniform centre. They'll see to you.' She pushed open a door to let me through, said briefly, 'Here's the actor,' to the staff inside, and with a nod abandoned me to fate.

The staff inside were good-natured and equally efficient. One was working a sewing machine, another a computer, and a third asked me what collar size I took.

There were shelves all round the room bearing hundreds of folded shirts of fine light grey and white vertical stripes, with striped collars, long striped sleeves and buttoned cuffs. 'The cuffs must remain buttoned at all times unless you are washing dishes.'

Catch me, I thought mildly, washing dishes.

There were two racks of the harvest gold waistcoats on hangers. 'All the buttons must be fastened at all times.'

DICK FRANCIS

There were row on row of mid-grey trousers and mid-grey jackets tidily hung, and boxes galore of grey, yellow and maroon striped ties.

My helper was careful that everything he gave me should fit perfectly. 'VIA Rail staff at all times are well turned out and spotlessly clean. We give everyone tips on how to care for the clothes.'

He gave me a grey jacket, two pairs of grey trousers, five shirts, two waistcoats (which he called vests), two ties and a grey raincoat to go over all, and as he passed each garment as suitable he called out the size to the man with the computer. 'We know the sizes of every VIA employee right across Canada.'

I looked at myself in the glass in my shirtsleeves and yellow waistcoat, and the waiter Tommy looked back. I smiled at my reflection. Tommy looked altogether too pleased with himself, I thought.

'Comfortable?' my helper asked.

'Very.'

'Don't vary the uniform at all,' he said. 'Any variation would mark you out straight away as an actor.'

'Thank you.'

'This uniform,' he said, 'trousers, shirt, tie and vest, is worn by all male service attendants and assistant service attendants when on duty. That's to say, the sleeping-car attendants and the dining-car staff, except that sometimes they wear aprons in the dining car.'

'Thank you,' I said again.

'The chief service attendant, who is in charge of the

dining car, wears a grey suit, not a vest or an apron. That's how you'll know him.'

'Right.'

He smiled. 'They'll teach you what to do. Now, we'll lend you a locker for these clothes until Sunday morning. Collect the clothes and put them on in the changing room here before boarding, and take your own clothes with you on to the train. When you've finished with the VIA uniform, please see that we get it back.'

'Right,' I said again.

When I'd put my own clothes on once more, he took me along a few passages into a room with ultra-narrow lockers into which Tommy's clothes barely slotted. He locked the metal door, gave me the key, showed me the way back into the Great Hall and smiled briefly.

'Good luck,' he said. 'Don't spill anything.'

'Thank you,' I said, 'very much.'

I went back to the hotel and had them arrange a car with a driver to take me to Woodbine, wait through the afternoon and bring me back. No trouble at all, they said, so as it was a nice bright autumn day with no forecast of rain I curled my hair and put on some sunglasses and a Scandinavian patterned sweater to merge into the crowd at the races.

It actually isn't easy to remember a stranger's face after a fleeting meeting unless one has a special reason for doing so, or unless there is something wholly distinctive about it, and I was reasonably certain no one going on the train would know me again even if I inadvertently stood next to them on the stands. I had spectacular proof of this, in fact, almost as soon as I'd paid my way into the paddock, because Bill Baudelaire was standing nearby, watching the throng coming in, and his eyes paused on me for a brief second and slid away. With his carroty hair and the acne scars, I thought, *he* would have trouble getting lost in a crowd.

I walked over to him and said, 'Could you tell me the time sir, please?'

He glanced at his watch but hardly at me and said, 'One twenty-five,' in his gravelly voice, and looked over my shoulder towards the gate.

'Thank you,' I said. 'I'm Tor Kelsey.'

His gaze sharpened abruptly on my face and he almost laughed.

'When Val told me about this I scarcely believed him.'

'Is Filmer here?' I asked.

'Yes. He arrived for the lunch.'

'OK,' I said. 'Thanks again.' I nodded and walked on past him and bought a racecard, and when in a moment or two I looked back, he had gone.

The racecourse was packed with people and there were banners everywhere announcing that this was the opening event of The Great Transcontinental Mystery Race Train's journey. Race Train Day, they economically said. There was a splendid colour photograph of a train crossing a prairie on the racecard's cover. There were stalls selling red and white Race Train T-shirts, with a horse face to face with a locomotive across the chest. There were Race Train flags and scarves and baseball caps; and a scatter of young ladies with Support Canadian Racing sashes across their bosoms were handing out information leaflets. The PR firm, I thought with amusement, were leaving no one in any doubt.

I didn't see Filmer until just before the Race Train's special race, which had been named without subtlety The Jockey Club Race Train Stakes at Woodbine. I'd spent some of the afternoon reading the information in the racecard about the owners and their horses and had seen that whereas all the owners were on the train's passenger list, none of the horses were. We would be taking fresh animals to Winnipeg and Vancouver.

Filmer wasn't on the racecard as an owner, but Mrs Daffodil Quentin was, and when she came down to see the saddling of her runner, Filmer was with her, assiduous and smiling.

Daffodil Quentin had a big puffball hair arrangement of blonde curls above a middle-aged face with intense shiny red lipstick. She wore a black dress with a striped chinchilla coat over it: too much fur, I briefly thought, for the warmth of the afternoon sun.

There was hardly time to identify all the other owners as the pre-race formalities were over much more quickly than in England, but I did particularly look for and sort out Mercer Lorrimore.

Mercer Lorrimore, darling of the glossy mags, was running two horses in the race, giving it his loyal support. He was a man of average height, average build, average weight, and was distinguishable chiefly because of his well-cut, well-brushed full head of white hair. His expression looked reasonable and pleasant, and he was being nice to his trainer.

Beside him was a thin well-groomed woman whom I supposed to be his wife, Bambi: and in attendance were a supercilious-looking young man and a sulking teenage girl. Son and daughter, Sheridan and Xanthe, no doubt.

The jockeys were thrown up like rainbow thistle-down on to the tiny saddles and let their skinny bodies move to the fluid rhythm of the walking thoroughbreds. Out on the track with the horses' gait breaking into a trot or canter they would be more comfortable standing up in the stirrups to let the bumpier rhythms flow beneath them, but on the way out from the parade ring they swayed languorously like a camel train. I loved to watch them: never grew tired of it. I loved the big beautiful animals with their tiny brains and their over-whelming instincts and I'd always, all over the world, felt at home tending them, riding them and watching them wake up and perform.

The Lorrimore colours were truly Canadian, bright red and white like the maple leaf flag. Daffodil Quentin's colours weren't daffodil yellow but pale blue and dark green, a lot more subdued than the lady.

She and Filmer and all the other owners disappeared upstairs behind glass to watch the race, and I went down towards the track to wait and watch from near where the lucky owner would come down to greet his winner.

There were fourteen runners for the mile-and-a-half race and I knew nothing about the form of any of them except for the information on the racecard. In England I knew the current scene like a magnified city map, knew the thoroughfares, the back alleys, the small turnings. Knew who people knew, who they would turn to and turn away from, who they lusted after. In Canada, I was without radar and felt blind.

The Race Train Stakes at Woodbine, turning out to be hot enough in the homestretch to delight the Ontario Jockey Club's heart, was greeted with roars and screams of encouragement from the stands. Lorrimore's scarlet-and-white favourite was beaten in the last stride by a streak in pale blue and dark green and a good many of the cheers turned to groans.

Daffodil Quentin came down and passed close by me in clouds of chinchilla, excitement and a musky scent. She preened coquettishly, receiving compliments and the trophy, and Filmer, ever at her side, gallantly kissed her hand.

A let-off murderer, I thought, kissing an unproven

insurance swindler. How very nice. Television cameras whirred and flash photographers outdid the sun.

I caught sight of Bill Baudelaire scowling, and I knew what John Millington would have said.

It was enough to make you sick.

CHAPTER SIX

On Saturday evening and early Sunday morning I packed two bags, the new suitcase from England and a softer holdall bought in Toronto.

Into the first I put the rich young owner's suit, cashmere pullover and showy shirts and into the second the new younger-looking clothes for off-duty Tommy, jeans, sweatshirts, woolly hat and trainers. I packed the Scandinavian jersey I'd worn at Woodbine into the suitcase just in case it jogged anyone's memory, and got dressed in dark trousers, open-necked shirt and a short zipped navy jacket with lighter blue bands round waist and wrists.

The rich young owner's expensive brown shoes went away. Tommy, following instructions from the uniform department, had shiny new black ones, with black socks.

Into Tommy's holdall went the binoculars-camera and the hair curler (one never knew), and I had the cigarette lighter-camera as always in my pocket. Tommy also had the rich young owner's razor and toothbrush, along with his underclothes, pyjamas and stock of fresh films. The suitcase, which held my passport, had a Merry & Co label on it addressed to the Vancouver Four Seasons Hotel; the holdall had no identification at all.

With everything ready, I telephoned Brigadier Catto in England and told him about Daffodil Quentin and the touching little scene in the winners' circle.

'Damn!' he said. 'Why does that sort of thing always happen? Absolutely the wrong person winning.'

'The general public didn't seem to mind. The horse was third favourite, quite well backed. Daffodil Quentin seems to be acceptable to the other owners, who of course probably don't know about her three dead horses. They're bound to take to Filmer too, you know how civilized he can seem, and I don't suppose news of the trial got much attention here since it collapsed almost before it began. Anyway, Filmer and Daffodil left the races together in what looked like her own car, with a chauffeur.'

'Pity you couldn't follow them.'

'Well, I did actually, in a hired car. They went to the hotel, where Filmer and the other owners from the train are staying, and they went into the bar for a drink. After that, Daffodil left in her Rolls and Filmer went upstairs. Nothing of note. He looked relaxed.'

The Brigadier said, 'You're sure they didn't spot you at the hotel?'

'Quite sure. The entrance hall of the hotel was as

big as a railway station itself. There were dozens of people sitting around waiting for other people. It was easy.'

It had even been easy following them from the race-course, as when I went out to where my driver had parked his car I had a clear view from a distance of Daffodil at the exit gate being spooned into a royal blue Rolls-Royce by Filmer and her chauffeur. My driver, with raised eyebrows but without spoken question, agreed to keep the Rolls in sight for as long as possible, which he did without trouble all the way back to the city. At the hotel I paid him in cash with a bonus and sent him on his way, and was in time to see Filmer's back view receding into a dark-looking bar as I walked into the big central hall lobby.

It had been an exercise without much in the way of results, but then many of my days were like that, and it was only by knowing the normal that the abnormal, when it happened, could be spotted.

'Would you mind telling me,' I said diffidently to the Brigadier, 'whether Filmer has made a positive threat to disrupt this train?'

There was a silence, then, 'Why do you ask?'

'Something Bill Baudelaire said.'

After a pause he answered, 'Filmer was seething with anger. He said the world's racing authorities could persecute him all they liked but he would find a spanner to throw in their works, and they'd regret it.'

'When did he say that?' I asked. 'And why . . . and who to?'

'Well . . . er . . .' He hesitated and sighed. 'Things go wrong, you know. After the acquittal, the Disciplinary Committee of the Jockey Club called Filmer to Portman Square to warn him as to his future behaviour, and Filmer said they couldn't touch him, and was generally unbearably arrogant. As a result, one of the committee lost his temper and told Filmer he was the scum of the earth and no one in racing would sleep well until he was warned off, which was the number one priority of the world's racing authorities.'

'That's a bit of an exaggeration,' I commented, sighing in my turn. 'I suppose you were there?'

'Yes. You could have cut the fury on both sides with a knife. Very vicious, all of it.'

'So,' I said regretfully, 'Filmer might indeed see the train as a target.'

'He might.'

The trouble and expense he had gone to to get himself on board looked increasingly ominous, I thought.

'There's one other thing you might care to know,' the Brigadier said. 'John saw Ivor Horfitz's son Jason hanging around outside the weighing-room at Newmarket yesterday and had a word with him.'

When Millington had a word with people they could take days to recover. In his own way, he could be as frightening as Derry Welfram or Filmer himself.

112

'What happened?' I asked.

'John spoke to him about the inadvisability of running errands on racecourses for his warned-off father, and said that if Jason had any information, he should pass it on to him, John Millington. And apparently Jason Horfitz then said he wouldn't be passing on the information he had to anybody else as he didn't want to end up in a ditch.'

'*What?*' I said.

'John Millington pounced on that but he couldn't get another word out of the wretched Jason. He turned to jelly and literally ran away, John says.'

'Does Jason really know,' I said slowly, 'what Paul Shacklebury knew? Did he *tell* Paul Shacklebury whatever it was he knew? Or was it just a figure of speech?'

'God knows. John's working on it.'

'Did he ask Jason what was in the briefcase?'

'Yes, he did, but Jason either didn't know or was too frightened to speak. John says he was terrified that we even knew about the briefcase. He couldn't believe we knew.'

'I wonder if he'll tell his father.'

'Not if he has any sense.'

He hadn't any sense, I thought, but he did have fear, which was almost as good a life preserver.

'If I hear anything more,' the Brigadier said, 'I'll leave a message with . . .' his voice still disapproved ' . . . with Mrs Baudelaire senior. Apart from that . . . good luck.'

I thanked him and hung up, and with considerable contentment took my two bags in a taxi to Union Station.

The train crew were already collecting in the locker room when I made my way there and introduced myself as Tommy, the actor.

They smiled and were generous. They always enjoyed the mysteries, they said, and had worked with an actor among them before. It would all go well, I would see.

The head waiter, head steward, chief service attendant, whatever one called him, was a neat small Frenchman named Emil. Late thirties, perhaps, I thought, with dark bright eyes.

'Do you speak French?' he asked first, shaking my hand. 'All VIA employees have to be able to speak French. It is a rule.'

'I do a bit,' I said.

'That is good. The last actor, he couldn't. This time the chef is from Montreal, and in the kitchen we may speak French.'

I nodded and didn't tell him that, apart from my school days, my working French had been learned in stables, not kitchens, and was likely to be rusty in any case. But I'd half-learned several languages on my travels, and somehow they each floated familiarly back at the first step on to the matching soil. Everything in bilingual Canada was written in both English and French and I realized that since my arrival I'd been reading the French quite easily.

'Have you ever worked in a restaurant?' Emil asked.

'No, I haven't.'

He shrugged good-humouredly. 'I will show you how to set the places, and to begin with, this morning, perhaps you will serve only water. When you pour anything, when the train is moving, you pour in small amounts at a time, and you keep the cup or glass close to you. Do you understand? It is always necessary to control, to use small movements.'

'I understand,' I said, and indeed I did.

He put a copy of the timetable into my hands and said, 'You will need to know where we stop. The passengers always ask.'

'OK. Thanks.'

He nodded with good humour.

I changed into Tommy's uniform and met some others of the crew: Oliver, who was a waiter in the special dining car, like myself, and several of the sleeping-car attendants, one to each car the whole length of the train. There was a smiling Chinese gentleman who cooked in the small forward dining car where the grooms, among others, would be eating, and an unsmiling Canadian who would be cooking in the main central dining car for the bulk of the racegoers and the crew themselves. The French chef from Montreal was not there, I soon discovered, because he was a she, and could only be found in the women's changing room.

Everyone put on the whole uniform including the grey raincoat on top, and I put on my raincoat also; I packed Tommy's spare garments and my own clothes into the holdall, and was ready.

Nell had said she would meet me this Sunday morning in the coffee shop in the Great Hall, and had told me that the crews often went there to wait for train time. Accordingly, accompanied by Emil and a few of the others, I carried my bags to the coffee shop where everyone immediately ordered huge carrot cakes, the speciality of the house, as if they were in fear of famine.

Nell wasn't there, but Zak and some of the other actors were, sitting four to a table, drinking pale-looking orange juice and not eating carrot cake because of the calories.

Zak said Nell was along with the passengers in the reception area, and that he wanted to go and see how things were shaping.

'She said something about you checking a suitcase through to Vancouver in the baggage car,' he added, standing up.

'Yes, this one.'

'Right. She said to tell you to bring it along to where the passengers are. I'll show you.'

I nodded, told Emil I'd be back, and followed Zak down the Great Hall and round a corner or two and came to a buzzing gathering of people in an area like an airport departure lounge.

An enormous banner across a latticed screen left no one in any doubt. Stretching for a good twelve feet it read in red on white THE GREAT TRANSCONTI-NENTAL MYSTERY RACE TRAIN, and in blue letters a good deal smaller underneath, THE ONTARIO JOCKEY CLUB, MERRY & CO AND VIA RAIL PRESENT A CELEBRATION OF CANADIAN RACING.

The forty or so passengers already gathered in happy anticipation wore name badges and carnations and held glasses of orange juice convivially.

'There was supposed to be champagne in the orange juice,' Zak said drily. 'There isn't. Something to do with the Sunday drink law.' He searched the throng with his eyes from where we stood a good twenty paces away out in the station. 'There's Ben doing his stuff, see? Asking Raoul to lend him money.'

I could indeed see. It looked incredibly real. People standing around them were looking shocked and embarrassed.

Zak was nodding his mop of curls beside me and had begun snapping his fingers rather fast. I could sense the energy starting to flow in him now that this fiction was coming alive, and I could see that he had used make-up on himself; not greasepaint or anything heavy, more a matter of darkening and thickening his eye-brows and darkening his mouth, emphasizing rather

117

than disguising. An actor in the wings, I thought, gathering up his power.

I spotted Mavis and Walter Bricknell being fussy and anxious as intended, and saw and heard Angelica asking if anyone had seen Steve.

'Who's Steve?' I asked Zak. 'I forget.'

'Her lover. He misses the train.'

Pierre and Donna began to have their row which made a different bunch of passengers uncomfortable. Zak laughed. 'Good,' he said, 'that's great.'

Giles-the-murderer, who had been in the coffee shop, strolled along into the mêlée and started being frightfully nice to old ladies. Zak snapped his fingers even faster and started humming.

The crowd parted and shifted a little and through the gap I saw Julius Apollo Filmer, another murderer, being frightfully nice to a not-so-old lady, Daffodil Quentin.

I took a deep breath, almost of awe, almost on a tremble. Now that it was really beginning, now that I was going to be near him, I felt as strung up and as energized as Zak, and no doubt suffered the same compelling anxiety that things shouldn't go wrong.

Daffodil was playfully patting Filmer's hand.

Yuk, I thought.

Ben the actor appeared beside them and started his piece, and I saw Filmer turn a bland face towards him and watched his mouth shape the unmistakable words, 'Go away.'

Ben backed off. Very wise, I thought. The crowd

came together again and hid Filmer and his flower and I felt the tension in my muscles subside, and realized I hadn't known I had tensed them. Have to watch that, I thought.

The Lorrimores had arrived, each wearing yesterday's expression: pleasant, aloof, supercilious, sulky. Mercer was entering into the spirit of things, Bambi also but more coolly. Sheridan looked as if he thought he was slumming. The young daughter, Xanthe, could have been quite pretty if she'd smiled.

James Winterbourne, actor, had discarded his red felt trilby and had shaved off the stubble and was drifting around being welcoming in his role as a member of the Jockey Club. And the real Jockey Club was there, I saw, in the person of Bill Baudelaire, who was known to one or two of the owners with whom he was chatting. I wondered how much he would fret if he didn't see me among the passengers, and I hoped not much.

Nell emerged from the noise of the crowd and came across towards us, a clipboard clasped to her chest, her eyes shining. She wore another severe suit, grey this time over a white blouse, but perhaps in honour of the occasion had added a long twisted rope of coral, pearls and crystal.

'It's all happening,' she said. 'I can hardly believe it, after all these months. I won't kiss you both, I'm not supposed to know you yet, but consider yourselves kissed. It's all going very well. Pierre and Donna are having a humdinger of a row. How does she manage to cry whenever she wants to? Is that the suitcase for Vancouver? Put it over there with those others which are being checked right through. Mercer Lorrimore is sweet, I'm so relieved. We haven't had any disasters yet, but there must be one on the way. I'm as high as a kite and there's no champagne in the orange juice.'

She stopped for breath and a laugh and I said, 'Nell, if Bill Baudelaire asks you if I'm here, just say yes, don't say where.'

She was puzzled but too short of time to argue. 'Well . . . OK.'

'Thanks.'

She nodded and turned to go and take care of the passengers, and the James Winterbourne character came out to meet her and also to talk to Zak.

'It's too much,' he complained, 'the real goddam Chairman of the Ontario Jockey Club has turned up to do the "bon voyage" bit himself. I'm out of a job.'

'We did ask him first,' Nell said. 'We suggested it right at the beginning, before it all grew so big. He's obviously decided he should be here after all.'

'Yes, but . . . what about my fee?'

'You'll get it,' Zak said resignedly. 'Just go back and jolly things along and tell everyone what a great trip they're going to have.'

'I've been doing that,' he grumbled, but returned obediently to his task.

'As a matter of fact,' Nell said, her brow wrinkling, 'I suppose I did get a message days ago to say the

Chairman was coming, but I didn't know it meant him. I didn't know who it meant. It was a message left for me while I was out. "The Colonel is coming." I didn't know any colonels. Is the Chairman a colonel?'

'Yes,' I said.

'Oh well, no harm done. I'd better go and see if he needs anything.' She hurried off, unperturbed.

Zak sighed. 'I could have saved myself that fee.'

'How do you mean?'

'Oh, Merry & Co pay me a lump sum to stage the mystery. I engage the actors and pay them, and whatever is left at the end is mine. Not much, sometimes.'

Voices were suddenly raised over in the crowd and people began scattering to the edges of the area, clearing the centre and falling silent. Zak and I instinctively went nearer, he in front, I in his shadow.

On the floor, sprawling, lay the actor Raoul, with Donna and Pierre bending down to help him up. Raoul dabbed at his nose with the back of his hand, and everyone could see the resulting scarlet streak.

Mavis Bricknell began saying loudly and indignantly, 'He hit him. He hit him. That young man hit our trainer in the face. He had no right to knock him down.'

She was pointing at Sheridan Lorrimore, who had turned his back on the scene.

I glanced at Zak for enlightenment.

'That,' he said blankly, 'wasn't in the script.'

*

121

Nell smoothed it over.

Sheridan Lorrimore could be heard saying furiously and fortissimo to his father, 'How the hell could I know they were acting? The fellow was being a bore. I just bopped him one. He deserved it. The girl was crying. And he was crowding me, pushing against me. I didn't like it.'

His father murmured something.

'Apologize?' Sheridan said in a high voice. 'Apol – oh, all right. I apologize. Will that do?'

Mercer drew him away to a corner, and slowly, haltingly, the general good humour resurfaced. Ironic compliments were paid to Pierre, Donna and Raoul for the potency and effect of their acting and Raoul played for sympathy and looked nobly forgiving, holding a handkerchief to his nose and peering at it for blood, of which there seemed to be not much.

Zak cursed and said that Pierre had in fact been going to knock Raoul to the ground at a slightly later time, and now that would have to be changed. I left him to his problems because it was coming up to the time when Emil had said the crew should board the train, and I was due back in the coffee shop.

The carrot cakes had been reduced to crumbs and the coffee cups were empty. The bussed consignment of grooms had arrived and were sitting in a group wearing Race Train T-shirts above their jeans. Emil looked at his watch and another crew member arrived and said the computer in the crew's room downstairs was showing that the special train had just pulled into the station, Gate 6, Track 7, as expected.

'*Bon*,' Emil said, smiling. 'Then, Tommy, your duties begin.'

Everyone picked up their travelling bags and in a straggle more than a group walked back towards the passengers' assembly area. As we approached we could hear the real Chairman of the Ontario Jockey Club welcoming everyone to the adventure and we could see Zak and the other actors waiting for him to finish so that they could get on with the mystery.

Jimmy the actor was dressed in a maroon VIA Rail station uniform, Zak was intent, and Ricky, due on in gory glory at any moment, was checking in a small handmirror that 'blood' was cascading satisfactorily from a gash on his head.

Zak flashed a glance at the crew, saw me and gave me a thumbs-up sign. The Chairman wound up to applause. Zak tapped Ricky, who had put the mirror in his pocket, and Ricky went into the 'I've been attacked' routine most convincingly.

Emil, the crew and I wasted no time watching. We went on past and came to Gate 6, which was basically a staircase leading to ground level, where the rails were. Even though it was high morning, the light was dim and artificial outside as acres of arched roof far above kept out the Canadian weather.

The great train was standing there, faintly hissing, silver, immensely heavy, stretching away in both directions for as far as one could see in the gloom. In the Merry & Co office, I'd learned that each carriage (built of strong unpainted corrugated aluminium with the corrugations lying horizontally) was eighty-five feet long; and there were fifteen carriages in all, counting the horses, the baggage and the Lorrimores. With the engines as well, this train covered more than a quarter of a mile standing still.

Two furlongs, I thought frivolously, to put it suitably. Three times round the train more than equalled the Derby.

There was another long banner, duplication of the one in the station, fastened to the side of the train, telling all the passengers what they were going on, if they were still in any doubt. The crew divided to right and left according to where their jobs were and, following Emil, I found myself climbing up not into the dining car but into one of the sleeping cars.

Emil briefly consulted a notebook, stowed his travel bag on a rack in a small bedroom and directed me to put my bag in the one next door. He said I should remove my raincoat and my jacket and hang them on the hangers provided. That done, he closed both doors and we descended again to the ground.

'It's easier to walk along outside while we are in the station,' he explained. He was ever precise. We walked along beside the wheels until the end of the train was in sight and finally walked past the dining car and at the end of it swung upwards through its rear door into the scene of operations.

The special dining car lived up to its name with a blue and red carpet, big blue padded leather chairs, polished wood gleaming in the lights and glass panels engraved with birds. There were windows all down both sides with blue patterned curtains at intervals and green plants lodged above, behind pelmets. Ten feet wide, the car was long enough to accommodate six oblong tables down each side of a wide aisle with four chairs at each: forty-eight seats, as promised. All quiet, all empty. All waiting.

'Come,' Emil said, leading the way forward through the splendour, 'I show you the kitchen.'

The long, silvery, all-metal kitchen was already occupied by two figures dressed in white trousers and jackets topped by high white paper hats: the diminutive lady chef from Montreal and a tall willowy young man who introduced himself as Angus, the special chef employed by the outside firm of top-class caterers who were providing for this journey the sort of food not usually served on trains.

It seemed to my amused eyes that the two chefs were in chilly unfriendliness, marking out their territories, each, in the normal course of events, being accustomed to being the boss.

Emil, who must have picked up the same signals, spoke with a true leader's decisiveness. 'In this kitchen this week,' he said to me, 'Angus is to command.

Simone will assist.' Angus looked relieved, Simone resentful. 'This is because,' Emil said, as if it clinched matters, which it did, 'Angus and his company have designed *le menu* and provided the food.'

The matter, everyone could see, was closed. Emil explained to me that on this trip the linen, cutlery and glasses had been provided by the caterers, and without more ado he showed me first, where to find everything and second, how to set a table.

He watched me do the second table in imitation of his manner. 'You learn fast,' he said approvingly. 'If you practise, they will not tell you are not a waiter.'

I practised on about half of the remaining tables while the two other dining-room stewards, the real regular service attendants, Oliver and Cathy, set the rest. They put things right with a smile when I got them wrong, and I fell into their ways and rhythm of working as well as I could. Emil surveyed the finished dining room with a critical eye and said that after a week I would probably be able to fold a napkin tidily. They all smiled: it seemed that my napkins were already OK, and I felt quite ridiculously pleased, and also reassured.

Outside the windows, the red hat of a porter trundling luggage went by, with, in its wake, the Lorrimores.

'They're boarding,' Emil said. 'When the train departs, our passengers will all come here for the champagne.' He bustled about with champagne flutes and ice and showed me how to fold a napkin round the neck of a bottle and how to pour without drips. He seemed to have forgotten about only letting me loose on water.

There were voices outside as the train came alive. I put my head out of the rear door of the dining car and, looking forward, saw all the passengers climbing upwards into the sleeping cars, with porters following after with their bags. Several people were embarking also into the car behind the dining car, into the car which comprised three bedrooms, a bar, a large lounge area and an upstairs glass-domed observation deck, the whole lot known, I'd discovered, as the dome car.

Forward by the gate through which the passengers were crowding, Nell was doing her stuff with bandages on the convincing bloodiness of Ricky. The little scene concluded, she walked aft, looking inward through the windows, searching for someone, who in fact turned out to be me.

'I wanted to tell you,' she said, 'the Conductor – he's like the captain of a ship – knows that you're our security guard, sort of, and he's agreed to help you with anything you want, and to let you go everywhere in the train without question, including the engines, as long as the two engineers – they're the train-drivers – permit it, which he says they will once he's talked to them. Say you are Tommy, when you see him.'

I gazed at her with admiration. 'You're marvellous,' I said.

'Yes, aren't I?' She smiled. 'Bill Baudelaire did ask about you. I said you were here and you'd boarded early. He seemed satisfied. Now I've got to sort out all the people who persist in putting themselves into the wrong bedrooms...' She had gone before she'd finished the sentence, climbing into the sleeping car forward of the kitchen and vanishing from view.

Filmer's bedroom was in that car.

It had been easy to get myself moved away from sleeping next door to him: it had happened naturally with my demotion to crew. However much I might want to keep tabs on him, bumping into him several times a day in the corridor hardly seemed the best route to anonymity.

People started coming into the dining room and sitting at the tables regardless of the fact that we were still in the station.

'Where do we sit?' a pleasant-faced woman asked Emil, and he said, 'Anywhere, madam.' The man with her demanded a double Scotch on the rocks and Emil told him that alcohol was available only after departure. Emil was courteous and helpful. I listened, and I learned.

Mercer Lorrimore came through into the dining car followed by his wife, who looked displeased.

'Where do we sit?' Lorrimore said to me, and I answered, 'Anywhere, sir,' in best Emil fashion, which drew a fast appreciative grin from Emil himself.

Mercer and Bambi chose a centrally located table and were soon joined by their less-than-happy offspring, Sheridan audibly saying, 'I don't see why we have to sit in here when we have our own private car.'

Both mother and daughter looked as if they agreed with him but Mercer, smiling round clenched molars, said with surprising bitterness, 'You will do what I ask or accept the consequences.' And Sheridan looked furious but also afraid.

They had spoken as if I weren't there, which in a way I wasn't, as other passengers were moving round me, all asking the same questions. 'Anywhere, madam. Anywhere, sir,' I said, and 'I'm afraid we can't serve alcohol before departure.'

Departure came from one instant to the next, without any whistles blowing, horns sounding or general ballyhoo. One moment we were stationary, the next sliding forward smoothly, the transition from rest to motion of a quarter of a mile of metal achieved as if on silk.

We emerged from the shadow of the station into the bright light of noon, and Daffodil Quentin under her sunburst of curls made an entrance from the dome car end, looking about her as if accustomed to people leaping up to help.

'Where do we sit?' she asked, not quite looking at me, and I said, 'Anywhere, madam. Wherever you like.'

She found two seats free not far from the Lorrimores and, putting herself on one chair and her handbag on the other, said with *bonhomie* to the elderly couple already occupying the table, 'I'm Daffodil Quentin.

Isn't this fun?' They agreed with her warmly. They knew who she was: she was yesterday's winner. They started talking with animation, like almost everyone else in the car. There was no cool period here of waiting for the ice to break. Any ice left after the previous day's racing had been broken conclusively in the scenes out in the station, and the party had already gelled and was in full swing.

Emil beckoned me towards the kitchen end, and I went up there into the small lobby with a serving counter, a space that made a needed gap between the hot glittering galley and the actual dining area. The lobby led on the left to the kitchen and on the right to the corridor to the rest of the train, along which desultory passengers were appearing, swaying gently now to the movement of gathering speed.

Behind the counter, Emil was opening bottles of Pol Roger. Oliver and Cathy were still taking glasses from a cardboard container and arranging them on small trays.

'Would you mind polishing some of these smeary glasses?' Emil said to me, pointing at a trayful. 'It would be of great help.'

'Just tell me,' I said.

'Polish them,' he said.

'That's better.'

They all laughed. I picked up a cloth and began polishing the tall flutes, and Filmer emerged from the corridor and crossed into the dining room without glancing our way.

I watched him walk towards Daffodil, who was waving to him vigorously, and take the place saved by her handbag. He had his back to me, for which I was grateful. Prepared for the closeness of him, I was still unprepared, still missing a breath. It wouldn't do, I thought. It was time for a bit of bottle, not for knocking knees.

Every seat in the dining car filled up and still people were coming. Nell, arriving, took it in her stride. 'Bound to happen. All the actors are here. Give everyone champagne.' She went on down the car, clipboard hugged to her chest, answering questions, nodding and smiling, keeping the class in order.

Emil gave me a tray of glasses. 'Put four on each table. Oliver will follow you to fill them. Start at the far end and work back.'

'OK.'

Carrying a tray of glasses would have been easier if the floor had been stable but I made it to the far end with only a lurch or two and delivered the goods as required. Three or four people without seats were standing at the far dome car end, including the actress Angelica. I offered them all glasses as well, and Angelica took one and went on bellyaching to all around her about how Steve had let her down and she should never have trusted the louse, and it was a tribute to her acting that there was a distinct drawing aside of skirts in the pursed mouths of those around her who were fed up with hearing about it.

Oliver, on my heels, was delivering them solace in Pol Roger's golden bubbles.

I came with acute awareness to the table where Filmer was sitting with Daffodil and, careful not to look directly at either of them, put my last four glasses in a row on the tablecloth.

At once Filmer said, 'Where have I seen you before?'

CHAPTER SEVEN

About fifty conclusions dashed through my head, all of them disastrous. I had been so sure he wouldn't know me. Stupid, arrogant mistake.

'I expect it was when we were over in Europe and went to the Derby Eve dinner in London,' the elderly woman said. 'We sat at the head table . . . We were guests of dear Ezra Gideon, poor man.'

I moved away, sending wordless prayers of thankfulness to anyone out there listening. Filmer hadn't even glanced at me, still less had known me. His head, when I'd finally looked at him, was turned away from me towards his companions, as was Daffodil's also.

Filmer's own thoughts must anyway have been thrown in a tangle. He was himself directly responsible for Gideon's suicide, and now he found himself sitting with Gideon's friends. Whether or not he felt an ounce of embarrassment (probably not), it had to be enough to make him unaware of waiters.

I fetched more glasses and dealt some of them to the Lorrimores who were an oasis of silence in the chattering mob and paid me absolutely no attention: and from then on I felt I had indeed chosen the right role and could sustain it indefinitely.

When everyone was served, Zak the investigator appeared like a gale-force wind and moved the mystery along through Scene Two, disclosing the details of the attempted kidnap of one of the horses and leaving a tantalizing question mark in the shape of *which one*? To the amusement of the audience, he quizzed several of the real passenger owners: 'Which is your horse, sir? Did you say Upper Gumtree?' He consulted a list. 'Ah yes. You must be Harvey Unwin from Australia? Do you have any reason to believe that your horse might be the target of international intrigue?'

It was skilfully and entertainingly acted. Mercer Lorrimore in his turn and with a smile said his horse was called Voting Right, and no, he'd had no advance notice of any attack. Bambi smiled thinly, and Sheridan said in a loud voice that he thought the whole thing was stupid; everyone knew there hadn't been any goddam kidnap attempt and why didn't Zak stop messing around and piss off.

Into a gasping horrified silence while Mercer struggled for words, Zak smiled brilliantly and said, 'Is it indigestion? We'll get you some tablets,' and he patted Sheridan compassionately on the shoulder.

It brought the house, or rather the train, down. People laughed and applauded and Sheridan looked truly murderous.

'Now, Sparrowgrass,' Zak said, consulting his list and very smoothly carrying on, 'who owns Sparrowgrass?'

The elderly gentleman sitting with Filmer said, 'I do. My wife and I.'

'So you are Mr and Mrs Young? Any relation to Brigham? No? Never mind. Isn't it true that someone tried to burn down the barn your Sparrowgrass was stabled in a month ago? Could the two attacks be linked, would you say?'

The Youngs looked astounded. 'How ever did you know that?'

'We have our sources,' Zak said loftily, and told me afterwards his source was the *Daily Racing Form*, busily read recently for background help with his story. It impressed the passengers most satisfactorily.

'I'm sure no one's trying to kidnap my horse,' Young said, but with a note of doubt in his voice that was a triumph for Zak.

'Let's hope not,' he said. 'And finally, who owns Calculator?'

The actors Walter and Mavis Bricknell put up their hands in agitation. 'We do. What's wrong with him? We must go at once to make sure. The whole thing's most upsetting. Have you proper guards now looking after the horses?'

'Calm down, sir, calm down, madam,' Zak said as to children. 'Merry & Co have a special horsemaster looking after them. They will all be safe from now on.'

He concluded the scene by saying that we would

soon be stopping at Newmarket, but that British owners shouldn't get off the train as they would find no races there. (Laughter.) Lunch was now on its way, he added, and he hoped everyone would return for drinks at five-thirty when there would be Interesting Developments as per their printed programmes. The passengers clapped very loudly, to encourage him. Zak waved, retreated and set off down the corridor, flat-footed almost at once after his bounce in the dining car, and already with drooping shoulders consulting his notebook about what he needed to do next. How often, I wondered, had he had to deal with the likes of Sheridan? From his demeanour, often enough.

Emil told me to collect the champagne glasses, pour the water and put a pot of breadsticks on each table. He himself was opening wine. Oliver and Cathy began bringing plates of smoked salmon and bowls of vichyssoise soup on trays from the kitchen and offering a choice.

The seating problem more or less sorted itself out. Mavis and Walter, pretending 'their horse's welfare meant more to them than eating', set off up the train to eat in the racegoers' dining car, and so did Angelica, 'too upset to sit down'. A few others like Raoul, Pierre and Donna, left discreetly, until Nell, counting heads, could match all paying passengers with a place. Giles-the-murderer, I was interested to see, was still in the dining room, still being overpoweringly nice: it was

136

apparently essential to the drama that he should be liked.

We stopped at Newmarket briefly. No British owners got off. (A pity.) The soup gave place to a fricassee of chicken with lemon and parsley.

I was promoted from Aquarius to Ganymede, forsaking water for wine. Emil quite rightly didn't trust me to clear dirty plates, which involved fancy juggling with knives and forks. I was allowed with the others to change ashtrays, to deliver maple hazelnut praline mousse and to take tea and coffee to the cups, already laid. Filmer ignored my presence throughout and I was extremely careful not to draw his attention by spilling things.

By the end I had a great admiration for Emil, Oliver and Cathy, who had neatly served and cleared three full courses with the floor swaying beneath their feet and who normally would have taken my few jobs also in their stride.

When nearly all the passengers (including Filmer) had left, heading for their own rooms or the observation car, we cleared the tables, spread fresh cloths and began thinking of food for ourselves. At least, I did. The others made for the kitchen with me following, but once there Oliver took off his waistcoat, donned an apron and long yellow gloves, and began washing dishes. A deep endless sinkful of three courses for forty-eight people.

I watched him in horror. 'Do you always do this?' I asked.

'Who else?'

Cathy took a cloth to do some drying.

'No machines?' I protested.

'We're the machines,' she said.

Catch me, I thought ruefully, washing dishes. I picked up one of the cloths and helped her.

'You don't have to,' she said. 'But thanks.'

Angus the chef was cleaning up his realm at the far end of the long hot kitchen and Simone was unpacking fat beef sandwiches which we all ate standing up while working. There was an odd sort of camaraderie about it all, as if we were the front-line troops in battle. They were entitled to eat after the last sitting in the central dining car, Emil said, rinsing glasses, but usually they went only for dinner, if then; I could see why, as after the sandwiches on that first day we ate the all-too-few left-over portions of the Lucullan lunch we had served. 'There's never anything thrown away,' Cathy said, 'when we do trips like this.'

The dishes finally finished and stowed in their racks, it appeared that we were free for a blessed couple of hours: reassembly on the dot of five-thirty.

I don't know what the others did but I made straight towards the front of the packed train, threading an unsteady way through seemingly endless sleeping cars (passing my own berth), through the still busy central dining car, the full and raucous open-seat dayniter, three more sleeping cars, the crowded dome car (dining room, kitchen, lounge, observation deck), another sleeping car, and finally reaching the horses. In all, a little less than a quarter of a mile's walk, though it felt like a marathon.

I was stopped at the horse-car entrance by a locked door and, in response to my repeated knocking, by a determined female who told me I wasn't welcome.

'You can't come in,' she said bluntly, physically barring my way. 'The train crew aren't allowed in here.'

'I'm working for Merry & Co,' I said.

She looked me up and down. 'You're an attendant,' she said flatly. 'You're not coming in.'

She was quivering with authority, the resolute governess guarding the pass. Maybe forty, I judged, with regular features, no make-up and a slim wiry figure in shirt, sweater and jeans. I knew an immovable object when I saw it, and I retreated through the first sleeping car, where grooms in T-shirts lolled in open day compartments (shut off by heavy felt curtains for sleeping), on my way to consult with the Chinese chef in the forward dome car's kitchen.

'The Conductor?' he said in answer to my question. 'He is here.' He pointed along the corridor towards the dining section. 'You're lucky.'

The Conductor, in his grey suit with gold bars of long service on his left sleeve, was sitting at the first table past the kitchen, finishing his lunch. There were other diners at other tables, but he was alone, using his lunch break to fill in papers laid out on the cloth. I slid into one of the seats opposite him and he raised his eyes enquiringly.

'I'm from Merry & Co,' I said. 'I believe you know about me.'

'Tommy?' he said, after thought.

'Yes.'

He put a hand across the table, which I shook.

'George Burley,' he said. 'Call me George.'

He was middle-aged, bulky, close cropped as to hair and moustache and with, I discovered, a nice line in irony.

I explained about the impasse at the door of the horse car.

His eyes twinkled, 'You've met the dragon-lady, eh? Ms Leslie Brown. They sent her to keep the grooms in order. Now she tries to rule the train, eh?'

He had the widespread Canadian habit of turning the most ordinary statement into a question. It's a nice day, eh?

'I hope,' I said politely, 'that your authority outranks hers.'

'You bet your life,' he said. 'Let me finish these papers and my lunch and we'll go along there, eh?'

I sat for a while watching the scenery slide by, wild uninhabited stretches of green and autumn-blazing trees, grey rocks and blue lakes punctuated by tiny hamlets and lonely houses, all vivid in the afternoon sunshine, a panoramic impression of the vastness of Canada and the smallness of her population.

'Right,' George said, shuffling his papers together. 'I'll just finish my coffee, eh?'

'Is there,' I asked, 'a telephone on the train?'

He chuckled. 'You bet your life. But it's a radio phone, eh? It only works near cities where they have receiver/ transmitters. At small stations, we have to get off and use the regular phones on the ground, like the passengers do at longer stops.'

'But can anyone use the train telephone?' I asked.

He nodded. 'It's a payphone by credit card, eh? Much more expensive. Most people stretch their legs and go into the stations. It's in my office.' He anticipated my question. 'My office is in the first sleeping car aft of the central dining car.'

'My roomette is there,' I said, working it out.

'There you are, then. Look for my name on the door.'

He finished his coffee, slid his papers into a folder and took me forward again to the horse car. The dragon answered belligerently to his knock and stared at me disapprovingly.

'He is Tommy,' George said. 'He is a security guard for Merry & Co, eh? He has the run of the *whole* train under my authority.'

She bowed in her turn to an irresistible force and let us in with raised eyebrows and an air of power suspended, not abdicated. She produced a clipboard with a sheet of ruled paper attached. 'Sign here,' she said. 'Everyone who comes in here has to sign. Put the date and time.'

I signed 'Tommy Titmouse' in a scrawl and put the time. Filmer, I was interested to see, had been to see his horse before departure.

We walked forward into the horse car with George pointing things out.

'There are eleven stalls, see? In the old days they carried twenty-four horses in a car, but there was no centre aisle, eh? No passage for anyone between stops. They don't carry horses by train much now. This car was built in 1958, eh? One of the last, one of the best.'

There was a single stall lengthwise against the wall on each side of the entrance door, then a space, then two more box-stalls, one on each side, then a space where big sliding doors gave access to the outer world for loading and unloading. Next came a wider central space with a single box on one side only. Then two more boxes and another space for loading, then two more boxes and a space, and finally another box on each side of the far forward door. Eleven boxes, as promised, with a central aisle.

The boxes were made of heavy green-painted panels of metal slotted and bolted together, dismantleable. In the wide centre space, where one box alone stood along one wall, there was a comfortable chair for the redoubtable Ms Brown, along with a table, equipment lockers, a refrigerator and a heavy plastic water tank with a tap

low down for the filling of buckets. George opened the
top lid of the tank and showed me a small plank floating
on the surface.

'It stops the water sloshing about so much, eh?'

Eh indeed, I thought.

There were dozens of bales of hay everywhere possible, and a filled hay-net swinging gently above each
horse's head. A couple of grooms sat around on bales
while their charges nibbled their plain fare and thought
mysterious equine thoughts.

Each box had the name of its occupant thoughtfully
provided on a typewritten card slotted into a holder on
the door. I peered at a few of them, identifying Filmer
and Daffodil's Laurentide Ice as a light grey colt with
brittle-looking bones, the Lorrimores' Voting Right as
an unremarkable bay, and the Youngs' Sparrowgrass
as a bright chestnut with a white star and sock.

'Come on,' George said. 'Meet the engineers, eh?'
He wasn't a horse man, himself.

'Yes. Thank you.'

He opened the forward door of the horse van with
a key, and with a key also let us through into the
baggage car.

'The doors are kept locked, eh?'

I nodded. We swayed down the long baggage car,
which was half empty of freight and very noisy, and
George, having told me to remove and lay aside my
waistcoat in case I got oil on it, unlocked the door at

the far end. If I'd thought it noisy where we were, where we went made talking impossible.

George beckoned and I followed through a door into the heat of the rear section of the engines, the section containing among other things the boiler which provided steam to heat the whole train. George pointed wordlessly to an immense tank of water and with amusement showed me the system for telling the quantity of the contents. At intervals up the huge cylinder there were normal taps, the sort found over sinks. George pointed to the figures beside each, which were in hundreds of gallons, and made tap-turning motions with his hands. One turned on the taps, I understood with incredulity, to discover the level of the contents. Supremely logical, I supposed, if one had never heard of gauges.

We went on forward into a narrow passage beside yards of hot hammering engine of more than head height, throbbingly painful to the senses, and then passed over a coupling into another engine, even longer, even noisier, even hotter, the very stuff of hell. At the forward end of that we came to a glass-panelled door, which needed no key, and suddenly we were in the comparative quietness of the drivers' cab, right at the front of the train.

There was fresh cool air there, as the right-hand window, next to the bank of controls in front of the engineer's seat, was wide open. When I commented on it, George said that that window was open always except in blizzards, eh?

Through the wide forward unopening windows there was a riveting view of the rails stretching ahead, signals shining green in the distance, trees flashing back at a useful seventy miles an hour. I'd never been in the cab of a moving train before, and I felt I could have stayed there all day.

At the controls sat a youngish man in no sort of uniform, and beside him sat an older man in cleanish overalls with grease on his fingers.

George made introductions. 'Robert', that was the younger, and 'Mike', the elder. They nodded and shook hands when George explained my position. 'Give him help, if he asks for it.'

They said they would. George patted Robert on the shoulder and pointed out to me a small white flag blowing stiffly outside to the right of the front windows.

'That flag shows this is a special train. Not in the timetable. It's so all railwaymen along the way don't think the Canadian is running thirty minutes early.'

They all thought it a great joke. Trains never ran early the world over. Late was routine.

Still chuckling, George led the way back through the glass door into the inferno. We inched again past the thundering monster and its second string to the rear, and emerged at last into the clattering reverberating peace of the baggage car where I was reunited with my waistcoat. My suitcase, I was interested to see, stood in a quiet row of others, accessible enough if I wanted it.

George locked the baggage car door behind us and we stood again in the quiet horse car which looked homely and friendly with the horses' heads poking forward over the doors. It was interesting, I thought, that as far as they were able in their maybe four-foot-wide stalls, most of them were standing diagonally across the space, the better to deal with the motion; and they all looked alert and interested, sure signs of contentment.

I rubbed the noses of one or two under the frowning suspicious gaze of Ms Brown who was not pleased to be told that she should let me in whenever I asked, eh?

George chuckled his way out of the horse car and we meandered back down the train together, George stopping to check for news with each sleeping-car attendant and to solve any problems. There was a sing-song in progress in the dome car and the racegoers in the dayniter had formed about four separate card schools with cash passing briskly.

The overworked and gloomy chef in the main dining car had not lost his temper altogether and only a few passengers had grumbled that the roomettes were too cramped; the most usual disgruntlement, George said.

No one was ill, no one was drunk, no one was fighting. Things, George said eventually, were going so smoothly that one should expect disaster any time now, eh?

We came at last to his office which was basically a roomette like my own: that is to say, it was a seven-by-four-foot space on one side of a central corridor, containing a washbasin, a folding table and two seats, one of which concealed what the timetable coyly called 'facilities'. One could either leave the sliding door open and see the world go by down the corridor, or close oneself into a private cocoon; and at night, one's bed descended from the ceiling and on to the seat of the facilities which effectively put them out of use.

George invited me in and left the door open.

'This train,' he said, settling himself into the armchair and indicating the facilities for me, 'is a triumph of diplomacy, eh?'

He had a permanent smile in his eyes, I thought, much as if he found the whole of life a joke. I learned later that he thought stupidity the norm for human behaviour, and that no one was as stupid as passengers, politicians, pressmen and the people who employed him.

'Why,' I asked, 'is it a triumph?'

'Common sense has broken out.'

I waited. He beamed and in a while went on, 'Except for the engineers, the same crew will stay with the train to Vancouver!'

I didn't to his eyes appear sufficiently impressed.

'It's unheard of, eh?' he said. 'The unions won't allow it.'

'Oh.'

'Also the horse car belongs to Canadian Pacific.'

I looked even blanker.

He chuckled. 'The Canadian Pacific and VIA Rail, who work so closely together, get along like sandpaper, good at friction. Canadian Pacific trains are freight trains, eh?, and VIA trains carry passengers, and never the two shall mix. This train is a mix. A miracle, eh?'

'Absolutely,' I said encouragingly.

He looked at me with twinkling pity for my lack of understanding of the really serious things in life.

I asked if his telephone would work at the next big stop which came under the heading of serious to me.

'Sudbury?' he said. 'Certainly. But we will be there for an hour. It's much cheaper from the station. A fraction of the price.'

'But more private here.'

He nodded philosophically. 'Come here as soon as we slow down coming to Sudbury, eh? I'll leave you here. I have to be busy in the station.'

I thanked him for everything and left the orbit of his beaming smile knowing that I was included in the universality of stupid behaviour. I could see a lot more of George, I thought, before I tired of him.

My own door, I found, was only two doors along from his, on the right-hand side of the train when facing forward. I went past without stopping, noting that there

were six roomettes altogether at the forward end of
the car: three each side. Then the corridor bent to the
side to accommodate four enclosed double bedrooms
and bent back again through the centre of open seating
with sleeping curtains, called sections. The six sections
of that car were allocated to twelve assorted actors and
crew, most of them at that point reading, talking or fast
asleep.

'How's it going?' Zak said, yawning.

'All quiet on the western front.'

'Pass, friend.'

I smiled and went on down the train, getting the feel
of it now, understanding the way it was put together,
beginning to wonder about things like electricity, water
supply and sewage. A small modern city on the move,
I thought, with all the necessary infrastructure.

All the doors were closed in the owners' sleeping
cars (there were almost no open sections in those), the
inhabitants there having the habit of privacy. The rooms
could have been empty, it was impossible to tell, and
in fact when I came to the special dining car I found a
good number of the passengers sitting at the unlaid
tables, just chatting. I went on through into the dome
car where there were three more bedrooms before one
came to the bar, which was furnished with tables,
seating and barman. A few people sat there also,
talking, and some again were sitting around in the long
lower lounge to the rear.

From there a short staircase went up to the

observation lounge, and I went up there briefly. The many seats there were almost full, the passengers enjoying their uninterrupted view of a million brilliant trees under blue skies and baking in the hot sunshine streaming through the glass roof.

Mr Young was up there, asleep. Julius Apollo wasn't, nor anywhere else in public view.

I hadn't seen Nell at all either. I didn't know where she'd put herself finally on her often-revised allocation of sleeping space, but wherever she was, it was behind a closed door.

To the rear of the dome car there was only the Lorrimores' private car, which I could hardly enter, so I retraced my steps, intending to retreat to my own roomette and watch the scenery do its stuff.

In the dining car I was stopped by Xanthe Lorrimore who was sitting alone at a table looking morose.

'Bring me some Coke,' she said.

'Yes, certainly,' I said, and went to fetch some from the cold locker in the kitchen, thanking my stars that I'd happened to see where the soft-drink cans were kept. I put the can and a glass on one of the small trays (Emil's voice in my ear saying, 'Never ever carry the object. Carry the tray.') and returned to Xanthe.

'I'm afraid this is on a cash bar basis,' I said, putting the glass on the table and preparing to open the can.

'What does that mean?'

'Things from the bar are extra. Not included in the fare.'

'How ridiculous. And I haven't any money.'

'You could pay later, I'm sure.'

'I think it's stupid.'

I opened the can and poured the Coke, and Mrs Young, who happened to be sitting alone at the next table, turned round and said to Xanthe sweetly that she, Mrs Young, would pay for the Coke, and wouldn't Xanthe come and join her?

Xanthe's first instinct was clearly to refuse but, sulky or not, she was also lonely, and there was an undemanding grandmotherliness about Mrs Young that promised an uncritical listening ear. Xanthe moved herself and her Coke and unburdened herself of her immediate thought.

'That brother of mine,' she said, 'is an asshole.'

'Perhaps he has his problems,' Mrs Young said equably, digging around in her capacious and disorganized handbag for some money.

'If he was anyone else's kid, he'd be in jail.'

The words came out as if propelled irresistibly from a well of compressed emotion. Even Xanthe herself looked shocked at what she'd let out, and feebly tried to weaken the impact. 'I didn't mean literally, of course,' she said. But she had.

Mrs Young, who had paused in her search, finally found her purse and gave me a dollar.

'If there's any change, keep it,' she said.

'Thank you, madam.'

I had no choice but to leave and I made for the

kitchen carrying the dollar on the tray like a trophy anchored by a thumb. From there I looked back to see Xanthe begin to talk to Mrs Young, at first slowly, with brakes on, and then faster and faster, until all the unhappiness was pouring out like a flood. I could see Xanthe's face and the back of Mrs Young's head. Xanthe, it seemed to me, was perhaps sixteen, but probably younger: certainly not older. She still had the facial contours of childhood, with a round chin and big-pupilled eyes: also chestnut hair in abundance and a growing figure hidden within a bulky white top with a pink glittering pop-slogan on the front, the badge of youth.

They were still talking when I continued on my way back to my roomette where I sat in comfortable privacy for a while reading the timetable and also reflecting that although I still had no answers to the old questions, I now had a whole crop of new ones, the most urgent being whether or not Filmer had already known the Youngs were friends of Ezra Gideon. Whether the Youngs were, in fact, a target of some kind. Yet Filmer hadn't chosen to sit at their table; it had been the random fortuitous decision of Daffodil. Perhaps if it hadn't happened so handily by chance, he would have engineered a meeting. Or was the fact of their friendship with Gideon just an unwelcome coincidence, as I had at first supposed? Time, perhaps, would tell.

Time told me more immediately that it was five-thirty, the hour of return to the dining room, and I returned to find every single seat already taken, the passengers having learned fast. Latecomers stood in the entrances, looking forlorn.

Filmer, I saw at once, was placed opposite Mercer Lorrimore. Daffodil, beside him, was opposite Bambi who was being coolly gracious.

Xanthe was still sitting across from Mrs Young, now rejoined by her husband. Sheridan, as far as I could see, was absent. Giles-the-murderer was present, sitting with the Youngs and Xanthe, being nice.

Emil, Oliver, Cathy and I went round the tables pouring wine, tea or coffee into glasses or cups on small trays with small movements, and when that was done Zak bounded into the midst of things, vibrating with fresh energy, to get on with the mystery.

I didn't listen in detail to it all, but it revolved round Pierre and Donna, and Raoul the racehorse trainer who wanted to marry her money. Zak had got round the pre-empted Pierre-hitting-Raoul-to-the-ground routine by having Donna slap Raoul's face instead, which she did with a gusto that brought gasps from the audience. Donna was clearly established as the wittering Bricknells' besotted daughter, with Raoul obviously Mavis's favourite, and Pierre despised as a no-good compulsive gambler. Mother and daughter went into a sharp slanging match, with Walter fussing and trying to stop them. Mavis, in the end, started crying.

I looked at the passengers' faces. Even though they knew this lot were all actors, they were transfixed. Soap opera had come to life within touching distance. Racing people, I'd always thought, were among the most cynical in the world, yet here some of the most experienced of them were moved and involved despite themselves.

Zak, keeping up the tension, said that at the last of our brief stops at minor stations he had been handed a telex about Angelica's missing friend Steve. Was Angelica present? Everyone looked around, and no, she wasn't. Never mind, Zak said, would someone please tell her that she must telephone Steve from Sudbury, as he had serious news for her.

A lot of people nodded. It was amazing.

Dressed in silk and ablaze with jewellery, apparently to prove that Donna's inheritance was no myth, Mavis Bricknell stumbled off towards the toilet room at the dome car's entrance saying she must repair the ravages to her face, and presently she came back, screaming loudly.

Angelica, it appeared, was lying on the lavatory floor, extremely dead. Zak naturally bustled to investigate, followed by a sizeable section of the audience. Some of them soon came back smiling weakly and looking unsettled.

'She can't really be dead,' someone said solemnly. 'But she certainly looks it.'

There was a lot of 'blood' all over the small compartment, it appeared, with Angelica's battered head in shadow beyond the essential facility. Angelica's eyes were just visible staring at the wall, unblinking. 'How can she do that?' several said.

Zak came back, looked around him, and beckoned to me.

'Stand in front of that door, will you, and don't let anyone go in?'

I nodded and went through the crowd towards the dome car. Zak himself was calling everyone back into the dining room, saying they should all stay together until we reached Sudbury, which would be soon. I could hear Nell's voice announcing calmly that everyone had time for another drink. There would be an hour's stop in Sudbury for everyone to stretch their legs if they wanted to, and dinner would be served as soon as the train started again.

I went across the clattering, windy linkage space between the dining and dome cars and stood outside the toilet room. I wasn't actually pleased with Zak as I didn't want to risk being identified as an actor, but that, I supposed, would be a great deal better than the truth.

It was boring in the passage but also, it proved, necessary, as one or two passengers came back for a look at the corpse. They were good-humoured enough when turned away. Meanwhile the corpse, who must have had to blink in the end, could be heard flushing water within.

When we began to slow down I knocked on the door. 'Message from Zak,' I said.

The door opened a fraction. Angelica's greasepaint make-up was a pale bluish grey, her hair a mass of tomato ketchup.

'Lock the door,' I said. 'Zak will be along. When you hear his voice outside, unlock it.'

'Right,' she said, sounding cheerfully alive. 'Have a nice trip.'

CHAPTER EIGHT

Angelica left the train on a stretcher in the dusk under bright station lights, her tomato head half covered by a blanket, and one lifeless hand, with red fingernails and sparkling rings, artistically drooping out of concealment on the side where the train's passengers were able to look on with fascination.

I watched the scene through the window of George Burley's office while I talked to Bill Baudelaire's mother on the telephone.

The conversation had been a surprise from the beginning, when a light young female voice had answered my call.

'Could I speak to Mrs Baudelaire, please?' I said.

'Speaking.'

'I mean . . . Mrs Baudelaire senior.'

'Any Mrs Baudelaire who is senior to me is in her grave,' she announced. 'Who are you?'

'Tor Kelsey.'

'Oh yes,' she replied instantly. 'The invisible man.'

I half laughed.

157

'How do you do it?' she asked. 'I'm dying to know.'

'Seriously?'

'Of course, seriously.'

'Well . . . say if someone serves you fairly often in a shop, you recognize them when you're in the shop, but if you meet them somewhere quite different, like at the races, you can't remember who they are.'

'Quite right. It's happened to me often.'

'To be easily recognized,' I said, 'you have to be in your usual environment. So the trick about invisibility is not to have a usual environment.'

There was a pause, then she said, 'Thank you. It must be lonely.'

I couldn't think of an answer to that, but was astounded by her perception.

'The interesting thing is,' I said, 'that it's quite different for the people who work in the shop. When they get to know their customers, they recognize them easily anywhere in the world. So the racing people I know, I recognize everywhere. They don't know that I exist . . . and that's invisibility.'

'You are,' she said, 'an extraordinary young man.'

She stumped me again.

'But Bill knew you existed,' she said, 'and he told me he didn't recognize you face to face.'

'He was looking for the environment he knew . . . straight hair, no sunglasses, a good grey suit, collar and tie.'

'Yes,' she said. 'If I meet you, will I know you?'

'I'll tell you.'

'Pact.'

This, I thought with relief and enjoyment, was some carrier pigeon.

'Would you give Bill some messages?' I asked.

'Fire away. I'll write them down.'

'The train reaches Winnipeg tomorrow evening at about seven-thirty, and everyone disembarks to go to hotels. Please would you tell Bill I will not be staying at the same hotel as the owners, and that I will again not be going to the President's lunch, but that I will be at the races, even if he doesn't see me.'

I paused. She repeated what I'd said.

'Great,' I said. 'And would you ask him some questions?'

'Fire away.'

'Ask him for general information on a Mr and Mrs Young who own a horse called Sparrowgrass.'

'It's on the train,' she said.

'Yes, that's right.' I was surprised, but she said Bill had given her a list to be a help with messages.

'Ask him,' I said, 'if Sheridan Lorrimore has ever been in any trouble that he knows of, apart from assaulting an actor at Toronto, that should have resulted in Sheridan going to jail.'

'Gracious me. The Lorrimores don't go to jail.'

'So I gathered,' I said dryly, 'and would you also ask which horses are running at Winnipeg and which at Vancouver, and which in Bill's opinion is the really best horse on the train, not necessarily on form, and which has the best chance of winning either race.'

'I don't need to ask Bill the first question, I can answer that for you right away, it's on this list. Nearly all the eleven horses, nine to be exact, are running at Vancouver. Only Upper Gumtree and Flokati run at Winnipeg. As for the second, in my own opinion neither Upper Gumtree nor Flokati will win at Winnipeg because Mercer Lorrimore is shipping his great horse Premiere by horse-van.'

'Um . . .' I said. 'You follow racing quite a bit?'

'My dear young man, didn't Bill tell you? His father and I owned and ran the *Ontario Raceworld* magazine for years before we sold it to a conglomerate.'

'I see,' I said faintly.

'And as for the Vancouver race,' she went on blithely, 'Laurentide Ice might as well melt right now, but Sparrowgrass and Voting Right are both in with a good chance. Sparrowgrass will probably start favourite as his form is consistently good, but as you ask, very likely the best horse, the one with most potential for the future, is Mercer Lorrimore's Voting Right, and I would give that one the edge.'

'Mrs Baudelaire,' I said, 'you are a gem.'

'Beyond the price of rubies,' she agreed. 'Anything else?'

'Nothing, except . . . I hope you are well.'

'No, not very. You're kind to ask. Goodbye, young man. I'm always here.'

She put the receiver down quickly as if to stop me from asking anything else about her illness, and it reminded me sharply of my Aunt Viv, bright, spirited and horse-mad to the end.

I went back to the dining car to find Oliver and Cathy laying the tables for dinner, and I helped them automatically, although they said I needn't. The job done, we repaired to the kitchen door to see literally what was cooking and to take the printed menus from Angus to put on the tables.

Blinis with caviare, we read, followed by rack of lamb or cold poached salmon, then chocolate mousse with cream.

'There won't be any over,' Cathy sighed, and she was right as far as the blinis went, though we all ate lamb in the end.

With ovens and gas burners roaring away, it was wiltingly hot even at the dining-room end of the kitchen. Down where the chef worked, a temperature gauge on the wall stood at 102° Fahrenheit, but tall willowy Angus, whose high hat nearly brushed the ceiling, looked cool and unperturbed.

'Don't you have air-conditioning?' I asked.

Angus said, 'In summer, I dare say. October is however officially winter, even though it's been warm this year. The air-conditioning needs freon gas, which has all leaked away, and it won't be topped up again until spring. So Simone tells me.'

Simone, a good foot shorter and with sweat trickling down her temples, mutely nodded.

The passengers came straggling back shedding over-coats and saying it was cold outside, and again the dining car filled up. The Lorrimores this time were all sitting together. The Youngs were with the Unwins from Australia and Filmer and Daffodil shared a table with a pair Nell later identified to me as the American owners of the horse called Flokati.

Filmer, extremely smooth in a dark suit and grey tie, solicitously removed Daffodil's chinchillas and hung them over the back of her chair. She shimmered in a figure-hugging black dress, diamonds sparkling when-ever she moved, easily outstripping the rest of the company (even Mavis Bricknell) in conspicuous expen-diture.

The train made its smooth inconspicuous departure and I did my stuff with water and breadsticks.

Bambi Lorrimore put her hand arrestingly on my arm as I passed. She was wearing a mink jacket and struggling to get out of it.

'Take this back into our private car, will you?' she said. 'It's too hot in here. Put it in the saloon, not the bedroom.'

'Certainly, madam,' I agreed, helping her with alac-rity. 'I'd be glad to.'

Mercer produced a key and gave it to me, explaining that I would come to a locked door.

'Lock it again when you come back.'

'Yes, sir.'

He nodded and, carrying the coat away over my arm, I went back through the dome car and with a great deal of interest into the private quarters of the Lorrimores.

There were lights on everywhere. I came first to a small unoccupied sleeping space, then a galley, cold and lifeless. Provision for private food and private crew, but no food, no crew. Beyond that was the locked door, and beyond that a small handsome dining room to seat eight. Through there, down a corridor, there were three bedrooms, two with the doors open. I took a quick peek inside: bed, drawers, small bathroom with shower. One was clearly Xanthe's, the other by inference Sheridan's. I didn't go into the parents' room but went on beyond it to find myself in the rear part of the carriage, at the very end of the train.

It was a comfortable drawing room with a television set and abundant upholstered armchairs in pastel blues and greens. I went over to the rear door and looked out, seeing a little open boarding platform with a polished brass-topped balustrade and, beyond, the Canadian Pacific's single pair of rails streaming away into darkness. The railroad across Canada, I'd learned, was single track for most of the way. Only in towns and at a few other places could trains going in opposite directions pass.

I put the mink coat on a chair and retraced my journey, locking the door again and eventually returning the key to Mercer who nodded without speech and put it in his pocket.

Emil was pouring wine. The passengers were scoffing the blinis. I eased into the general picture again and became as unidentifiable as possible. Few people, I discovered, looked directly at a waiter's eyes, even when they were talking to him.

About an hour after we'd left Sudbury we stopped briefly for under five minutes at a place called Cartier and then went on again. The passengers, replete with the lamb and chocolate mousse, lingered over coffee, and began to drift away to the dome car's bar lounge. Xanthe Lorrimore got up from the table after a while and went that way, and presently came back screaming.

This time, the real thing. She came stumbling back into the dining car followed by a commotion of people yelling behind her.

She reached her parents who were bewildered as well as worried.

'I was nearly killed,' she said frantically. 'I nearly stepped off into space. I mean, I was *nearly killed.*'

'Darling,' Mercer said calmly, 'what has exactly happened?'

'You don't understand.' She was screaming, trembling, hysterical. 'I nearly stepped into space because our private car *isn't there.*'

It brought both of the Lorrimores to their feet in an incredulous rush, but they had only to look at the faces crowding behind her to know it was true.

'And they say, all those people say . . .' she was gasping, half unable to get the words out, terribly frightened, ' . . . they say the other train, the regular Canadian, is only half an hour behind us, and will smash into . . . will smash into . . . don't you *see*?'

The Lorrimores, followed by everyone still in the dining room, went dashing off into the dome car, but Emil and I looked at each other, and I said, 'How do we warn that train?'

'Tell the Conductor. He has a radio.'

'I'll go,' I said. 'I know where his office is. I'll find him.'

'Hurry then.'

'Yes.'

I hurried. Ran. Reached George's office.

No one there.

I went on, running where I could, and found him walking back towards me through the dayniter. He instantly took in that I brought bad news and steered me at once into the noisy outside coupling space between the dayniter and the central dining car.

'What is it?' he shouted.

'The Lorrimores' private car is unhitched . . . it's

somewhere back on the track, and the Canadian is coming.'

He moved faster than I would have thought anyone could on a train and was already talking into a radio headset when I reached his office.

'The private car was there at Cartier,' he said. 'I was off the train there and saw it. Are you sure it's not in sight?' He listened. 'Right, then radio to the Canadian and warn the Conductor he'll not be leaving Cartier, eh? I'll get this train stopped and we'll go back for the lost car. See what's what. You'd better inform Toronto and Montreal. They won't think this is very funny on a Sunday evening, eh?' He chuckled and looked at me assessingly as I stood in his doorway. 'I'll leave someone here manning the radio,' he continued. 'Tell him when you've got the Canadian understanding the situation, eh?'

He nodded at the reply he heard, took off the headset and gave it to me.

'You are talking to the despatcher in Schreiber,' he said, ' – that's ahead of us, this side of Thunder Bay – and he can radio straight to the Canadian following us. You can hear the despatcher without doing anything. To transmit, press the button.' He pointed, and was gone.

I put on the headset and sat in his chair and presently into my ears a disembodied voice said, 'Are you there?'

I pressed the button. 'Yes.'

'Tell George I got the Canadian and it will stop in

Cartier. There's a CP freight train due behind it but I got Sudbury in time and it isn't leaving there. No one is happy. Tell George to pick up that car and get the hell out.'

I pressed the button. 'Right,' I said.

'Who are you?' asked the voice.

'One of the attendants.'

He said, 'Huh,' and was quiet.

The Great Transcontinental Mystery Race Train began to slow down and soon came to a smooth stop. Almost in the same instant, George was back in his doorway.

'Tell the despatcher we've stopped and are going back,' he said, when I'd relayed the messages. 'We're eleven point two miles out of Cartier, between Benny and Stralak, which means in an uninhabited wilderness. You stay here, eh?' And he was gone again, this time towards the excitement in the tail.

I gave his message to the despatcher and added, 'We're reversing now, going slowly.'

'Let me know when you find the car.'

'Yes.'

It was pitch dark through the windows; no light in the wilderness. I heard afterwards from a lot of excited chattering in the dining room that George had stood alone outside the rear door of the dome car on the brink of space, directing a bright hand-held torch beam down the track. Heard that he had a walkie-talkie radio

167

on which he could give the engineer instructions to slow down further, and to stop.

He found the Lorrimores' car about a mile and a half out of Cartier. The whole train stopped while he jumped down from the dome car and went to look at the laggard. There was a long pause from my point of view, while the lights began flickering in the office and the train exceedingly slowly reversed, before stopping again and going into a sudden jerk. Then we started forward slowly, and then faster, and the lights stopped flickering, and soon after that George appeared in his office looking grim, all chuckles extinguished.

'What's the matter?' I said.

'*Nothing*,' he said violently, 'that's what's the matter.' He stretched out a hand for the headset which I gave him.

He spoke into it. 'This is George. We picked up the Lorrimores' car at one point three miles west of Cartier. There was no failure in the linkage.' He listened. 'That's what I said. Who the hell do they have working in Cartier, eh? Someone uncoupled that car at Cartier and rigged some way of pulling it out of the station into the darkness before releasing it. The brakes weren't on. You tell Cartier to send someone right away down the track looking for a rope or some such, eh? The steam heat pipe wasn't broken, it had been unlocked. That's what I said. The valve was closed. It was no goddam accident, no goddam mechanical failure, someone deliberately unhitched that car. If the Lorrimore girl hadn't found out, the Canadian would have crashed into it. No, maybe not at high speed, but at twenty-five, thirty miles an hour the Canadian can do a lot of damage. Would have made matchsticks of the private car. Might have killed the Canadian engineers, or even derailed the train. You tell them to start looking, eh?'

He took off the headset and stared at me with rage.

'Would you,' he said, 'know how to uncouple one car from another?'

'No, of course not.'

'It takes a railwayman.' He glared. 'A railwayman! It's like a mechanic letting someone drive off in a car with loose wheel nuts. It's criminal, eh?'

'Yes.'

'A hundred years ago,' he said furiously, 'they designed a system to prevent cars that had broken loose from running backwards and crashing into things. The brakes go on automatically in a runaway.' He glared. 'That system had been bypassed. The Lorrimores' brakes weren't on. That car was deliberately released on level ground, eh? I don't understand it. What was the point?'

'Maybe someone doesn't like the Lorrimores,' I suggested.

'We'll find the bastard,' he said, not listening. 'There can't be many in Cartier who know trains.'

'Do you get much sabotage?' I asked.

'Not like this. Not often. Once or twice in the past.

169

But it's mostly vandals. A kid or two throwing rocks off a bridge. Some stealing, eh?'

He was affronted, I saw, by the treachery of one of his own kind. He took it personally. He was in a way ashamed, as one is if one's countrymen behave badly abroad.

I asked him about his communication system with the engineer. Why had he gone up the train himself to get it stopped if he had a walkie-talkie?

'It crackles if we're going at any speed. It's better to talk face to face.'

A light flashed on the ship-to-shore radio and he replaced his headset.

'George here,' he said, and listened. He looked at his watch and frowned. 'Yes. Right. Understood.' He took off the headset, shaking his head. 'They're not going to go along the track looking for a rope until both the Canadian and the freight train have been through. If our saboteur's got an ounce of sense, by that time there won't be anything incriminating to find.'

'Probably not already,' I said. 'It's getting on for an hour since we left Cartier.'

'Yeah,' he said. His good humour was trickling back despite his anger, the gleam of irony again in his eye. 'Better than that fellow's fake mystery, eh?'

'Yes . . .' I said, thinking. 'Is the steam pipe the only thing connecting one car to the next? Except the links, of course.'

'That's right.'

'What about electricity . . . and water?'

He shook his head. 'Each car makes its own electricity. Self-contained. They have generators under the floors . . . like dynamos on bicycles . . . that make electricity from the wheels going round. The problem is that when we're going slowly, the lights flicker. Then there are batteries for when we're stopped, but they'd only last for forty-five minutes, eh?, if we weren't plugged into the ground supply at a station. After that we're down to emergency lighting, just the aisle lights and not much else for about four hours, then we're in the dark.'

'And water?' I asked.

'It's in the roof.'

'Really?' I said, surprised.

He patiently explained. 'At city stations, we have water hydrants every eighty-five feet, the length of the cars. One to each car. Also the main electricity, same thing, eh? Anyway, the water goes up under pressure into the tanks in the roof and feeds down again to the washrooms by gravity.'

Fascinating, I thought. And it had made unhitching the Lorrimores' car a comparatively quick and easy job.

'The new cars,' George said, 'will be heated by electricity, not steam, so we'll be doing away with the steam pipe, eh? And they'll have tanks for the sewage, which now drops straight down on to the tracks, of course.'

171

'Canada's railways,' I said politely, 'will be the envy of the world.'

He chuckled. 'The trains between Montreal and Toronto are late three-quarters of the time and the new engines break down regularly. The old rolling stock, like this train, is great.'

He picked up the headset again. I raised a hand in farewell and went back to the dining room where the real mystery had easily usurped Zak's, though some were sure it was part of the plot.

Xanthe had cheered up remarkably through being the centre of sympathetic attention, and Filmer was telling Mercer Lorrimore he should sue the railway company for millions of dollars for negligence. The near-disaster had galvanized the general consciousness to a higher adrenalin level, probably because Xanthe had not, in fact, been carried off like Angelica.

Nell was sitting at a table with a fortyish couple who she later told me owned one of the horses in the box-car, a dark bay called Redi-Hot. The man beckoned to me as I stood around vaguely, and asked me to fetch cognac for him, vodka with ice for his wife and . . . what for Nell?

'Just Coke, please,' she said.

I went to the kitchen where I knew the Coke was, but made frantic question mark signals to Nell about the rest. Emil, the chefs, Oliver and Cathy had finished cleaning up and had all gone off duty. I had no alcohol-divining rod to bend a twig in the direction of brandy or Smirnoff.

Nell said something to the owners and came to join me, stifling laughter.

'Yes, very funny,' I said, 'but what the hell do I do?'

'Take one of the small trays and get the drinks from the bar. I'll explain they have to pay for them.'

'I haven't seen you for five minutes alone today,' I complained.

'You're downstairs, I'm up.'

'I could easily hate you.'

'But do you?'

'Not yet,' I said.

'If you're a good little waiter, I'll leave you a tip.'

She went back to her place with a complacent bounce to her step, and with a curse, but not meaning it, I took the Coke and a glass to her table and went on into the dome car for the rest. After I'd returned and delivered the order someone else asked for the same service, which I willingly performed again, and yet again.

On each trip I overheard snatches of the bar-room conversations and could hear the louder buzz of continuing upheaval along in the lounge, and I thought that after I'd satisfied everyone in the dining room I might drift along to the far end with my disarming little tray.

The only person not wholly in sympathy with this plan was the bartender who complained that I was supposed to be off duty and that the passengers should come to the bar to buy the drinks themselves; I was siphoning off his tips. I saw the justice of that and offered to split fifty-fifty. He knew very well that, without my running to and fro, the passengers mostly wouldn't be bothered to move to drink, so he accepted fast, no doubt considering me a mug as well as an actor.

Sheridan Lorrimore, who was sitting at a table apart from his parents, demanded I bring him a double Scotch at once. He had a carrying voice, and his sister from two tables away turned round in disapproval.

'No, no, you're not supposed to,' she said.

'Mind your own business.' He turned his head slightly towards me and spoke in the direction of my tie. 'Double Scotch, at the double.'

'Don't get it,' Xanthe said.

I stood irresolute.

Sheridan stood up, his ready anger rising. He put out a hand and pushed my shoulder fiercely.

'Go on,' he said. 'Damn well do as I say. Go and get my drink.'

He pushed again quite hard and as I turned away I heard him snigger and say, 'You have to kick 'em, you know.'

I went into the dome car and stood behind the bar with the bartender, and felt furious with Sheridan, not for his outrageous behaviour but because he was getting me noticed. Filmer had been sitting with his back to me, it was true, but near enough to overhear.

Mercer Lorrimore appeared tentatively in the bar doorway and came in when he saw me.

'I apologize for my son,' he said wearily, and I had a convincing impression that he'd apologized countless times before. He pulled out his wallet, removed a twenty-dollar note from it and offered me the money.

'Please don't,' I said. 'There's no need.'

'Yes, yes. Take it.'

I saw he would feel better if I did, as if paying money would somehow excuse the act. I thought he should stop trying to buy pardons for his son and pay for mental treatment instead. But then, perhaps he had. There was more wrong with Sheridan than ill temper, and it had been obvious to his father for a long time.

I didn't approve of what he was doing, but if I refused his money I would be more and more visible, so I took it, and when he had gone off in relief back towards the dining car I gave it to the barman.

'What was that all about?' he asked curiously, pocketing the note without hesitation. When I explained, he said, 'You should have kept the money. You should have charged him triple.'

'He would have felt three times as virtuous,' I said, and the barman looked at me blankly.

I didn't go back to the dining car but forward into the lounge, where again the sight of my yellow waistcoat stirred a few thirsts, which I did my best to accommodate. The barman was by now mellow and helpful and said we were rapidly running out of the ice that had come aboard in bags in Sudbury.

Up in the dome, the uncoupling of the private car had given way to speculation about whether the northern lights would oblige: the weather was right, apparently. I took a few drinks up there (including some for Zak and Donna, which amused them), and on my way down the stairs saw the backs of Mercer and Bambi, Filmer and Daffodil, as they walked through the lounge towards the door to the private car. Mercer stood aside to let Bambi lead the other two through the short noisy joining section, and then, before going himself, he looked back, saw me and beckoned.

'Bring a bowl of ice, will you?' he said when I reached him. 'To the saloon.'

'Yes, sir,' I said.

He nodded and departed, and I relayed the request to the barman who shook his head and said he was down to six cubes. I knew there were other bags of cubes in the kitchen refrigerator, so, feeling that I had been walking the train for a lifetime, I went along through the dining room to fetch some.

There weren't many people still in there, though Xanthe was still being comforted and listened to by Mrs Young. Nell sat opposite Sheridan Lorrimore who seemed to be telling her that he had wrapped his Lamborghini round a tree recently and had ordered a new one.

'Tree?' Nell said, smiling.

He looked at her uncomprehendingly. Sheridan wasn't a great one for jokes. I fetched a bag of ice and a bowl from the kitchen, swayed back to the bar and in due course took the bowl of ice (on a tray) to the saloon.

The four of them were sitting in armchairs, Bambi talking to Daffodil, Mercer to Filmer.

Mercer said to me, 'You'll find glasses and cognac in the cupboard in the dining room. And Benedictine. Bring them along here, will you?'

'Yes, sir.'

Filmer paid me no attention. In the neat dining room, the cupboards had glass fronts with pale green curtains inside them. In one I found the bottles and glasses as described, and took them aft.

Filmer was saying, 'Will Voting Right go on to the Breeders' Cup if he wins at Winnipeg?'

'He's not running at Winnipeg,' Mercer said. 'He runs at Vancouver.'

'Yes, I meant Vancouver.'

Daffodil with enthusiasm was telling a cool Bambi that she should try some face cream or other that helped with wrinkles.

'Just leave everything,' Mercer said to me. 'We'll pour.'

'Yes, sir,' I said, and retreated as he began the ultimate heresy of sloshing Rémy Martin's finest on to rocks.

Mercer would know me everywhere on the train, I thought, but none of the other three would. I hadn't met Filmer's eyes all day; had been careful not to; and it seemed to me that his attention had been exclusively focused upon what he had now achieved, a visiting-terms acquaintanceship with Mercer Lorrimore.

There was now loud music in the lounge, with two couples trying to dance and falling over with giggles from the perpetual motion of the dance floor. Up in the dome, the aurora borealis was doing its flickering fiery best on the horizon, and in the bar there was a group playing poker in serious silent concentration. Playing for thousands, the barman said.

Between the bar and the dining room there were three bedrooms, and in one of those, with the door open, was a sleeping-car attendant, dressed exactly like myself.

'Hello,' he said, as I paused in the doorway. 'Come to help?'

'Sure,' I said. 'What do I do?'

'You're the actor, aren't you?' he asked.

'It's hush-hush.'

He nodded. 'I won't say a word.'

He was of about my own age, perhaps a bit older, pleasant-looking and cheerful. He showed me how to fold up the ingenious mechanism of the daytime arm-chairs and slide them under a bed which pulled out from the wall. A top bunk was then pulled down from the ceiling, complete with ladder. He straightened the bedclothes and laid a wrapped chocolate truffle on each pillow, a goodnight blessing.

'Neat,' I said.

He had only one more room to do, he said, and he should have finished long before this but he'd been badly delayed in the car on the other side of the dining car, which he had in his care also.

I nodded – and several thoughts arrived simultaneously in a rush on my mental doorstep. They were that Filmer's bedroom was in that car. Filmer was at that moment with the Lorrimores. The only locks on the bedroom doors were inside, in the form of bolts to ensure privacy. There was no way of preventing anyone from walking in if a room were empty.

I went along to the sleeping car on the far side of the kitchen and opened the door of the abode of Julius Apollo.

CHAPTER NINE

By virtue of having paid double and possibly treble, Filmer had a double bedroom all to himself. Only the lower bunk had been prepared for the night: the upper was still in the ceiling.

For all that he could be expected to stay in the Lorrimores' car for at least fifteen more minutes I felt decidedly jittery, and I left the door open so that if he did come back unexpectedly I could say I was merely checking that everything was in order. My uniform had multiple advantages.

The bedrooms were small, as one would expect, though in the daytime, with the beds folded away, there was comfortable space. There was a washbasin in full view, with the rest of the plumbing in a discreet little closet. For hanging clothes there was a slot behind the bedheads about eight inches wide, enough in Filmer's case for two suits. Another two jackets hung on hangers on pegs on the wall.

I searched quickly through all the pockets, but they were mostly empty. There was only, in one inner pocket, a receipt for a watch repair which I replaced where I found it.

There were no drawers: more or less everything else had to be in his suitcase which stood against the wall. With an eye on the corridor outside, I tried one of the latches and wasn't surprised to find it locked.

That left only a tiny cupboard above the hanging space, in which Julius Apollo had stored a black leather toilet bag and his brushes.

On the floor below his suits, pushed to the back of the hanging space, I found his briefcase.

I put my head out of the door which was directly beside the hanging space, and looked up and down the corridor.

No one in sight.

I went down on hands and knees, half in and half out of the doorway, with an excuse ready of looking for a coin I'd dropped. I put a hand into the hanging space and drew the briefcase to the front; and it was of black crocodile skin with gold clasps, as I'd seen at Nottingham races.

The fact of its presence was all I was going to learn, however, as it had revolving combination locks which were easy enough to undo, but only if one had two hours to spend on each lock, which I hadn't. Whether or not the briefcase still contained whatever Horfitz had given Filmer at Nottingham was anyone's guess, and dearly though I would have liked to look at the contents, I didn't want to risk any more at that point.

I pushed the black case deep into the hanging space again, stood up outside the door, closed it and went back to the scenes of jollity to the rear.

It was, by this time, nearly midnight. The Youngs were standing up in the dining room, ready to go to bed. Xanthe, however, alarmed by the departure of her new-found friend, was practically clinging to Mrs Young and with an echo of the earlier hysteria was saying that she couldn't possibly sleep in the private car, she would have nightmares, she would be too scared to stay, she was sure whoever had uncoupled the car before would do it again in the middle of the night, and they would all be killed when the Canadian crashed into them, because the Canadian was still there behind us, wasn't it, wasn't it?

Yes, it was.

Mrs Young did her best to soothe her, but it was impossible not to respect her fears. She had undoubtedly nearly been killed. Mrs Young told her that the madman who had mischievously unhitched the car was hours behind us in Cartier, but Xanthe was beyond reassurance.

Mrs Young appealed to Nell, asking if there was anywhere else that Xanthe could sleep, and Nell, consulting the ever-present clipboard, shook her head doubtfully.

'There's an upper berth in a section,' she said slowly, 'but it only has a curtain, and no facilities except at the end of the car, and it's hardly what Xanthe's used to.'

'I don't care,' Xanthe said passionately. 'I'll sleep on the floor or on the seats in the lounge, or *anywhere*. I'll sleep in that upper berth . . . please let me.'

'I don't see why not, then,' Nell said. 'What about night things?'

'I'm not going into our car to fetch them. I'm *not*.'

'All right,' Nell said. 'I'll go and ask your mother.'

Mrs Young stayed with Xanthe, who was again faintly trembling, until at length Nell returned with both a small grip and Bambi.

Bambi tried to get her daughter to change her mind, but predictably without success. I thought it unlikely that Xanthe would ever sleep in that car again, so strong was her present reaction. She, Bambi, Nell and the Youngs made their way past me without looking at me and continued on along the corridor beside the kitchen, going to inspect the revised quarters which I knew were in the sleeping car forward of Filmer's.

After a while Bambi and Nell returned alone, and Bambi with an unexcited word of gratitude to Nell walked a few paces forward and stopped beside her son, who had done nothing to comfort or help his sister and was now sitting alone.

'Come along, Sheridan,' she said, her tone without peremptoriness but also without affection. 'Your father asks you to come.'

Sheridan gave her a look of hatred which seemed not in the least to bother her. She stood patiently waiting until, with exceedingly bad grace, he got to his feet and followed her homewards.

Bambi, it seemed to me, had taught herself not to care for Sheridan so as not to be hurt by him. She too, like Mercer, must have suffered for years from his boorish behaviour in public, and she had distanced herself from it. She didn't try to buy the toleration of the victims of his rudeness, as Mercer did: she ignored the rudeness instead.

I wondered which had come first, the chill and disenchantment of her worldly sophistication, or the lack of warmth in her son: and perhaps there was ice in both of them, and the one had reinforced the other. Bambi, I thought, was a highly inappropriate name for her; she was no innocent wide-eyed smooth-skinned fawn but an experienced, aloof, good-looking woman in the skin of minks.

Nell, watching them go, sighed and said, 'She didn't kiss Xanthe goodnight, you know, or give her even a hug to comfort her. Nothing. And Mercer's so nice.'

'Forget them.'

'Yes. . . . You do realize the press will be down on this train like a pack of hunting lions at the next stop?'

'Lionesses,' I said.

'What?'

'It's the females who hunt in a pack. One male sits by, watching, and takes the lion's share of the kill.'

'I don't want to know that.'

'Our next stop,' I said, 'will be fifteen minutes at

White River in the middle of the night. After the delay, we'll aim to arrive at four-oh-five, depart four-twenty.'

'And after that?'

'Except for a three-minute pause in a back-of-beyond, we stop at Thunder Bay for twenty-five minutes at ten-fifty tomorrow morning.'

'Do you know the whole timetable by heart?'

'Emil told me to learn it. He was right when he said the question I would have to answer most was "When do we reach so and so?" ... and if I were a regular waiter he said I would know the answers, even though we're thirty-five minutes earlier everywhere than the regular Canadian.'

'Emil is cute,' she said.

I looked at her in surprise. I wouldn't have thought of Emil as cute. Small, neat, bright and generous, yes. 'Cute?' I asked.

'I would hope,' she said, 'that you don't think so.'

'No.'

'Good.' She was relieved, I saw.

'Weren't you sure?' I asked curiously. 'Am I so ... ambivalent?'

'Well ...' There was a touch of embarrassment. 'I didn't mean to get into this sort of conversation, really I didn't. But if you want to know, there's something about you that's secret ... ultra-private ... as if you didn't want to be known too well. So I just wondered. I'm sorry ...'

'I shall shower you with ravening kisses.'

185

She laughed. 'Not your style.'

'Wait and see.' And two people didn't, I thought, drift into talking like that after knowing each other for such a short while unless there was immediate trust and liking.

We were standing in the tiny lobby between the kitchen and the dining room, and she still had the clipboard clasped to her chest. She would have to put it down, I thought fleetingly, before any serious ravening could take place.

'You always have jokes in your eyes,' she said. 'And you never tell them.'

'I was thinking about how you use your clipboard as chain-mail.'

Her own eyes widened. 'A lousy man in the magazine office squeezed my breast ... Why am I telling you? It was years ago. Why should I care? Anyway, where else would you carry a clipboard?'

She put it down, all the same, on the counter, but we didn't talk much longer as the revellers from the rear began coming through to go to the bedrooms. I retreated into the kitchen and I could hear people asking Nell what time they could have breakfast.

'Between seven and nine-thirty,' she said. 'Sleep well, everybody.' She put her head into the kitchen. 'Same to you, sleep well. I'm off to bed.'

'Goodnight,' I said, smiling.

'Aren't you going?'

'Yes, in a while.'

'When everything's . . . safe?'

'You might say so.'

'What exactly does the Jockey Club expect you to *do*?'

'See trouble before it comes.'

'But that's practically impossible.'

'Mm,' I said. 'I didn't foresee anyone uncoupling the Lorrimores.'

'You'll be fired for that,' she said drily, 'so if you sleep, sleep well.'

'Tor would kiss you,' I said. 'Tommy can't.'

'I'll count it done.'

She went away blithely, the clipboard again in place: a habit, I supposed, as much as a defence.

I walked back to the bar and wasted time with the barman. The intent poker school looked set for an all-night session, the dancing was still causing laughter in the lounge and the northern lights were entrancing the devotees in the dome. The barman yawned and said he'd be closing the bar soon. Alcohol stopped at midnight.

I heard Daffodil's voice before I saw her, so that when Filmer came past the door of the bar I was bending down with my head below the counter as if to be tidying things there. I had the impression they did no more than glance in as they passed, as Filmer was saying ' . . . when we get to Winnipeg.' 'You mean Vancouver,' Daffodil said. 'Yes, Vancouver.' 'You always get them mixed . . .' Her voice, which had been raised, as his had been, so as to be heard while one of them walked ahead of the other, died away as they passed down the corridor, presumably en route to bed.

Giving them time to say goodnight, as Daffodil's room was one of the three just past the bar, I slowly followed. They were nowhere in sight as I went through to the dining car, and Filmer seemed to have gone straight to his room, as there was a thread of light shining along the bottom of his door; but Daffodil, I discovered, had after all not. Instead of being cosily tucked up in her bunk near the bar, she surprisingly came walking towards me from the sleeping car forward of Filmer's, her diamonds lighting small bright fires with every step.

I stood back to let her pass, but she shimmered to a stop before me and said, 'Do you know where Miss Lorrimore is sleeping?'

'In the car you've just come from, madam,' I answered helpfully.

'Yes, but where? I told her parents that I would make sure she was all right.'

'The sleeping-car attendant will know,' I said. 'If you would like to follow me?'

She nodded assent and as I turned to lead the way I thought that at close quarters she was probably younger than I'd assumed, or else that she was older but immature: an odd impression, fleeting and gone.

The middle-aged sleeping-car attendant was dozing but dressed. He obligingly showed Daffodil the upper berth where Xanthe was sleeping, but the thick felt curtains were closely fastened, and when Daffodil called the girl's name quietly, there was no response. The slightly fatherly attendant said he was sure she was safely asleep, as he'd seen her returning from the washroom at the end of the car and climbing up to her bunk.

'I guess that will do,' Daffodil said, shrugging off someone else's problem. 'Goodnight, then, and thank you for your help.'

We watched her sway away holding on to the rails, her high curls shining, her figure neat, her intense musky scent lingering like a memory in the air after she herself had gone. The sleeping-car attendant sighed deeply at so much opulent femininity and philosophically returned to his roomette, and I went on up the train into the next car, where my own bed lay.

George Burley's door, two along from mine, was wide open, and I found he was in residence, dressed but asleep, quietly snoring in his armchair. He jerked awake as if with a sixth sense as I paused in his doorway and said, 'What's wrong, eh?'

'Nothing that I know of,' I said.

'Oh, it's you.'

'I'm sorry I woke you.'

'I wasn't asleep . . . well, napping, then. I'm used to that. I've been on the railways all my life, eh?'

'A love affair?' I said.

'You can bet your life.' He rubbed his eyes, yawning.

'In the old days there were many big railway families. Father to son . . . cousins, uncles . . . it got handed down. My father, my grandfather, they were railwaymen. But my sons, eh? They're behind desks in big cities tapping at computers.' He chuckled. 'They run the railways too now from behind desks, eh? They sit in Montreal making decisions and they've never heard a train's call at night across the prairie. They've missed all that. These days the top brass fly everywhere, eh?' His eyes twinkled. Anyone who wasn't a wheels-on railwayman was demonstrably stupid. 'I'll tell you,' he said, 'I hope to die on the railways.'

'Not too soon, though.'

'Not before White River, at any rate.'

I said goodnight and went to my own room where I found the sleeping-car attendant had duly lowered my bed and laid a chocolate truffle on the pillow.

I ate the chocolate. Very good.

I took off the yellow waistcoat with its white lining and hung it on a hanger, and I took off my shoes, but rather like George I still felt myself to be on duty, so I switched off the light and lay on top of the bedclothes watching the black Canadian land slide by, while the free northern show went on above for hours in the sky. There seemed to be wide horizontal bands of light which slowly changed in intensity, with brighter spots growing and fading in places mysteriously against the deeps of eternity. It was peaceful more than frenetic, a mirage of slow dawns and sunsets going back to the

Fluted Point people: humbling. In the context of ten
thousand years, I thought, what did Filmer and his sins
matter? Yet all we had was here and now, and here
and now . . . always through time . . . was where the
struggle towards goodness had to be fought. Towards
virtue, morality, uprightness, order: call it what one
liked. A long, ever-recurring battle.

In the here and now we stopped without incident at
White River. I saw George outside under the station
lights and watched him set off towards the rear of the
train. Apparently the Lorrimores were still safely with
us as he came back presently without haste or alarm,
and after a while the train made its usual unobtrusive
departure westwards.

I slept for a couple of hours and was awakened while
it was still dark by a gentle rapping on my door: it
proved to be Emil, fully dressed and apologetic.

'I didn't know if I should wake you. If you are
serious about this, it is time to set the tables for
breakfast.'

'I'm serious,' I said.

He smiled with seeming satisfaction. 'It is much
easier with four of us.'

I said I would come at once and made it, washed,
shaved and tidy, in roughly ten minutes. Oliver and
Cathy were already there, wide awake. The kitchen was
filled with glorious smells of baking and Angus, with
languid largesse, said he wouldn't notice if we ate a
slice or two of his raisin bread, or of his apple and

walnut. Simone said dourly that we were not to eat the croissants as there wouldn't be enough. It was all rather like school.

We set the plates, put fresh water and carnations in bud vases, one flower to each table, and folded pink napkins with precision. By seven-fifteen, the first break-fasters were addressing themselves to eggs Benedict and I was pouring tea and coffee as to the service born.

At seven-thirty, in struggling daylight, we stopped briefly in a place identified in suitably small letters on the small station as Schreiber.

It was from here, I reflected, looking through the windows at a small scattered town, that the despatcher had spoken to George and me the previous evening: and while I watched, George appeared outside and was met by a man who came from the station. They con-ferred for a while, then George returned to the train, and the train went quietly on its way.

A spectacular way: all through breakfast, the track ran along the north shore of Lake Superior, so close that at times the train seemed to be overhanging the water. The passengers oohed and aahed, the Unwins (Upper Gumtree) sitting with the owners of Flokati, the Redi-Hots with a couple talking incessantly of the prowess of their horse, Wordmaster, also on the train.

Filmer came alone to sit at an untenanted table, ordering eggs and coffee from Oliver without looking at him. Presently the Youngs appeared and with smiling acquaintanceship joined Filmer. I wondered if he thought immediately of Ezra Gideon, the Youngs' dear friend, but his face showed nothing but politeness.

Xanthe ambled in in a tousled yawning state and yesterday's clothes and flopped into the empty chair beside Filmer. Interestingly he made no attempt to save the seat for Daffodil, but seemed to echo Mrs Young's enquiries about how Xanthe had slept.

Like a log, it appeared, although she seemed to regret not reporting constant nightmares. Mr Young looked bored, as if he had tired of the subject a long time ago, but his wife retained her sweet comforting expression without any visible effort.

I waited with hovering impatience for Nell to arrive, which she did at length in a straight black skirt (worse and worse) with a prim coffee blouse and unobtrusive gold earrings. She had drawn her fair hair high into an elaborate plait down the back of her head and fastened it at the bottom with a wide tortoiseshell clasp: it looked distinguished and competent, but nowhere near cuddly.

People I hadn't yet identified beckoned her eagerly to join them, which she did with the ravishing smile she had loosed once or twice in my direction. She told Cathy she would pass on the eggs but would like croissants and coffee, and presently I was bringing them to her as she sat with eyes demurely downwards, studiously ignoring my existence. I set butter, jam and breads before her. I poured into her cup. She told her table companions it was nice having hand-picked attendants all the way to Vancouver.

I knew it was a game but I could cheerfully have strangled her. I didn't want them noticing me even a little. I went away and looked back, and met her eyes, which were laughing. It was the sort of look between us which would have started alert interest in me if I'd spotted it between others, and I thought I was near to losing my grip on what I was supposed to be doing, and that I'd better be more careful. I hadn't needed to serve her: I'd taken the tray from Cathy. Temptation will be your downfall, Tor, I thought.

Except for Xanthe, Mercer was the only Lorrimore to surface for breakfast, and he came not to eat but to ask Emil to send trays through to his own private dining room. Emil himself and Oliver delivered the necessary, although Emil on his return said he hoped this wasn't going to happen at lunch and dinner also, because it took too much time. Room service was strictly not available, yet one didn't disoblige the Lorrimores if one could help it.

Daffodil arrived after everyone else with each bright curl in place and pleasantly sat across the aisle from the Filmer/Young table, asking for news of Xanthe's night. The only people not bothering to ask, it seemed, were the near-victim's own family. Xanthe chattered and could be heard telling Daffodil she felt snug and safe behind her curtain. The next time I went slowly past their table, refill coffee pot at the ready, the conversation was back to the journey, with Xanthe this time saying she basically thought horse racing boring and she wouldn't have come on this trip if her father hadn't made her.

'How did he make you?' Filmer said interestedly.

'Oh!' She sounded suddenly flustered and evaded an answer. 'He made Sheridan come, too.'

'But why, if you both didn't want to?' That was Daffodil's voice, behind my back.

'He likes us where he can see us, he says.' There was a note of grudge and bitterness but also, it seemed to me, a realistic acknowledgement that father knew best: and judging from Sheridan's behaviour to date, under his father's long-suffering eye was certainly the son's safest place.

The conversation faded into the distance and I paused to refill the Unwins' cups, where the talk was about Upper Gumtree having the edge over Mercer's Premiere that was coming to Winnipeg by road.

George Burley presently came into the dining car and spoke for a while to Nell, who subsequently went from table to table, clipboard in place, repeating what he'd said.

'We're stopping at Thunder Bay for longer than scheduled, as there'll be an investigation there about the Lorrimores' car being uncoupled. We'll be there about an hour and a half, as we're not going on until after the regular Canadian has gone through. The Canadian will be ahead of us then all the way to Winnipeg.'

'What about lunch?' Mr Young asked. Mr Young, though thinnish, had a habit of eating half his wife's food as well as his own.

'We'll leave Thunder Bay at about a quarter to one,' Nell said, 'so we'll have lunch soon after. And a more leisurely dinner before we get to Winnipeg, instead of having to crowd it in early. It will all fit in quite well.' She was smiling, reassuring, keeping the party from unravelling. 'You'll be glad to stretch your legs for a bit longer in Thunder Bay, and some of you might visit your horses.'

The owner of Redi-Hot, who seemed to spend most of his time reading a guide book, told Mr and Mrs Wordmaster, who looked suitably impressed, that Thunder Bay, one of Canada's largest ports, was at the far west end of the St Lawrence–Great Lakes Seaway and should really be called what the locals called it, The Lakehead. Grain from the prairies was shipped from there to throughout the world, he said.

'Fancy that,' said Mrs Wordmaster, who was English.

I retreated from this scintillating conversation and helped Oliver and Cathy clear up in the kitchen, and shortly before eleven we slid to a halt in the port that was halfway across Canada on some rails parallel with but a little removed from the station buildings.

Immediately a waiting double posse of determined-looking men advanced from the station across two intervening tracks, one lot sprouting press cameras, the other notebooks. George stepped down from the train to meet the notebook people, and the others fanned out and began clicking. One of the notebook crowd climbed aboard and came into the dining car, inviting anyone who had seen anyone or anything suspicious the previous evening to please unbutton, but of course no one had, or no one was saying, because otherwise the whole train would have known about it by now.

The investigator said he would try his luck with the scenery-watchers in the dome car, with apparently the same result, and from there he presumably went in to see the Lorrimores, who apart from Xanthe were still in seclusion. He then reappeared in the dining car with an interested crowd of people following him and asked to speak to Xanthe, who up until then had kept palely quiet.

He identified her easily because everyone looked her way. Filmer was still beside her: the passengers tended all the time to linger at the tables, talking, after the meals had been cleared, rather than return to the solitude of their bedrooms. Nearly everyone, I would have guessed, had been either in the dining room or the dome car all morning.

Mrs Young squeezed Xanthe's hand encouragingly from across the table while the half-child half-young-woman shivered her way through the dangerous memory.

'No,' she said, with everyone quiet and attentively

listening, 'no one suggested I went to our car . . . I just wanted to go to the bathroom. And I could . . . I . . . could have been killed.'

'Yes . . .' The investigator, middle-aged and sharp-eyed, was sympathetic but calming, speaking in a distinct voice that carried easily through the dining car, now that we weren't moving. 'Was there anyone in the dome car lounge when you went through?'

'Lots of people.' Xanthe's voice was much quieter than his.

'Did you know them?'

'No. I mean, they were on this trip. Everyone there was.' She was beginning to speak more loudly, so that all could hear.

A few heads nodded.

'No one you now know was a stranger?'

'No.'

Mrs Young, intelligent besides comforting, asked, 'Do you mean it's possible to uncouple a car while you're actually on the train? You don't have to be on the ground to do it?'

The investigator gave her his attention and everyone leaned forward slightly to hear the answer.

'It's possible. It can be done also while the train is moving, which is why we want to know if there was anyone in the dome car who was unknown to you all. Unknown to any of you, I should say.'

There was a long, respectful, understanding silence.

Nell said, 'I suppose I know most of our passengers by sight by now. I identified them all at Toronto station when I was allocating their sleeping quarters. I didn't see anyone yesterday evening who puzzled me.'

'You don't think,' Mrs Young said, putting her finger unerringly on the implication, 'that the car was unhitched by *someone in our party*?'

'We're investigating all possibilities,' the investigator said without pompousness. He looked around at the ranks of worried faces and his slightly severe expression softened. 'The private car was deliberately uncoupled,' he said, 'but we're of the preliminary opinion that it was an act of mischief committed by someone in Cartier, the last place you stopped before Miss Lorrimore found the car was missing. But we do have to ask if the saboteur could have been on the train, just in case any of you noticed anything wrong.'

A man at the back of the crowd said, 'I was sitting in the dome car lounge when Xanthe came through, and I can tell you that no one had come the other way. I mean, we all knew that only the Lorrimores' car was behind the dome car. If anyone except the Lorrimores had gone that way and come back again . . . well . . . we would have noticed.'

Another nodding of heads. People noticed everything to do with the Lorrimores.

I was watching the scene from the kitchen end of the dining car, standing just behind Emil, Cathy and

199

Oliver. I could see Xanthe's troubled face clearly, and also Filmer's beside her. He seemed to me to be showing diminishing interest in the enquiry, turning his tidily brushed head away to look out of the window instead. There was no tension in him: when he was tense there was a rigidity in his neck muscles, a rigidity I'd watched from the depths of the crowd during the brief day of his trial and seen a few times since, as at Nottingham. When Filmer felt tense, it showed.

Even as I watched him, his neck went rigid.

I looked out of a window to see what he was looking at, but there seemed to be nothing of great note, only the racegoing passengers streaming off their forward carriages en route to write postcards home from the station.

Filmer looked back towards Xanthe and the investigator and made a small gesture of impatience, and it seemed to trigger a response from the investigator because he said that if anyone remembered any helpful detail, however small, would they please tell him or one of his colleagues, but meanwhile everyone was free to go.

There was a communal sigh as the real-life investigation broke up. Zak, I thought, would be finding the competition too stiff, the fiction an anti-climax after the fact. He hadn't appeared for this scene: none of the actors had.

Most of the passengers went off to don coats against what appeared to be a cold wind outside, but Filmer climbed down from the door of the dome-car end of the dining car without more protection than his carefully casual shirt and aristocratic tweed jacket. He paused irresolutely, not scrunching, as the others were beginning to, across the two sets of rails between our train and the station but meandering at an angle forward in the direction of the engine.

Inside, I followed him, easily keeping pace with his slow step. I thought at first that he was merely taking an open-air path to his own bedroom, but he went straight past the open door at the end of his sleeping car, and straight on past the next car also. Going to see his horse, no doubt. I went on following: it had become a habit.

At the end of the third car, just past George Burley's office, he stopped, because someone was coming out from the station to meet him: a gaunt man in a padded short coat with a fur collar, with grey hair blowing in disarray in the wind.

They met between George's window and the open door at the end of the car and although at first they looked moderately at peace with each other, the encounter deteriorated rapidly.

I risked them seeing me so as to try to hear, but in fact by the time I could hear them they were shouting, which meant I could listen through the doorway without seeing them or being seen.

Filmer was yelling furiously, 'I said before Vancouver!'

The gaunt man with a snarl in his Canadian voice said, 'You said before Winnipeg, and I've done it and I want my money.'

'Coo-ee,' trilled Daffodil, teetering towards them in chinchillas and high-heeled boots. 'Are we going to see Laurentide Ice?'

CHAPTER TEN

Blast her, I thought intensely. Triple bloody shit, and several other words to that effect.

I watched through George's window as Filmer made great efforts to go towards her with a smile, drawing attention away from the gaunt-faced man, who returned to the station.

Before Winnipeg, before Vancouver. Julius Apollo had mixed them up yet again. 'You said before Winnipeg, and I've done it and I want my money.' Heavy words, full of threat.

What before Winnipeg? What had he done?

What indeed.

It couldn't have been the Lorrimores' car, I thought. Filmer had shown no interest and no tension; had been obviously uninvolved. But then he would have been calm, I supposed, if he hadn't been expecting anything to happen except before Vancouver. He hadn't been expecting the Lorrimores' car to be uncoupled before either city, of that I was certain. He had instead been cultivating his acquaintanceship with Mercer, a game plan that would have come to an abrupt end if the Lorrimores had deserted the trip, which they would have done at once if the Canadian had ploughed into their home-from-home.

If not the Lorrimores' car, what else had happened? What had happened before Winnipeg that Filmer had intended to happen before Vancouver? In what way had the gaunt man already earned his money?

Anyone's guess, I thought.

He could have robbed someone, bribed a stable lad, nobbled a horse . . .

Nobbled a horse that was going to run at Winnipeg, instead of one running at Vancouver?

From the fury in their voices, the mistake had been devastating.

Only Flokati and Upper Gumtree were due to run at Winnipeg . . . Laurentide Ice was running at Vancouver against Voting Right and Sparrowgrass. . . . Could Filmer have been so stupid as to get the horses' names wrong in addition to the cities? No, he couldn't.

Impasse. Yet . . . gaunt-face had done *something*.

Sighing, I watched the Youngs walk past the window en route, I supposed, to the horse car. Soon after, the Unwins followed. I would have liked to have checked at once on the state of the horses, but I supposed if there were something wrong with any of them I would hear soon enough.

I wished I'd been able to take a photograph of gaunt-face, but I'd been more keen to listen.

If he'd done something to or around the horses, I thought, then he had to have travelled with us on the train. He hadn't just met us in Thunder Bay. If he'd been on the train and had walked with the other race-goers towards the station, Filmer could have seen him through the window . . . and just the sight of him had caused the tensing of the neck muscles . . . and if Filmer hadn't yet paid him for whatever . . . then he would come back to the train . . .

I left George's office and went two doors along to my roomette to dig my telescopic-lens binoculars-camera out of Tommy's holdall, and I sat and waited by the window for gaunt-face's return.

What happened instead was that after a while Filmer and Daffodil appeared in my view, making a diagonal course towards the station buildings, and pretty soon afterwards, accompanied by a lot of bell-ringing and warning hooters, a huge bright yellow diesel engine came grinding and groaning past my window followed by long corrugated silver coaches as the whole of the regular Canadian rolled up the track next to the race train and stopped precisely alongside.

Instead of a nice clear photographic view of the station, I now faced the black uninformative window of someone else's roomette.

Frustration and damnation, I thought. I tucked the binoculars into the holdall again and without any sensible plans wandered back towards the dining car. If I went on like this, I would fulfil the gloomiest fears of Bill Baudelaire, the Brigadier and, above all, John Millington. 'I *told* you we should have sent an ex-policeman . . .' I could hear his voice in my ear.

It occurred to me, when I reached Julius Apollo's door, that the Canadian would be standing where it was for the whole of the twenty-five minutes of its daily scheduled stop. For twenty-five minutes . . . say twenty-two by now . . . Filmer would stay over in the station. He would not walk round either end of the lengthy Canadian to return to his room.

Would he?

No, he would not. Why should he? He had only just gone over there. I had twenty minutes to see what I could do about his combination locks.

If I'd paused for more thought I perhaps wouldn't have had the nerve, but I simply opened his door, checked up and down the corridor for observers (none) and went inside, shutting myself in.

The black briefcase was still on the floor at the back of the hanging space, under the suits. I pulled it out, sat on one of the armchairs, and with a feeling of unreality started on the right-hand lock. If anyone should come in, I thought confusedly . . . if the sleeping-car attendant for instance came in . . . whatever excuse could I possibly find?

None at all.

The right-hand combination wheels were set at one-three-seven. I methodically went on from there, one-three-eight, one-three-nine, one-four-zero, trying the latch after each number change.

My heart hammered and I felt breathless. I was used to long-distance safety in my work, and in the past to many physical dangers, but never to this sort of risk.

One-four-one, one-four-two, one-four-three.... I tried the latch over and over and looked at my watch. Only two minutes had gone. It felt like a lifetime. One-four-four, one-four-five.... There were a thousand possible combinations ... one-four-six, one-four-seven ... in twenty minutes I could perhaps try a hundred and fifty numbers.... I had done this process before, once, but not under pressure, when Aunt Viv had set a combination on a new suitcase and then forgotten it ... one-four-eight, one-four-nine ... my face sweating, my fingers slipping on the tiny wheels from haste ... one-five-zero, one-five-one ...

With a snap the latch flew open.

It was incredible. I could hardly believe it. I had barely started. All I needed now was double the luck.

The left-hand combination numbers stood at seven-three-eight. I tried the latch. Nothing.

With just a hope that both locks opened to the same sesame, I turned the wheels to one-five-one and tried it. Nothing. Not so easy. I tried reversing it to five-one-five. Nothing. I tried comparable numbers, one-two-one, two-one-two, one-three-one, three-one-three, one-four-one, four-one-four ... six ... seven ... eight ... nine ... three zeros.

Zilch.

My nerve deserted me. I rolled the left-hand wheels back to seven-three-eight and with the latch closed again set the right-hand lock to one-three-seven. I polished the latches a bit with my shirtsleeve, then I put the briefcase back exactly as I'd found it and took my leaf-trembling self along to the dining car, already regretting, before I got there, that I hadn't stayed until the Canadian left, knowing that I'd wasted some of the best and perhaps the only chance I would get of seeing what Filmer had brought with him on the train.

Perhaps if I'd tried one-one-five, or five-five-one . . . or five-one-one, or five-five-five . . .

Nell was sitting alone at a table in the dining car working on her interminable lists (those usually clipped to the clipboard) and I sat down opposite her feeling ashamed of myself.

She glanced up. 'Hello,' she said.

'Hi.'

She considered me. 'You look hot. Been running?'

I'd been indulging in good heart exercise while sitting still. I didn't think I would confess.

'Sort of,' I said. 'How's things?'

She glanced sideways with disgust at the Canadian.

'I was just about to go over to the station when *that* arrived.'

That, as if taking the hint, began quietly to roll, and within twenty seconds, we again had a clear view of the station. Most of the train's passengers, including

Filmer and Daffodil, immediately started across the tracks to reboard. Among them, aiming for the race-goers' carriages, was gaunt-face.

God in heaven, I thought. I forgot about him. I forgot about photographing him. My wits were scattered.

'What's the matter?' Nell said, watching my face.

'I've earned a D minus. A double D minus.'

'You probably expect too much of yourself,' she said dispassionately. 'No one's perfect.'

'There are degrees of imperfection.'

'How big is the catastrophe?'

I thought it over more coolly. Gaunt-face was on the train, and I might have another opportunity. I could undo one of the latches of Filmer's briefcase and, given time, I might do the other. Correction: given nerve, I might do the other.

'OK,' I said, 'let's say C minus, could do better. Still not good.' Millington would have done better.

Zak and Emil arrived together at that point, Emil ready to set the tables for lunch, Zak in theatrical exasperation demanding to know if the actors were to put on the next scene before the meal as originally planned, and if not, when?

Nell looked at her watch and briefly thought. 'Couldn't you postpone it until cocktail time this evening?'

'We're supposed to do the following scene then,' he objected.

'Well . . . couldn't you run them both together?'

He rather grumpily agreed and went away saying they would have to rehearse. Nell smiled sweetly at his departing back and asked if I'd ever noticed how *important* everything was to actors? Everything except the real world, of course.

'Pussycat,' I said.

'But I have such tiny, indulgent claws.'

Oliver and Cathy arrived and with Emil began spreading tablecloths and setting places. I got to my feet and helped them, and Nell with teasing amusement watched me fold pink napkins into water lilies and said, 'Well, well, hidden depths,' and I answered, 'You should see my dishwashing,' which were the sort of infantile surface remarks of something we both guessed might suddenly become serious. The surface meanwhile was safe and shimmering and funny, and would stay that way until we were ready for change.

As usual, the passengers came early into the dining car, and I faded into the scenery in my uniform and avoided Nell's eyes.

The passengers hadn't over-enjoyed their sojourn in the station, it appeared, as they had been fallen upon by the flock of pressmen who had taken Xanthe back again to the brink of hysteria, and had asked Mercer whether it wasn't unwise to flaunt the privilege of wealth in his private car, and hadn't he invited trouble by adding it to the train? Indignation on his behalf was thick in the air. Everyone knew he was public-spiritedly on the trip For the Sake of Canadian Racing.

The Lorrimores, all four of them, arrived together to murmurs of sympathy, but the two young ones split off immediately from their parents and from each other, all of them gravitating to their various havens: the parents went to join Filmer and Daffodil of their own free will, Xanthe made a straight piteous line to Mrs Young, and Sheridan grabbed hold of Nell, who was by this time standing, saying that he needed her to sit with him, she was the only decent human being on the whole damn train.

Nell, unsure of the worth of his compliment, nevertheless sat down opposite him, even if temporarily. Keeping Sheridan on a straight or even a wavy line definitely came into the category of crisis control.

Sheridan had the looks which went with Julius's name, Apollo: he was tall, handsome, nearly blond, a child of the sun. The ice, the arrogance, the lack of common sense and of control, these were the darkside tragedy. A mini psychopath, I thought, and maybe not so mini, at that, if Xanthe thought he should be in jail.

The Australian Unwins, sitting with the rival owners of Flokati, were concerned about a lifelessness they had detected in Upper Gumtree due to the fact that on the train their horse had been fed a restricted diet of compressed food nuts and high-grade hay and the Flokati people were cheerfully saying that on so long a stretch without exercise, good hay was best. Hay was calming. 'We don't want them climbing the walls,' Mr Flokati said. Upper Gumtree had looked asleep, Mrs Unwin remarked with disapproval. The Flokati people beamed wide, trying to look sympathetic. If Upper Gumtree proved listless, so much the better for Flokati's chances.

It seemed that all of the owners had taken the opportunity of visiting the horses while the train was standing still, and listen though I might I could hear no one else reporting trouble.

Upper Gumtree, it seemed to me, might revive spectacularly on the morrow, given oats, fresh air and exercise. His race was still more than forty-eight hours away. If gaunt-face had in fact given Upper Gumtree something tranquillizing, the effects would wear off long before then.

On reflection, I thought it less and less probable that he had done any such thing: he would have to have bypassed the dragon-lady, Leslie Brown, for a start. Yet presumably at times she left her post . . . to eat and sleep.

'I said,' Daffodil said to me distinctly, 'would you bring me a clean knife? I've dropped mine on the floor.'

'Certainly, madam,' I said, coming back abruptly to the matter in hand and, realizing with a shock that she had already asked me once, I fetched her a knife fast. She merely nodded, her attention again on Filmer, and he, I was mightily relieved to see, had taken no notice of the small matter. But how could I, I thought ruefully, how could I have possibly stopped concentrating when I was so close to him? Only one day ago the proximity had had my pulse racing.

The train had made its imperceptible departure and was rolling along again past the uninhabited infinity of rocks and lakes and conifers that seemed to march on to the end of the world. We finished serving lunch and coffee and cleared up, and as soon as I decently could I left the kitchen and set off forward up the train.

George, whom I looked for first, was in his office eating a fat ragged beef sandwich and drinking diet Coke.

'How did it go,' I asked, 'in Thunder Bay?'

He scowled, but half-heartedly. 'They found out nothing I hadn't told them. There was nothing to see. They're thinking now that whoever uncoupled the private car was on it when the train left Cartier.'

'On the private car?' I said in surprise.

'That's right. The steam tube could have been disconnected in the station, eh? Then the train leaves Cartier with the saboteur in the Lorrimores' car. Then less than a mile out of Cartier, eh?, our saboteur pulls up the rod that undoes the coupling. Then the private car rolls to a stop, and he gets off and walks back to Cartier.'

'But why should anyone do that?'

'Grow up, sonny. There are people in this world who cause trouble because it makes them feel important. They're ineffective, eh?, in their lives. So they burn

213

things ... and smash things ... paint slogans on walls ... leave their mark on something, eh? And wreck trains. Put slabs of concrete on the rails. I've seen it done. Power over others, that's what it's about. A grudge against the Lorrimores, most like. Power over them, over their possessions. That's what those investigators think.'

'Hm,' I said. 'If that's the case, the saboteur wouldn't have walked back to Cartier but up to some vantage point from where he could watch the smash.'

George looked startled. 'Well ... I suppose he might.'

'Arsonists often help to put out the fires they've started.'

'You mean he would have waited around ... to help with the wreck? Even to help with casualties?'

'Sure,' I said. 'Pure, heady power, to know you'd caused such a scene.'

'I didn't see anyone around,' he said thoughtfully, 'when we went back to the car. I shone the lamp ... there wasn't anyone moving, eh?, or anything like that.'

'So, what are the investigators going to do?' I asked.

His eyes crinkled and the familiar chuckle escaped. 'Write long reports, eh? Tell us never to take private cars. Blame me for not preventing it, I dare say.'

He didn't seem worried at the idea. His shoulders and his mind were broad.

I left him with appreciation and went forward into the central dining car where all the actors were sitting in front of coffee cups and poring over typed sheets of stage directions, muttering under their breaths and sometimes exclaiming aloud.

Zak raised his eyes vaguely in my direction but it would have been tactless to disrupt the thoughts behind them, so I pressed on forward, traversing the dayniter and the sleeping cars and arriving at the forward dome car. There were a lot of people about everywhere, but no one looked my way twice.

I knocked eventually on the door of the horse-car and, after inspection and formalities that would have done an Iron Curtain country proud, was admitted again by Ms Brown to the holy of holies.

Rescrawling 'Tommy Titmouse' on her list I was interested to see how long it had grown, and I noticed that even Mercer hadn't been let in without signing. I asked the dragon-lady if anyone had come in who wasn't an owner or a groom, and she bridled like a thin turkey and told me that she had conscientiously checked every visitor against her list of bona fide owners, and only they had been admitted.

'But you wouldn't know them all by sight,' I said.

'What do you mean?' she demanded.

'Supposing for instance someone came and said they were Mr Unwin, you would check that his name was on the list and let him in?'

'Yes, of course.'

'And suppose he wasn't Mr Unwin, although he said he was?'

'You're just being difficult,' she said crossly. 'I cannot refuse entry to the owners. They were given the right to visit, but they don't have to produce passports. Nor do their wives or husbands.'

I looked down her visitors' list. Filmer appeared on it twice, Daffodil once. Filmer's signature was large and flamboyant, demanding attention. No one had written Filmer in any other way: it seemed that gaunt-face hadn't gained entry by giving Filmer's name, at least. It didn't mean he hadn't given someone else's.

I gave Leslie Brown her list back and wandered around under her eagle eye looking at the horses. They swayed peacefully to the motion, standing diagonally across the stalls, watching me incuriously, seemingly content. I couldn't perceive that Upper Gumtree looked any more sleepy than any of the others: his eyes were as bright, and he pricked his ears when I came near him.

All of the grooms, except one who was asleep on some hay bales, had chosen not to sit in the car with their charges, and I imagined it was because of Leslie Brown's daunting presence: racing lads on the whole felt a companionable devotion to their horses, and I would have expected more of them to be sitting on the hay bales during the day.

'What happens at night on the train?' I asked Leslie Brown. 'Who guards the horses then?'

'I do,' she said tartly. 'They've given me a roomette or some such, but I take this thing seriously. I slept in here last night, and will do so again after Winnipeg, and after Lake Louise. I don't see why you're so worried about anyone slipping past me.' She frowned at me, not liking my suspicions. 'When I go to the bathroom, I leave one groom in here and lock the horses' car door behind me. I'm never away more than a few minutes. I insist on one of the grooms being in here at all times. I am very well aware of the need for security, and I assure you that the horses are well guarded.'

I regarded her thin obstinate face and knew she believed to her determined soul in what she said.

'As for the barns at Winnipeg and the stabling at Calgary,' she added righteously, 'they are someone else's responsibility. I can't answer for what happens to the horses there.' She was implying, plain enough, that no one else could be trusted to be as thorough as herself.

'Do you ever have any fun, Ms Brown?' I asked.

'What do you mean?' she said, raising surprised eyebrows. 'All this is fun.' She waved a hand in general round the horse car. 'I'm having the time of my life.' And she wasn't being ironic: she truly meant it.

'Well,' I said a little feebly, 'then that's fine.'

She gave two sharp little nods, as if that finished the matter, which no doubt it did, except that I still looked for gaps in her defences. I wandered one more time round the whole place, seeing the sunlight slant in through the barred unopenable windows (which would

217

keep people out as well as horses in), smelling the sweet hay and the faint musty odour of the horses themselves, feeling the swirls of fresh air coming from the rows of small ventilators along the roof, hearing the creaking and rushing noises in the car's fabric and the grind of the electricity-generating wheels under the floor.

In that long, warm, friendly space there were animals worth at present a total of many millions of Canadian dollars: worth more if any of them won at Winnipeg or Vancouver. I stood for a long while looking at Voting Right. If Bill Baudelaire's mother knew her onions, in this undistinguished-looking bay lay the dormant seed of greatness.

Maybe she was right. Vancouver would tell.

I turned away, cast a last assessing glance at Laurentide Ice, who looked coolly back, thanked the enthusiastic dragon for her co-operation (prim acknowledgement) and began a slow walk back through the train, looking for gaunt-face.

I didn't see him. He could have been behind any of the closed doors. He wasn't in the forward dome car, upstairs or down, nor in the open dayniter. I sought out and consulted separately with three of the sleeping-car attendants in the racegoers' sleeping cars who frowned in turn and said that first, the sort of jacket I was describing was worn by thousands, and second, everyone tended to look gaunt outside in the cold air. All the same, I said, if they came across anyone fitting that description in their care, please would they tell George Burley his name and room number.

Sure, they each said, but wasn't this an odd thing for an actor to be asking? Zak, I improvised instantly at the first enquiry, had thought the gaunt man had an interesting face and he wanted to ask if he could use him in a scene. Ah, yes, that made sense. If they found him, they would tell George.

When I got back to George, I told him what I'd asked. He wrinkled his brow. 'I saw a man like that at Thunder Bay,' he said. 'But I probably saw several men like that in all this trainload. What do you want him for?'

I explained that I'd told the sleeping-car attendants that Zak wanted to use him in a scene.

'But you?' George said. 'What do you want him for yourself?'

I looked at him and he looked back. I was wondering how far I should trust him and had an uncomfortable impression that he knew what I was thinking.

'Well,' I said finally, 'he was talking to someone I'm interested in.'

I got a long bright beam from the shiny eyes.

'Interested in . . . in the line of duty?'

'Yes.'

He didn't ask who it was and I didn't tell him. I asked him instead if he himself had talked to any of the owners' party.

'Of course I have,' he said. 'I always greet passengers

eh?, when they board. I tell them I'm the Conductor, tell them where my office is, tell them if they've any problems to bring them to me.'

'And do they? Have they?'

He chuckled. 'Most of the complaints go to your Miss Richmond, and she brings them to me.'

'Miss Richmond . . .' I repeated.

'She's your boss, isn't she? Tall pretty girl with her hair in a plait today, eh?'

'Nell,' I said.

'That's right. Isn't she your boss?'

'Colleague.'

'Right, then. The sort of problems the owners' party have had on this trip so far are a tap that won't stop dripping, a blind that won't stay down in one of the bedrooms, eh?, and a lady who thought one of her suitcases had been stolen, only it turned up in someone else's room.' He beamed. 'Most of the owners have been along to see the horses. When they see me, they stop to talk.'

'What do they say?' I asked. 'What sort of things?'

'Only what you'd expect. The weather, the journey, the scenery. They ask what time we get to Sudbury, eh? Or Thunder Bay, or Winnipeg, or whatever.'

'Has anyone asked anything that was different, or surprised you?'

'Nothing surprises me, sonny.' He glowed with irony and bonhomie. 'What would you expect them to ask?'

I shrugged in frustration. 'What happened before Thunder Bay that shouldn't have?'

'The Lorrimores' car, eh?'

'Apart from that.'

'You think something happened?'

'Something happened, and I don't know what, and it's what I'm here to prevent.'

He thought about it, then said, 'When it turns up, you'll know, eh?'

'Maybe.'

'Like if someone put something in the food, eh?, sooner or later everyone will be ill.'

'George!' I was dumbstruck.

He chuckled. 'We had a waiter once years ago who did that. He had a grudge against the world. He put handfuls of ground-up laxative pills into the chocolate topping over ice cream and watched the passengers eat it, and they all had diarrhoea. Dreadful stomach pains. One woman had to go to hospital. She'd had two helpings. What a to-do, eh?'

'You've frightened me stiff,' I said frankly. 'Where do they keep the fodder for the horses?'

He stared, his perpetual smile fading.

'Is that what you're afraid of? Something happening to the horses?'

'It's a possibility.'

'All the fodder is in the horse car,' he said, 'except for some extra sacks of those cubes most of the horses are having, which are in the baggage car. Some of the horses have their own special food brought along with them, sent by their trainers. One of the grooms had a whole set of separate bags labelled "Sunday evening", "Monday morning" and so on. He was showing them to me.'

'Which horse was that for?'

'Um . . . the one that belongs to that Mrs Daffodil Quentin, I think. The groom said one of her horses died of colic or some such recently, from eating the wrong things, and the trainer didn't want any more accidents, so he'd made up the feeds himself.'

'You're brilliant, George.'

His ready laugh came back.

'Don't forget the water tank, eh? You can lift the lid . . . where the plank floats, remember? You could dope all those horses at once with one quick cupful of mischief, couldn't you?'

CHAPTER ELEVEN

Leslie Brown told us adamantly that no one could possibly have tampered with either the fodder or the water.

'When did the grooms last fill the buckets?' I asked.

During the morning, she said. Each groom filled the bucket for his own horse, when he wanted to. All of them had been in there, seeing to their charges.

The horses' drinking-water tank had been topped up, she said, by a hosepipe from the city's water supply during the first twenty minutes of our stop in Thunder Bay, in a procedure that she herself had supervised.

George nodded and said the whole train had been re-watered at that point.

'Before Thunder Bay,' I said, 'could anyone have put anything in the water?'

'Certainly not. I've told you over and over again, I am here all the time.'

'And how would you rate all the grooms for trustworthiness?' I said.

She opened her mouth and closed it again and gave me a hard look.

'I am here to supervise them,' she said. 'I didn't know any of them before yesterday. I don't know if any of them could be bribed to poison the water. Is that what you want?'

'It's realistic,' I said with a smile.

She was unsoftened, unsoftenable.

'My chair, as you see,' she said carefully, 'is next to the water tank. I sit there and watch. I do not think . . . I repeat, I do not believe, that anyone has tampered with the water.'

'Mm,' I said calmingly. 'But you could ask the grooms, couldn't you, if they've seen anything wrong?'

She began to shake her head automatically, but then stopped and shrugged. 'I'll ask them, but they won't have.'

'And just in case,' I said, 'in case the worst happens and the horses prove to have been interfered with, I think I'll take a sample of what's in the tank and also what's in their buckets at this moment. You wouldn't object to that, Ms Brown, would you?'

She grudgingly said she wouldn't. George elected himself to go and see what could be done in the way of sample jars and presently returned with gifts from the Chinese cook in the dome car, in the shape of four rinsed-out plastic tomato-sauce bottles rescued from the rubbish bin.

George and Leslie Brown took a sample from the

tank, draining it, at the dragon's good suggestion, from the tap lower down, where the buckets were filled. I visited Voting Right, Laurentide Ice and Upper Gumtree, who all graciously allowed me to dip into their drink. With Leslie Brown's pen, we wrote the provenance of each sample on the sauce label and put all four containers into a plastic carrier bag which Leslie Brown happened to have handy.

Carrying the booty, I thanked her for her kindness in answering our questions, and helping, and George and I retreated.

'What do you think?' he said, as we started back through the train.

'I think she now isn't as sure as she says she is.'

He chuckled. 'She'll be doubly careful from now on.'

'As long as it's not already too late.'

He looked as if it were a huge joke. 'We could get the tank emptied, scrubbed and refilled at Winnipeg,' he said.

'Too late. If there's anything in it, it was there before Thunder Bay, and the horses will have drunk some of it. Some horses drink a lot of water . . . but they're a bit fussy. They won't touch it if they don't like the smell. If there're traces of soap in it, for instance, or oil. They'd only drink doped water if it smelled all right to them.'

'You know a lot about it,' George commented.

'I've spent most of my life near horses, one way and another.'

We reached his office where he said he had some paperwork to complete before we stopped fairly soon for ten minutes at Kenora. We would be there at five-twenty, he said. We were running thirty minutes behind the Canadian. There were places the race train didn't really need to stop, he said, except to keep pace with the Canadian. We needed always to stop where the trains were serviced for water, trash and fuel.

I had nowhere on our journey to and from the horse car seen the man with the gaunt face. George had pointed someone out to me in the dayniter, but he was not the right person: grey-haired, but too ill-looking, too old. The man I was looking for, I thought, was fifty-something, maybe less, still powerful; not in decline.

In a vague way, I thought, he had reminded me of Derry Welfram. Less bulky than the dead frightener, and not as smooth, but the same stamp of man. The sort Filmer seemed to seek out naturally.

I sat for an hour in my roomette looking out at the unvarying scenery and trying to imagine anything else that Filmer might have paid to have done. It was all the wrong way round, I thought: it was more usual to know the crime and seek the criminal, than to know the criminal and seek his crime.

The four sample bottles of water stood in their plastic carrier on my roomette floor. To have introduced something noxious into that tank, gaunt-face would certainly have to have bribed a groom. He wasn't one of the grooms himself, though perhaps he had been one, somewhere, sometime. The grooms on the train were all younger, thinner and from what I'd seen of them in their uniform T-shirts less positive. I couldn't imagine any of them having the nerve to stand up to Filmer and demand their money.

I spent the brief stop at the small town of Kenora hanging out of the open doorway past George's office, watching him, on the station side of the train, walk a good way up and down outside while he checked that all looked well. The Lorrimores' car, it appeared, was still firmly tacked on. Up behind the engine, two baggage handlers were loading a small pile of boxes. I hung out of the door on the other side of the train for a while, but no one was moving out there at all.

George climbed back on board and closed the doors, and presently we set off again to our last stop before Winnipeg.

I wished intensely that I had the power to see into Filmer's mind. I ached to foresee what he was planning. I felt blind, and longed for second sight. Failing such superhuman qualities, however, there was only as usual ordinary observation and patience, and they both seemed inadequate and tame.

I went along to the dining car where I found that Zak had already positioned some of the actors at the tables for the cocktail-hour double-length scene. He and Nell were agreeing that after the scene the actors would leave again (all except Giles-the-murderer), even though they didn't like being banished all the time and were complaining about it.

Emil, laying tablecloths, said that wine alone was included in the fare, all other cocktails having to be paid for, and perhaps I'd better just serve the wine; he and Oliver and Cathy would do the rest. Fine by me, I said, distributing ashtrays and bud vases. I could set the wine glasses also, Emil said. Glasses for red wine and for white at each place.

The passengers drifted in from their rooms and the dome car and fell into by now predictable patterns of seating. Even though to my mind Bambi Lorrimore and Daffodil Quentin were as compatible as salt and strawberries, the two women were again positioned opposite each other, bound there by the attraction between their men. When I put the wineglasses on their table, Mercer and Filmer were discussing world-wide breeding in terms of exchange rates.

Daffodil told Bambi there was a darling little jewellery store in Winnipeg.

Xanthe was still clinging to Mrs Young. Mr Young looked exceedingly bored.

Sheridan had struck up an acquaintanceship with the actor-murderer Giles, a slightly bizarre eventuality which might have odd consequences.

The Upper Gumtree Unwins and the Flokati couple seemed locked in common interest: whether the instant friendship would wither after their mutual race would be Wednesday evening's news.

Most of the other passengers I knew only vaguely, by face more than by name. I'd learned their names only to the extent that they owned horses in the horse car or had touched bases with Filmer, which came to only about half. They were all in general pleasant enough, although one of the men sent nearly everything back to the kitchen to be reheated, and one of the women pushed the exceptional food backwards and forwards across her plate with flicking movements of her fork, sternly remarking that plain fare was all anyone needed for godliness. What she was doing among the racing fraternity, I never found out.

Zak's long scene began with impressive fireworks as soon as everyone in the dining car had been served with a drink.

A tall man dressed in the full scarlet traditional uniform of the Royal Canadian Mounted Police strode into the dining car and in a conversation-stopping voice said he had some serious information for us. He had come aboard at Kenora, he said, because the body of a groom from this train called Ricky had been found lying beside the railway lines near Thunder Bay. He had been wearing his Race Train T-shirt, and he had identification in his pocket.

The passengers looked horrified. The Mountie's impressive presence dominated the whole place and he sounded undoubtedly authentic. He understood, he said, that the groom had been attacked earlier, in Toronto, when he foiled the kidnapping of a horse, but he had insisted on making the journey nevertheless, having been bandaged by a Miss Richmond. Was that correct?

Nell demurely said that it was.

Among the actual owners of the horses, disbelief had set in the quickest. Mercer Lorrimore enjoyed the joke. Mounties, when investigating, didn't nowadays go around dressed for parades.

'But we are in Manitoba,' Mercer could be heard saying in a lull, 'they've got that right. We passed the boundary with Ontario a moment ago. The Mounted Police's territory starts right there.'

'You seem to know all about it,' our Mountie said. 'What do you know about this dead groom?'

'Nothing,' Mercer said cheerfully.

I glanced briefly at Filmer. His face was hard, his neck rigid, his eyes narrow; and I thought in a flash of Paul Shacklebury, the lad dead in his ditch. Stable lads in England . . . grooms in Canada: same job. What had Paul Shacklebury known about Filmer . . . ? Same old unanswerable question.

'And why was he killed?' the Mountie asked. 'What did he know?'

I risked a glance, looked away, Filmer's mouth was a tight line. The answer to the question had to be in his tautly-held head at that moment and it was as inaccessible to me as Alpha Centauri.

Zak suggested that Ricky had identified one of the hijackers. Perhaps, he said, the hijackers had come on the train. Perhaps they were among the racegoers, waiting another chance to kidnap their quarry.

Filmer's neck muscles slowly relaxed, and I realized that for a moment he must have suspected that the scene had been specifically aimed at him. Perhaps he spent a lot of his time reacting in that way to the most innocent of remarks.

Mavis and Walter Bricknell demanded that the Mountie should keep their own precious horse safe.

The Mountie brushed them aside. He was taking over the enquiry into the death of Angelica Standish, he said. Two deaths connected to the same train could be no coincidence. What was the connection between Angelica and Ricky?

Zak said that *he* was in charge of the Angelica investigation.

No longer, said the Mountie. We were now in the province of Manitoba, not Ontario. His territory, exclusively.

Zak's intended scene of investigation into Angelica's murder had been upstaged by the reality of the Lorrimores' car and then aborted by the long stop at Thunder Bay. Passing the questioning to the Mountie bridged the void neatly, and the Mountie told us that the reason that Steve, Angelica's business manager, also her lover, had not turned up at Toronto station was because he too was dead, struck down in his apartment by blows to the head with a mallet.

The audience received the news of still more carnage

with round eyes. The said Steve, the Mountie went on, seemed to have been in bed asleep at the time of his murder, and the Ontario police were wanting to interview Angelica Standish as a suspect.

'But she's dead!' Mavis Bricknell said.

After a pause, Donna said she and Angelica had talked for maybe two hours between Toronto and Sudbury, and Donna was sure Angelica couldn't have murdered Steve, she was lost without him.

Maybe, the Mountie said, but if she was as upset as all that, why had she come on the train at all? Couldn't it have been to escape from having to realize that she'd killed her lover?

Giles-the-murderer calmly enquired whether any murder weapon had been found after Angelica had been killed.

Also, Pierre asked, wouldn't Angelica's murderer have been covered with blood? The whole toilet compartment had been splashed.

Zak and the Mountie exchanged glances. The Mountie said grudgingly that a blood-covered rolled-up sheet of plastic had been found on the track near the area where Angelica must have been battered, and it could have been used as a poncho, and it was being investigated for blood type and fingerprints.

Donna said couldn't Steve and Angelica both have been killed by a mallet? That would make her innocent, wouldn't it? She couldn't believe that anyone as nice as Angelica could have been mixed up in an insurance swindle.

What? What insurance swindle?

I glanced involuntarily at Daffodil, but if there had been a flicker of her eyelids, I had missed it.

Donna in confusion said she didn't know what insurance swindle. Angelica had just mentioned that Steve was mixed up in an insurance swindle, and she was afraid that was why he had missed the train. Donna hadn't liked to probe any further.

Sheridan Lorrimore, saying loudly that Angelica had been a bitch, made a lunging grab at the pistol sitting prominently in a holster on the Mountie's hip. The Mountie, feeling the tug, turned fast and put his hand down on Sheridan's wrist. It was a movement in a way as dextrous as John Millington on a good day, speaking of razor-sharp reactions, more like an athlete than an actor.

'That gun's mine, sir,' he said, lifting Sheridan's wrist six inches sideways and releasing it. 'And, everybody, it's not loaded.'

There was a general laugh. Sheridan, universally unpopular and having made a boorish fool of himself yet again, looked predictably furious. His mother, I noticed, had turned her head away. Mercer was shaking his.

The Mountie, unperturbed, said he would be proceeding vigorously with the enquiries into both Angelica's and Ricky's deaths and perhaps he would have news for everyone in Winnipeg. He and Zak went away together, and Donna drifted around from table to table for a while telling everyone that poor Angelica had really been very sweet, not a murderess, and she, Donna, was dreadfully upset at the suggestion. She wrung out a real tear or two. She was undoubtedly an effective actress.

'What do you care?' Sheridan asked her rudely. 'You only met her yesterday morning and she was dead before dinner.'

Donna looked at him uncertainly. He'd sounded as if he really believed in Angelica's death.

'Er . . .' she said, 'some people you know at once.' She moved on gently and presently disappeared with disconsolate-looking shoulders down the corridor beside the kitchen. Sheridan muttered under his breath several times, making the people he was sitting with uncomfortable.

Emil and his crew, including me, immediately began setting the tables round the passengers for dinner, and were soon serving warm goat's cheese and radicchio salads followed by circles of rare Chateaubriand with snow peas and matchstick carrots and finally rich orange sorbets smothered in fluffy whipped cream and nuts. Most of the passengers persevered to the end and looked as though it were no torture.

My suggestion to Angus, while we were dishwashing after the battle, that maybe his food could have been injected somehow with a substance that even now could be working away to the detriment of everyone's health was received by him with frosty amusement. Absolutely impossible, he assured me. I had surely noticed that nearly all the ingredients had come on to the train *fresh*? He was *cooking* this food, not bringing it in pre-frozen packs.

I assured him truthfully that I had been impressed by his skill and speed, and I thought his results marvellous.

'You actors,' he said more indulgently, 'will think of any impossible thing for a plot.'

Everyone got off the train at Winnipeg, one thousand, four hundred and thirteen miles along the rails from Toronto.

Two large motor horseboxes were waiting for the horses, which were unloaded down and loaded up ramps. The grooms and Leslie Brown led the horses across from train to van and saw them installed and then, carrying holdalls, themselves trooped on to a bus which followed the horseboxes away towards the racetrack.

A row of buses waited outside the station to take the racegoers away to a variety of outlying motels, and a long new coach with darkly tinted windows was set aside for the owners. A few of the owners, like the Lorrimores and Daffodil and Filmer, had arranged their own transport separately in the shape of chauffeur-driven limousines, their chauffeurs coming over to the train to carry their bags.

The crew, after everyone else had left, tidied away into secure lockers every movable piece of equipment and goods, and then joined the actors in the last waiting bus. The Mountie, I was interested to see, was among us, tall and imposing even with his scarlet and brass buttons tucked away in his bag.

George came last, carrying an attaché case of papers and looking over his shoulder at the train as if wondering if he'd forgotten anything. He sat in the seat across the aisle from me and said the cars would be backed into a siding for two days, the engine would be removed and used elsewhere, and there would be a security guard on duty. In the siding, the carriages would be unheated and unlit and would come to life again only about an hour before we left on the day after tomorrow. We'd been able to keep the same crew from coast to coast, he said, only because of the two rest breaks along the way.

The owners and some of the actors were staying in the Westin Hotel which had, Nell had told everyone during dinner, a ballroom and an indoor pool on the roof. There was a breakfast room set aside for the train party where a piece of the mystery would unravel each morning. Apart from that, everyone was on their own: there were good shops, good restaurants and good racing. Transport had been arranged to and from the racecourse. We would all come back to reboard the train after the Jockey Club Race Train Stakes on Wednesday, and cocktails and dinner would be served as soon as we'd rolled out of the station. The party, in good humour, applauded.

I had decided not to stay in the same hotel as any of the groups of owners, actors, racegoers or crew, and asked Nell if she knew of anywhere else. A tall order, it seemed.

'We've put people almost everywhere,' she said doubtfully, 'but only a few actors will be at the Holiday Inn . . . why don't you try there? Although actually . . . there *is* one place we haven't booked anyone into, and that's the Sheraton. But it's like the Westin – expensive.'

'Never mind, I'll find somewhere,' I said, and when the crew bus, after a short drive, stopped and disgorged its passengers, I took my grip and vanished on foot and, after asking directions, made a homing line to where no one else was staying.

In my buttoned-up grey VIA raincoat, I was unexceptional to the receptionists of the Sheraton: the only problem, they said, was that they were full. It was late in the evening. The whole city was full.

'An annexe?' I suggested.

Two of them shook their heads and consulted with each other in low voices. Although they had no single rooms left, they said finally, they had had a late cancellation of a suite. They looked doubtful. I wouldn't be interested in that, they supposed.

'Yes, I would,' I said and gave them my American

Express card with alacrity. So Tommy the waiter carefully hung up his yellow waistcoat with its white lining and ordered some wine from room service and in a while after a long easing shower slept for eight solid hours and didn't dream about Filmer.

In the morning, I telephoned Mrs Baudelaire and listened again to the almost girlish voice on the wire.

'Messages for the invisible man,' she said cheerfully. 'Er . . . are you still invisible?'

'Mostly, yes, I think.'

'Bill says Val Catto would like to know if you are still invisible to the quarry. Does that make sense to you?'

'It makes sense, and the answer is yes.'

'They're both anxious.'

'And not alone,' I said. 'Will you tell them the quarry has an ally on the train, travelling I think with the racegoers. I've seen him once and will try to photograph him.'

'Goodness!'

'Also will you ask them whether certain numbers, which I'll tell you, have any significance in the quarry's life.'

'Intriguing,' she said. 'Fire away.'

'Well . . . three numbers I don't know. Three question marks, say. Then one-five-one.'

'Three question marks, then one-five-one. Right?'

'Right. I know it's not his car's number plate, or not the car he usually travels in, but ask if it fits his birthday in any way, or his phone number, or anything at all they can think of. I want to know what the first three digits are.'

'I'll ask Bill right away, when I've finished talking to you. He gave me some answers to give you about your questions yesterday evening.'

'Great.'

'The answers are that Mr and Mrs Young who own Sparrowgrass are frequent and welcome visitors to England and are entertained by the Jockey Club at many race meetings. They were friends of Ezra Gideon. Val Catto doesn't know if they know that Ezra Gideon sold two horses to Mr J. A. Filmer. Does that make sense?'

'Yes,' I said.

'I'm glad you understand what I'm talking about. How about this one, then?' She paused for breath. 'Sheridan Lorrimore was sent down – expelled – from Cambridge University last May, amid some sort of hushed-up scandal. Mercer Lorrimore was over in England at that time, and stayed and went racing at Newmarket in July, but the Jockey Club found him grimmer than his usual self and understood it was something to do with his son, although he didn't say what. Val Catto is seeing what he can find out from Cambridge.'

'That's fine,' I said.

'Sheridan Lorrimore!' she said, sounding shocked. 'I hope it's not true.'

'Brace yourself,' I said drily.

'Oh dear.'

'How well do you know him?' I asked.

'Hardly at all. But it does no good, does it, for one of our golden families to hit the tabloids.'

I loved the expression, and remembered she'd owned a magazine.

'It demeans the whole country,' she went on. 'I just hope whatever it was will stay hushed up.'

'Whatever it was?'

'Yes,' she said firmly. 'For his family's sake. For his mother's sake. I know Bambi Lorrimore. She's a proud woman. She doesn't deserve to be disgraced by her son.'

I wasn't so sure about that: didn't know to what extent she was responsible for his behaviour. But perhaps not much. Perhaps no one deserved a son like Sheridan. Perhaps people like Sheridan were born that way, as if without arms.

'Are you still there?' Mrs Baudelaire asked.

'I sure am.'

'Bill says the Lorrimores' private car got detached from the train on Sunday evening. Is that really true? There's a great fuss going on, isn't there? It's been on the television news and it's all over the papers this morning. Bill says it was apparently done by some lunatic for reasons unknown, but he wants to know if you have any information about it that he doesn't have.'

I told her what had happened: how Xanthe had casually nearly walked off into space.

'Tell Bill the quarry sat relaxed and unconcerned throughout both the incident and the enquiry held at Thunder Bay yesterday morning, and I'm certain he didn't plan the uncoupling. I think he did plan *something* though, with his ally on the train, and I think Bill should see that they guard the train's horses very carefully out at the track.'

'I'll tell him.'

'Tell him there's a slight possibility that the horses' drinking water was tampered with on the train, before it got to Thunder Bay. But I think that if it had been, the horses should have been showing distress by last night, which they weren't. I can't check them this morning. I suppose if there's anything wrong with them, Bill will know pretty soon. Anyway, I took four samples of the drinking water which I will take to the races this evening.'

'Good heavens.'

'Tell Bill I'll get them to him somehow. They'll be in a package with his name on it.'

'Let me write some of this down. Don't go away.'

There was a quiet period while she put down the receiver and wrote her notes. Then she came back on the line and faithfully repeated everything I'd told her, and everything I'd asked.

'Is that right?' she demanded, at the end.

'Perfect,' I said fervently. 'When in general is it a good time for me to phone you? I don't like to disturb you at bad moments.'

'Phone any time. I'll be here. Have a good day. Stay invisible.'

I laughed, and she'd gone off the line before I could ask her about her health.

A complimentary copy of a Winnipeg newspaper had been slipped under my sitting-room door. I picked it up and checked on what news it gave of the train. The story wasn't exactly all over the front page, but it started there with photographs of Mercer and Bambi and continued inside, with a glamorous backlit formal shot of Xanthe, which made her look a lot older than her published age, fifteen.

I suspected ironically that the extra publicity given to the Great Transcontinental Mystery Race Train hadn't hurt the enterprise in the least. Blame hadn't been fastened on anyone except some unknown nutter back in the wilds of Ontario. Winnipeg was full of racegoing visitors who were contributing handsomely to the local economy. Winnipeg was pleased to welcome them. Don't forget, the paper prominently said, that the first of the two Celebration of Canadian Racing meetings would be held this evening with the regular post time of 7 p.m., while the second meeting, including the running of the Jockey Club Race Train Stakes would be tomorrow afternoon, post time 1.30. The afternoon had been declared a local holiday, as everyone knew, and it would be a fitting finale to the year's thoroughbred racing programme at Assiniboia Downs. (Harness racing, it said in brackets, would hold the first meeting of its winter season the following Sunday.)

I spent most of the day mooching around Winnipeg, seeing a couple of owners once in a shop selling Eskimo sculptures, but never coming face to face with anyone who might know me. I didn't waste much time trying to see what Filmer did or where he went, because I'd quickly discovered that the Westin Hotel was sitting over an entrance to a subterranean shopping mall that stretched like a rabbit warren in all directions. Shopping, in Canada, had largely gone underground to defeat the climate. Filmer could go in and out of the Westin without a sniff of fresh air, and probably had.

There were racetrack express buses, I found, going from the city to the Downs, so I went on one at about six o'clock and strolled around at ground level looking for some way of conveying to Bill Baudelaire the water samples which were now individually wrapped inside the nondescript plastic carrier.

It was made easy for me. A girl of about Xanthe's age bounced up to my side as I walked slowly along in front of the grandstand, and said, 'Hi! I'm Nancy. If that's for Clarrie Baudelaire, I'll take it up if you like.'

'Where is she?' I asked.

'Dining with her dad up there by a window in the

Clubhouse.' She pointed to a part of the grandstand. 'He said you were bringing her some thirst quenchers, and he asked me to run down and collect them. Is that right?'

'Spot on,' I said appreciatively.

She was pretty, with freckles, wearing a bright blue tracksuit with a white and gold studded belt. I gave her the carrier and watched her jaunty back view disappear with it into the crowds, and I was more and more sure that what she was carrying was harmless. Bill Baudelaire wouldn't be calmly eating dinner with his daughter if there were a multi-horse crisis going on over in the racecourse stables.

The Clubhouse, from where diners could watch the sport, took up one whole floor of the grandstand, glassed in along its whole length to preserve summer indoors. I decided not to go in there on the grounds that Tommy would not, and Tommy off duty in Tommy's off-duty clothes was what I most definitely wanted to be at that moment. I made some Tommy-sized bets and ate very well in the (literally) below-stairs bar, and in general walked around, racecard in hand, binoculars around neck, exactly as usual.

The daylight faded almost imperceptibly into night, electricity taking over the sun's job smoothly. By seven, when the first race was run, it was under floodlighting, the jockeys' colours brilliant against the backdrop of night.

There were a lot of half-familiar faces in the crowds;

the enthusiastic racegoers from the train. The only one of them that I was interested in, though, was either extremely elusive, or not there. All the techniques I knew of finding people were to no avail: the man with his gaunt face, grey hair and fur-collared parka was more invisible than myself.

I did see Nell.

In her plain blue suit she came down from the Club-house with two of the owners who seemed to want to be near the horses at ground level. I drifted after the three of them to watch the runners come out for the third race and wasn't far behind them when they walked right down to the rails to see the contest from the closest possible quarters. When it was over, the owners turned towards the stands, talking animatedly about the result, and I contrived to be where Nell would see me, with any luck, making a small waving motion with my racecard.

She noticed the card, noticed me with widening eyes, and in a short while detached herself from the owners and stood and waited. When without haste I reached her side, she gave me a sideways grin.

'Aren't you one of the waiters from the train?' she said.

'I sure am.'

'Did you find somewhere to sleep?'

'Yes, thank you. How's the Westin?'

She was staying with the owners; their shepherd, their smoother-of-the-way, their information booth.

'The hotel's all right – but someone should strangle that rich . . . that arrogant . . . that *insufferable* Sheridan.' Disgust vibrated in her voice as she suddenly let go of some clearly banked-up and held-back emotion. 'He's unbearable. He's spoiling it for others. They all paid a fortune to come on this trip and they're entitled not to be upset.'

'Did something happen?' I asked.

'Yes, at breakfast.' The memory displeased her. 'Zak put on the next scene of the mystery and Sheridan shouted him down *three* times. I went over to Sheridan to ask him to be quiet and he grabbed my wrist and tried to pull me on to his lap, and I overbalanced and fell and hit the table hard where he was sitting, and I caught the cloth somehow and pulled it with me and everything on it landed on the floor. So you can imagine the fuss. I was on my knees, there was orange juice and broken plates and food and coffee everywhere and Sheridan was saying loudly it was my fault for being clumsy.'

'And I can imagine,' I said, seeing resignation more than indignation now in her face, 'that Bambi Lorrimore took no notice, that Mercer hurried to help you up and apologize, and Mrs Young enquired if you were hurt.'

She looked at me in amazement. 'You were there!'

'No. It just figures.'

'Well . . . that's exactly what happened. A waiter came to deal with the mess, and while he was kneeling there Sheridan said loudly that the waiter was sneering at him and he would get him fired.' She paused. 'And I suppose you can tell me again what happened next?'

She was teasing, but I answered, 'I'd guess Mercer assured the waiter he wouldn't be fired and took him aside and gave him twenty dollars.'

Her mouth opened. 'You *were* there.'

I shook my head. 'He gave me twenty dollars when Sheridan shoved me the other evening.'

'But that's awful.'

'Mercer's a nice man caught in an endless dilemma. Bambi's closed her mind to it. Xanthe seeks comfort somewhere else.'

Nell thought it over and delivered her judgement, which was much like my own.

'One day, beastly Sheridan will do something his father can't pay for.'

'He's a very rich man,' I said.

CHAPTER TWELVE

'It's nothing to do with his birthday, nor with his telephone numbers, nor addresses, past or present, nor his bank accounts, nor his national insurance.'

Mrs Baudelaire's light voice in my ear, passing on the bad news on Wednesday morning.

'Val Catto is working on your quarry's credit card numbers now,' she said. 'And he wants to know why he's doing all this research. He says he's looked up your quarry's divorced wife's personal numbers also and he cannot see one-five-one anywhere, with or without three unknown digits in front.'

I sighed audibly, disappointed.

'How important is it?' she asked.

'It's impossible to tell. It could be pointless, it could solve all our problems. Empty box or jackpot, or anywhere in between. Please would you tell the Brigadier that one-five-one is the combination that unlocks the right-hand latch of a black crocodile briefcase. We have three unknowns on the left.'

'Good gracious,' she said.

'Could you say I would appreciate his instructions?'

'I could, young man. Why don't you just steal the briefcase and take your time?'

I laughed. 'I've thought of that, but I'd better not. Or not yet, anyway. If the numbers have any logic, this way is safest.'

'Val would presumably prefer you didn't get arrested.'

Or murdered, perhaps, I thought.

'I would say,' I agreed, 'that getting myself arrested would lose me my job.'

'You'd no longer be invisible?'

'Quite right.'

'And I'm afraid,' she said, 'that I have some more negative news for you.'

'What is it?' I asked.

'Bill says the samples of water you sent him were just that, water.'

'That's good news, actually.'

'Oh? Well, good, then.'

I reflected. 'I think I'll phone you again this evening before we leave Winnipeg.'

'Yes, do,' she agreed. 'The further west you go the bigger the time change and the longer it takes to get replies from Val Catto.'

'Mm.'

Mrs Baudelaire couldn't ring the Brigadier in the middle of his night, nor in the middle of hers. Toronto, where she lived, was five hours behind London,

Winnipeg six, Vancouver eight. At breakfast time in Vancouver, London's office workers began travelling home. Confusing for carrier pigeons.

'Good luck,' she said. 'I'll talk to you later.'

I was used by now to her abrupt disappearances. I put my receiver down, hearing only silence on the line, and wondered what she looked like, and how deeply she was ill. I would go back to Toronto, I thought, and see her.

I sped again on the bus to the races and found that overnight Assiniboia Downs had sprouted all the ballyhoo of Woodbine: T-shirt stalls, banners and be-sashed bosoms saying 'Support Canadian Racing' included.

I again spent most of the afternoon looking for gaunt-face, coming in the end to the conclusion that whatever he was doing on the train he wasn't travelling because of an overpowering interest in racing. The racegoers from the train were on the whole easily identifiable as they all seemed to have been issued with large red and white rosettes with 'Race Train Passenger' emblazoned on them in gold: and the rosettes proved not to be confined to those in the front half of the train because I came across Zak wearing one too, and he told me that everyone had been given one, the owners included, and where was mine?

I didn't know about them, I said. Too bad, he said, because they entitled everyone to free entry, free racecards and free food. They were gifts from the racecourse, he said. Nell should have one for me, he thought.

I asked him how the scene from the mystery had fared that morning, as Nell had described what had happened the day before.

'A lot better without that bastard Sheridan.'

'Wasn't he there?'

'I got Nell to tell his father that if Sheridan came to breakfast we wouldn't be putting on our scene, and it did the trick. No Sheridan.' He grinned. 'No Lorrimores at all, in fact.' He looked around. 'But they're all here, Sheridan included. They were getting out of a stretch limo when we rolled up in our private bus. That's where we were given these rosettes; on the bus. How did you get here, then?'

'On a public bus.'

'Too bad.'

His batteries were running at half-speed, neither highly charged up nor flat. Under the mop of curls his face, without the emphasizing make-up he wore perpetually on the train, looked younger and more ordinary: it was David Flynn who was at the races, not Zak.

'Are all the actors here?' I asked.

'Oh, sure. We have to know what happens here today. Have to be able to talk about it to the owners tonight. Don't forget, it's a racing mystery, after all.'

I thought that I had forgotten, in a way. The real

mystery that I was engaged in tended to crowd the fiction out.

'What are you betting on in our race?' he asked. 'I suppose Premiere will win. What do you think?'

'Upper Gumtree,' I said.

'It's supposed to be half asleep,' he objected.

'It's got a nice face,' I said.

He looked at me sideways. 'You're crazy, you know that?'

'I am but mad north-north-west.'

'When the wind is southerly,' he said promptly, 'I know a hawk from a handsaw.' He laughed. 'There isn't an actor born who doesn't hope to play Hamlet.'

'Have you ever?'

'Only in school. But once learned, never forgotten. Shall I give you my "To be or not to be"?'

'No.'

'You slay me. See you tonight.'

He went off with a medium spring to his step and I saw him later with his arms round Donna's shoulders, which wasn't (as far as I knew) in his script.

Most of the owners came down from the Clubhouse to watch the saddling of the runners in the Jockey Club Race Train Stakes, and all the sportier of them wore the rosettes.

Filmer didn't: there was no light-heartedness in him. Daffodil, however, had fastened hers to her cleavage, the red, white and gold popping out now and again past the long-haired chinchillas. Mrs Young wore hers boldly on her lapel. Mr Young's wasn't in sight.

The Unwins, rosetted, were showing uninhibited pleasure in Upper Gumtree, who did in fact have a nice face, and wasn't unacceptably sleepy. Upper Gumtree's trainer hadn't made the journey from Australia, and nor had his usual jockey: Canadian substitutes had been found. The Unwins beamed and patted everyone within reach including the horse, and Mr Unwin in his great antipodean accent could be heard calling his jockey 'son', even though the rider looked older by far than the owner.

In the next stall along things were a great deal quieter. Mercer Lorrimore, unattended by the rest of his family, talked pleasantly with his trainer, who had come from Toronto, and shook hands with his jockey, the same one who had ridden for him at Woodbine. Premiere, the favourite, behaved like a horse that had had a fuss made of him all his life; almost, I thought fancifully, as arrogantly as Sheridan.

The owners of Flokati were showing Mavis and Walter Bricknell-type behaviour, fluttering about in a nervous anxiety that would be bound to affect the horse if it went on too long. Their ineffective-looking trainer was trying to stop the owners from straightening the number cloth, tidying the forelock over the headband, tweaking at the saddle and shoving their big rosettes with every ill-judged movement near the horse's affronted nostrils. A riot, really. Poor Mr and Mrs Flokati; owning the horse looked an agony, not a joy.

Mr and Mrs Young, like Mercer Lorrimore, had shipped their Winnipeg runners, two of them, by road. They, old hands at the owning game, stood by with calm interest while their pair, Soluble and Slipperclub, were readied, Mrs Young speaking with her sweet expression to one of the jockeys, Mr Young more impassively to the other.

Daffodil Quentin's runner, Pampering, had been flown in with five others owned by people on the train, all of whom were strolling around with rosettes and almost permanently smiling faces. This was, after all, one of the highlights of their journey, the purpose behind the pizzazz. I learned that the Manitoba Racing Commission had moreover by mid-afternoon given each of them not only a champagne reception and a splendid lunch but also, as a memento, a framed group photograph of all the owners on the trip. They were living their memories, I thought, here and now.

Television cameras all over the place recorded everything both for news items that evening and for the two-hour Support Canadian Racing programme which posters everywhere announced was being made for a gala showing coast to coast after the triple had been completed in Vancouver.

The Winnipeg runners went out on to the track to bugle fanfares and cheers from the stands and were pony-escorted to the starting gate.

Mercer Lorrimore's colours, red and white like the rosette he had pinned on gamely 'For the Sake of Canadian Racing', could be seen entering the outermost stall. Daffodil's pale blue and dark green were innermost. Upper Gumtree, carrying orange and black, started dead centre of the eleven runners and came out of the stalls heading a formation like an arrow.

I was watching from high up, from the upper part of the grandstand, above the Clubhouse floor to which the owners had returned in a chattering flock to watch the race. Through my binoculars-camera the colours down on the track in the chilly sunshine looked sharp and bright, the race easy on that account to read.

The arrow formation soon broke up into a ragged line, with Premiere on the outside, Pampering on the inner and Upper Gumtree still just in front. The Youngs' pair, split by the draw, nevertheless came together and raced the whole way side by side like twins. Flokati, in pink, made for the rails as if needing them to steer by, and four of the other runners boxed him in.

Going past the stands for the first time, the Unwins' Upper Gumtree still showed in front but with Premiere almost alongside; Pampering was on the inside tugging his jockey's arms out. Doing their best for the glory of Canada, the whole field of eleven swept round the bend and went down the far side as if welded together, and it still seemed when they turned for home that that was how they might finish, in a knot.

They split apart in the straight, one group swinging wide, the red and white of Premiere spurting forward with the Youngs' pair at his quarters and Upper Gumtree swerving dramatically through a gap to take the rails well ahead of Pampering.

The crowd bounced up and down. The money was on Premiere. The yelling could have been heard in Montreal. The Canadian racing authorities were again getting a rip-roaring brilliant finish to a Race Train Stakes ... and Mercer, putting his brave face on it, again came in second.

It was the Unwins, in the stratosphere of ecstasy, who led Upper Gumtree into the winners' circle. The Unwins from Australia who were hugging and kissing everyone near enough (including the horse). The Unwins who had their photographs taken each side of their panting winner, now covered across the shoulders by a long, triumphant blanket of flowers. The Unwins who received the trophy, the cheque and the speeches from the President of the racecourse and the top brass of the Jockey Club; whose memories of the day would be the sweetest.

Feeling pleased for them, I lowered the binoculars through which I'd been able to see even the tears on Mrs Unwin's cheeks, and there below me and in front of the grandstand was the man with the gaunt face looking up towards the Clubhouse windows.

Almost trembling with haste, I put the binoculars up again, found him, activated the automatic focus, pressed the button, heard the quiet click of the shutter: had him in the bag.

It had been my only chance. Even before the film had wound on, he'd looked down and away, so that I could see only his forehead and his grey hair; and within two seconds, he'd walked towards the grandstand and out of my line of vision.

I had no idea how long he'd been standing there. I'd been too diverted by the Unwins' rejoicings. I went down from the upper grandstand as fast as I could, which was far too slowly because everyone else was doing the same thing.

Down on ground level again, I couldn't see gaunt-face anywhere. The whole crowd was on the move: one could get no length of view. The Race Train event had been the climax of the programme and although there was one more race on the card, no one seemed to be much interested. A great many red and white rosettes, baseball caps, T-shirts and balloons were on their way out of the gates.

The Unwins' entourage was disappearing into the Clubhouse entrance, no doubt for more champagne and Press interviews, and probably all the other owners would be in there with them. If gaunt-face had been looking up at the Clubroom windows in the hope of seeing Filmer – or of Filmer seeing him – maybe Filmer would come down to talk to him and maybe I could photograph them both together, which might one day prove useful. If I simply waited, it might happen.

I simply waited.

Filmer did eventually come down, but with Daffodil. They weren't approached by gaunt-face. They climbed into their chauffeured car and were whisked away to heaven-knew-where, and I thought frustratedly about time and the little of it there was left in Winnipeg. It was already nearly six o'clock, and I wouldn't be able to find a one-hour photo lab open anywhere that evening; and I had to return to the Sheraton to collect my bag, and be back on the train by seven-thirty or soon after.

I retreated to the men's room and took the film out of the binoculars-camera, and wrote a short note to go with it. Then I twisted the film and note together into a paper towel and went out to try to find Bill Baudelaire, reckoning it might be all right to speak to him casually down on ground level since Filmer wasn't there to see. I'd caught sight of him in the distance from time to time all afternoon, but now when I wanted him his red hair wasn't anywhere around.

Zak came up to me with Donna and offered me a lift back to the city in their bus, and at that exact moment I saw not Bill Baudelaire himself but someone who might go among the owners, where Tommy couldn't.

'When does the bus go?' I asked Zak rapidly, preparing to leave him.

'Twenty minutes . . . out front. It's got a banner on.

'I'll come . . . thanks.'

258

I covered a good deal of ground rapidly but not running and caught up with the shapely back view of a dark-haired girl in a red coat with a wide gold and white studded belt.

'Nancy?' I said from behind her.

She turned, surprised, and looked at me enquiringly.

'Er . . .' I said, 'yesterday you collected some thirst quenchers from me for Bill Baudelaire's daughter.'

'Oh, yes.' She recognized me belatedly.

'Do you happen to know where I could find him now?'

'He's up in the Clubhouse, drinking with the winners.'

'Could you . . . could you possibly deliver something else to him?'

She wrinkled her freckled teenage nose. 'I just came down, for some fresh air.' She sighed. 'Oh, all right. I guess he'd want me to, if you asked. You seem to be OK with him. What do you want me to give him this time?'

I passed over the paper-towel bundle.

'Instructions?' she asked.

'There's a note inside.'

'Real cloak and dagger goings-on.'

'Thanks, truly, and . . . er . . . give it to him quietly.'

'What's in it?' she asked.

'A film, with photos of today's events.'

She didn't know whether or not to be disappointed.

'Don't lose it,' I said.

She seemed to be more pleased with that, and flashing me a grin from over her shoulder went off towards the Clubhouse entrance. I hoped she wouldn't make a big production out of the delivery upstairs, but just in case she did I thought I wouldn't go anywhere where she could see me and point me out to any of the owners, so I left through the front exit gates and found the actors' bus with its 'Mystery Race Train' banner and faded inside into the reassembling troupe.

In general, the cast had backed Premiere (what else?) but were contented to have been interviewed on television at some length. A lot of Winnipeg's race crowd, Zak said, had asked how they could get on the train. 'I must say,' he said, yawning, 'with all the publicity it's had, it's really caught on.'

In the publicity and the success, I thought, lay the danger. The more the eyes of Canada and Australia and England were directed to the train, the more Filmer might want to discredit it. Might . . . might. I was guarding a moving shadow; trying to prevent something that might not happen, searching for the intention so as to stop it occurring.

The bus letting me off at a convenient corner in the city, I walked to the Sheraton and from a telephone there spoke to Mrs Baudelaire.

'Bill called me ten minutes ago from the track,' she said. 'He said you sent him a film and you didn't say where you wanted the pictures sent.'

'Is he calling you back?' I asked.

'Yes, I told him I'd be speaking to you soon.'

'Right, well, there's only one picture on the film. The rest is blank. Please tell Bill the man in the photo is the ally of our quarry. His ally on the train. Would you ask if Bill knows him? Ask if anyone knows him. And if there's something about him that would be useful if I knew, please will he tell you, to tell me.'

'Heavens,' she said. 'Let me get that straight.' She paused, writing. 'Basically, who is he, what does he do, and is what he does likely to be of help.'

'Yes,' I said.

'And do you want a copy of the photo?'

'Yes, please. Ask if there's any chance of his getting it to Nell Richmond at Chateau Lake Louise by tomorrow night or the next morning.'

'Difficult,' she commented. 'The mail is impossible.'

'Well, someone might be flying to Calgary tomorrow morning,' I suggested. 'They might even meet our train there. We get there at twelve-forty, leave at one-thirty. I suppose the time's too tight, but if it's possible, get Bill to address the envelope to the Conductor of the train, George Burley. I'll tell George it might come.'

'Dear young man,' she said, 'let me write it all down.'

I waited while she did it.

'Let me check,' she said. 'Either George Burley on the train or Nell Richmond at Chateau Lake Louise.'

'Right. I'll call you soon.'

'Don't go,' she said. 'I have a message for you from Val Catto.'

'Oh good.'

'He said ... now these are his exact words ... "Stolen evidence cannot be used in court but facts learned can be verified." ' The understanding amusement was light in her voice. 'What he means is, have a look-see but hands off.'

'Yes.'

'And he said to tell you to remember his motto.'

'OK,' I said.

'What is his motto?' she asked curiously, obviously longing to know.

'Thought before action, if you have time.'

'Nice,' she said, pleased. 'He said to tell you he was working hard on the unknown numbers, and you are not to put yourself in danger of arrest.'

'All right.'

'Phone me from Calgary tomorrow,' she said. 'By then it will be evening in England. Val will have had a whole day on the numbers.'

'You're marvellous.'

'And I'll be able to tell you when you'll get your photos.'

There was a click and she'd gone, and I could hardly believe that I'd ever doubted her as a relay post.

The train had come in from the sidings and stood in the station, warm and pulsing, its engines reattached, the horses and grooms on board and fresh foods and ice loaded.

It was like going back to an old friend, familiar and almost cosy. I changed into Tommy's uniform in my roomette and went along to the dining car where Emil, Oliver and Cathy welcomed me casually as if I were an accepted part of the crew. We began immediately laying the pink cloths and putting fresh flowers in the vases, and Angus in his tall white hat, whistling 'Speed Bonny Boat' amid clouds of steam, addressed his talents to wild rice and scallops in Parmesan sauce while Simone rather grimly chopped lettuce.

The passengers returned well before eight o'clock in very good spirits, Mercer bringing with him a porter wheeling a case of highly superior bubbles for toasting the Unwins' success. The Unwins themselves – and it was impossible for anyone to grudge them their moment – said over and over that it was great, just great that one of the horses actually on the train had won one of the races, it made the whole thing worth-while, and the whole party, drifting into the dining car in true party mood, agreed and applauded.

Filmer, I was interested to see as I distributed glasses, was smiling pleasantly in all directions, when the last thing he probably wanted was the enormous smash-hit the train enterprise was proving.

Daffodil had changed into a sparkling crimson dress and showed no pique over Pampering finishing fifth.

She was being friendly as usual to Bambi, frostier in pale turquoise with pearls.

Mercer came to Emil and worried that the wine wasn't cold enough, but Emil assured him he had lodged all twelve bottles among the many plastic bags of ice cubes: by the time the train left the station, all would be well.

The Youngs, whose Slipperclub had finished third, were embraced by the hyperjoyous Unwins and were invited to their table, leaving the poor Flokatis to seek solace with others whose hopes had died on the last bend. Sheridan Lorrimore was telling a long-suffering good-natured couple all about his prowess at ice hockey and Xanthe, pouting and put out at having been temporarily deserted by Mrs Young, had ended up next to Giles-the-murderer whose real-life preference, I'd gathered, was for boys.

The train slid out of Winnipeg on time at eight-twenty and I put all my energies and attention into being an unexceptional and adequate waiter, even though always conscious of the ominous presence in the aisle seat, facing forward, three tables back from the kitchen end. I never met his eyes and I don't think he noticed me much, but we were all, Emil, Oliver, Cathy and I, becoming slowly and inevitably more recognizable to the passengers. Several of them enquired if we'd been to the races (we all had) and had backed the winner (no, we hadn't). Fortunately Mercer himself had had this conversation with Emil, which meant he felt no need to ask me also, so I escaped having to speak too much in my English accent at his table.

The party atmosphere went on all through dinner, prevailed through a short scene put on by Zak to explain that the Mountie had been left behind in Winnipeg for investigations on the ground and heated up thoroughly afterwards with more unsteady dancing and laughter in the dome car.

Nell wandered about looking slightly less starchy in a fuller-cut black skirt with her tailored white silk blouse, telling me in passing that Cumber and Rose wanted to give a similar party at Chateau Lake Louise.

'Who?' I said.

'Cumber and Rose. Mr and Mrs Young.'

'Oh.'

'I've spent most of the day with them.' She smiled briefly and went on her way. No clipboard, I noticed.

Cumber and Rose, I thought, collecting ashtrays. Well, well. Rose suited Mrs Young fine. Cumber was appropriate also, I supposed, though Mr Young wasn't cumbersome; perhaps a shade heavy in personality, but not big, not awkward.

Mercer and Bambi again invited Filmer and Daffodil into their private car, although it was Oliver, this time, who obliged them with a bowl of ice. Mercer came back after a while to collect the Unwins and the Youngs, and the general jollifications everywhere wore on without any alarms.

After midnight Nell said she was going to bed, and

I walked up the train with her to her roomette, almost opposite mine. She paused in the doorway.

'It's all going well, don't you think?' she said.

'Terrific.' I meant it. 'You've worked very hard.'

We looked at each other, she in executive black and white, I in my yellow waistcoat.

'What are you really?' she said.

'Twenty-nine.'

Her lips twitched. 'One day I'll crack your defences.'

'Yours are half down.'

'What do you mean?'

I made a hugging movement across my own chest. 'No clipboard,' I said.

'Oh . . . well . . . I didn't need it this evening.'

She wasn't exactly confused. Her eyes were laughing.

'You can't,' she said.

'Can't what?'

'Kiss me.'

I'd wanted to. She'd seen it unerringly.

'If you come into my parlour, I can,' I said.

She shook her head, smiling. 'I am not going to lose my credibility on this train by being caught coming out of the help's bedroom.'

'Talking in the corridor is almost as bad.'

'Yes, it is,' she said, nodding. 'So goodnight.'

I said with regret, 'Goodnight,' and she went abruptly into her own domain and closed the door.

With a sigh I went on a few steps further to George's office and found him as I'd expected, fully dressed, lightly napping, with worked-on forms pushed to one side beside an empty coffee cup.

'Come in,' he said, fully alert in an instant. 'Sit down. How's it going?'

'So far, so good.'

I sat on the facilities, and told him that the water samples from the horse car had been pure and simple H_2O.

'That'll please the dragon-lady, eh?' he said.

'Did you go to the races?' I asked.

'No, I've got family in Winnipeg, I went visiting. And I slept most of today, as I'll be up all night, with the stops.' He knew, however, that Upper Gumtree had won. 'You should see the party going on in the forward dome car. All the grooms are drunk. The dragon-lady's in a sober tizzy, eh?, because they tried to give a bucket of beer to the horse. They're singing gold-rush songs at the tops of their voices in the dayniter and it's a wonder they haven't all rocked the train right off the rails, with the noise and the booze.'

'I guess it wouldn't be easy to rock the train off the rails,' I said thoughtfully.

'Easy?' George said. 'Of course it is. Go too fast round the curves.'

'Well . . . suppose it was one of the passengers who wanted to stop the train getting happily to Vancouver, what could he do?'

He looked at me with bright eyes, unperplexed. 'Besides doping the horses' water? Do what they're

267

doing in the mystery, I'd say. Throw a body off the train, eh? That would stop the parties pretty quick.' He chuckled. 'You could throw someone off the Stoney Creek bridge – that's a high curved bridge over Roger's Pass. It's a long way down into the gulch. Three hundred feet and a bit more. If the fall didn't kill them, the bears would.'

'Bears!' I exclaimed.

He beamed. 'Grizzly bears, eh? The Rocky Mountains aren't anyone's tame backyard. They're raw nature. So are the bears. They kill people, no trouble.' He put his head on one side. 'Or you could throw someone out into the Connaught Tunnel. That tunnel's five miles long with no lights. There's a species of blind mice that live in there, eating the grain that falls from the grain trains.'

'Jolly,' I said.

'There's a wine storage under the floor of your dining car,' he said with growing relish. 'They decided not to use it on this trip because opening it might disrupt the passengers. It's big enough to hide a body in.'

His imagination, I saw, was of a scarier dimension than my own.

'Hiding a body in the wine store,' I said politely, 'might indeed disrupt the passengers.'

He laughed. 'Or how about someone alive and tied up in there, writhing in agony?'

'Shouting his head off?'

'Gagged.'

'If we miss anyone,' I promised, 'that's where we'll look.' I stood up and prepared to go. 'Where exactly is the Stoney Creek bridge,' I asked, pausing in the doorway, 'over Roger's Pass?'

His eyes gleamed, the lower lids pouching with enjoyment. 'About a hundred miles further on from Lake Louise. High up in the mountains. But don't you worry, eh?, you'll be going across it in the dark.'

CHAPTER THIRTEEN

Everyone survived the night, although there were a few obvious hangovers at breakfast. Outside the windows, the seemingly endless rock, lake and conifer scenery had dramatically given way to the wide sweeping rolling prairies, not yellow with the grain that had already been harvested, but greenish grey, resting before winter.

There was a brief stop during breakfast at the town of Medicine Hat which lay in a valley and looked a great deal more ordinary than its name. The passengers dutifully put back their watches when Nell told them we were now in Mountain Time, but where, they asked, were the mountains?

'This afternoon,' she answered, and handed out the day's printed programme which promised 'Dreadful Developments in The Mystery' at eleven-thirty a.m., followed by an early lunch. We would reach Calgary at twelve-forty, where the horse car would be detached, and leave at one-thirty, heading up into the Rockies to Banff and Lake Louise. At Lake Louise, the owners would disembark and be ferried by bus to the Chateau, the huge hotel sitting on the lake's shore, amid 'Snowy Scenes of Breathtaking Beauty'. 'Cocktails and Startling Discoveries' would be offered at six-thirty in a private conference room in the hotel. Have a nice day.

Several people asked if we were now in front or behind the regular Canadian.

'We're in front,' I said.

'If we break down,' Mr Unwin said facetiously, 'it will be along to help us out.'

Xanthe, sitting next to him, didn't laugh. 'I wish we were behind it,' she said. 'I'd feel safer.'

'Behind the Canadian there are freight trains,' Mr Unwin said reasonably, 'and ahead of us there are freight trains. And coming the other way there are freight trains. We're not all alone on these rails.'

'No, I suppose not.' She seemed doubtful still and said she had slept much better again that past night in her upper bunk than she would have done in her family's own quarters.

I brought her the French toast and sausages she ordered from the menu and filled her coffee cup, and Mr Unwin, holding out his own cup for a refill, asked if I had backed his horse to win at Winnipeg.

'I'm afraid not, sir,' I said regretfully. I put his cup on the tray and poured with small movements. 'But congratulations, sir.'

'Did you go to the races?' Xanthe asked me without too much interest.

'Yes, miss,' I said.

I finished pouring Mr Unwin's coffee and put it by his place, then took my tray and coffee pot along to the next table where the conversation seemed to be about Zak's mystery rather than directly about horses.

'I think the trainer killed Angelica. And the groom too.'

'Why ever should he?'

'He wants to marry Donna for her money. Angelica knew something that would make the marriage impossible, so he killed her.'

'Knew what?'

'Maybe that he's already married.'

'To Angelica?'

'Well . . . why not?'

'But where does the dead groom come in?'

'He saw the murderer getting rid of the blood-spattered plastic.'

They laughed. I filled their cups and moved on and poured for Daffodil, who had an empty place on her far side. Daffodil, smoking with deep sucking lungfuls, sat with the Flokatis, and nobody else.

No Filmer.

I glanced back along the whole dining car, but couldn't see him anywhere. He hadn't come in while I was serving others, and he hadn't been at the kitchen and when I'd started.

Daffodil said to me, 'Can you bring me some vodka? Ice and lemon.'

'I'll ask, madam,' I said, and asked Emil, and it was he who civilly explained to her that the barman wouldn't be back on duty until eleven, and meanwhile everything was locked up.

Daffodil received the bad news without speaking but jabbed the fire out of her cigarette with some violent stabs and a long final grind. The Flokatis looked at her uncertainly and asked if they could help.

She shook her head. She seemed angry and near to tears, but determinedly in control.

'Give me some coffee,' she said to me, and to the Flokatis she said, 'I think I'll get off the train at Calgary. I think I'll go home.'

Small movements saved the day, as I would have spilled the brown liquid all over her hand.

'Oh no!' exclaimed the Flokatis, instantly distressed. 'Oh, don't do that. Your horse ran splendidly yesterday, even if it was only fifth. Ours was nearly last . . . and we are going on. You can't give up. And you have Laurentide Ice, besides, for Vancouver.'

Daffodil looked at them as if bemused. 'It's not because of yesterday,' she said.

'But why, then?'

Daffodil didn't tell them. Maybe wouldn't; maybe couldn't. She merely pursed her lips tight, shook her curly head, and dug out another cigarette.

The Flokatis having declined more coffee, I couldn't stay to listen any further. I moved across the aisle and stretched my ears, but the Flokatis seemed to get

273

nothing extra from Daffodil except a repeated and stronger decision to go home.

Nell in her straight grey skirt, clipboard in attendance, was still talking to passengers up by the kitchen end. I took my nearly empty coffee pot up there and made a small gesture onwards to the lobby, to where presently she came with enquiring eyebrows.

'Daffodil Quentin,' I said, peering into the coffee pot, 'is upset to the point of leaving the train. She told the Flokatis, not me . . . so you don't know, OK?'

'Upset about what?' Nell was alarmed.

'She wouldn't tell them.'

'Thanks,' she said. 'I'll see what I can do.'

Smoothing ruffled feelings, keeping smiles in place; all in her day's work. She started casually on her way through the dining car and I went into the kitchen to complete my mission. By the time I was out again with a full pot, Nell had reached Daffodil and was standing by her, listening. Nell appealed to the Youngs and the Unwins at adjacent tables for help, and presently Daffodil was out of sight in a bunch of people trying to persuade her to change her mind.

I had to wait quite a while to hear what was happening, but finally the whole little crowd, Daffodil among them, went out at the far end into the dome car and Nell returned to the lobby, relaying the news to me in snatches as I paused beside her on to-and-fro journeys to clear away the breakfast debris.

'Cumber and Rose . . .' The Youngs, I thought.

274

'Cumber and Rose and also the Unwins say there was nothing wrong last night, they all had a splendid time in the Lorrimores' car. Daffodil finally said she'd had a disagreement with Mr Filmer after the party had broken up. She said she had hardly slept and wasn't sure what to do, but there was no fun left in taking Laurentide Ice to Vancouver, and she couldn't face the rest of the journey. The Youngs have persuaded her to go up into the dome with them to think things over, but I honestly think she's serious. She's very upset.'

'Mm.' I put the last of the debris into the kitchen and excused myself apologetically from washing the dishes.

'How can Mr Filmer have upset Daffodil so much?' Nell exclaimed. 'She's obviously been enjoying herself, and he's such a nice man. They were getting on together so well, everyone thought.' She paused. 'Mr Unwin believes it's a lovers' quarrel.'

'Does he?' I pondered. 'I think I'll make a recce up the train. See if anything else is happening.'

Maybe Daffodil had made advances and been too roughly repulsed, I thought. And maybe not.

'Mr Filmer hasn't been in to breakfast,' Nell said. 'It's all very worrying. And last night everyone was so happy.'

If Daffodil's leaving the train was the worst thing that happened, I thought, we would have got off lightly. I left Nell and set off up the corridor, coming pretty soon to Filmer's bedroom door, which was uninformatively closed.

I checked with the sleeping-car attendant further along the car who was in the midst of folding up the bunks for the day and unfolding the armchairs.

'Mr Filmer? He's in his room still, as far as I know. He was a bit short with me, told me to hurry up. And he's not usually like that. He was eating something, and he had a thermos too. But then we do get passengers like that sometimes. Can't get through the night without raiding the icebox, that sort of thing.'

I nodded noncommittally and went onwards, but I thought that if Filmer had brought food and a thermos on board for breakfast, he must have known in Winnipeg that he would need them, which meant that last night's quarrel had been planned and hadn't been caused by Daffodil.

George Burley was in his office, writing his records.

'Morning,' he said, beaming.

'How's the train?'

'The forward sleeping-car attendants are threatening to resign, eh?, over the vomit in the bathrooms.'

'Ugh.'

He chuckled. 'I brought extra disinfectants aboard in Winnipeg,' he said. 'Train-sickness gets them, you know.'

I shook my head at his indulgence and pressed forward, looking as always for gaunt-face but chiefly aiming for the horses.

Leslie Brown, hollow-eyed from lack of sleep, regarded me with only half the usual belligerence.

'Come in,' she said, stepping back from her door. 'To be honest, I could do with some help.'

As I'd just passed several green-looking grooms being sorry for themselves in their section, I supposed at first she meant simply physical help in tending the horses, but it appeared that she didn't.

'Something's going on that I don't understand,' she said, locking the entrance door behind me and leading the way to the central space where her chair stood beside the innocent water tank.

'What sort of thing?' I asked, following her.

She mutely pointed further forward up the car, and I walked on until I came to the final space between the stalls, and there, in a sort of nest made of hay bales, one of the grooms half lay, half sat, curled like an embryo and making small moaning noises.

I went back to Leslie Brown. 'What's the matter with him?' I said.

'I don't know. He was drunk last night, they all were, but this doesn't look like an ordinary hangover.'

'Did you ask the others?'

She sighed. 'They don't remember much about last night. They don't care what's the matter with him.'

'Which horse is he with?'

'Laurentide Ice.'

I'd have been surprised, I supposed, if she'd said anything else.

'That's the horse, isn't it,' I asked, 'whose trainer sent separate numbered individual bags of food, because another of Mrs Quentin's horses had died because of eating the wrong things?'

She nodded. 'Yes.'

'And this boy was with the horse all the time in the barns at Winnipeg?'

'Yes, of course. They exercised the horses and looked after them, and they all came back to the train in horse vans yesterday after the races, while the train was still in the siding. I came with them. There's nothing wrong with any of the horses, I assure you.'

'That's good,' I said. 'Laurentide Ice as well?'

'See for yourself.'

I walked round looking at each horse but in truth they all appeared healthy and unaffected, even Upper Gumtree and Flokati who would have been excused seeming thin and fatigued after their exertions. Most of them had their heads out over the stall doors, a sure sign of interest: a few were a pace or two back, semi-dreaming. Laurentide Ice watched me with a bright glacial eye, in far better mental health than his attendant.

I returned to Leslie Brown and asked her the groom's name.

'Lenny,' she said. She consulted a list. 'Leonard Higgs.'

'How old is he?'

'About twenty, I should think.'

278

'What's he like, usually?'

'Like the others. Full of foul language and dirty jokes.' She looked disapproving. 'Every other word beginning with f.'

'When did all this moaning and retreating start?'

'He was lying there all night. The other boys said it was his turn to be in here, but it wasn't really, only he was paralytic, and they just dumped him in the hay and went back to the party. He started the moaning about an hour ago and he won't answer me at all.' She was disturbed by him, and worried, I thought, that his behaviour might be held to be her responsibility.

Rather to her surprise, I took off my yellow waistcoat and striped tie and gave them to her to hold. If she would sit down for a while, I suggested, I would try to sort Lenny out.

Meekly for her, she agreed. I left her perching with my badges of office across her trousered knees and returned to the total collapse in the hay.

'Lenny,' I said, 'give it a rest.'

He went on with the moaning, oblivious.

I sat down beside him on one of the hay bales and put my mouth near his one visible ear.

'Shut up,' I said, very loudly.

He jumped and he gasped and after a short pause he went back to moaning, though artificially now, it seemed to me.

'If you're sick from beer,' I said forcefully, 'it's your

own bloody fault, but I'll get you something to make you feel better.'

He curled into a still tighter ball, tucking his head down into his arms as if shielding it from a blow. It was a movement impossible to misconstrue: what he felt, besides alcohol sickness, was fear.

Fear followed Julius Apollo Filmer like a spoor; the residue of his passing. Lenny, frightened out of his wits, was a familiar sight indeed.

I undid the top buttons of my shirt, loosening the collar, and rolled up my cuffs, aiming for informality, and I slid down until I was sitting on the floor with my head on the same level as Lenny's.

'If you're shit-scared,' I said distinctly, 'I can do something about that, too.'

Nothing much happened. He moaned a couple of times and fell silent and after a long while, I said, 'Do you want help, or don't you? This is a good offer. If you don't take it, whatever you're afraid of will probably happen.'

After a lengthy pause he rolled his head round, still wrapped in his arms, until I could see his face. He was red-eyed, bony, unshaven and dribbling, and what came out of his slack mouth wasn't a groan but a croak.

'Who the bleeding hell are you?' He had an English accent and a habitual pugnacity of speech altogether at odds with his present state.

'Your bit of good luck,' I said calmly.

'Piss off,' he said.

'Right.' I got to my feet. 'Too bad,' I said. 'Go on feeling sorry for yourself, and see where it gets you.'

I walked away from him, out of his sight.

'Here,' he said, croaking, making it sound like an order.

I stayed where I was.

'Wait,' he said urgently.

I did wait, but I didn't go back to him. I heard the hay rustling and then a real groan as the hangover hit him, and finally he came staggering into view, keeping his balance with both hands on the green outside of Flokati's stall. He stopped when he saw me. Blinking, swaying, the Race Train T-shirt torn and filthy, he looked stupid, pathetic and spineless.

'Go back and sit down,' I said neutrally. 'I'll bring you something.'

He sagged against the green stall but finally turned round and shuffled back the way he'd come. I went down to Leslie Brown and asked if she had any aspirins.

'Not aspirins, but these,' she said, proffering a box from a canvas holdall. 'These might do.'

I thanked her, filled a polystyrene cup with water and went back to see how Lenny was faring: he was sitting on the hay with his head in his hands looking a picture of misery and a lot more normal.

'Drink,' I said, giving him the water. 'And swallow these.'

'You said you could help me.'

'Yes. Take the pills for a start.'

He was accustomed, on the whole, to doing what he was told, and he must have been reasonably good at his job, I supposed, to have been sent across Canada with Laurentide Ice. He swallowed the pills and drank the water and not surprisingly they made no immediate difference to his physical woes.

'I want to get out of here,' he said with a spurt of futile violence. 'Off this bleeding train. Off this whole effing trip. And I've got no money. I lost it. It's gone.'

'All right,' I said. 'I can get you off.'

'Straight up?' He was surprised.

'Straight up.'

'When?'

'At Calgary. In a couple of hours. You can leave then. Where do you want to go?'

He stared. 'You're having me on,' he said.

'No. I'll get you taken care of, and I'll see you get a ticket to wherever you want.'

The dawning hope in his face became clouded with confusion.

'What about old Icy?' he said. 'Who'll look after him?'

It was the first thought he'd had which hadn't been raw self-pity, and I felt the first flicker of compassion.

'We'll get another groom for old Icy,' I promised. 'Calgary's full of horse people.'

It wasn't exactly true. The Calgary I'd known had been one of the six biggest cities in Canada, half the size of Montreal and on a population par with central

Toronto. Time might have changed the statistics slightly, but probably not much. Calgary was no dusty old-west cattle town, but a skyscrapered modern city set like a glittering oasis in the skirts of the prairies: and the Stampede, in which one July I'd worked as a bronco rider, was a highly organized ten-day rodeo with a stadium, adjacent art and stage shows and all the paraphernalia and razzamatazz of big-time tourist entertainment. But Calgary, even in October, definitely had enough horse people around to provide a groom for Laurentide Ice.

I watched Lenny Higgs decide to jettison his horse, his job and his unbearable present. Fearful that I would bungle the whole business because I'd never before actually tried this sort of unscrambling myself, I strove to remember John Millington's stated methods with people like the chambermaid at Newmarket. Offer protection, make any promise that might get results, hold out carrots, be supportive, ask for help.

Ask for help.

'Could you tell me why you don't want to go on to Vancouver?' I said.

I made the question sound very casual, but it threw him back into overall panic, even if not into the foetal position.

'No.' He shivered with intense alarm. 'Piss off. It's none of your effing business.'

Without fuss I withdrew from him again, but this

time I went further away, beyond Leslie Brown, right down to the exit door.

'Stay there,' I said to her, passing. 'Don't say anything to him, will you?'

She shook her head, folding her thin arms over my waistcoat and across her chest. The dragon, I thought fleetingly, with the fire in abeyance.

'Here,' Lenny shouted behind me. 'Come back.'

I didn't turn round.

He wailed despairingly at the top of his voice, 'I want to get off this train.'

It was, I thought, a serious cry for help.

I went back slowly. He was standing between Flokati's stall and Sparrowgrass's, swaying unsteadily, watching me with haggard eyes.

When I was near him, I said simply, 'Why?'

'He'll kill me if I tell you.'

'That's rubbish,' I said.

'It isn't.' His voice was high. 'He said I'd effing die.'

'Who said?'

'Him.' He was trembling. The threat had been of sufficient power for him to believe it.

'Who is him?' I asked. 'One of the owners?'

He looked blank, as if I were talking gibberish.

'Who is him?' I asked again.

'Some bloke . . . I never saw him before.'

'Look,' I said calmingly, 'let's go back, sit on the hay, and you tell me why he said he'd kill you.' I pointed over his shoulders towards the bales and with a sort of exhausted compliance he stumbled that way and flopped into a huddled mess.

'How did he frighten you?' I asked.

'He . . . came to the barns . . . asked for me.'

'Asked for you by name?'

He nodded glumly.

'When was this?'

'Yesterday,' he said hoarsely. 'During the races.'

'Go on.'

'He said he knew all about old Icy's food being in numbered bags.' Lenny sounded aggrieved. 'Well, it wasn't a secret, was it?'

'No,' I said.

'He said he knew why . . . because Mrs Quentin's other horse died . . .' Lenny stopped and looked as if an abyss had opened before him. 'He started saying I done it . . .'

'Done what?'

Lenny was silent.

'Said you'd poisoned Mrs Quentin's other horse?' I suggested.

'I never did it. I didn't.' He was deeply agitated. 'I never.'

'But this man said you did?'

'He said I would go to jail for it, and "they do bad things to boys like you in jail", he said.' He shivered. 'I know they do. And he said . . . "Do you want AIDS, because you'll get it in jail, a pretty boy like you." '

Pretty, at that moment, he did not look.

285

'So what next?' I prompted.

'Well, I . . . Well, I . . .' he gulped. 'I said I never did it, it wasn't me . . . and he went on saying I'd go to jail and get AIDS and he went on and on . . . and I told him . . . I told him . . .'

'Told him what?'

'She's a nice lady,' he wailed. 'I didn't want to . . . he made me . . .'

'Was it Mrs Quentin,' I asked carefully, 'who poisoned her horse?'

He said miserably, 'Yes, No. See . . . she gave me this bag of treats . . . that's what she said they were, treats . . . and to give them to her horse when no one was looking . . . See, I didn't look after that horse of hers, it was another groom. So I gave her horse the bag of treats private, like . . . and it got colic and blew up and died . . . Well, I asked her, after. I was that scared . . . but she said it was all dreadful, she'd no idea her darling horse would get colic, and let's not say anything about it, she said, and she gave me a hundred dollars, and I didn't . . . I didn't want to be blamed, see?'

I did see.

I said, 'So when you told this man about the treats, what did he say?'

Lenny looked shattered. 'He grinned like a shark . . . all teeth . . . and he says . . . if I say anything about him to anybody . . . he'll see I get . . . I get . . .' He finished in a whisper, 'AIDS.'

I sighed. 'Is that how he threatened to kill you?'

He nodded weakly, as if spent.

'What did he look like?' I asked.

'Like my dad.' He paused. 'I hated my dad.'

'Did he sound like your dad?' I asked.

He shook his head. 'He wasn't a Brit.'

'Canadian?'

'Or American.'

'Well,' I said, running out of questions, 'I'll see you don't get AIDS.' I thought things over. 'Stay in the car until we get to Calgary. Ms Brown will get one of the other grooms to bring your bag here. The horse car is going to be unhitched from the train, and the horses are going by motor van to some stables for two days. All the grooms are going with them, as I expect you know. You go with the other grooms. And don't worry. Someone will come to find you and take you away, and bring another groom for Icy.' I paused to see if he understood, but it seemed he did. 'Where do you want to go from Calgary?'

'I don't know,' he said dully. 'Have to think.'

'All right. When the someone comes for you, tell him then what you want to do.'

He looked at me with a sort of wonderment. 'Why are you bothering?' he asked.

'I don't like frighteners.'

He shuddered. 'My dad frightened the living daylights out of people . . . and me and Mum . . . and someone stabbed him, killed him . . . served him right.' He paused. 'No one ever helped the people he frightened.' He paused again, struggling for the unaccustomed word, and came up with it. 'Thanks.'

With tie and buttons all correctly fastened, Tommy went back to the dining car. Zak was just finishing a scene in which old Ben, the groom who had been importuning Raoul for money on Toronto station, had been brought in from the racegoers' part of the train to give damning (false) evidence against Raoul for having doped the Bricknells' horses, a charge flatly denied by Raoul who contrived to look virtuous and possibly guilty, both at the same time. Sympathy on the whole ended on Raoul's side because of Ben's whining nastiness, and Zak told everyone that a Most Important Witness would be coming to Chateau Lake Louise that evening to give Damaging Testimony. Against whom? some people asked. Ah, said Zak mysteriously, vanishing towards the corridor, only time would tell.

Emil, Oliver, Cathy and I set the tables for lunch and served its three courses. Filmer didn't materialize, but Daffodil did, still shaken and angry as at breakfast. Her suitcase was packed, it appeared, and she was adamant about leaving the party at Calgary. No one, it seemed, had been able to find out from her exactly what the matter was, and the lovers' tiff explanation had gained ground.

I served wine carefully and listened, but it was the

appealing prospect of two days in the mountains rather than Daffodil's troubles that filled most of the minds.

When Calgary appeared like sharp white needles on the prairie horizon and everyone began pointing excitedly, I told Emil I would do my best to return for the dishwashing and sloped off up the train to George's office.

Would the credit-card telephone work in Calgary? Yes, it would. He waved me towards it as the train slowed and told me I'd got fifty minutes. He himself, as usual, would be outside, supervising.

I got through to Mrs Baudelaire, who sounded care-free and sixteen.

'Your photograph is on its way,' she said without preamble. 'But it won't get to Calgary in time. Someone will be driving from Calgary to Chateau Lake Louise later this afternoon, and they are going to take it to your Miss Richmond.'

'That's great,' I said. 'Thank you.'

'But I'm afraid there's been no word from Val Catto about your numbers.'

'It can't be helped.'

'Anything else?' she asked.

'Yes,' I said. 'I need to talk to Bill direct.'

'What a shame. I've been enjoying this.'

'Oh,' I said. 'Please . . . so have I. It's only that it's more than a message and question and answer. It's long . . . and complicated.'

'My dear young man, don't apologize. Bill was still

in Winnipeg ten minutes ago. I'll call him straight away. Do you have a number?'

'Um, yes.' I read her the number on the train's handset. 'The sooner the better, would you tell him?'

'Talk to you later,' she said, and went away.

I waited restlessly through ten wasted minutes before the phone rang.

Bill's deep voice reverberated in my ear. 'Where are you?'

'On the train in Calgary station.'

'My mother says it's urgent.'

'Yes, but chiefly because this cellular telephone is in the Conductor's office and only works in cities.'

'Understood,' he said. 'Fire away.'

I told him about Daffodil's departure and Lenny Higgs's frightened collapse; about what she had not said, and he had.

Bill Baudelaire at length demanded, 'Have I got this straight? This Lenny Higgs said Daffodil Quentin got him to give her horse something to eat, from which the horse got colic and died?'

'Strong supposition of cause and effect, but unprovable, I should think.'

'Yes. They had an autopsy and couldn't find what caused the colic. It was the third of her dead horses. The insurers were very suspicious, but they had to pay.'

'Lenny says she told him she would never do any harm to her darling horses, but she gave him a hundred dollars to keep quiet.'

Bill groaned.

'But,' I said, 'it might have been because she'd had two dead horses already and she was afraid everyone would think exactly what they did think anyway.'

'I suppose so,' he said. 'So where are we now?'

'Going on past experience,' I said, 'I would think – and this is just guessing – that after midnight last night, our quarry told Daffodil that her groom had spilled the beans, and would spill them again to order in public, and that he would see she was warned off at the very least if she didn't sell him . . . or give him . . . her remaining share in Laurentide Ice.'

He said gloomily, 'You all know him better than I do, but on form I'd think you may be right. We'll know for sure, won't we, if he applies to change the partnership registration before the Vancouver race.'

'Mm,' I agreed. 'Well, if you – the Ontario Racing Commission – feel like giving Daffodil the benefit of the doubt over her horses . . . and of course you know her better than I do, but it seems to me she may not be intentionally wicked, but more silly . . . I mean there's something immature about her, for all her fifty years or so . . . and some people don't think it's all that wicked to defraud insurance companies, perfectly respectable people sometimes do it . . . and I believe all three horses would have been put down sooner or later, wouldn't they? Anyway, I'm not excusing her if she's guilty, but explaining how she might feel about it . . .'

'You've got to know her remarkably well.'

'Er . . . I've just . . . noticed . . .'

'Mm,' he said dryly. 'Val Catto said you notice things.'

'Well . . . I, er, don't know how you feel about this, but I thought that if we spirited Lenny Higgs away, sort of, he wouldn't be around to be threatened, or to be a threat to Daffodil, and if you could tell her somehow that Lenny Higgs had vanished and will not be spilling any beans whatsoever . . . if you could square it with your conscience to do that . . . then she doesn't need to part with her half-share and we will have foiled at least one of our quarry's rotten schemes. And that's my brief, isn't it?'

He breathed out lengthily, as a whistle.

I held the line and waited.

'Is Lenny Higgs still on the train?' he asked eventually.

'Unless he panics, he's going with the other grooms and horses to their stabling here. I told him someone would come to fetch him and look after him and give him a free ticket to wherever he wants to go.'

'Now, hold on . . .'

'It's the least we can do. But I think we should follow it up, and positively know his exact ultimate destination, even fix him up with a job, because we in our turn may want him to give evidence against the man who frightened him. If we do, we don't want to have to find him worldwide. And if you can send someone to help him, get them to take along a copy of the photo you've had printed for me, because I'm pretty certain that's the man who frightened him. Lenny should turn to jelly, if it is.'

CHAPTER FOURTEEN

There was unfortunately a fair amount of dishwashing still to do when I returned to the kitchen so I lent a slightly guilty hand but kept walking out with glasses and cloths into the dining car so that I could see what was going on outside the windows.

Daffodil, attended by Nell and Rose and Cumber Young (he carrying her two suitcases), was helped down from the dome car by station staff and went off slowly into the main part of the station. Daffodil's curls were piled as perkily high as usual but her shoulders drooped inside the chinchillas, and the glimpse I had of her face showed a forlorn lost-child expression rather than a virago bent on revenge. Nell was being helpful. Rose Young exuded comfort: Cumber Young looked grim.

'Are you drying glasses or are you not?' Cathy demanded. She was pretty, bright-eyed and quick, and also, at that moment, tired.

'Intermittently,' I said.

Her momentary ill-temper dissolved. 'Then get an

intermittent move on or I won't be able to go over to the station before we leave.'

'Right,' I said, and dried and polished several glasses devotedly.

Cathy giggled. 'How long are you going to keep this up?'

'To the end, I guess.'

'But when is your scene?'

'Ah . . .' I said, 'that's the trouble. Right at the end. So I'll be drying dishes to Vancouver.'

'Are you the murderer?' she asked teasingly.

'Most definitely not.'

'The last time we had an actor pretending to be a waiter, he was the murderer.'

'The murderer,' I said, 'is that passenger you give the best portions to. That good-looking single man who's nice to everyone.'

Her eyes stretched wide. 'He's an owner,' she said.

'He's an actor. And don't give him away.'

'Of course I won't.' She looked slightly dreamy-eyed, though, as if I'd passed on good news. I didn't like to disillusion her about her or any girl's prospects with the gorgeous Giles; she would find out soon enough.

The chores finally done, Cathy skipped away to the delights of the station and in her place I helped Emil and Oliver stow and lock up all the equipment, as when everyone disembarked at Lake Louise the train was again going to be standing cold and silent in sidings for two days before the last stretch westwards to the Pacific.

Some but not all of the passengers had gone ashore, so to speak, at Calgary, and those who had been in the station came wandering back in good time, including the Youngs. Of Filmer there was no sign, nor of the gaunt-faced man. The dining car half filled again with people who simply preferred sitting there, and from those I heard that the horse car had been safely detached from the train and had been towed away by the engine, leaving the rest of us temporarily stranded.

The regular Canadian, they told each other, which had arrived on time thirty-five minutes after us, was the train standing three tracks away, its passengers stretching their legs like our own. The Canadian, it seemed, had changed from threat to friend in the general perception; our *doppelgänger* and companion on the journey. The passengers from both had mingled and compared notes. The Conductors had met for a talk.

There was a jerk and a shudder through the train as the engine returned and reattached, and soon afterwards we were on our way again, with passengers crowding now towards the dome car's observation deck to enjoy the ascent into the mountains.

Filmer, slightly to my surprise, was among those going through the dining car, and right behind him came Nell who looked over Filmer's shoulder at me and said, 'I've got a message for you from George Burley.'

'Excuse me, miss,' I said abruptly, standing well back between two tables to let Filmer go by, 'I'll be right with you.'

'What?' She was puzzled, but paused and stepped sideways also to let others behind her walk on through the car. Filmer himself had gone on without stopping, without paying Nell or me the least attention, and when his back was way down the car and well out of earshot of a quiet conversation, I turned back to Nell with enquiry.

'It's a bit of a mix-up,' she said. She was standing on the far side of the table from me, and speaking across it. 'Apparently the telephone in George Burley's office was ringing when he got back on board, and it was a woman wanting to speak to a Mr Kelsey. George Burley consulted his lists and said there was no Mr Kelsey on board. So whoever it was asked him to give a message to me, which he did.'

It must have been Mrs Baudelaire phoning, I thought: no one else knew the number. Bill himself could never be mistaken for a woman. Not his secretary . . .? Heaven forbid.

'What's the message?' I asked.

'I don't know if between us George Burley and I have got it right.' She was frowning. 'It's meaningless, but . . . zero forty-nine. That's the whole message, zero

297

forty-nine.' She looked at my face. 'You look happy enough about it, anyway.'

I was also appalled, as a matter of fact, at how close Filmer had come to hearing it.

I said, 'Yes, well . . . please don't tell anyone else about the message, and please forget it if you can.'

'I can't.'

'I was afraid not.' I hunted around if not for explanations at least for a reasonable meaning. 'It's to do,' I said, 'with the border between Canada and America, with the Forty-Ninth Parallel.'

'Oh, sure.' She was unsure by the look of things, but willing to let it go.

I said, 'Someone will bring a letter to the Chateau sometime this evening addressed to you. It will have a photo in it. It's for me, from Bill Baudelaire. Will you see that I get it?'

'Yes, OK.' She briefly glanced at her clipboard. 'I wanted to talk to you anyway about rooms.' A passenger or two walked past, and she waited until they had gone. 'The train crew are staying in the staff annexe at Chateau Lake Louise and the actors will be in the hotel itself. Which do you want? I have to write the list.'

'Our passengers will be in the hotel?'

'Ours, yes, but not the racegoers. They're all getting off in Banff. That's the town before Lake Louise. The owners are all staying in the Chateau. So am I. Which do you want?'

'To be with you,' I said.

'Seriously.'

I thought briefly. 'Is there anywhere else?'

'There's a sort of village near the station about a mile from the Chateau itself, but it's just a few shops, and they're closing now at this time of the year, ready for winter. A lot of places are closed by this time, in the mountains.' She paused. 'The Chateau stands by itself on the lake shore. It's beautiful there.'

'Is it big?' I asked.

'Huge.'

'OK. I'll stay there and risk it.'

'Risk what?'

'Being stripped of my waistcoat.'

'But you won't wear it there,' she assured me.

'No . . . metaphorically.'

She lowered the clipboard and clicked her pen for writing.

'Tommy Titmouse,' I said.

Her lips curved. 'T. Titmuss.' She spelled it out. 'That do?'

'Fine.'

'What are you really?'

'Wait and see,' I said.

She gave me a dry look but no answer because some passengers came by with questions, and I went forward into the dome car to see how firmly Julius Apollo would appear to be seated, wondering whether it would be safe to try to look inside his briefcase or whether I should most stringently obey the command not to risk being arrested. If he hadn't hoped I would look, the Brigadier wouldn't have relayed the number. But if I looked and got caught looking, it would blow the whole operation.

Filmer was nowhere to be seen.

From the top of the staircase, I searched again through the rows of backs of heads under the dome. No thick black well-brushed thatch with a scattering of grey hairs. Bald, blond, tangled and trimmed, but no Filmer.

He wasn't in the downstairs lounge, and he wasn't in the bar where the poker school was as usual in progress, oblivious to the scenery. That left only the Lorrimores' car. . . . He had to be with Mercer, Bambi and Sheridan. Xanthe was with Rose and Cumber Young, watching the approach of the distant white peaks under a cloudless sky.

I walked irresolutely back towards Filmer's bedroom, wondering whether the disinclination I felt to enter it was merely prudence or otherwise plain fear, and being afraid it was the latter.

I would have to do it, I thought, because if I didn't I'd spend too much of my life regretting it. A permanent D minus in the balance sheet. By the time I left the dining room and started along the corridor past the kitchen, I was already feeling breathless, already conscious of my heart, and it was not in any way good for self-confidence. With a dry mouth I crossed the chilly shifting join between cars, opening and closing the doors, every step bringing me nearer to the risky commitment.

Filmer's was the first room in the sleeping car beyond the kitchen. I rounded the corner into the corridor with the utmost reluctance and was just about to put my hand to the door handle when the sleeping-car attendant, dressed exactly as I was, came out of his roomette at the other end of the car, saw me, waved and started walking towards me. With craven relief I went slowly towards him, and he said, 'Hi,' and how was I doing.

He was the familiar one who'd told me about Filmer's private breakfast, who'd shown me how to fold and unfold the armchairs and bunks, the one who looked after both the car we were in and the three bedrooms, Daffodil's among them, in the dome car. He had all afternoon and nothing to do and was friendly and wanted to talk, and he made it impossible for me to shed him and get back to my nefarious business.

He talked about Daffodil and the mess she had made of her bedroom.

Mess?

'If you ask me,' he said, nodding, 'she'd had a bottle of vodka in her suitcase. . . . There was broken glass all over the place. Broken vodka bottle. And the mirror over the washbasin. In splinters. All over the place. I'd guess she threw the vodka bottle at the mirror and they both broke.'

'A bore for you to have to clear that up,' I said.

He seemed surprised. 'I didn't clear it. It's still like that. George can take a look at it.' He shrugged. 'I don't know if the company will charge her for it. Shouldn't be surprised.'

He looked over my shoulder at someone coming into the car from the dining car.

'Afternoon, sir,' he said.

There was no reply from behind me. I turned my head and saw Filmer's back view going into his bedroom.

Dear God, I thought in horror: I would have been in there with his briefcase open, reading his papers. I felt almost sick.

I sensed more than saw Filmer come out of his bedroom again and walk towards us.

'Can I help you, sir?' the sleeping-car attendant said, going past me, towards him.

'Yes. What do we do about our bags at Lake Louise?'

'Leave it to me, sir. We're collecting everyone's cases and transporting them to the Chateau. They'll be delivered to your room in the Chateau, sir.'

'Good,' Filmer said, and went back into his lair, closing the door. Beyond the merest flicker of a glance at about waist level, he hadn't looked at me at all.

'We did the same with the bags at Winnipeg,' the sleeping-car attendant said to me resignedly. 'You'd think they'd learn.'

'Perhaps they will by Vancouver.'

'Yeah.'

I left him after a while and went and sat in my own roomette and did some deep breathing and thanked every guardian angel in the firmament for my deliverance, and in particular the angel in the sleeping-car attendant's yellow waistcoat.

Outside the window, the promise of the mountains became an embrace, rocky hillsides covered with tall narrow pines crowding down to the railway line winding through the valley of the Bow River. There were thick untidy collections of twigs sitting like Ascot hats on the top of a good many telegraph poles, which looked quite extraordinary; one of the passengers had said the hats were osprey nests, and that the poles were made with platforms on especially to accommodate them. Brave birds, I thought, laying their eggs near to the roaring trains. Hair-raising entertainment for the hatchlings.

Our speed had slowed from the brisk prairie rattle to a grunting uphill slither, the train taking two hours to cover the seventy miles from Calgary to Banff. When it stopped there, in the broad part of the valley, the snow-topped peaks were suddenly revealed as standing around in a towering, glistening, uneven ring, the quintessential mountains rising in bare majestic rocky grandeur from the thronging forested courtier foothills. I felt then, as most people do, the strong lure of high mysterious frozen places and, Filmer or not, I found myself smiling with pleasure, light-hearted to the bone.

It had been noticeably warm in Calgary, owing, it

was said, to the föhn winds blowing down from the
mountains, but in Banff it was suitably cold. The engine
huffed and puffed about and split the train in two,
taking the racegoers and all the front part off to a
siding and coming back to pick up just the owners'
quarters; the three sleeping cars, the dining car, the
dome car and the Lorrimores'. Abbreviated and much
lighter, these remains of the train climbed at good
speed for another three-quarters of an hour and tri-
umphantly drew up beside the log-cabin station of Lake
Louise.

With great cheerfulness the passengers disembarked,
shivering even in their coats after the warmth of the
cars, but full of expectation, Daffodil forgotten. They
filed on to a waiting bus, while their suitcases were
loaded into a separate truck. I clung to a fraction of
hope that Filmer would leave his briefcase to be ferried
in that fashion, but when he emerged from the train
the case went with him, clutched firmly in his fist.

I told Nell I would walk up the mile or so from the
station so as not to arrive until everyone had booked
in and cleared the lobby. She said I could travel up
anyway with the crew in their own bus, but I entrusted
my bag to her keeping and in my grey regulation raincoat, buttoned to the neck, I enjoyed the fresh cold air
and the deepening harvest gold of the late afternoon
sunlight. When I reached the lobby of the grand
Chateau, it was awash with polite young Japanese

couples on honeymoon, not the Unwins, the Youngs and the Flokatis.

Nell was sprawled in a lobby armchair as if she would never be able to summon the energy to rise again, and I went and sat beside her before she'd realized I was there.

'Is everyone settled?' I asked.

She sighed deeply and made no attempt at moving. 'The suite I had reserved for the Lorrimores had been given to someone else half an hour before we got here. The people are not budging, the management are not apologizing, and Bambi is not pleased.'

'I can imagine.'

'On the other hand, we are sitting with our backs to one of the greatest views on earth.'

I twisted round and looked over the back of the chair, and saw, between thronging Japanese, black and white mountains, a turquoise blue lake, green pines and an advancing glacier, all looking like painted stage scenery, awesomely close and framed by the windows.

'Wow,' I said, impressed.

'It won't go away,' Nell said, after a while. 'It'll all still be there tomorrow.'

I flopped back into the chair. 'It's amazing.'

'It's why people have been coming here to stare for generations.'

'I expected altogether more snow,' I said.

'It'll be knee-deep by Christmas.'

'Do you have any time off here?' I asked.

She looked at me sideways. 'Five seconds now and then, but almost no privacy.'

I sighed lightly, having expected nothing else. She was the focus, the centre round which the tour revolved: the most visible person, her behaviour vivisected.

'Your room is in one of the wings,' she said, handing me a card with a number on it. 'You just have to sign in at the desk and they'll give you the key. Your bag should be up there already. Most of the actors are in that wing. None of the owners.'

'Are you?'

'No.'

She didn't say where her room was, and I didn't ask. 'Where will you eat?' she said doubtfully. 'I mean . . . will you sit with the actors in the dining room?'

I shook my head.

'But not with the owners . . .'

'It's a lonely old life,' I said.

She looked at me with sudden sharp attention, and I thought ruefully that I'd told her a good deal too much.

'Do you mean,' she asked slowly, 'that you do this all the time? Play a part? Not just on the train?'

'No,' I smiled. 'I work alone. That's all I meant.'

She almost shivered. 'Are you ever yourself?'

'Sundays and Mondays.'

'Alone?'

'Well . . . yes.'

Her eyes, steady and grey, looked only moderately

troubled. 'You don't seem unhappy,' she observed, 'being lonely.'

'Of course not. I choose it, mostly. But not when there's an alluring alternative hiding behind a clipboard.'

The armour lay on her lap at that moment, off duty. She smoothed a hand over it, trying not to laugh.

'Tomorrow,' she said, retreating into common sense, 'I'm escorting a bus load of passengers to a glacier, then to lunch in Banff, then up a mountain in cable cars.'

'And may it keep fine for you.'

'The Lorrimores have a separate chauffeur-driven car.'

'Has anyone else?'

'Not since Mrs Quentin's left.'

'Poor old Daffodil,' I said.

'Poor?' Nell exclaimed. 'Did you know she smashed the mirror in her room?'

'Yes, I heard. Is Mr Filmer going on the bus trip?'

'I don't know yet. He wanted to know if there's an exercise gym because he likes lifting weights. The bus is simply available for anyone who wants to go. I won't know everyone who'll be on it until we set off.'

I would have to watch the departure, I thought, and that could be difficult as I would be half familiar to all of them by now and could hardly stand around invisibly for very long.

'The Unwins have come down into the hall and are heading towards me,' Nell said, looking away from me.

'Right.'

I stood up without haste, took the card she'd given me to the desk, and signed the register. Behind me, I could hear the Unwins' Australian voices telling her they were going for a stroll by the shore and it was the best trip they'd ever taken. When I turned round, holding my own key, they were letting themselves out through the glass doors to the garden.

I paused again beside Nell who was now standing up. 'Maybe I'll see you,' I said.

'Maybe.'

I smiled at her eyes. 'If anything odd happens . . .'

She nodded. 'You're in room six sixty-two.'

'After Vancouver,' I said, 'what then?'

'After the races I'm booked straight back to Toronto on the red-eye special.'

'What's the red-eye special?'

'The overnight flight.'

'So soon?'

'How was I to know I wouldn't want to?'

'That'll do fine,' I said, 'for now.'

'Don't get ideas,' Nell said sedately, 'above your lowly station.'

She moved away with a mischievous glint and I went contentedly up to the sixth floor in the wing where there were no owners, and found that the room allocated to me was near the end of the passage and next door to Zak's.

His door was wide open with Donna and Pierre standing half in, half out.

'Come on in,' Donna said, seeing me. 'We're just walking through tonight's scene.'

'And we've a hell of a crisis on our hands,' Pierre said. 'We need all the input we can get.'

'But Zak might not . . .' I began.

He came to the door himself. 'Zak is taking suggestions from chimpanzees,' he said.

'OK. I'll just take off my coat.' I pointed. 'I'm in the room next along.'

I went into my room which proved to have the same sweeping view of the mountains, the lake, the trees, and the glacier, and it was if anything more spectacular than in the lobby from being higher up. I took off the raincoat and the uniform it had hidden, put on a track-suit and trainers, and returned to Zak's fray.

The crisis was the absence of an actor who was supposed to have arrived but had sent apologies instead.

'Apologies!' Zak fumed. 'He broke his goddam arm this morning and he's not coming. I ask you! Is a broken arm any sort of excuse?'

The others, the whole troupe, were inclined to think not.

'He was supposed to be Angelica's husband,' Zak said.

'What about Steve?' I asked.

'He was her lover, and her business partner. They were both killed by Giles because they had just found out he had embezzled all the capital and the bloodstock business was bankrupt. Now Angelica's husband comes on the scene to ask where her money is, as she hasn't changed her will and he inherits. He decided to investigate her death himself because he doesn't think either the Mounties or I have done a good enough job. And now he isn't even *here*.'

'Well,' I said, 'why don't you discover that it is *Raoul* who is really Angelica's husband and who stands to inherit, which gives him a lot of motive as he doesn't know yet that Giles has embezzled the money, does he? No one does. And Raoul is only free to marry Donna because Angelica is dead, which can give the Bricknells hysterics. And how about if Raoul says the Bricknells themselves have been doping their horses, not Raoul, but they deny it and are very pleased that he should be judged guilty of everything now they know he can't marry their daughter because he is probably a murderer and will go to jail? And how about if it was the Bricknells' horse that was really supposed to be kidnapped, but by Giles, as you can later discover, so that he could sell it and gain enough to skip the country once he got safely to Vancouver?'

They opened their mouths.

'I don't know that it actually makes sense,' Zak said eventually.

'Never mind, I don't suppose they'll notice.'

'You cynical son-of-a . . .'

'I don't see why not,' Donna said. 'And I can have a nice weepy scene with Pierre.'

'Why?' Zak said.

'I like doing them.'

They all fell about, and in a while walked through dramatic revelations (received by Zak from Outside Sources) of Raoul's marriage to Angelica five years earlier, which neither had acknowledged at Toronto station because, Raoul said unconvincingly, they were both shocked to find the other there, as he wanted to meld with Donna as she with Steve.

They all went away presently to get into their character clothes, and from Zak, very much later, I heard that the whole thing, played at the tops of their voices, had been a galvanic riot. He came to my door with a bottle in each hand, Scotch for him, red wine for me, and sank exhaustedly into an armchair with an air of having nobly borne the weight of the world on his shoulders and bravely survived.

'Did you have any dinner?' he said, yawning. 'Didn't see you.'

'I had some sent up.'

He looked at the television programme with which I'd passed the time.

'Rotten reception in these mountains,' he said. 'Look at that idiot.' He stared at the screen. 'Couldn't act his way out of a paper bag.'

311

We drank companionably and I asked if the party were all generally happy without Daffodil Quentin.

'The dear in the Mont Blanc curls?' he said. 'Oh, sure. They were all in a great mood. That man who used to be with her all the time was dripping charm all over Bambi Lorrimore and that nutter of a son of hers didn't open his mouth once. Those Australians are still in the clouds . . .'

He described the reactions of some of the others to the evening's scene and then said he would rely on me for another scintillating bit of scrambled plot for the next night. Not to mention, he added, a denouement and finale for the night after, our last on the train. The mystery had to be solved then before a gala dinner of epic proportions comprising five courses produced by Angus by sleight of hand.

'But I only said it all off the top of my head,' I said.

'The top of your head will do us all fine.' He yawned. 'Tell you the truth, we need a fresh mind.'

'Well . . . all right.'

'So how much do I pay you?'

I was surprised. 'I don't want money.'

'Don't be silly.'

'Um,' I said. 'I do earn more than Tommy.'

He looked at me over his whisky glass. 'You don't really surprise me.'

'So thanks a lot,' I said, meaning it, 'but no thanks.'

He nodded and left it: the offer honourably made, realistically declined. Anything he would have paid me would have come directly out of his own pocket: impossible to accept.

'Oh!' he said, clearly hit by a shaft of memory, 'Nell asked me to give you this.' He dug into a pocket and produced a sealed envelope which he handed over. It said 'Nell Richmond' on the outside, and 'Photographs, do not bend.'

'Thanks,' I said, relieved. 'I was beginning to think it hadn't got here.'

I opened the envelope and found three identical prints inside, but no letter. The pictures were clear, sharp and in black and white owing to the fast high-definition film I habitually used in the binoculars-camera. The subject, taken from above, was looking upwards and to one side to a point somewhere below the lens, so that one couldn't see his eyes clearly; but the sharply jutting cheekbones, the narrow nose, the deep eye sockets, the angled jawbone and the hairline retreating from the temples, all were identifiable at a glance. I handed one of the prints to Zak, and he looked at it curiously.

'Who is it?' he said.

'That's the point. Who is he? Have you seen him on the train?'

He looked again at the picture which showed, below the head, the shoulders and neck, with the sheepskin collar of the padded jacket over a sweater of some sort and a checked shirt unbuttoned at the top.

'A tough-looking man,' Zak said. 'Is he a militant union agitator?'

I was startled. 'Why do you say that?'

'Don't know. He has the look. All intensity and aggression. That's what I'd cast him as.'

'And is that how you'd also act a union agitator?'

'Sure.' He grinned. 'If he was described in the script as a troublemaker.' He shook his head. 'I haven't seen him on the train or anywhere else that I know of. Is he one of the racegoers, then?'

'I don't know for sure, but he was at Thunder Bay station and also at Winnipeg races.'

'The sleeping-car attendants will know.'

I nodded. 'I'll ask them.'

'What do you want him for?'

'Making trouble.'

He handed back the photograph with a smile. 'Type-cast,' he said, nodding.

He ambled off to bed, and early the next morning I telephoned Mrs Baudelaire who sounded as if she rose with the lark.

I asked her to tell Bill the photos had arrived safely.

'Oh, good,' she said blithely. 'Did you get my message with the numbers?'

'Yes, I did, thank you very much.'

'Val called with them from London, sounding very pleased. He said he wasn't having so much success with whatever it was that Sheridan Lorrimore did at Cambridge. No one's talking. He thinks the gag is cash for the new library being built at Sheridan's old college. How immoral can academics get? And Bill said to tell you that they went round to the Winnipeg barns with that photo, but no one knew who the man was, except that he did go there asking for Lenny Higgs. Bill says they will ask all the Ontario racing people they can reach and maybe print it in the racing papers coast to coast.'

'Great.'

'Bill wants to know what name you're using on the train.'

I hesitated, which she picked up at once with audible hurt. 'Don't you trust us?'

'Of course I do. But I don't trust everyone on the train.'

'Oh, I see.'

'You were right to send the message to Nell.'

'Good, then.'

'Are you well?' I asked.

The line said, 'Have a nice day, young man,' and went dead.

I listened to her silence with regret. I should have known better. I did know better, but it seemed discourteous never to ask.

With her much in mind I dressed for outdoors, hopped down the fire stairs and found an inconspicuous way out so as not to come face to face with any passengers who were en route to breakfast. In my woolly hat, well pulled down, and my navy zipped jacket, I found a good vantage point for watching the front door, then wandered round a bit and returned to the watching point a little before bus-boarding time for the joy-trip to Banff. Under the jacket I had slung the binoculars, just in case I could get nowhere near, but in fact, from leaning against the boot of an empty, parked, locked car where I hoped I looked as if I was waiting for the driver to return, I had a close enough view not to need them.

A large ultra-modern bus with tinted windows rolled in and stationed itself obligingly so that I could see who walked from the hotel to board it, and very soon after, when the driver had been into the hotel to report his arrival, Nell appeared in a warm jacket, trousers and boots and shepherded her flock with smiles into its depths. Most of the passengers were going sightseeing, it seemed, but not all.

Filmer didn't come out. I willed him to: to appear without his briefcase and roll away for hours: to give me a chance of thinking of some way to get into his room in safety. Willing didn't work. Julius Apollo didn't seem to want to walk on a glacier or dangle in a cable car, and stayed resolutely indoors.

Mercer, Bambi and Sheridan came out of the hotel together, hardly looking a light-hearted little family, and inserted themselves into a large waiting chauffeur-driven car which carried them off immediately.

No Xanthe. No Xanthe on the bus either. Rose and

Cumber Young had boarded without her. Xanthe, I surmised, was back in the sulks.

Nell, making a note on her clipboard and looking at her watch, decided there were no more customers for the bus. She stepped inside it and closed the door and I watched it roll away.

CHAPTER FIFTEEN

I walked about on foot in the mountains thinking of the gifts that had been given me.

Lenny Higgs. The combinations of the locks of the briefcase. Nell's friendship. Mrs Baudelaire. The chance to invent Zak's scripts.

It was the last which chiefly filled my mind as I walked round the path which circled the little lake; and the plans I began forming for the script had a lot to do with the end of my conversation with Bill Baudelaire, which had been disturbing.

After he'd agreed to arrange a replacement groom for Laurentide Ice, he said he'd tried to talk to Mercer Lorrimore at Assiniboia Downs but hadn't had much success.

'Talk about what?' I asked.

'About our quarry. I was shocked to find how friendly he had become with the Lorrimores. I tried to draw Mercer Lorrimore aside and remind him about the trial, but he was quite short with me. If a man was found innocent, he said, that was an end of it. He thinks good of everyone, it seems – which is saintly but not sensible.' Bill's voice went even deeper with disillusion. 'Our quarry can be overpoweringly pleasant, you know, if he puts his mind to it, and he had certainly been doing that. He had poor Daffodil Quentin practically eating out of his hand, too, and I wonder what she thinks of him now.'

I could hear the echo of his voice in the mountains. 'More saintly than sensible.' Mercer was a man who saw good where no good existed. Who longed for goodness in his son, and would pay for ever because it couldn't be achieved.

The path round the lake wound up hill and down, sometimes through close-thronging pines, sometimes with sudden breath-stopping views of the silent giants towering above, sometimes with clear vistas of the deep turquoise water below in its perfect bowl. It had rained during the night so that the whole scene in the morning sunshine looked washed and glittering; and the rain had fallen as snow on the mountaintops and the glacier which now appeared whiter, cleaner and nearer than the day before.

The air was cold, descending perceptibly like a tide from the frozen peaks, but the sun, at its autumn highest in the sky, still kept enough warmth to make walking a pleasure, and when I came to a place where a bench had been placed before a stunning panorama of lake, the Chateau and the mountain behind it, it was warm enough also to pause and sit down. I brushed some raindrops off the seat and slouched on the bench, hands in pockets, gazed vaguely on the picture-postcard spectacle, mind in second gear on Filmer.

I could see figures walking about by the shore in the Chateau garden, and thought without hurry of perhaps bringing out the binoculars to see if any of them was Julius Apollo. Not that it would have been of much help, I supposed, if he'd been there. He wouldn't be doing anything usefully criminal under the gaze of the Chateau's serried ranks of windows.

Someone with quiet footsteps came along the path from the shelter of the trees and stopped, looking down at the lake. Someone female.

I glanced at her incuriously, seeing a backview of jeans, blue parka, white trainers and a white woollen hat with two scarlet pompoms: and then she turned round, and I saw that it was Xanthe Lorrimore.

She looked disappointed to find the bench already occupied.

'Do you mind if I sit here?' she said. 'It's a long walk. My legs are tired.'

'No, of course not.' I stood up and brushed the raindrops off the rest of the bench, making a drier space for her.

'Thanks.' She flopped down in adolescent gawkiness and I took my own place again, with a couple of feet between us.

She frowned. 'Haven't I seen you before?' she asked. 'Are you on the train?'

'Yes, miss,' I said, knowing that there was no point in denying it, as she would see me again and more clearly in the dining room. 'I'm one of the crew.'

'Oh.' She began as if automatically to get to her feet, and then, after a moment, decided against it out of tiredness, and relaxed. 'Are you,' she said slowly, keeping her distance, 'one of the waiters?'

'Yes, Miss Lorrimore.'

'The one who told me I had to pay for a Coke?'

'Yes, I'm sorry.'

She shrugged and looked down at the lake. 'I suppose,' she said in a disgruntled voice, 'all this is pretty special, but what I really feel is *bored*.'

She had thick almost straight chestnut hair which curved at the ends over her shoulders, and she had clear fine skin and marvellous eyebrows. She was going to be beautiful, I thought, with maturity, unless she let the sulky cast of her mouth spoil not just her face but her life.

'I sometimes wish I was poor like you,' she said. 'It would make everything simple.' She glanced at me. 'I suppose you think I'm crazy to say that.' She paused. 'My mother would say I shouldn't be talking to you anyway.'

I moved as if to stand up. 'I'll go away, if you like,' I said politely.

'No, don't.' She was unexpectedly vehement and surprised even herself. 'I mean ... there's no one else to talk to. I mean ... well.'

'I do understand,' I said.

'Do you?' She was embarrassed. 'I was going to go on the bus, really. My parents think I'm on the bus. I was going with Rose . . . Mrs Young . . . and Mr Young. But he . . .' She almost stopped, but the childish urge in her to talk was again running strong, sweeping away discretion. 'He's never as nice to me as she is. I think he's tired of me. Cumber, isn't that a stupid name? It's Cumberland, really. That's somewhere in England where his parents went on their honeymoon, Rose says. Albert Cumberland Young, that's what his name is. Rose started calling him Cumber when they met because she thought it sounded cosier, but he isn't cosy at all, you know, he's stiff and stern.' She broke off and looked down towards the Chateau. 'Why do all those Japanese go on their honeymoons together?'

'I don't know,' I said.

'Perhaps they'll all call their children Lake Louise.'

'They could do worse.'

'What's your name?' she asked.

'Tommy, Miss Lorrimore.'

She made no comment. She was only half easy in my company, too conscious of my job. But above all, she wanted to talk.

'You know my brother, Sheridan?' she said.

I nodded.

'The trouble with Sheridan is that we're too rich. He thinks he's better than everyone else because he's richer.' She paused. 'What do you think of that?' It

322

was part a challenge, part a desperate question, and I answered her from my own heart.

'I think it's very difficult to be very rich very young.'

'Do you really?' She was surprised. 'It's what everyone wants to be.'

'If you can have everything, you forget what it's like to need. And if you're given everything, you never learn to save.'

She brushed that aside. 'There's no point in saving. My grandmother left me millions. And Sheridan too. I suppose you think that's awful. He thinks he deserves it. He thinks he can do anything he likes because he's rich.'

'You could give it away,' I said, 'if you think it's awful.'

'Would you?'

I said regretfully, 'No.'

'There you are, then.'

'I'd give some of it away.'

'I've got trustees and they won't let me.'

I smiled faintly. I'd had Clement Cornborough. Trustees, he'd told me once austerely, were there to preserve and increase fortunes, not to allow them to be squandered, and no, he wouldn't allow a fifteen-year-old boy to fund a farm for pensioned-off racehorses.

'Why do you think it's difficult to be rich?' she demanded. 'It's easy.'

I said neutrally, 'You said just now that if you were poor, life would be simple.'

'I suppose I did. I suppose I didn't mean it. Or not really. I don't know if I meant it. Why is it difficult to be rich?'

'Too much temptation. Too many available corruptions.'

'Do you mean drugs?'

'Anything. Too many pairs of shoes. Self-importance.'

She put her feet up on the bench and hugged her knees, looking at me over the top. 'No one will believe this conversation.' She paused. 'Do you wish you were rich?'

It was an unanswerable question. I said truthfully in evasion, 'I wouldn't like to be starving.'

'My father says,' she announced, 'that one's not better because one's richer, but richer because one's better.'

'Neat.'

'He always says things like that. I don't understand them sometimes.'

'Your brother Sheridan,' I said cautiously, 'doesn't seem to be happy.'

'Happy!' She was scornful. 'He's never happy. I've hardly seen him happy in his whole life. Except that he does laugh at people sometimes.' She was doubtful. 'I suppose if he laughs, he must be happy. Only he despises them, that's why he laughs. I wish I *liked* Sheridan. I wish I had a terrific brother who would look after me and take me places. That would be fun.

Only it wouldn't be with Sheridan, of course, because it would end in trouble. He's been terrible on this trip. Much worse than usual. I mean, he's embarrassing.' She frowned, disliking her thoughts.

'Someone said,' I said without any of my deep curiosity showing, 'that he had a bit of trouble in England.'

'Bit of trouble! I shouldn't tell you, but he ought to be in jail, only they didn't press charges. I think my father bought them off ... and anyway, that's why Sheridan does what my parents say, right now, because they threatened to let him be prosecuted if he as much as squeaks.'

'Could he still be prosecuted?' I asked without emphasis.

'What's a statute of limitations?'

'A time limit,' I said, 'after which one cannot be had up for a particular bit of law-breaking.'

'In England?'

'Yes.'

'You're English, aren't you?' she asked.

'Yes.'

'He said, "Hold your breath, the statute of limitations is out of sight." '

'Who said?'

'An attorney, I think. What did he mean? Did he mean Sheridan is ... is ...'

'Vulnerable?'

She nodded. ' ... for ever?'

'Maybe for a long time.'

'Twenty years?' An unimaginable time, her voice said.

'It would have to have been bad.'

'I don't know what he did,' she said despairingly. 'I only know it's ruined this summer. Absolutely ruined it. And I'm supposed to be in school right now, only they made me come on this train because they wouldn't leave me in the house alone. Well, not alone, but alone except for the servants. And that's because my cousin Susan Lorrimore, back in the summer, she's seventeen, she ran off with their chauffeur's son and they got married and there was an *earthquake* in the family. And I can see why she did, they kept leaving her alone in that huge house and going to Europe and she was bored out of her skull and, anyway, it seems their chauffeur's son is all brains and cute, too, and she sent me a card saying she didn't regret a thing. My mother is scared to death that I'll run off with some . . .'

She stopped abruptly, looked at me a little wildly and sprang to her feet.

'I forgot,' she said. 'I sort of forgot you are . . .'

'It's all right,' I said, standing also. 'Really all right.'

'I guess I talk too much.' She was worried and unsure. 'You won't . . .'

'No. Not a word.'

'Cumber told me I ought to mind my tongue,' she said resentfully. 'He doesn't know what it's like living in a mausoleum with everyone glowering at each other

326

and Daddy trying to smile.' She swallowed. 'What would you do,' she demanded, 'if you were me?'

'Make your father laugh.'

She was puzzled. 'Do you mean ... make him happy?'

'He needs your love,' I said. I gestured to the path back to the Chateau. 'If you'd like to go on first, I'll follow after.'

'Come with me,' she said.

'No. Better not.'

In an emotional muddle that I hadn't much helped, she tentatively set off, looking back twice until a bend in the path took her out of sight, and I sat down again on the bench, although growing cold now, and thought about what she'd said, and felt grateful, as ever and always, for Aunt Viv.

There wasn't much wrong with Xanthe, I thought. Lonely, worried, only half understanding the adult world, needing reassurance, she longed primarily for exactly what Mercer himself wanted, a friendly united family. She hadn't thought of affronting her parents by cuddling up to a waiter; very much the reverse. She hadn't tried to put me into a difficult position: had been without guile or tricks. I wouldn't have minded having a younger sister like her that I could take places for her to have fun. I hoped she would learn to live in peace with her money, and thought that a month or so of serving other people in a good crew like Emil, Oliver and Cathy would be the best education she could get.

After a while I scanned the whole Chateau and its gardens with the binoculars but I couldn't see Filmer, which wasn't really surprising, and in the end I set off again to walk, and detoured up on to the foot of the glacier, trudging on the cracked, crunchy, grey-brown-green fringe of the frozen river.

Laurentide Ice, one of the passengers had know-ledgeably said early on, was the name given to one of the last great polar ice sheets to cover most of Canada twenty thousand years before. Daffodil, nodding, had said her husband had named the horse because he was interested in prehistory, and she was going to call her next horse Cordilleran Ice, the sheet that had covered the Rockies. Her husband would have been pleased, she said. I could be standing at that moment on prehis-toric Cordilleran ice perhaps, I thought, but if glaciers moved faster than history, perhaps not. Anyway, it gave a certain perspective to the concerns of Julius Apollo.

Back at the Chateau, I went upstairs and drafted a new scene for the script, and I'd barely finished when Zak came knocking to enquire for it. We went into his room where the cast had already gathered for the rehearsal, and I looked round at their seven faces and asked if we still had the services of begging Ben, who was missing from the room. No, we didn't, Zak said. He had gone back to Toronto. Did it matter?

'No, not really. He might have been useful as a messenger, but I expect you can pretend a messenger.'

They nodded.

'Right,' Zak said, looking at his watch. 'We're on stage in two and a half hours. What do we do?'

'First,' I said, 'Raoul starts a row with Pierre. Raoul is furious to have been discovered to be Angelica's husband, and he says he positively knows Pierre owes thousands in gambling debts which he can't pay, and he knows who he owes it to, and he says that that man is known to beat people up who don't pay.'

Raoul and Pierre nodded. 'I'll put in some detail,' Raoul said. 'I'll say the debts are from illegal racing bets, and I've been told because they were on the Bricknells' horses, OK?'

'OK?' Zak said to me.

'Yes, OK. Then Raoul taunts Pierre that his only chance of getting the money is to marry Donna, and Walter Bricknell says that if Donna's so stupid as to marry Pierre, he will not give her a penny. He will in no circumstances pay Pierre's debts.'

They all nodded.

'At that point, Mavis Bricknell comes screaming into the cocktail room saying that all her beautiful jewels have been stolen.'

They all literally sat up. Mavis laughed and clapped her hands. 'Who's stolen them?' she said.

'All in good time,' I smiled. 'Raoul accuses Pierre, Pierre accuses Raoul, and they begin to shove each other around, letting all their mutual hatred hang out. Finally Zak steps in, breaks it up, and says they will all go and search both Pierre's room and Raoul's room for the jewels. Zak, Raoul, Pierre and Mavis go off.'

They nodded.

'That leaves,' I said. 'Donna, Walter Bricknell and Giles in the cocktail room. Donna and Walter have another argument about Pierre, Donna stifles a few tears and then Giles comes out of the audience to support Donna and say she's been having a bad experience, and he thinks it's time for a little good feeling all round.'

Giles said, 'OK, good. Here we go.'

'Then,' I said, 'Zak and the others return. They haven't found the jewels. Giles begins to comfort Mavis as well. Mavis says she lived for her collection, she loved every piece. She's distraught. She goes on a bit.'

'Lovely,' Mavis said.

'Walter,' I went on, 'says he can't see any point in jewellery. His jewellery is his horses. He lives for his horses. He says extravagantly that if he couldn't go racing to watch his horses, he'd rather die. He'd kill himself if he couldn't have horses.'

Walter frowned but eagerly nodded. He hadn't had much of a part so far: it would give him a big scene of his own, even if one difficult to make convincing.

'Walter then says Raoul is ruining his pleasure in his horses, and ruining the journey for everyone, and he gives him the formal sack as his trainer. Raoul protests, and says he hasn't deserved to be fired. Walter says Raoul is probably a murderer and a jewel thief and has been cheating him with his horses. Raoul in a rage tries to attack Walter. Zak hauls him off. Zak tells everyone to cool down. He says he will organize a search of everyone's bedrooms to see if the jewels can be found, and he will consult with the hotel's detective and call in the police if necessary. Everyone looks as if they don't want the police. End of scene.'

I waited for their adverse comments and altering suggestions, but there were very few. I handed my outline to Zak who went over it again bit by bit with the actors concerned, and they all started murmuring, making up their own words.

'And what happens tomorrow?' Zak asked finally. 'How do we sort it all out?'

'I haven't written it down yet,' I said.

'But you do have it in mind? Could you write it this evening?'

I nodded twice.

'Right,' he said. 'We'd better all meet here tomorrow after breakfast. We'll have to do a thorough walk through, maybe two or even three, to make sure we get it all right. Tie up the loose ends, that sort of thing. And don't forget, everybody, tomorrow we'll be back in the dining car. Not so much room for fighting and so on, so make it full of action tonight.'

'Tomorrow Pierre gets shot,' I said.

'Oh boy, oh boy,' Pierre said.

'But not fatally. You can go on talking.'

'Better and better.'

'But you'll need some blood.'

'Great,' Pierre said. 'How much?'

'Well . . .' I laughed. 'I'll let you decide where the bullet goes, and how much gore you think the passengers can stand, but you'd better be going to live, at the end of it.'

They wanted to know what else I had in store, but I wouldn't tell them: I said they might give the future away by accident if they knew, and they protested they were too professional to do that. But I didn't altogether trust their improvising tongues, and they shrugged and gave way with fair grace.

I watched the walk through which seemed to go pretty well, but it was nothing, Zak assured me afterwards, to the actual live performance among the cocktails.

He came back to my room at eleven, as on the previous night, drinking well-earned whisky exhaustedly.

'Those two, Raoul and Pierre, they really gave it a go,' he said. 'They both learned stage fighting and stunts at drama school, you know. They'd worked out the fight beforehand, and it was a humdinger. All over the place. It was a shame to break it up. Half the passengers spilled their cocktails with Raoul and Pierre rolling and slogging on the floor near their feet and we had to give everyone free refills.' He laughed. 'Dear Mavis put on the grand tragedy for reporting the theft of the jewels and poured on some tremendous pathos later over losing all her happy memories of the gifts that were bound up in them. Had half the audience in tears. Marvellous. Then Walter did his thing quite well considering he complained to me that no one in their right mind would kill themselves because they couldn't go racing. And afterwards, would you believe it, one of the passengers asked me where we got the idea from, about someone killing themselves because they couldn't go racing.'

'What did you say?' I asked with a jerk of anxiety.

'I said I picked it out of the air.' He watched me relax a shade and asked, 'Where *did* you get it from?'

'I knew of someone not long ago who did just that.' Thirteen days ago . . . a lifetime.

'Crazy.'

'Mm.' I paused. 'Who asked you?'

'Can't remember.' He thought. 'It might have been Mr Young.'

Indeed it might, I thought. Ezra Gideon had been his friend.

It might have been Filmer. Ezra Gideon had been his victim.

'Are you sure?' I asked.

He thought some more. 'Yep, Mr Young. He was sitting with that sweet wife of his, and he got up and came across the room to ask.'

I drank some wine and said conversationally, 'Did anyone else react?'

Zak's attention, never far below the surface, came to an intuitive point.

'Do I detect,' he said, 'a hint of Hamlet?'

'How do you mean?' I asked, although I knew exactly what he meant.

'The play's the thing, wherein I'll catch the conscience of the King? Right? Is that what you were up to?'

'In a mild way.'

'And tomorrow?'

'Tomorrow too,' I agreed.

He said broodingly, 'You're not going to get any of us into trouble, are you? Not sued for slander, or anything?'

'I promise not.'

'Perhaps I shouldn't let you write tomorrow's script.'

'You must do what you think best.' I picked the finished script off the table beside me and stretched forward to hand it to him. 'Read it first, then decide.'

'OK.'

He put his glass down and began reading. He read to the end and finally raised a smiling face.

'It's great,' he said. 'All my original ideas with yours on top.'

'Good.' I was much relieved that he liked it, and thought him generous.

'Where's the Hamlet bit?' he asked.

'In loving not wisely but too well.'

'That's Othello.'

'Sorry.'

He thought it over. 'It seems harmless enough to me, but . . .'

'All I want to do,' I said, 'is open a few specific eyes. Warn a couple of people about the path they're treading. I can't, you see, just walk up to them and say it, can I? They wouldn't take it from Tommy. They probably wouldn't take it from anybody. But if they see something acted . . . they can learn from it.'

'Like Hamlet's mother.'

'Yes.'

He sipped his whisky. 'Who do you want to warn about what?' he said.

'Better I don't tell you, then nothing's your fault.'

'What are you really on the train for?' he asked, frowning.

'You know what. To keep everyone happy and foil the wicked.'

'And this scene will help?'

'I hope so.'

'All right.' He made up his mind. 'I don't object to foiling the wicked. We'll give it our best shot.' He grinned suddenly. 'The others will love the Hamlet angle.'

I was alarmed. 'No . . . please don't tell them.'

'Why ever not?'

'I want the passengers to think that any similarity of the plot to their own lives is purely coincidental. I don't want the actors telling them afterwards that it was all deliberate.'

He smiled twistedly. 'Are we back to slander?'

'No. There's no risk of that. It's just . . . I don't want them identifying me as the one who knows so much about them. If anyone asks the actors where the plot came from, I'd far rather they said it was you.'

'And dump me in the shit?' He was good-humoured, however.

'No one could have suspicions about you.' I smiled faintly. 'Apart from foiling villainy, success for me means hiding behind Tommy to the end and getting off the train unexposed.'

'Are you some sort of spy?'

'A security guard, that's all.'

'Can I put you in my next plot? In my next train mystery?'

'Be my guest.'

He laughed, yawned, put down his glass and stood up.

'Well, pal, whoever you are,' he said, 'it's been an education knowing you.'

Nell telephoned to my room at seven in the morning. 'Are you awake?' she said.

'Wide.'

'It snowed again in the night. The mountains are white.'

'I can see them,' I said, 'from my bed.'

'Do you sleep with your curtains open?'

'Always. Do you?'

'Yes.'

'Are you dressed?' I asked.

'Yes, I am. What's that to do with anything?'

'With defences, even over the telephone.'

'I hate you.'

'One can't have everything.'

'Listen,' she said severely, smothering a laugh. 'Be sensible. I phoned to ask if you wanted to walk down again to the station this afternoon when we board the train, or go down on the crew bus?'

I reflected. 'On the bus, I should think.'

'OK. That bus goes from outside the staff annexe at three-thirty-five. Take your bag with you.'

'All right. Thanks.'

'The whole train, with the horses and racegoers and everything, comes up from Banff to arrive at Lake Louise station at four-fifteen. That gives the passengers plenty of time to board and go to their bedrooms again and begin to unpack comfortably before we leave Lake Louise on the dot of four-thirty-five. The regular Canadian comes along behind us as before and leaves Lake Louise at ten past five, so we have to make sure everyone is boarded early so that our train can leave right on time.'

'Understood.'

'I'm going to tell all this to the passengers at breakfast, and also that at five-thirty we're serving champagne and canapés to everyone in the dining car, and at six we'll have the solution to the mystery, and after that cocktails for those who want them, and then the gala banquet. Then the actors return for photos and post-mortems over cognac. It all sounds like hell.'

I laughed. 'It will all work beautifully.'

'I'm going into a nunnery after this.'

'There are better places.'

'Where, for instance?'

'Hawaii?'

There was a sudden silence on the line. Then she said, 'I have to be back at my desk . . .'

'We could take the desk too.'

She giggled. 'I'll find out about shipment.'

'Done, then?'

'No . . . I don't know . . . I'll let you know in Vancouver.'

'Vancouver,' I said, 'is tomorrow morning.'

'After the race, then.'

'And before the red-eye special.'

'Do you ever give up?'

'It depends,' I said, 'on the signals.'

CHAPTER SIXTEEN

Filmer clung closely to his briefcase during the transit from Chateau to train at Lake Louise, although he had allowed his larger suitcase to be brought down with everyone else's to be arranged side by side in a long line at the station, waiting to be lifted aboard by porters.

From among the bunch of crew members, Emil, Oliver, Cathy, Angus, Simone, the barman and the sleeping-car attendants, I watched Filmer and most of the passengers disembark from the bus and check that their bags were in the line-up. The Lorrimores, arriving separately with their chauffeur, brought their cases with them, the chauffeur stacking them in an aloof little group.

A freight train clanked by, seemingly endless. A hundred and two grain cars, Cathy said, counting. A whole lot of bread.

I thought about Mrs Baudelaire to whom I'd been talking just before leaving the Chateau.

'Bill said to tell you,' she said, 'that Lenny Higgs did turn to jelly and is being safely taken care of, and a new groom has been engaged for Laurentide Ice with the approval, by telephone, of his trainer. They told the trainer that Lenny Higgs had done a bunk. Bill has left Winnipeg and has come back to Toronto. He says he has been consulting with the Colonel as a matter of urgency, and they agree that Bill will see Mrs Daffodil Quentin as soon as possible. Does that all make sense?'

'Indeed it does,' I said fervently.

'Good, then.'

'Is Bill still going to Vancouver?' I asked.

'Oh, yes, I think so. Monday evening, I believe, ready for the race on Tuesday. He said he would be back here again on Wednesday. All these time changes can't be good for anybody.'

'Canada is so huge.'

'Five thousand five hundred and fourteen kilometres from side to side,' she said primly.

I laughed. 'Try me in miles.'

'You'll have to do your own sums, young man.'

I did them later, out of curiosity: three thousand four hundred and twenty-six miles, and a quarter.

She asked if I had any more questions, but I couldn't think of any, and I said I would talk to her again from Vancouver in the morning.

'Sleep well,' she said cheerfully.

'You too.'

'Yes.' There was reservation in her voice, and I realized that she probably never slept well herself.

'Sweet dreams, then,' I said.

340

'Much easier. Goodnight.'

She gave me no time, as usual, to answer.

The train hooted in the distance: one of the most haunting of seductive sounds to a wanderer. That, and the hollow breathy boom of departing ships. If I had any addiction, it was to the setting off, not the arrival.

Headlights bright in the ripening afternoon sunlight, the huge yellow-fronted engine slowed into the station with muted thunder, one of the engineers, as he passed us, looking down from his open window. The engineers were the only crew that hadn't come the whole way from Toronto, each stretch of track having its own specialists.

There being no sidings at Lake Louise, the abbreviated train that had brought us there had been returned to Banff for the two mountain days, with George Burley going with it, in charge. He returned now with the whole train, his cheerful round figure climbing down in the station and greeting the passengers like long-lost friends.

With a visible lifting of spirits and freshening enjoyment, the whole party returned upwards to their familiar quarters; the Lorrimores, a glum quartet stepping on to their private railed platform entrance at the very rear of everything, being the only sad note. Nell went along to speak to them, to try to cheer them up. Mercer stopped, answered, smiled: the others simply went on inside. Why bother with them, I thought. One would get no thanks. Yet one would always bother, somehow, for Mercer, the blind saint.

Filmer boarded through the open door at the end of his sleeping car and through his window I saw him moving about in his room. Hanging up jackets. Washing his hands. Ordinary things. What made one man good, I wondered, and another man bad: one man to seek to build, the other to frighten and destroy? The acid irony was that the bad might feel more satisfied and fulfilled than the good.

I walked along to the car where my roomette was, dumped my bag there and took off my raincoat to reveal the familiar livery beneath. Only one more night of Tommy. One dinner, one breakfast. Pity, I thought; I'd been getting quite fond of him.

George came swinging aboard as the train moved off in its quiet way, and he greeted me with a pleased chuckle.

'We're lucky to have heat on this train, eh?' he said.

'Why?' I asked. 'It's very warm.'

'They couldn't start the boiler.' He seemed to think it a great joke. 'You know why?'

I shook my head.

'No fuel.'

I looked blank. 'Well . . . they could surely fill up?'

'You bet your life,' he said. 'Only the tank had been filled two days ago, eh?, when we went down to Banff. Or was supposed to have been. So we had a look, and there were a few drips trickling from the bottom drain which is only opened for sluicing through the tank, which isn't done often, eh?' He looked at me expectantly, his eyes bright.

'Someone stole the fuel?'

He chuckled. 'Either stole it from the tank, or never loaded it in the first place, and opened the drain to be misleading.'

'Was there a lot of oil on the ground?' I asked.

'Not a bad detective, are you? Yes, there was.'

'What do you think, then?'

'I think they never loaded the right amount, probably just enough to get us a fair way out of Lake Louise, then they opened the drain a bit to persuade us the fuel had run away by accident along the track, eh? Only they got it wrong. Opened the drain too much.' The laugh vibrated in his throat. 'What a fuss, eh?, if the train went cold in the mountains! The horses would freeze. What a panic!'

'You don't seem too worried.'

'It didn't happen, did it?'

'No, I guess it didn't.'

'We would have filled the tank again at Revelstoke, anyway,' he said. 'It would have ruined this gala banquet of yours, eh? But no one would have died. Doubt if they'd even have got frostbite, not like they might in January. The air temperature up here will fall below zero after sunset, soon, but the track goes through the valleys, not up the peaks, eh? And there'd be no wind chill factor, inside the cars.'

'Very uncomfortable, though.'

'Very.' His eyes gleamed. 'I left them all buzzing around like a wasp's nest in Banff, trying to find out who did it.'

I wasn't as insouciant as he was. I said, 'Is there anything else that can go wrong with this train? Is there for instance any *water* in the boiler?'

'Never you mind,' he said comfortingly. 'We checked the water. The top tap ran. That tank's full, just as it should be. The boiler won't blow up.'

'What about the engine?'

'We checked every inch of everything, eh? But it was just some greedy ordinary crook stealing that oil.'

'Like the ordinary crook who unhitched the Lorri-mores' car?'

He thought it over sceptically. 'I'll grant you that this particular train might attract psychos, as the publicity would be that much greater, and more pleasing to them, but there is no visible connection between the two things.' He chuckled. 'People will steal anything, not just oil. Someone stole eight of those blue leather chairs in the dining car, once. Drove up to the dining car while it was standing unused in the sidings at Mimico in Toronto, drove up in a van saying "Furniture Repairs" on the side, and simply loaded up eight good chairs, eh? Last that was ever seen of them.'

He turned away towards the paperwork spread out on his table, and I left him to go along to the dining car, but I'd taken only two paces when I remembered

gaunt-face, and I fetched his photograph and went back
to George.

'Who is he?' he asked, frowning slightly. 'Yes, I'd
say he might be on the train. He was down in Banff,
in the sidings . . .' He thought, trying to remember. 'This
afternoon, eh?' he exclaimed suddenly. 'That's it. While
they were joining up the train. See, the horses had
come up from Calgary this morning as the first car of
a freight train. They dropped the horse car in the
sidings. Then our engine picked up the horse car and
then the racegoers' cars . . .' He concentrated. 'This
man, he was down on the ground, rapping on the horse-
car door with a stick, and when the dragon-lady came
to the door and asked what he wanted, he said he had
a message for the groom looking after the grey horse,
so the dragon-lady told him to wait and she came back
with a groom, only he said it wasn't the right groom,
and he, the groom, eh?, said the other groom had left
in Calgary and he had taken over, and then your man in
the photo walked off. I didn't see where he went to. I
mean, it wasn't important.'

I sighed. 'Did the man look angry, or anything?'

'I didn't notice. I was there to ask Ms Brown if
everything was in order in the horse car before we set
off, and she said it was. She said all the grooms were
in the horse car with their horses, looking after them,
as they had been all day, and they would stay there
until after we left. She looks after the horses well, eh?,
and the grooms, too. Can't fault her, eh?'

'No.'

He held out the photograph for me to take back, but I told him to keep it, and asked diffidently if he would check with the racegoers' sleeping-car attendants, if he had time, to find out for sure whether or not gaunt-face had come all the way from Toronto among the passengers.

'What's he done? Anything yet?'

'Frightened a groom into leaving.'

He stared. 'Not much of a crime, eh?' His eyes laughed. 'He won't do much jail time for that.'

I had to agree with him. I left him to his enjoyment of human failures and went towards the dining car, passing as I did so the friendly sleeping-car attendant who was again resting himself in the corridor, watching the changing perspectives of the snowy giants.

'I don't see this usually,' he said in greeting. 'I don't usually come further west than Winnipeg. Grand, isn't it?'

I agreed. Indeed it was.

'What time do you bring the beds down?' I asked.

'Any time after the passengers have all gone along to the dining car. Half of them are in their rooms here, now, changing. I've just taken extra towels to two of them.'

'I'll give you a hand with the beds later, if you like.'

'Really?' He was surprised and pleased. 'That would be great.'

'If you do your dome-car rooms first,' I said, 'then

when you come back through the dining car, I'll follow
you and we can do these.'

'You don't have to, you know.'

'Makes a nice change from waiting at table.'

'And your scene,' he said, smiling in understanding,
'what about that?'

'That comes later,' I promised him.

'All right, then. Thanks very much.'

'Pleasure,' I said, and swung along past Filmer's
closed door, through the heavy doors of the cold and
draughty join, into the heat of the corridor beside the
kitchen, and finally to the little lobby between kitchen
door and tables where Emil, Oliver and Cathy were
busy unboxing the champagne flutes.

I picked up a cloth and began polishing. The other
three smiled.

In the hissing heat of the kitchen, Angus and Simone
were arguing, Angus having asked Simone to shell a
bowlful of hard-boiled eggs which she refused to do,
saying he must do it himself.

Emil raised amused eyebrows. 'She is getting crosser
as time goes by. Angus is a genius and she doesn't
like it.'

Angus, as usual seeming to have six hands all busy
at once, proved to be making dozens of fresh canapés
on baking trays ready for ten minutes in a scorching
oven. Crab and Brie together in thin layers of pastry,
he said of one batch, and chicken and tarragon in
another, cheese and bacon in a third. Simone stood

with her hands on her hips, a hoity-toity tilt to her chin. Angus had begun ignoring her completely, which was making things worse.

The passengers as usual came to the dining car well before the appointed hour, but seemed perfectly happy just to sit and wait. The theatrical entertainment outside the windows anyway claimed all eyes and tongues until the shadows grew long in the valleys and only the peaks were lit with slowly fading intensity, until they too were extinguished into darkness. Evening came swift and early in the mountains, twilight being a matter of a lingering lightness in the sky, night growing upwards from the earth.

A real shame, most of the passengers complained to Nell, that the train went through the best scenery in Canada in the dark. Someone in a newspaper, they were saying as I distributed the champagne glasses, had said that it was as if the French kept the lights off in the Louvre, in Paris. Nell said she was really sorry, she didn't write the timetables, and she hoped everyone had been able to see a mountain or two at Lake Louise, which everyone had, of course. Most had gone up one, Sulphur Mountain, to the windy summit, in four-seater glass containers on wires. Others had said no way, and stayed at the bottom. Filmer, sitting this time with the ultra-rich owners of Redi-Hot, was saying pleasantly that no, he hadn't been on the bus tour, he'd been content to take his exercise in the gym at Lake Louise.

Filmer had come into the dining room from the

dome-car end, not from his bedroom, and he arrived wearing a private smirk which sent uncomfortable shivers along my nerves. Any time Julius Apollo looked as pleased with himself as that, it was sure to mean trouble.

The Lorrimores arrived in a group and sat together at one table, the offspring both looking mutinous and the parents glum. Xanthe, it was clear, hadn't yet made Mercer laugh. Rose and Cumber Young were with the Upper Gumtree Unwins and the Flokati people were with the owners of Wordmaster. It was interesting, I thought, that the owners of the horses tended to be attracted to each other, much as if they belonged to a brotherhood which clung naturally together.

Perhaps Filmer had understood that. Perhaps it was why he had made such efforts to go on the train as an owner: because being an owner of one of the horses gave him standing, gave him credibility, gave him a power base. If that was what he intended, he had achieved it. Everyone on the train knew Mr Julius Filmer.

Emil popped the champagne corks. Angus whizzed his succulent hot appetizers from oven to serving trays, seeming to summon from nowhere the now peeled and sliced eggs topped with caviare and lemonskin twists on Melba toast circles. We set off from the kitchen in a small procession, Emil and I pouring the bubbles, Oliver and Cathy doing the skilful stuff with silver serving tongs, giving everyone little platefuls of the hors-d'oeuvre they preferred.

Nell was laughing at me silently. Well, she would. I kept a totally straight face while filling her glass and also that of Giles who was sitting beside her in the aisle seat, ready for action.

'Thank you,' Giles said in a bored voice when his glass was full.

'My pleasure, sir,' I said.

He nodded. Nell smothered her laughing mouth against her glass and the people sitting opposite her noticed nothing at all.

When I reached the Lorrimores, Xanthe was perceptibly anxious. I poured into Bambi's glass and said to Xanthe, 'For you, miss?'

She gave me a flicker of a glance. 'Can I have Coke?'

'Certainly, miss.'

I poured champagne for Mercer and for Sheridan, and went back to the kitchen for the Coke.

'You have to pay for it,' Xanthe said jerkily to her father when I returned.

'How much?' Mercer asked. I told him, and he paid. 'Thank you,' he said.

'A pleasure, sir.'

He looked abstracted, not his usual placatory self. Xanthe risked another semi-frightened glance at me and seemed to be greatly reassured when I didn't refer in any way to our encounter above the lake. The most I gave her was the faintest of deferential smiles, which even her mother couldn't have disapproved of, if she had seen it: but she, like Mercer, seemed more than usually preoccupied.

I went on to the next table and hoped that Filmer's smirk and Mercer's gloom were not connected, although I was afraid that they might be. The smirk had been followed into the dining room by the gloom.

When Angus's canapés had been devoured to the last melting morsel and the champagne glasses refilled, Zak arrived with a flourish for the long wrap-up scene. First of all, he said, he had to announce that a thorough search of the rooms in the Chateau had produced no sign of Mavis Bricknell's jewels.

Commiserations were expressed for Mavis, the passengers entering into the fantasy with zest. Mavis accepted them gratefully.

Raoul came bursting into the dining car, furious with Walter Bricknell who was looking upset enough already.

It was too much, Raoul loudly said. It was bad enough Walter firing him as his trainer when he had done nothing to deserve it, but now he had found out that Walter had sent a letter from the Chateau to the racing authorities saying his horse, Calculator, wouldn't be running in his, Walter's, name at Vancouver, and that Raoul wouldn't be credited as trainer.

'It's unfair,' he shouted. 'I've trained the horse to the minute for that race. I've won five races with him for you. You're cheating me. You're damned ungrateful. I'm going to complain to the Jockey Club.'

Walter looked stony. Raoul had another go. Walter said he would do what he liked, Calculator was his. If he wanted to sell it ... or give it away ... that was entirely his own business and nobody else's.

'You said yesterday,' Raoul yelled, 'that if you didn't have horses, if you couldn't go racing, you'd kill yourself. So kill yourself. Is that what you're going to do?'

Everyone looked at Walter in shocked disbelief.

Zak invited Walter to explain. Walter said it was none of Zak's business. Everything on the train was his business, Zak said. 'Could we all please know,' he asked Walter, 'who the new owner of Calculator is going to be?'

No, no one could ask. Mavis, bewildered, did ask. Walter was rude to her, which no one liked. Walter realized that no one liked it, but said he couldn't help it, he was getting rid of Calculator, and since the horse was in his name only, not Mavis's, she couldn't do anything about it. Mavis began to cry.

Donna went to her mother's defence and verbally attacked her father.

'You be quiet,' he said angrily. 'You've done enough harm.'

Pierre put his arm round Donna's shoulders and told Walter not to talk to his daughter that way. He, Pierre, would borrow some money to pay his gambling debts, he said, and really work this time and save until it was paid off, and he would never let Donna take a penny from her father, and when he was out of debt he and Donna would get married and there was nothing Walter could do to stop them.

'Oh, Pierre,' Donna wailed, and hid her face against his chest. Pierre, in snow-white shirtsleeves, put both arms round her, stroked her hair and looked very manly, handsome and protective. The audience approved of him with applause.

'Oh, goody,' Cathy said from beside me. 'Isn't he cute?'

'He sure is.'

We were standing in the little lobby, watching from the shadows and, by a malign quirk of fate, all the faces I was most interested in were sitting with their backs to me. Filmer's neck, not far off, was rigid with tension, and Cumber Young, one table further along, had got compulsively to his feet when Raoul had told Walter to kill himself, and only slowly subsided, with Rose talking to him urgently. Mercer, just over midway along, sitting against the far right-hand side wall, had his head bowed, not watching the action. He couldn't help but hear, however. The actors were all courting laryngitis, making sure that those in the furthest corners weren't left out.

Mavis had a go at Walter, first angry, then pleading, then saying she might as well leave him, she obviously didn't count with him any more. She prepared to go.

Walter, stung beyond bearing, muttered something to her that stopped her dead.

'*What?*' she said.

Walter muttered again.

'He says he's being *blackmailed*,' Mavis said in a high voice. 'How can anyone blackmail someone into getting rid of a horse?'

Filmer, pinned against the left-hand wall by the Unwins in the aisle seats, sat as if with a rod up his backbone. Mercer turned his head to stare at Walter. Mercer had his back towards Filmer, and I wondered whether he'd sat that way round on purpose so as not to see his recent friend. He was sitting beside Sheridan and opposite Bambi. Xanthe sat opposite her brother, both in aisle seats. I could see both of the female faces, where I wanted to see the male. I would have done better, I supposed, to have watched from the far end, but on the other hand they might have seen me watching: watching them instead of the action.

Walter, under pressure, said loudly that yes, he was being blackmailed, and by the very nature of blackmail he couldn't say what about . . . he categorically refused to discuss it further. He had good and sufficient reasons and he was angry and upset enough about losing his horse without everyone attacking him.

And who was he losing it to? Zak asked. Because whoever's name turned up on the race card at Vancouver as the owner, he or she would be the blackmailer.

Heads nodded. Walter said it wasn't so. The black-mailer had just said he must give the horse away.

'Who to?' Zak asked insistently. 'Tell us. We'll soon know. We'll know at the races on Tuesday.'

Walter, defeated, said, 'I'm giving the horse to Giles.'

General consternation followed. Mavis objected. Giles was a very nice, comforting fellow, but they hardly knew him, she said.

Raoul said bitterly that Walter should have given *him* the horse. He'd worked so hard . . .

Giles said that Walter had asked him, Giles, to have the horse, and of course he'd said yes. After the race on Tuesday, he would decide Calculator's future.

Walter looked stony. Giles was being frightfully nice.

Donna suddenly detached herself from Pierre and said rather wildly, 'No, Daddy, I won't let you do it. I understand what's happening . . . I won't let it happen.'

Walter told her thunderously to shut up. Donna wouldn't be stopped. It was her fault that her father was being blackmailed and she wouldn't let him give his horse away.

'Be quiet,' Walter ordered.

'I stole Mother's jewels,' she said miserably to everyone. 'I stole them to pay Pierre's debts. They said he would be beaten up if he didn't pay. Those jewels were going to be mine anyway, one day, they're in Mother's will . . . so I was only stealing from myself really . . . but then, he guessed . . .'

'Who guessed?' Zak demanded.

'Giles,' she said. 'He saw me coming out of Mother's room. I suppose I looked scared . . . maybe guilty. I had her jewels in a tote bag. I suppose it was afterwards, when Mother came to say someone had stolen them, that he guessed. . . . He made me give them to him . . . he said he'd have me arrested otherwise, and my parents wouldn't like that . . .'

'Stop him!' Zak yelled peremptorily as Giles made a dash for the lobby, and Raoul, a big fellow, intercepted him and twisted his arm up behind his back. Giles displayed pain.

Zak invited Walter to talk.

Walter, distressed, said that Giles had threatened to prove publicly that Donna had stolen the jewels if Walter wouldn't give him the horse. Even if Walter refused to press charges against his daughter, Giles had said, everyone would know she was a thief. Walter confessed that Giles had said, 'What is one horse against your daughter's reputation?' Walter thought he'd had no choice.

Donna wept. Mavis wept. Half the audience wept.

Filmer was rigid. Also Mercer, Bambi and Sheridan; all unmoving in their seats.

'It wasn't sensible to love your daughter so much,' Raoul said. 'She stole the jewels. You shouldn't cover up for her. Look where it got you. Into the hands of a blackmailer, and losing the horse you love. And did you think it would stop there, with just one horse? You've got two more in my care, don't forget.'

'Stop it,' Mavis said, defending Walter now. 'He's a wonderful man to give up his dearest possession to save his daughter.'

'He's a fool,' Raoul said.

During this bit, Zak came to the lobby as if to receive a message and went back into the centre of the dining car opening an envelope and reading the contents.

He said the letter was from Ben, who had begged for money, did they remember? They remembered.

Ben, Zak said, had run away off the train because he was frightened, but he had left this letter to be opened after he'd gone. Zak read the letter portentously aloud.

'I know who killed Ricky. I know who threw him off the train. Ricky told me he knew who killed that lady, Angelica someone. Ricky saw the murderer with a lot of plastic rolled into a ball. He didn't know he was a murderer then, like. This man came up the train into the part where the grooms are and he was in the join part between two sleeping cars and he pushed the plastic out through one of the gaps, until it fell from the train, and then he saw Ricky looking at him. Ricky didn't think much of it until we were told about Angelica someone, and the plastic with her blood on, and then he was afraid, and told me. And then he was thrown off the train. I know who it was, I knew who must have did it, but I wasn't saying. I didn't want to end up dead beside the railway tracks. But now I'm safe out of here I'll tell you, and it's that good-looking one they was calling Giles on Toronto station. I saw him there too, same as Ricky. It was him.'

Zak stopped reading and Giles, struggling in Raoul's grip, shouted that it was rubbish. Lies. All made up.

Raoul showed signs of breaking Giles's arm on account of him having killed Angelica, who was his wife, even if they had separated.

How could a groom like Ben make up anything like this? Zak said, waving the note. He said it was time someone searched Giles's room on the train for the jewels, and for anything else incriminating.

'You've no right. You've no search warrant. And this man is breaking my arm.'

'You murdered his wife, what do you expect?' Zak said, 'and I don't need a search warrant. I'm chief of the railway detectives, don't forget. On trains, I investigate and search where I like.' He marched off past me and went swaying down the corridor, pausing down at the end of the kitchen wall where he'd left a sports bag full of props, and soon came marching back. The other actors, meanwhile, had been emoting in character over the disclosure of Giles as murderer as well as blackmailer. Zak took the sports bag, it seemed to me by accident, to the table across from the Lorrimores. The people sitting at the table cleared the glasses and empty plates into a stack and Zak, dumping the bag on the pink cloth, unfastened a few zips.

To no one's surprise, he produced the jewels. Mavis was reunited with them, with joy slightly dampened by knowing who had stolen them. Reproachful looks, and so on.

Zak then discovered a folder of papers.

'*A-HAH!*' he said.

Giles struggled, to no avail.

Zak said, 'Here we have the motive for Angelica's murder. Here's a letter to Giles from Steve, Angelica's lover and business partner, complaining accusingly that he has been checking up, and Giles, in his capacity of bloodstock agent, has not bought the horses that he says he has, that Angelica and Steve have given him the money for. Steve is saying that unless Giles comes up with a very good explanation he is going to the police.'

'Lies,' Giles shouted.

'It's all here.' Zak waved the letter, which everyone later inspected, along with Ben's note. They were accurately written: Zak's props were thorough. 'Giles embezzled Angelica and Steve's money,' he said, 'and when they threatened him with disgrace, he killed them. Then he killed the groom, who knew too much. Then he blackmailed Walter Bricknell, who was too fond of his daughter. This man Giles is beneath contempt. I will get the conductor of the train to arrange for him to be arrested and taken away in Revelstoke, where we stop in two hours.'

He walked towards the lobby again.

Giles, finally breaking free of Raoul, snatched a gun

that Zak was wearing in a holster on his hip and waved it about. Zak warned, 'Put it down. This gun is loaded.'

Giles shouted at Donna, 'It's all your fault, you shouldn't have confessed. You spoiled it all. And I'll spoil you.'

He pointed the gun at Donna. Pierre leapt in front of her to save her. Giles shot Pierre, who had, it transpired, chosen a romantic shoulder for the affected part. He clapped a hand to his snow-white shirt which suddenly blossomed bright red. He fell artistically.

The audience truly gasped. Donna knelt frantically beside Pierre, having a grand dramatic time. Giles tried to escape and was subdued, none too gently, by Zak and Raoul. George Burley appeared on the scene, chuckling non-stop, waving a pair of stage handcuffs. As Zak later said, it was a riot.

CHAPTER SEVENTEEN

Emil said there was enough champagne for everyone to have half a glass more, so he and I went around pouring while Oliver and Cathy cleared the hors d'oeuvre plates, straightened the cloths and began setting the places for the banquet.

I glanced very briefly at Filmer. He looked exceedingly pale, with sweat on his forehead. One hand, lying on the tablecloth, was tightly clenched. Beside him, the Redi-Hots were enthusing over Zak who was standing beside their table agreeing that Pierre was a redeemable character who would make good. Zak gave me a smile and stepped to one side to let me fill the Redi-Hots' glasses.

Filmer said, in a harsh croaking voice, 'Where did you get that story?'

As if accepting a compliment, Zak answered, 'Made it up.'

'You must have got it from somewhere.' He was positive and angry. The Redi-Hots looked at him in surprise.

'I always make them up,' Zak said lightly. 'Why . . . didn't you enjoy it?'

'Champagne, sir?' I said to Filmer. I'd grown very bold, I thought.

Filmer didn't hear. Mrs Redi-Hot passed me his glass which I replenished. She passed it back. He didn't notice.

'I thought it a great story,' she said. 'What a wicked revolting murderer. And he was so nice all along . . .'

I stepped around Zak with a glimmer of eye contact in which I gave him my devout thanks for his discretion, and he accepted them with amusement.

At the next table Rose Young was protesting to Cumber that it had to have been a coincidence about committing suicide after getting rid of your best horse . . . and Ezra had sold his horse, she said, not given it away because he was being blackmailed.

'How do we know he wasn't?' Cumber demanded.

The Unwins were listening open-mouthed. I filled all their glasses quietly, unnoticed in their general pre-occupation.

'Who now has Ezra's horses, that's what I want to know,' Cumber said truculently. 'And it'll be easy enough to find out.' He spoke loudly: loudly enough, I thought, for Filmer to hear him, if he were listening.

Emil had beaten me to it with the Lorrimores, but they made a remarkable picture. Mercer's forearms rested on the table as he sat with his head bowed. Bambi, a glitter of tears in the frosty eyes, stretched out a hand, closed it over one of Mercer's fists, and stroked his knuckles with comforting affection. Xanthe was saying anxiously, 'What's the matter with every-body?' and Sheridan looked blank. Not supercilious, not arrogant, not even alarmed: a wiped blank slate.

There were a good many people in the aisle, not only the service crew but also the actors who, still in character, were finishing off the drama in the ways they felt happy with: Walter and Mavis, for instance, agreeing that Pierre had saved Donna's life and couldn't be all bad, and maybe he would marry Donna . . . if he stopped gambling.

Threading his way through all this came the sleeping-car attendant on his way to do the bunks in the dome car. He nodded to me with a smile as he passed, and I nodded back: and I thought that my main problem would probably be that the play had been all too suc-cessful, and that the people most upset by it wouldn't stay sitting down for dinner.

I wandered back to the kitchen where Angus's octopus act was reaching new heights and hoped especially that Filmer's physical reactions wouldn't get him restlessly to his feet and force him to leave.

He didn't move. The rigidity in his body very slowly relaxed. The impact of the play seemed to be lessening, and perhaps he really believed that Zak had made it all up.

I set the two tables nearest to the kitchen: automatic-ally folded the napkins and arranged knives and forks.

The sleeping-car attendant came back eventually from the dome car, and I left my place settings unfinished and followed him.

'Are you sure?' he asked over his shoulder. 'They seem pretty busy in the dining car.'

'It's a good time,' I assured him. 'Fifteen minutes to dinner. How about if I start from this end, then I'll just stop and go back if I feel guilty.'

'Right,' he said. 'Do you remember how to fold the chairs?'

He knocked on Filmer's door.

'The people are all along in the dining car, but knock first just in case,' he said.

'OK.'

We went into Filmer's room.

'Fold the chair while I'm here, so I can help if you need it.'

'OK.'

I folded, a shade slowly, Julius Apollo's armchair. The sleeping-car attendant gave me a pat on the shoulder and left, saying he would start from the far end, as he usually did, and we might meet in the middle.

'And thanks a lot,' he said.

I waved a hand. The thanks, did he but know it, were all mine. I left the door open and pulled Filmer's bed down into the night position, smoothing the bottom sheet, folding down a corner of the top sheet, as I'd been shown.

I groped into Filmer's wardrobe space, gripped the black crocodile briefcase and rested it on the bed.

Zero-four-nine. One-five-one.

My fingers trembled with the compulsion for speed.

I aligned the little wheels, fumbling where I needed precision. Zero-four-nine . . . press the catch.

Click!

One-five-one. Press the catch. Click! The latches were open.

I laid the case flat on the bottom sheet, pushing the upper sheet back a little to accommodate it, and I lifted the lid. Heart thumping, breathing stopped.

The first thing inside was Filmer's passport. I looked at it briefly and then more closely, getting my suspended breath back in a jerky sort of silent laugh. The number of Filmer's passport was H049151. Hooray for the Brigadier.

I laid the passport on the bed, and looked through the other papers without removing them or changing their order. They were mainly a boring lot: all the bumf about the train trip, a few newspaper pages about the races, then a newspaper cutting from a Cambridge local paper about the building of a new library in one of the colleges, thanks to the generosity of Canadian philanthropist Mercer P. Lorrimore.

My God, I thought.

Beneath the clipping was a letter – a photocopy of a letter. I read it at breakneck speed, feeling danger creep up my spine, feeling my skin flood with heat.

It was short. Typewritten. There was no address at the top, no date, no salutation and no signature. It said:

> As requested I examined the cadavers of the seven cats found pegged out, eviscerated and beheaded in the College gardens. I can find nothing except for wilful wickedness. These were not cult killings, in my opinion. The cats were killed over a period of perhaps three weeks, the last one yesterday. Each one, except the last, had been hidden under leaves, and had been attacked after death by insects and scavengers. They were all alive when they were pegged out, and during evisceration. Most, if not all, were alive at decapitation. I have disposed of the remains, as you asked.

I could see my hand trembling. I tipped up the next few sheets of paper which were reports from stock-brokers, and then, at the very bottom, I came across a small yellow memo sticking to a foolscap-size paper headed CONVEYANCE.

The memo said, 'You will have to sign this, not Ivor Horfitz, but I think we can keep it quiet.'

I looked a shade blankly at the legal words on the deed: ' . . . all that parcel of land known as SF 90155 on the west side of . . .' and heard the sleeping-car attendant's voice coming nearer along the corridor.

'Tommy . . . where are you?'

I flicked the case shut and pushed it under the bed's

top sheet. The passport was still in view. I shoved it under the pillow, walked out of the door hastily and closed it behind me.

'You've been ages in there,' he said, but tolerantly. 'Couldn't you undo the bed?'

'Managed it finally,' I said, dry-mouthed.

'Right. Well, I didn't give you any chocolates.' He handed me a box of big silver-wrapped bonbons. 'Put one on each pillow.'

'Yes,' I said.

'Are you all right?' he asked curiously.

'Oh, yes. It was hot in the dining car.'

'True.' He went back towards his end of the car, unsuspicious. Heart still thumping I returned to Filmer's room, retrieved his passport from under the pillow, replaced it in the briefcase, shut the locks, twirled the combination wheels, realized I hadn't noticed where they'd been set when I came in, hoped to hell that Filmer didn't set them deliberately, put the case back as I'd found it, straightened the bed and put the chocolate tidily where it belonged.

I went out of the room, closed the door and walked two paces towards the next door along.

'Hey, you,' Filmer's voice said angrily from close behind me. 'What were you doing in there?'

I turned. Looked innocent . . . felt stunned.

'Making your bed ready for the night, sir.'

'Oh.' He shrugged, accepting it.

I held the box of sweets towards him. 'Would you like an extra chocolate, sir?'

'No, I wouldn't,' he said, and went abruptly into his bedroom.

I felt weak. I waited for him to come out exploding that I'd meddled with his belongings.

Nothing . . . nothing . . . happened.

I went into the room next door, folded the armchairs, lowered both beds, turned back the sheets, delivered the sweets. All automatic, with a feeling of total unreality. I'd twice come too close to discovery. I had no great taste, I found, for the risks of a spy.

I was disturbed, in a way, by my pusillanimity. I supposed I'd never thought much about courage: had taken it for granted . . . physical courage, or physical endurance, anyway. I'd been in hard places in the past, but these risks were different and more difficult, at least for me.

I did the third bedroom, by which time the sleeping-car attendant, much faster, had almost finished the rest.

'Thanks a lot,' he said cheerfully. 'Appreciate it.'

'Any time.'

'Did you do your scene?' he asked.

I nodded. 'It went fine.'

Filmer came out of his room and called, 'Hey, you.'

The sleeping-car attendant went towards him. 'Yes, sir?'

Filmer spoke to him, his voice obliterated, as far as

I was concerned, by rail noise, and went back into his room.

'He's not feeling well,' the sleeping-car attendant reported, going back towards his own roomette. 'He asked for something to settle his stomach.'

'Do you have things like that?'

'Antacids, sure. A few simple things.'

I left him to his mission and went back to the dining car, where Emil greeted me with raised eyebrows and thrust into my hands a trayful of small plates, each bearing a square of pâté de foie gras with a thin slice of black truffle on top.

'We missed you. You're needed,' Emil said. 'The crackers for the pâté are on the tables.'

'Right.'

I went ahead with the delivery, going to the Redi-Hots' table first. I asked Mrs Redi-Hot if Mr Filmer would be coming back: should I put his pâté in his place?

She looked a little bewildered. 'He didn't say if he was coming back. He went out in a hurry... he trampled on my feet.'

'Leave the pâté,' Mr Redi-Hot said. 'If he doesn't come back, I'll eat it.'

With a smile I put some pâté in Filmer's place and went on to the Youngs' table, where Cumber had stopped talking about Ezra Gideon but looked dour and preoccupied. Rose received her pâté with a smile and made attempts not to let Cumber's moroseness spoil the occasion for the Unwins.

Cathy had taken pâté to the Lorrimores who sat in glum silence except for Xanthe who could be heard saying exasperatedly, 'This is supposed to be a *party*, for God's sakes.'

For the rest of the passengers, that was true. The faces were bright, the smiles came easily, the euphoria of the whole journey bonded them in pleasure. It was the last night on the train and they were determined to make it a good one.

Nell was moving down the aisle handing out mementos: silver bracelets made of tiny gleaming railway carriages for the women, onyx paperweights set with miniature engines for the men. Charming gifts, received with delight. Xanthe clipped on her bracelet immediately and forgot to look sullen.

Emil and I collected the wrapping-paper debris. 'Miss Richmond might have waited until after dinner,' Emil said.

We served and cleared the rest of the banquet: a salad of sliced yellow tomatoes and fresh basil, a scoop of champagne sorbet, rare roast rib of beef with julienned vegetables and finally apple snowballs appearing to float on raspberry purée. About six people, including Rose Young, asked how to make the apple snowballs, so I enquired of Angus.

He was looking languid and exhausted, but obliging. 'Tell them it's sieved apple purée, sugar, whipped cream, whipped white of egg. Combine at the last minute. Very simple.'

'Delicious,' Rose said, when I relayed the information. 'Do bring out the chef for us to congratulate him.'

Emil brought out and introduced Angus to prolonged applause. Simone sulked determinedly in the kitchen. Rose Young said they should all thank the rest of the dining-car crew who had worked so hard throughout. Everyone clapped: all most affecting.

Xanthe clapped, I noticed. I had great hopes for Xanthe.

I managed to stop beside Nell's ear.

'Xanthe's longing to have a good time,' I said. 'Couldn't you rescue her?'

'What's the matter with the others?' she asked, frowning.

'Xanthe might tell you, if she knows.'

Nell flashed me an acutely perceptive glance. 'And you want me to tell you?'

'Yes, please, since you ask.'

'One day you'll explain all this.'

'One day soon.'

I went back to the kitchen with the others to tackle the mountainous dishwashing and to eat anything left over, which wasn't much. Angus produced a bottle of Scotch from a cupboard and drank from it deeply without troubling a glass. Apart from Simone, who had disappeared altogether, there was very good feeling in the kitchen. I wouldn't have missed it, I thought, for a fieldful of mushrooms.

When everything was scoured, polished and put away, we left Angus unbelievably beginning to make breads for breakfast. I stood in the lobby for a while, watching the dining-car slowly clear as everyone drifted off to the dome-car lounge for laughter and music. The Lorrimores had all gone, and so had Nell and the Unwins and the Youngs. Out of habit I began to collect, with Oliver, the used napkins and tablecloths, ready to put out clean ones for breakfast, and presently Nell came back and sat down wearily where I was working.

'For what it's worth,' she said, 'Xanthe doesn't know what has thrown her parents into such a tizzy. She says it can't have been something Mr Filmer said in the lounge before cocktails because it sounded so silly.'

'Did she tell you what he said?'

Nell nodded. 'Xanthe said Mr Filmer asked her father if he would let him have Voting Right, and her father said he wouldn't part with the horse for anything, and they were both smiling, Xanthe said. Then Mr Filmer, still smiling, said, "We'll have to have a little talk about cats." And that was all. Mr Filmer went into the dining car. Xanthe said she asked her father what Mr Filmer meant, and he said, "Don't bother me, darling." ' Nell shook her head in puzzlement. 'So anyway, Xanthe is now having a good time in the dome-car lounge and the rest of the family have gone off into their own car, and I'm deadly tired, if you want to know.'

'Go to bed, then.'

'The actors are all along in the lounge having their photos taken,' she said, dismissing my suggestion as frivolous. 'They came up trumps tonight, didn't they?'

'Brilliant,' I said.

'Someone was asking Zak who had tried to kidnap which horse at Toronto station.'

'What did he say?' I asked, amused. It was the loosest of the loose ends.

'He said it had seemed a good idea at the time.' She laughed. 'He said they'd had to change the script because the actor who was supposed to play the part of the kidnapper had broken his arm and couldn't appear. Everyone seemed to be satisfied. They're all very happy with the way it ended. People are kissing Donna and Mavis. Mavis is wearing the jewels.' She yawned and reflected. 'Mr Filmer didn't have any dinner, did he? Perhaps I'd better go and see if he's all right.'

I dissuaded her. Antacids were taking care of it, I said. What one could give a man for a sick soul was another matter.

From his point of view, he had made his move a fraction too early, I thought. If he hadn't already made the threat, the play wouldn't have had such a cataclysmic effect either on him or on Mercer. Mercer might have been warned, as I'd intended, might have been made to think: but I couldn't have foreseen that it would happen the way it had, even though Filmer's smirk and Mercer's gloom had made me wonder. Just as well, perhaps, that I hadn't known about the cats when I invented the theft of the jewels. I might have been terribly tempted to hit even closer to home. Tortured horses, perhaps?

'What are you hatching now?' Nell demanded. 'You've got that distant look.'

'I haven't done a thing,' I said.

'I'm not so sure.' She stood up. She was wearing, in honour of the banquet, a boat-necked black blouse above the full black skirt, a pearl choker round her neck. Her fair hair was held back high in a comb, but not plaited, falling instead in informal curls. I thought with unnerving intensity that I didn't want to lose her, that for me it was no longer a game. I had known her for a week and a day. Reason said it wasn't long enough. Instinct said it was.

'Where are you staying in Vancouver?' I asked.

'At the Four Seasons Hotel, with all the passengers.'

She gave me a small smile and went off towards the action. Oliver had finished clearing the cloths and was laying clean ones, to leave the place looking tidy, he said. I left him to finish and made my way up the train to talk to George Burley, passing Filmer's closed door on the way.

The sleeping-car attendant was sitting in his roomette with the door open. I poked my head in and asked how the passenger was, who'd asked for the antacid.

'He went up the train a while ago, and came back. He didn't say anything, just walked past. He must be all right, I guess.'

I nodded and went on, and came to George sitting at his table with his endless forms.

'Come in,' he invited, and I took my accustomed seat. 'I showed that photo,' he said. 'Is that what you want to know about?'

'Yes.'

'He's definitely on the train. Name of Johnson, according to the passenger list. He has a roomette right forward, and he stays in it most of the time. He eats in the forward dome-car dining room, but only dinner, eh? He was in there just now when I went up to the engine, but he'd gone when I came back. A fast eater, they say. Never goes for breakfast or lunch. Never talks to anyone, eh?'

'I don't like it,' I said.

George chuckled. 'Wait till you hear the worst.'

'What's the worst?'

'My assistant conductor – he's one of the sleeping-car attendants up front – he says he's seen him before, eh?'

'Seen him where?'

George watched me for effect. 'On the railways.'

'On the – do you mean he's a *railwayman*?'

'He can't be sure. He says he looks like a baggage

handler he once worked with on the Toronto to Montreal sector, long time ago. Fifteen years ago. Twenty. Says if it's him, he had a chip on his shoulder all the time, no one liked him. He could be violent. You didn't cross him. Might not be him, though. He's older. And he doesn't remember the name Johnson, though I suppose it's forgettable, it's common enough.'

'Would a baggage handler,' I said slowly, 'know how to drain a fuel tank . . . and uncouple the Lorrimores' car?'

George's eyes gleamed with pleasure. 'The baggage handlers travel on the trains, eh? They're not fools. They take on small bits of freight at the stops and see the right stuff gets off. If you live around trains, you get to know how they work.'

'Is there a baggage handler on this train?'

'You bet your life. He's not always in the baggage car, not when we're going along. He eats, eh? He's always there in the stations, unlocking the doors. This one's not the best we've got, mind. A bit old, a bit fat.' He chuckled. 'He said he'd never seen this man Johnson, but then he's always worked Vancouver to Banff, never Toronto to Montreal.'

'Has the baggage handler or your assistant talked to Johnson?'

'My assistant conductor says the only person Johnson talks to is one of the owners who raps on Johnson's door when he goes along to see his horse. He went up there this evening not long ago, and they had some sort of row in the corridor outside my assistant's roomette.'

'George! Did your assistant hear what it was about?'

'Important, is it?' George said, beaming.

'Could be, very.'

'Well, he didn't.' He shook his head regretfully. 'He said he thought the owner told Johnson not to do something Johnson wanted to. They were shouting, he said, but he didn't really listen, eh? He wasn't interested. Anyway, the owner came back down here, he said, and he heard Johnson say, "I'll do what I frigging like," very loudly, but he doesn't think the owner heard, as he'd gone by then.'

'That's not much help,' I said.

'It's easier to start a train going downhill than to stop it, eh?'

'Mm.'

'It's the best I can do for you.'

'Well,' I said. 'We do know he's on the train, and we know his name may or may not be Johnson, and we know he may or may not be a railwayman, and I know for certain he has a violent personality. It sounds as if he's still planning something and we don't know what. I suppose you are certain he can't get past the dragon-lady?'

'Nothing is certain.'

'How about if you asked the baggage handler to sit in with her, with the horses?'

He put his head on one side. 'If you think she'd stand for it?'

'Tell her it's to keep the horses safe, which it is.'

He chuckled. 'Don't see why not.' He looked at his watch. 'Sicamous is coming up. I'll go up there outside, when we stop. Three or five minutes there. Then it'll be time to put the clocks back an hour. Did your Miss Richmond remember to tell everyone?'

'Yes. They're all on Pacific time already, I think. Getting on for midnight.'

We had stopped towards the end of dinner in a small place called Revelstoke for half an hour for all the cars to be refilled with water. At Kamloops, a far larger town, we would stop at two in the morning very briefly. Then it was North Bend at five-forty, then the last stretch to Vancouver, arriving at five past ten on Sunday morning, a week from the day we set off.

We slowed towards Sicamous while I was still with George.

'After here, though you won't see it,' he said, 'we follow the shoreline of Shuswap Lake. The train goes slowly.'

'It hasn't exactly been whizzing along through the Rockies.'

He nodded benignly. 'We go at thirty, thirty-five miles an hour. Fast enough, eh? Uphill, downhill, round hairpin bends. There are more mountains ahead.'

He swung down on to the ground when the train

stopped and crunched off forward to arrange things with the baggage handler.

It was snowing outside: big dry flakes settling on others that had already fallen, harbingers of deep winter. The trains almost always went through, George had said.

I thought I might as well see how the revelries were going but it seemed that, unlike after the Winnipeg race, most people were feeling the long evening was dying. The lounge in the dome car was only half full. The observation deck was scarcely populated. The poker school, in shirtsleeves, were counting their money. The actors had vanished. Nell was walking towards me with Xanthe whom she was seeing safely to bed in the upper bunk behind the felt curtains.

'Goodnight,' Nell said softly.

'Sleep well,' I replied.

'Goodnight,' Xanthe said.

I smiled. 'Goodnight.'

I watched them go along the corridor beside the bar. Nell turned round, hesitated, and waved. Xanthe turned also, and waved. I waved back.

Gentle was the word, I thought. Go gentle into this good night . . . No, no! It should be, 'Do not go gentle into that good night.' Odd how poets' words stuck in one's head. Dylan Thomas, wasn't it it? *Do not go gentle into that good night* . . . because that good night was death.

*

The train was slowly going to sleep.

There would be precious little peace, I thought, in the minds of the Lorrimores, father, mother and son. Little peace also in Filmer who would know now from Johnson that the departure of Lenny Higgs had robbed him of the lever to be used against Daffodil; who could have doubts at the very least about Mercer's future reactions; who would know that Cumber Young would find out soon who had taken Ezra Gideon's horses; who would realize he was riding a flood tide of contempt. I wished him more than an upset stomach. I wished him remorse, which was the last thing he would feel.

I wandered back through the train past George's office, which was empty, and stretched out in my own room on the bed, still dressed, with the door open and the light on, meaning just to rest but stay awake: and not surprisingly I went straight to sleep.

I awoke to the sound of someone calling 'George . . . George . . .' Woke with a start and looked at my watch. I hadn't slept long, not more than ten minutes, but in that time the train had stopped.

That message got me off the bed in a hurry. The train should have been moving; there was no stop scheduled for almost an hour. I went out into the passage and found an elderly man in a VIA grey suit like George's peering into the office. The elderly man looked at my uniform and said urgently, 'Where's George?'

'I don't know,' I said. 'What's the matter?'

'We've got a hot box.' He was deeply worried. 'George must radio to the despatcher to stop the Canadian.'

Not again, I thought wildly. I went into George's office, following the VIA Rail man who said he was the assistant conductor, George's deputy.

'Can't you use the radio?' I said.

'The Conductor does it.'

The assistant conductor was foremost a sleeping-car attendant, I supposed. I thought I might see if I could raise someone myself, as George would have already tuned in the frequency, but when I pressed the transmit switch, nothing happened at all, not even a click, and then I could see why it wouldn't work . . . the radio was soaking wet.

There was an empty coffee cup beside it.

With immense alarm, I said to George's assistant, 'What's a hot box?'

'A hot axle, of course,' he said. 'A journal-box that holds the axle. It's under the horse car, and it's glowing dark red. We can't go on until it cools down and we put more oil in.'

'How long does that take?'

'Too long. They're putting snow on it.' He began to understand about the radio. 'It's wet . . .'

'It won't work,' I said. Nor would the cellular telephone, not out in the mountains. 'How do we stop the Canadian? There must be ways, from before radio.'

'Yes, but . . .' He looked strained, the full enormity

of the situation sinking in. 'You'll have to go back along the track and plant fusees.'

'Fusees?'

'Flares, of course. You're younger than me . . . you'll have to go . . . you'll be faster.'

He opened a cupboard in George's office and pulled out three objects, each about a foot in length, with a sharp metal spike at one end, the rest being tubular with granulations on the tip. They looked like oversized matches, which was roughly what they were.

'You strike them on any rough or hard surface,' he said. 'Like a rock, or the rails. They burn bright red . . . they burn for twenty minutes. You stick the spike . . . throw it . . . into the wooden ties, in the middle of the track. The driver of the Canadian will stop at once when he sees it.' His mind was going faster almost than his tongue. 'You'll have to go half a mile, it'll take the Canadian that much time to stop . . . Hurry, now . . . half a mile at least. And if the engineers are not in the cab . . .'

'What do you mean,' I asked aghast, 'if they're not in the cab?'

'They aren't always there. One of them regularly flushes out the boiler . . . the other could be in the bathroom . . . If they aren't there, if they haven't seen the fusees and the train isn't stopping, you must light another flare and throw it through the window into the cab. Then when they come back, they'll stop.'

I stared at him. 'That's impossible.'

'They'll be there, they'll see the flares. Go now. Hurry. But that's what you do if you have to. Throw one through the window.' He suddenly grabbed a fourth flare from the cupboard. 'You'd better take another one, just in case.'

'In case of what?' What else could there be?

'In case of bears,' he said.

CHAPTER EIGHTEEN

With a feeling of complete unreality I set off past the
end of the train and along the single railway track in
the direction of Toronto.

With one arm I clasped the four flares to my chest,
in the other hand I carried George's bright-beamed
torch, to show me the way.

Half a mile. How long was half a mile?

Hurry, George's assistant had said. Of all unnecessary instructions . . .

I half walked, half ran along the centre of the track,
trying to step on the flat wood of the ties, the sleepers,
because the stones in between were rough and speed-
inhibiting.

Bears . . . my God.

It was cold. It had stopped snowing, but some snow
was lying . . . not enough to give me problems. I hadn't
thought to put on a coat. It didn't matter, movement
would keep me warm. Urgency and fierce anxiety
would keep me warm.

I began to feel it wasn't totally impossible. After all,

it must have been done often in the old days. Standard procedure still, one might say. The flares had been there, ready. All the same, it was fairly eerie running through the night with snow-dusted rocky tree-dotted hillsides climbing away on each side and the two rails shining silver into the distance in front.

I didn't see the danger in time, and it didn't growl; it wasn't a bear, it had two legs and it was human. He must have been hiding behind rocks or trees in the shadow thrown by my torch. I saw his movement in the very edge of my peripheral vision after I'd passed him. I sensed an upswept arm, a weapon, a blow coming.

There was barely a hundredth of a second for instinctive evasion. All I did as I ran was to lean forward a fraction so that the smash came across my shoulders, not on my head.

It felt as if I had cracked apart, but I hadn't. Feet, hands, muscles were all working. I staggered forward, dropped the flares and the torch, went down on one knee, knew another bang was travelling. Thought before action . . . I didn't have time. I turned towards him, not away. Turned inside and under the swinging arm, rising, butting upwards with my head to find the aggressive chin, jerking my knee fiercely to contact between the braced legs, punching with clenched fist and the force of fury into the Adam's apple in his throat. One of the many useful things I'd learned on my travels was how to fight dirty, and never had I needed the knowledge more.

He grunted and wheezed with triple unexpected pain and dropped to his knees on the ground, and I wrenched the long piece of wood from his slackening hand and hit his own head with it, hoping I was doing it hard enough to knock him out, not hard enough to kill him. He fell quietly face down in the snow between the rails, and I rolled him over with my foot, and in the deflected beam of the torch which lay unbroken a few paces away, saw the gaunt features of the man called Johnson.

He had got, I reckoned, a lot more than he was used to, and I felt intense satisfaction which was no doubt reprehensible but couldn't be helped.

I bent down, lifted one of his wrists and hauled him unceremoniously over the rail and into the shadows away from the track. He was heavy. Also the damage he'd done me, when it came to lugging unconscious persons about, was all too obvious. He might not have broken my back, which was what it had sounded like, but there were some badly squashed muscle fibres somewhere that weren't in first-class working order and were sending stabbing messages of protest besides.

I picked up the torch and looked for the flares, filled with an increased feeling of urgency, of time running out. I found three of the flares, couldn't see the fourth, decided not to waste time, thought the bears would have to lump it.

Must be light-headed, I thought. Got to get moving. I hadn't come anything like half a mile away from the train. I swung the beam back the way I'd come, but the train was out of sight round a corner that I hadn't noticed taking. For a desperate moment I couldn't remember which direction I'd come from: too utterly stupid if I ran the wrong way.

Think, for God's sake.

I swung the torch both ways along the track. Trees, rocks, silver parallel rails, all exactly similar.

Which way? *Think.*

I walked one way and it felt wrong. I turned and went back. That was right. It felt right. It was the wind on my face, I thought. I'd been running before into the wind.

The rails, the ties seemed to stretch to infinity. I was going uphill also, I thought. Another bend to the right lay ahead.

How long did half a mile take? I stole a glance at my watch, rolling my wrist round which hurt somewhere high up, but with remote pain, not daunting. Couldn't believe the figures. Ten minutes only . . . or twelve . . . since I'd set off.

A mile in ten minutes was ordinarily easy . . . but not a mile of sleepers and stones.

Johnson had been waiting for me, I thought. Not for me personally, but for whomever would come running from the train with the flares.

Which meant he knew the radio wouldn't work.

I began actively to worry about George being missing.

Perhaps Johnson had fixed the hot box, to begin with.

Johnson had meant the trains to crash with himself safely away to the rear. Johnson was darned well not going to succeed.

With renewed purpose, with perhaps at last a feeling that all this was really happening and that I could indeed stop the Canadian, I pressed on along the track.

George's voice floated into my head, telling me about the row between Johnson and Filmer. Filmer told Johnson not to do something; Johnson said, 'I'll do what I frigging like.' Filmer could have told him not to try any more sabotage tricks on the train, realizing that trouble was anyway mounting up for him, trouble from which he might not be able to extricate himself if anything disastrous happened.

Johnson, once started, couldn't be stopped. 'Easier to start a train running downhill than to stop it, eh?' Johnson with a chip on his shoulder from way back; the ex-railwayman, the violent frightener.

I had to have gone well over half a mile, I thought. Half a mile hadn't sounded far enough: the train itself was a quarter-mile long. I stopped and looked at my watch. The Canadian would come in a very few minutes. There was another curve just ahead. I mustn't leave it too late.

I ran faster, round the curve. There was another

curve in a further hundred yards, but it would have to do. I put the torch down beside the track, rubbed the end of one of the flares sharply against one of the rails, and begged it, implored it, to ignite.

It lit with a huge red rush for which I was not prepared. Nearly dropped it. Rammed the spike into the wood of one of the ties.

The flare burned in a brilliant fiery scarlet that would have been visible for a mile, if only the track had been straight.

I picked up the torch and ran on round the next bend, the red fire behind me washing all the snow with pink. Round that bend there was a much longer straight: I ran a good way, then stopped again and lit a second flare, jamming its point into the wood as before.

The Canadian had to be almost there. I'd lost count of the time. The Canadian would come with its bright headlights and see the flare and stop with plenty of margin in hand.

I saw pinpoint lights in the distance. I hadn't known we were anywhere near habitation. Then I realized the lights were moving, coming. The Canadian seemed to be advancing slowly at first . . . and then faster . . . and *it wasn't stopping*. . . . There was no screech of brakes urgently applied.

With a feeling of dreadful foreboding, I struck the third flare forcefully against the rail, almost broke it, felt it whoosh, stood waving it beside the track, beside the other flare stuck in the wood.

The Canadian came straight on. I couldn't bear it, couldn't *believe* it. . . . It was almost impossible to throw the flare through the window . . . the window was too small, too high up, and moving at thirty-five miles an hour. I felt puny on the ground beside the huge roaring advance of the yellow bulk of the inexorable engine with its blinding lights and absence of brain.

It was there. Then or never. There were no faces looking out from the cab. I yelled in a frenzy, 'Stop', and the sound blew away futilely on the bow wave of parting air.

I threw the flare. Threw it high, threw it too soon, missed the empty black window.

The flare flew forward of it and hit the outside of the windscreen, and fell on to the part of the engine sticking out in front; and then all sight of it was gone, the whole long heavy silver train rolling past me at a constant speed, making the ground tremble, extinguishing beneath it the second flare I'd planted in its path. It went on its mindless way, swept round the curve, and was gone.

I felt disintegrated and sick, failure flooding back in the pain I'd disregarded. The trains would fold into each other, would concertina, would heap into killing chaos. . . . In despair, I picked up the torch and began to jog the way the Canadian had gone. I would have to face what I hadn't been able to prevent . . . have to help

even though I felt wretchedly guilty . . . couldn't bear
the thought of the Canadian ploughing into the Lorrimores' car . . . someone would have warned the
Lorrimores . . . oh God, oh God . . . someone *must* have
warned the Lorrimores . . . and everyone else. They
would all be out of the train, away from the track . . .
Nell . . . Zak . . . everybody.

I ran round the curve. Ahead, lying beside the track,
still burning, was the flare I'd thrown. Fallen off the
engine. The first flare that I'd planted a hundred yards
ahead before the next curve had vanished altogether,
swept away by the Canadian.

There was nothing. No noise, except the sighing
wind. I wondered helplessly when I would hear the
crash. I had no idea how far away the race train was;
how far I'd run.

Growing cold and with leaden feet, I plodded past
the fallen flare and along and round the next bend, and
round the long curve following. I hadn't heard the
screech of a metal tearing into metal, though it reverberated in my head. They must have warned the
Lorrimores, they must. . . . I shivered among the
freezing mountains from far more than frost.

There were two red lights on the rails far ahead.
Not bright and burning like the flares, but small and
insignificant, like reflectors. I wondered numbly what
they were, and it wasn't until I'd gone about five more
paces that I realized that they weren't reflectors, they
were *lights* . . . stationary lights . . . and I began running

faster again, hardly daring to hope, but then seeing that they were indeed the rear lights of a train . . . a train . . . it could be only one train . . . there had been no night-tearing crash. . . . The Canadian had stopped. I felt swamped with relief, near to tears, breathless. It had stopped . . . there was no collision . . . no tragedy . . . it had *stopped*.

I ran towards the lights, seeing the bulk of the train now in the torch's beam, unreasonably afraid that the engineers would set off again and accelerate away. I ran until I was panting, until I could touch the train. I ran alongside it, sprinting now, urgent to tell them not to go on.

There were several people on the ground up by the engine. They could see someone running towards them with a torch, and when I was fairly near to them, one of them shouted out authoritatively, 'Get back on the train, there's no need for people to be out there.'

I slowed to a walk, very out of breath. 'I . . . er . . .' I called, 'I came from the train in front.' I gestured along the rails ahead, which were vacant as far as one could see in the headlights of the Canadian.

'What train?' one of them said, as I finally reached them.

'The race train.' I tried to breathe. Air came in gasps. 'Transcontinental . . . mystery . . . race train.'

There was a silence. One of them said, 'It's supposed to be thirty-five minutes ahead of us.'

'It had . . .' I said, dragging in oxygen, 'a hot box.'

It meant a great deal to them. It explained everything.

'Oh.' They took note of my uniform. 'It was you who lit the fusees?'

'Yes.'

'How far ahead is the other train?'

'I don't know. . . . Can't remember . . . how far I ran.'

They consulted. One, from his uniform, was the Conductor. Two, from their lack of it, were the engineers. There was another man there; perhaps the Conductor's assistant. They decided – the Conductor and the train driver himself decided to go forward slowly. They said I'd better come with them in the cab.

Gratefully, lungs settling, I climbed up and stood watching as the engineer released the brakes, put on power and set the train going at no more than walking pace, headlights bright on the empty track ahead.

'Did you *throw* one of the fusees?' the engineer asked me.

'I didn't think you were going to stop.' It sounded prosaic, unemotional.

'We weren't in the cab,' he said. 'The one you threw hit the windscreen and I could see the glare all the way down inside the engine where I was checking a valve. Just as well you threw it . . . I came racing up here just in time to see the one on the track before we ran over it. Bit of luck, you know.'

'Yes.' Bit of luck . . . deliverance from a lifetime's regret.

'Why didn't the Conductor radio?' the Conductor said crossly.

'It's out of order.'

He tut-tutted a bit. We rolled forward slowly. There was a bend ahead to the right.

'I think we're near now,' I said. 'Not far.'

'Right.' The pace slowed further. The engineer inched carefully round the bend and it was as well he did, because when he braked at that point to a halt, we finished with twenty yards between the front of the Canadian's yellow engine and the shining brass railing along the back platform of the Lorrimores' car.

'Well,' the engineer said phlegmatically, 'I wouldn't have wanted to come round the corner unawares to see *that*.'

It wasn't until then that I remembered that Johnson was somewhere out on the track. I certainly hadn't spotted him lying unconscious or dead on the ground on the return journey, and nor obviously had the Canadian's crew. I wondered briefly where he'd got to, but at that moment I didn't care. Everyone climbed down from the Canadian's cab, and the crew walked forward to join their opposite numbers ahead.

I went with them. The two groups greeted each other without fuss. The race train lot seemed to take it for granted that the Canadian would stop in time. They didn't discuss flares, but hot boxes.

The journal-box which held the nearside end of the rear-most of the six axles of the horse car had overheated, and it had overheated because, they surmised, the oil inside had somehow leaked away. That's what was usually wrong, when this happened. They hadn't yet opened it. It no longer glowed red, but was too hot to touch. They were applying fresh snow all the time. Another ten minutes, perhaps.

'Where's George Burley?' I asked.

The race train baggage handler said no one could find him, but two sleeping-car attendants were still searching for him. He told the others that it was a good thing he'd happened to be travelling in the horse car. He had smelled the hot axle, he said. He'd smelled that smell once before. Terrible smell, he said. He'd gone straight forward to tell the engineer to stop at once. 'Otherwise the axle would have broken and we could have had a derailment.'

The others nodded. They all knew.

'Did you warn any of the passengers?' I asked.

'What? No, no, no need to wake them up.'

'But . . . the Canadian might not have stopped . . .'

'Of course it would, when it saw the fusees.'

Their faith amazed and frightened me. The Conductor of the Canadian said that he would radio ahead to Kamloops and both trains would stop there again, where there were multiple tracks, not just the one. Kamloops, he thought, would be getting worried soon that the race train hadn't arrived, and he went off to inform them.

I walked back behind the horse car and boarded

the race train, and almost immediately met George's assistant who was walking forward.

'Where's George?' I said urgently.

He was worried. 'I can't find him.'

'There's one place he might be.' And please let him be there, I thought. Please don't let him be lying miles back in some dreadful condition beside the track.

'Where?' he said.

'In one of the bedrooms. Look up the list. In Johnson's bedroom.'

'Who?'

'Johnson.'

Another sleeping-car attendant happened to arrive at that point.

'I still can't find him,' he said.

'Do you know where Johnson's room is?' I asked anxiously.

'Yes, nearly next to mine. Roomette, it is.'

'Then let's look there.'

'You can't go into a passenger's room in the middle of the night,' he protested.

'If Johnson's there, we'll apologize.'

'I can't think why you think George might be there,' he grumbled, but he led the way back and pointed to a door. 'That's his.'

I opened it. George was lying on the bed, squirming in ropes, fighting against a gag. Very much alive.

Relieved beyond measure, I pulled off the gag which was a wide band of adhesive plaster firmly stuck on.

'Dammit, that hurt, eh?' George said. 'What took you so long?'

George sat in his office, grimly drinking hot tea and refusing to lie down. He was concussed, one could see from his eyes, but he would not admit that the blow to his head that had knocked him out had had any effect. As soon as he was free of the ropes and had begun to understand about the hot box, he had insisted that he and the Conductor from the Canadian had a talk together in the forward dome car of the race train, a meeting attended by various other crew members and myself.

The despatcher in Kamloops, the Canadian's Conductor reported, had said that as soon as the race train could set off again, it would proceed to Kamloops. The Canadian would follow ten minutes later. They would also alert a following freight train. The race train would remain at Kamloops for an hour. The Canadian would leave Kamloops first so that it fell as little behind its timetable as possible. After all the journalboxes of the race train had been checked for heat, it would go on its way to Vancouver. There wouldn't be any enquiry at Kamloops as it would be past three in the morning – Sunday morning – by then. The enquiry would take place at Vancouver.

Everyone nodded. George looked white, as if he wished he hadn't moved his head.

The race train's engineer came to say that the box had been finally opened, it had been dry and the oily waste had burned away, but all was now well, it was cool and filled again, it was not dripping out underneath, and the train could go on.

They wasted no time. The Canadian's crew left and the race train was soon on the move again as if nothing had happened. I went with George to his office and then fetched him the tea, and he groggily demanded I tell him from start to finish what was going on.

'You tell me first how you came to be knocked out,' I said.

'I can't remember. I was walking up to see the engineers.' He looked puzzled. 'First thing I knew, I was lying there trussed up. I was there for ages. Couldn't understand it.' He hadn't a chuckle left in him. 'I was in Johnson's roomette, they said. Johnson did it, I suppose. Jumped me.'

'Yes.'

'Where is he now?'

'Heaven knows.' I told George about Johnson's attacking me and how I'd left him, and how I hadn't seen him anywhere on the way back.

'Two possibilities,' George said. 'Three, I suppose. Either he buggered off somewhere or he's getting a ride on the Canadian right now.'

I stared. Hadn't thought of that. 'What's the third?' I asked.

A tired gleam crept into George's disorientated eyes.

'The mountain where we stopped,' he said. 'That was Squilax Mountain. Squilax is the Indian word for black bear.'

I swallowed. 'I didn't see any bears.'

'Just as well.'

I didn't somehow think Johnson had been eaten by a bear. I couldn't believe in it. I thought I must have been crazy, but I hadn't believed in bears all the time I'd been out there on Black Bear Mountain.

'Know something?' George said. 'The new rolling stock can't easily get hot boxes, the axles run on ball-bearings, eh?, not oily waste. Only old cars like the horse car will always be vulnerable. Know what? You bet your life Johnson took most of the waste out of that box when we stopped in Revelstoke.'

'Why do you say oily waste?' I asked.

'Rags. Rags in the oil. Makes a better cushion for the axle than plain oil. I've known one sabotaged before, mind. Only that time they didn't just take the rags out, they put iron filings in, eh? Derailed the train. Another railwayman with a grudge, that was. But hot boxes do happen by accident. They've got heat sensors with alarm systems beside the track in some places, because of that. How did that Johnson ever think he'd get away with it?'

'He doesn't know we have a photo of him.'

George began to laugh and thought better of it. 'You kill me, Tommy. But what was my assistant thinking of, sending you off with the fusees? It was his job, eh? He should have gone.'

'He said I'd go faster.'

'Well, yes, I suppose he was right. But you weren't really crew.'

'He'd forgotten,' I said. 'But I thought he might have warned the Lorrimores . . . and everyone else . . . to get them out of danger.'

George considered it. 'I'm not going to say he should. I'm not going to say he shouldn't.'

'Railwaymen stick together?'

'He's coming up to his pension. And no one was as much as jolted off their beds, eh?'

'Lucky.'

'Trains always stop for flares,' he said comfortably.

I left it. I supposed one couldn't lose a man his pension for not doing something that had proved unnecessary.

We ran presently into Kamloops where the axles were all checked, the radio was replaced, and everything else went according to plan. Once we were moving again, George finally agreed to lie down in his clothes and try to sleep; and two doors along from him I tried the same.

Things always start hurting when one has time to think about them. The dull ache where Johnson's piece of wood had landed on the back of my left shoulder was intermittently sharply sore: all right when I was standing up, not so good lying down. A bore. It would be stiffer still, I thought, in the morning. A pest for serving breakfast.

I smiled to myself finally. In spite of Johnson's and Filmer's best efforts, the great Transcontinental Mystery Race Train might yet limp without disaster to Vancouver.

Complacency, I should have remembered, was never a good idea.

CHAPTER NINETEEN

It was discomfort as much as anything which had me on my feet again soon after six. Emil wouldn't have minded if I'd been late, as few of the passengers were early breakfasters, but I thought I'd do better in the dining car. I stripped off the waistcoat and shirt for a wash and a shave, and inspected in the mirror as best I could the fairly horrifying bruise already colouring a fair-sized area across my back. Better than on my head, I thought resignedly. Look on the bright side.

I put on a clean shirt and the spare clean waistcoat and decided that this was one VIA Rail operative who was not going to polish his shoes that morning, despite the wear and tear on them from the night's excursions. I brushed my hair instead. Tommy looked tidy enough, I thought, for his last appearance.

It wasn't yet light. I went forward through the sleeping train to the kitchen where Angus was not only awake but singing Scottish ballads at the top of his voice while filling the air with the fragrant yeasty smell of his baking. The dough, it seemed, had risen satisfactorily during the night.

Emil, Oliver, Cathy and I laid the tables and set out fresh flowers in the bud vases, and in time, with blue skies appearing outside, poured coffee and ferried sausages and bacon. The train stopped for a quarter of an hour in a place called North Bend, our last stop before Vancouver, and ran on down what the passengers were knowledgeably calling Fraser Canyon. Hell's Gate, they said with relish, lay ahead.

The track seemed to me to be clinging to the side of a cliff. Looking out of the window by the kitchen door, one could see right down to a torrent rushing between rocky walls, brownish tumbling water with foam-edged waves. The train, I was pleased to note, was negotiating this extraordinary feat of engineering at a suitably circumspect crawl. If it went too fast round these bends, it would fly off into space.

I took a basket of bread down to the far end just as Mercer Lorrimore came through from the dome car. Although Cathy was down there also, he turned from her to me and asked if I could possibly bring hot tea through to his own car.

'Certainly, sir. Any breads?'

He looked vaguely at the basket. 'No. Just tea. For three of us.' He nodded, turned and went away. Cathy raised her eyebrows and said with tolerance, 'Chauvinist pig.'

Emil shook his head a bit over the private order but

made sure the tray I took looked right from his point of view, and I swayed through on the mission.

The lockable door in the Lorrimores' car was open. I knocked on it, however, and Mercer appeared in the far doorway to the saloon at the rear.

'Along here, please.'

I went along there. Mercer, dressed in a suit and tie, gestured to me to put the tray on the coffee table. Bambi wasn't there. Sheridan sprawled in an armchair in jeans, trainers and a big white sweatshirt with the words MAKE WAVES on the front.

I found it difficult to look at Sheridan pleasantly. I could think of nothing but cats. He himself still wore the blank look of the evening before, as if he had opted out of thinking.

'We'll pour,' Mercer said. 'Come back in half an hour for the tray.'

'Yes, sir.'

I left them and returned to the dining car. The chill within Bambi, I thought, was because of the cats.

Nell and Xanthe had arrived during my absence.

'My goodness, you look grim,' Nell exclaimed, then, remembering, said more formally, 'Er . . . what's for breakfast?'

I got rid of the grimness and handed her the printed menu. Xanthe said she would have everything that was going.

'Has George told you that we're running late?' I asked Nell.

'No. His door was shut. Are we? How much?'

'About an hour and a half.' I forestalled her question. 'We had to stop in the night at Kamloops to get George's radio fixed, and then we had to wait there for the Canadian to go ahead of us.'

'I'd better tell everyone, then. What time do we get to Vancouver?'

'About eleven-thirty, I think.'

'Right. Thanks.'

I almost said, 'Be my guest,' but not quite. Tommy wouldn't. Nell's eyes were smiling, all the same. Cathy chose that exact moment to go past me with a tray of breakfasts: or not exactly past, but rather against me where it seemed to hurt most.

'Sorry,' she said contritely, going on her way.

'It's OK.'

It was difficult always to pass in the swaying aisle without touching. Couldn't be helped.

Filmer came into the dining room and sat at the table nearest to the kitchen, normally the least favourite with the passengers. He looked as if he'd spent a bad night. 'Here, you,' he said abruptly at my approach, having apparently abandoned the Mister-Nice-Guy image.

'Yes, sir?' I said.

'Coffee,' he said.

'Yes, sir.'

'Now.'

'Yes, sir.'

I gave Xanthe's order to Simone who was stiffly

laying a baking sheet of sausages in the oven in silent protest at life in general, and I took the coffee pot, on a tray, to Filmer.

'Why did we stop in the night?' he demanded.

'I believe it was to fix the radio, sir.'

'We stopped twice,' he said accusingly. 'Why?'

'I don't know, sir. I expect the Conductor could tell you.'

I wondered what he'd do if I said, 'Your man Johnson nearly succeeded in wrecking the train with you in it.' It struck me then that perhaps his enquiry was actually anxiety: that he wanted to be told that nothing dangerous had happened. He did seem marginally relieved by my answer and I resisted the temptation of wiping out all that relief by telling him that the radio had been sabotaged, because the people at the next table were listening also. Spreading general gloom and fright was not in my brief. Selective gloom, selective fright . . . sure.

Others, it seemed, had noticed the long stops in the night, but no one seriously complained. No one minded letting the Canadian go on in front. The general good humour and the party atmosphere prevailed and excused everything. The train ride might be coming to an end, but meanwhile there was the spectacular gorge outside to be exclaimed over, the city of Vancouver to be looked forward to, the final race to promise a sunburst of a conclusion. The Great Transcontinental Race Train, they were saying, had been just that: great.

After half an hour or so, I went back to the Lorri-mores' car to fetch the tray of teacups. I knocked on the door, but as there was no answer I went anyway along to the saloon.

Mercer was standing there looking bewildered. Looking haggard. Stricken with shock.

'Sir?' I said.

His eyes focused on me vaguely.

'My son,' he said.

'Sir?'

Sheridan wasn't in the saloon. Mercer was alone.

'Stop the train,' he said. 'We must go back.'

Oh *God*, I thought.

'He went out ... on to the platform ... to look at the river ...' Mercer could hardly speak. 'When I looked up ... he wasn't there.'

The door to the platform was closed. I went past Mercer, opened the door and went out. There was no one on the platform, as he'd said.

There was wind in plenty. The polished brass top of the railings ran round at waist height, with both of the exit gates still firmly bolted.

Over the right-hand side, from time to time, there were places which offered a straight unimpeded hundred-foot drop to the fearsome frothing rocky river below. Death beckoned there. A quick death.

I went into the saloon and closed the door.

Mercer was swaying with more than the movement of the train.

'Sit down, sir,' I said, taking his arm. 'I'll tell the Conductor. He'll know what to do.'

'We must go back.' He sat down with buckling legs. 'He went out . . . and when I looked . . .'

'Will you be all right while I go to the Conductor?'

He nodded dully. 'Yes. Hurry.'

I hurried, myself feeling much of Mercer's bewildered shock, if not his complicated grief. Half an hour earlier, Sheridan hadn't looked like someone about to jump off a cliff; but then I supposed that I'd never seen anyone else at that point, so how would I know? Perhaps the blank look, I thought, had been a sign, if anyone could have read it.

I hurried everywhere except through the dining car, so as not to be alarming, and when I reached George's room I found the door still shut. I knocked. No reply. I knocked again harder and called his name with urgency. '*George!*'

There was a grunt from inside. I opened the door without more ado and found him still lying on the bed in his clothes, waking from a deep sleep.

I closed his door behind me and sat on the edge of his bed, and told him we'd lost a passenger.

'Into Fraser Canyon,' he repeated. He shunted himself up into a sitting position and put both hands to his head, wincing. 'When?'

'About ten minutes ago, I should think.'

He stretched out a hand to the radio, looking out of the window to get his bearings. 'It's no use going back, you know. Not if he went into the water from this height. And the river's bitter cold, and you can see how fast it is . . . and there's a whirlpool.'

'His father will go, though.'

'Of course.'

The despatcher he got through to this time was in Vancouver. He explained that Mercer Lorrimore's son – that was right, *the* Mercer Lorrimore – his twenty-year-old son had fallen from the rear of the race train into Fraser Canyon somewhere between Hell's Gate and a mile or two south of Yale. Mercer Lorrimore wanted the train stopped so that he could go back to find his son. He, George Burley, wanted instructions from Montreal. The despatcher, sounding glazed, told him to hang on.

There was no chance now, I thought, of reaching Vancouver without a disaster. Sheridan was a disaster of major proportions, and the Press would be at Vancouver station for all the wrong reasons.

'I think I'd better go back to Mercer,' I said.

George nodded gingerly. 'Tell him I'll come to talk to him when I get instructions from Montreal, eh?' He rubbed a hand over his chin. 'He'll have to put up with stubble.'

I returned to the dining car and found Nell still sitting beside Xanthe. I said into Nell's ear, 'Bring Xanthe into the private car.'

She looked enquiringly into my face and saw nothing comforting, but she got Xanthe to move without alarming her. I led the way through the dome car and through the join into the rear car, knocking again on the unlocked door.

Mercer came out of his and Bambi's bedroom further up the corridor looking grey and hollow-eyed, a face of unmistakable calamity.

'Daddy!' Xanthe said, pushing past me. 'What's the matter?'

He folded his arms round her and hugged her, and took her with him towards the saloon. Neither Nell nor I heard the words he murmured to her, but we both heard her say sharply, 'No! He couldn't!'

'Couldn't what?' Nell said to me quietly.

'Sheridan went off the back platform into the canyon.'

'Do you mean . . .' she was horrified ' . . . that he's *dead*?'

'I would think so.'

'Oh *shit*,' Nell said.

My feelings exactly, I thought.

We went on into the saloon. Mercer said almost mechanically, 'Why don't we stop? We have to go back.' He no longer sounded, I thought, as if he expected or even hoped to find Sheridan alive.

'Sir, the Conductor is radioing for instructions,' I said.

He nodded. He was a reasonable man in most circumstances. He had only to look out of the window to know that going back wouldn't help. He knew that it was practically impossible for anyone to fall off the platform by accident. He certainly believed, from his demeanour, that Sheridan had jumped.

Mercer sat on the sofa, his arm around Xanthe beside him, her head on his shoulder. Xanthe wasn't crying. She looked serious, but calm. The tragedy for Xanthe hadn't happened within that half-hour, it had been happening all her life. Her brother had been lost to her even when alive.

Nell said, 'Shall we go, Mr Lorrimore?' meaning herself and me. 'Can I do anything for Mrs Lorrimore?'

'No, no,' he said. 'Stay.' He swallowed. 'You'll have to know what's decided . . . what to tell everyone . . .' He shook his head helplessly. 'We must make some decisions.'

George arrived at that point and sat down in an armchair near Mercer, leaning forward with his forearms on his knees and saying how sorry he was, how very sorry.

'We have to go back,' Mercer said.

'Yes, sir, but not the whole train, sir. Montreal says the train must go on to Vancouver as scheduled.'

Mercer began to protest. George interrupted him. 'Sir, Montreal say that they are already alerting all the authorities along the canyon to look out for your son. They say they will arrange transport for you to return, you and your family, as soon as we reach Vancouver. You can see . . .' he glanced out of the window ' . . . that the area is unpopulated, eh?, but there are often people working by the river. There is a road running along quite near the canyon, as well as another railway line on the other side. There's a small town over there called . . . er . . .' he coughed ' . . . Hope. It's at the south end of the canyon, eh?, where the river broadens out and runs more slowly. We're almost at that point now, as you'll see. If you go to Hope, Montreal says, you will be in the area if there is any news.'

'How do I get there?' Mercer said. 'Is there a train back?'

George said, 'There is, yes, but only one a day. It's the Super-continental. It leaves Vancouver at four in the afternoon, passes through Hope at seven.'

'That's useless,' Mercer said. 'How far is it by road?'

'About a hundred and fifty kilometres.'

He reflected. 'I'll get a helicopter,' he said.

There was absolutely no point in being rich, I thought, if one didn't know how to use it.

The logistics of the return were making Mercer feel better, one could see. George told him that the train we were on would speed up considerably once we were clear of the canyon, and that we'd be in Vancouver in two hours and a half. They discussed how to engage a helicopter; Mercer already had a car meeting him at the station. Nell said Merry & Co would arrange everything, as they had indeed already arranged the car. No problem, if she could reach her office by telephone. George shook his head. He would relay the message by radio through Montreal. He brought out a notepad to write down Merry & Co's number and the instruction 'Arrange helicopter, Nell will phone from Vancouver.'

'I'll phone from the train,' she said.

George stood up. 'I'll get moving then, Mr Lorrimore. We'll do everything possible.' He looked big, awkward and unshaven, but Mercer had taken strength from him and was grateful. 'My sympathy,' George said, 'to Mrs Lorrimore.'

The tray of empty teacups still lay where I'd left it on the coffee table. I picked it up and asked if there was anything I could bring them, but Mercer shook his head.

'I'll come and find you,' Xanthe said, 'if they need anything.' She sounded competent and grown up, years older than at breakfast. Nell gave her a swift, sweet glance of appreciation, and she, George and I made our way back into the dome car, George hurrying off to his radio and Nell sighing heavily over what to say to the other passengers.

'It'll spoil the end of their trip,' she said.

'Try them.'

'You're cynical.'

'Pretty often.'

She shook her head as if I were a lost cause and went into the dining room with the bad news, which was predictably greeted with shock but no grief.

'Poor Xanthe,' Rose Young exclaimed, and Mrs Unwin said, 'Poor Bambi.' The sympathy stage lasted ten seconds. The deliciously round-eyed 'Isn't it dreadful?' stage went on all morning.

Julius Apollo Filmer was no longer in the dining room and I wished he had been as I would like to have seen his reactions. Chance would seem to have robbed him of his lever against Mercer; or would he reckon that Mercer would still sacrifice one horse to preserve the reputation of the dead? Filmer could read it wrong, I thought.

There was a cocktail party scheduled for that evening in the Four Seasons Hotel for Vancouver's racing bigwigs to meet the owners: would it still be held, several anxiously asked.

'Certainly,' Nell answered robustly. 'The party and the race will go on.'

No one, not even I, was cynical enough to say, 'Sheridan would have wished it.'

I helped clear away the breakfast and wash the dishes and pack everything into boxes for sending back to the caterers in Toronto, and when we'd finished I found that Nell had collected gratuities from the passengers to give to the waiters, and Emil, Cathy and Oliver had split it four ways. Emil put a bundle of notes into my hand, and he and the others were smiling.

'I can't take it,' I said.

Emil said, 'We know you aren't a waiter, and we

know you aren't an actor, but you have worked for it. It's yours.'

'And we know you've worked all morning although it's obvious you've hurt your arm,' Cathy said. 'I made it worse . . . I'm real sorry.'

'And it would all have been very much harder work without you,' Oliver said. 'So we thought we'd like to give you a present.'

'And that's it,' Cathy added, pointing to the notes.

They waited expectantly, wanting my thanks.

'I . . . er, I don't know . . .' I kissed Cathy suddenly; hugged her. 'All right. I'll buy something to remember us by. To remember the journey. Thank you all very much.'

They laughed, pleased. 'It's been fun,' Cathy said, and Emil added ironically, 'But not every week.'

I shook Emil's hand, and Oliver's. Kissed Cathy again. Shook hands with Angus. Was offered Simone's cheek for a peck. I looked round at their faces, wanting to hold on to the memory.

'See you again,' I said, and they said, 'Yes,' and we all knew it was doubtful. I went away along the swaying corridor, taking Tommy to extinction and, as often in the past, not looking back. Too many regrets in looking back.

In the sleeping cars everyone was packing and holding impromptu parties in each other's rooms, walking in and out of the open doors. Filmer's door was shut.

Nell was in her roomette, with the door open, packing.

'What's wrong with your arm?' she said, folding one of the straight skirts.

'Is it so obvious?'

'Most obvious when Cathy bumped into you with her tray. The shock went right through you.'

'Yes, well, it's not serious.'

'I'll get you a doctor.'

'Don't be silly.'

'I suppose,' she said, 'Mercer won't run his horse now on Tuesday. Such a shame. That *damned* Sheridan.'

The biblical description, I thought, was accurate.

'Xanthe,' Nell said, putting the skirt in her suitcase, 'says you were kind to her at Lake Louise. Did you really say something about the corruption of self-importance? She said she learned a lot.'

'She grew up this morning,' I said.

'Yes, didn't she?'

'If we go to Hawaii,' I said, 'you can wear a sarong and a hibiscus behind your ear.'

She paused in the packing. 'They wouldn't really go,' she said judiciously, 'with a clipboard.'

George came out of his office and told her the cellular telephone was now working, if she wanted to make her calls, and I went into my roomette and changed out of uniform into Tommy's outdoor clothes, and packed everything away. The train journey might be finished, I was thinking, but my real job wasn't.

There was much to be done. Filmer might be sick, but it was sick sharks that attacked swimmers, and there could still be a dorsal fin unseen below the surface.

Nell came out of George's office and along to my door.

'No helicopter needed,' she said. 'They've found Sheridan already.'

'That was quick.'

'Apparently he fell on to a fish ladder.'

'You're kidding me.'

'No, actually.' She stifled a laugh, as improper to the occasion. 'George says the ladders are a sort of staircase hundreds of metres long that are built in the river because the salmon can't swim upstream to spawn against the strength of the water, because the water flows much faster than it used to because a huge rock-fall constricted it.'

'I'll believe it,' I said.

'Some men were working on the lower ladder,' she said, 'and Sheridan was swept down in the water.'

'Dead?' I asked.

'Very.'

'You'd better tell Mercer.'

She made a reluctant face. 'You do it.'

'I can't. George could.'

George agreed to go with the good bad news and hurried off so as to be back at his post when we reached the station.

'Did you know,' I said to Nell, 'that Emil, Cathy and Oliver wanted to share their tips with me?'

'Yes, they asked me if I thought it would be all right. I do hope,' she said with sudden anxiety, 'that you accepted? They said you'd been great. They wanted to thank you. They were so pleased with themselves.'

'Yes,' I said, relieved to be able to. 'I accepted. I told them I'd buy something to remind me of them and the trip. And I will.'

She relaxed. 'I should have warned you. But then, I guess . . . no need.' She smiled. 'What are you really?'

'Happy,' I said.

'Yuk.'

'I try hard, but it keeps breaking out. My boss threatens to fire me for it.'

'Who's your boss?'

'Brigadier Valentine Catto.'

She blinked. 'I never know when you're telling the truth.'

Catto, I thought. Cats. Sobering.

'I have just,' I said slowly, 'been struck by a blinding idea.'

'Yes, you rather look like it.'

Time, I thought. Not enough of it.

'Come back,' Nell said. 'I've lost you.'

'You don't happen to have a world air timetable with you, do you?'

'There are several in the office. What do you want?'

'A flight from London to Vancouver tomorrow.'

She raised her eyebrows, went into George's office, consulted on the telephone and came out again.

'Air Canada leaves Heathrow 3 p.m., arrives Vancouver 4.25.'

'Consider yourself kissed.'

'Are you still a waiter, then, in the eyes of the passengers?'

There were passengers all the time in the corridor.

'Mm,' I said thoughtfully, 'I think so. For another two days. To the end.'

'All right.'

George returned and reported that all three of the Lorrimores had received the news of Sheridan calmly and would go to the hotel as planned, and make arrangements from there.

'Poor people,' Nell said. 'What a mess.'

I asked George what he would be doing. Going back to Toronto, of course, possibly by train, as soon as the various VIA enquiries were completed, which would be tomorrow. Couldn't he stay for the race, I asked, and go back on the Tuesday evening? He wasn't sure. I took him into his office and convinced him, and he was chuckling again as the train slowed to a crawl and inched into the terminus at Vancouver.

The wheels stopped. Seven days almost to the hour since they'd set off, the passengers climbed down from the travelling hotel and stood in little groups outside, still smiling and still talking. Zak and the other actors moved among them, shaking farewell hands. The

419

actors had commitments back in Toronto and weren't staying for the race.

Zak saw me through the window and bounced up again into the sleeping car to say goodbye.

'Don't lose touch, now,' he said. 'Any time you want a job writing mysteries, let me know.'

'OK.'

'Bye, guy,' he said.

'Bye.'

He jumped off the train again and trailed away beneath his mop of curls towards the station buildings, with Donna, Pierre, Raoul, Mavis, Walter and Giles following like meteorites after a comet.

I waited for Filmer to pass. He walked on his own, looking heavy and intent. He was wearing an overcoat and carrying the briefcase and not bothering to be charming. There was a firmness of purpose in his step that I didn't much like, and when Nell took a pace forward to ask him something he answered her with a brief turn of his head but no break in his stride.

When he'd gone, I jumped down beside Nell who was carefully checking other passengers off against a list on the clipboard as they passed. It was a list, I discovered by looking over her shoulder, of the people catching the special bus to check into the Four Seasons Hotel. Against Filmer's name, as against all the others, I was relieved to see a tick.

'That's everyone,' Nell said finally. She looked

towards the rear of the train. 'Except the Lorrimores, of course. I'd better go and help them.'

I stepped back on board to collect my gear and through the window watched the little solemn party pass by outside: Mercer, head up, looking sad, Bambi expressionless, Xanthe caring, Nell concerned.

Some way after them I walked forward through the train. It was quiet and empty, the racegoers having flooded away, the surly cook gone from the centre diner, the dayniter no longer alive with singing, the doors of the empty bedrooms standing open, the Chinese cook vanished with his grin. I climbed down again and went on forward, past the baggage car where I collected my suitcase from the handler, and past the horse car, where Leslie Brown was leaning out of the window, still a dragon.

'Bye,' I said.

She looked at me, as if puzzled for a second, and then recognized me: Calgary and Lenny Higgs were three days back.

'Oh, yes . . . goodbye.'

The train was due to shunt out backwards, to take the horses and the grooms to a siding, from where they would go by road to Exhibition Park. Ms Brown was going with them, it seemed.

'Good luck at the races,' I said.

'I never bet.'

'Well . . . have a good time.'

She looked as if that were an unthinkable suggestion.

I waved to her, the stalwart custodian, and went on past the engine where the engineer was a shadowy figure high up beyond his impossibly small window, went on into the station.

The Lorrimores had been interrupted by people with notebooks, cameras and deadlines. Mercer was being civil. Nell extricated the family and ushered them to their car, and herself climbed into the long bus with the owners. I hung back until they'd all gone, then travelled in a taxi, booked in at the Hyatt and telephoned England.

The Brigadier wasn't at home in Newmarket. I could try his club in London, a voice said, giving me the familiar number, and I got connected to the bar of the Hobbs Sandwich where the Brigadier, I was relieved to hear, was at that moment receiving his first-of-the-evening well-watered Scotch.

'Tor!' he said. 'Where are you?'

'Vancouver.' I could hear the clink of the glasses and the murmurings in the background. I pictured the dark oak walls with the gentlemen in the pictures with side-whiskers, big pads and little caps, and it all seemed far back in time, not just in distance.

'Um,' I said. 'Can I phone you again when you're alone? This is going to take some time. I mean, soon, really.'

'Urgent?'

'Fairly.'

'Hold on. I'll go upstairs to my bedroom and get them to transfer the call. Don't go away.'

I waited through a few clicks until his voice came quietly on the line again without sound effects.

'Right. What's happened?'

I talked for what seemed a very long time. He punctuated my pauses with grunts to let me know he was still listening, and at the end he said, 'You don't ask much, do you? Just for miracles.'

'There's an Air Canada flight from Heathrow at three tomorrow afternoon,' I said, 'and they'll have all day and all Tuesday to find the information, because when it's only eleven in the morning in Vancouver on Tuesday, it'll be seven in the evening in England. And they could send it by fax.'

'Always supposing,' he said drily, 'that there's a fax machine in the Jockey Club in Exhibition Park.'

'I'll check,' I said. 'If there isn't, I'll get one.'

'What does Bill Baudelaire think of all this?' he asked.

'I haven't talked to him yet. I had to get your reaction first.'

'What's your phone number?' he asked. 'I'll think it over and ring you back in ten minutes.'

'Thought before action?'

'You can't fault it, if there's time.'

He thought for twice ten minutes, until I was itchy. When the bell rang, I took a deep breath and answered.

'We'll attempt it,' he said, 'as long as Bill Baudelaire

423

agrees, of course. If we can't find the information in the time available, we may have to abort.'

'All right.'

'Apart from that,' he said, 'well done.'

'Good staff work,' I said.

He laughed. 'Flattery will get you no promotion.'

CHAPTER TWENTY

I was looking forward to talking to Mrs Baudelaire. I dialled her number and Bill himself answered.

'Hello,' I said, surprised. 'It's Tor Kelsey. How's your mother?'

There was a long, awful pause.

'She's ill,' I said with anxiety.

'She . . . er . . . she died . . . early this morning.'

'Oh . . . no.' She couldn't have, I thought. It couldn't be true. 'I talked to her yesterday,' I said.

'We knew . . . she knew . . . it would only be weeks. But yesterday evening there was a crisis.'

I was silent. I felt her loss as if she'd been Aunt Viv restored to me and snatched away. I'd wanted so very much to meet her.

'Tor?' Bill's voice said.

I swallowed. 'Your mother . . . was great.'

He would hear the smothered tears in my voice, I thought. He would think me crazy.

'If it's of any use to you,' he said, 'she felt like that about you, too. You made her last week a good one.

She wanted to live to find out what happened. One of the last things she said was ... "I don't want to go before the end of the story. I want to see that invisible young man ..." She was slipping away ... all the time.'

> Do not go gentle into that good night,
> Old age should burn and rave at close of day:
> Rage, rage against the dying of the light ...

'Tor?' Bill said.

'I'm so very sorry,' I said with more control. 'So sorry.'

'Thank you.'

'I don't suppose ...' I said, and paused, feeling helpless.

'You suppose wrong,' he replied instantly. 'I've been waiting here for you to phone. We would both fail her if we didn't go straight on. I've had hours to think this out. The last thing she would want would be for us to give up. So I'll start things off by telling you we've had a telex from Filmer announcing that he is the sole owner of Laurentide Ice, but we are going to inform him that the Ontario Racing Commission are rescinding his licence to own horses. We're also telling him he won't be admitted to the President's lunch at Exhibition Park.'

'I'd ... er ... like to do it differently,' I said.

'How do you mean?'

I sighed deeply and talked to him also for a long

time. He listened as the Brigadier had, with intermittent throat noises, and at the end he said simply, 'I do wish she'd been alive to hear all this.'

'Yes, so do I.'

'Well,' he paused. 'I'll go along with it. The real problem is time.'

'Mm.'

'You'd better talk to Mercer Lorrimore yourself.'

'But . . .'

'No buts. You're there. I can't get there until tomorrow late afternoon, not with all you want me to do here. Talk to Mercer without delay, you don't want him coming back to Toronto.'

I said with reluctance, 'All right.' But I had known that I would have to.

'Good. Use all the authority you need. Val and I will back you.'

'Thank you . . . very much.'

'See you tomorrow,' he said.

I put the receiver down slowly. Death could be colossally unfair, one knew that, but rage, rage . . . I felt anger for her as much as grief. Do not go gentle into that good night . . . I thought it probable, if I remembered right, that the last word she'd said to me was 'Good night'. Good night dear, dear Mrs Baudelaire. Go gentle. Go sweetly into that good night.

I sat for a while without energy, feeling the lack of sleep, feeling the nagging pain, feeling the despondency her death had opened the door to: feeling unequal to the next two days, even though I'd set them up myself.

With an effort, after an age I got through to the Four Seasons Hotel and asked for Mercer, but found myself talking to Nell.

'All the calls are being re-routed to me,' she said. 'Bambi is lying down. Mercer and Xanthe are on their way to Hope in the helicopter, which was reordered for him, so that he can identify Sheridan's body which is being taken there by road.'

'It all sounds so clinical.'

'The authorities want to make sure it's Sheridan before they make any arrangements.'

'When will Mercer and Xanthe be back, do you know?'

'About six, they expected.'

'Um . . . the Jockey Club asked me to fix up a brief meeting. Do you think Mercer would agree to that?'

'He's being terrifically helpful to everyone. Almost too calm.'

I thought things over. 'Can you get hold of him in Hope?'

She hesitated. 'Yes, I suppose so. I have the address and the phone number of where he was going, but I think it's a police station . . . or a mortuary.'

'Could you . . . could you tell him that on their return to the hotel, a car will be waiting to take him straight on to a brief meeting with the Jockey Club? Tell him the Jockey Club send their sincere condolences and ask for just a little of his time.'

'I guess I could,' she said doubtfully. 'What about Xanthe?'

'Mercer alone,' I said positively.

'Is it important?' she asked, and I could imagine her frowning.

'I think it's important for Mercer.'

'All right.' She made up her mind. 'Xanthe can take the phone calls for her mother, then, because I have to go to this cocktail party.' A thought struck her. 'Aren't some of the Jockey Club coming to the party?'

'Mercer won't want to go. They want a quiet talk with him alone.'

'OK then, I'll try to arrange it.'

'Very many thanks,' I said fervently. 'I'll call back to check.'

I called back at five o'clock. The helicopter was in the air on its way back, Nell said, and Mercer had agreed to being picked up at the hotel.

'You're brilliant.'

'Tell the Jockey Club not to keep him long. He'll be tired . . . and he's identified Sheridan.'

'I could kiss you,' I said. 'The way to a man's heart is through his travel agent.'

She laughed. 'Always supposing that's where one wants to go.'

She put her receiver down with a delicate click. I did not want to lose her, I thought.

The car I sent for Mercer picked him up successfully and brought him to the Hyatt, the chauffeur telling him, as requested, the room to go straight up to. He rang the doorbell of the suite I'd engaged more or less in his honour, and I opened the door to let him in.

He came in about two paces and then stopped and peered with displeasure at my face.

'What is this?' he demanded with growing anger, preparing to depart.

I closed the door behind him.

'I work for the Jockey Club,' I said. 'The British Jockey Club. I am seconded here with the Canadian Jockey Club for the duration of the race train Celebration of Canadian Racing.'

'But you're ... you're ...'

'My name is Tor Kelsey,' I said. 'It was judged better that I didn't go openly on the train as a sort of security agent for the Jockey Club, so I went as a waiter.'

He looked me over. Looked at the rich young owner's good suit that I'd put on for the occasion. Looked at the expensive room.

'My God,' he said weakly. He took a few paces forward. 'Why am I here?'

'I work for Brigadier Valentine Catto in England,' I said, 'and Bill Baudelaire over here. They are the heads of the Jockey Club Security Services.'

He nodded. He knew them.

'As they cannot be here, they have both given me their authority to speak to you on their behalf.'

'Yes, but . . . what about?'

'Would you sit down? Would you like . . . a drink?'

He looked at me with a certain dry humour. 'Do you have any identification?'

'Yes.' I fetched my passport. He opened it. Looked at my name, at my likeness, and at my occupation: investigator.

He handed it back. 'Yes, I'll have a drink,' he said, 'as you're so good at serving them. Cognac if possible.'

I opened the cupboard that the hotel had supplied at my request with wine, vodka, Scotch and brandy, and poured the amount I knew he'd like, even adding the heretical ice. He took the glass with a twist of a smile, and sat in one of the armchairs.

'No one guessed about you,' he said. 'No one came anywhere near it.' He took a sip reflectively. 'Why were you on the train?'

'I was sent because of one of the passengers. Because of Julius Filmer.'

The ease that had been growing in him fled abruptly. He put the glass down on the table beside him and stared at me.

'Mr Lorrimore,' I said, sitting down opposite him, 'I am sorry about your son. Truly sorry. All of the Jockey Club send their sympathy. I think though that I should tell you straight away that Brigadier Catto, Bill Baudelaire and myself all know about the . . . er . . . incident . . . of the cats.'

He looked deeply shocked. 'You can't know!'

'I imagine that Julius Filmer knows also.'

He made a hopeless gesture with one hand. 'However did he find out?'

'The Brigadier is working on that in England.'

'And how did *you* find out?'

'Not from anyone you swore to silence.'

'Not from the college?'

'No.'

He covered his face briefly with one hand.

'Julius Filmer may still suggest you give him Voting Right in exchange for his keeping quiet,' I said.

He lowered the hand to his throat and closed his eyes. 'I've thought of that,' he said. He opened his eyes again. 'Did you see the last scene of the mystery?'

'Yes,' I said.

'I haven't known what to do . . . since then.'

'It's you who has to decide,' I said. 'But . . . can I tell you a few things?'

He gave a vague gesture of assent, and I talked to him, also, for quite a long time. He listened with total concentration, mostly watching my face. People who were repudiating in their minds every word one said didn't look at one's face but at the floor, or at a table, at anything else. I knew, by the end, that he would do what I was asking, and I was grateful because it wouldn't be easy for him.

When I'd finished, he said thoughtfully, 'That mystery was no coincidence, was it? The father blackmailed because of his child's crime, the groom

432

murdered because he knew too much, the man who would kill himself if he couldn't keep his racehorses . . . Did you write it yourself?'

'All that part, yes. Not from the beginning.'

He smiled faintly. 'You showed me what I was doing . . . was prepared to do. But beyond that . . . you showed Sheridan.'

'I wondered,' I said.

'Did you? Why?'

'He looked different afterwards. He had changed.'

Mercer said, 'How could you see that?'

'It's my job.'

He looked startled. 'There isn't such a job.'

'Yes,' I said, 'there is.'

'Explain,' he said.

'I watch . . . for things that aren't what they were, and try to understand, and find out why.'

'All the time?'

I nodded. 'Yes.'

He drank some brandy thoughtfully. 'What change did you see in Sheridan?'

I hesitated. 'I just thought that things had shifted in his mind. Like seeing something from a different perspective. A sort of revelation. I didn't know if it would last.'

'It might not have done.'

'No.'

'He said,' Mercer said, ' "Sorry, Dad." '

It was my turn to stare.

'He said it before he went out on to the platform.' Mercer swallowed with difficulty and eventually went on. 'He had been so quiet. I couldn't sleep. I went out to the saloon about dawn, and he was sitting there. I asked him what was the matter, and he said, "I fucked things up, didn't I?" We all knew he had. It wasn't anything new. But it was the first time he'd said so. I tried ... I tried to comfort him, to say we would stand by him, no matter what. He knew about Filmer's threat, you know. Filmer said in front of all of us that he knew about the cats.' He looked unseeingly over his glass. 'It wasn't the only time it had happened. Sheridan killed two cats like that in our garden when he was fourteen. We got therapy for him. ... They said it was the upheaval of adolescence.' He paused. 'One psychiatrist said Sheridan was psychopathic, he couldn't help what he did ... but he could, really, most of the time. He could help being discourteous, but he thought being rich gave him the right ... I told him it didn't.'

'Why did you send him to Cambridge?' I asked.

'My father was there, and established a scholarship. They gave it to Sheridan as thanks – as a gift. He couldn't concentrate long enough to get into college otherwise. But then ... the Master of the college said they couldn't keep him, scholarship or not, and I understood ... of course they couldn't. We thought he would be all right there ... we so hoped he would.'

They'd spent a lot of hope on Sheridan, I thought.

'I don't know if he meant to jump this morning when

he went out on the platform,' Mercer said. 'I don't know if it was just an impulse. He gave way to impulses very easily. Unreasonable impulses . . . almost insane, sometimes.'

'It was seductive, out there,' I said. 'Easy to jump.'

Mercer looked at me gratefully. 'Did you feel it?'

'Sort of.'

'Sheridan's revelation lasted until this morning,' he said.

'Yes,' I said. 'I saw . . . when I brought your tea.'

'The waiter . . .' He shook his head, still surprised.

'I'd be grateful,' I said, 'if you don't tell anyone else about the waiter.'

'Why not?'

'Because most of my work depends on anonymity. My bosses don't want people like Filmer to know I exist.'

He nodded slowly, with comprehension. 'I won't tell.'

He stood up and shook my hand. 'What do they pay you?' he asked.

I smiled. 'Enough.'

'I wish Sheridan had been able to have a job. He couldn't stick at anything.' He sighed. 'I'll believe that what he did this morning was for us. "Sorry, Dad . . ." '

Mercer looked me in the eyes and made a simple statement, without defensiveness, without apology.

'I loved my son,' he said.

On Monday morning, I went to Vancouver station to back up George Burley in the rail company's dual enquiry into the hot box and the suicide.

I was written down as 'T. Titmuss, Acting Crew', which amused me and seemed to cover several interpretations. George was stalwart and forthright, with the ironic chuckles subdued to merely a gleam. He was a railwayman of some prestige, I was glad to see, who was treated with respect if not quite deference, and his were the views they listened to.

He gave the railway investigators a photograph of Johnson and said that while he hadn't actually seen him pour liquid into the radio, he could say that it was in this man's roomette that he had awakened bound and gagged, and he could say that it was this man who had attacked Titmuss, when he, Titmuss, went back to plant the flares.

'Was that so?' they asked me. Could I identify him positively?

'Positively,' I said.

They moved on to Sheridan's death. A sad business, they said. Apart from making a record of the time of the occurrence and the various radio messages, there was little to be done. The family had made no complaint to or about the railway company. Any other conclusions would have to be reached at the official inquest.

'That wasn't too bad, eh?' George said afterwards.

'Would you come in uniform to the races?' I asked.

'If that's what you want.'

'Yes, please.' I gave him a card with directions and instructions and a pass cajoled from Nell to get him in through the gates.

'See you tomorrow, eh?'

I nodded. 'At eleven o'clock.'

We went our different ways, and with some reluctance but definite purpose I sought out a doctor recommended by the hotel and presented myself for inspection.

The doctor was thin, growing old and inclined to make jokes over his half-moon glasses.

'Ah,' he said, when I'd removed my shirt. 'Does it hurt when you cough?'

'It hurts when I do practically anything, as a matter of fact.'

'We'd better have a wee X-ray then, don't you think?'

I agreed to the X-ray and waited around for ages until he reappeared with a large sheet of celluloid which he clipped in front of a light.

'Well, now,' he said, 'the good news is that we don't have any broken ribs or chipped vertebrae.'

'Fine.' I was relieved and perhaps a bit surprised.

'What we do have is a fractured shoulder blade.'

I stared at him. 'I didn't think that was possible.'

'Anything's possible,' he said. 'See that,' he pointed, 'that's a real granddaddy of a break. Goes right across, goes right through. The bottom part of your left scapula,' he announced cheerfully, 'is to all intents and purposes detached from the top.'

'Um,' I said blankly. 'What do we do about it?'

He looked at me over the half-moons. 'Rivets,' he said, 'might be extreme, don't you think? Heavy strapping, immobility for two weeks, that'll do the trick.'

'What about,' I said, 'if we do nothing at all? Will it mend?'

'Probably. Bones are remarkable. Young bones especially. You could try a sling. You'd be more comfortable though, if you let me strap your arm firmly skin to skin to your side and chest, under your shirt.'

I shook my head and said I wanted to go on a sort of honeymoon to Hawaii.

'People who go on honeymoons with broken bones,' he said with a straight face, 'must be ready to giggle.'

I giggled there and then. I asked him for a written medical report and the X-ray, and paid him for them, and bore away my evidence.

Stopping at a pharmacy on my way back to the hotel, I bought an elbow-supporting sling made of wide black ribbon, which I tried on for effect in the shop, and which made things a good deal better. I was wearing it when I opened my door in the evening, first to the Brigadier on his arrival from Heathrow, and then to Bill Baudelaire, from Toronto.

Bill Baudelaire looked around the sitting room and commented to the Brigadier about the lavishness of my expense account.

'Expense account, my foot!' the Brigadier said, drinking my Scotch. 'He's paying for it himself.'

Bill Baudelaire looked shocked. 'You can't let him,' he said.

'Didn't he tell you?' the Brigadier laughed. 'He's as rich as Croesus.'

'No . . . he didn't tell me.'

'He never tells anybody. He's afraid of it.'

Bill Baudelaire, with his carroty hair and pitted skin, looked at me with acute curiosity.

'Why do you do this job?' he said.

The Brigadier gave me no time to answer. 'What else would he do to pass the time? Play backgammon? This game is better. Isn't that it, Tor?'

'This game is better,' I agreed.

The Brigadier smiled. Although shorter than Bill Baudelaire, and older and leaner, and with fairer, thinning hair, he seemed to fill more of the room. I might be three inches taller than he, but I had the impression always of looking up to him, not down.

'To work, then,' he suggested. 'Strategy, tactics, plan of attack.'

He had brought some papers from England, though some were still to come, and he spread them out on the coffee table so that all of us, leaning forward, could see them.

'It was a good guess of yours, Tor, that the report on the cats was a computer print-out, because of its lack of headings. The Master of the college had a call

from Mercer Lorrimore at eight this morning . . . must
have been midnight here . . . empowering him to tell us
everything, as you'd asked. The Master gave us the
name of the veterinary pathology lab he'd employed
and sent us a fax of the letter he'd received from them.
Is that the same as the one in Filmer's briefcase, Tor?'

He pushed a paper across and I glanced at it. 'Identical, except for the headings.'

'Good. The path lab confirmed they kept the letter
stored in their computer but they don't know yet how
anyone outside could get a printout. We're still trying.
So are they. They don't like it happening.'

'How about a list of their employees,' I said,
'including temporary secretaries or wizard hacker office
boys?'

'Where do you get such language?' the Brigadier
protested. He produced a sheet of names. 'This was the
best they could do.'

I read the list. None of the names was familiar.

'Do you really need to know the connection?' Bill
Baudelaire asked.

'It would be neater,' I said.

The Brigadier nodded. 'John Millington is working
on it. We're talking to him by telephone before tomorrow's meeting. Now, the next thing,' he turned to me.
'That conveyance you saw in the briefcase. As you
suggested, we checked the number SF 90155 with the
Land Registry.' He chuckled with all George Burley's

enjoyment. 'That alone would have been worth your trip.'

He explained why. Bill Baudelaire said, 'We've got him, then,' with great satisfaction: and the joint Commanders-in-Chief began deciding in which order they would fire off their accumulated salvoes.

Julius Apollo walked into a high-up private room in Exhibition Park racecourse on Tuesday morning to sign and receive, as he thought, certification that he was the sole owner of Laurentide Ice, which would run in his name that afternoon.

The room was the President of the racecourse's conference room, having a desk attended by three comfortable armchairs at one end, with a table surrounded by eight similar chairs at the other. The doorway from the passage was at mid-point between the groupings, so that one turned right to the desk, left to the conference table. A fawn carpet covered the floor, horse pictures covered the walls, soft yellow leather covered the armchairs: a cross between comfort and practicality, without windows but with interesting spotlighting from recesses in the ceiling.

When Filmer entered, both of the Directors of Security were sitting behind the desk, with three senior members of the Vancouver Jockey Club and the British Columbia Racing Commission seated at the conference table. They were there to give weight to the proceedings and to bear witness afterwards, but they had chosen to be there simply as observers, and they had agreed not to interrupt with questions. They would take notes, they said, and ask questions afterwards, if necessary.

Three more people and I waited on the other side of a closed door which led from the conference table end of the room into a serving pantry, and from there out again into the passage.

When Filmer arrived I went along the passage and locked the door he had come in by, and put the key in the pocket of my grey raincoat, which I wore buttoned to the neck. Then I walked back along the passage and into the serving pantry where I stood quietly behind the others waiting there.

A microphone stood on the desk in front of the Directors, with another on the conference table, both of them leading to a tape recorder. Out in the serving pantry, an amplifier quietly relayed everything that was said inside.

Bill Baudelaire's deep voice greeted Filmer, invited him to sit in the chair in front of the desk, and said, 'You know Brigadier Catto, of course?'

As the two men had glared at each other times without number, yes, he knew him.

'And these other gentlemen are from the Jockey Club and Racing Commission here in Vancouver.'

'What *is* this?' Filmer asked truculently. 'All I want is some paperwork. A formality.'

The Brigadier said, 'We are taking this opportunity

442

to make some preliminary enquiries into some racing matters, and it seemed best to do it now, as so many of the people involved are in Vancouver at this time.'

'What are you talking about?' Filmer said.

'We should explain,' the Brigadier said smoothly, 'that we are recording what is said in this room this morning. This is not a formal trial or an official enquiry, but what is said here may be repeated at any trial or enquiry in the future. We would ask you to bear this in mind.'

Filmer said strongly, 'I object to this.'

'At any future trial or Jockey Club enquiry,' Bill Baudelaire said, 'you may of course be accompanied by a legal representative. We will furnish you with a copy of the tape of this morning's preliminary proceedings which you may care to give to your lawyer.'

'You can't do this,' Filmer said. 'I'm not staying.'

When he went to the door he had entered by, he found it locked.

'Let me out,' Filmer said furiously. 'You can't do this.'

In the serving pantry Mercer Lorrimore took a deep breath, opened the door to the conference room, went through and closed it behind him.

'Good morning, Julius,' he said.

'What are you doing here?' Filmer's voice was surprised but not overwhelmingly dismayed. 'Tell them to give me my paper and be done with it.'

'Sit down, Julius,' Mercer said. He was speaking into

the conference table microphone, his voice sounding much louder than Filmer's. 'Sit down by the desk.'

'The preliminary enquiry, Mr Filmer,' the Brigadier's voice said, 'is principally into your actions before and during, and in conjunction with, the journey of the race train.' There was a pause, presumably a wait for Filmer to settle. Then the Brigadier's voice again, 'Mr Lorrimore . . . may I ask you . . .?'

Mercer cleared his throat. 'My son Sheridan,' he said evenly, 'who died two days ago, suffered intermittently from a mental instability which led him sometimes to do bizarre . . . and unpleasant . . . things.'

There was a pause. No words from Filmer.

Mercer said, 'To his great regret, there was an incident of that sort, back in May. Sheridan killed . . . some animals. The bodies were taken from where they were found by a veterinary pathologist who then performed private autopsies on them.' He paused again. The strain was clear in his voice, but he didn't falter. 'You, Julius, indicated to my family on the train that you knew about this incident, and three of us . . . my wife Bambi, my son Sheridan and myself . . . all understood during that evening that you would use Sheridan's regrettable act as leverage to get hold of my horse, Voting Right.'

Filmer said furiously, 'That damned play!'

'Yes,' Mercer said. 'It put things very clearly. After Sheridan died, I gave permission to the Master of my son's college, to the British Jockey Club Security Service, and to the veterinary pathologist himself, to find out how that piece of information came into your possession.'

'We did find out,' the Brigadier said, and repeated what a triumphant John Millington had relayed to us less than an hour ago. 'It happened by chance ... by accident. You, Mr Filmer, owned a horse, trained in England at Newmarket, which died. You suspected poison of some sort and insisted on a post-mortem, making your trainer arrange to have some organs sent to the path lab. The lab wrote a letter to your trainer saying there was no foreign substance in the organs, and at your request they later sent a copy of the letter to you. One of their less bright computer operators had meanwhile loaded your letter on to a very private disk which she shouldn't have used, and in some way chain-loaded it, so that you received not only a copy of your letter but copies of three other letters besides, letters which were private and confidential.' The Brigadier paused. 'We know this is so,' he said, 'because when one of our operators asked the lab to print out a copy for us, your own letter and the others came out attached to it, chain-loaded into the same secret document name.'

The pathologist, Millington had said, was in total disarray and thinking of scrapping the lab's computer for a new one. 'But it wasn't the computer,' he said. 'It was a nitwit girl, who apparently thought the poison enquiry on the horse was top secret also, and put it on the top-secret disk. They can't sack her, she left weeks ago.'

'Could the pathologist be prosecuted for the cover-up?' the Brigadier had asked.

'Doubtful,' Millington had said, 'now that Sheridan's dead.'

Filmer's voice, slightly hoarse, came out of the loud-speaker into the pantry. 'This is rubbish.'

'You kept the letter,' the Brigadier said. 'It was dynamite, if you could find who it referred to. No doubt you kept all three of the letters, though the other two didn't concern criminal acts. Then you saw one day in your local paper that Mercer Lorrimore was putting up money for a new college library. And you would have had to ask only one question to find out that Mercer Lorrimore's son had left that college in a hurry during May. After that, you would have found that no one would say why. You became sure that the letter referred to Sheridan Lorrimore. You did nothing with your information until you heard that Mercer Lorrimore would be on the Transcontinental Race Train, and then you saw an opportunity of exploring the possibility of blackmailing Mr Lorrimore into letting you have his horse, Voting Right.'

'You can't prove any of this,' Filmer said defiantly.

'We all believe,' said Bill Baudelaire's voice, 'that with you, Mr Filmer, it is the urge to crush people and make them suffer that sets you going. We know you could afford to buy good horses. We know that for you simply owning horses isn't enough.'

'Save me the sermon,' Filmer said. 'And if you can't put up, shut up.'

'Very well,' the Brigadier said. 'We'll ask our next visitor to come in, please.'

Daffodil Quentin, who was standing beside George in the pantry and had been listening with parted mouth and growing anger, opened the dividing door dramatically and slammed it shut behind her.

'You unspeakable toad,' her voice said vehemently over the loudspeaker.

Attagirl, I thought.

She was wearing a scarlet dress and a wide shiny black belt and carrying a large shiny black handbag. Under the high curls and in a flaming rage, she attacked as an avenging angel in full spate.

'I will never give you or sell you my half of Laurentide Ice,' she said forcefully, 'and you can threaten and blackmail until you're blue in the face. You can frighten my stable lad until you think you're God Almighty, but you can't from now on frighten *me* – and I think you're contemptible and should be put in a zoo.'

CHAPTER TWENTY-ONE

Bill Baudelaire, who had persuaded her to come with him to Vancouver, cleared his throat and sounded as if he were trying not to laugh.

'Mrs Quentin,' he said to the world at large, 'is prepared to testify . . .'

'You bet I am,' Daffodil interrupted.

' . . . that you threatened to have her prosecuted for killing one of her own horses if she didn't give . . . *give* . . . you her remaining share of Laurentide Ice.'

'You used me,' Daffodil said furiously. 'You bought your way on to the train and you were all charm and smarm and all you were aiming to do was ingratiate yourself with Mercer Lorrimore so you could sneer at him and cause him pain and take away his horse. You make me puke.'

'I don't have to listen to this,' Filmer said.

'Yes, you damned well do. It's time someone told you to your face what a slimy putrid blob of spit you are and gave you back some of the hatred you sow.'

'Er,' Bill Baudelaire said. 'We have here a letter from

Mrs Quentin's insurance company, written yesterday, saying that they made exhaustive tests on her horse that died of colic and they are satisfied that they paid her claim correctly. We also have here an affidavit from the stable lad, Lenny Higgs, to the effect that you learned about the colic and the specially numbered feeds for Laurentide Ice from him during one of your early visits to the horse car. He goes on to swear that he was later frightened into saying that Mrs Quentin gave him some food to give to her horse who died of colic.' He cleared his throat. 'As you have heard, the insurance company are satisfied that whatever she gave her horse didn't cause its death. Lenny Higgs further testifies that the man who frightened him, by telling him he would be sent to prison where he would catch AIDS and die, that man is an ex-baggage handler once employed by VIA Rail, name of Alex Mitchell McLachlan.'

'*What*?' For the first time there was fear in Filmer's voice, and I found it sweet.

'Lenny Higgs positively identifies him from this photograph.' There was a pause while Bill Baudelaire handed it over. 'This man travelled in the racegoers' part of the train under the name of Johnson. During yesterday, the photograph was shown widely to VIA employees in Toronto and Montreal, and he was several times identified as Alex McLachlan.'

There was silence where Filmer might have spoken.

'You were observed to be speaking to McLachlan . . .'

'You bet you were,' Daffodil interrupted. 'You were talking to him . . . arguing with him . . . at Thunder Bay, and I didn't like the look of him. This is his picture. I identify it too. You used him to frighten Lenny, and you told me Lenny would give evidence against me, and I didn't know you'd *frightened* the poor boy with such a terrible threat. You told me he hated me and would be glad to tell lies about me . . .' The enormity of it almost choked her. 'I don't know how you can live with yourself. I don't know how anyone can be so full of *sin*.'

Her voice resonated with the full old meaning of the word: an offence against God. It was powerful, I thought, and it had silenced Filmer completely.

'It may come as an anticlimax,' the Brigadier said after a pause, 'but we will now digress to another matter entirely. One that will be the subject of a full stewards' enquiry at the Jockey Club, Portland Square, in the near future. I refer to the ownership of a parcel of land referred to in the Land Registry as SF 90155.'

The Brigadier told me later that it was at that point that Filmer turned grey and began to sweat.

'This parcel of land,' his military voice went on, 'is known as West Hillside Stables, Newmarket. This was a stables owned by Ivor Horfitz and run by his paid private trainer in such a dishonest manner that Ivor Horfitz was barred from racing – and racing stables –

for life. He was instructed to sell West Hillside Stables, as he couldn't set foot there, and it was presumed that he had. However, the new owner in his turn wants to sell and has found a buyer, but the buyer's lawyers' searches have been very thorough, and they have discovered that the stables were never Horfitz's to sell. They belonged, and they still do legally belong, to you, Mr Filmer.'

There was a faint sort of groan which might have come from Filmer.

'That being so, we will have to look into your relationship with Ivor Horfitz and with the illegal matters that were carried on for years at West Hillside Stables. We also have good reason to believe that Ivor Horfitz's son, Jason, knows you owned the stables and were concerned in its operation, and that Jason let that fact out to his friend, the stable lad Paul Shacklebury who, as you will remember, was the subject of your trial for conspiracy to murder, which took place earlier this year.'

There was a long long silence.

Daffodil's voice said, murmuring, 'I don't understand any of this, do you?'

Mercer, as quietly, answered: 'They've found a way of warning him off for life.'

'Oh good, but it sounds so dull.'

'Not to him,' Mercer murmured.

'We'll now return,' Bill Baudelaire's voice said more loudly, 'to the matter of your attempt to wreck the train.' He coughed. 'Will you please come in, Mr Burley?'

I smiled at George who had been listening to the Horfitz part in non-comprehension and the rest in horrified amazement.

'We're on,' I said, removing my raincoat and laying it on a serving counter. 'After you.'

He and I, the last in the pantry, went through the door. He was wearing his grey uniform and carrying his conductor's cap. I was revealed in Tommy's grey trousers, grey and white shirt, deep-yellow waistcoat and tidy striped tie. Polished, pressed, laundered, brushed: a credit to VIA Rail.

Julius Filmer saw the Conductor and a waiter he'd hardly noticed in his preoccupation with his own affairs. The Brigadier and Bill Baudelaire saw the waiter for the first time, and there was an awakening and realization on each of their faces. Although I'd told them by now that I'd worked with the crew, they hadn't truly understood how perfect had been the bright camouflage.

'Oh, that's who you are!' exclaimed Daffodil who was sitting now in one of the chairs round the conference table. 'I couldn't place you, outside.'

Mercer patted her hand which lay on the table, and gave me the faintest of smiles over her head. The three Vancouver bigwigs took me at face value, knowing no different.

'Would you come forward, please?' Bill Baudelaire said.

George and I both advanced past the conference table until we were nearer the desk. The two Directors were seated behind the desk, Filmer in the chair in front of it. Filmer's neck was rigid, his eyes were dark, and the sweat ran down his temples.

'The Conductor, George Burley,' Bill Baudelaire said, 'yesterday gave VIA Rail an account of three acts of sabotage against the race train. Disaster was fortunately averted on all three occasions, but we believe that all these dangerous situations were the work of Alex McLachlan who was acting on your instructions and was paid by you.'

'No,' Filmer said dully.

'Our enquiries are not yet complete,' Bill Baudelaire said, 'but we know that the VIA Rail offices in Montreal were visited three or four weeks ago by a man answering in general to your description who said he was researching for a thesis on the motivations of industrial sabotage. He asked for the names of any railroad saboteurs so that he could interview them and see what made them tick. He was given a short list of people no longer to be employed on the railroads in any capacity.'

Heads would roll, the VIA Rail executive had said. That list, although to be found in every railway station office in the country, should *never* have been given to an outsider.

'McLachlan's name is on that list,' Bill Baudelaire observed.

Filmer said nothing. The realization of total disaster showed in every line of his body, in every twitch in his face.

'As we said,' Bill Baudelaire went on, 'McLachlan travelled on the train under the name of Johnson. During the first evening, at a place called Cartier, he uncoupled Mr Lorrimore's private car and left it dead and dark on the track. The railroad investigators believe he waited in the vicinity to see the next train along, the regular transcontinental Canadian, come and crash into the Lorrimores' car. He had always been around to watch the consequences of his sabotage in the past: acts he had been sent to prison for committing. When the race train returned to pick up the Lorrimores' car, he simply reboarded and continued on the journey.'

'He shouldn't have done it,' Filmer said.

'We know that. We also know that in speech you continually mixed up Winnipeg with Vancouver. You instructed McLachlan to wreck the train before Winnipeg, when you meant before Vancouver.'

Filmer looked dumbfounded.

'That's right,' Daffodil said, sitting up straight, 'Winnipeg and Vancouver. He got them mixed up all the time.'

'In Banff,' Bill Baudelaire said, 'someone loosened the drain plug on the fuel tank for the boiler that provides steam heat for the train. If it hadn't been discovered, the train would have had to go through a freezing evening in the Rockies without heat for horses or passengers. Mr Burley, would you tell us at first hand about both of these occurrences, please?'

George gave his accounts of the uncoupling and the missing fuel with a railwayman's outrage quivering in his voice.

Filmer looked shrunken and sullen.

'During that last evening,' Bill Baudelaire said, 'you decided to cancel your instructions to McLachlan and you went forward to speak to him. You had a disagreement with him. You told him to do no more, but you had reckoned without McLachlan. He really is a perpetual saboteur. You misunderstood his mentality. You could start him off, but you couldn't stop him. You were responsible for putting him on the train to wreck it, and we will make that responsibility stick.'

Filmer began weakly to protest, but Bill Baudelaire gave him no respite.

'Your man McLachlan,' he said, 'knocked out the Conductor and left him tied up and gagged in the roomette he had been given in the name of Johnson. McLachlan then put the radio out of order by pouring liquid into it. These acts were necessary, as he saw it, because he had already, at a place called Revelstoke, removed oily waste from the journal-box holding one of the axles under the horse car. One of two things could then happen: if the train crew failed to notice the axle getting red hot, the axle would break, cause damage, possibly derail the train. If it were discovered, the train would stop for the axle to be cooled. In either case, the Conductor would radio to the despatcher in Vancouver, who would radio to the Conductor of the regular train, the Canadian, coming along behind, to tell him to stop, so that there shouldn't be a collision. Is that clear?'

It was pellucid to everyone in the room.

'The train crew,' he went on, 'did discover the hot axle and the engineers stopped the train. No one could find the Conductor, who was tied up in Johnson's roomette. No one could radio to Vancouver as the radio wouldn't work. The only recourse left to the crew was to send a man back along the line to light flares, to stop the Canadian in the old historic way.' He paused briefly. 'McLachlan, a railwayman, knew this would happen, so when the train stopped he went himself along the track, armed himself with a piece of wood and lay in wait for whoever came with the flares.'

Filmer stared darkly, hearing it for the first time.

'McLachlan attacked the man with the flares, but by good fortune failed to knock him out. It was this man here who was sent with the flares.' He nodded in my direction. 'He succeeded in lighting the flares and stopping the Canadian.' He paused and said to me, 'Is that correct?'

'Yes, sir,' I said. Word-perfect, I thought.

He went on, 'The race-train engineers cooled the

journal-box with snow and refilled it with oil, and the train went on its way. The Conductor was discovered in McLachlan's roomette. McLachlan did not reboard the train that time, and there will presently be a warrant issued for his arrest. You, Mr Filmer, are answerable with McLachlan for what happened.'

'I told him not to.' Filmer's voice was a rising shout of protest. 'I didn't want him to.'

His lawyers would love that admission, I thought.

'McLachlan's assault was serious,' Bill Baudelaire said calmly. He picked up my X-ray and the doctor's report, and waved them in Filmer's direction. 'McLachlan broke this crewman's shoulder blade. The crewman has positively identified McLachlan as the man who attacked him. The Conductor has positively identified McLachlan as the passenger known to him as Johnson. The Conductor has suffered concussion, and we have here another doctor's report on that.'

No doubt a good defence lawyer might have seen gaps in the story, but at that moment Filmer was beleaguered and confounded and hampered by the awareness of guilt. He was past thinking analytically, past asking how the crewman had escaped from McLachlan and been able to complete his mission, past wondering what was conjecture with the sabotage and what was provable fact.

The sight of Filmer reduced to sweating rubble was the purest revenge that any of us – Mercer, Daffodil, Val Catto, Bill Baudelaire, George Burley or I – could have envisaged, and we had it in full measure. Do unto others, I thought drily, what they have done to your friends.

'We will proceed against you on all counts,' the Brigadier said magisterially.

Control disintegrated in Filmer. He came up out of his chair fighting mad, driven to lashing out, to raging against his defeat, to pushing someone else for his troubles, even though it could achieve no purpose.

He made me his target. It couldn't have been a subconscious awareness that it was I who had been his real enemy all along: much the reverse, I supposed, in that he saw me as the least of the people there, the one he could best bash with most impunity.

I saw him coming a mile off. I also saw the alarm on the Brigadier's face and correctly interpreted it.

If I fought back as instinct dictated, if I did to Filmer the sort of damage I'd told the Brigadier I'd done to McLachlan, I would weaken our case.

Thought before action; if one had time.

Thought could be flash fast. I had time. *It would be an unexpected bonus for us if the damage were the other way round.*

He had iron-pumping muscle power. It would indeed be damage.

Oh well . . .

I rolled my head a shade sideways and he punched me twice, quite hard, on the cheek and the jaw. I went back with a crash against the nearby wall, which wasn't all that good for the shoulder blade, and I slid the bottom of my spine down the wall until I was sitting on the floor, knees bent up, my head back against the paintwork.

Filmer was above me, lunging about and delivering another couple of stingingly heavy cuffs, and I thought, come on, guys, it's high time for the arrival of the cavalry, and the cavalry – the Mounties – in the shape of George Burley and Bill Baudelaire obligingly grabbed Filmer's swinging arms and hauled him away.

I stayed where I was, feeling slightly pulped, watching the action.

The Brigadier pressed a button on the desk which soon resulted in the arrival of two large racecourse security guards, one of whom, to Filmer's furious astonishment, placed a manacle upon the Julius Apollo wrist.

'You can't do this,' he shouted.

The guard phlegmatically fastened the hanging half of the metal bracelet to his own thick wrist.

One of the Vancouver top brass spoke for the first time, in an authoritative voice. 'Take Mr Filmer to the security office and detain him until I come down.'

The guards said, 'Yes, sir.'

They moved like tanks. Filmer, humiliated to his socks, was tugged away between them as if of no account. One might almost have felt sorry for him . . . if one hadn't remembered Paul Shacklebury and Ezra Gideon for whom he had had no pity.

Daffodil Quentin's eyes were stretched wide open.

She came over and looked down at me with compassion.

'You poor boy,' she said, horrified. 'How perfectly *dreadful.*'

'Mr Burley,' Bill Baudelaire said smoothly, 'would you be so kind as to escort Mrs Quentin for us? If you turn right in the passage, you'll find some double doors ahead of you. Through there is the reception room where the passengers and the other owners from the train are gathering for cocktails and lunch. Would you take Mrs Quentin there? We'll look after this crewman . . . get him some help. . . . And we would be pleased if you could yourself stay for lunch.'

George said to me, 'Are you all right, Tommy?' and I said, 'Yes, George,' and he chuckled with kind relief and said it would be a pleasure, eh?, to stay for lunch.

He stood back to let Daffodil lead the way out of the far door, and when she reached there she paused and looked back.

'The poor boy,' she said again. 'Julius Filmer's a *beast.*'

The Vancouver Jockey Club men rose and made courteous noises of sympathy in my direction; said they would hand Filmer on to the police with a report of the assault; said we would no doubt be needed to make statements later. They then followed Daffodil, as they were the hosts of the party.

When they'd gone, the Brigadier switched off the machine that had recorded every word.

'Poor boy, my foot,' he said to me. 'You chose to let him hit you. I saw you.'

I smiled a little ruefully, acknowledging his perception.

'He couldn't!' Mercer protested, drawing nearer. 'No one could just let himself be . . .'

'He could and he did.' The Brigadier came round from behind the desk. 'Quick thinking. Brilliant.'

'But why?' Mercer said.

'To tie the slippery Mr Filmer in tighter knots.' The Brigadier stood in front of me, put a casual hand down to mine and pulled me to my feet.

'Did you truly?' Mercer said to me in disbelief.

'Mm.' I nodded and straightened a bit, trying not to wince.

'Don't worry about him,' the Brigadier said. 'He used to ride bucking broncos, and God knows what else.'

The three of them stood as in a triumvirate, looking at me in my uniform, as if I'd come from a different planet.

'I sent him on the train,' the Brigadier said, 'to stop Filmer doing whatever he was planning.' He smiled briefly. 'A sort of match . . . a two-horse race.'

'It seems to have been neck and neck now and then,' Mercer said.

The Brigadier considered it. 'Maybe. But our runner had the edge.'

*

Mercer Lorrimore and I watched the races from a smaller room next to the large one where the reception was taking place. We were in the racecourse President's private room, to which he could retire with friends if he wanted to, and it was furnished accordingly in extreme comfort and soft turquoise and gold.

The President had been disappointed but understanding that Mercer felt he couldn't attend the lunch party so soon after his son's death, and had offered this room instead. Mercer had asked if I might join him, so he and I drank the President's champagne and looked down from his high window to the track far below, and talked about Filmer, mostly.

'I liked him, you know,' Mercer said, wonderingly.

'He can be charming.'

'Bill Baudelaire tried to warn me at Winnipeg,' he said, 'but I wouldn't listen. I really thought that his trial had been a travesty, and that he was innocent. He told me about it himself . . . he said he didn't bear the Jockey Club any malice.'

I smiled. 'Extreme malice,' I said. 'He threatened them to their faces that he would throw any available spanner into their international works. McLachlan was some spanner.'

Mercer sat down in one of the huge armchairs. I stayed standing by the window.

'Why was Filmer prosecuted,' he asked, 'if there was such a poor case?'

'There was a cast-iron case,' I said. 'Filmer sent a

particularly vicious frightener to intimidate all four prosecution witnesses, and the cast iron became splinters. This time . . . this morning . . . we thought we'd stage a sort of preliminary trial, at which the witnesses couldn't have been reached, and have it all on record in case anyone retracted afterwards.'

He looked at me sceptically. 'Did you think I could be intimidated? I assure you I can't. Not any more.'

After a pause I said, 'You have Xanthe. Ezra Gideon had daughters and grandchildren. One of the witnesses in the Paul Shacklebury case backed away because of what she was told would happen to her sixteen-year-old daughter if she gave evidence.'

'Dear God,' he said, dismayed. 'Surely he'll be sent to prison?'

'He'll be warned off, anyhow, and that's what he wants least. He had Paul Shacklebury killed to prevent it. I think we will have got rid of him from racing. For the rest . . . we'll have to see what the Canadian police and VIA Rail can do, and hope they'll find McLachlan.'

Let McLachlan not be eaten by a bear, I thought. (And he hadn't been: he was picked up for stealing tools from a railway yard in Edmonton a week later, and subsequently convicted with Filmer of the serious ancient offence of attempted train-wrecking, chiefly on the evidence of a temporary crew member in his VIA Rail clothes. VIA put me on their personnel list retroactively, and shook my hand. Filmer was imprisoned despite his defence that he had not given specific instructions to McLachlan on any count and had tried to stop him before the end. It was proved that he had actively recruited a violent saboteur: any later possible change of mind was held to be irrelevant. Filmer never did find out that I wasn't a waiter, because it wasn't a question his lawyers ever thought to ask, and it went much against him with the jury that he'd violently attacked a defenceless rail employee without provocation in front of many witnesses even though he knew of the broken scapula. The Brigadier kept a straight face throughout. 'It worked a treat,' he said afterwards. 'Wasn't Daffodil Quentin a trouper, convincing them the poor boy had been brutally beaten for no reason except that he'd saved them all from being killed in their beds? Lovely stuff. It made nonsense of the change-of-heart defence. They couldn't wait to find Filmer guilty after that.' McLachlan in his turn swore that I'd nearly murdered him, out on the track. I said he'd tripped and knocked himself out on the rails. McLachlan could produce no X-rays and wasn't believed, to his fury. 'Broken bone or not, that waiter can fight like a goddam tiger,' he said. 'No way could Filmer beat him up.' Filmer, however, had done so. It had been seen, and was a fact.)

On the Tuesday of the Jockey Club Race Train Stakes at Exhibition Park, with the trial still months ahead, and the feel of Filmer's fists a reality not a memory, the racecourse President came into his private room to see Mercer and me and to show us that if we drew the curtains along the right-hand side wall, we could see into the reception room.

'They can't see into here,' he said. 'It's one-way glass.' He pulled strings and revealed the party. 'I hear the meeting went well this morning except for the end.' He looked at me questioningly. 'Mr Lorrimore and Bill Baudelaire asked that you be treated as a most honoured guest . . . but shouldn't you be resting?'

'No point, sir,' I said, 'and I wouldn't miss the great race for anything.'

Through the window one could fascinatingly see all the faces grown so familiar during the past ten days. The Unwins, the Redi-Hots, the Youngs . . .

'If I might ask you – ?' I said.

'Ask the world, according to Bill Baudelaire and Brigadier Catto.'

I smiled. 'Not the world. That young woman over there in the grey suit, with the fair hair in a plait and a worried expression.'

'Nell Richmond,' Mercer said.

'Would you mind if she came in here for a while?'

'Not in the least,' the President said, and within minutes could be seen talking to her. He couldn't have told her who to expect in his room, though, because when she came in and saw me she was surprised and, I had to think, joyful.

'You're on your feet! Daffodil said the waiter was hurt badly.' Her voice died away and she swallowed. 'I was afraid . . .'

'That we wouldn't get to Hawaii?'

'Oh.' It was a sound somewhere between a laugh and a sob. 'I don't think I like you.'

'Try harder.'

'Well . . .' She opened her handbag and began to look inside it, and glanced up and saw all the people next door. 'How great,' she said to Mercer. 'You're both with us, even if you're not.' She produced a folded piece of paper and gave it to me. 'I have to go back to sort out the lunch places.'

I didn't want her to go. I said, 'Nell . . .' and heard it sound too full of anxiety, too full of plain physical battering, but it was past calling back.

Her face changed. The games died away.

'Read that when I've gone,' she said. 'And I'll be there . . . through the glass.'

She went out of the President's room without looking back and soon reappeared among the others. I unfolded the paper slowly, not wanting it to be bad news, and found it was a telex.

It said:

RICHMOND, FOUR SEASONS HOTEL, VAN-COUVER. CONFIRM YOUR TWO WEEKS VACATION STARTING IMMEDIATELY.
MERRY. HAVE A GOOD TIME.

I closed my eyes.

'Is that despair?' Mercer said.

I opened my eyes. The telex still read the same way. I handed it to him, and he read it also.

'I dare say,' he said ironically, 'that Val Catto will match this.'

'If he doesn't, I'll resign.'

We spent the afternoon companionably and watched the preliminary races with the interest of devotees. When it was time for the Jockey Club Race Train Stakes Mercer decided that, Sheridan or not, he would go down to see Voting Right saddled, as he could go and return by express elevator to our eyrie to watch the race.

When he'd gone and the room next door had mostly emptied, I looked down on the flags and the banners and the streamers and balloons and the razzamatazz with which Exhibition Park had met the challenge of Assiniboia Downs and Woodbine and thought of all that had happened on the journey across Canada, and I wondered whether I would find flat-footing round British racecourses in the rain a relaxation or a bore, wondered if I would go on doing it; thought that time would show me the way, as it always had.

I thought of Mrs Baudelaire, whom I would never meet, and wished she could have watched this next race; thought of Aunt Viv with gratitude.

Mercer came back looking happy: happier in a peaceful way, as if he had settled ghosts.

'Daffodil is amazing,' he said. 'She's down there

holding court, kissing Laurentide Ice, laughing, on top of the world. There seems to be no difficulty in the horse running, even though half still presumably belongs to Filmer.'

'It's in Daffodil's name on the racecard,' I said.

'So it is. And the Youngs . . . Rose and Cumber . . . with Sparrowgrass, and the people with Redi-Hot. It's like a club, down there. They were pleased, they said, that I had come.'

They genuinely would be, I thought. The party was incomplete without Mercer.

There was a large television set in the President's room, through which one could hear the bugles preceding the runners to the track and hear crowd noises and the commentary. Nothing like being down near the action, but better than silence. The race was being broadcast live throughout Canada and recorded for the rest of the world, and there was a long spiel going on about the Growing International Flavour of Canadian Racing, and how the Great Transcontinental Mystery Race Train had awakened enormous interest everywhere and was altogether A Good Thing For Canada.

Mercer, who had been prepared to do a lot for Canadian racing, watched Voting Right lead the pre-race parade, the horse on the screen appearing larger to us than the real one far down on the track.

'He's looking well,' he told me. 'I do hope . . .' He

stopped. 'I think he may be the best of all my horses. The best to come. But he may not be ready today. It's perhaps too soon. Sparrowgrass is favourite. It would be nice for the Youngs . . .'

We watched Sparrowgrass prance along in his turn.

'Cumber Young has found out it was Filmer who bought . . . or took . . . Ezra Gideon's horses. If Cumber had been up here this morning, he'd have torn Filmer limb from limb.'

'And been in trouble himself,' I said.

'As Filmer is now?'

'Yes, roughly speaking.'

'Rough is the word.' He looked at me sideways, but made no further comment.

'Watch the horses,' I said mildly. Not the lumps that were swelling.

With a wry twitch of the lips, he turned his attention back to Redi-Hot who looked fit to scorch the dirt, and to Laurentide Ice, the colour of his name.

Nine of the ten runners had travelled on the train. The tenth was a local Vancouver horse bought by the Unwins for the occasion. Not as good a prospect as Upper Gumtree, but the Unwins had wanted to take their part in the climax.

All of the owners and Nell, precious Nell, came to watch the race in the glassed-in part of the stands slanting down in front of the window of the President's room, so that it was over their excited heads that

Mercer and I saw the horses loaded into the stalls and watched the flashing colours sprint out.

'All the way across Canada,' Mercer said as if to himself, 'for the next two minutes.'

All the way across Canada, I thought, in worry and love and grief for his son.

Voting Right shot out of the gate and took a strong lead.

Mercer groaned quietly, 'He's running away.'

Laurentide Ice and Sparrowgrass, next, weren't in a hurry but kept a good pace going, their heads together, not an inch in it. Behind them came five or six in a bunch, with Redi-Hot last.

The sing-song commentary on the television read off the time of the first quarter-mile covered by Voting Right.

'Too fast,' Mercer groaned.

At the half-mile, Voting Right was still in front, still going at high speed, ahead by a full twenty lengths.

'It's hopeless,' Mercer said. 'He'll blow up in the home stretch. He's never been ridden this way before.'

'Didn't you discuss it with the jockey?'

'I just wished him luck. He knows the horse.'

'Maybe the horse has been inspired by the train travel,' I said flippantly.

'To come all this way . . .' Mercer said, taking no notice. 'Oh well, that's racing.'

'He hasn't exactly blown up yet,' I pointed out.

Voting Right was far in front, going down the back stretch a good deal faster than the race train had gone through the Rockies, and he didn't know he was going too fast, he simply kept on going.

The jockeys on Sparrowgrass, Laurentide Ice, Redi-Hot and the others left their move on the leader until they'd come round the last bend and spread out across the track to give themselves a clear run home.

Then Laurentide Ice melted away as Mrs Baudelaire had said he would, and Redi-Hot produced a spurt, and Sparrowgrass with determination began to close at last on Voting Right.

'He's going to lose,' Mercer said despairingly.

It looked like it. One couldn't say for certain, but his time was too fast.

Voting Right kept right on going. Sparrowgrass raced hard to the finish, but it was Voting Right, as Mrs Baudelaire had predicted, Voting Right who had the edge, who went floating past the post in a record time for the track; the best horse Mercer would ever own, the target kept safe from Filmer.

Sheridan lay in untroubled eternity, and who was to say that Mercer wasn't right, that in his impulsive way the son hadn't died to give his father this moment.

Mercer turned towards me, speechless, brimming to overflowing with inexpressible emotion, wanting to laugh, wanting to cry, like all owners at the fulfilment of a dreamed-of success. The sheen in his eyes was the

same the world over: the love of the flying thoroughbred, the perfection of winning a great race.

He found his voice. Looked at me with awakening
humour and a good deal of understanding.

'Thank you,' he said.

IN THE FRAME

My thanks to two professional artists Michael Jeffrey of Australia and Josef Jira of Czechoslovakia who generously showed me their studios, their methods, their minds and their lives.

Also to the many art galleries whose experts gave me information and help and particularly to Peter Johnson of Oscar and Peter Johnson, London SW1, and to the Stud and Stable Gallery, Ascot.

for Caroline
sound asleep

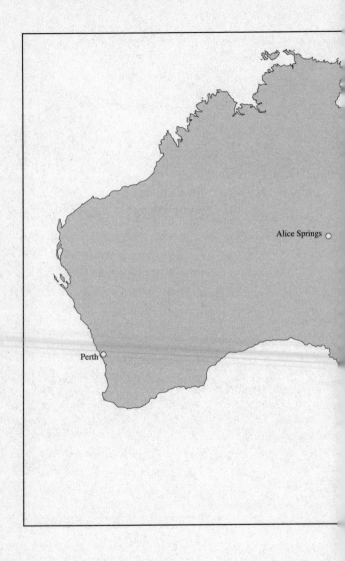

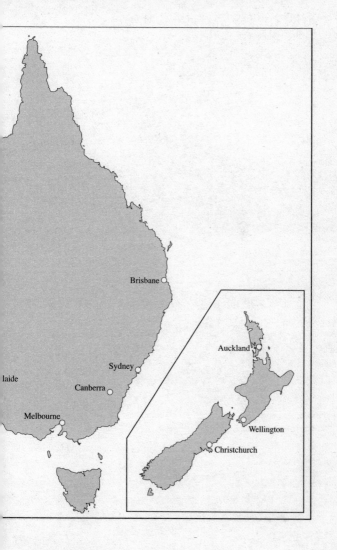

IN THE FRAME

In the Frame was conceived in Czechoslovakia, incubated in Australia and New Zealand and written in England.

We (my wife, Mary, and I) were with the remarkable lady burns-specialist doctor who translates my books into the Czech language in her spare time, when she had business to attend to with a painter friend of hers. She took us briefly to his studio, where our eyes and emotions were bombarded by massed canvases of extraordinary passion and vigorous jumbled colour, chiefly on the subject – if deciphering were possible – of the feeding of the multitude with five fishes. As the painter spoke no English nor we a word of Czech, asking for meaning was impracticable, especially as (according to my translator) he couldn't explain them to her either.

We visited her apartment and found another of his paintings on her wall: again the fishes, the thick brilliant and dark colours, the unfathomable urgent mysterious message.

I began unexpectedly to want to write about a painter, and I asked if we could go back and watch him work. To my translator's surprise he agreed, and for two fascinating silent hours the three of us watched him sticking paint on to canvas with a sort of violent divine energy, using brushes, fingers and even at one point his elbow to satisfy his vision.

I came away shaken. I couldn't imagine being *him*. I needed a less driven artist for my protagonist. I thought I could manage a painter of horses.

Later that year we went to Australia and New Zealand on a book-promotion tour, and there – arranged in advance – I met Michael Jeffrey, one of Australia's foremost horse painters. He, too, generously let me into his studio and gave great advice about the use and mixing of colours.

Back home in England, Mary and I read books about the chemical composition of oil paints and how they adhere to wood and canvas, and we filled our sunroom with easels, linseed, turps and other tools of the trade. Primed by this little knowledge, I put Charles Todd to paper as a painter of horses, alongside the flamboyant abstract genius of his long-time friend, Jik.

Mary finally painted a horse. Its neck was too long. We both learned we were never destined to be artists ourselves, but, nevertheless, *In the Frame* taught us a lot about Art.

CHAPTER ONE

I stood on the outside of disaster, looking in.

There were three police cars outside my cousin's house, and an ambulance with its blue turret light revolving ominously, and people bustling in seriously through his open front door. The chill wind of early autumn blew dead brown leaves sadly on to the driveway, and harsh scurrying clouds threatened worse to come. Six o'clock, Friday evening, Shropshire, England.

Intermittent bright white flashes from the windows spoke of photography in progress within. I slid my satchel from my shoulder and dumped both it and my suitcase on the grass verge, and with justifiable foreboding completed my journey to the house.

I had travelled by train to stay for the weekend. No cousin with car to meet me as promised, so I had started to walk the mile and a half of country road, sure he would come tearing along soon in his muddy Peugeot, full of jokes and apologies and plans.

No jokes.

He stood in the hall, dazed and grey. His body inside

1

his neat business suit looked limp, and his arms hung straight down from the shoulders as if his brain had forgotten they were there. His head was turned slightly towards the sitting-room, the source of the flashes, and his eyes were stark with shock.

'Don?' I said. I walked towards him. 'Donald!'

He didn't hear me. A policeman, however, did. He came swiftly from the sitting-room in his dark blue uniform, took me by the arm and swung me strongly and unceremoniously back towards the door.

'Out of here, sir,' he said. 'If you please.'

The strained eyes slid uncertainly our way.

'Charles . . .' His voice was hoarse.

The policeman's grip loosened very slightly. 'Do you know this man, sir?' he asked Donald.

'I'm his cousin,' I said.

'Oh.' He took his hand off, told me to stay where I was and look after Mr Stuart, and returned to the sitting-room to consult.

'What's happened?' I said.

Don was past answering. His head turned again towards the sitting-room door, drawn to a horror he could no longer see. I disobeyed the police instructions, took ten quiet steps, and looked in.

The familiar room was unfamiliarly bare. No pictures, no ornaments, no edge-to-edge floor covering of oriental rugs. Just bare grey walls, chintz-covered sofas, heavy furniture pushed awry, and a great expanse of dusty wood-block flooring.

And on the floor, my cousin's young wife, bloody and dead.

The big room was scattered with busy police, measuring, photographing, dusting for fingerprints. I knew they were there; didn't see them. All I saw was Regina lying on her back, her face the colour of cream.

Her eyes were half open, still faintly bright, and her lower jaw had fallen loose, outlining brutally the shape of the skull. A pool of urine lay wetly on the parquet around her sprawled legs, and one arm was flung out sideways with the dead white fingers curling upwards as if in supplication.

There had been no mercy.

I looked at the scarlet mess of her head and felt the blood draining from my own.

The policeman who had grabbed me before turned round from his consultation with another, saw me swaying in the doorway, and took quick annoyed strides back to my side.

'I told you to wait outside, sir,' he said with exasperation, stating clearly that my faintness was my own fault.

I nodded dumbly and went back into the hall. Donald was sitting on the stairs, looking at nothing. I sat abruptly on the floor near him and put my head between my knees.

'I . . . f . . . found . . . her,' he said.

I swallowed. What could one say? It was bad enough for me, but he had lived with her, and loved her. The faintness passed away slowly, leaving a sour feeling of sickness. I leaned back against the wall behind me and wished I knew how to help him.

'She's . . . never . . . home . . . on F . . . Fridays,' he said.

'I know.'

'S . . . six. S . . . six o'clock . . . she comes b . . . back. Always.'

'I'll get you some brandy,' I said.

'She shouldn't . . . have been . . . here . . .'

I pushed myself off the floor and went into the dining-room, and it was there that the significance of the bare sitting-room forced itself into consciousness. In the dining-room too there were bare walls, bare shelves, and empty drawers pulled out and dumped on the floor. No silver ornaments. No silver spoons or forks. No collection of antique china. Just a jumble of table mats and napkins and broken glass.

My cousin's house had been burgled. And Regina . . . Regina, who was never home on Fridays . . . had walked in . . .

I went over to the plundered sideboard, flooding with anger and wanting to smash in the heads of all greedy, callous, vicious people who cynically devastated the lives of total strangers. Compassion was all right for saints. What I felt was plain hatred, fierce and basic.

I found two intact glasses, but all the drink had gone. Furiously I stalked through the swing door into the kitchen and filled the electric kettle.

In that room too, the destruction had continued, with stores swept wholesale off the shelves. What valuables, I wondered, did thieves expect to find in kitchens? I jerkily made two mugs of tea and rummaged in Regina's spice cupboard for the cooking brandy, and felt unreasonably triumphant when it proved to be still there. The sods had missed that, at least.

Donald still sat unmoving on the stairs. I pressed the cup of strong sweet liquid into his hands and told him to drink, and he did, mechanically.

'She's never home . . . on Fridays,' he said.

'No,' I agreed, and wondered just how many people knew there was no one home on Fridays.

We both slowly finished the tea. I took his mug and put it with mine on the floor, and sat near him as before. Most of the hall furniture had gone. The small Sheraton desk . . . the studded leather chair . . . the nineteenth-century carriage clock . . .

'Christ, Charles,' he said.

I glanced at his face. There were tears, and dreadful pain. I could do nothing, nothing, to help him.

The impossible evening lengthened to midnight, and beyond. The police, I suppose, were efficient, polite, and not unsympathetic, but they left a distinct impression that they felt their job was to catch criminals, not to succour the victims. It seemed to me that there was also, in many of their questions, a faint hovering doubt, as if it were not unknown for householders to arrange their own well-insured burglaries, and for smooth-seeming swindles to go horrifically wrong.

Donald didn't seem to notice. He answered wearily, automatically, with long pauses sometimes between question and answer.

Yes, the missing goods were well insured.

Yes, they had been insured for years.

Yes, he had been to his office all day as usual.

Yes, he had been out to lunch. A sandwich in a pub.

He was a wine shipper.

His office was in Shrewsbury.

He was thirty-seven years old.

Yes, his wife was much younger. Twenty-two.

He couldn't speak of Regina without stuttering, as if his tongue and lips were beyond his control. She always s . . . spends F . . . Fridays . . . working . . . in a f . . . friend's . . . flower . . . shop.

'Why?'

Donald looked vaguely at the Detective Inspector, sitting opposite him across the dining-room table. The matched antique dining chairs had gone. Donald sat in a garden armchair brought from the sunroom. The Inspector, a constable and I sat on kitchen stools.

'What?'

'Why did she work in a flower shop on Fridays?'

'She . . . she . . . I . . . likes . . .'

I interrupted brusquely. 'She was a florist before she

6

married Donald. She liked to keep her hand in. She used to spend Fridays making those table arrangement things for dances and weddings and things like that . . .'

And wreaths, too, I thought, and couldn't say it.

'Thank you, sir, but I'm sure Mr Stuart can answer for himself.'

'And I'm sure he can't.'

The Detective Inspector diverted his attention my way.

'He's too shocked,' I said.

'Are you a doctor, sir?' His voice held polite disbelief, which it was entitled to, no doubt. I shook my head impatiently. He glanced at Donald, pursed his lips, and turned back to me. His gaze wandered briefly over my jeans, faded denim jacket, fawn polo-neck, and desert boots, and returned to my face, unimpressed.

'Very well, sir. Name?'

'Charles Todd.'

'Age?'

'Twenty-nine.'

'Occupation?'

'Painter.'

The constable unemotionally wrote down these scintillating details in his pocket-sized notebook.

'Houses or pictures?' asked the Inspector.

'Pictures.'

'And your movements today, sir?'

'Caught the two-thirty from Paddington and walked from the local station.'

'Purpose of visit?'

'Nothing special. I come here once or twice a year.'

'Good friends, then?'

'Yes.'

He nodded non-committally. Turned his attention again to Donald and asked more questions, but patiently and without pressure.

'And what time do you normally reach home on Fridays, sir?'

Don said tonelessly, 'Five. About.'

'And today?'

'Same.' A spasm twitched the muscles of his face. 'I saw . . . the house had been broken into . . . I telephoned . . .'

'Yes, sir. We received your call at six minutes past five. And after you had telephoned, you went into the sitting-room, to see what had been stolen?'

Donald didn't answer.

'Our sergeant found you there, sir, if you remember.'

'*Why?*' Don said in anguish. 'Why did she come home?'

'I expect we'll find out, sir.'

The careful exploratory questions went on and on, and as far as I could see achieved nothing except to bring Donald ever closer to all-out breakdown.

I, with a certain amount of shame, grew ordinarily hungry, having not bothered to eat earlier in the day. I thought with regret of the dinner I had been looking forward to, with Regina tossing in unmeasured ingredients and herbs and wine and casually producing a gourmet feast. Regina with her cap of dark hair and ready smile, chatty and frivolous and anti-blood-sports. A harmless girl, come to harm.

At some point during the evening her body was loaded into the ambulance and driven away. I heard it happen, but Donald gave no sign of interpreting the sounds. I thought that probably his mind was raising barriers against the unendurable, and one couldn't blame him.

The Inspector rose finally and stretched the kinks caused by the kitchen stool out of legs and spine. He said he would be leaving a constable on duty at the house all night, and that he would return himself in the morning. Donald nodded vaguely, having obviously not listened properly to a word, and when the police had gone still sat like an automaton in the chair, with no energy to move.

'Come on,' I said. 'Let's go to bed.'

I took his arm, persuaded him to his feet, and steered him up the stairs. He came in a daze, unprotesting.

His and Regina's bedroom was a shambles, but the twin-bedded room prepared for me was untouched. He flopped full-length in his clothes and put his arm up over his eyes, and in appalling distress asked the unanswerable question of all the world's sufferers.

'*Why?* Why did it have to happen to *us*?'

I stayed with Donald for a week, during which time some questions, but not that one, were answered.

One of the easiest was the reason for Regina's premature return home. She and the flower-shop friend, who had been repressing annoyance with each other for weeks, had erupted into a quarrel of enough bitterness to make Regina leave at once. She had driven away at about two-thirty, and had probably gone straight home, as it was considered she had been dead for at least two hours by five o'clock.

This information, expressed in semi-formal sentences, was given to Donald by the Detective Inspector on Saturday afternoon. Donald walked out into the autumnal garden and wept.

The Inspector, Frost by name and cool by nature, came quietly into the kitchen and stood beside me watching Donald with his bowed head among the apple trees.

'I would like you to tell me what you can about the relationship between Mr and Mrs Stuart.'

'You'd like *what*?'

'How did they get on?'

'Can't you tell for yourself?'

He answered neutrally after a pause. 'The intensity of grief shown is not always an accurate indication of the intensity of love felt.'

'Do you always talk like that?'

A faint smile flickered and died. 'I was quoting from a book on psychology.'

' "Not always" means it usually is,' I said.

He blinked.

'Your book is bunk,' I said.

'Guilt and remorse can manifest themselves in an excess of mourning.'

'Dangerous bunk,' I added. 'And as far as I could see, the honeymoon was by no means over.'

'After three years?'

'Why not?'

He shrugged and didn't answer. I turned away from the sight of Donald and said, 'What are the chances of getting back any of the stuff from this house?'

'Small, I should think. Where antiques are involved, the goods are likely to be halfway across the Atlantic before the owner returns from his holidays.'

'Not this time, though,' I objected.

He sighed. 'Next best thing. There have been hundreds of similar break-ins during recent years and very little has been recovered. Antiques are big business these days.'

'Connoisseur thieves?' I said sceptically.

'The prison library service reports that all their most requested books are on antiques. All the little chummies boning up to jump on the bandwagon as soon as they get out.'

He sounded suddenly quite human. 'Like some coffee?' I said.

He looked at his watch, raised his eyebrows, and accepted. He sat on a kitchen stool while I fixed the

11

mugs, a fortyish man with thin sandy hair and a well-worn grey suit.

'Are you married?' he asked.

'Nope.'

'In love with Mrs Stuart?'

'You do try it on, don't you?'

'If you don't ask, you don't find out.'

I put the milk bottle and a sugar basin on the table and told him to help himself. He stirred his coffee reflectively.

'When did you visit this house last?' he said.

'Last March. Before they went off to Australia.'

'Australia?'

'They went to see the vintage there. Donald had some idea of shipping Australian wine over in bulk. They were away for at least three months. Why didn't their house get robbed *then*, when they were safely out of the way?'

He listened to the bitterness in my voice. 'Life is full of nasty ironies.' He pursed his lips gingerly to the hot coffee, drew back, and blew gently across the top of the mug. 'What would you all have been doing today? In the normal course of events?'

I had to think what day it was. Saturday. It seemed totally unreal.

'Going to the races,' I said. 'We always go to the races when I come to stay.'

'Fond of racing, were they?' The past tense sounded

wrong. Yet so much was now past. I found it a great deal more difficult than he did, to change gear.

'Yes . . . but I think they only go . . . went . . . because of me.'

He tried the coffee again and managed a cautious sip. 'In what way do you mean?' he asked.

'What I paint,' I said, 'is mostly horses.'

Donald came in through the back door, looking red-eyed and exhausted.

'The Press are making a hole in the hedge,' he said leadenly.

Inspector Frost clicked his teeth, got to his feet, opened the door to the hall and the interior of the house, and called out loudly.

'Constable? Go and stop those reporters from breaking into the garden.'

A distant voice replied 'Sir', and Frost apologized to Donald. 'Can't get rid of them entirely, you know, sir. They have their editors breathing down their necks. They pester the life out of us at times like these.'

All day long the road outside Donald's house had been lined with cars, which disgorged crowds of reporters, photographers and plain sensation-seekers every time anyone went out of the front door. Like a hungry wolf pack they lay in wait, and I supposed that they would eventually pounce on Donald himself. Regard for his feelings was nowhere in sight.

'Newspapers listen to the radio on the police fre-quencies,' Frost said gloomily. 'Sometimes the Press arrive at the scene of a crime before we can get there ourselves.'

At any other time I would have laughed, but it wouldn't have been much fun for Donald if it had happened in his case. The police, of course, had thought at first that it more or less had, because I had heard that the constable who had tried to eject me forcibly had taken me for a spearheading scribbler.

Donald sat down heavily on a stool and rested his elbows wearily on the table.

'Charles,' he said, 'if you wouldn't mind heating it, I'd like some of that soup now.'

'Sure,' I said, surprised. He had rejected it earlier as if the thought of food revolted him.

Frost's head went up as if at a signal, and his whole body straightened purposefully, and I realized he had merely been coasting along until then, waiting for some such moment. He waited some more while I opened a can of Campbell's condensed, sloshed it and some water and cooking brandy into a saucepan, and stirred until the lumps dissolved. He drank his coffee and waited while Donald disposed of two platefuls and a chunk of brown bread. Then, politely, he asked me to take myself off, and when I'd gone he began what Donald afterwards referred to as 'serious digging'.

It was three hours later, and growing dark, when the Inspector left. I watched his departure from the upstairs landing window. He and his attendant plain-clothes constable were intercepted immediately outside the front door by a young man with wild hair and a microphone, and before they could dodge round him to reach their car the pack on the road were streaming in full cry into the garden and across the grass.

I went methodically round the house drawing curtains, checking windows, and locking and bolting all the outside doors.

'What are you doing?' Donald asked, looking pale and tired in the kitchen.

'Pulling up the drawbridge.'

'Oh.'

In spite of his long session with the Inspector he seemed a lot calmer and more in command of himself, and when I had finished Fort-Knoxing the kitchen-to-garden door he said, 'The police want a list of what's gone. Will you help me make it?'

'Of course.'

'It'll give us something to do . . .'

'Sure.'

'We did have an inventory, but it was in that desk in the hall. The one they took.'

'Damn silly place to keep it,' I said.

'That's more or less what *he* said. Inspector Frost.'

'What about your insurance company? Haven't they got a list?'

'Only of the more valuable things, like some of the paintings, and her jewellery.' He sighed. 'Everything else was lumped together as "contents".'

We started on the dining-room and made reasonable

15

progress, with him putting the empty drawers back in the sideboard while trying to remember what each had once contained, and me writing down to his dictation. There had been a good deal of solid silver tableware, acquired by Donald's family in its affluent past and handed down routinely. Donald, with his warmth for antiques, had enjoyed using it, but his pleasure in owning it seemed to have vanished with the goods. Instead of being indignant over its loss, he sounded impersonal, and by the time we had finished the sideboard, decidedly bored.

Faced by the ranks of empty shelves where once had stood a fine collection of early nineteenth-century porcelain, he baulked entirely.

'What does it matter?' he said drearily, turning away. 'I simply can't be bothered . . .'

'How about the paintings, then?'

He looked vaguely round the bare walls. The site of each missing frame showed unmistakably in lighter oblong patches of palest olive. In this room they had mostly been works of modern British painters: a Hockney, a Bratby, two Lowrys, and a Spear for openers, all painted on what one might call the artists' less exuberant days. Donald didn't like paintings which he said 'jumped off the wall and made a fuss'.

'You probably remember them better than I do,' he said. 'You do it.'

'I'd miss some.'

'Is there anything to drink?'

'Only the cooking brandy,' I said.

'We could have some of the wine.'

'What wine?'

'In the cellar.' His eyes suddenly opened wide. 'Good God, I'd forgotten about the cellar.'

'I didn't even know you had one.'

He nodded. 'Reason I bought the house. Perfect humidity and temperature for long-term storage. There's a small fortune down there in claret and port.'

There wasn't, of course. There were three floor-to-ceiling rows of empty racks, and a single cardboard box on a plain wooden table.

Donald merely shrugged. 'Oh well . . . that's that.'

I opened the top of the cardboard box and saw the elegant corked shapes of the tops of wine bottles.

'They've left these, anyway,' I said. 'In their rush.'

'Probably on purpose,' Don smiled twistedly. 'That's Australian wine. We brought it back with us.'

'Better than nothing,' I said disparagingly, pulling out a bottle and reading the label.

'Better than most, you know. A lot of Australian wine is superb.'

I carried the whole case up to the kitchen and dumped it on the table. The stairs from the cellar led up into the utility room among the washing machines and other domesticities, and I had always had an unclear impression that its door was just another cupboard. I looked at it thoughtfully, an unremarkable

17

white painted panel merging inconspicuously into the general scenery.

'Do you think the burglars *knew* the wine was there?' I asked.

'God knows.'

'I would never have found it.'

'You're not a burglar, though.'

He searched for a corkscrew, opened one of the bottles, and poured the deep red liquid into two kitchen tumblers. I tasted it and it was indeed a marvellous wine, even to my untrained palate. *Wynn's Coonawarra Cabernet Sauvignon.* You could wrap the name round the tongue as lovingly as the product. Donald drank his share absent-mindedly as if it were water, the glass clattering once or twice against his teeth. There was still an uncertainty about many of his movements, as if he could not quite remember how to do things, and I knew it was because with half his mind he thought all the time of Regina, and the thoughts were literally paralysing.

The old Donald had been a man of confidence, capably running a middle-sized inherited business and adding his share to the passed-on goodies. He had a blunt uncompromising face lightened by amber eyes which smiled easily, and he had considered his money well spent on shapely haircuts.

The new Donald was a tentative man shattered with shock, a man trying to behave decently but unsure where his feet were when he walked upstairs.

We spent the evening in the kitchen, talking desultorily, eating a scratch meal, and tidying all the stores back on to the shelves. Donald made a good show of being busy but put half the tins back upside down.

The front door bell rang three times during the evening but never in the code pre-arranged with the police. The telephone, with its receiver lying loose beside it, rang not at all. Donald had turned down several offers of refuge with local friends and visibly shook at the prospect of talking to anyone but Frost and me.

'Why don't they go away?' he said despairingly, after the third attempt on the front door.

'They will, once they've seen you,' I said. And sucked you dry, and spat out the husk, I thought.

He shook his head tiredly. 'I simply can't.'

It felt like living through a siege.

We went eventually again upstairs to bed, although it seemed likely that Donald would sleep no more than the night before, which had been hardly at all. The police surgeon had left knock-out pills, which Donald wouldn't take. I pressed him again on that second evening, with equal non-results.

'No, Charles. I'd feel I'd deserted her. D . . . ducked out. Thought only of myself, and not of . . . of how awful it was for her . . . dying like that . . . with n . . . no one near who l . . . loved her.'

He was trying to offer her in some way the comfort

of his own pain. I shook my head at him, but tried no more with the pills.

'Do you mind,' he said diffidently, 'if I sleep alone tonight?'

'Of course not.'

'We could make up a bed for you in one of the other rooms.'

'Sure.'

He pulled open the linen-cupboard door on the upstairs landing and gestured indecisively at the contents. 'Could you manage?'

'Of course,' I said.

He turned away and seemed struck by one particular adjacent patch of empty wall.

'They took the Munnings,' he said.

'What Munnings?'

'We bought it in Australia. I hung it just there ... only a week ago. I wanted you to see it. It was one of the reasons I asked you to come.'

'I'm sorry,' I said. Inadequate words.

'Everything,' he said helplessly. 'Everything's gone.'

CHAPTER TWO

Frost arrived tirelessly again on Sunday morning with his quiet watchful eyes and non-committal manner. I opened the front door to his signal, and he followed me through to the kitchen, where Donald and I seemed to have taken up permanent residence. I gestured him to a stool, and he sat on it, straightening his spine to avoid future stiffness.

'Two pieces of information you might care to have, sir,' he said to Donald, his voice at its most formal. 'Despite our intensive investigation of this house during yesterday and the previous evening, we have found no fingerprints for which we cannot account.'

'Would you expect to?' I asked.

He flicked me a glance. 'No, sir. Professional house-breakers always wear gloves.'

Donald waited with a grey patient face, as if he would find whatever Frost said unimportant. Nothing, I judged, was of much importance to Donald any more.

'Second,' said Frost, 'our investigations in the district

reveal that a removal van was parked outside your front door early on Friday afternoon.'

Donald looked at him blankly.

'Dark-coloured, and dusty, sir.'

'Oh,' Donald said, meaninglessly.

Frost sighed. 'What do you know of a bronze statuette of a horse, sir? A horse rearing up on its hind legs?'

'It's in the hall,' Donald said automatically; and then, frowning slightly, 'I mean, it used to be. It's gone.'

'How do you know about it?' I asked Frost curiously, and guessed the answer before I'd finished the question. 'Oh no . . .' I stopped, and swallowed. 'I mean, perhaps you found it . . . fallen off the van . . .?'

'No, sir.' His face was calm. 'We found it in the sitting-room, near Mrs Stuart.'

Donald understood as clearly as I had done. He stood up abruptly and went to the window, and stared out for a while at the empty garden.

'It is heavy,' he said at last. 'The base of it.'

'Yes, sir.'

'It must have been . . . quick.'

'Yes, sir,' Frost said again, sounding more objective than comforting.

'P . . . poor Regina.' The words were quiet, the desolation immense. When he came back to the table, his hands were trembling. He sat down heavily and stared into space.

Frost started another careful speech about the sitting-room being kept locked by the police for a few days yet and please would neither of us try to go in there.

Neither of us would.

Apart from that, they had finished their enquiries at the house, and Mr Stuart was at liberty to have the other rooms cleaned, if he wished, where the finger-print dust lay greyish-white on every polished surface.

Mr Stuart gave no sign of having heard.

Had Mr Stuart completed the list of things stolen?

I passed it over. It still consisted only of the dining-room silver and what I could remember of the paintings. Frost raised his eyebrows and pursed his lips.

'We'll need more than this, sir.'

'We'll try again today,' I promised. 'There's a lot of wine missing, as well.'

'Wine?'

I showed him the empty cellar and he came up looking thoughtful.

'It must have taken hours to move that lot,' I said.

'Very likely, sir,' he said primly.

Whatever he was thinking, he wasn't telling. He suggested instead that Donald should prepare a short statement to read to the hungry reporters still waiting outside, so that they could go away and print it.

'No,' Don said.

'Just a short statement,' Frost said reasonably. 'We can prepare it here and now, if you like.'

He wrote it himself, more or less, and I guessed it

was as much for his own sake as Donald's that he wanted the Press to depart, as it was he who had to push through them every time. He repeated the statement aloud when he had finished. It sounded like a police account, full of jargon, but because of that so distant from Donald's own raw grief that my cousin agreed in the end to read it out.

'But no photographs,' he said anxiously, and Frost said he would see to it.

They crowded into the hall, a collection of dry-eyed fact-finders, all near the top of their digging profession and inured from sensitivity by a hundred similar intrusions into tragedy. Sure, they were sorry for the guy whose wife had been bashed, but news was news and bad news sold papers, and if they didn't produce the goods they'd lose their jobs to others more tenacious. The Press Council had stopped the brutal bullying of the past, but the leeway still allowed could be a great deal too much for the afflicted.

Donald stood on the stairs, with Frost and myself at the foot, and read without expression, as if the words applied to someone else.

'... I returned to the house at approximately five p.m. and observed that during my absence a considerable number of valuable objects had been removed ... I telephoned immediately for assistance ... My wife, who was normally absent from the house on Fridays, returned unexpectedly ... and, it is presumed, disturbed the intruders.'

He stopped. The reporters dutifully wrote down the stilted words and looked disillusioned. One of them, clearly elected by pre-arrangement, started asking questions for them all, in a gentle, coaxing, sympathetic tone of voice.

'Could you tell us which of these closed doors is the one to the room where your wife . . .'

Donald's eyes slid briefly despite himself towards the sitting-room. All the heads turned, the eyes studied the uninformative white painted panels, the pencils wrote.

'And could you tell us what exactly was stolen?'

'Silver. Paintings.'

'Who were the paintings by?'

Donald shook his head and began to look even paler.

'Could you tell us how much they were worth?'

After a pause Don said, 'I don't know.'

'Were they insured?'

'Yes.'

'How many bedrooms are there in your house?'

'What?'

'How many bedrooms?'

Donald looked bewildered. 'I suppose . . . five.'

'Do you think you could tell us anything about your wife? About her character, and about her job? And could you let us have a photograph?'

Donald couldn't. He shook his head and said, 'I'm sorry,' and turned and walked steadily away upstairs.

'That's all,' Frost said with finality.

'It's not much,' they grumbled.

'What do you want? Blood?' Frost said, opening the front door and encouraging them out. 'Put yourselves in his position.'

'Yeah,' they said cynically; but they went.

'Did you see their eyes?' I said. 'Sucking it all in?'

Frost smiled faintly. 'They'll write long stories from that little lot.'

The interview, however, produced to a great extent the desired results. Most of the cars departed, and the rest, I supposed, would follow as soon as fresher news broke.

'Why did they ask about the bedrooms?' I said.

'To estimate the value of the house.'

'Good grief.'

'They'll all get it different.' Frost was near to amusement. 'They always do.' He looked up the stairs in the direction Donald had taken, and, almost casually, said, 'Is your cousin in financial difficulties?'

I knew his catch-them-off-guard technique by now.

'I wouldn't think so,' I said unhurriedly. 'You'd better ask him.'

'I will, sir.' He switched his gaze sharply to my face and studied my lack of expression. 'What do you know?'

I said calmly, 'Only that the police have suspicious minds.'

He disregarded that. 'Is Mr Stuart worried about his business?'

'He's never said so.'

'A great many middle-sized private companies are going bankrupt these days.'

'So I believe.'

'Because of cash flow problems,' he added.

'I can't help you. You'll have to look at his company's books.'

'We will, sir.'

'And even if the firm turns out to be bust, it doesn't follow that Donald would fake a robbery.'

'It's been done before,' Frost said dryly.

'If he needed money he could simply have sold the stuff,' I pointed out.

'Maybe he had. Some of it. Most of it, maybe.'

I took a slow breath and said nothing.

'That wine, sir. As you said yourself, it would have taken a long time to move.'

'The firm is a limited company,' I said. 'If it went bankrupt, Donald's own house and private money would be unaffected.'

'You know a good deal about it, don't you?'

I said neutrally, 'I live in the world.'

'I thought artists were supposed to be unworldly.'

'Some are.'

He peered at me with narrowed eyes as if he were trying to work out a possible way in which I too might have conspired to arrange the theft.

I said mildly, 'My cousin Donald is an honourable man.'

'That's an out-of-date word.'

'There's quite a lot of it about.'

He looked wholly disbelieving. He saw far too much in the way of corruption, day in, day out, all his working life.

Donald came hesitantly down the stairs and Frost took him off immediately to another private session in the kitchen. I thought that if Frost's questions were to be as barbed as those he'd asked me, poor Don was in for a rough time. While they talked I wandered aimlessly round the house, looking into storage spaces, opening cupboards, seeing the inside details of my cousin's life.

Either he or Regina had been a hoarder of empty boxes. I came across dozens of them, all shapes and sizes, shoved into odd corners of shelves or drawers: brown cardboard, bright gift-wrap, beribboned chocolate boxes, all too potentially useful or too pretty to be thrown away. The burglars had opened a lot but had thrown more unopened on the floor. They must, I thought, have had a most frustrating time.

They had largely ignored the big sunroom, which held few antiques and no paintings, and I ended up there sitting on a bamboo armchair among sprawling potted plants looking out into the windy garden. Dead leaves blew in scattered showers from the drying trees and a few late roses clung hardily to thorny stems.

I hated autumn. The time of melancholy, the time of death. My spirits fell each year with the soggy leaves and revived only with crisp winter frost. Psychiatric statistics proved that the highest suicide rate occurred in the spring, the time for rebirth and growth and stretching in the sun. I could never understand it. If ever I jumped over a cliff, it would be in the depressing months of decay.

The sunroom was grey and cold. No sun, that Sunday.

I went upstairs, fetched my suitcase, and brought it down. Over years of wandering journeys I had reversed the painter's traditional luggage: my suitcase now contained the tools of my trade, and my satchel, clothes. The large toughened suitcase, its interior adapted and fitted by me, was in fact a sort of portable studio, containing besides paints and brushes a light collapsible metal easel, unbreakable containers of linseed oil and turpentine, and a rack which would hold four wet paintings safely apart. There were also a dust sheet, a large box of tissues and generous amounts of white spirit, all designed for preventing mess and keeping things clean. The organization of the suitcase had saved and made the price of many a sandwich.

I untelescoped the easel and set out my palette, and on a middling-sized canvas laid out the beginnings of a melancholy landscape, a mixture of Donald's garden as I saw it, against a sweep of bare fields and gloomy woods. Not my usual sort of picture, and not, to be honest, the sort to make headline news a century hence; but it gave me at least something to do. I worked steadily, growing ever colder, until the chillier Frost chose to depart; and he went without seeing me again, the front door closing decisively on his purposeful footsteps.

Donald, in the warm kitchen, looked torn to rags. When I went in he was sitting with his arms folded on the table and his head on his arms, a picture of absolute despair. When he heard me he sat up slowly and wearily, and showed a face suddenly aged and deeply lined.

'Do you know what he thinks?' he said.

'More or less.'

He stared at me sombrely. 'I couldn't convince him. He kept on and on. Kept asking the same questions, over and over. Why doesn't he believe me?'

'A lot of people lie to the police. I think they grow to expect it.'

'He wants me to meet him in my office tomorrow. He says he'll be bringing colleagues. He says they'll want to see the books.'

I nodded. 'Better be grateful he didn't drag you down there today.'

'I suppose so.'

I said awkwardly, 'Don, I'm sorry. I told him the wine was missing. It made him suspicious . . . It was a good deal my fault that he was so bloody to you.'

He shook his head tiredly. 'I would have told him myself. I wouldn't have thought of not telling him.'

'But . . . I even pointed out that it must have taken a fair time to move so many bottles.'

'Mm. Well, he would have worked that out for himself.'

'How long, in fact, do you think it would have taken?'

'Depends how many people were doing it,' he said, rubbing his hand over his face and squeezing his tired eyes. 'They would have to have had proper wine boxes in any case. That means they had to know in advance that the wine was there, and didn't just chance on it. And that means . . . Frost says . . . that I sold it myself some time ago and am now saying it is stolen so I can claim fraudulent insurance, or, if it was stolen last Friday, that I told the thieves they'd need proper boxes, which means that I set up the whole frightful mess myself.'

We thought it over in depressed silence. Eventually, I said, 'Who *did* know you had the wine there? And who knew the house was always empty on Fridays? And was the prime target the wine, the antiques, or the paintings?'

'God, Charles, you sound like Frost.'

'Sorry.'

'Every business nowadays,' he said defensively, 'is going through a cash crisis. Look at the nationalized industries, losing money by the million. Look at the

31

wage rises and the taxes and the inflation . . . How can any small business make the profit it used to? Of *course* we have a cash flow problem. Whoever hasn't?'

'How bad is yours?' I said.

'Not critical. Bad enough. But not within sight of liquidation. It's illegal for a limited company to carry on trading if it can't cover its costs.'

'But it could . . . if you could raise more capital to prop it up?'

He surveyed me with the ghost of a smile. 'It surprises me still that you chose to paint for a living.'

'It gives me a good excuse to go racing whenever I like.'

'Lazy sod.' He sounded for a second like the old Donald, but the lightness passed. 'The absolutely last thing I would do would be to use my own personal assets to prop up a dying business. If my firm was that rocky, I'd wind it up. It would be mad not to.'

I sucked my teeth. 'I suppose Frost asked if the stolen things were insured for more than their worth?'

'Yes, he did. Several times.'

'Not likely you'd tell him, even if they were.'

'They weren't, though.'

'No.'

'Under-insured, if anything.' He sighed. 'God knows if they'll pay up for the Munnings. I'd only arranged the insurance by telephone. I hadn't actually sent the premium.'

'It should be all right, if you can give them proof of purchase, and so on.'

He shook his head listlessly. 'All the papers to do with it were in the desk in the hall. The receipt from the gallery where I bought it, the letter of provenance, and the customs and excise receipt. All gone.'

'Frost won't like that.'

'He doesn't.'

'Well ... I hope you pointed out that you would hardly be buying expensive pictures and going on world trips if you were down to your last farthing.'

'He said it might be *because* of buying expensive pictures and going on world trips that I might be down to my last farthing.'

Frost had built a brick wall of suspicion for Donald to batter his head against. My cousin needed hauling away before he was punch drunk.

'Have some spaghetti,' I said.

'What?'

'It's about all I can cook.'

'Oh ...' He focused unclearly on the kitchen clock. It was half past four and long past feeding time according to my stomach.

'If you like,' he said.

The police sent a car the following morning to fetch him to his ordeal in the office. He went lifelessly, having more or less made it clear over coffee that he wouldn't defend himself.

'Don, you must,' I said. 'The only way to deal with the situation is to be firm and reasonable, and decisive, and accurate. In fact, just your own self.'

He smiled faintly. 'You'd better go instead of me. I haven't the energy. And what does it matter?' His smile broke suddenly and the ravaging misery showed deeply like black water under cracked ice. 'Without Regina . . . there's no point in making money.'

'We're not talking about making money, we're talking about suspicion. If you don't defend yourself, they'll assume you can't.'

'I'm too tired. I can't be bothered. They can think what they like.'

'Don,' I said seriously, 'they'll think what you let them.'

'I don't really care,' he said dully: and that was the trouble. He really didn't.

He was gone all day. I spent it painting.

Not the sad landscape. The sunroom seemed even greyer and colder that morning, and I had no mind any more to sink into melancholy. I left the half-finished canvas on the table there and removed myself and trappings to the source of warmth. Maybe the light wasn't so good in the kitchen, but it was the only room in the house with the pulse of life.

I painted Regina standing beside her cooker, with a wooden spoon in one hand and a bottle of wine in the other. I painted the way she held her head back to smile, and I painted the smile, shiny-eyed and guileless and unmistakably happy. I painted the kitchen behind her as I literally saw it in front of my eyes, and I painted Regina herself from the clearest of inner visions. So easily did I see her that I looked up once or twice from her face on the canvas to say something to her, and was disconcerted to find only empty space. An extraordinary feeling of the real and unreal disturbingly tangled.

I seldom ever worked for more than four hours at a stretch because for one thing the actual muscular control required was tiring, and for another the concentration always made me cold and hungry; so I knocked off at around lunch-time and dug out a tin of corned beef to eat with pickles on toast, and after that went for a walk, dodging the front-gate watchers by taking to the apple trees and wriggling through the hedge.

I tramped aimlessly for a while round the scattered shapeless village, thinking about the picture and working off the burst of physical energy I often felt after the constraint of painting. More burnt umber in the folds of the kitchen curtains, I thought; and a purplish shadow on the saucepan. Regina's cream shirt needed yellow ochre under the collar, and probably a touch of green. The cooking stove needed a lot more attention, and I had broken my general rule of working the picture as a whole, background and subject pace by pace.

This time, Regina's face stood out clearly, finished except for a gloss on the lips and a line of light along inside the lower eyelids, which one couldn't do until the under paint was dry. I had been afraid of seeing her less clearly if I took too long, but because of it the picture was now out of balance and I'd have to be very careful to get the kitchen into the same key, so that the whole thing looked harmonious and natural and as if it couldn't have been any other way.

The wind was rawly cold, the sky a hurrying jumbled mass of darkening clouds. I huddled my hands inside my anorak pockets and slid back through the hedge with the first drops of rain.

The afternoon session was much shorter because of the light, and I frustratingly could not catch the right mix of colours for the tops of the kitchen fitments. Even after years of experience, what looked right on the palette looked wrong on the painting. I got it wrong three times and decided to stop.

I was cleaning the brushes when Donald came back. I heard the scrunch of the car, the slam of the doors, and, to my surprise, the ring of the front door bell. Donald had taken his keys.

I went through and opened the door. A uniformed policeman stood there, holding Don's arm. Behind, a row of watching faces gazed on hungrily. My cousin, who had looked pale before, now seemed bloodlessly white. The eyes were as lifeless as death.

'Don!' I said, and no doubt looked as appalled as I felt.

He didn't speak. The policeman leaned forward, said, 'There we are, sir,' and transferred the support of my cousin from himself to me: and it seemed to me that the action was symbolic as much as practical, because he turned immediately on his heel and methodically drove off in his waiting car.

I helped Donald inside and shut the door. I had never seen anyone in such a frightening state of disintegration.

'I asked,' he said, 'about the funeral.'

His face was stony, and his voice came out in gasps.

'They said . . .' He stopped, dragged in air, tried again. 'They said . . . no funeral.'

'Donald . . .'

'They said . . . she couldn't be buried until they had finished their enquiries. They said . . . it might be months. They said . . . they will keep her . . . refrigerated . . .'

The distress was fearful.

'They said . . .' He swayed slightly. 'They said . . . the body of a murdered person belongs to the State.'

I couldn't hold him. He collapsed at my feet in a deep and total faint.

CHAPTER THREE

For two days Donald lay in bed, and I grew to understand what was meant by prostration.

Whether he liked it or not, this time he was heavily sedated, his doctor calling morning and evening with pills and injections. No matter that I was a hopeless nurse and a worse cook, I was appointed, for lack of anyone else, to look after him.

'I want Charles,' Donald in fact told the doctor. 'He doesn't *fuss*.'

I sat with him a good deal when he was awake, seeing him struggle dazedly to face and come to terms with the horrors in his mind. He lost weight visibly, the rounded muscles of his face slackening and the contours changing to the drawn shape of illness. The grey shadows round his eyes darkened to a permanent charcoal, and all normal strength seemed to have vanished from arms and legs.

I fed us both from tins and frozen packets, reading the instructions and doing what they said. Donald thanked me punctiliously and ate what he could, but I doubt if he tasted a thing.

In between times, while he slept, I made progress with both the paintings. The sad landscape was no longer sad but merely Octoberish, with three horses standing around in a field, one of them eating grass. Pictures of this sort, easy to live with and passably expert, were my bread and butter. They sold quite well, and I normally churned one off the production line every ten days or so, knowing that they were all technique and no soul.

The portrait of Regina, though, was the best work I'd done for months. She laughed out of the canvas, alive and glowing, and to me at least seemed vividly herself. Pictures often changed as one worked on them, and day by day the emphasis in my mind had shifted, so that the kitchen background was growing darker and less distinct and Regina herself more luminous. One could still see she was cooking, but it was the girl who was important, not the act. In the end I had painted the kitchen, which was still there, as an impression, and the girl, who was not, as the reality.

I hid that picture in my suitcase whenever I wasn't working on it. I didn't want Donald to come face to face with it unawares.

Early Wednesday evening he came shakily down to the kitchen in his dressing-gown, trying to smile and pick up the pieces. He sat at the table, drinking the

Scotch I had that day imported, and watching while I cleaned my brushes and tidied the palette.

'You're always so neat,' he said.

'Paint's expensive.'

He waved a limp hand at the horse picture which stood drying on the easel. 'How much does it cost, to paint that?'

'In raw materials, about ten quid. In heat, light, rates, rent, food, Scotch and general wear and tear on the nervous system, about the amount I'd earn in a week if I chucked it in and went back to selling houses.'

'Quite a lot, then,' he said seriously.

I grinned. 'I don't regret it.'

'No. I see that.'

I finished the brushes by washing them in soap and water under the tap, pinching them into shape, and standing them upright in a jar to dry. Good brushes were at least as costly as paint.

'After the digging into the company accounts,' Donald said abruptly, 'they took me along to the police station and tried to prove that I had actually killed her myself.'

'I don't believe it!'

'They'd worked out that I could have got home at lunch-time and done it. They said there was time.'

I picked up the Scotch from the table and poured a decent-sized shot into a tumbler. Added ice.

'They must be crazy,' I said.

'There was another man, besides Frost. A superintendent. I think his name was Wall. A thin man, with fierce eyes. He never seemed to blink. Just stared and said over and over again that I'd killed her because she'd come back and found me supervising the burglary.'

'For God's sake!' I said disgustedly. 'And anyway, she didn't leave the flower shop until half past two.'

'The girl in the flower shop now says she doesn't know to the minute when Regina left. Only that it was soon after lunch. And I didn't get back from the pub until nearly three. I went to lunch late. I was hung up with a client all morning . . .' He stopped, gripping his tumbler as if it were a support to hold on to. 'I can't tell you . . . how awful it was.'

The mild understatement seemed somehow to make things worse.

'They said,' he nodded, 'that eighty per cent of murdered married women are killed by their husbands.'

That statement had Frost stamped all over it.

'They let me come home, in the end, but I don't think . . .' His voice shook. He swallowed, visibly trying to keep tight control on his hard-won calm. 'I don't think they've finished.'

It was five days since he'd walked in and found Regina dead. When I thought of the mental hammerings he'd taken on top, the punishing assault on his emotional reserves, where common humanity would have suggested kindness and consoling help, it seemed marvellous that he had remained as sane as he had.

'Have they got anywhere with catching the thieves?'
I said.

He smiled wanly. 'I don't even know if they're
trying.'

'They must be.'

'I suppose so. They haven't said.' He drank some
whisky slowly. 'It's ironic, you know. I've always had
a regard for the police. I didn't know they could
be . . . the way they are.'

A quandary, I thought. Either they leaned on a
suspect in the hope of breaking him down, or they
asked a few polite questions and got nowhere: and
under the only effective system the innocent suffered
more than the guilty.

'I see no end to it,' Donald said. 'No end at all.'

By midday Friday the police had called twice more at
the house, but for my cousin the escalation of agony
seemed to have slowed. He was still exhausted, apa-
thetic, and as grey as smoke, but it was as if he were
saturated with suffering and could absorb little more.
Whatever Frost and his companion said to him, it
rolled off without destroying him further.

'You're supposed to be painting someone's horse,
aren't you?' he said suddenly, as we shaped up to
lunch.

'I told them I'd come later.'

He shook his head. 'I remember you saying, when

I asked you to stay, that it would fit in fine before your next commission.' He thought a bit. 'Tuesday. You should have gone to Yorkshire on Tuesday.'

'I telephoned and explained.'

'All the same, you'd better go.'

He said he would be all right alone, now, and thanks for everything. He insisted I look up the times of trains, order a taxi, and alert the people at the other end. I could see in the end that the time had indeed come for him to be by himself, so I packed up my things to depart.

'I suppose,' he said diffidently, as we waited for the taxi to fetch me, 'that you never paint portraits? People, that is, not horses.'

'Sometimes,' I said.

'I just wondered . . . Could you, one day . . . I mean, I've got quite a good photograph of Regina . . .'

I looked searchingly at his face. As far as I could see, it could do no harm. I unclipped the suitcase and took out the picture with its back towards him.

'It's still wet,' I warned. 'And not framed, and I can't varnish it for at least six months. But you can have it, if you like.'

'Let me see.'

I turned the canvas round. He stared and stared, but said nothing at all. The taxi drove up to the front door.

'See you,' I said, propping Regina against a wall.

He nodded and punched my arm, opened the door

43

for me, and sketched a farewell wave. Speechlessly, because his eyes were full of tears.

I spent nearly a week in Yorkshire doing my best to immortalize a patient old steeplechaser, and then went home to my noisy flat near Heathrow airport, taking the picture with me to finish.

Saturday I downed tools and went to the races, fed up with too much nose-to-the-grindstone.

Jump racing at Plumpton, and the familiar swelling of excitement at the liquid movement of racehorses. Paintings could never do justice to them: never. The moment caught on canvas was always second best.

I would love to have ridden in races, but hadn't had enough practice or skill; nor, I dare say, nerve. Like Donald, my childhood background was of middlesized private enterprise, with my father an auctioneer in business on his own account in Sussex. I had spent countless hours in my growing years watching the horses train on the Downs round Findon, and had drawn and painted them from about the age of six. Riding itself had been mostly a matter of begging the wherewithal for an hour's joy from indulgent aunts, never of a pony of my own. Art school later had been fine, but at twenty-two, alone in the world with both parents newly dead, I'd had to face the need to eat. It had been a short meant-to-be-temporary step to the estate agent's across the street, but I'd liked it well enough to stay.

Half the horse painters in England seemed to have turned up at Plumpton, which was not surprising, as the latest Grand National winner was due to make his first appearance of the new season. It was a commercial fact that a picture called, for instance, *Nijinsky on Newmarket Heath* stood a much better chance of being sold than one labelled *A Horse on Newmarket Heath*, and *The Grand National Winner at the Start* won hands down over *A Runner at Plumpton Before the Off.* The economic facts of life had brought many a would-be Rembrandt down to market research.

'Todd!' said a voice in my ear. 'You owe me fifteen smackers.'

'I bloody don't,' I said.

'You said Seesaw was a certainty for Ascot.'

'Never take sweets from a stranger.'

Billy Pyle laughed extravagantly and patted me heavily on the shoulder. Billy Pyle was one of those people you met on racecourses who greeted you as a bosom pal, plied you with drinks and bonhomie, and bored you to death. On and off I'd met Billy Pyle at the races for umpteen years, and had never yet worked out how to duck him without positive rudeness. Ordinary evasions rolled off his thick skin like mercury off glass, and I found it less wearing on the whole to get the drink over quickly than dodge him all afternoon.

I waited for him to say 'how about a beverage', as he always did.

'How about a beverage?' he said.

'Er . . . sure,' I agreed, resignedly.

'Your father would never forgive me if I neglected you.' He always said that, too. They had been business acquaintances, I knew, but I suspected the reported friendship was posthumous.

'Come along, laddie.'

I knew the irritating routine by heart. He would meet his Auntie Sal in the bar, as if by accident, and in my turn I would buy them both a drink. A double brandy and ginger for Auntie Sal.

'Why, there's Auntie Sal,' Billy said, pushing through the door. Surprise, surprise.

Auntie Sal was a compulsive racegoer in her seventies with a perpetual cigarette dangling from the corner of her mouth and one finger permanently inserted in her form book, keeping her place.

'Know anything for the two-thirty?' she demanded.

'Hello,' I said.

'What? Oh, I see. Hello. How are you? Know anything for the two-thirty?'

''Fraid not.'

'Huh.'

She peered into the form book. 'Treetops is well in at the weights, but can you trust his leg?' She looked up suddenly and with her free hand prodded her

46

nephew, who was trying to attract service from the bar. 'Billy, get a drink for Mrs Matthews.'

'Mrs Who?'

'Matthews. What do you want, Maisie?'

She turned to a large middle-aged woman who had been standing in the shadows behind her.

'Oh . . . gin and tonic, thanks.'

'Got that, Billy? Double brandy and ginger for me, gin and tonic for Mrs Matthews.'

Maisie Matthews' clothes were noticeably new and expensive, and from lacquered hair via crocodile handbag to gold-trimmed shoes she shouted money without saying a word. The hand which accepted the drink carried the weight of a huge opal set in diamonds. The expression on her expertly painted face showed no joy at all.

'How do you do?' I said politely.

'Eh?' said Auntie Sal. 'Oh, yes, Maisie, this is Charles Todd. What do you think of Treetops?'

'Moderate,' I said.

Auntie Sal peered worriedly into the form book and Billy handed round the drinks.

'Cheers,' Maisie Matthews said, looking cheerless.

'Down the hatch,' said Billy, raising his glass.

'Maisie's had a bit of bad luck,' Auntie Sal said.

Billy grinned. 'Backed a loser, then, Mrs Matthews?'

'Her house burned down.'

As a light conversation stopper, it was a daisy.

47

'Oh ... I say ...' said Billy uncomfortably. 'Hard luck.'

'Lost everything, didn't you, Maisie?'

'All but what I stand up in,' she agreed gloomily.

'Have another gin,' I suggested.

'Thanks, dear.'

When I returned with the refills she was in full descriptive flood.

'... I wasn't there, of course, I was staying with my sister Betty up in Birmingham, and there was this policeman on the doorstep telling me what a job they'd had finding me. But by that time it was all over, of course. When I got back to Worthing there was just a heap of cinders with the chimney-breast sticking up in the middle. Well, I had a real job finding out what happened, but anyway they finally said it was a flash fire, whatever that is, but they didn't know what started it, because there'd been no one in the house for two days.'

She accepted the gin, gave me a brief unseeing smile, and returned to her story.

'Well, I was spitting mad, I'll tell you, over losing everything like that, and I said why hadn't they used sea water, what with the sea being only the other side of the tamarisk and down the shingle, because of course they said they hadn't been able to save a thing because they hadn't enough water, and this fireman, the one I was complaining to, he said they couldn't use sea water because for one thing it corroded everything and for another the pumps sucked up seaweed and shells and things, and in any case the tide was out.'

I smothered an unseemly desire to laugh. She sensed it, however.

'Well, dear, it may seem funny to you, of course, but then you haven't lost all of your treasures that you'd been collecting since heaven knows when.'

'I'm really sorry, Mrs Matthews. I don't think it's funny. It was just . . .'

'Yes, well, dear. I suppose you can see the funny side of it, all that water and not a drop to put a fire out with, but I was that mad, I can tell you.'

'I think I'll have a bit on Treetops,' Auntie Sal said thoughtfully.

Maisie Matthews looked at her uncertainly and Billy Pyle, who had heard enough of disaster, broke gratefully into geniality, clapped me again on the shoulder, and said yes, it was time to see the next contest.

Duty done, I thought with a sigh, and took myself off to watch the race from the top of the stands, out of sight and earshot.

Treetops broke down and finished last, limping. Too bad for its owner, trainer, and Auntie Sal. I wandered down to the parade ring to see the Grand National winner walk round before his race, but without any thought of drawing him. I reckoned he was just about played out as a subject, and there would shortly be a glut.

The afternoon went quickly, as usual. I won a little,

lost a little, and filled my eyes with something better than money. On the stands for the last race, I found myself approached by Maisie Matthews. No mistaking the bright red coat, the air of gloss, and the big, kind-looking, worldly face. She drew to a halt on the step below me, looking up. Entirely self-confident, though registering doubt.

'Aren't you,' she said, 'the young man I had a drink with, with Sal and Billy?'

'Yes, that's right.'

'I wasn't sure,' she said, the doubt disappearing. 'You look older out here.'

'Different light,' I said, agreeing. She too looked older, by about ten years. Fifty-something, I thought. Bar-light always flattered.

'They said you were an artist.' Their mild disapproval coloured the way she spoke.

'Mm,' I said, watching the runners canter past on the way to the post.

'Not very well paid, is it, dear?'

I grinned at her, liking her directness. 'It depends who you are. Picasso didn't grumble.'

'How much would you charge to paint a picture for me?'

'What sort of picture?'

'Well, dear, you may say it sounds morbid and I dare say it is, but I was just thinking this morning when I went over there, and really it makes me that mad every time I see it, I was thinking actually that it makes a crazy picture, that burnt ruin with the chimney sticking up, and the burnt hedge behind and all that sea, and I was thinking of getting the local photographer who does all the weddings and things to come along and take a colour picture, because when it's all cleared away and rebuilt, no one will believe how awful it was, and I want to hang it in the new house, just to show them.'

'But . . .'

'So how much would you charge? Because I dare say you can see I am not short of the next quid but if it would be hundreds I might as well get the photographer of course.'

'Of course,' I agreed gravely. 'How about if I came to see the house, or what's left of it, and gave you an estimate?'

She saw nothing odd in that. 'All right, dear. That sounds very businesslike. Of course, it will have to be soon, though, because once the insurance people have been I am having the rubble cleared up.'

'How soon?'

'Well, dear, as you're halfway there, could you come today?'

We discussed it. She said she would drive me in her Jaguar as I hadn't a car, and I could go home by train just as easily from Worthing as from Plumpton.

So I agreed.

One takes the most momentous steps unawares.

*

51

The ruin was definitely paintagenic, if there is such a word. On the way there, more or less non-stop, she had talked about her late husband, Archie, who had looked after her very well, dear.

'Well, that's to say, I looked after him too, dear, because of course I was a nurse. Private, of course. I nursed his first wife all through her illness, cancer it was, dear, of course, and then I stayed on for a bit to look after him, and, well, he asked me to stay on for life, dear, and I did. Of course he was much older, he's been gone more than ten years now. He looked after me very well, Archie did.'

She glanced fondly at the huge opal. Many a man would have liked to have been remembered as kindly.

'Since he went, and left me so well off, dear, it seemed a shame not to get some fun out of it, so I carried on with what we were doing when we were together those few years, which was going round to auction sales in big houses, dear, because you pick up such nice things there, quite cheap sometimes, and of course it's ever so much more interesting when the things have belonged to someone well known or famous.' She changed gear with a jerk and aggressively passed an inoffensive little van. 'And now all those things are burnt to cinders, of course, and all the memories of Archie and the places we went together, and I'll tell you, dear, it makes me mad.'

'It's really horrid for you.'

'Yes, dear, it is.'

I reflected that it was the second time in a fortnight that I'd been cast in the role of comforter, and I felt as inadequate for her as I had for Donald.

She stamped on the brakes outside the remains of her house and rocked us to a standstill. From the opulence of the minor mansions on either side, her property had been far from a slum; but all that was left was an extensive sprawling black heap, with jagged pieces of outside wall defining its former shape, and the thick brick chimney, as she'd said, pointing sturdily skywards from the centre. Ironic, I thought fleetingly, that the fireplace alone had survived the flames.

'There you are, dear,' Maisie said. 'What do you think?'

'A very hot fire.'

She raised her pencilled eyebrows. 'But yes, dear, all fires are hot, aren't they? And of course there was a lot of wood. So many of these old seaside houses were built with a lot of wood.'

Even before we climbed out of her big pale blue car, I could smell the ash.

'How long ago . . .?' I asked.

'Last weekend, dear. Sunday.'

While we surveyed the mess for a moment in silence a man walked slowly into view from behind the chimney. He was looking down, concentrating, taking a step at a time and then bending to poke into the rubble.

Maisie, for all her scarlet-coated bulk, was nimble on her feet.

'Hey,' she called, hopping out of the car and advancing purposefully. 'What do you think you're doing?'

The man straightened up, looking startled. About forty, I judged, with a raincoat, a crisp-looking trilby and a down-turning moustache.

He raised his hat politely. 'Insurance, madam.'

'I thought you were coming on Monday.'

'I happened to be in the district. No time like the present, don't you think?'

'Well, I suppose not,' Maisie said. 'And I hope there isn't going to be any shilly-shallying over you paying up, though of course nothing is going to get my treasures back and I'd rather have them than any amount of money, as I've got plenty of that in any case.'

The man was unused to Maisie's brand of chat.

'Er . . .' he said. 'Oh yes. I see.'

'Have you found out what started it?' Maisie demanded.

'No, madam.'

'Found anything at all?'

'No, madam.'

'Well, how soon can I get all this cleared away?'

'Any time you like, madam.'

He stepped carefully towards us, picking his way round clumps of blackened debris. He had steady greyish eyes, a strong chin, and an overall air of intelligence.

'What's your name?' Maisie asked.

'Greene, madam.' He paused slightly, and added 'With an "e".'

'Well, Mr Greene with an "e",' Maisie said good-humouredly. 'I'll be glad to have all that in writing.'

He inclined his head. 'As soon as I report back.'

Maisie said, 'Good,' and Greene, lifting his hat again, wished her good afternoon and walked along to a white Ford parked a short way along the road.

'That's all right, then,' Maisie said with satisfaction, watching him go. 'Now, how much for that picture?'

'Two hundred plus two nights' expenses in a local hotel.'

'That's a bit steep, dear. *One* hundred, and two nights, and I've got to like the results, or I don't pay.'

'No foal, no fee?'

The generous red mouth smiled widely. 'That's it, dear.'

We settled on one-fifty if she liked the picture, and fifty if she didn't, and I was to start on Monday unless it was raining.

CHAPTER FOUR

Monday came up with a bright breezy day and an echo of summer's warmth. I went to Worthing by train and to the house by taxi, and to the interest of the neighbours set up my easel at about the place where the front gates would have been, had they not been unhinged and transplanted by the firemen. The gates themselves lay flat on the lawn, one of them still pathetically bearing a neat painted nameboard.

Treasure Holme.

Poor Archie. Poor Maisie.

I worked over the whole canvas with an unobtrusive coffee-coloured underpainting of raw umber much thinned with turpentine and linseed oil, and while it was still wet drew in, with a paintbrushful of a darker shade of the same colour, the shape of the ruined house against the horizontals of hedges, shingle, sea and sky. It was easy with a tissue to wipe out mistakes of composition at that stage, and try again: to get the proportions right, and the perspective, and the balance of the main masses.

That done and drying, I strolled right round the whole garden, looking at the house from different angles, and staring out over the blackened stumps of the tamarisk hedge which had marked the end of the grass and the beginning of the shingle. The sea sparkled in the morning sunshine, with the small hurrying cumulus clouds scattering patches of dark slate-grey shadow. All the waves had white frills: distant, because the tide again had receded to the far side of a deserted stretch of wet-looking, wave-rippled sand.

The sea wind chilled my ears. I turned to get back to my task and saw two men in overcoats emerge from a large station wagon and show definite signs of interest in what was left of *Treasure Holme*.

I walked back towards them, reaching them where they stood by the easel appraising my handiwork.

One, heavy and fiftyish. One lean, in the twenties. Both with firm self-confident faces and an air of purpose.

The elder raised his eyes as I approached.

'Do you have permission to be here?' he asked. An enquiry; no belligerence in sight.

'The owner wants her house painted,' I said obligingly.

'I see.' His lips twitched a fraction.

'And you?' I enquired.

He raised his eyebrows slightly. 'Insurance,' he said, as if surprised that anyone should ask.

'Same company as Mr Greene?' I asked.

57

'Mr Who?'

'Greene. With an "e".'

'I don't know who you mean,' he said. 'We
here by arrangement with Mrs Matthews to inspect
damage to her house, which is insured with us.'
looked with some depression at the extent of the
called damage, glancing about as if expecting Ma
to materialize phoenix-like from the ashes.

'No Greene?' I repeated.

'Neither with nor without an "e".'

I warmed to him. Half an ounce of a sense
humour, as far as I was concerned, achieved res
where thumb-screws wouldn't.

'Well ... Mrs Matthews is no longer expecting y
because the aforesaid Mr Greene, who said he wa
insurance, told her she could roll in the demolit
squad as soon as she liked.'

His attention sharpened like a tightened vi
string.

'Are you serious?'

'I was here, with her. I saw him and heard him,
that's what he said.'

'Did he show you a card?'

'No, he didn't.' I paused. 'And ... er ... nor h
you.'

He reached into an inner pocket and did so, v
the speed of a conjuror. Producing cards from poc
was a reflex action, no doubt.

'Isn't it illegal to insure the same property with two companies?' I asked idly, reading the card.

FOUNDATION LIFE AND SURETY
D. J. Lagland   Area Manager

'Fraud.' He nodded.

'Unless of course Mr Greene with an "e" had nothing to do with insurance.'

'Much more likely.'

I put the card in my trouser pocket, Arran sweaters not having been designed noticeably for business transactions. He looked at me thoughtfully, his eyes observant but judgment suspended. He was the same sort of man my father had been, middle-aged, middle-of-the-road, expert at his chosen job but unlikely to set the world on fire.

Or *Treasure Holme*, for that matter.

'Gary,' he said to his younger side-kick, 'go and find a telephone and ring the Beach Hotel. Tell Mrs Matthews we're here.'

'Will do,' Gary said. He was that sort of man.

While he was away on the errand, D. J. Lagland turned his attention to the ruin, and I, as he seemed not to object, tagged along at his side.

'What do you look for?' I asked.

He shot me a sideways look. 'Evidence of arson. Evidence of the presence of the goods reported destroyed.'

'I didn't expect you to be so frank.'

'I indulge myself, occasionally.'

I grinned. 'Mrs Matthews seems pretty genuine.'

'I've never met the lady.'

Treat in store, I thought. 'Don't the firemen,' I said, 'look for signs of arson?'

'Yes, and also the police, and we ask them for guidance.'

'And what did they say?'

'None of your business, I shouldn't think.'

'Even for a wooden house,' I said, 'it is pretty thoroughly burnt.'

'Expert, are you?' he said with irony.

'I've built a lot of Guy Fawkes bonfires, in my time.'

He turned his head.

'They burn a lot better,' I said, 'if you soak them in paraffin. Especially round the edges.'

'I've been looking at fires since before you were born,' he said. 'Why don't you go over there and paint?'

'What I've done is still wet.'

'Then if you stay with me, shut up.'

I stayed with him, silent, and without offence. He was making what appeared to be a preliminary reconnaissance, lifting small solid pieces of debris, inspecting them closely, and carefully returning them to their former positions. None of the things he chose in that way were identifiable to me from a distance of six feet, and as far as I could see none of them gave him much of a thrill.

'Permission to speak?' I said.

'Well?'

'Mr Greene was doing much what you are, though in the area behind the chimney-breast.'

He straightened from replacing yet another black lump. 'Did he take anything?' he said.

'Not while we were watching, which was a very short time. No telling how long he'd been there.'

'No.' He considered. 'Wouldn't you think he was a casual sightseer, poking around out of curiosity?'

'He hadn't the air.'

D. J. frowned. 'Then what did he want?'

A rhetorical question. Gary rolled back, and soon after him, Maisie. In her Jaguar. In her scarlet coat. In a temper.

'What do you mean,' she said, advancing upon D. J. with eyes flashing fortissimo, 'the question of arson isn't yet settled? Don't tell me you're trying to wriggle out of paying my cheque, now. Your man said on Saturday that everything was all right and I could start clearing away and rebuilding, and anyway even if it had been arson you would still have to pay up because the insurance covered arson of course.'

D. J. opened and shut his mouth several times and finally found his voice.

'Didn't our Mr Robinson tell you that the man you saw here on Saturday wasn't from us?'

Our Mr Robinson, in the shape of Gary, nodded vigorously.

'He . . . Mr Greene . . . distinctly said he *was*,' Maisie insisted.

'Well . . . what did he look like?'

'Smarmy,' said Maisie without hesitation. 'Not as young as Charles . . .' she gestured towards me, 'or as old as you.' She thought, then shrugged. 'He looked like an insurance man, that's all.'

D. J. swallowed the implied insult manfully.

'About five feet ten,' I said. 'Suntanned skin with a sallow tinge, grey eyes with deep upper eyelids, widish nose, mouth straight under heavy drooping dark moustache, straight brown hair brushed back and retreating from the two top corners of his forehead, ordinary eyebrows, greeny-brown trilby of smooth felt, shirt, tie, fawn unbuttoned raincoat, gold signet ring on little finger of right hand, suntanned hands.'

I could see him in memory as clearly as if he still stood there in the ashes before me, taking off his hat and calling Maisie 'madam'.

'Good God,' D. J. said.

'An artist's eye, dear,' said Maisie admiringly. 'Well I never.'

D. J. said he was certain they had no one like that in their poking-into-claims department, and Gary agreed.

'Well,' said Maisie, with a resurgence of crossness, 'I suppose that still means you are looking for arson, though why you think that anyone in his right senses would want to burn down my lovely home and all my treasures is something I'll never understand.'

Surely Maisie, worldly Maisie, could not be so naïve. I caught a deep glimmer of intelligence in the glance she gave me, and knew that she certainly wasn't. D. J. however, who didn't know, made frustrated little motions with his hands and voted against explaining. I smothered a few more laughs, and Maisie noticed.

'Do you want your picture,' I asked, 'to be sunny like today, or cloudy and sad?'

She looked up at the bright sky.

'A bit more dramatic, dear,' she said.

D. J. and Gary inch-by-inched over the ruin all afternoon, and I tried to infuse it with a little Gothic romance. At five o'clock, on the dot, we all knocked off.

'Union hours?' said D. J. sarcastically, watching me pack my suitcase.

'The light gets too yellow in the evenings.'

'Will you be here tomorrow?'

I nodded. 'And you?'

'Perhaps.'

I went by foot and bus along to the Beach Hotel, cleaned my brushes, thought a bit, and at seven met Maisie downstairs in the bar, as arranged.

'Well, dear,' she said, as her first gin and tonic gravitated comfortably. 'Did they find anything?'

'Nothing at all, as far as I could see.'

'Well, that's good, dear.'

I tackled my pint of draught. Put the glass down carefully.

'Not altogether, Maisie.'

'Why not?'

'What exactly were your treasures, which were burned?'

'I dare say you wouldn't think so much of them of course, but we had ever such fun buying them, and so have I since Archie's gone, and well, dear, things like an antique spear collection that used to belong to old Lord Stequers whose niece I nursed once, and a whole wall of beautiful butterflies, which professors and such came to look at, and a wrought-iron gate from Lady Tythe's old home, which divided the hall from the sitting-room, and six warming pans from a castle in Ireland, and two tall vases with eagles on the lids signed by Angelica Kaufman, which once belonged to a cousin of Mata Hari, they really did, dear, and a copper firescreen with silver bosses which was a devil to polish, and a marble table from Greece, and a silver tea urn which was once used by Queen Victoria, and really, dear, that's just the beginning, if I tell you them all I'll go on all night.'

'Did the Foundation insurance company have a full list?'

'Yes, they did, dear, and why do you want to know?'

'Because,' I said regretfully, 'I don't think many of

those things were inside the house when it burned down.'

'*What?*' Maisie, as far as I could tell, was genuinely astounded. 'But they must have been.'

'D. J. as good as told me that they were looking for traces of them, and I don't think they found any.'

'D. J.?'

'Mr Lagland. The elder one.'

Alternate disbelief and anger kept Maisie going through two more double gins. Disbelief, eventually, won.

'You got it wrong, dear,' she said finally.

'I hope so.'

'Inexperience of youth, of course.'

'Maybe.'

'Because of course everything was in its place, dear, when I went off last Friday week to stay with Betty, and I only went to Betty's with not having seen her for so long while I'd been away, which is ironic when you think of it, but of course you can't stay at home for ever on the off chance your house is going to catch fire and you can save it, can you dear, or you'd never go anywhere and I would have missed my trip to Australia.'

She paused for breath. Coincidence, I thought.

'All I can say, dear, is that it's a miracle I took most of my jewellery with me to Betty's, because I don't always, except that Archie always said it was safer and of course he was always so sensible and thoughtful and sweet.'

'Australia?' I said.

'Well, yes, dear, wasn't that nice? I went out there for a visit to Archie's sister who's lived there since heaven knows when and was feeling lonely since she'd been widowed, poor dear, and I went out for a bit of fun, dear, because of course I'd never really met her, only exchanged postcards of course, and I was out there for six weeks with her. She wanted me to stay, and of course we got on together like a house on fire . . . oh dear, I didn't mean that exactly . . . well, anyway, I said I wanted to come back to my little house by the sea and think it over, and of course I took my jewellery with me on that trip too, dear.'

I said idly, 'I don't suppose you bought a Munnings while you were there.'

I didn't know why I'd said it, apart from thinking of Donald in Australia. I was totally unprepared for her reaction.

Astounded she had been before: this time, pole-axed. Before, she had been incredulous and angry. This time, incredulous and frightened.

She knocked over her gin, slid off her bar stool, and covered her open mouth with four trembling red-nailed fingers.

'You didn't!' I said disbelievingly.

'How do you know?'

'I don't . . .'

'Are you from Customs and Excise?'

'Of course not.'

'Oh dear. Oh dear . . .' She was shaking, almost as shattered as Donald.

I took her arm and led her over to an armchair beside a small bar table.

'Sit down,' I said coaxingly, 'and tell me.'

It took ten minutes and a refill double gin.

'Well, dear, I'm not an art expert, as you can probably guess, but there was this picture by Sir Alfred Munnings, signed and everything, dear, and it was such a bargain really, and I thought how tickled Archie would have been to have a real Munnings on the wall, what with us both liking the races, of course, and, well, Archie's sister egged me on a bit, and I felt quite . . . I suppose you might call it *high*, dear, so I bought it.'

She stopped.

'Go on,' I said.

'Well, dear, I suppose you've guessed from what I said just now.'

'You brought it into this country without declaring it?'

She sighed. 'Yes, dear, I did. Of course it was silly of me but I never gave customs duty a thought when I bought the painting, not until just before I came home, a week later, that was, and Archie's sister asked if I was going to declare it, and well, dear, I really *resent* having to pay duty on things, don't you? So anyway I thought I'd better find out just how much the duty would be, and I found it wasn't duty at all in the ordinary way, dear, there isn't duty on second-hand pictures being brought in from Australia, but would you believe it, they said I would have to pay Value Added Tax, sort of tax on buying things, you know, dear, and I would have to pay eight per cent on whatever I had bought the picture for. Well, I ask you! I was that mad, dear, I can tell you. So Archie's sister said why didn't I leave the painting with her, because then if I went back to Australia I would have paid the tax for nothing, but I wasn't sure I'd go back and anyway I did want to see Sir Alfred Munnings on the wall where Archie would have loved it, so, well, dear, it was all done up nicely in boards and brown paper so I just camouflaged it a bit with my best nightie and popped it in my suitcase, and pushed it through the "Nothing to Declare" lane at Heathrow when I got back, and nobody stopped me.'

'How much would you have had to pay?' I said.

'Well, dear, to be precise, just over seven hundred pounds. And I know that's not a fortune, dear, but it made me so mad to have to pay tax here because I'd bought something nice in Australia.'

I did some mental arithmetic. 'So the painting cost about nine thousand?'

'That's right, dear. Nine thousand.' She looked anxious. 'I wasn't done, was I? I've asked one or two people since I got back and they say lots of Munningses cost fifteen or more.'

'So they do,' I said absently. And some could be got for fifteen hundred, and others, I dared say, for less.

'Well, anyway, dear, it was only when I began to think about insurance that I wondered if I would be found out, if say, the insurance people wanted a *receipt* or anything, which they probably would, of course, so I didn't do anything about it, because of course if I *did* go back to Australia I could just take the picture with me and no harm done.'

'Awkward,' I agreed.

'So now it's burnt, and I dare say you'll think it serves me right, because the nine thousand's gone up in smoke and I won't see a penny of it back.'

She finished the gin and I bought her another.

'I know it's not my business, Maisie, but how did you happen to have nine thousand handy in Australia? Aren't there rules about exporting that much cash?'

She giggled. 'You don't know much about the world, do you, dear? But anyway, this time it was all hunky-dory. I just toddled along with Archie's sister to a jeweller's and sold him a brooch I had, a nasty sort of *toad*, dear, with a socking big diamond in the middle of its forehead, something to do with Shakespeare, I think, though I never got it clear, anyway I never wore it, it was so ugly, but of course I'd taken it with me because of it being worth so much, and I sold it for nine thousand five, though in Australian dollars of course, so there was no problem, was there?'

Maisie took it for granted I would be eating with

her, so we drifted in to dinner. Her appetite seemed healthy, but her spirits were damp.

'You won't *tell* anyone, will you, dear, about the picture?'

'Of course not, Maisie.'

'I could get into such trouble, dear.'

'I know.'

'A fine, of course,' she said. 'And I suppose that might be the least of it. People can be so beastly about a perfectly innocent little bit of smuggling.'

'No one will find out, if you keep quiet.' A thought struck me. 'Unless, that is, you've told anyone already that you'd bought it?'

'No, dear, I didn't, because of thinking I'd better pretend I'd had it for years, and of course I hadn't even hung it on the wall yet because one of the rings was loose in the frame and I thought it might fall down and be damaged, and I couldn't decide who to ask to fix it.' She paused for a mouthful of prawn cocktail. 'I expect you'll think me silly, dear, but I suppose I was feeling a bit scared of being found out, not guilty exactly because I really don't see why we *should* pay that irritating tax but anyway I didn't not only not hang it up, I hid it.'

'You hid it? Still wrapped up?'

'Well, yes, dear, more or less wrapped up. Of course I'd opened it when I got home, and that's when I found the ring coming loose with the cord through it, so I wrapped it up again until I'd decided what to do.'

I was fascinated. 'Where did you hide it?'

She laughed. 'Nowhere very much, dear. I mean, I was only keeping it out of sight to stop people asking about it, of course, so I slipped it behind one of the radiators in the lounge, and don't look so horrified dear, the central heating was turned off.'

I painted at the house all the next day, but neither D. J. nor anyone else turned up.

In between stints at the easel I poked around a good deal on my own account, searching for Maisie's treasures. I found a good many recognizable remains, durables like bed-frames, kitchen machines and radiators, all of them twisted and buckled not merely by heat but by the weight of the whole edifice from roof downwards having collapsed inwards. Occasional remains of heavy rafters lay blackly in the thick ash, but apart from these, everything combustible had totally, as one might say, combusted.

Of all the things Maisie had described, and of all the dozens she hadn't, I found only the wrought-iron gate from Lady Tythe's old home, which had divided the hall from the sitting-room. Lady Tythe would never have recognized it.

No copper warming pans, which after all had been

designed to withstand red-hot coals. No metal fire-screen. No marble table. No antique spears.

Naturally, no Munnings.

When I took my paint-stained fingers back to the Beach at five o'clock I found Maisie waiting for me in the hall. Not the kindly, basically cheerful Maisie I had come to know, but a belligerent woman in a full-blown state of rage.

'I've been waiting for you,' she said, fixing me with a furious eye.

I couldn't think how I could have offended her.

'What's the matter?' I said.

'The bar's shut,' she said. 'So come upstairs to my room. Bring all your stuff with you.' She gestured to the suitcase. 'I'm so *mad* I think I'll absolutely *burst*.'

She did indeed, in the lift, look in danger of it. Her cheeks were bright red with hard outlines of colour against the pale surrounding skin. Her blonde-rinsed hair, normally lacquered into sophistication, stuck out in wispy spikes, and for the first time since I'd met her her mouth was not glistening with lipstick.

She threw open the door of her room and stalked in. I followed, closing it after me.

'You'll never believe it,' she said forcefully, turning to face me and letting go with all guns blazing. 'I've had the police here half the day, and those insurance men here the other half, and *do you know what they're saying?'*

'Oh, Maisie.' I sighed inwardly. It had been inevitable.

'What do you think I am, I asked them,' she said. 'I was so *mad*. There they were, having the nerve to suggest I'd sold all my treasures and over-insured my house, and was trying to take the insurance people for a ride. I told them, I told them over and over, that everything was in its place when I went to Betty's and if it was over-insured it was to allow for inflation and anyway the brokers had advised me to put up the amount pretty high, and I'm glad I took their advice, but that Mr Lagland says they won't be paying out until they have investigated further and he was proper sniffy about it, and no sympathy at all for me having lost everything. They were absolutely *beastly*, and I *hate* them all.'

She paused to regather momentum, vibrating visibly with the strength of her feelings. 'They made me feel so *dirty*, and maybe I *was* screaming at them a bit, I was so mad, but they'd no call to be so *rude*, and making out I was some sort of criminal, and just what *right* have they to tell me to pull myself together when it is because of *them* and their bullying that I am yelling at them at the top of my voice?'

It must, I reflected, have been quite an encounter. I wondered in what state the police and D. J. had retired from the field.

'They say it was definitely arson and I said why did they think so now when they hadn't thought so at first, and it turns out that it was because that Lagland couldn't find any of my treasures in the ashes or any trace of them at all, and they said even if I hadn't sold the things first I had arranged for them to be stolen and the house burnt to cinders while I was away at Betty's, and they kept on and on asking me who I'd paid to do it, and I got more and more furious and if I'd had anything handy I would have *hit* them, I really would.'

'What you need is a stiff gin,' I said.

'I told them they ought to be out looking for who-ever had done it instead of hounding helpless women like me, and the more I thought of someone walking into *my* house and stealing *my* treasures and then callously setting fire to everything the madder I got, and somehow that made me even *madder* with those stupid men who couldn't see any further than their stupid noses.'

It struck me after a good deal more of similar dia-tribe that genuine though Maisie's anger undoubtedly was, she was stoking herself up again every time her temper looked in danger of relapsing to normal. For some reason, she seemed to need to be in the position of the righteous wronged.

I wondered why; and in a breath-catching gap in the flow of hot lava, I said, 'I don't suppose you told them about the Munnings.'

The red spots on her cheeks burned suddenly brighter.

'I'm not *crazy*,' she said bitingly. 'If they found out about that, there would have been a fat chance of convincing them I'm telling the truth about the rest.'

'I've heard,' I said tentatively, 'that nothing infuriates a crook more than being had up for the one job he didn't do.'

It looked for a moment as if I'd just elected myself as the new target for hatred, but suddenly as she glared at me in rage her sense of humour reared its battered head and nudged her in the ribs. The stiffness round her mouth relaxed, her eyes softened and glimmered, and after a second or two, she ruefully smiled.

'I dare say you're right, dear, when I come to think of it.' The smile slowly grew into a giggle. 'How about that gin?'

Little eruptions continued all evening through drinks and dinner, but the red-centred volcano had subsided to manageable heat.

'You didn't seem surprised, dear, when I told you what the police thought I'd done.' She looked sideways at me over her coffee cup, eyes sharp and enquiring.

'No.' I paused. 'You see, something very much the same has just happened to my cousin. Too much the same, in too many ways. I think, if you will come, and he agrees, that I'd like to take you to meet him.'

'But why, dear?'

I told her why. The anger she felt for herself burned up again fiercely for Donald.

'How *dreadful*. How *selfish* you must think *me*, after all that that poor man has suffered.'

'I don't think you're selfish at all. In fact, Maisie, I think you're a proper trouper.'

She looked pleased and almost kittenish, and I had a vivid impression of what she had been like with Archie.

'There's one thing, though, dear,' she said awkwardly. 'After today, and all that's been said, I don't think I want that picture you're doing. I don't any more want to remember the house as it is now, only like it used to be. So if I give you just the fifty pounds, do you mind?'

CHAPTER FIVE

We went to Shropshire in Maisie's Jaguar, sharing the driving. Donald on the telephone had sounded unenthusiastic at my suggested return, but also too lethargic to raise objections. When he opened his front door to us, I was shocked.

It was two weeks since I'd left him to go to Yorkshire. In that time he had shed at least fourteen pounds and aged ten years. His skin was tinged with bluish shadows, the bones in his face showed starkly, and even his hair seemed speckled with grey.

The ghost of the old Donald put an obvious effort into receiving us with good manners.

'Come in,' he said. 'I'm in the dining-room now. I expect you'd like a drink.'

'That would be very nice, dear,' Maisie said.

He looked at her with dull eyes, seeing, as I saw, a large good-natured lady with glossy hair and expensive clothes, her smart appearance walking a tightrope between vulgarity and elegance and just making it to the safer side.

He waved to me to pour the drinks, as if it would be too much for him, and invited Maisie to sit down. The dining-room had been roughly refurnished, containing now a large rug, all the sunroom armchairs, and a couple of small tables from the bedrooms. We sat in a fairly close group round one of the tables, because I had come to ask questions, and I wanted to write down the answers. My cousin watched the production of notebook and ballpoint with no show of interest.

'Don,' I said, 'I want you to listen to a story.'

'All right.'

Maisie, for once, kept it short. When she came to the bit about buying a Munnings in Australia, Donald's head lifted a couple of inches and he looked from her to me with the first stirring of attention. When she stopped, there was a small silence.

'So,' I said finally, 'you both went to Australia, you both bought a Munnings, and soon after your return you both had your houses burgled.'

'Extraordinary coincidence,' Donald said: but he meant simply that, nothing more. 'Did you come all this way just to tell me that?'

'I wanted to see how you were.'

'Oh. I'm all right. Kind of you, Charles, but I'm all right.'

Even Maisie, who hadn't known him before, could see that he wasn't.

'Where did you buy your picture, Don? Where exactly, I mean.'

'I suppose . . . Melbourne. In the Hilton Hotel. Opposite the cricket ground.'

I looked doubtful. Although hotels quite often sold pictures by local artists, they seldom sold Munnings.

'Fellow met us there,' Don added. 'Brought it up to our room. From the gallery where we saw it first.'

'Which gallery?'

He made a slight attempt to remember. 'Might have been something like Fine Arts.'

'Would you have it on a cheque stub, or anything?'

He shook his head. 'The wine firm I was dealing with paid for it for me, and I sent a cheque to their British office when I got back.'

'Which wine firm?'

'Monga Vineyards Proprietary Limited of Adelaide and Melbourne.'

I wrote it all down.

'And what was the picture like? I mean, could you describe it?'

Donald looked tired. 'One of those "Going down to the start" things. Typical Munnings.'

'So was mine,' said Maisie, surprised. 'A nice long row of jockeys in their colours against a darker sort of sky.'

'Mine had only three horses,' Donald said.

'The biggest, I suppose you might say the *nearest* jockey in my picture had a purple shirt and green cap,' Maisie said, 'and I expect you'll think I was silly but that was one of the reasons I bought it, because when

Archie and I were thinking what fun it would be to buy a horse and go to the races as owners, we decided we'd like purple with a green cap for our colours, if no one else already had that, of course.'

'Don?' I said.

'Mm? Oh . . . three bay horses cantering . . . in profile . . . one in front, two slightly overlapping behind. Bright colours on the jockeys. I don't remember exactly. White racetrack rails and a lot of sunny sky.'

'What size?'

He frowned slightly. 'Not very big. About twenty-four inches by eighteen, inside the frame.'

'And yours, Maisie?'

'A bit smaller, dear, I should think.'

'Look,' Donald said. 'What are you getting at?'

'Trying to make sure that there are no more coincidences.'

He stared, but without any particular feeling.

'On the way up here,' I said, 'Maisie told me everything' (but *everything*) 'of the way she came to buy her picture. So could you possibly tell us how you came to buy yours? Did you, for example, deliberately go looking for a Munnings?'

Donald passed a weary hand over his face, obviously not wanting the bother of answering.

'Please, Don,' I said.

'Oh . . .' A long sigh. 'No. I wasn't especially wanting to buy anything at all. We just went into the Melbourne

Art Gallery for a stroll round. We came to the Munnings they have there . . . and while we were looking at it we just drifted into conversation with a woman near us, as one does in art galleries. She said there was another Munnings, not far away, for sale in a small commercial gallery, and it was worth seeing even if one didn't intend to buy it. We had time to spare, so we went.'

Maisie's mouth had fallen open. 'But dear,' she said, recovering, 'that was *just* the same as us, my sister-in-law and me, though it was Sydney Art Gallery, not Melbourne. They have this marvellous picture there, *The Coming Storm*, and we were admiring it when this man sort of drifted up to us and joined in . . .'

Donald suddenly looked a great deal more exhausted, like a sick person overdone by healthy visitors.

'Look . . . Charles . . . you aren't going to the police with all this? Because I . . . I don't think . . . I could stand . . . a whole new lot . . . of questions.'

'No, I'm not,' I said.

'Then what . . . does it matter?'

Maisie finished her gin and tonic and smiled a little too brightly.

'Which way to the girls' room, dear?' she asked, and disappeared to the cloakroom.

Donald said faintly, 'I can't concentrate . . . I'm sorry, Charles, but I can't seem to do anything . . . while they still have Regina . . . unburied . . . just *stored* . . .'

81

Time, far from dulling the agony, seemed to have preserved it, as if the keeping of Regina in a refrigerated drawer had stopped dead the natural progression of mourning. I had been told that the bodies of murdered people could be held in that way for six months or more in unsolved cases. I doubted whether Donald would last that long.

He stood suddenly and walked away out of the door to the hall. I followed. He crossed the hall, opened the door of the sitting-room, and went in.

Hesitantly, I went after him.

The sitting-room still contained only the chintz-covered sofas and chairs, now ranged over-tidily round the walls. The floor where Regina had lain was clean and polished. The air was cold.

Donald stood in front of the empty fireplace looking at my picture of Regina, which was propped on the mantelpiece.

'I stay in here with her, most of the time,' he said. 'It's the only place I can bear to be.'

He walked to one of the armchairs and sat down, directly facing the portrait.

'You wouldn't mind seeing yourselves out, would you Charles?' he said. 'I'm really awfully tired.'

'Take care of yourself.' Useless advice. One could see he wouldn't.

'I'm all right,' he said. 'Quite all right. Don't you worry.'

I looked back from the door. He was sitting immobile, looking at Regina. I didn't know whether it would have been better or worse if I hadn't painted her.

Maisie was quiet for the whole of the first hour of the return journey, a record in itself.

From Donald's house we had driven first to one of the neighbours who had originally offered refuge, because he clearly needed help more now than ever.

Mrs Neighbour had listened with sympathy, but had shaken her head.

'Yes, I know he should have company and get away from the house, but he won't. I've tried several times. Called. So have lots of people round here. He just tells us he's all right. He won't let anyone help him.'

Maisie drove soberly, mile after mile. Eventually she said, 'We shouldn't have bothered him. Not so soon after . . .'

Three weeks, I thought. Only three weeks. To Donald it must have seemed like three months, stretched out in slow motion. You could live a lifetime in three weeks' pain.

'I'm going to Australia,' I said.

'You're very fond of him, dear, aren't you?' Maisie said.

Fond? I wouldn't have used that word, I thought: but perhaps after all it was accurate.

'He's eight years older than me, but we've always got on well together.' I looked back, remembering. 'We were both only children. His mother and mine were sisters. They used to visit each other, with me and Donald in tow. He was always pretty patient about having a young kid under his feet.'

'He looks very ill, dear.'

'Yes.'

She drove another ten miles in silence. Then she said, 'Are you sure it wouldn't be better to tell the police? About the paintings, I mean? Because you do think they had something to do with the burglaries, don't you, dear, and the police might find out things more easily than you.'

I agreed. 'I'm sure they would, Maisie. But how can I tell them? You heard what Donald said, that he couldn't stand a new lot of questions. Seeing him today, do you think he could? And as for you, it wouldn't just be confessing to a bit of smuggling and paying a fine, but of having a conviction against your name for always, and having the customs search your baggage every time you travelled, and all sorts of other complications and humiliations. Once you get on any black-list nowadays it is just about impossible to get off.'

'I didn't know you cared, dear.' She tried a giggle, but it didn't sound right.

We stopped after a while to exchange places. I liked driving her car, particularly as for the last three years, since I'd given up a steady income, I'd owned no wheels myself. The power purred elegantly under the pale blue bonnet and ate up the southward miles.

'Can you afford the fare, dear?' Maisie said. 'And hotels, and things?'

'I've a friend out there. Another painter. I'll stay with him.'

She looked at me doubtfully. 'You can't get there by hitch-hiking, though.'

I smiled. 'I'll manage.'

'Yes, well, dear, I dare say you can, but all the same, and I don't want any silly arguments, I've got a great deal of this world's goods thanks to Archie, and you haven't, and as it's partly because of me having gone in for smuggling that you're going yourself at all, I am insisting that you let me buy your ticket.'

'No, Maisie.'

'Yes, dear. Now be a good boy, dear, and do as I say.'

You could see, I thought, why she'd been a good nurse. Swallow the medicine, dear, there's a good boy. I didn't like accepting her offer but the truth was that I would have had to borrow anyway.

'Shall I paint your picture, Maisie, when I get back?'

'That will do very nicely, dear.'

I pulled up outside the house near Heathrow whose attic was my home, and from where Maisie had picked me up that morning.

'How do you stand all this noise, dear?' she said, wincing as a huge jet climbed steeply overhead.

'I concentrate on the cheap rent.'

She smiled, opening the crocodile handbag and producing her chequebook. She wrote out and gave me the slip of paper which was far more than enough for my journey.

'If you're fussed, dear,' she said across my protests, 'you can give me back what you don't spend.' She gazed at me earnestly with grey-blue eyes. 'You will be careful dear, won't you?'

'Yes, Maisie.'

'Because of course, dear, you might turn out to be a nuisance to some really *nasty* people.'

I landed at Mascot airport at noon five days later, wheeling in over Sydney and seeing the harbour bridge and the opera house down below, looking like postcards.

Jik met me on the other side of Customs with a huge grin and a waving bottle of champagne.

'Todd the sod,' he said. 'Who'd have thought it?' His voice soared easily over the din. 'Come to paint Australia red!'

He slapped me on the back with an enthusiastic horny hand, not knowing his own strength. Jik Cassavetes, long-time friend, my opposite in almost everything.

Bearded, which I was not. Exuberant, noisy, extravagant, unpredictable; qualities I envied. Blue eyes and sun-blond hair. Muscles which left mine gasping. An outrageous way with girls. An abrasive tongue; and a wholehearted contempt for the things I painted.

We had met at art school, drawn together by mutual truancy on racetrains. Jik compulsively went racing, but strictly to gamble, never to admire the contestants, and certainly not to paint them. Horse painters, to him, were the lower orders. No *serious* artist, he frequently said, would be seen dead painting horses.

Jik's paintings, mostly abstract, were the dark reverse of the bright mind: fruits of depression, full of despair at the hatred and pollution destroying the fair world.

Living with Jik was like a toboggan run, downhill, dangerous, and exhilarating. We'd spent the last two years at art school sharing a studio flat and kicking each other out for passing girls. They would have chucked him out of school except for his prodigious talent, because he'd missed weeks in the summer for his other love, which was sailing.

I'd been out with him, deep sea, several times in the years afterwards. I reckoned he'd taken us on several occasions a bit nearer death than was strictly necessary, but it had been a nice change from the office. He was a great sailor, efficient, neat, quick and strong, with an instinctive feeling for wind and waves. I had been sorry when one day he had said he was setting off single-handed round the world. We'd had a paralytic farewell party on his last night ashore; and the next day, when he'd gone, I'd given the estate agent my notice.

He had brought a car to fetch me: his car, it turned out. A British M.G. Sports, dark blue. Both sides of him right there, extrovert and introvert, the flamboyant statement in a sombre colour.

'Are there many of these here?' I asked, surprised, loading suitcase and satchel into the back. 'It's a long way from the birth pangs.'

He grinned. 'A few. They're not popular now because petrol passes through them like salts.' The engine roared to life, agreeing with him, and he switched on the windscreen wiper against a starting shower. 'Welcome to sunny Australia. It rains all the time here. Puts Manchester in the sun.'

'But you like it?'

'Love it, mate. Sydney's like rugger, all guts and go and a bit of grace in the line-out.'

'And how's business?'

'There are thousands of painters in Australia. It's a flourishing cottage industry.' He glanced at me sideways. 'A hell of a lot of competition.'

'I haven't come to seek fame and fortune.'

'But I scent a purpose,' he said.

'How would you feel about harnessing your brawn?'

'To your brain? As in the old days?'

'Those were pastimes.'

His eyebrows rose. 'What are the risks?'

'Arson and murder, to date.'

'Jesus.'

The blue car swept gracefully into the centre of the city. Sky-scrapers grew like beanstalks.

'I live right out on the other side,' Jik said. 'God, that sounds banal. Suburban. What has become of me?'

'Contentment oozing from every pore,' I said smiling.

'Yes. So. O.K., for the first time in my life I've been actually happy. I dare say you'll soon put that right.'

The car nosed on to the expressway, pointing towards the bridge.

'If you look over your right shoulder,' Jik said, 'You'll see the triumph of imagination over economics. Like the Concorde. Long live madness, it's the only thing that gets us anywhere.'

I looked. It was the opera house, glimpsed, grey with rain.

'Dead in the day,' Jik said. 'It's a night bird. Fantastic.'

The great arch of the bridge rose above us, intricate as steel lace. 'This is the only flat bit of road in Sydney,' Jik said. We climbed again on the other side.

To our left, half seen at first behind other familiar-looking high-rise blocks, but then revealed in its full glory, stood a huge shiny red-orange building, all its sides set with regular rows of large curve-cornered square windows of bronze-coloured glass.

Jik grinned. 'The shape of the twenty-first century. Imagination and courage. I love this country.'

'Where's your natural pessimism?'

'When the sun sets, those windows glow like gold.' We left the gleaming monster behind. 'It's the water-board offices,' Jik said sardonically. 'The guy at the top moors his boat near mine.'

The road went up and down out of the city through close-packed rows of one-storey houses, whose roofs, from the air, had looked like a great red-squared carpet.

'There's one snag,' Jik said. 'Three weeks ago, I got married.'

The snag was living with him aboard his boat, which was moored among a colony of others near a headland he called the Spit: and you could see why, temporarily at least, the glooms of the world could take care of themselves.

She was not plain, but not beautiful. Oval-shaped face, mid-brown hair, so-so figure and a practical line in clothes. None of the style or instant vital butterfly quality of Regina. I found myself the critically inspected target of bright brown eyes which looked out with impact-making intelligence.

'Sarah,' Jik said. 'Todd. Todd, Sarah.'

We said hi and did I have a good flight and yes I did. I gathered she would have preferred me to stay at home.

Jik's thirty-foot ketch, which had set out from England as a cross between a studio and a chandler's warehouse, now sported curtains, cushions, and a flowering plant. When Jik opened the champagne he poured it into shining tulip glasses, not plastic mugs.

'By God,' he said. 'It's good to see you.'

Sarah toasted my advent politely, not sure that she agreed. I apologized for gatecrashing the honeymoon.

'Nuts to that,' Jik said, obviously meaning it. 'Too much domestic bliss is bad for the soul.'

'It depends,' said Sarah neutrally, 'on whether you need love or loneliness to get you going.'

For Jik, before, it had always been loneliness. I wondered what he had painted recently: but there was no sign, in the now comfortable cabin, of so much as a brush.

'I walk on air,' Jik said. 'I could bound up Everest and do a handspring on the summit.'

'As far as the galley will do,' Sarah said, 'if you remembered to buy the crayfish.'

Jik, in our shared days, had been the cook; and times, it seemed, had not changed. It was he, not Sarah, who with speed and efficiency chopped open the cray-fish, covered them with cheese and mustard, and set them under the grill. He who washed the crisp lettuce and assembled crusty bread and butter. We ate the feast round the cabin table with rain pattering on port-holes and roof and the sea water slapping against the sides in the freshening wind. Over coffee, at Jik's insist-ence, I told them why I had come to Australia.

They heard me out in concentrated silence. Then Jik, whose politics had not changed much since student pink, muttered darkly about 'pigs', and Sarah looked nakedly apprehensive.

'Don't worry,' I told her. 'I'm not asking for Jik's help, now that I know he's married.'

'You have it. You have it,' he said explosively.

I shook my head. 'No.'

Sarah said, 'What precisely do you plan to do first?'

'Find out where the two Munningses came from.'

'And after?'

'If I knew what I was looking for I wouldn't need to look.'

'That doesn't follow,' she said absently.

'Melbourne,' Jik said suddenly. 'You said one of the pictures came from Melbourne. Well, that settles it. Of course we'll help. We'll go there at once. It couldn't be better. Do you know what next Tuesday is?'

'No,' I said. 'What is it?'

'The day of the Melbourne Cup!'

His voice was triumphant. Sarah stared at me darkly across the table.

'I wish you hadn't come,' she said.

CHAPTER SIX

I slept that night in the converted boathouse which constituted Jik's postal address. Apart from a bed alcove, new-looking bathroom, and rudimentary kitchen, he was using the whole space as studio.

A huge old easel stood in the centre, with a table to each side holding neat arrays of paints, brushes, knives, pots of linseed and turpentine and cleaning fluid: all the usual paraphernalia.

No work in progress. Everything shut and tidy. Like its counterpart in England, the large rush mat in front of the easel was black with oily dirt, owing to Jik's habit of rubbing his roughly rinsed brushes on it between colours. The tubes of paint were characteristically squeezed flat in the middles, impatience forbidding an orderly progress from the bottom. The palette was a small oblong, not needed any larger because he used most colours straight from the tube and got his effects by overpainting. A huge box of rags stood under one table, ready to wipe clean everything used to apply paint to picture, not just brushes and knives, but fingers, palms, nails, wrists, anything which took his fancy. I smiled to myself. Jik's studio was as identifiable as his pictures.

Along one wall a two-tiered rack held rows of canvases, which I pulled out one by one. Dark, strong, dramatic colours, leaping to the eye. Still the troubled vision, the perception of doom. Decay and crucifixions, obscurely horrific landscapes, flowers wilting, fish dying, everything to be guessed, nothing explicit.

Jik hated to sell his paintings and seldom did, which I thought was just as well, as they made uncomfortable room-mates, enough to cause depression in a skylark. They had a vigour, though, that couldn't be denied. Everyone who saw his assembled work remembered it, and had their thoughts modified, and perhaps even their basic attitudes changed. He was a major artist in a way I would never be, and he would have looked upon easy popular acclaim as personal failure.

In the morning I walked down to the boat and found Sarah there alone.

'Jik's gone for milk and newspapers,' she said. 'I'll get you some breakfast.'

'I came to say goodbye.'

She looked at me levelly. 'The damage is done.'

'Not if I go.'

'Back to England?'

I shook my head.

'I thought not.' A dim smile appeared briefly in her eyes. 'Jik told me last night that you were the only person he knew who had a head cool enough to calculate a ship's position for a mayday call by dead reckoning at night after tossing around violently for four hours in a force ten gale with a hole in the hull and the pumps packed up, and get it right.'

I grinned. 'But he patched the hull and mended the pump, and we cancelled the mayday when it got light.'

'You were both stupid.'

'Better to stay safely at home?' I said.

She turned away. '*Men*,' she said. 'Never happy unless they're risking their necks.'

She was right, to some extent. A little healthy danger wasn't a bad feeling, especially in retrospect. It was only the nerve-breakers which gave you the shakes and put you off repetition.

'Some women, too,' I said.

'Not me.'

'I won't take Jik with me.'

Her back was still turned. 'You'll get him killed,' she said.

Nothing looked less dangerous than the small suburban gallery from which Maisie had bought her picture. It was shut for good. The bare premises could be seen nakedly through the shopfront window, and a succinct and unnecessary card hanging inside the glass door said 'Closed'.

The little shops on each side shrugged their shoulders.

'They were only open for a month or so. Never seemed to do much business. No surprise they folded.'

Did they, I asked, know which estate agent was handling the letting? No, they didn't.

'End of enquiry,' Jik said.

I shook my head. 'Let's try the local agents.'

We split up and spent a fruitless hour. None of the firms on any of the 'For Sale' boards in the district admitted to having the gallery on its books.

We met again outside the uninformative door.

'Where now?'

'Art Gallery?'

'In the Domain,' Jik said, which turned out to be a chunk of park in the city centre. The Art Gallery had a suitable façade of six pillars outside and the Munnings, when we ran it to earth, inside.

No one else was looking at it. No one approached to fall into chat and advise us we could buy another one cheap in a little gallery in an outer suburb.

We stood there for a while with me admiring the absolute mastery which set the two grey ponies in the shaft of pre-storm light at the head of the darker herd, and Jik grudgingly admitted that at least the man knew how to handle paint.

Absolutely nothing else happened. We drove back to the boat in the M.G., and lunch was an anti-climax.

'What now?' Jik said.

'A spot of work with the telephone, if I could borrow the one in the boathouse.'

It took nearly all afternoon, but alphabetically systematic calls to every estate agent as far as Holloway & Son in the classified directory produced the goods in the end. The premises in question, said Holloway & Son, had been let to North Sydney Fine Arts on a short lease.

How short?

Three months, dating from September first.

No, Holloway & Son did not know the premises were now empty. They could not re-let them until December first, because North Sydney Fine Arts had paid all the rent in advance; and they did not feel able to part with the name of any individual concerned. I blarneyed a bit, giving a delicate impression of being in the trade myself, with a client for the empty shop. Holloway & Son mentioned a Mr John Grey, with a post-office box number for an address. I thanked them. Mr Grey, they said, warming up a little, had said he wanted the gallery for a short private exhibition, and they were not really surprised he had already gone.

How could I recognize Mr Grey if I met him? They really couldn't say: all the negotiations had been done by telephone and post. I could write to him myself, if my client wanted the gallery before December first.

Ta ever so, I thought.

All the same, it couldn't do much harm. I unearthed a suitable sheet of paper, and in twee and twirly lettering

in black ink told Mr Grey I had been given his name
and box number by Holloway & Son, and asked him
if he would sell me the last two weeks of his lease so
that I could mount an exhibition of a friend's *utterly
meaningful* watercolours. Name his own price, I said,
within reason. Yours sincerely, I said; Peregrine Smith.

I walked down to the boat to ask if Jik or Sarah
would mind me putting their own box number as a
return address.

'He won't answer,' Sarah said, reading the letter. 'If
he's a crook. I wouldn't.'

'The first principle of fishing,' Jik said, 'is to dangle
a bait.'

'This wouldn't attract a starving piranha.'

I posted it anyway, with Sarah's grudging consent.
None of us expected it to bring forth any result.

Jik's own session on the telephone proved more
rewarding. Melbourne, it seemed, was crammed to the
rooftops for the richest race meeting of the year, but
he had been offered last-minute cancellations. Very
lucky indeed, he insisted, looking amused.

'Where?' I asked suspiciously.

'In the Hilton,' he said.

I couldn't afford it, but we went anyway. Jik in his
student days had lived on cautious hand-outs from a
family trust, and it appeared that the source of bread

was still flowing. The boat, the boathouse, the M.G. and the wife were none of them supported by paint.

We flew south to Melbourne the following morning, looking down on the Snowy Mountains en route and thinking our own chilly thoughts. Sarah's disapproval from the seat behind froze the back of my head, but she had refused to stay in Sydney. Jik's natural bent and enthusiasm for dicey adventure looked like being curbed by love, and his reaction to danger might not henceforth be uncomplicatedly practical. That was, if I could find any dangers for him to react to. The Sydney trail was dead and cold, and maybe Melbourne too would yield an unlooked-at public Munnings and a gone-away private gallery. And if it did, what then? For Donald the outlook would be bleaker than the strange puckered ranges sliding away underneath.

If I could take home enough to show beyond doubt that the plundering of his house had its roots in the sale of a painting in Australia, it should get the police off his neck, the life back to his spirit, and Regina into a decent grave.

If.

And I would have to be quick, or it would be too late to matter. Donald, staring hour after hour at a portrait in an empty house ... Donald, on the brink.

Melbourne was cold and wet and blowing a gale. We checked gratefully into the warm plushy bosom of the

Hilton, souls cossetted from the door onwards by rich reds and purples and blues, velvety fabrics, copper and gilt and glass. The staff smiled. The lifts worked. There was polite shock when I carried my own suitcase. A long way from the bare boards of home.

I unpacked, which is to say, hung up my one suit, slightly crumpled from the squashy satchel, and then went to work again on the telephone.

The Melbourne office of the Monga Vineyards Proprietary Limited cheerfully told me that the person who dealt with Mr Donald Stuart from England was the Managing Director, Mr Hudson Taylor, and he could be found at present in his office at the vineyard itself, which was north of Adelaide. Would I like the number?

Thanks very much.

'No sweat,' they said, which I gathered was Australian shorthand for 'It's no trouble, and you're welcome.'

I pulled out the map of Australia I'd acquired on the flight from England. Melbourne, capital of the state of Victoria, lay right down in the south-east corner. Adelaide, capital of South Australia, lay about four hundred and fifty miles north-west. Correction, seven hundred and thirty kilometres: the Australians had already gone metric, to the confusion of my mental arithmetic.

Hudson Taylor was not in his vineyard office. An equally cheerful voice there told me he'd left for Melbourne to go to the races. He had a runner in the Cup. Reverence, the voice implied, was due.

Could I reach him anywhere, then?

Sure, if it was important. He would be staying with friends. Number supplied. Ring at nine o'clock.

Sighing a little I went two floors down and found Jik and Sarah bouncing around their room with gleeful satisfaction.

'We've got tickets for the races tomorrow and Tuesday,' he said, 'And a car pass, and a car. And the West Indies play Victoria at cricket on Sunday opposite the hotel and we've tickets for that too.'

'Miracles courtesy of the Hilton,' Sarah said, looking much happier at this programme. 'The whole package was on offer with the cancelled rooms.'

'So what do you want us to do this afternoon?' finished Jik expansively.

'Could you bear the Arts Centre?'

It appeared they could. Even Sarah came without forecasting universal doom, my lack of success so far having cheered her. We went in a taxi to keep her curled hair dry.

The Victoria Arts Centre was huge, modern, inventive and endowed with the largest stained-glass roof in the world. Jik took deep breaths as if drawing the living spirit of the place into his lungs and declaimed at the top of his voice that Australia was the greatest, the greatest, the only adventurous country left in the corrupt, stagnating, militant, greedy, freedom-hating, mean-minded, strait-jacketed, rotting, polluted world. Passers-by stared in amazement and Sarah showed no surprise at all.

We ran the Munnings to earth, eventually, deep in the labyrinth of galleries. It glowed in the remarkable light which suffused the whole building; the *Departure of the Hop Pickers*, with its great wide sky and the dignified gypsies with their ponies, caravans and children.

A young man was sitting at an easel slightly to one side, painstakingly working on a copy. On a table beside him stood large pots of linseed oil and turps, and a jar with brushes in cleaning fluid. A comprehensive box of paints lay open to hand. Two or three people stood about, watching him and pretending not to, in the manner of gallery-goers the world over.

Jik and I went round behind him to take a look. The young man glanced at Jik's face, but saw nothing there except raised eyebrows and blandness. We watched him squeeze flake white and cadmium yellow from tubes on to his palette and mix them together into a nice pale colour with a hogshair brush.

On the easel stood his study, barely started. The outlines were there, as precise as tracings, and a small amount of blue had been laid on the sky.

Jik and I watched in interest while he applied the pale yellow to the shirt of the nearest figure.

'Hey,' Jik said loudly, suddenly slapping him on the shoulder and shattering the reverent gallery hush into kaleidoscopic fragments, 'You're a fraud. If you're an artist I'm a gas-fitter's mate.'

Hardly polite, but not a hanging matter. The faces of the scattered onlookers registered embarrassment, not affront.

On the young man, though, the effect was galvanic. He leapt to his feet, overturning the easel and staring at Jik with wild eyes: and Jik, with huge enjoyment, put in the clincher.

'What you're doing is *criminal*,' he said.

The young man reacted to that with ruthless reptilian speed, snatching up the pots of linseed and turps and flinging the liquids at Jik's eyes.

I grabbed his left arm. He scooped up the paint-laden palette in his right and swung round fiercely, aiming at my face. I ducked instinctively. The palette missed me and struck Jik, who had his hands to his eyes and was yelling very loudly.

Sarah rushed towards him, knocking into me hard in her anxiety and loosening my grip on the young man. He tore his arm free, ran precipitously for the exit, dodged round behind two open-mouthed middle-aged spectators who were on their way in, and pushed them violently into my chasing path. By the time I'd disentangled myself, he had vanished from sight. I ran through several halls and passages, but couldn't find him. He knew his way, and I did not: and it took me long enough, when I finally gave up the hunt, to work out the route back to Jik.

A fair-sized crowd had surrounded him, and Sarah was in a roaring fury based on fear, which she unleashed on me as soon as she saw me return.

'Do something,' she screamed. 'Do something, he's going blind . . . He's going *blind* . . . I knew we should never have listened to you . . .'

I caught her wrists as she advanced in near hysteria to do at least some damage to my face in payment for Jik's. Her strength was no joke.

'Sarah,' I said fiercely. 'Jik is *not* going blind.'

'He is. He is,' she insisted, kicking my shins.

'Do you *want* him to?' I shouted.

She gasped sharply in outrage. What I'd said was at least as good as a slap in the face. Sense reasserted itself suddenly like a drench of cold water, and the manic power receded back to normal angry girl proportions.

'Linseed oil will do no harm at all,' I said positively. 'The turps is painful, but that's all. It absolutely will not affect his eyesight.'

She glared at me, pulled her wrists out of my grasp, and turned back to Jik, who was rocking around in agony and cupping his fingers over his eyes with rigid knuckles. Also, being Jik, he was exercising his tongue.

'The slimy little bugger . . . wait till I catch him . . . Jesus Christ Almighty I can't bloody see . . . Sarah . . . where's that bloody Todd . . . I'll strangle him . . . get an ambulance . . . my eyes are burning out . . . bloody buggering hell . . .'

I spoke loudly in his ear. 'Your eyes are O.K.'

'They're my bloody eyes and if I say they're not O.K. they're bloody not.'

'You know damn well you're not going blind, so stop hamming it up.'

'They're not your eyes, you sod.'

'And you're frightening Sarah,' I said.

That message got through. He took his hands away and stopped rolling about.

At the sight of his face a murmur of pleasant horror rippled through the riveted audience. Blobs of bright paint from the young man's palette had streaked one side of his jaw yellow and blue: and his eyes were red with inflammation and pouring with tears, and looked very sore indeed.

'Jesus, Sarah,' he said blinking painfully. 'Sorry, love. The bastard's right. Turps never blinded anybody.'

'Not permanently,' I said, because to do him justice he obviously couldn't see anything but tears at the moment.

Sarah's animosity was unabated. 'Get him an ambulance, then.'

I shook my head. 'All he needs is water and time.'

'You're a stupid heartless *pig*. He obviously needs a doctor, and hospital care.'

Jik, having abandoned histrionics, produced a handkerchief and gently mopped his streaming eyes.

'He's right, love. Lots of water, as the man said. Washes the sting away. Lead me to the nearest gents.'

With Sarah unconvinced but holding one arm, and a sympathetic male spectator the other, he was solicitously helped away like an amateur production of *Samson*. The chorus in the shape of the audience bent reproachful looks on me, and cheerfully awaited the next act.

I looked at the overturned mess of paints and easel which the young man had left. The onlookers looked at them too.

'I suppose,' I said slowly, 'that no one here was talking to the young artist before any of this happened?'

'We were,' said one woman, surprised at the question.

'So were we,' said another.

'What about?'

'Munnings,' said one, and 'Munnings,' said the other, both looking immediately at the painting on the wall.

'Not about his own work?' I said, bending down to pick it up. A slash of yellow lay wildly across the careful outlines, result of Jik's slap on the back.

Both of the ladies, and also their accompanying husbands, shook their heads and said they had talked with him about the pleasure of hanging a Munnings on their own walls, back home.

I smiled slowly.

'I suppose,' I said, 'that he didn't happen to know where you could get one?'

'Well, yeah,' they said. 'As a matter of fact, he sure did.'

'Where?'

'Well, look here, young fellow . . .' The elder of the husbands, a seventyish American with the unmistakable stamp of wealth, began shushing the others to silence with a practised damping movement of his right hand. Don't give information away, it said, you may lose by it. '. . . You're asking a lot of questions.'

'I'll explain,' I said. 'Would you like some coffee?'

They all looked at their watches and said doubtfully they possibly would.

'There's a coffee shop just down the hall,' I said. 'I saw it when I was trying to catch that young man . . . to make him tell why he flung turps in my friend's eyes.'

Curiosity sharpened in their faces. They were hooked.

The rest of the spectators drifted away, and I, asking the others to wait a moment, started moving the jumbled painting stuff off the centre of the floor to a tidier wallside heap.

None of it was marked with its owner's name. All regulation kit, obtainable from art shops. Artists' quality, not students' cheaper equivalents. None of it new, but not old, either. The picture itself was on a standard-sized piece of commercially prepared hardboard, not on stretched canvas. I stacked everything together, added the empty jars which had held linseed and turps, and wiped my hands on a piece of rag.

'Right,' I said. 'Shall we go?'

*

They were all Americans, all rich, retired, and fond of racing. Mr and Mrs Howard K. Petrovitch of Ridgeville, New Jersey, and Mr and Mrs Wyatt L. Minchless from Carter, Illinois.

Wyatt Minchless, the one who had shushed the others, called the meeting to order over four richly creamed iced coffees and one plain black. The black was for himself. Heart condition, he murmured, patting the relevant area of suiting. A white-haired man, black-framed specs, pale indoor complexion, pompous manner.

'Now, young fellow, let's hear it from the top.'

'Um,' I said. Where exactly was the top? 'The artist boy attacked my friend Jik because Jik called him a criminal.'

'Yuh,' Mrs Petrovitch nodded, 'I heard him. Just as we were leaving the gallery. Now why would he do that?'

'It isn't criminal to copy good painting,' Mrs Minchless said knowledgeably. 'In the Louvre in Paris, France, you can't get near the *Mona Lisa* for those irritating students.'

She had blue-rinsed puffed-up hair, uncreasable navy and green clothes, and enough diamonds to attract a top-rank thief. Deep lines of automatic disapproval ran downwards from the corner of her mouth. Thin body. Thick mind.

'It depends what you are copying *for*,' I said. 'If

you're going to try to pass your copy off as an original, then that definitely is a fraud.'

Mrs Petrovitch began to say, 'Do you think the young man was *forging* . . .' but was interrupted by Wyatt Minchless, who smothered her question both by the damping hand and his louder voice.

'Are you saying that this young artist boy was painting a Munnings he later intended to sell as the real thing?'

'Er . . .' I said.

Wyatt Minchless swept on. 'Are you saying that the Munnings picture he told us we might be able to buy is itself a forgery?'

The others looked both horrified at the possibility and admiring of Wyatt L. for his perspicacity.

'I don't know,' I said. 'I just thought I'd like to see it.'

'You don't want to buy a Munnings yourself? You are not acting as an agent for anyone else?' Wyatt's questions sounded severe and inquisitorial.

'Absolutely not,' I said.

'Well, then.' Wyatt looked round the other three, collected silent assents. 'He told Ruthie and me there was a good Munnings racing picture at a very reasonable price in a little gallery not far away . . .' He fished with forefinger and thumb into his outer breast pocket. 'Yes, here we are. Yarra River Fine Arts. Third turning off Swanston Street, about twenty yards along.'

Mr and Mrs Petrovitch looked resigned. 'He told us exactly the same.'

'He seemed such a nice young man,' Mrs Petrovitch added sadly. 'So interested in our trip. Asked us what we'd be betting on in the Cup.'

'He asked where we would be going after Melbourne,' Mr Petrovitch nodded. 'We told him Adelaide and Alice Springs, and he said Alice Springs was a Mecca for artists and to be sure to visit the Yarra River gallery there. The same firm, he said. Always had good pictures.'

Mr Petrovitch would have misunderstood if I had leaned across and hugged him. I concentrated on my fancy coffee and kept my excitement to myself.

'We're going on to Sydney,' pronounced Wyatt L. 'He didn't offer any suggestions for Sydney.'

The tall glasses were nearly empty. Wyatt looked at his watch and swallowed the last of his plain black.

'You didn't tell us,' Mrs Petrovitch said, looking puzzled, 'why your friend called the young man a criminal. I mean . . . I can see why the young man attacked your friend and ran away if he *was* a criminal, but why did your friend *think* he was?'

'Just what I was about to ask,' said Wyatt, nodding away heavily. Pompous liar, I thought.

'My friend Jik,' I said, 'is an artist himself. He didn't think much of the young man's effort. He called it criminal. He might just as well have said lousy.'

'Is that all?' said Mrs Petrovitch, looking disappointed.

'Well . . . the young man was painting with paints

110

which won't really mix. Jik's a perfectionist. He can't stand seeing paint misused.'

'What do you mean, won't mix?'

'Paints are chemicals,' I said apologetically. 'Most of them don't have any effect on each other, but you have to be careful.'

'What happens if you aren't?' demanded Ruthie Minchless.

'Um . . . nothing explodes,' I said, smiling. 'It's just that . . . well, if you mix flake white, which is lead, with cadmium yellow, which contains sulphur, like the young man was doing, you get a nice pale colour to start with but the two minerals react against each other and in time darken and alter the picture.'

'And your friend called this criminal?' Wyatt said in disbelief. 'It couldn't possibly make that much difference.'

'Er . . .' I said. 'Well, Van Gogh used a light bright new yellow made of chrome when he painted a picture of sunflowers. Cadmium yellow hadn't been developed then. But chrome yellow has shown that over a couple of hundred years it decomposes and in the end turns greenish black, and the sunflowers are already an odd colour, and I don't think anyone has found a way of stopping it.'

'But the young man wasn't painting for posterity,' said Ruthie with irritation. 'Unless he's another Van Gogh, surely it doesn't matter.'

I didn't think they'd want to hear that Jik hoped for

111

recognition in the twenty-third century. The permanence of colours had always been an obsession with him, and he'd dragged me along once to a course on their chemistry.

The Americans got up to go.

'All very interesting,' Wyatt said with a dismissive smile. 'I guess I'll keep my money in regular stocks.'

CHAPTER SEVEN

Jik had gone from the gents, gone from the whole Arts Centre. I found him back with Sarah in their hotel room, being attended by the Hilton's attractive resident nurse. The door to the corridor stood open, ready for her to leave.

'Try not to rub them, Mr Cassavetes,' she was saying. 'If you have any trouble, call the reception desk, and I'll come back.'

She gave me a professional half-smile in the open doorway and walked briskly away, leaving me to go in.

'How are the eyes?' I said, advancing tentatively.

'Ruddy awful.' They were bright pink, but dry. Getting better.

Sarah said with tight lips, 'This has all gone far enough. I know that this time Jik will be all right again in a day or two, but we are not taking any more risks.'

Jik said nothing and didn't look at me.

It wasn't exactly unexpected. I said, 'O.K. . . . Well, have a nice weekend, and thanks anyway.'

'Todd . . .' Jik said.

Sarah leapt in fast. 'No, Jik. It's not our responsibility. Todd can think what he likes, but his cousin's troubles are nothing to do with us. We are not getting involved any further. I've been against all this silly poking around all along, and this is where it stops.'

'Todd will go on with it,' Jik said.

'Then he's a fool.' She was angry, scornful, biting.

'Sure,' I said. 'Anyone who tries to right a wrong these days is a fool. Much better not to meddle, not to get involved, not to think it's your responsibility. I really ought to be painting away safely in my attic at Heathrow, minding my own business and letting Donald rot. Much more sensible, I agree. The trouble is that I simply can't do it. I see the hell he's in. How can I just turn my back? Not when there's a chance of getting him out. True enough, I may not manage it, but what I can't face is not having tried.'

I came to a halt.

A blank pause.

'Well,' I said, raising a smile. 'Here endeth the lesson according to the world's foremost nit. Have fun at the races. I might go too, you never know.'

I sketched a farewell and eased myself out. Neither of them said a word. I shut the door quietly and took the lift up to my own room.

A pity about Sarah, I thought. She would have Jik in cotton-wool and slippers if he didn't look out; and he'd never paint those magnificent brooding pictures any more, because they sprang from a torment he

114

would no longer be allowed. Security, to him, would be a sort of abdication; a sort of death.

I looked at my watch and decided the Yarra River Fine Arts set-up might still have its doors open. Worth trying.

I wondered, as I walked along Wellington Parade and up Swanston Street, whether the young turps-flinger would be there, and if he was, whether he would know me. I'd seen only glimpses of his face, as I'd mostly been standing behind him. All one could swear to was light-brown hair, acne on the chin, a round jaw-line and a full-lipped mouth. Under twenty. Perhaps not more than seventeen. Dressed in blue jeans, white tee-shirt, and tennis shoes. About five-foot-eight, a hundred and thirty pounds. Quick on his feet, and liable to panic. And no artist.

The gallery was open, brightly lit, with a horse painting on a gilt display easel in the centre of the window. Not a Munnings. A portrait picture of an Australian horse and jockey, every detail sharp-edged, emphatic, and, to my taste, overpainted. Beside it a notice, gold embossed on black, announced a special display of distinguished equine art; and beside that, less well-produced but with larger letters, stood a display card saying 'Welcome to the Melbourne Cup'.

The gallery looked typical of hundreds of others round the world; narrow frontage, with premises stretching back a good way from the street. Two or three people were wandering about inside, looking at the merchandise on the well-lit neutral grey walls.

I had gone there intending to go in. To go in was still what I intended, but I hesitated outside in the street feeling as if I were at the top of a ski jump. Stupid, I thought. Nothing ventured, nothing gained, and all that. If you don't look, you won't see.

I took a ruefully deep breath and stepped over the welcoming threshold.

Greeny-grey carpet within, and an antique desk strategically placed near the door, with a youngish woman handing out small catalogues and large smiles.

'Feel free to look around,' she said. 'More pictures downstairs.'

She handed me a catalogue, a folded glazed white card with several typed sheets clipped into it. I flipped them over. One hundred and sixty-three items, numbered consecutively, with titles, artists' names, and asking price. A painting already sold, it said, would have a red spot on the frame.

I thanked her. 'Just passing by,' I said.

She nodded and smiled professionally, eyes sliding in a rapid summing-up over my denim clothes and general air of not belonging to the jet set. She herself wore the latest trendy fashion with careless ease and radiated tycoon-catching sincerity. Australian, assured, too big a personality to be simply a receptionist.

'You're welcome anyway,' she said.

I walked slowly down the long room, checking the

pictures against their notes. Most were by Australian artists, and I could see what Jik had meant about the hot competition. The field was just as crowded as at home, if not more so, and the standard in some respects better. As usual when faced with other people's flourishing talents I began to have doubts of my own.

At the far end of the ground-floor display there was a staircase leading downwards, adorned with a large arrow and a notice repeating 'More Pictures Downstairs'.

I went down. Same carpet, same lighting, but no scatter of customers looking from pictures to catalogues and back again.

Below stairs, the gallery was not one straight room but a series of small rooms off a long corridor, apparently the result of not being able to knock down all the dividing and load-bearing walls. A room to the rear of the stairs was an office, furnished with another distinguished desk, two or three comfortable chairs for prospective clients, and a civilized row of teak-faced filing cabinets. Heavily framed pictures adorned the walls, and an equally substantial man was writing in a ledger at the desk.

He raised his head, conscious of my presence outside his door.

'Can I help you?' he said.

'Just looking.'

He gave me an uninterested nod and went back to his work. He, like the whole place, had an air of permanence and respectability quite unlike the fly-by-night suburban affair in Sydney. This reputable business, I thought, could not be what I was looking for. I had got the whole thing wrong. I would have to wait until I could get Hudson Taylor to look up Donald's cheque and point me in a new direction.

Sighing, I continued down the line of rooms, thinking I might as well finish taking stock of the opposition. A few of the frames were adorned with red spots, but the prices on everything good were a mile from a bargain and a deterrent to all but the rich.

In the end room, which was larger than the others, I came across the Munningses. Three of them. All with horses: one racing scene, one hunting, one of gypsies.

They were not in the catalogue.

They hung without ballyhoo in a row of similar subjects, and to my eyes stuck out like thoroughbreds among hacks.

Prickles began up my spine. It wasn't just the workmanship, but one of the pictures itself. Horses going down to the start. A long line of jockeys, bright against a dark sky. The silks of the nearest rider, purple with a green cap.

Maisie's chatty voice reverberated in my inner ear, describing what I saw. '... I expect you'll think I was silly but that was one of the reasons I bought it ... because Archie and I decided we'd like purple with a green cap for our colours, if no one already had that ...'

118

Munnings had always used a good deal of purple and green in shadows and distances. All the same . . . This picture, size, subject, and colouring, was exactly like Maisie's, which had been hidden behind a radiator, and, presumably, burned.

The picture in front of me looked authentic. The right sort of patina for the time since Munnings' death, the right excellence of draughtsmanship, the right indefinable something which separated the great from the good. I put out a gentle finger to feel the surface of canvas and paint. Nothing there that shouldn't be.

An English voice from behind me said, 'Can I help you?'

'Isn't that a Munnings?' I said casually, turning round.

He was standing in the doorway, looking in, his expression full of the guarded helpfulness of one whose best piece of stock is being appraised by someone apparently too poor to buy it.

I knew him instantly. Brown receding hair combed back, grey eyes, down-drooping moustache, suntanned skin: all last on view thirteen days ago beside the sea in Sussex, England, prodding around in a smoky ruin.

Mr Greene. With an 'e'.

It took him only a fraction longer. Puzzlement as he glanced from me to the picture and back, then the shocking realization of where he'd seen me. He took a sharp step backwards and raised his hand to the wall outside.

I was on my way to the door, but I wasn't quick enough. A steel mesh gate slid down very fast in the doorway and clicked into some sort of bolt in the floor. Mr Greene stood on the outside, disbelief still stamped on every feature and his mouth hanging open. I revised all my easy theories about danger being good for the soul and felt as frightened as I'd ever been in my life.

'What's the matter?' called a deeper voice from up the corridor.

Mr Greene's tongue was stuck. The man from the office appeared at his shoulder and looked at me through the imprisoning steel.

'A thief?' he asked with irritation.

Mr Greene shook his head. A third person arrived outside, his young face bright with curiosity, and his acne showing like measles.

'Hey,' he said in loud Australian surprise. 'He was the one at the Arts Centre. The one who chased me. I swear he didn't follow me. I swear it.'

'Shut up,' said the man from the office briefly. He stared at me steadily. I stared back.

I was standing in the centre of a brightly lit room of about fifteen feet square. No windows. No way out except through the guarded door. Nowhere to hide, no weapons to hand. A long way down the ski jump and no promise of a soft landing.

'I say,' I said plaintively. 'Just what is all this about?' I walked up to the steel gate and tapped on it. 'Open this up, I want to get out.'

'What are you doing here?' the office man said. He was bigger than Greene and obviously more senior in the gallery. Heavy dark spectacle frames over unfriendly eyes, and a blue bow tie with polka dots under a double chin. Small mouth with a full lower lip. Thinning hair.

'Looking,' I said, trying to sound bewildered. 'Just looking at pictures.' An innocent at large, I thought, and a bit dim.

'He chased me in the Arts Centre,' the boy repeated.

'You threw some stuff in that man's eyes,' I said indignantly. 'You might have blinded him.'

'Friend of yours, was he?' the office man said.

'No,' I said. 'I was just there, that was all. Same as I'm here. Just looking at pictures. Nothing wrong in that, is there? I go to lots of galleries, all the time.'

Mr Greene got his voice back. 'I saw him in England,' he said to the office man. His eyes returned to the Munnings, then he put his hand on the office man's arm and pulled him up the corridor out of my sight.

'Open the door,' I said to the boy, who still gazed in.

'I don't know how,' he said. 'And I don't reckon I'd be popular, somehow.'

The two other men returned. All three gazed in. I began to feel sympathy for creatures in cages.

'Who *are* you?' said the office man.

'Nobody. I mean, I'm just here for the racing, of course, and the cricket.'

'Name?'

'Charles Neil.' Charles Neil Todd.

'What were you doing in England?'

'I live there!' I said. 'Look,' I went on, as if trying to be reasonable under great provocation. 'I saw this man here,' I nodded to Greene, 'at the home of a woman I know slightly in Sussex. She was giving me a lift home from the races, see, as I'd missed my train to Worthing and was thumbing along the road from the Members' car park. Well, she stopped and picked me up, and then said she wanted to make a detour to see her house which had lately been burnt, and when we got there, this man was there. He said his name was Greene and that he was from an insurance company, and that's all I know about him. So what's going on?'

'It is a coincidence that you should meet here again so soon.'

'It certainly is,' I agreed fervently. 'But that's no bloody reason to lock me up.'

I read indecision on all their faces. I hoped the sweat wasn't running visibly down my own.

I shrugged exasperatedly. 'Fetch the police or something, then,' I said. 'If you think I've done anything wrong.'

The man from the office put his hand to the switch on the outside wall and carefully fiddled with it, and the steel gate slid up out of sight, a good deal more slowly than it had come down.

'Sorry,' he said perfunctorily. 'But we have to be careful, with so many valuable paintings on the premises.'

'Well, I see that,' I said, stepping forward and resisting a strong impulse to make a dash for it. 'But all the same . . .' I managed an aggrieved tone. 'Still, no harm done, I suppose.' Magnanimous, as well.

They all walked behind me along the corridor and up the stairs and through the upper gallery, doing my nerves no slightest good. All the other visitors seemed to have left. The receptionist was locking the front door.

My throat was dry beyond swallowing.

'I thought everyone had gone,' she said in surprise.

'Slight delay,' I said, with a feeble laugh.

She gave me the professional smile and reversed the locks. Opened the door. Held it, waiting for me.

Six steps.

Out in the fresh air.

God almighty, it smelled good. I half turned. All four stood in the gallery watching me go. I shrugged and nodded and trudged away into the drizzle, feeling as weak as a fieldmouse dropped by a hawk.

I caught a passing tram and travelled a good way into unknown regions of the huge city, conscious only of an urgent desire to put a lot of distance between myself and that basement prison.

They would have second thoughts. They were bound to. They would wish they had found out more about me before letting me go. They couldn't be certain it wasn't a coincidence that I'd turned up at their gallery because far more amazing coincidences did exist, like Lincoln at the time of his assassination having a secretary called Kennedy and Kennedy having a secretary called Lincoln; but the more they thought about it the less they would believe it.

If they wanted to find me, where would they look? Not at the Hilton, I thought in amusement. At the races: I had told them I would be there. On the whole I wished I hadn't.

At the end of the tramline I got off and found myself opposite a small interesting-looking restaurant with B.Y.O. in large letters on the door. Hunger as usual rearing its healthy head, I went in and ordered a steak, and asked for a look at the wine list.

The waitress looked surprised. 'It's B.Y.O.,' she said.

'What's B.Y.O.?'

Her eyebrows went still higher. 'You are a stranger? Bring Your Own. We don't sell drinks here, only food.'

'Oh.'

'If you want something to drink, there's a drive-in bottle shop a hundred yards down the road that'll still be open. I could hold the steak until you get back.'

I shook my head and settled for a teetotal dinner, grinning all through coffee at a notice on the wall saying 'We have an arrangement with our bank. They don't fry steaks and we don't cash cheques.'

When I set off back to the city centre on the tram, I passed the bottle shop, which at first sight looked so like a garage that if I hadn't known I would have thought the line of cars was queuing for petrol. I could see why Jik liked the Australian imagination: both sense and fun.

The rain had stopped. I left the tram and walked the last couple of miles through the bright streets and dark parks, asking the way. Thinking of Donald and Maisie and Greene with an 'e', and of paintings and burglaries and violent minds.

The overall plan had all along seemed fairly simple: to sell pictures in Australia and steal them back in England, together with everything else lying handy. As I had come across two instances within three weeks, I had been sure there had to be more, because it was surely impossible that I could have stumbled on the *only* two, even given the double link of racing and painting. Since I'd met the Petrovitches and the Minchlesses, it seemed I'd been wrong to think of all the robberies taking place in England. Why not in America? Why not anywhere that was worth the risk?

Why not a mobile force of thieves shuttling containerfuls of antiques from continent to continent, selling briskly to a ravenous market? As Inspector Frost had said, few antiques were ever recovered. The demand was insatiable and the supply, by definition, limited.

Suppose I were a villain, I thought, and I didn't want to waste weeks in foreign countries finding out exactly which houses were worth robbing. I could just stay quietly at home in Melbourne selling paintings to rich visitors who could afford an impulse-buy of ten thousand pounds or so. I could chat away with them about their picture collections back home, and I could shift the conversation easily to their silver and china and objets d'art.

I wouldn't want the sort of customers who had Rembrandts or Fabergés or anything well-known and unsaleable like that. Just the middling wealthy with Georgian silver and lesser Gauguins and Chippendale chairs.

When they bought my paintings, they would give me their addresses. Nice and easy. Just like that.

I would be a supermarket type of villain, with a large turnover of small goods. I would reckon that if I kept the victims reasonably well scattered, the fact that they had been to Australia within the past year or so would mean nothing to each regional police force. I would reckon that among the thousands of burglary claims they had to settle, Australian visits would bear no significance to insurance companies.

I would not, though, reckon on a crossed wire like Charles Neil Todd.

If I were a villain, I thought, with a well-established

business and a good reputation, I wouldn't put myself at risk by selling fakes. Forged oil paintings were almost always detectable under a microscope, even if one discounted that the majority of experienced dealers could tell them at a glance. A painter left his signature all over a painting, not just in the corner, because the way he held his brush was as individual as handwriting. Brush strokes could be matched as conclusively as grooves on bullets.

If I were a villain I'd wait in my spider's web with a real Munnings, or maybe a real Picasso drawing, or a genuine work by a recently dead good artist whose output had been voluminous, and along would come the rich little flies, carefully steered my way by talkative accomplices who stood around in the states' capitals' art galleries for the purpose. Both Donald and Maisie had been hooked that way.

Supposing when I'd sold a picture to a man from England and robbed him, and got my picture back again, I then sold it to someone from America. And then robbed him, and got it back, and so on and round.

Suppose I sold a picture to Maisie in Sydney, and got it back, and started to sell it again in Melbourne . . . My supposing stopped right there, because it didn't fit.

If Maisie had left her picture in full view it would have been stolen like her other things. Maybe it even had been, and was right now glowing in the Yarra

127

River Fine Arts, but if so, why had the house been burnt, and why had Mr Greene turned up to search the ruins?

It only made sense if Maisie's picture had been a copy, and if the thieves hadn't been able to find it. Rather than leave it around, they'd burned the house. But I'd just decided that I wouldn't risk fakes. Except that ... would Maisie know an expert copy if she saw one? No, she wouldn't.

I sighed. To fool even Maisie you'd have to find an accomplished artist willing to copy instead of pressing on with his own work, and they weren't that thick on the ground. All the same, she'd bought her picture in the short-lived Sydney gallery, not in Melbourne, so maybe in other places besides Melbourne they would take a risk with fakes.

The huge bulk of the hotel rose ahead of me across the last stretch of park. The night air blew cool on my head. I had a vivid feeling of being disconnected, a stranger in a vast continent, a speck under the stars. The noise and warmth of the Hilton brought the expanding universe down to imaginable size.

Upstairs, I telephoned Hudson Taylor at the number his secretary had given me. Nine o'clock on the dot. He sounded mellow and full of good dinner, his voice strong, courteous and vibrantly Australian.

'Donald Stuart's cousin? Is it true about little Regina being killed?'

'I'm afraid so.'

'It's a real tragedy. A real nice lass, that Regina.'

'Yes.'

'Lookee here, then, what can I do for you? Is it tickets for the races?'

'Er, no,' I said. 'It was just that since the receipt and provenance letter of the Munnings had been stolen along with the picture, Donald would like to get in touch with the people who had sold it to him, for insurance purposes, but he had forgotten their name. And as I was coming to Melbourne for the Cup . . .'

'That's easy enough,' Hudson Taylor said pleasantly. 'I remember the place well. I went with Donald to see the picture there, and the guy in charge brought it along to the Hilton afterwards, when we arranged the finance. Now let's see . . .' There was a pause for thought. 'I can't remember the name of the place just now. Or the manager. It was some months ago, do you see? But I've got him on record here in the Melbourne office, and I'm calling in there anyway in the morning, so I'll look them up. You'll be at the races tomorrow?'

'Yes,' I said.

'How about meeting for a drink, then? You can tell me about poor Donald and Regina, and I'll have the information he wants.'

I said that would be fine, and he gave me detailed instructions as to where I would find him, and when. 'There will be a huge crowd,' he said. 'But if you stand on that exact spot I shouldn't miss you.'

The spot he had described sounded public and exposed. I hoped that it would only be he who found me on it.

'I'll be there,' I said.

CHAPTER EIGHT

Jik called through on the telephone at eight next morning.

'Come down to the coffee shop and have breakfast.'

'O.K.'

I went down in the lift and along the foyer to the hotel's informal restaurant. He was sitting at a table alone, wearing dark glasses and making inroads into a mountain of scrambled egg.

'They bring you coffee,' he said, 'but you have to fetch everything else from that buffet.' He nodded towards a large well-laden table in the centre of the breezy blue and sharp green decor. 'How's things?'

'Not what they used to be.'

He made a face. 'Bastard.'

'How are the eyes?'

He whipped off the glasses with a theatrical flourish and leaned forward to give me a good look. Pink, they were, and still inflamed, but on the definite mend.

'Has Sarah relented?' I asked.

'She's feeling sick.'

'Oh?'

'God knows,' he said. 'I hope not. I don't want a kid yet. She isn't overdue or anything.'

'She's a nice girl,' I said.

He slid me a glance. 'She says she's got nothing against you personally.'

'But,' I said.

He nodded. 'The mother hen syndrome.'

'Wouldn't have cast you as a chick.'

He put down his knife and fork. 'Nor would I, by God. I told her to cheer up and get this little enterprise over as soon as possible and face the fact she hadn't married a marshmallow.'

'And she said?'

He gave a twisted grin. 'From my performance in bed last night, that she had.'

I wondered idly about the success or otherwise of their sex life. From the testimony of one or two past girls who had let their hair down to me while waiting hours in the flat for Jik's unpredictable return, he was a moody lover, quick to arousal and easily put off. 'It only takes a dog barking, and he's gone.' Not much, I dared say, had changed.

'Anyway,' he said. 'There's this car we've got. Damned silly if you didn't come with us to the races.'

'Would Sarah . . .', I asked carefully, '. . . scowl?'

'She says not.'

I accepted this offer and inwardly sighed. It looked as if he wouldn't take the smallest step henceforth without the nod from Sarah. When the wildest ones got married, was it always like that? Wedded bliss putting nets over the eagles.

'Where did you get to, last night?' he said.

'Aladdin's cave,' I said. 'Treasures galore and damned lucky to escape the boiling oil.'

I told him about the gallery, the Munnings, and my brief moment of captivity. I told him what I thought of the burglaries. It pleased him. His eyes gleamed with humour and the familiar excitement rose.

'How are we going to prove it?' he said.

He heard the 'we' as soon as he said it. He laughed ruefully, the fizz dying away. 'Well, how?'

'Don't know yet.'

'I'd like to help,' he said apologetically.

I thought of a dozen sarcastic replies and stifled the lot. It was I who was the one out of step, not them. The voice of the past had no right to break up the future.

'You'll do what pleases Sarah,' I said with finality, and as an order, not a prodding satire.

'Don't sound so bloody bossy.'

We finished breakfast amicably trying to build a suitable new relationship on the ruins of the old, and both knowing well what we were about.

When I met them later in the hall at setting-off time it was clear that Sarah too had made a reassessment and put her mind to work on her emotions. She greeted me with an attempted smile and an outstretched hand.

I shook the hand lightly and also gave her a token kiss on the cheek. She took it as it was meant.

Truce made, terms agreed, pact signed. Jik the mediator stood around looking smug.

'Take a look at him,' he said, flapping a hand in my direction. 'The complete stockbroker. Suit, tie, leather shoes. If he isn't careful they'll have him in the Royal Academy.'

Sarah looked bewildered. 'I thought that was an honour.'

'It depends,' said Jik, sneering happily. 'Passable artists with polished social graces get elected in their thirties. Masters with average social graces, in their forties; masters with no social graces, in their fifties. Geniuses who don't give a damn about being elected are ignored as long as possible.'

'Putting Todd in the first category and yourself in the last?' Sarah said.

'Of course.'

'Stands to reason,' I said. 'You never hear about young masters. Masters are always old.'

'For God's sake,' Sarah said. 'Let's go to the races.'

We went slowly, on account of a continuous stream of traffic going the same way. The car park at Flemington racecourse, when we arrived, looked like a giant picnic ground, with hundreds of full-scale lunch parties going on between the cars. Tables, chairs, cloths, china, silver, glass. Sun umbrellas optimistically raised in defiance of the rain-clouds threatening above. A lot of gaiety and booze and a giant overall statement that 'This Was The Life.'

To my mild astonishment Jik and Sarah had come prepared. They whipped out table, chairs, drinks and food from the rented car's boot and said it was easy when you knew how, you just ordered the whole works.

'I have an uncle,' Sarah said, 'who holds the title of Fastest Bar in the West. It takes him roughly ten seconds from putting the brakes on to pouring the first drink.'

She was really trying, I thought. Not just putting up with an arrangement for Jik's sake, but actually trying to make it work. If it was an effort, it didn't show. She was wearing an interesting olive-green linen coat, with a broad-brimmed hat of the same colour, which she held on from time to time against little gusts of wind. Overall, a new Sarah, prettier, more relaxed, less afraid.

'Champagne?' Jik offered, popping the cork. 'Steak and oyster pie?'

'How will I go back to cocoa and chips?'

'Fatter.'

We demolished the goodies, repacked the boot, and with a sense of taking part in some vast semi-religious ritual, squeezed along with the crowd through the gate to the holy of holies.

'It'll be much worse than this on Tuesday,' observed Sarah, who had been to these junkets several times in the past. 'Melbourne Cup day is a public holiday. The

city has three million inhabitants and half of them wil
try to get here.' She was shouting above the crowd
noises and holding grimly on to her hat against the
careless buffeting all around.

'If they've got any sense they'll stay at home and
watch it on the box,' I said breathlessly, receiving a
hefty kidney punch from the elbow of a man fighting
his way into a can of beer.

'It won't be on the television in Melbourne, only on
the radio.'

'Good grief. Why ever not?'

'Because they want everyone to come. It's televised
all over the rest of Australia, but not on its own
doorstep.'

'Same with the golf and the cricket,' Jik said with a
touch of gloom. 'And you can't even have a decent bet
on those.'

We went through the bottleneck and, by virtue of
the inherited badges, through a second gate and round
into the calmer waters of the green oblong of Mem
bers' lawn. Much like on many a Derby Day at home
I thought. Same triumph of will over weather. Brigh
faces under grey skies. Warm coats over the pretty
silks, umbrellas at the ready for the occasional top hat
When I painted pictures of racegoers in the rain, whicl
I sometimes did, most people laughed. I neve
minded. I reckoned it meant they understood that the
inner warmth of a pleasure couldn't be externally

damped; that they too might play a trumpet in a thunderstorm.

Come to think of it, I thought, why didn't I paint a racegoer playing a trumpet in a thunderstorm? It might be symbolic enough even for Jik.

My friends were deep in a cross-talking assessment of the form of the first race. Sarah, it appeared, had a betting pedigree as long as her husband's, and didn't agree with him.

'I know it was soft going at Randwick last week. But it's pretty soft here too after all this rain, and he likes it on top.'

'He was only beaten by Boyblue at Randwick, and Boyblue was out of sight in the Caulfield Cup.'

'Please your silly self,' Sarah said loftily. 'But it's still too soft for Grapevine.'

'Want to bet?' Jik asked me.

'Don't know the horses.'

'As if that mattered.'

'Right.' I consulted the racecard. 'Two dollars on Generator.'

They both looked up, and they both said 'Why?'

'If in doubt, back number eleven. I once went nearly through the card on number eleven.'

They made clucking and pooh-poohing noises and told me I could make a gift of my two dollars to the bookies or the T.A.B.

'The what?'

'Totalizator Agency Board.'

137

The bookmakers, it seemed, were strictly on-course only, with no big firms as in England. All off-course betting shops were run by the T.A.B., which returned a good share of the lolly to racing. Racing was rich, rock-solid, and flourishing. Bully for Australia, Jik said.

We took our choice and paid our money, and Generator won at twenty-fives.

'Beginner's luck,' Sarah said.

Jik laughed. 'He's no beginner. He got kicked out of playschool for running a book.'

They tore up their tickets, set their minds to race two, and made expeditions to place their bets. I settled for four dollars on number one.

'Why?'

'Double my stake on half of eleven.'

'Oh God,' said Sarah. 'You're something else.'

One of the more aggressive clouds started scattering rain, and the less hardy began to make for shelter.

'Come on,' I said. 'Let's go and sit up there in the dry.'

'You two go,' Sarah said. 'I can't.'

'Why not?'

'Because those seats are only for men.'

I laughed. I thought she was joking, but it appeared it was no joke. Very unfunny, in fact. About two thirds of the best seats in the Members' stands were reserved for males.

'What about their wives and girlfriends?' I said incredulously.

'They can go up on the roof.'

Sarah, being Australian, saw nothing very odd in it. To me, and surely to Jik, it was ludicrous.

He said with a carefully straight face, 'On a lot of the bigger courses the men who run Australian racing give themselves leather armchairs behind glass to watch from, and thick-carpeted restaurants and bars to eat and drink like kings in, and let their women eat in the cafeterias and sit on hard plastic chairs on the open stands among the rest of the crowd. They consider this behaviour quite normal. All anthropological groups consider their most bizarre tribal customs quite normal.'

'I thought you were in love with all things Australian.'

Jik sighed heavily. 'Nowhere's perfect.'

'I'm getting wet,' Sarah said.

We escalated to the roof which had a proportion of two women to one man and was windy and damp, with bench seating.

'Don't worry about it,' Sarah said, amused at my aghastness on behalf of womankind. 'I'm used to it.'

'I thought this country made a big thing about equality for all.'

'For all except half the population,' Jik said.

We could see the whole race superbly from our eyrie. Sarah and Jik screamed encouragement to their fancies but number one finished in front by two lengths, at eight to one.

'It's disgusting,' Sarah said, tearing up more tickets. 'What number do you fancy for the third?'

'I won't be with you for the third. I've got an appointment to have a drink with someone who knows Donald.'

She took it in, and the lightness went out of her manner. 'More . . . investigating?'

'I have to.'

'Yes.' She swallowed and made a visible effort. 'Well . . . Good luck.'

'You're a great girl.'

She looked surprised that I should think so and suspicious that I was intending sarcasm, and also partly pleased. I returned earthwards with her multiple expression amusing my mind.

The Members' lawn was bounded on one long side by the stands and on the opposite side by the path taken by the horses on their way from the saddling boxes to the parade ring. One short side of the lawn lay alongside part of the parade ring itself: and it was at the corner of lawn where the horses' path reached the parade ring that I was to meet Hudson Taylor.

The rain had almost stopped, which was good news for my suit. I reached the appointed spot and stood there waiting, admiring the brilliant scarlet of the long bedful of flowers which lined the railing between horse-walk and lawn. Cadmium red mixtures with highlights of orange and white and maybe a streak or two of expensive vermilion . . .

'Charles Todd?'

'Yes . . . Mr Taylor?'

'Hudson. Glad to know you.' He shook hands, his grip dry and firm. Late forties, medium height, comfortable build, with affable, slightly sad eyes sloping downwards at the outer corners. He was one of the minority of men in morning suits, and he wore it as comfortably as a sweater.

'Let's find somewhere dry,' he said. 'Come this way.'

He led me steadily up the bank of steps, in through an entrance door, down a wide interior corridor running the whole length of the stands, past a uniformed guard and a notice saying 'Committee Only', and into a large square comfortable room fitted out as a small-scale bar. The journey had been one long polite push through expensively dressed cohorts, but the bar was comparatively quiet and empty. A group of four, two men, two women, stood chatting with half-filled glasses held close to their chests, and two women in furs were complaining loudly of the cold.

'They love to bring out the sables,' Hudson Taylor chuckled, fetching two glasses of Scotch and gesturing to me to sit by a small table. 'Spoils their fun, the years it's hot for this meeting.'

'Is it usually hot?'

'Melbourne's weather can change twenty degrees in an hour.' He sounded proud of it. 'Now then, this business of yours.' He delved into an inner breast pocket and surfaced with a folded paper. 'Here you

141

are, typed out for Donald. The gallery was called Yarra
River Fine Arts.'

I would have been astounded if it hadn't been.

'And the man we dealt with was someone called
Ivor Wexford.'

'What did he look like?' I asked.

'I don't remember very clearly. It was back in April,
do you see?'

I thought briefly and pulled a small slim sketch-
book out of my pocket.

'If I draw him, might you know him?'

He looked amused. 'You never know.'

I drew quickly in soft pencil a reasonable likeness
of Greene, but without the moustache.

'Was it him?'

Hudson Taylor looked doubtful. I drew in the moustache. He shook his head decisively. 'No, that wasn't
him.'

'How about this?'

I flipped over the page and started again. Hudson
Taylor looked pensive as I did my best with the man
from the basement office.

'Maybe,' he said.

I made the lower lip fuller, added heavy-framed
spectacles, and a bow tie with spots.

'That's him,' said Hudson in surprise. 'I remember
the bow tie, anyway. You don't see many of those these
days. How did you know? You must have met him.'

'I walked round a couple of galleries yesterday afternoon.'

'That's quite a gift you have there,' he said with interest, watching me put the notebook away.

'Practice, that's all.' Years of seeing people's faces as matters of shapes and proportions and planes, and remembering which way the lines slanted. I could already have drawn Hudson's eyes from memory. It was a knack I'd had from childhood.

'Sketching is your hobby?' Hudson asked.

'And my work. I mostly paint horses.'

'Really?' He glanced at the equine portraits decorating the wall. 'Like these?'

I nodded, and we talked a little about painting for a living.

'Maybe I can give you a commission, if my horse runs well in the Cup.' He smiled, the outer edges of his eyes crinkling finely. 'If he's down the field, I'll feel more like shooting him.'

He stood up and gestured me still to follow. 'Time for the next race. Care to watch it with me?'

We emerged into daylight in the prime part of the stands, overlooking the big square enclosure which served both for parading the runners before the race and unsaddling the winners after. I was amused to see that the front rows of seats were all for men: two couples walking in front of us split like amoebas, the husbands going down left, the women up right.

'Down here,' Hudson said, pointing.

'May we only go up there if accompanied by a lady?'
I asked.

He glanced at me sideways, and smiled. 'You find
our ways odd? We'll go up, by all means.'

He led the way and settled comfortably among the
predominantly female company, greeting several
people and introducing me companionably as his friend
Charles from England. Instant first names, instant
acceptance, Australian style.

'Regina hated all this division of the sexes, poor
lass,' he said. 'But it has interesting historical roots.'
He chuckled. 'Australia was governed nearly all last
century with the help of the British Army. The officers
and gentlemen left their wives back in England, but
such is nature, they all set up liaisons here with women
of low repute. They didn't want their fellow officers to
see the vulgarity of their choice, so they invented a
rule that the officers' enclosures were for men only,
which effectively silenced their popsies' pleas to be
taken.'

I laughed. 'Very neat.'

'It's easier to establish a tradition,' Hudson said,
'than to get rid of it.'

'You're establishing a great tradition for fine wines,
Donald says.'

The sad-looking eyes twinkled with civilized pleasure. 'He was most enthusiastic. He travelled round all
the big vineyards, of course, besides visiting us.'

The horses for the third race cantered away to the

start, led by a fractious chestnut colt with too much white about his head.

'Ugly brute,' Hudson said. 'But he'll win.'

'Are you backing it?'

He smiled. 'I've a little bit on.'

The race started and the field sprinted, and Hudson's knuckles whitened so much from his grip as he gazed intently through his binoculars that I wondered just how big the little bit was. The chestnut colt was beaten into fourth place. Hudson put his raceglasses down slowly and watched the unsatisfactory finish with a blank expression.

'Oh well,' he said, his sad eyes looking even sadder. 'Always another day.' He shrugged resignedly, cheered up, shook my hand, told me to remember him to Donald, and asked if I could find my own way out.

'Thank you for your help,' I said.

He smiled. 'Any time. Any time.'

With only a couple of wrong turnings I reached ground level, listening on the way to fascinating snippets of Australian conversation.

'. . . They say he's an embarrassment as a Committee man. He only opens his mouth to change feet . . .'

'. . . a beastly stomach wog, so he couldn't come . . .'

'. . . told him to stop whingeing like a bloody Pommie, and get on with it . . .'

'. . . won twenty dollars? Good on yer, Joanie . . .'

And everywhere the diphthong vowels which gave the word 'No' about five separate sounds, defying my attempts to copy it. I'd been told on the flight over, by an Australian, that all Australians spoke with one single accent. It was about as true as saying all Americans spoke alike, or all British. English was infinitely elastic; and alive, well and living in Melbourne.

Jik and Sarah, when I rejoined them, were arguing about their fancies for the Victoria Derby, next race on the card.

'Ivory Ball is out of his class and has as much chance as a blind man in a blizzard.'

Sarah ignored this. 'He won at Moonee Valley last week and two of the tipsters picked him.'

'Those tipsters must have been drunk.'

'Hello Todd,' Sarah said. 'Pick a number, for God's sake.'

'Ten.'

'Why ten?'

'Eleven minus one.'

'Jesus,' Jik said. 'You used to have more sense.'

Sarah looked it up. 'Royal Road. Compared with Royal Road, Ivory Ball's a certainty.'

We bought our tickets and went up to the roof, and none of our bets came up. Sarah disgustedly yelled at Ivory Ball who had at least managed fifth, but Royal Road fell entirely by the wayside. The winner was number twelve.

'You should have *added* eleven and one,' Sarah said. 'You make such silly mistakes.'

'What are you staring at?' Jik said.

I was looking attentively down at the crowd which had watched the race from ground level on the Members' lawn.

'Lend me your raceglasses . . .'

Jik handed them over. I raised them, took a long look, and slowly put them down.

'What is it?' Sarah said anxiously. 'What's the matter?'

'That,' I said, 'has not only torn it, but ripped the bloody works apart.'

'What has?'

'Do you see those two men . . . about twenty yards along from the parade ring railing . . . one of them in a grey morning suit?'

'What about them?' Jik said.

'The man in the morning suit is Hudson Taylor, the man I just had a drink with. He's the Managing Director of a wine-making firm, and he saw a lot of my cousin Donald when he was over here. And the other man is called Ivor Wexford, and he's the Manager of the Yarra River Fine Arts Gallery.'

'So what?' Sarah said.

'So I can just about imagine the conversation that's going on down there,' I said. 'Something like, "Excuse me, sir, but didn't I sell a picture to you recently?" "Not to me, Mr Wexford, but to my friend Donald Stuart." "And who was that young man I saw you talking to just now?" "That was Donald Stuart's cousin, Mr Wexford." "And what do you know about him?"

"That he's a painter by trade and drew a picture of you, Mr Wexford, and asked me for your name." '

I stopped. 'Go on,' Jik said.

I watched Wexford and Hudson Taylor stop talking, nod casually to each other, and walk their separate ways.

'Ivor Wexford now knows he made a horrible mistake in letting me out of his gallery last night.'

Sarah looked searchingly at my face. 'You really do think that's very serious.'

'Yes I really do.' I loosened a few tightened muscles and tried a smile. 'At the least, he'll be on his guard.'

'And at the most,' Jik said, 'he'll come looking for you.'

'Er . . .' I said thoughtfully. 'What do either of you feel about a spot of instant travel?'

'Where to?'

'Alice Springs?' I said.

CHAPTER NINE

Jik complained all the way to the airport on various counts. One, that he would be missing the cricket. Two, that I hadn't let him go back to the Hilton for his paints. Three, that his Derby clothes would be too hot in Alice. Four, that he wasn't missing the Melbourne Cup for any little ponce with a bow tie.

None of the colourful gripes touched on the fact that he was paying for all our fares with his credit card, as I had left my traveller's cheques in the hotel.

It had been Sarah's idea not to go back there.

'If we're going to vanish, let's get on with it,' she said. 'It's running back into fires for handbags that gets people burnt.'

'You don't have to come,' I said tentatively.

'We've been through all that. What do you think the rest of my life would be like if I stopped Jik helping you, and you came to grief?'

'You'd never forgive me.'

She smiled ruefully. 'You're dead right.'

As far as I could tell we had left the racecourse

unobserved, and certainly no one car had followed us to the airport. Neither Greene with an 'e' nor the boy non-artist appeared underfoot to trip us up, and we travelled uneventfully on a half-full aircraft on the first leg to Adelaide, and an even emptier one from there to Alice Springs.

The country beneath us from Adelaide northwards turned gradually from fresh green to grey-green, and finally to a fierce brick red.

'Gaba,' said Jik, pointing downwards.

'What?'

'G.A.B.A.,' he said. 'Gaba. Stands for Great Australian Bugger All.'

I laughed. The land did indeed look baked, deserted, and older than time, but there were track-like roads here and there, and incredibly isolated homesteads. I watched in fascination until it grew dark, the purple shadows rushing in like a tide as we swept north into the central wastelands.

The night air at Alice was hot, as if someone had forgotten to switch off the oven. The luck which had presented us with an available flight as soon as we reached Melbourne airport seemed still to be functioning: a taciturn taxi driver took us straight to a new-looking motel which proved to have room for us.

'The season is over,' he grunted, when we congratulated and thanked him. 'It will soon be too hot for tourists.'

Our rooms were air-conditioned, however. Jik and

Sarah's was down on the ground floor, their door opening directly on to a shady covered walk which bordered a small garden with a pool. Mine, in an adjacent wing across the car park, was two tall floors up, reached by an outside tree-shaded staircase and a long open gallery. The whole place looked greenly peaceful in the scattered spotlights which shone unobtrusively from palms and gums.

The motel restaurant had closed for the night at eight o'clock, so we walked along the main street to another. The road surface itself was tarmacked, but some of the side roads were not, nor were the footpaths uniformly paved. Often enough we were walking on bare fine grit, and we could see from the dust haze in the headlights of passing cars that the grit was bright red.

'Bull dust,' Sarah said. 'I've never seen it before. My aunt swore it got inside her locked trunk once when she and my uncle drove out to Ayers Rock.'

'What's Ayers Rock?' I said.

'Ignorant Pommie,' Sarah said. 'It's a chunk of sandstone two miles long and a third of a mile high left behind by some careless glacier in the ice age.'

'Miles out in the desert,' Jik added. 'A place of ancient magic regularly desecrated by the plastic society.'

'Have you been there?' I asked dryly.

He grinned. 'Nope.'

'What difference does that make?' Sarah asked.

'He means,' Jik said, 'our pompous friend here means that one shouldn't make judgments from afar.'

'You haven't actually got to be swallowed up by a shark before you believe it's got sharp teeth,' Sarah said. 'You can believe what other people see.'

'It depends from where they're looking.'

'Facts are not judgments, and judgments are not facts,' Jik said. 'A bit of Todd's Law from way back.'

Sarah gave me a glance. 'Have you got iced water in that head?'

'Emotion is a rotten base for politics. He used to say that too,' Jik said. 'Envy is the root of all evil. What have I left out?'

'The most damaging lies are told by those who believe they're true.'

'There you are,' Jik said. 'Such a pity you can't paint.'

'Thanks very much.'

We reached the restaurant and ate a meal of such excellence that one wondered at the organization it took to bring every item of food and clothing and everyday life to an expanding town of thirteen and a half thousand inhabitants surrounded by hundreds of miles of desert in every direction.

'It was started here, a hundred years ago, as a relay station for sending cables across Australia,' Sarah said. 'And now they're bouncing messages off the stars.'

Jik said, 'Bet the messages aren't worth the technology. Think of "See you Friday, Ethel", chattering round the eternal spheres.'

With instructions from the restaurant we walked back a different way and sought out the Yarra River Fine Arts gallery, Alice Springs variety.

It was located in a paved shopping arcade closed to traffic, one of several small but prosperous-looking boutiques. There were no lights on in the gallery, nor in the other shops. From what we could see in the single dim street light, the merchandise in the gallery window consisted of two bright orange landscapes of desert scenes.

'Crude,' said Jik, whose own colours were not noted for pastel subtlety.

'The whole place,' he said, 'will be full of local copies of Albert Namatjira. Tourists buy them by the ton.'

We strolled back to the motel more companionably than at any time since my arrival. Maybe the desert distances all around us invoked their own peace. At any rate when I kissed Sarah's cheek to say goodnight it was no longer as a sort of pact, as in the morning, but with affection.

At breakfast she said, 'You'll never guess. The main street here is Todd Street. So is the river. Todd River.'

'Such is fame,' I said modestly.

'And there are eleven art galleries.'

'She's been reading the Alice Springs Tourist Promotion Association Inc.'s handout,' Jik explained.

'There's also a Chinese takeaway.'

Jik made a face. 'Just imagine all this lot dumped down in the middle of the Sahara.'

The daytime heat, in fact, was fierce. The radio was cheerfully forecasting a noon temperature of thirty-nine, which was a hundred and two in the old Fahrenheit shade. The single step from a cool room to the sun-roasting balcony was a sensuous pleasure, but the walk to the Yarra River gallery, though less than half a mile, was surprisingly exhausting.

'I suppose one would get used to it, if one lived here,' Jik said. 'Thank God Sarah's got her hat.'

We dodged in and out of the shadows of overhanging trees and the local inhabitants marched around bareheaded as if the branding-iron in the sky was pointing another way. The Yarra River gallery was quiet and air-conditioned and provided chairs near the entrance for flaked-out visitors.

As Jik had prophesied, all visible space was knee-deep in the hard clear watercolour paintings typical of the disciples of Namatjira. They were fine if you liked that sort of thing, which on the whole I didn't. I preferred the occasional fuzzy outline, indistinct edge, shadows encroaching, suggestion, impression, and ambiguity. Namatjira, given his due as the first and greatest of the Aboriginal artists, had had a vision as sharp as a diamond. I vaguely remembered reading somewhere that he'd produced more than two thousand paintings himself, and certainly his influence on the town where he'd been born had been extraordinary.

154

Eleven art galleries. Mecca for artists. Tourists buying pictures by the ton. He had died, a plaque on the wall said, in Alice Springs hospital on August 8th 1959.

We had been wandering around for a good five minutes before anyone came. Then the plastic strip curtain over a recessed doorway parted, and the gallery keeper came gently through.

'See anything you fancy?' he said.

His voice managed to convey an utter boredom with tourists and a feeling that we should pay up quickly and go away. He was small, languid, long-haired and pale, and had large dark eyes with drooping tired-looking lids. About the same age as Jik and myself, though a lot less robust.

'Do you have any other pictures?' I asked.

He glanced at our clothes. Jik and I wore the trousers and shirts in which we'd gone to the races: no ties and no jackets, but more promising to picture-sellers than denims. Without discernible enthusiasm he held back half the strip curtain, inviting us to go through.

'In here,' he said.

The inner room was bright from skylights, and its walls were almost entirely covered with dozens of pictures which hung closely together. Our eyes opened wide. At first sight we were surrounded by an incredible feast of Dutch interiors, French impressionists and Gainsborough portraits. At second blink one could see that although they were original oil paintings, they were basically second rate. The sort sold as 'school of' because the artists hadn't bothered to sign them.

'All European, in this room,' the gallery keeper said. He still sounded bored. He wasn't Australian, I thought. Nor British. Maybe American. Difficult to tell.

'Do you have any pictures of horses?' I asked.

He gave me a long steady peaceful gaze. 'Yes we do, but this month we are displaying works by native Australians and lesser Europeans.' His voice had the faintest of lisps. 'If you wish to see horse paintings, they are in racks through there.' He pointed to a second plastic strip curtain directly opposite the first. 'Are you looking for anything in particular?'

I murmured the names of some of the Australians whose work I had seen in Melbourne. There was a slight brightening of the lack-lustre eyes.

'Yes, we do have a few by those artists.'

He led us through the second curtain into the third, and from our point of view, most interesting room. Half of it, as promised, was occupied by well-filled double tiers of racks. The other half was the office and packing and framing department. Directly ahead a glass door led out to a dusty parched-looking garden, but most of the lighting in here too came from the roof.

Beside the glass door stood an easel bearing a small canvas with its back towards us. Various unmistakable signs showed work currently in progress and recently interrupted.

'Your own effort?' asked Jik inquisitively, walking over for a look.

The pale gallery keeper made a fluttering movement with his hand as if he would have stopped Jik if he could, and something in Jik's expression attracted me to his side like a magnet.

A chestnut horse, three-quarters view, its elegant head raised as if listening. In the background, the noble lines of a mansion. The rest, a harmonious composition of trees and meadow. The painting, as far as I could judge, was more or less finished.

'That's great,' I said with enthusiasm. 'Is that for sale? I'd like to buy that.'

After the briefest hesitation he said, 'Sorry. That's commissioned.'

'What a pity! Couldn't you sell me that one, and paint another?'

He gave me a small regretful smile. 'I'm afraid not.'

'Do tell me your name,' I said earnestly.

He was unwillingly flattered. 'Harley Renbo.'

'Is there anything else of yours here?'

He gestured towards the racks. 'One or two. The horse paintings are all in the bottom row, against the wall.'

We all three of us pulled out the paintings one by one, making amateur-type comments.

'That's nice,' said Sarah, holding a small picture of

a fat grey pony with two old-fashioned country boys. 'Do you like that?' She showed it to Jik and me.

We looked at it.

'Very nice,' I said kindly.

Jik turned away as if uninterested. Harley Renbo stood motionless.

'Oh well,' Sarah said, shrugging. 'I just thought it looked nice.' She put it back in the rack and pulled out the next. 'How about this mare and foal? I think it's pretty.'

Jik could hardly bear it. 'Sentimental tosh,' he said.

Sarah looked downcast. 'It may not be Art, but I like it.'

We found one with a flourishing signature; Harley Renbo. Large canvas, varnished, unframed.

'Ah,' I said appreciatively. 'Yours.'

Harley Renbo inclined his head. Jik, Sarah and I gazed at his acknowledged work.

Derivative Stubbs-type. Elongated horses set in a Capability Brown landscape. Composition fair, anatomy poor, execution good, originality nil.

'Great,' I said. 'Where did you paint it?'

'Oh . . . here.'

'From memory?' Sarah said admiringly. 'How clever.'

Harley Renbo, at our urging, brought out two more examples of his work. Neither was better than the first, but one was a great deal smaller.

'How much is this?' I asked.

Jik glanced at me sharply, but kept quiet.

Harley Renbo mentioned a sum which had me shaking my head at once.

'Awfully sorry,' I said. 'I like your work, but . . .'

The haggling continued politely for quite a long time, but we came to the usual conclusion, higher than the buyer wanted, lower than the painter hoped. Jik resignedly lent his credit card and we bore our trophy away.

'Jesus Christ,' Jik exploded when we were safely out of earshot. 'You could paint better than that when you were in your cradle. Why the hell did you want to buy that rubbish?'

'Because,' I said contentedly, 'Harley Renbo is the copier.'

'But this,' Jik pointed to the parcel under my arm, 'is his own abysmal original work.'

'Like fingerprints?' Sarah said. 'You can check other things he paints against this?'

'Got brains, my wife,' Jik said. 'But that picture he wouldn't sell was nothing like any Munnings I've ever seen.'

'You never look at horse paintings if you can help it.'

'I've seen more of your pathetic daubs than I care to.'

'How about Raoul Millais?' I said.

'Jesus.'

We walked along the scorching street almost without feeling it.

'I don't know about you two,' Sarah said, 'but I'm going to buy a bikini and spend the rest of the day in the pool.'

We all bought swimming things, changed into them, splashed around for ages, and laid ourselves out on towels to dry. It was peaceful and quiet in the shady little garden. We were the only people there.

'That picture of a pony and two boys, that you thought was nice,' I said to Sarah.

'Well, it was,' she repeated defensively. 'I liked it.'

'It was a Munnings.'

She sat up abruptly on her towel.

'Why ever didn't you say so?'

'I was waiting for our friend Renbo to tell us, but he didn't.'

'A real one?' Sarah asked. 'Or a copy?'

'Real,' Jik said, with his eyes shut against the sun dappling through palm leaves.

I nodded lazily. 'I thought so, too,' I said. 'An old painting. Munnings had that grey pony for years when he was young, and painted it dozens of times. It's the same one you saw in Sydney in *The Coming Storm*.'

'You two do know a lot,' Sarah said, sighing and lying down again.

'Engineers know all about nuts and bolts,' Jik said. 'Do we get lunch in this place?'

I looked at my watch. Nearly two o'clock. 'I'll go and ask,' I said.

I put shirt and trousers on over my sun-dried trunks

160

and ambled from the outdoor heat into the refrigerated air of the lobby. No lunch, said the reception desk. We could buy lunch nearby at a takeaway and eat in the garden. Drink? Same thing. Buy your own at a bottle shop. There was an ice-making machine and plastic glasses just outside the door to the pool.

'Thanks,' I said.

'You're welcome.'

I looked at the ice-making machine on the way out. Beside it swung a neat notice. 'We don't swim in your toilet. Please don't pee in our pool.' I laughed across to Jik and Sarah and told them the food situation.

'I'll go and get it,' I said. 'What do you want?'

Anything, they said.

'And drink?'

'Cinzano,' Sarah said, and Jik nodded. 'Dry White.'

'O.K.'

I picked up my room key from the grass and set off to collect some cash for shopping. Walked along to the tree-shaded outside staircase, went up two storeys, and turned on to the blazing hot balcony.

There was a man walking along it towards me, about my own height, build and age; and I heard someone else coming up the stairs at my back.

Thought nothing of it. Motel guests like me. What else?

I was totally unprepared for both the attack itself, and for its ferocity.

CHAPTER TEN

They simply walked up to me, one from in front, one from behind.

They reached me together. They sprang into action like cats. They snatched the dangling room key out of my hand.

The struggle, if you could call it that, lasted less than five seconds. Between them, with Jik's type of strength, they simply picked me up by my legs and armpits and threw me over the balcony.

It probably takes a very short time to fall two storeys. I found it long enough for thinking that my body, which was still whole, was going to be smashed. That disaster, not yet reached, was inevitable. Very odd, and very nasty.

What I actually hit first was one of the young trees growing round the staircase. Its boughs bent and broke and I crashed on through them to the hard driveway beneath.

The monstrous impact was like being wiped out. Like fusing electrical circuits. A flash into chaos. I lay in a semi-conscious daze, not knowing if I were alive or dead.

I felt warm. Simply a feeling, not a thought.

I wasn't aware of anything else at all. I couldn't move any muscle. Couldn't remember I had muscles to move. I felt like pulp.

It was ten minutes, Jik told me later, before he came looking for me: and he came only because he wanted to ask me to buy a lemon to go with the Cinzano, if I had not gone already.

'Jesus Christ Almighty,' Jik's voice, low and horrified, near my ear.

I heard him clearly. The words made sense.

I'm alive, I thought. I think, therefore I exist.

Eventually, I opened my eyes. The light was brilliant. Blinding. There was no one where Jik's voice had been. Perhaps I'd imagined it. No I hadn't. The world began coming back fast, very sharp and clear.

I knew also that I hadn't imagined the fall. I knew, with increasing insistence, that I hadn't broken my neck and hadn't broken my back. Sensation, which had been crushed out, came flooding back with vigour from every insulted tissue. It wasn't so much a matter of which bits of me hurt, as of finding out which didn't. I remembered hitting the tree. Remembered the ripping of its branches. I felt both torn to shreds and pulverized. Frightfully jolly.

After a while I heard Jik's voice returning. 'He's alive,' he said, 'and that's about all.'

'It's impossible for anyone to fall off our balcony. It's more than waist-high.' The voice of the reception desk, sharp with anger and anxiety. A bad business for motels, people falling off their balconies.

'Don't . . . panic,' I said. It sounded a bit croaky.

'Todd!' Sarah appeared, kneeling on the ground and looking pale.

'If you give me time . . .' I said, '. . . I'll fetch . . . the Cinzano.' How much time? A million years should be enough.

'You sod,' Jik said, standing at my feet and staring down. 'You gave us a shocking fright.' He was holding a broken-off branch of tree.

'Sorry.'

'Get up, then.'

'Yeah . . . in a minute.'

'Shall I cancel the ambulance?' said the reception desk hopefully.

'No,' I said. 'I think I'm bleeding.'

Alice Springs hospital, even on a Sunday, was as efficient as one would expect from a Flying Doctor base. They investigated and X-rayed and stitched, and presented me with a list.

One broken shoulder blade. (Left.)
Two broken ribs. (Left side, no lung puncture.)

Large contusion, left side of head. (No skull
fracture.)
Four jagged tears in skin of trunk, thigh, and left
leg. (Stitched.)
Several other small cuts.
Grazes and contusions on practically all of left
side of body.

'Thanks,' I said, sighing.

'Thank the tree. You'd've been in a right mess if
you'd missed it.'

They suggested I stop there for the rest of the day
and also all night. Better, they said, a little too mean-
ingfully.

'O.K.' I said resignedly. 'Are my friends still here?'

They were. In the waiting-room. Arguing over my
near-dead body about the favourite for the Melbourne
Cup.

'Newshound *stays* . . .'

'Stays in the same place . . .'

'Jesus,' Jik said, as I shuffled stiffly in. 'He's on his
feet.'

'Yeah.' I perched gingerly on the arm of a chair,
feeling a bit like a mummy, wrapped in bandages from
neck to waist with my left arm totally immersed, as it
were, and anchored firmly inside.

'Don't damn well laugh,' I said.

'No one but a raving lunatic would fall off that
balcony,' Jik said.

'Mm,' I agreed. 'I was pushed.'

Their mouths opened like landed fish. I told them exactly what had happened.

'Who were they?' Jik said.

'I don't know. Never seen them before. They didn't introduce themselves.'

Sarah said, definitely, 'You must tell the police.'

'Yes,' I said. 'But . . . I don't know your procedures here, or what the police are like. I wondered . . . if you would explain to the hospital, and start things rolling in an orderly and unsensational manner.'

'Sure,' she said, 'if anything about being pushed off a balcony could be considered orderly and unsensational.'

'They took my room key first,' I said. 'Would you see if they've pinched my wallet?'

They stared at me in awakening unwelcome awareness.

I nodded. 'Or that picture,' I said.

Two policemen came, listened, took notes, and departed. Very non-committal. Nothing like that had happened in The Alice before. The locals wouldn't have done it. The town had a constant stream of visitors so, by the law of averages, some would be muggers. I gathered that there would have been much more fuss if I'd been dead. Their downbeat attitude suited me fine.

By the time Jik and Sarah came back I'd been given a bed, climbed into it, and felt absolutely rotten. Shivering. Cold deep inside. Gripped by the system's aggrieved reaction to injury, or in other words, shock.

'They did take the painting,' Jik said. 'And your wallet as well.'

'And the gallery's shut,' Sarah said. 'The girl in the boutique opposite said she saw Harley close early today, but she didn't see him actually leave. He goes out the back way, because he parks his car out there.'

'The police've been to the motel,' Jik said. 'We told them about the picture being missing, but I don't think they'll do much more about it unless you tell them the whole story.'

'I'll think about it,' I said.

'So what do we do now?' Sarah asked.

'Well . . . there's no point in staying here any more. Tomorrow we'll go back to Melbourne.'

'Thank God,' she said, smiling widely. 'I thought you were going to want us to miss the Cup.'

In spite of a battery of pills and various ministering angels I spent a viciously uncomfortable and wide-awake night. Unable to lie flat. Feverishly hot on the pendulum from shock. Throbbing in fifteen places. Every little movement screechingly sticky, like an engine without oil. No wonder the hospital had told me it would be better to stay.

I counted my blessings until daybreak. It could have been so very much worse.

What was most alarming was not the murderous nature of the attackers, but the speed with which they'd found us. I'd known ever since I'd seen Regina's head that the directing mind was ruthlessly violent. The acts of the team always reflected the nature of the boss. A less savage attitude would have left Regina gagged and bound, not brutally dead.

I had to conclude that it was chiefly this pervading callousness which had led to my being thrown over the balcony. As a positive means of murder, it was too chancy. It was quite possible to survive a fall from such a height, even without a cushioning tree. The two men had not as far as I could remember bothered to see whether I was alive or dead, and they had not, while I lay half-unconscious and immobile, come along to finish the job.

So it had either been simply a shattering way of getting rid of me while they robbed my room, or they'd had the deliberate intention of injuring me so badly that I would have to stop poking my nose into their affairs.

Or both.

And how had they found us?

I puzzled over it for some time but could arrive at no definite answer. It seemed most likely that Wexford or Greene had telephoned from Melbourne and told Harley Renbo to be on his guard in case I turned

up. Even the panic which would have followed the
realization that I'd seen the Munnings and the fresh
Millais copy, and actually carried away a specimen of
Renbo's work, could not have transported two toughs
from Melbourne to Alice Springs in the time available.

There had only been about four hours between purchase and attack, and some of that would have had to
be spent on finding out which motel we were in, and
which rooms, and waiting for me to go upstairs from
the pool.

Perhaps we had after all been followed all the way
from Flemington racecourse, or traced from the aeroplane passenger lists. But if that were the case, surely
Renbo would have been warned we were on our way,
and would never have let us see what we had.

I gave it up. I didn't even know if I would recognize
my attackers again if I saw them. Certainly not the
one who had been behind me, because I hadn't had a
single straight look at him.

They could, though, reasonably believe they had
done a good job of putting me out of action: and
indeed, if I had any sense, they had.

If they wanted time, what for?

To tighten up their security, and cover their tracks,
so that any investigation I might persuade the police
to make into a paintings–robbery link would come up
against the most respectable of brick walls.

Even if they knew I'd survived, they would not
expect any action from me in the immediate future:

169

therefore the immediate future was the best time to act.

Right.

Easy enough to convince my brain. From the neck down, a different story.

Jik and Sarah didn't turn up until eleven, and I was still in bed. Sitting up, but not exactly perky.

'God,' Sarah said, 'You look much worse than yesterday.'

'So kind.'

'You're never going to make it to Melbourne.' She sounded despondent. 'So goodbye Cup.'

'Nothing to stop you going,' I said.

She stood beside the bed. 'Do you expect us just to leave you here ... like this ... and go and enjoy ourselves?'

'Why not?'

'Don't be so bloody stupid.'

Jik sprawled in a visitor's chair. 'It isn't our responsibility if he gets himself thrown from heights,' he said.

Sarah whirled on him. 'How *can* you say such a thing?'

'We don't want to be involved,' Jik said.

I grinned. Sarah heard the sardonic echo of what she'd said so passionately herself only three days ago. She flung out her arms in exasperated realization.

'You absolutely bloody beast,' she said.

Jik smiled like a cream-fed cat. 'We went round to the gallery,' he said. 'It's still shut. We also found our way round into the back garden, and looked in through the glass door, and you can guess what we saw.'

'Nothing.'

'Dead right. No easel with imitation Millais. Everything dodgy carefully hidden out of sight. Everything else, respectable and normal.'

I shifted a bit to relieve one lot of aches, and set up protests from another. 'Even if you'd got in, I doubt if you'd've found anything dodgy. I'll bet everything the least bit incriminating disappeared yesterday afternoon.'

Jik nodded. 'Sure to.'

Sarah said, 'We asked the girl in the reception desk at the motel if anyone had been asking for us.'

'And they had?'

She nodded. 'A man telephoned. She thought it was soon after ten o'clock. He asked if a Mr Charles Todd was staying there with two friends, and when she said yes, he asked for your room number. He said he had something to deliver to you.'

'Christ.' Some delivery. Express. Downwards.

'She told him the room number but said if he left the package at the desk, she would see you got it.'

'He must have laughed.'

'He wouldn't have that much sense of humour,' Jik said.

'Soon after ten?' I said, considering.

'While we were out,' Sarah said, nodding. 'It must

have been fairly soon after we'd left the gallery . . . and
while we were buying the swimming things.'

'Why didn't the girl tell us someone had been
enquiring for us?'

'She went off for a coffee break, and didn't see
us when we came back. And after that, she forgot. She
hadn't anyway thought it of any importance.'

'There aren't all that many motels in Alice,' Jik said.
'It wouldn't have taken long to find us, once they knew
we were in the town. I suppose the Melbourne lot
telephoned Renbo, and that set the bomb ticking.'

'They must have been apoplectic when they heard
you'd bought that picture.'

'I wish I'd hidden it,' I said. The words reminded
me briefly of Maisie, who had hidden her picture, and
had her house burnt.

Sarah sighed. 'Well . . . what are we going to do?'

'Last chance to go home,' I said.

'Are you going?' she demanded.

I listened briefly to the fierce plea from my battered
shell, and I thought too of Donald in his cold house. I
didn't actually answer her at all.

She listened to my silence. 'Quite,' she said. 'So what
do we do next?'

'Well . . .' I said. 'First of all, tell the girl on the
reception desk at the motel that I'm in a pretty poor
state and likely to be in hospital for at least a week.'

'No exaggeration,' Jik murmured.

'Tell her it's O.K. to pass on that news, if anyone

172

enquires. Tell her you're leaving for Melbourne, pay all our bills, confirm your bookings on the afternoon flight, and cancel mine, and make a normal exit to the airport bus.'

'But what about you?' Sarah said. 'When will you be fit to go?'

'With you,' I said. 'If between you you can think of some unobtrusive way of getting a bandaged mummy on to an aeroplane without anyone noticing.'

'Jesus,' Jik said. He looked delighted. 'I'll do that.'

'Telephone the airport and book a seat for me under a different name.'

'Right.'

'Buy me a shirt and some trousers. Mine are in the dustbin.'

'It shall be done.'

'And reckon all the time that you may be watched.'

'Put on sad faces, do you mean?' Sarah said.

I grinned. 'I'd be honoured.'

'And after we get to Melbourne, what then?' Jik said.

I chewed my lip. 'I think we'll have to go back to the Hilton. All our clothes are there, not to mention my passport and money. We don't know if Wexford and Greene ever knew we were staying there, so it may well be a hundred per cent safe. And anyway, where else in Melbourne are we likely to get beds on the night before the Melbourne Cup?'

'If you get thrown out of the Hilton's windows, you won't be alive to tell the tale,' he said cheerfully.

'They don't open far enough,' I said. 'It's impossible.'

'How reassuring.'

'And tomorrow,' Sarah said. 'What about tomorrow?'

Hesitantly, with a pause or two, I outlined what I had in mind for Cup day. When I had finished, they were both silent.

'So now,' I said. 'Do you want to go home?'

Sarah stood up. 'We'll talk it over,' she said soberly. 'We'll come back and let you know.'

Jik stood also, but I knew from the jut of his beard which way he'd vote. It had been he who'd chosen the bad-weather routes we'd taken into the Atlantic and the North Sea. At heart he was more reckless than I.

They came back at two o'clock lugging a large fruit-shop carrier with a bottle of Scotch and a pineapple sticking out of the top.

'Provisions for hospitalized friend,' said Jik, whisking them out and putting them on the end of the bed. 'How do you feel?'

'With every nerve ending.'

'You don't say. Well, Sarah says we go ahead.'

I looked searchingly at her face. Her dark eyes stared steadily back, giving assent without joy. There was no antagonism, but no excitement. She was committed, but from determination, not conviction.

'O.K.,' I said.

'Item,' said Jik, busy with the carrier, 'one pair of medium grey trousers. One light blue cotton shirt.'

'Great.'

'You won't be wearing those, though, until you get to Melbourne. For leaving Alice Springs, we bought something else.'

I saw the amusement in both their faces. I said with misgiving, 'What else?'

With rising glee they laid out what they had bought for my unobtrusive exit from Alice Springs.

Which was how I came to stroll around the little airport, in the time-gap between signing in and boarding, with the full attention of everyone in the place. Wearing faded jeans cut off and busily frayed at mid-calf. No socks. Flip-flop rope-soled sandals. A brilliant orange, red and magenta poncho-type garment which hung loosely over both arms like a cape from shoulders to crutch. A sloppy white T-shirt underneath. A large pair of sunglasses. Artificial suntan on every bit of skin. And to top it all, a large straw sunhat with a two-inch raffia fringe round the brim, the sort of hat in favour out in the bush for keeping flies away. Flies were the torment of Australia. The brushing-away-of-flies movement of the right hand was known as the great Australian salute.

175

On this hat there was a tourist-type hat-band, bright and distinctly legible. It said 'I Climbed Ayers Rock'.

Accompanying all this jazz I carried the Trans-Australian airline bag Sarah had bought on the way up. Inside it, the garments of sanity and discretion.

'No one,' Jik had said with satisfaction, laying out my wardrobe, 'will guess you're a walking stretcher case, if you're wearing these.'

'More like a nutcase.'

'Not far out,' Sarah said dryly.

They were both at the airport, sitting down and looking glum, when I arrived. They gave me a flickering glance and gazed thereafter at the floor, both of them, they told me later, fighting off terrible fits of giggles at seeing all that finery on the march.

I walked composedly down to the postcard stand and waited there on my feet, for truth to tell it was more comfortable than sitting. Most of the postcards seemed to be endless views of the huge crouching orange monolith out in the desert: Ayers Rock at dawn, at sunset, and every five minutes in between.

Alternatively with inspecting the merchandise I took stock of the room. About fifty prospective passengers, highly assorted. Some airline ground staff, calm and unhurried. A couple of Aborigines with shadowed eyes and patient black faces, waiting for the airport bus back to dreamtime. Air-conditioning doing fine, but everyone inside still moving with the slow walk of life out in the sun.

No one remotely threatening.

The flight was called. The assorted passengers, including Jik and Sarah, stood up, picked up their hand luggage and straggled out to the tarmac.

It was then, and then only, that I saw him.

The man who had come towards me on the balcony to throw me over.

I was almost sure at once, and then certain. He had been sitting among the waiting passengers, reading a newspaper which he was now folding up. He stood still, watching Jik and Sarah present their boarding passes at the door and go through to the tarmac. His eyes followed them right across to the aircraft. When they'd filed up the steps and vanished, he peeled off and made a bee-line in my direction.

My heart lurched painfully. I absolutely could not run.

He looked just the same. Exactly the same. Young, strong, purposeful, as well co-ordinated as a cat. Coming towards me.

As Jik would have said, *Jesus*.

He didn't even give me a glance. Three yards before he reached me he came to a stop beside a wall tele-phone, and fished in his pocket for coins.

My feet didn't want to move. I was still sure he would see me, look at me carefully, recognize me ... and do something I would regret. I could feel the sweat prickling under the bandages.

'Last call for flight to Adelaide and Melbourne.'

I would have to, I thought. Have to walk past him to get to the door.

I unstuck my feet. Walked. Waiting for every awful step to hear his voice shouting after me. Or even worse, his heavy hand.

I got to the door, presented the boarding pass, made it out on to the tarmac.

Couldn't resist glancing back. I could see him through the glass, earnestly telephoning, and not even looking my way.

The walk to the aircraft was all the same quite far enough. God help us all, I thought, if the slightest fright is going to leave me so weak.

CHAPTER ELEVEN

I had a window seat near the rear of the aircraft, and spent the first part of the journey in the same sort of fascination as on the way up, watching the empty red miles of the ancient land roll away underneath. A desert with water underneath it in most places; with huge lakes and many rock pools. A desert which could carry dormant seed for years in its burning dust, and bloom like a garden when it rained. A place of pulverizing heat, harsh and unforgiving, and in scattered places, beautiful.

Gaba, I thought. I found it awesome, but it didn't move me in terms of paint.

After a while I took off the exaggerated hat, laid it on the empty seat beside me, and tried to find a comfortable way to sit, my main frustration being that if I leaned back in the ordinary way my broken shoulder blade didn't care for it. You wouldn't think, I thought, that one *could* break a shoulder blade. Mine, it appeared, had suffered from the full thud of my five-eleven frame hitting terra extremely firma.

179

Oh well . . . I shut my eyes for a bit and wished I didn't still feel so shaky.

My exit from hospital had been the gift of one of the doctors, who had said he couldn't stop me if I chose to go, but another day's rest would be better.

'I'd miss the Cup,' I said, protesting.

'You're crazy.'

'Yeah . . . Would it be possible for you to arrange that the hospital said I was "satisfactory", and "progressing" if anyone telephones to ask, and not on any account to say that I'd left?'

'Whatever for?'

'I'd just like those muggers who put me here to think I'm still flat out. For several days, if you don't mind. Until I'm long gone.'

'But they won't try again.'

'You never know.'

He shrugged. 'You mean you're nervous?'

'You could say so.'

'All right. For a couple of days, anyway. I don't see any harm in it, if it will set your mind at rest.'

'It would indeed,' I said gratefully.

'Whatever are these?' He gestured to Jik's shopping, still lying on the bed.

'My friend's idea of suitable travelling gear.'

'You're having me on?'

'He's an artist,' I said, as if that explained any excesses.

He returned an hour later with a paper for me to

180

sign before I left, Jik's credit card having again come up trumps, and at the sight of me, nearly choked. I had struggled slowly into the clothes and was trying on the hat.

'Are you going to the airport dressed like that?' he said incredulously.

'I sure am.'

'How?'

'Taxi, I suppose.'

'You'd better let me drive you,' he said, sighing. 'Then if you feel too rotten I can bring you back.'

He drove carefully, his lips twitching. 'Anyone who has the courage to go around like that shouldn't worry about a couple of thugs.' He dropped me solicitously at the airport door, and departed laughing.

Sarah's voice interrupted the memory.

'Todd?'

I opened my eyes. She had walked towards the back of the aeroplane and was standing in the aisle beside my seat.

'Are you all right?'

'Mm.'

She gave me a worried look and went on into the toilet compartment. By the time she came out, I'd assembled a few more wits, and stopped her with the flap of the hand. 'Sarah ... You were followed to the airport. I think you'll very likely be followed from Melbourne. Tell Jik ... tell Jik to take a taxi, spot the

181

tail, lose him, and take a taxi back to the airport to collect the hired car. O.K?'

'Is this . . . this tail . . . on the aeroplane?' She looked alarmed at the thought.

'No. He telephoned . . . from Alice.'

'All right.'

She went away up front to her seat. The aeroplane landed at Adelaide, people got off, people got on, and we took off again for the hour's flight to Melbourne. Halfway there, Jik himself came back to make use of the facilities.

He too paused briefly beside me on the way back.

'Here are the car keys,' he said. 'Sit in it, and wait for us. You can't go into the Hilton like that, and you're not fit enough to change on your own.'

'Of course I am.'

'Don't argue. I'll lose any tail, and come back. You wait.'

He went without looking back. I picked up the keys and put them in my jeans pocket, and thought grateful thoughts to pass the time.

I dawdled a long way behind Jik and Sarah at disembarkation. My gear attracted more scandalized attention in this solemn financial city, but I didn't care in the least. Nothing like fatigue and anxiety for killing off embarrassment.

Jik and Sarah, with only hand baggage, walked without ado past the suitcase-unloading areas and straight out towards the waiting queue of taxis. The whole airport was bustling with Cup eve arrivals, but only one person, that I could see, was bustling exclusively after my fast-departing friends.

I smiled briefly. Young and eel-like, he slithered through the throng, pushing a young woman with a baby out of the way to grab the next taxi behind Jik's. They'd sent him, I supposed, because he knew Jik by sight. He'd flung turps in his eyes at the Arts Centre.

Not too bad, I thought. The boy wasn't over-intelligent, and Jik should have little trouble in losing him. I wandered around for a bit looking gormless, but as there was no one else who seemed the remotest threat, I eventually eased out to the car park.

The night was chilly after Alice Springs. I unlocked the car, climbed into the back, took off the successful hat, and settled to wait for Jik's return.

They were gone nearly two hours, during which time I grew stiffer and ever more uncomfortable and started swearing.

'Sorry,' Sarah said breathlessly, pulling open the car door and tumbling into the front seat.

'We had the devil's own job losing the little bugger,' Jik said, getting in beside me in the back. 'Are you all right?'

'Cold, hungry, and cross.'

'That's all right, then,' he said cheerfully. 'He stuck like a bloody little leech. That boy from the Arts Centre.'

'Yes, I saw him.'

'We hopped into the Victoria Royal, meaning to go straight out again by the side door and grab another cab, and there he was following us in through the front. So we peeled off for a drink in the bar and he hovered around in the lobby looking at the bookstall.'

'We thought it would be better not to let him know we'd spotted him, if we could,' Sarah said. 'So we did a re-think, went outside, called another taxi, and set off to the Naughty Ninety, which is about the only noisy big dine, dance and cabaret place in Melbourne.'

'It was absolutely packed,' Jik said. 'It cost me ten dollars to get a table. Marvellous for us, though. All dark corners and psychedelic coloured lights. We ordered and paid for some drinks, and read the menu, and then got up and danced.'

'He was still there, when we saw him last, standing in the queue for tables just inside the entrance door. We got out through an emergency exit down a passage past some cloakrooms. We'd dumped our bags there when we arrived, and simply collected them again on the way out.'

'I don't think he'll know we ducked him on purpose,' Jik said. 'It's a proper scrum there tonight.'

'Great.'

With Jik's help I exchanged Tourist, Alice Style, for Racing Man, Melbourne Cup. He drove us all back to the Hilton, parked in its car park, and we walked into the front hall as if we'd never been away.

No one took any notice of us. The place was alive

with pre-race excitement. People in evening dress flooding downstairs from the ballroom to stand in loud-talking groups before dispersing home. People returning from eating out, and calling for one more nightcap. Everyone discussing the chances of the next day's race.

Jik collected our room keys from the long desk.

'No messages,' he said. 'And they don't seem to have missed us.'

'Fair enough.'

'Todd,' Sarah said. 'Jik and I are going to have some food sent up. You'll come as well?'

I nodded. We went up in the lift and along to their rooms, and ate a subdued supper out of collective tiredness.

'Night,' I said eventually, getting up to go. 'And thanks for everything.'

'Thank us tomorrow,' Sarah said.

The night passed. Well, it passed.

In the morning I did a spot of one-handed shaving and some highly selective washing, and Jik came up, as he'd insisted, to help with my tie. I opened the door to him in underpants and dressing-gown and endured his comments when I took the latter off.

'Jesus God Almighty, is there any bit of you neither blue nor patched?'

'I could have landed face first.'

He stared at the thought. '*Jesus.*'

'Help me rearrange these bandages,' I said.

'I'm not touching that lot.'

'Oh come on, Jik. Unwrap the swaddling bands. I'm itching like hell underneath and I've forgotten what my left hand looks like.'

With a variety of blasphemous oaths he undid the expert handiwork of the Alice hospital. The outer bandages proved to be large strong pieces of linen fastened with clips, and placed so as to support my left elbow and hold my whole arm statically in one position, with my hand across my chest and pointing up towards my right shoulder. Under the top layer there was a system of crêpe bandages tying my arm in that position. Also a sort of tight cummerbund of adhesive strapping, presumably to deal with the broken ribs. Also, just below my shoulder blade, a large padded wound dressing, which, Jik kindly told me after a delicate inspection from one corner, covered a mucky looking bit of darning.

'You damn near tore a whole flap of skin off. There are four lots of stitching. Looks like Clapham Junction.'

'Fasten it up again.'

'I have, mate, don't you worry.'

There were three similar dressings, two on my left thigh and one, a bit smaller, just below the knee: all fastened both with adhesive strips and tapes with clips. We left them all untouched.

'What the eye doesn't see doesn't scare the patient,' Jik said. 'What else do you want done?'

'Untie my arm.'

'You'll fall apart.'

'Risk it.'

He laughed and undid another series of clips and knots. I tentatively straightened my elbow. Nothing much happened except that the hovering ache and soreness stopped hovering and came down to earth.

'That's not so good,' Jik observed.

'It's my muscles as much as anything. Protesting about being stuck in one position all that time.'

'What now, then?'

From the bits and pieces we designed a new and simpler sling which gave my elbow good support but was less of a strait-jacket. I could get my hand out easily, and also my whole arm, if I wanted. When we'd finished, we had a small heap of bandages and clips left over.

'That's fine,' I said.

We all met downstairs in the hall at ten-thirty.

Around us a buzzing atmosphere of anticipation pervaded the chattering throng of would-be winners, who were filling the morning with celebratory drinks. The hotel, I saw, had raised a veritable fountain of champagne at the entrance to the bar-lounge end of the lobby, and Jik, his eyes lighting up, decided it was too good to be missed.

'Free booze,' he said reverently, picking up a glass and holding it under the prodigal bubbly which flowed in delicate gold streams from a pressure-fed height. 'Not bad, either,' he added, tasting. He raised his glass. 'Here's to Art. God rest his soul.'

'Life's short. Art's long,' I said.

'I don't like that,' Sarah said, looking at me uneasily.

'It was Alfred Munnings's favourite saying. And don't worry, love, he lived to be eighty plus.'

'Let's hope you do.'

I drank to it. She was wearing a cream dress with gold buttons; neat, tailored, a touch severe. An impression of the military for a day in the front line.

'Don't forget,' I said. 'If you think you see Wexford or Greene, make sure they see you.'

'Give me another look at their faces,' she said.

I pulled the small sketch book out of my pocket and handed it to her again, though she'd studied it on and off all the previous evening through supper.

'As long as they look like this, maybe I'll know them,' she said, sighing. 'Can I take it?' She put the sketch book in her handbag.

Jik laughed. 'Give Todd his due, he can catch a likeness. No imagination, of course. He can only paint what he sees.' His voice as usual was full of disparagement.

Sarah said, 'Don't you mind the awful things Jik says of your work, Todd?'

I grinned. 'I know exactly what he thinks of it.'

'If it makes you feel any better,' Jik said to his wife, 'he was the star pupil of our year. The art school lacked judgment, of course.'

'You're both crazy.'

I glanced at the clock. We all finished the champagne and put down the glasses.

'Back a winner for me,' I said to Sarah, kissing her cheek.

'Your luck might run out.'

I grinned. 'Back number eleven.'

Her eyes were dark with apprehension. Jik's beard was at the bad-weather angle for possible storms ahead.

'Off you go,' I said cheerfully. 'See you later.'

I watched them through the door and wished strongly that we were all three going for a simple day out to the Melbourne Cup. The effort ahead was something I would have been pleased to avoid. I wondered if others ever quaked before the task they'd set themselves, and wished they'd never thought of it. The beginning, I supposed, was the worst. Once you were in, you were committed. But before, when there was still time to turn back, to rethink, to cancel, the temptation to retreat was demoralizing.

Why climb Everest if at its foot you could lie in the sun?

Sighing, I went to the cashier's end of the reception desk and changed a good many traveller's cheques into cash. Maisie's generosity had been far-sighted. There would be little enough left by the time I got home.

Four hours to wait. I spent them upstairs in my room calming my nerves by drawing the view from the window. Black clouds still hung around the sky like cobwebs, especially in the direction of Flemington race course. I hoped it would stay dry for the Cup.

Half an hour before it was due to be run I left the Hilton on foot, walking unhurriedly along towards Swanston Street and the main area of shops. They were all shut, of course. Melbourne Cup Day was a national public holiday. Everything stopped for the Cup.

I had taken my left arm out of its sling and threaded it gingerly through the sleeves of my shirt and jacket. A man with his jacket hunched over one shoulder was too memorable for sense. I found that by hooking my thumb into the waistband of my trousers I got quite good support.

Swanston Street was far from its usual bustling self. People still strode along with the breakneck speed which seemed to characterize all Melbourne pedestrians, but they strode in tens, not thousands. Trams ran up and down the central tracks with more vacant seats than passengers. Cars sped along with the drivers' eyes down, fiddling dangerously with radio dials. Fifteen minutes to the race which annually stopped Australia in its tracks.

Jik arrived exactly on time, driving up Swanston Street in the hired grey car and turning smoothly around the corner where I stood waiting. He stopped outside the Yarra River Fine Arts gallery, got out, opened the boot, and put on a brown coat-overall, of the sort worn by storemen.

I walked quietly along towards him. He brought out a small radio, switched it on, and stood it on top of the car. The commentator's voice emerged tinnily, giving details of the runners currently walking round the parade ring at Flemington races.

'Hello,' he said unemotionally, when I reached him. 'All set?' I nodded, and walked to the door of the gallery. Pushed it. It was solidly shut. Jik dived again into the boot, which held further fruits of his second shopping expedition in Alice Springs.

'Gloves,' he said, handing me some, and putting some on himself. They were of white cotton, with ribbed wristbands, and looked a lot too new and clean. I wiped the backs of mine along the wings of Jik's car, and he gave me a glance and did the same with his.

'Handles and impact adhesive.'

He gave me the two handles to hold. They were simple chromium-plated handles, with flattened pieces at each end, pierced by screw holes for fixing. Sturdy handles, big enough for gripping with the whole hand. I held one steady, bottom side up, while Jik covered the screw-plate areas at each end with adhesive. We couldn't screw these handles where we wanted them. They had to be stuck.

'Now the other. Can you hold it in your left hand?'

I nodded. Jik attended to it. One or two people passed, paying no attention. We were not supposed to park there, but no one told us to move.

We walked across the pavement to the gallery. Its frontage was not one unbroken line across its whole width, but was recessed at the right-hand end to form a doorway. Between the front-facing display window and the front-facing glass door, there was a joining window at right angles to the street.

To this sheet of glass we stuck the handles, or rather, Jik did, at just above waist height. He tested them after a minute, and he couldn't pull them off. We returned to the car.

One or two more people passed, turning their heads to listen to the radio on the car roof, smiling in brotherhood at the universal national interest. The street was noticeably emptying as the crucial time drew near.

'. . . *Vinery carries the colours of Mr Hudson Taylor of Adelaide and must be in with a good outside chance. Fourth in the Caulfield Cup and before that, second at Randwick against Brain-Teaser, who went on to beat Afternoon Tea . . .*'

'Stop listening to the damn race!' Jik said sharply.

'Sorry.'

'Ready?'

'Yes.'

We walked back to the entrance to the gallery, Jik carrying the sort of glass-cutter used by, among others, picture framers. Without casting a glance around for possible onlookers, he applied the diamond cutting edge to the matter in hand, using considerable strength as he pushed the professional tool round the outside of the pane. I stood behind him to block any passing curious glances.

'Hold the right-hand handle,' he said, as he started on the last of the four sides, the left-hand vertical.

I stepped past him and slotted my hand through the grip. None of the few people left in the street paid the slightest attention.

'When it goes,' Jik said, 'for God's sake don't drop it.'

'No.'

'Put your knee against the glass. Gently, for God's sake.'

I did what he said. He finished the fourth long cut.

'Press smoothly.'

I did that. Jik's knee, too, was firmly against the glass. With his left hand he gripped the chromium handle, and with the palm of his right he began jolting the top perimeter of the heavy pane.

Jik had cut a lot of glass in his time, even if not in exactly these circumstances. The big flat sheet cracked away evenly all round under our pressure and parted with hardly a splinter. The weight fell suddenly on to the handle I held in my right hand, and Jik steadied the now free sheet of glass with hands and knees and blasphemy.

'Jesus, don't let go.'

'No.'

The heavy vibrations set up in the glass by the breaking process subsided, and Jik took over the right-hand handle from me. Without any seeming inconvenience he pivoted the sheet of glass so that it opened like a door. He stepped through the hole, lifted the glass up wholesale by the two handles, carried it several feet, and propped it against the wall to the right of the more conventional way in.

He came out, and we went over to the car. From there, barely ten feet away, one could not see that the gallery was not still securely shut. There were by now in any case very few to look.

'... *Most jockeys have now mounted and the horses will soon be going out on to the course . . .*'

I picked up the radio. Jik exchanged the glass-cutter for a metal saw, a hammer and a chisel, and shut the boot, and we walked through the unorthodox entrance as if it was all in the day's work. Often only the furtive manner gave away the crook. If you behaved as if you had every right, it took longer for anyone to suspect.

It would really have been best had we next been able to open the real door, but a quick inspection proved it impossible. There were two useful locks, and no keys.

'The stairs are at the back,' I said.

'Lead on.'

We walked the length of the plushy green carpet and down the beckoning stairs. There was a bank of electric switches at the top: we pressed those lighting the basement and left the upstairs lot off.

Heart-thumping time, I thought. It would take only a policeman to walk along and start fussing about a car parked in the wrong place to set Cassavetes and Todd on the road to jail.

'... *horses are now going out on to the course. Four-square in front, sweating up and fighting jockey Ted Nester for control* ...'

We reached the front of the stairs. I turned back towards the office, but Jik took off fast down the corridor.

'Come back,' I said urgently. 'If that steel gate shuts down ...'

'Relax,' Jik said. 'You told me.' He stopped before reaching the threshold of the furthest room. Stood still, and looked. Came back rapidly.

'O.K. The Munningses are all there. Three of them. Also something else which will stun you. Go and look while I get this door open.'

'... *cantering down to the start, and the excitement is mounting here now* ...'

With a feeling of urgency I trekked down the passage, stopped safely short of any electric gadgets which might trigger the gate and set off alarms, and looked into the Munnings room. The three paintings still hung

195

there, as they had before. But along the row from them was something which, as Jik had said, stunned me. Chestnut horse with head raised, listening. Stately home in the background. The Raoul Millais picture we'd seen in Alice.

I went back to Jik who with hammer and chisel had bypassed the lock on the office door.

'Which is it?' he said. 'Original or copy?'

'Can't tell from that distance. Looks like real.'

He nodded. We went into the office and started work.

'. . . *Derriby and Special Bet coming down to the start now, and all the runners circling while the girths are checked . . .*'

I put the radio on Wexford's desk, where it sat like an hourglass, ticking away the minutes as the sands ran out.

Jik turned his practical attention to the desk drawers, but they were all unlocked. One of the waist-high line of filing cabinets, however, proved to be secure. Jik's strength and know-how soon ensured that it didn't remain that way.

In his wake I looked through the drawers. Nothing much in them except catalogues and stationery.

In the broken-open filing cabinet, a gold mine.

Not that I realized it at first. The contents looked merely like ordinary files with ordinary headings.

'. . . *moved very freely coming down to the start and*

is prime fit to run for that hundred-and-ten-thousand-dollar prize . . .'

There were a good many framed pictures in the office, some on the walls but even more standing in a row on the floor. Jik began looking through them at high speed, almost like flicking through a rack of record albums.

'. . . handlers are beginning to load the runners into the starting stalls, and I see Vinery playing up . . .'

Half of the files in the upper of the two drawers seemed to deal in varying ways with insurance. Letters, policies, revaluations and security. I didn't really know what I was looking for, which made it all a bit difficult.

'Jesus Almighty,' Jik said.

'What is it?'

'Look at this.'

'. . . more than a hundred thousand people here today to see the twenty-three runners fight it out over the three thousand two hundred metres . . .'

Jik had reached the end of the row and was looking at the foremost of three unframed canvases tied loosely together with string. I peered over his shoulder. The picture had Munnings written all over it. It had Alfred Munnings written large and clear in the right-hand bottom corner. It was a picture of four horses with jockeys cantering on a racecourse: and the paint wasn't dry.

'What are the others?' I said.

Jik ripped off the string. The two other pictures were exactly the same.

'God Almighty,' Jik said in awe.

'. . . *Vinery carries only fifty-one kilograms and has a good barrier position so it's not impossible . . .*'

'Keep looking,' I said, and went back to the files.

Names. Dates. Places. I shook my head impatiently. We needed more than those Munnings copies and I couldn't find a thing.

'Jesus!' Jik said.

He was looking inside the sort of large flat two-foot by three-foot folder which was used in galleries to store prints.

'. . . *only Derriby now to enter the stalls . . .*'

The print-folder had stood between the end of the desk and the nearby wall. Jik seemed transfixed.

Overseas Customers. My eyes flicked over the heading and then went back. Overseas Customers. I opened the file. Lists of people, sorted into countries. Pages of them. Names and addresses.

England.

A long list. Not alphabetical. Too many to read through in the shortage of time.

A good many of the names had been crossed out.

'. . . *They're running! This is the moment you've all been waiting for, and Special Bet is out in front . . .*'

'Look at this,' Jik said.

Donald Stuart. Donald Stuart, crossed out. Shropshire, England. Crossed out.

I practically stopped breathing.

'... *as they pass the stands for the first time it's Special Bet, Foursquare, Newshound, Derriby, Wonderbug, Vinery ...*'

'Look at this,' Jik said again, insistently.

'Bring it,' I said. 'We've got less than three minutes before the race ends and Melbourne comes back to life.'

'But—'

'Bring it,' I said. 'And also those three copies.'

'... *Special Bet still making it, from Newshound close second, then Wonderbug ...*'

I shoved the filing-drawer shut.

'Put this file in the print-folder and let's get out.'

I picked up the radio and Jik's tools, as he himself had enough trouble managing all three of the untied paintings and the large print-folder.

'... *down the back stretch by the Maribyrnong River it's still Special Bet with Vinery second now ...*'

We went up the stairs. Switched off the lights. Eased round into a view of the car.

It stood there, quiet and unattended, just as we'd left it. No policeman. Everyone elsewhere, listening to the race.

Jik was calling on the Deity under his breath.

'... *rounding the turn towards home Special Bet is dropping back now and it's Derriby with Newshound ...*'

We walked steadily down the gallery.

199

The commentator's voice rose in excitement against a background of shouting crowds.

'. . . *Vinery in third with Wonderbug, and here comes Ringwood very fast on the stands side* . . .'

Nothing stirred out on the street. I went first through our hole in the glass and stood once more, with a great feeling of relief, on the outside of the beehive. Jik carried out the plundered honey and stacked it in the boot. He took the tools from my hands and stored them also.

'Right?'

I nodded with a dry mouth. We climbed normally into the car. The commentator was yelling to be heard.

'. . . *Coming to the line it's Ringwood by a length from Wonderbug, with Newshound third, then Derriby, then Vinery* . . .'

The cheers echoed inside the car as Jik started the engine and drove away.

'. . . *Might be a record time. Just listen to the cheers. The result again. The result of the Melbourne Cup. In the frame* . . . *first Ringwood, owned by Mr Robert Khami* . . . *second Wonderbug* . . .'

'Phew,' Jik said, his beard jaunty and a smile stretching to show an expanse of gum. 'That wasn't a bad effort. We might hire ourselves out some time for stealing politicians' papers.' He chuckled fiercely.

'It's an overcrowded field,' I said, smiling broadly myself.

We were both feeling the euphoria which follows

the safe deliverance from danger. 'Take it easy,' I said. 'We've a long way to go.'

He drove to the Hilton, parked, and carried the folder and pictures up to my room. He moved with his sailing speed, economically and fast, losing as little time as possible before returning to Sarah on the race-course and acting as if he'd never been away.

'We'll be back here as soon as we can,' he promised, sketching a farewell.

Two seconds after he'd shut my door there was a knock on it.

I opened it. Jik stood there.

'I'd better know,' he said, 'what won the Cup?'

CHAPTER TWELVE

When he'd gone I looked closely at the spoils.

The more I saw, the more certain it became that we had hit the absolute jackpot. I began to wish most insistently that we hadn't wasted time in establishing that Jik and Sarah were at the races. It made me nervous, waiting for them in the Hilton with so much dynamite in my hands. Every instinct urged immediate departure.

The list of Overseas Customers would to any other eyes have seemed the most harmless of documents. Wexford would not have needed to keep it in better security than a locked filing-cabinet, for the chances of anyone seeing its significance in ordinary circumstances were millions to one against.

Donald Stuart, Wrenstone House, Shropshire.

Crossed out.

Each page had three columns, a narrow one at each side with a broad one in the centre. The narrow left-hand column was for dates and the centre for names and addresses. In the narrow right-hand column, against each name, was a short line of apparently random letters and numbers. Those against Donald's entry, for instance, were MM3109T: and these figures had not been crossed out with his name. Maybe a sort of stock list, I thought, identifying the picture he'd bought.

I searched rapidly down all the other crossed-out names in the England sector. Maisie Matthews' name was not among them.

Damn, I thought. Why wasn't it?

I turned all the papers over rapidly. As far as I could see all the overseas customers came from basically English-speaking countries, and the proportion of crossed-out names was about one in three. If every crossing-out represented a robbery, there had been literally hundreds since the scheme began.

At the back of the file I found there was a second and separate section, again divided into pages for each country. The lists in this section were much shorter.

England.

Halfway down. My eyes positively leapt at it.

Mrs M. Matthews, Treasure Holme, Worthing, Sussex.

Crossed out.

I almost trembled. The date in the left-hand column looked like the date on which Maisie had bought her picture. The uncrossed-out numbers in the right-hand column were SMC29R.

I put down the file and sat for five minutes staring unseeingly at the wall, thinking.

My first and last conclusions were that I had a great deal to do before Jik and Sarah came back from the races, and that instincts were not always right.

The large print-folder, which had so excited Jik, lay on my bed. I opened it flat and inspected the contents.

I dare say I looked completely loony standing there with my mouth open. The folder contained a number of simplified line drawings like the one the boy-artist had been colouring in the Arts Centre. Full-sized outline drawings, on flat white canvas, as neat and accurate as tracings.

There were seven of them, all basically of horses. As they were only black and white line drawings I couldn't be sure, but I guessed that three were Munnings, two Raoul Millais, and the other two . . . I stared at the old-fashioned shapes of the horses . . . They couldn't be Stubbs, he was too well documented . . . How about Herring? Herring, I thought, nodding. The last two had a look of Herring.

Attached to one of these two canvases by an ordinary paper clip was a small handwritten memo on a piece of scrap paper.

'Don't forget to send the original. Also find out what palette he used, if different from usual.'

I looked again at the three identical finished paintings which we had also brought away. These canvases, tacked on to wooden stretchers, looked very much as if they might have started out themselves as the same sort of outlines. The canvas used was of the same weave and finish.

The technical standard of the work couldn't be faulted. The paintings did look very much like Munnings' own, and would do much more so after they had dried and been varnished. Different-coloured paints dried at different speeds, and also the drying time of paints depended very much on the amount of oil or turps used to thin them, but at a rough guess all three pictures had been completed between three and six days earlier. The paint was at the same stage on all of them. They must, I thought, have all been painted at once, in a row, like a production line. Red hat, red hat, red hat . . . It would have saved time and paint.

The brushwork throughout was painstaking and controlled. Nothing slapdash. No time skimped. The quality of care was the same as in the Millais copy at Alice.

I was looking, I knew, at the true worth of Harley Renbo.

All three paintings were perfectly legal. It was never illegal to copy: only to attempt to sell the copy as real.

I thought it all over for a bit longer, and then set rapidly to work.

The Hilton, when I went downstairs an hour later, were most amiable and helpful.

Certainly, they could do what I asked. Certainly, I

could use the photocopying machine, come this way. Certainly, I could pay my bill now, and leave later.

I thanked them for their many excellent services.

'Our pleasure,' they said: and, incredibly, they meant it.

Upstairs again, waiting for Jik and Sarah, I packed all my things. That done, I took off my jacket and shirt and did my best at rigging the spare bandages and clips back into something like the Alice shape, with my hand inside across my chest. No use pretending that it wasn't a good deal more comfortable that way than the dragging soreness of letting it all swing free. I buttoned my shirt over the top and calculated that if the traffic was bad Jik might still be struggling out of the racecourse.

A little anxiously, and still feeling faintly unwell, I settled to wait.

I waited precisely five minutes. Then the telephone by the bed rang, and I picked up the receiver.

Jik's voice, sounding hard and dictatorial.

'Charles, will you please come down to our room at once.'

'Well . . .' I said hesitantly. 'Is it important?'

'Bloody chromic oxide!' he said explosively. 'Can't you do anything without arguing?'

Christ, I thought.

I took a breath. 'Give me ten minutes,' I said. 'I

need ten minutes. I'm ... er ... I've just had a shower. I'm in my underpants.'

'Thank you, Charles,' he said. The telephone clicked as he disconnected.

A lot of Jik's great oaths galloped across my mind, wasting precious time. If ever we needed divine help, it was now.

Stifling a gut-twisting lurch of plain fear I picked up the telephone and made a series of internal calls.

'Please could you send a porter up right away to room seventeen-eighteen to collect Mr Cassavetes' bags?'

'Housekeeper ...? Please will you send someone along urgently to seventeen-eighteen to clean the room as Mr Cassavetes has been sick ...'

'Please will you send the nurse along to seventeen-eighteen at once as Mr Cassavetes has a severe pain ...'

'Please will you send four bottles of your best champagne and ten glasses up to seventeen-eighteen immediately ...'

'Please bring coffee for three to seventeen-eighteen at once ...'

'Electrician? All the electrics have fused in room seventeen-eighteen, please come at once.'

'... the water is overflowing in the bathroom, please send the plumber urgently.'

Who else was there? I ran my eye down the list of possible services. One wouldn't be able to summon chiropodists, masseuses, secretaries, barbers or clothes-pressers in a hurry . . . but television, why not?

'. . . Please would you see to the television in room seventeen-eighteen. There is smoke coming from the back and it smells like burning . . .'

That should do it, I thought. I made one final call for myself, asking for a porter to collect my bags. Right on, they said. Ten-dollar tip I said if the bags could be down in the hall within five minutes. No sweat, an Australian voice assured me happily. Coming right that second.

I left my door ajar for the porter and rode down two storeys in the lift to floor seventeen. The corridor outside Jik and Sarah's room was still a broad empty expanse of no one doing anything in a hurry.

The ten minutes had gone.

I fretted.

The first to arrive was the waiter with the champagne, and he came not with a tray but a trolley, complete with ice buckets and spotless white cloths. It couldn't possibly have been better.

As he slowed to a stop outside Jik's door, two other figures turned into the corridor, hurrying, and behind them, distantly, came a cleaner slowly pushing another trolley of linen and buckets and brooms.

I said to the waiter, 'Thank you so much for coming so quickly.' I gave him a ten-dollar note, which surprised him. 'Please go and serve the champagne straight away.'

He grinned, and knocked on Jik's door.

After a pause, Jik opened it. He looked tense and strained.

'Your champagne, sir,' said the waiter.

'But I didn't . . .' Jik began. He caught sight of me suddenly, where I stood a little back from his door. I made waving-in motions with my hand, and a faint grin appeared to lighten the anxiety.

Jik retreated into the room followed by trolley and waiter.

At a rush, after that, came the electrician, the plumber and the television man. I gave them each ten dollars and thanked them for coming so promptly. 'I had a winner,' I said. They took the money with more grins and Jik opened the door to their knock.

'Electrics . . . plumbing . . . television . . .' His eyebrows rose. He looked across to me in rising comprehension. He flung wide his door and invited them in with all his heart.

'Give them some champagne,' I said.

'God Almighty.'

After that, in quick succession, came the porter, the man with the coffee, and the nurse. I gave them all ten dollars from my mythical winnings and invited them to join the party. Finally came the cleaner, pushing her top-heavy-looking load. She took the ten dollars, congratulated me on my good fortune, and entered the crowded and noisy fray.

It was up to Jik, I thought. I couldn't do any more.

He and Sarah suddenly popped out like the corks from the gold-topped bottles, and stood undecided in the corridor. I gripped Sarah's wrist and tugged her towards me.

'Push the cleaning trolley through the door, and turn it over,' I said to Jik.

He wasted no time deliberating. The brooms crashed to the carpet inside the room, and Jik pulled the door shut after him.

Sarah and I were already running on ourselves to the lifts. She looked extremely pale and wild-eyed, and I knew that whatever had happened in their room had been almost too much for her.

Jik sprinted along after us. There were six lifts from the seventeenth floor, and one never had to wait more than a few seconds for one to arrive. The seconds this time seemed like hours but were actually very few indeed. The welcoming doors slid open, and we leapt inside and pushed the 'doors closed' button like maniacs.

The doors closed.

The lift descended, smooth and fast.

'Where's the car?' I said.

'Car park.'

'Get it and come round to the side door.'

'Right.'

'Sarah . . .'

She stared at me in fright.

210

'My satchel will be in the hall. Will you carry it for me?'

She looked vaguely at my one-armed state, my jacket swinging loosely over my left shoulder.

'Sarah!'

'Yes . . . all right.'

We erupted into the hall, which had filled with people returning from the Cup. Talkative groups mixed and mingled, and it was impossible to see easily from one side to the other. All to the good, I thought.

My suitcase and satchel stood waiting near the front entrance, guarded by a young man in porter's uniform.

I parted with the ten dollars. 'Thank you very much,' I said.

'No sweat,' he said cheerfully. 'Can I get you a taxi?'

I shook my head. I picked up the suitcase and Sarah the satchel and we headed out of the door.

Turned right. Hurried. Turned right again, round to the side where I'd told Jik we'd meet him.

'He's not here,' Sarah said with rising panic.

'He'll come,' I said encouragingly. 'We'll just go on walking to meet him.'

We walked. I kept looking back nervously for signs of pursuit, but there were none. Jik came round the corner on two wheels and tore millimetres off the tyres stopping beside us. Sarah scrambled into the front and I and my suitcase filled the back. Jik made a hair-raising U-turn and took us away from the Hilton at an illegal speed.

'Wowee,' he said, laughing with released tension. 'Whatever gave you that idea?'

'The Marx Brothers.'

He nodded. 'Pure crazy comedy.'

'Where are we going?' Sarah said.

'Have you noticed,' Jik said, 'how my wife always brings us back to basics?'

The city of Melbourne covered a great deal of land.

We drove randomly north and east through seemingly endless suburban developments of houses, shops, garages and light industry, all looking prosperous, haphazard, and, to my eyes, American.

'Where are we?' Jik said.

'Somewhere called Box Hill,' I said, reading it on shop fronts.

'As good as anywhere.'

We drove a few miles further and stopped at a modern middle-rank motel which had bright coloured strings of triangular flags fluttering across the forecourt. A far cry from the Hilton, though the rooms we presently took were cleaner than nature intended.

There were plain divans, a square of thin carpet nailed at the edges, and a table lamp screwed to an immovable table. The looking glass was stuck flat to the wall and the swivelling armchair was bolted to the floor. Apart from that, the curtains were bright and the hot tap ran hot in the shower.

'They don't mean you to pinch much,' Jik said. 'Let's paint them a mural.'

'No!' Sarah said, horror-struck.

'There's a great Australian saying,' Jik said. 'If it moves, shoot it, and if it grows, chop it down.'

'What's that got to do with it?' Sarah said.

'Nothing. I just thought Todd might like to hear it.'

'Give me strength.'

We were trying to, in our inconsequential way.

Jik sat in the armchair in my room, swivelling. Sarah sat on one of the divans, I on the other. My suitcase and satchel stood side by side on the floor.

'You do realize we skipped out of the Hilton without paying,' Sarah said.

'No we didn't,' Jik said. 'According to our clothes, we are still resident. I'll ring them up later.'

'But Todd . . .'

'I did pay,' I said. 'Before you got back.'

She looked slightly happier.

'How did Greene find you?' I said.

'God knows,' Jik said gloomily.

Sarah was astonished. 'How did you know about Greene? How did you know there was anyone in our room besides Jik and me? How did you know we were in such awful trouble?'

'Jik told me.'

'But he couldn't! He couldn't risk warning you. He just had to tell you to come. He really did . . .' Her

213

voice quivered. The tears weren't far from the surface. 'They made him . . .'

'Jik told me,' I said matter-of-factly. 'First, he called me Charles, which he never does, so I knew something was wrong. Second, he was rude to me, and I know you think he is most of the time, but he isn't, not like that. And third, he told me the name of the man who I was to guess was in your room putting pressure on you both to get me to come down and walk into a nasty little hole. He told me it was chromic oxide, which is the pigment in green paint.'

'Green paint!' The tearful moment passed. 'You really are both extraordinary,' she said.

'Long practice,' Jik said cheerfully.

'Tell me what happened,' I said.

'We left before the last race, to avoid the traffic, and we just came back normally to the Hilton. I parked the car, and we went up to our room. We'd only been there about a minute when there was this knock on the door, and when I opened it they just pushed in . . .'

'They?'

'Three of them. One was Greene. We both knew him straightaway, from your drawing. Another was the boy from the Arts Centre. The third was all biceps and beetle brows, with his brains in his fists.'

He absent-mindedly rubbed an area south of his heart.

'He punched you?' I said.

'It was all so quick . . .' he said apologetically. 'They

just crammed in . . . and biff bang . . . The next thing I knew they'd got hold of Sarah and were twisting her arm and saying that she wouldn't just get turps in her eyes if I didn't get you to come at once.'

'Did they have a gun?' I asked.

'No . . . a cigarette lighter. Look, I'm sorry, mate. I guess it sounds pretty feeble, but Beetle-brows had her in a pretty rough grasp and the boy had this ruddy great cigarette lighter with a flame like a blowtorch just a couple of inches from her cheek . . . and I was a bit groggy . . . and Greene said they'd burn her if I didn't get you . . . and I couldn't fight them all at once.'

'Stop apologizing,' I said.

'Yeah . . . well, so I rang you. I told Greene you'd be ten minutes because you were in your underpants, but I think he heard you anyway because he was standing right beside me, very wary and sharp. I didn't know really whether you'd cottoned on, but I hoped to God . . . and you should have seen their faces when the waiter pushed the trolley in. Beetle-brows let go of Sarah and the boy just stood there with his mouth open and the cigarette lighter flaring up like an oil refinery . . .'

'Greene said we didn't want the champagne and to take it away,' Sarah said. 'But Jik and I said yes we did, and Jik asked the waiter to open it at once.'

'Before he got the first cork out the others all began coming . . . and then they were all picking up glasses . . . and the room was filling up . . . and Greene and the boy and Beetle-brows were all on the window side of the room, sort of pinned in by the trolley and all those people ... and I just grabbed Sarah and we ducked round the edge. The last I saw, Greene and the others were trying to push through, but our guests were pretty thick on the ground by then and keen to get their champagne ... and I should think the cleaning trolley was just about enough to give us that start to the lift.'

'I wonder how long the party lasted,' I said.

'Until the bubbles ran out.'

'They must all have thought you mad,' Sarah said.

'Anything goes on Cup day,' I said, 'and the staff of the Hilton would be used to eccentric guests.'

'What if Greene had had a gun?' Sarah said.

I smiled at her twistedly. 'He would have had to wave it around in front of a hell of a lot of witnesses.'

'But he might have done.'

'He might ... but he was a long way from the front door.' I bit my thumbnail. 'Er ... how did he know I was in the Hilton?'

There was a tangible silence.

'I told him,' Sarah said finally, in a small mixed outburst of shame and defiance. 'Jik didn't tell you it all, just now. At first they said ... Greene said ... they'd burn my face if Jik didn't tell them where you were. He didn't want to ... but he had to ... so I told them, so that it wouldn't be him ... I suppose that sounds stupid.'

I thought it sounded extraordinarily moving. Love of an exceptional order, and a depth of understanding.

I smiled at her. 'So they didn't know I was there, to begin with?'

Jik shook his head. 'I don't think they knew you were even in Melbourne. They seemed surprised when Sarah said you were upstairs. I think all they knew was that you weren't still in hospital in Alice Springs.'

'Did they know about our robbery?'

'I'm sure they didn't.'

I grinned. 'They'll be schizophrenic when they find out.'

Jik and I both carefully shied away from what would have happened if I'd gone straight down to their room, though I saw from his eyes that he knew. With Sarah held as a hostage I would have had to leave the Hilton with Greene and taken my chance. The uncomfortably slim chance that they would have let me off again with my life.

'I'm hungry,' I said.

Sarah smiled. 'Whenever are you not?'

We ate in a small Bring Your Own restaurant nearby, with people at tables all around us talking about what they'd backed in the Cup.

'Good heavens,' Sarah exclaimed. 'I'd forgotten about that.'

'About what?'

217

'Your winnings,' she said. 'On Ringwood.'

'But . . .' I began.

'It was number eleven!'

'I don't believe it.'

She opened her handbag and produced a fat wad ￼
notes. Somehow, in all the mêlée in the Hilton, sh￼
had managed to emerge from fiery danger with th￼
cream leather pouch swinging from her arm. Th￼
strength of the instinct which kept women attached ￼
their handbags had often astounded me, but neve￼
more than that day.

'It was forty to one,' she said. 'I put twenty dolla￼
on for you, so you've got eight hundred dollars, and ￼
think it's disgusting.'

'Share it,' I said, laughing.

She shook her head. 'Not a cent . . . To be honest, ￼
thought it had no chance at all, and I thought I'd teac￼
you not to bet that way by losing you twenty dolla￼
otherwise I'd only have staked you ten.'

'I owe most of it to Jik, anyway,' I said.

'Keep it,' he said. 'We'll add and subtract later. D￼
you want me to cut your steak?'

'Please.'

He sliced away neatly at my plate, and pushed ￼
back with the fork placed ready.

'What else happened at the races?' I said, speari￼
the first succulent piece. 'Who did you see?' The stea￼
tasted as good as it looked, and I realized that in spi￼
of all the sore patches I had at last lost the overa￼

eling of unsettled shaky sickness. Things were on the
mend, it seemed.

'We didn't see Greene,' Jik said. 'Or the boy, or
Beetle-brows.'

'I guess they saw you.'

'Do you think so?' Sarah said worriedly.

'I'd guess,' I said, 'that they saw you at the races
and simply followed you back to the Hilton.'

'Jesus,' Jik groaned. 'We never spotted them. There
was a whole mass of traffic.'

I nodded. 'And all moving very slowly. If Greene
was perhaps three cars behind you, you'd never have
seen him, but he could have kept you in sight easily.'

'I'm bloody sorry, Todd.'

'Don't be silly. And no harm done.'

'Except for the fact,' Sarah said, 'that I've still got
no clothes.'

'You look fine,' I said absently.

'We saw a girl I know in Sydney,' Sarah said. 'We
watched the first two races together and talked to her
aunt. And Jik and I were talking to a photographer
we both knew just after he got back . . . so it would be
pretty easy to prove Jik was at the races all afternoon,
like you wanted.'

'No sign of Wexford?'

'Not if he looked like your drawing,' Sarah said.
'Though of course he might have been there. It's
awfully difficult to recognize a complete stranger just
from a drawing, in a huge crowd like that.'

'We talked to a lot of people,' Jik said. 'To everyon
Sarah knew even slightly. She used the excuse of intro
ducing me as her newly bagged husband.'

'We even talked to that man you met on Saturday
Sarah agreed, nodding. 'Or rather, he came over an
talked to us.'

'Hudson Taylor?' I asked.

'The one you saw talking to Wexford,' Jik said.

'He asked if you were at the Cup,' Sarah said. 'H
said he'd been going to ask you along for anothe
drink. We said we'd tell you he'd asked.'

'His horse ran quite well, didn't it?' I said.

'We saw him earlier than that. We wished him luc
and he said he'd need it.'

'He bets a bit,' I said, remembering.

'Who doesn't?'

'Another commission down the drain,' I said. 'H
would have had Vinery painted if he'd won.'

'You hire yourself out like a prostitute,' Jik sai
'It's obscene.'

'And anyway,' added Sarah cheerfully, 'you wo
more on Ringwood than you'd've got for the painting

I looked pained, and Jik laughed.

We drank coffee, went back to the motel, an
divided to our separate rooms. Five minutes later Ji
knocked on my door.

'Come in,' I said, opening it.

He grinned. 'You were expecting me.'

'Thought you might come.'

He sat in the armchair and swivelled. His gaze fell on my suitcase, which lay flat on one of the divans.

'What did you do with all the stuff we took from the gallery?'

I told him.

He stopped swivelling and sat still.

'You don't mess about, do you?' he said eventually.

'A few days from now,' I said, 'I'm going home.'

'And until then?'

'Um . . . until then, I aim to stay one jump ahead of Wexford, Greene, Beetle-brows, the Arts Centre boy, and the toughs who met me on the balcony at Alice.'

'Not to mention our copy artist, Harley Renbo.'

I considered it. 'Him too,' I said.

'Do you think we can?'

'Not we. Not from hereon. This is where you take Sarah home.'

He slowly shook his head. 'I don't reckon it would be any safer than staying with you. We're too easy to find. For one thing, we're in the Sydney phone book. What's to stop Wexford from marching on to the boat with a bigger threat than a cigarette lighter?'

'You could tell him what I've just told you.'

'And waste all your efforts.'

'Retreat is sometimes necessary.'

He shook his head. 'If we stay with you, retreat may never be necessary. It's the better of two risks. And anyway . . .' the old fire gleamed in his eye . . . 'It will be a great game. Cat and mouse. With cats who don't know they are mice chasing a mouse who knows he's a cat.'

More like a bull fight, I thought, with myself waving the cape to invite the charge. Or a conjuror, attracting attention to one hand while he did the trick with the other. On the whole I preferred the notion of the conjuror. There seemed less likelihood of being gored.

CHAPTER THIRTEEN

spent a good deal of the night studying the list of
Overseas Customers, mostly because I still found it
difficult to lie comfortably to sleep, and partly because
had nothing else to read.

It became more and more obvious that I hadn't
really pinched *enough*. The list I'd taken was fine in its
way, but would have been doubly useful with a stock
list to match the letters and numbers in the right-hand
column.

On the other hand, all stock numbers were a form
of code, and if I looked at them long enough, maybe
some sort of recognizable pattern might emerge.

By far the majority began with the letter M, particularly in the first and much larger section. In the smaller
section, which I had found at the back of the file, the
M prefixes were few, and S, A, W and B were much
commoner.

Donald's number began with M. Maisie's began
with S.

Suppose, I thought, that the M simply stood for

Melbourne, and the S for Sydney, the cities where each
had bought their pictures.

Then A, W and B were where? Adelaide, Wagga
Wagga and Brisbane?

Alice?

In the first section the letters and numbers following
the initial M seemed to have no clear pattern. In the
second section, though, the third letter was always C
the last letter always R, and the numbers, divided
though they were between several countries, pro
gressed more or less consecutively. The highest number
of all was 54, which had been sold to a Mr Norman
Updike, living in Auckland, New Zealand. The stock
number against his name was WHC54R. The date in
the left-hand column was only a week old, and Mr
Updike had not been crossed out.

All the pictures in the shorter section had been sold
within the past three years. The first dates in the long
first section were five and a half years old.

I wondered which had come first, five and a half
years ago: the gallery or the idea. Had Wexford ori
ginally been a full-time crook deliberately setting up
an imposing front, or a formerly honest art dealer
struck by criminal possibilities? Judging from the
respectable air of the gallery and what little I'd seen
of Wexford himself, I would have guessed the latter
But the violence lying just below the surface didn't
match.

I sighed, put down the lists, and switched off the

ight. Lay in the dark, thinking of the telephone call
'd made after Jik had gone back to Sarah.

It had been harder to arrange from the motel than
t would have been from the Hilton, but the line had
een loud and clear.

'You got my cable?' I said.

'I've been waiting for your call for half an hour.'

'Sorry.'

'What do you want?'

'I've sent you a letter,' I said. 'I want to tell you
what's in it.'

'But . . .'

'Just listen,' I said. 'And talk after.' I spoke for quite
a long time to a response of grunts from the far end.

'Are you sure of all this?'

'Positive about most,' I said. 'Some of it's a guess.'

'Repeat it.'

'Very well.' I did so, at much the same length.

'I have recorded all that.'

'Good.'

'Hm . . . What do you intend doing now?'

'I'm going home soon. Before that, I think I'll keep
looking into things that aren't my business.'

'I don't approve of that.'

I grinned at the telephone. 'I don't suppose you do,
but if I'd stayed in England we wouldn't have got this
far. There's one other thing . . . Can I reach you by
telex if I want to get a message to you in a hurry?'

'Telex? Wait a minute.'

I waited.

'Yes, here you are.' A number followed. I wrote it down. 'Address any message to me personally and head it urgent.'

'Right,' I said. 'And could you get answers to three questions for me?' He listened and said he could. 'Thank you very much,' I said. 'And goodnight.'

Sarah and Jik both looked heavy-eyed and languorous in the morning. A successful night, I judged.

We checked out of the motel, packed my suitcase into the boot of the car, and sat in the passenger seat to plan the day.

'Can't we please get our clothes from the Hilton?' Sarah said, sounding depressed.

Jik and I said 'No' together.

'I'll ring them now,' Jik said. 'I'll get them to pack all our things and keep them safe for us, and I'll tell them I'll send a cheque for the bill.' He levered himself out of the car again and went off on the errand.

'Buy what you need out of my winnings,' I said to Sarah.

She shook her head. 'I've got some money. It's not that. It's just . . . I wish all this was over.'

'It will be, soon,' I said neutrally. She sighed heavily. 'What's your idea of a perfect life?' I asked.

'Oh . . .' she seemed surprised. 'I suppose right now

I just want to be with Jik on the boat and have fun, like before you came.'

'And for ever?'

She looked at me broodingly. 'You may think, Todd, that I don't know Jik is a complicated character, but you've only got to look at his paintings . . . They make me shudder. They're a side of Jik I don't know because he hasn't painted anything since we met. You may think that this world will be worse off if Jik is happy for a bit, but I'm no fool, I know that in the end whatever it is that drives him to paint like that will come back again . . . I think these first few months together are frantically precious . . . and it isn't just the physical dangers you've dragged us into that I hate, but the feeling that I've lost the rest of that golden time . . . that you remind him of his painting, and that after you've gone he'll go straight back to it . . . weeks and weeks before he might have done.'

'Get him to go sailing,' I said. 'He's always happy at sea.'

'You don't care, do you?'

I looked straight into her clouded brown eyes. 'I care for you both, very much.'

'Then God help the people you hate.'

And God help me, I thought, if I become any fonder of my oldest friend's wife. I looked away from her, out of the window. Affection wouldn't matter. Anything else would be a mess.

Jik came back with a satisfied air. 'That's all fixed.

They said there's a letter for you, Todd, delivered by hand a few minutes ago. They asked me for a forwarding address.'

'What did you say?'

'I said you'd call them yourself.'

'Right . . . Well, let's get going.'

'Where to?'

'New Zealand, don't you think?'

'That should be far enough,' Jik said dryly.

He drove us to the airport, which was packed with people going home from the Cup.

'If Wexford and Greene are looking for us,' Sarah said, 'they will surely be watching at the airport.'

If they weren't, I thought, we'd have to lay a trail: but Jik, who knew that, didn't tell her.

'They can't do much in public,' he said comfortingly.

We bought tickets and found we could either fly to Auckland direct at lunch-time, or via Sydney leaving within half an hour.

'Sydney,' said Sarah positively, clearly drawing strength from the chance of putting her feet down on her own safe doorstep.

I shook my head. 'Auckland direct. Let's see if the restaurant's still open for breakfast.'

We squeezed in under the waitresses' pointed consultation of clocks and watches and ordered bacon and eggs lavishly.

'Why are we going to New Zealand?' Sarah said.

'To see a man about a painting and advise him to take out extra insurance.'

'Are you actually making sense?'

'Actually,' I said, 'yes.'

'I don't see why we have to go so far, when Jik said you found enough in the gallery to blow the whole thing wide open.'

'Um . . .' I said. 'Because we don't want to blow it wide open. Because we want to hand it to the police in full working order.'

She studied my face. 'You are very devious.'

'Not on canvas,' Jik said.

After we'd eaten we wandered around the airport shops, buying yet more toothbrushes and so on for Jik and Sarah, and another airline bag. There was no sign of Wexford or Greene or the boy or Beetle-brows or Renbo, or the tough who'd been on watch at Alice Springs. If they'd seen us without us seeing them, we couldn't tell.

'I think I'll ring the Hilton,' I said.

Jik nodded. I put the call through with him and Sarah sitting near, within sound and sight.

'I called about a forwarding address . . .' I told the reception desk. 'I can't really give you one. I'll be in New Zealand. I'm flying to Auckland in an hour or two.'

They asked for instructions about the hand-delivered letter.

'Er . . , Would you mind opening it, and reading it
to me?'

Certainly, they said. Their pleasure. The letter was
from Hudson Taylor saying he was sorry to have
missed me at the races, and that if while I was in
Australia I would like to see round a vineyard, he
would be pleased to show me his.

Thanks, I said. Our pleasure, sir, they said. If anyone
asked for me, I said, would they please mention where
I'd gone. They would. Certainly. Their pleasure.

During the next hour Jik called the car-hire firm
about settling their account and leaving the car in the
airport car park, and I checked my suitcase through
with Air New Zealand. Passports were no problem: I
had mine with me in any case, but for Jik and Sarah
they were unnecessary, as passage between New Zealand and Australia was as unrestricted as between
England and Ireland.

Still no sign of Wexford or Greene. We sat in the
departure bay thinking private thoughts.

It was again only when our flight was called that I
spotted a spotter. The prickles rose again on my skin.
I'd been blind, I thought. Dumb and blind.

Not Wexford, nor Greene, nor the boy, nor Renbo,
nor any rough set of muscles. A neat day dress, neat
hair, unremarkable handbag and shoes. A calm concentrated face. I saw her because she was staring at Sarah.
She was standing outside the departure bay, looking
in. The woman who had welcomed me into the Yarra

River Fine Arts, and given me a catalogue, and let me out again afterwards.

As if she felt my eyes upon her she switched her gaze abruptly to my face. I looked away instantly, blankly, hoping she wouldn't know I'd seen her, or wouldn't know at least that I'd recognized her.

Jik, Sarah and I stood up and drifted with everyone else towards the departure doors. In their glass I could see the woman's reflection: standing still, watching us go. I walked out towards the aircraft and didn't look back.

Mrs Norman Updike stood in her doorway, shook her head, and said that her husband would not be home until six.

She was thin and sharp-featured and talked with tight New Zealand vowels. If we wanted to speak to her husband, we would have to come back.

She looked us over; Jik with his rakish blond beard, Sarah in her slightly crumpled but still military cream dress, I with my arm in its sling under my shirt, and jacket loose over my shoulder. Hardly a trio one would easily forget. She watched us retreat down her front path with a sharply turned-down mouth.

'Dear gentle soul,' murmured Jik.

We drove away in the car we had hired at the airport.

'Where now?' Jik said.

'Shops.' Sarah was adamant. 'I must have some clothes.'

The shops, it appeared, were in Queen Street, and still open for another half-hour. Jik and I sat in the car, waiting and watching the world go by.

'The dolly-birds fly out of their office cages about now,' Jik said happily.

'What of it?'

'I sit and count the ones with no bras.'

'And you a married man.'

'Old habits die hard.'

We had counted eight definites and one doubtful by the time Sarah returned. She was wearing a light olive skirt with a pink shirt, and reminded me of pistachio ice cream.

'That's better,' she said, tossing two well-filled carriers on to the back seat. 'Off we go, then.'

The therapeutic value of the new clothes lasted all the time we spent in New Zealand and totally amazed me. She seemed to feel safer if she looked fresh and clean, her spirits rising accordingly. Armour-plated cotton, I thought. Drip-dry bullet-proofing. Security is a new pin.

We dawdled back to the hill overlooking the bay where Norman Updike's house stood in a crowded suburban street. The Updike residence was large but squashed by neighbours, and it was not until one was inside that one realized that the jostling was due to the view. As many houses as could be crammed on

232

to the land had been built to share it. The city itself
seemed to sprawl endlessly round miles of indented
coastline, but all the building plots looked tiny.

Norman Updike proved as expansive as his wife was
closed in. He had a round shiny bald head on a round
short body, and he called his spouse Chuckles without
apparently intending satire.

We said, Jik and I, that we were professional artists
who would be intensely interested and grateful if we
could briefly admire the noted picture he had just
bought.

'Did the gallery send you?' he asked, beaming at
the implied compliments to his taste and wealth.

'Sort of,' we said, and Jik added: 'My friend here is
well known in England for his painting of horses, and
is represented in many top galleries, and has been hung
often at the Royal Academy . . .'

I thought he was laying it on a bit too thick, but
Norman Updike was impressed and pulled wide his
door.

'Come in then. Come in. The picture's in the lounge.
This way, lass, this way.'

He showed us into a large over-stuffed room with
dark ankle-deep carpet, big dark cupboards, and the
glorious view of sunlit water.

Chuckles, sitting solidly in front of a television busy
with a moronic British comic show, gave us a sour look
and no greeting.

'Over here,' Norman Updike beamed, threading his

portly way round a battery of fat armchairs. 'Wha
do you think of that, eh? He waved his hand with
proprietorial pride at the canvas on his wall.

A smallish painting, fourteen inches by eighteen. A
black horse, with an elongated neck curving against a
blue and white sky; a chopped-off tail; the grass in the
foreground yellow; and the whole covered with an old
looking varnish.

'Herring,' I murmured reverently.

Norman Updike's beam broadened. 'I see you know
your stuff. Worth a bit, that is.'

'A good deal,' I agreed.

'I reckon I got a bargain. The gallery said I'd always
make a profit if I wanted to sell.'

'May I look at the brushwork?' I asked politely.

'Go right ahead.'

I looked closely. It was very good. It did look like
Herring, dead since 1865. It also, indefinably, looked
like the meticulous Renbo. One would need a micro
scope and chemical analysis to make sure.

I stepped back and glanced round the rest of the
room. There was nothing of obvious value, and the few
other pictures were all prints.

'Beautiful,' I said admiringly, turning back to the
Herring. 'Unmistakable style. A real master.'

Updike beamed.

'You'd better beware of burglars,' I said.

He laughed. 'Chuckles, dear, do you hear what this

young man says? He says we'd better beware of
burglars!'

Chuckles' eyes gave me two seconds' sour attention
and returned to the screen.

Updike patted Sarah on the shoulder. 'Tell your
friend not to worry about burglars.'

'Why not?' I said.

'We've got alarms all over this house,' he beamed.
'Don't you worry, a burglar wouldn't get far.'

Jik and Sarah, as I had done, looked round the
room and saw nothing much worth stealing. Nothing,
certainly, worth alarms all over the house. Updike
watched them looking and his beam grew wider.

'Shall I show these young people our little treasures,
Chuckles?' he said.

Chuckles didn't even reply. The television cackled
with tinned laughter.

'We'd be most interested,' I said.

He smiled with the fat anticipatory smirk of one
about to show what will certainly be admired. Two or
three steps took him to one of the big dark cupboards
which seemed built into the walls, and he pulled open
the double doors with a flourish.

Inside, there were about six deep shelves, each bearing several complicated pieces of carved jade. Pale
pink, creamy-white and pale green, smooth, polished,
intricate, expensive; each piece standing upon its own
heavy-looking black base-support. Jik, Sarah and I

235

made appreciative noises and Norman Updike smiled even wider.

'Hong Kong, of course,' he said. 'I worked there for years, you know. Quite a nice little collection, eh?' He walked along to the next dark cupboard and pulled open a duplicate set of doors. Inside, more shelves more carvings, as before.

'I'm afraid I don't know much about jade,' I said apologetically. 'Can't appreciate your collection to the full.'

He told us a good deal more about the ornate good-ies than we actually wanted to know. There were four cupboards full in the lounge and overflows in bedroom and hall.

'You used to be able to pick them up very cheap in Hong Kong,' he said. 'I worked there more than twenty years, you know.'

Jik and I exchanged glances. I nodded slightly.

Jik immediately shook Norman Updike by the hand put his arm round Sarah, and said we must be leaving Updike looked enquiringly at Chuckles, who was still glued to the telly and still abdicating from the role of hostess. When she refused to look our way he shrugged good-humouredly and came with us to his front door Jik and Sarah walked out as soon as he opened it, and left me alone with him in the hall.

'Mr Updike,' I said. 'At the gallery ... which man was it who sold you the Herring?'

'Mr Grey,' he said promptly.

Mr Grey . . . Mr Grey . . .

I frowned.

'Such a pleasant man,' nodded Updike, beaming. 'I told him I knew very little about pictures, but he assured me I would get as much pleasure from my little Herring as from all my jade.'

'You did tell him about your jade, then?'

'Naturally I did. I mean . . . if you don't know anything about one thing, well . . . you try and show you do know about something else. Don't you? Only human, isn't it?'

'Only human,' I agreed, smiling. 'What was the name of Mr Grey's gallery?'

'Eh?' He looked puzzled. 'I thought you said he sent you, to see my picture.'

'I go to so many galleries, I've foolishly forgotten which one it was.'

'Ruapehu Fine Arts,' he said. 'I was down there last week.'

'Down . . .?'

'In Wellington.' His smile was slipping. 'Look here, what is all this?' Suspicion flitted across his rounded face. 'Why did you come here? I don't think Mr Grey sent you at all.'

'No,' I said. 'But Mr Updike, we mean you no harm. We really are painters, my friend and I. But . . . now we've seen your jade collection . . . we do think we must warn you. We've heard of several people who've bought paintings and had their houses burgled soon

after. You say you've got burglar alarms fitted, so if
were you I'd make sure they are working properly.'

'But . . . good gracious . . .'

'There's a bunch of thieves about,' I said. 'Wh
follow up the sales of paintings and burgle the house
of those who buy. I suppose they reckon that if anyon
can afford, say, a Herring, they have other things wort
stealing.'

He looked at me with awakening shrewdness. 'Yo
mean, young man, that I told Mr Grey about m
jade . . .'

'Let's just say,' I said, 'that it would be sensible t
take more precautions than usual.'

'But . . . for how long?'

I shook my head. 'I don't know, Mr Updike. Mayb
for ever.'

His round jolly face looked troubled.

'Why did you bother to come and tell me all this'
he said.

'I'd do a great deal more to break up this bunch.'

He asked 'Why?' again, so I told him. 'My cousi
bought a painting. My cousin's house was burgled. M
cousin's wife disturbed the burglars, and they kille
her.'

Norman Updike took a long slow look at my fac
I couldn't have stopped him seeing the abiding ange
even if I'd tried. He shivered convulsively.

'I'm glad you're not after *me*,' he said.

I managed a smile. 'Mr Updike . . . please take car

And one day, perhaps, the police may come to see your picture, and ask where you bought it ... anyway, they will if I have anything to do with it.'

The round smile returned with understanding and conviction. 'I'll expect them,' he said.

CHAPTER FOURTEEN

Jik drove us from Auckland to Wellington; eight hours in the car.

We stopped overnight in a motel in the town of Hamilton, south of Auckland, and went on in the morning. No one followed us, molested us or spied on us. As far as I could be, I was sure no one had picked us up in the northern city, and no one knew we had called at the Updikes.

Wexford must know, all the same, that I had the Overseas Customers list, and he knew there were several New Zealand addresses on it. He couldn't guess which one I'd pick to visit, but he could and would guess that any I picked with the prefix W would steer me straight to the gallery in Wellington.

So in the gallery in Wellington, he'd be ready...

'You're looking awfully grim, Todd,' Sarah said.

'Sorry.'

'What were you thinking?'

'How soon we could stop for lunch.'

She laughed. 'We've only just had breakfast.'

We passed the turning to Rotorua and the land of hot springs. Anyone for a boiling mud pack? Jik asked. There was a power station further on run by steam jets from underground, Sarah said, and horrid black craters stinking of sulphur, and the earth's crust was so thin in places that it vibrated and sounded hollow. She had been taken round a place called Waiotapu when she was a child, she said, and had had terrible nightmares afterwards, and she didn't want to go back.

'Pooh,' Jik said dismissively. 'They only have earthquakes every other Friday.'

'Somebody told me they have so many earthquakes in Wellington that all the new office blocks are built in cradles,' Sarah said.

'Rock-a-bye sky-scraper . . .' sang Jik, in fine voice.

The sun shone bravely, and the countryside was green with leaves I didn't know. There were fierce bright patches and deep mysterious shadows; gorges and rocks and heaven-stretching tree trunks; feathery waving grasses, shoulder-high. An alien land, wild and beautiful.

'Get that chiaroscuro,' Jik said, as we sped into one particularly spectacular curving valley.

'What's chiaroscuro?' Sarah said.

'Light and shade,' Jik said. 'Contrast and balance. Technical term. All the world's a chiaroscuro, and all the men and women merely blobs of light and shade.'

'Every life's a chiaroscuro,' I said.

'And every soul.'

'The enemy,' I said, 'is grey.'

'And you get grey,' Jik nodded, 'by muddling together red, white and blue.'

'Grey lives, grey deaths, all levelled out into equal grey nothing.'

'No one,' Sarah sighed, 'would ever call you two grey?'

'Grey!' I said suddenly. 'Of bloody course.'

'What are you on about?' Jik said.

'Grey was the name of the man who hired the suburban art gallery in Sydney, and Grey is the name of the man who sold Updike his quote Herring unquote.'

'Oh dear.' Sarah's sigh took the lift out of the spirit and the dazzle from the day.

'Sorry,' I said.

There were so many of them, I thought. Wexford and Greene. The boy. The woman. Harley Renbo. Two toughs at Alice Springs, one of whom I knew by sight and one (the one who'd been behind me) whom I didn't. The one I didn't know might, or might not, be Beetle-brows. If he wasn't, Beetle-brows was extra.

And now Grey. And another one, somewhere.

Nine at least. Maybe ten. How could I possibly tangle all that lot up without getting crunched? Or worse, getting Sarah crunched, or Jik. Every time I moved, the serpent grew another head.

I wondered who did the actual robberies. Did the

send their own two (or three) toughs overseas, or did they contract out to local labour, so to speak?

If they sent their own toughs, was it one of them who had killed Regina?

Had I already met Regina's killer? Had he thrown me over the balcony at Alice?

I pondered uselessly, and added one more twist . . .

Was he waiting ahead in Wellington?

We reached the capital in the afternoon and booked into the Townhouse Hotel because of its splendid view over the harbour. With such marvellous coastal scenery, I thought, it would have been a disgrace if the cities of New Zealand had been ugly. I still thought there were no big towns more captivating than flat old marshy London, but that was another story. Wellington, new and cared for, had life and character to spare.

I looked up the Ruapehu Fine Arts in the telephone directory and asked the hotel's reception desk how to get there. They had never heard of the gallery, but the road it was in, that must be up past the old town, they thought: past Thorndon.

They sold me a local area road map, which they said would help, and told me that Mount Ruapehu was a (with luck) extinct volcano, with a warm lake in its crater. If we'd come from Auckland, we must have passed nearby.

I thanked them and carried the map to Jik and Sarah upstairs in their room.

'We could find the gallery,' Jik said. 'But what would we do when we got there?'

'Make faces at them through the window?'

'You'd be crazy enough for that, too,' Sarah said.

'Let's just go and look,' I said. 'They won't see us in the car, if we simply drive past.'

'And after all,' Jik said incautiously, 'we do want them to know we're here.'

'Why?' asked Sarah in amazement.

'Oh Jesus,' Jik said.

'Why?' she demanded, the anxiety crowding back.

'Ask Todd, it's his idea.'

'You're a sod,' I said.

'Why, Todd?'

'Because,' I said, 'I want them to spend all their energies looking for us over here and not clearing away every vestige of evidence in Melbourne. We do want the police to deal with them finally, don't we, because we can't exactly arrest them ourselves? Well ... when the police start moving, it would be hopeless if there was no one left for them to find.'

She nodded. 'That's what you meant by leaving it all in working order. But ... you didn't say anything about deliberately enticing them to follow us.'

'Todd's got that list, and the pictures we took,' Jik said, 'and they'll want them back. Todd wants them to concentrate exclusively on getting them back, because if they think they can get them back and shut us up . . .'

'Jik,' I interrupted. 'You do go on a bit.'

Sarah looked from me to him and back again. A sort of hopeless calm took over from the anxiety.

'If they think they can get everything back and shut us up,' she said, 'they will be actively searching for us in order to kill us. And you intend to give them every encouragement. Is that right?'

'No,' I said. 'Or rather, yes.'

'They'd be looking for us anyway,' Jik pointed out.

'And we are going to say "Coo-ee, we're over here"?'

'Um,' I said. 'I think they may know already.'

'God give me strength,' she said. 'All right. I see what you're doing, and I see why you didn't tell me. And I think you're a louse. But I'll grant you you've been a damn sight more successful than I thought you'd be, and here we all still are, safe and moderately sound, so all right, we'll let them know we're definitely here. On the strict understanding that we then keep our heads down until you've fixed the police in Melbourne.'

I kissed her cheek. 'Done,' I said.

'So how do we do it?'

I grinned at her. 'We address ourselves to the telephone.'

In the end Sarah herself made the call, on the basis that her Australian voice would be less remarkable than Jik's Englishness, or mine.

'Is that the Ruapehu Fine Arts gallery? It is? I wonder if you can help me . . .' she said. 'I would like to speak to whoever is in charge. Yes, I know, but it is important. Yes, I'll wait.' She rolled her eyes and put her hand over the mouthpiece. 'She sounded like a secretary. New Zealand, anyway.'

'You're doing great,' I said.

'Oh . . . Hello? Yes. Could you tell me your name, please?' Her eyes suddenly opened wide. '*Wexford*. Oh, er . . . Mr Wexford, I've just had a visit from three extraordinary people who wanted to see a painting I bought from you some time ago. Quite extraordinary people. They said you'd sent them. I didn't believe them. I wouldn't let them in. But I thought perhaps I'd better check with you. Did you send them to see my painting?'

There was some agitated squawking from the receiver.

'Describe them? A young man with fair hair and a beard, and another young man with an injured arm, and a bedraggled-looking girl. I sent them away. I didn't like the look of them.'

She grimaced over the phone and listened to some more squawks.

'No of course I didn't give them any information. I told you I didn't like the look of them. Where do I live? Why, right here in Wellington. Well, thank you so much Mr Wexford, I am so pleased I called you.'

She put the receiver down while it was still quawking.

'He was asking me for my name,' she said.

'What a girl,' Jik said. 'What an actress, my wife.'

Wexford. Wexford himself.

It had *worked*.

I raised a small internal cheer.

'So now that they know we're here,' I said, 'would you like to go off somewhere else?'

'Oh no,' Sarah said instinctively. She looked out of the window across the busy harbour. 'It's lovely here, and we've been travelling all day already.'

I didn't argue. I thought it might take more than a single telephone call to keep the enemy interested in Wellington, and it had only been for Sarah's sake that I would have been prepared to move on.

'They won't find us just by checking the hotels by telephone,' Jik pointed out. 'Even if it occurred to them to try the Townhouse, they'd be asking for Cassavetes and Todd, not Andrews and Peel.'

'Are we Andrews and Peel?' Sarah asked.

'We're Andrews. Todd's Peel.'

'So nice to know,' she said.

Mr and Mrs Andrews and Mr Peel took dinner in the hotel restaurant without mishap, Mr Peel having discarded his sling for the evening on the grounds that it was in general a bit too easy to notice. Mr Andrews had declined, on the same consideration, to remove his beard.

We went in time to our separate rooms, and so to bed. I spent a jolly hour unsticking the Alice bandages from my leg and admiring the hemstitching. The tree had made tears that were far from the orderly cuts of operations, and as I inspected the long curving railway lines on a ridged backing of crimson, black and yellow skin, I reckoned that those doctors had done an expert job. It was four days since the fall, during which time I hadn't exactly led an inactive life, but none of their handiwork had come adrift. I realized I had progressed almost without noticing it from feeling terrible all the time to scarcely feeling anything worth mentioning. It was astonishing, I thought, how quickly the human body repaired itself, given the chance.

I covered the mementoes with fresh adhesive plaster bought that morning in Hamilton for the purpose, and even found a way of lying in bed that drew no strike action from mending bones. Things, I thought complacently as I drifted to sleep, were altogether looking up.

I suppose one could say that I underestimated on too many counts. I underestimated the desperation with which Wexford had come to New Zealand. Underestimated the rage and the thoroughness with which he searched for us.

Underestimated the effect of our amateur robbery on professional thieves. Underestimated our success. Underestimated the fear and the fury we had unleashed.

My picture of Wexford tearing his remaining hair in almost comic frustration was all wrong. He was pursuing us with a determination bordering on obsession, grimly, ruthlessly, and fast.

In the morning I woke late to a day of warm windy spring sunshine and made coffee from the fixings provided by the hotel in each room; and Jik rang through on the telephone.

'Sarah says she must wash her hair today. Apparently it's sticking together.'

'It looks all right to me.'

His grin came down the wire. 'Marriage opens vast new feminine horizons. Anyway, she's waiting down in the hall for me to drive her to the shops to buy some shampoo, but I thought I'd better let you know we were going.'

I said uneasily, 'You will be careful . . .'

'Oh sure,' he said. 'We won't go anywhere near the gallery. We won't go far. Only as far as the nearest shampoo shop. I'll call you as soon as we get back.'

He disconnected cheerfully, and five minutes later the bell rang again. I lifted the receiver.

It was the girl from the reception desk. 'Your friends say would you join them downstairs in the car.'

'O.K.,' I said.

I went jacketless down in the lift, left my room key at the desk, and walked out through the front door to the sun-baked and windy car park. I looked around for Jik and Sarah; but they were not, as it happened, the friends who were waiting.

It might have been fractionally better if I hadn't had my left arm slung up inside my shirt. As it was they simply clutched my clothes, lifted me off balance and off my feet, and ignominiously bundled me into the back of their car.

Wexford was sitting inside it; a one-man reception committee. The eyes behind the heavy spectacles were as hostile as forty below, and there was no indecision this time in his manner. This time he as good as had me again behind his steel mesh door, and this time he was intent on not making mistakes.

He still wore a bow tie. The jaunty polka dots went oddly with the unfunny matter in hand.

The muscles propelling me towards him turned out to belong to Greene with an 'e', and to a thug I'd never met but who answered the general description of Beetle-brows.

My spirits descended faster than the Hilton lifts. I ended up sitting between Beetle-brows and Wexford, with Greene climbing in front into the driving seat.

'How did you find me?' I said.

Greene, with a wolfish smile, took a Polaroid photograph from his pocket and held it for me to see. It was a picture of the three of us, Jik, Sarah and me, standing by the shops in Melbourne airport. The woman from the gallery, I guessed, had not been wasting the time she spent watching us depart.

'We went round asking the hotels,' Greene said. 'It was easy.'

There didn't seem to be much else to say, so I didn't say anything. A slight shortage of breath might have had something to do with it.

None of the others, either, seemed over-talkative. Greene started the car and drove out into the city. Wexford stared at me with a mixture of anger and satisfaction: and Beetle-brows began twisting my free right arm behind my back in a grip which left no room for debate. He wouldn't let me remain upright. My head went practically down to my knees. It was all most undignified and excruciating.

Wexford said finally, 'We want our list back.'

There was nothing gentlemanly in his voice. He wasn't making light conversation. His heavy vindictive rage had no trouble at all in communicating itself to me without possibility of misunderstanding.

Oh Christ, I thought miserably; I'd been such a bloody fool, just walking into it like that.

'Do you hear? We want our list back, and everything else you took.'

I didn't answer. Too busy suffering.

From external sounds I guessed we were travelling through busy workaday Friday-morning city streets, but as my head was below window level, I couldn't actually see.

After some time the car turned sharply left and ground uphill for what seemed like miles. The engine sighed from overwork at the top, and the road began to descend.

Almost nothing was said on the journey. My thoughts about what very likely lay at the end of it were so unwelcome that I did my best not to allow them houseroom. I could give Wexford his list back, but what then? What then, indeed.

After a long descent the car halted briefly and then turned to the right. We had exchanged city sounds for those of the sea. There were also no more Doppler effects from cars passing us from the opposite direction. I came to the sad conclusion that we had turned off the highway and were on our way along an infrequently used side road.

The car stopped eventually with a jerk.

Beetle-brows removed his hands. I sat up stiffly, wrenched and unenthusiastic.

They could hardly have picked a lonelier place. The road ran along beside the sea so closely that it was more or less part of the shore, and the shore was a jungle of sharply pointed rough black rocks, with frothy white waves slapping among them, a far cry from the gentle beaches of home.

On the right rose jagged cliffs, steeply towering. Ahead, the road ended blindly in some workings which looked like a sort of quarry. Slabs had been cut from the cliffs, and there were dusty clearings, and huge heaps of small jagged rocks, and graded stones and sifted chips. All raw and harsh and blackly volcanic.

No people. No machinery. No sign of occupation.

'Where's the list?' Wexford said.

Greene twisted round in the driving seat and looked seriously at my face.

'You'll tell us,' he said. 'With or without a beating. And we won't hit you with our fists, but with pieces of rock.'

Beetle-brows said aggrievedly, 'What's wrong with fists?' But what was wrong with Greene's fists was the same as with mine: I would never have been able to hit anyone hard enough to get the desired results. The local rocks, by the look of them, were something else.

'What if I tell you?' I said.

They hadn't expected anything so easy. I could see the surprise on their faces, and it was flattering, in a way. There was also a furtiveness in their expressions which boded no good at all. Regina, I thought. Regina, with her head bashed in.

I looked at the cliffs, the quarry, the sea. No easy exit. And behind us, the road. If I ran that way, they would drive after me, and mow me down. If I could run. And even that was problematical.

I swallowed and looked dejected, which wasn't awfully difficult.

'I'll tell you . . .' I said. 'Out of the car.'

There was a small silence while they considered it; but as they weren't anyway going to have room for much crashing around with rocks in that crowded interior, they weren't entirely against it.

Greene leaned over towards the glove compartment on the passenger side, opened it, and drew out a pistol. I knew just about enough about firearms to distinguish a revolver from an automatic, and this was a revolver, a gun whose main advantage, I had read, was that it never jammed.

Greene handled it with a great deal more respect than familiarity. He showed it to me silently, and returned it to the glove compartment, leaving the hinged flap door open so that we all had a clear view of his ultimate threat.

'Get out, then,' Wexford said.

We all got out, and I made sure that I ended up on the side of the sea. The wind was much stronger on this exposed coast, and chilling in the bright sunshine. It lifted the thin carefully combed hair away from Wexford's crown, and left him straggly bald, and intensified the stupid look of Beetle-brows. Greene's eyes stayed as watchful and sharp as the harsh terrain around us.

'All right then,' Wexford said roughly, shouting a little to bring his voice above the din of sea and sky. 'Where's the list?'

I whirled away from them and did my best to sprint for the sea.

I thrust my right hand inside my shirt and tugged at the sling-forming bandages.

Wexford, Greene and Beetle-brows shouted furiously and almost trampled on my heels.

I pulled the lists of Overseas Customers out of the sling, whirled again with them in my hand, and flung them with a bowling action as far out to sea as I could manage.

The pages fluttered apart in mid-air, but the offshore winds caught most of them beautifully and blew them like great leaves out to sea.

I didn't stop at the water's edge. I went straight on into the cold inhospitable battlefield of shark-teeth rocks and green water and white foaming waves. Slipping, falling, getting up, staggering on, finding that the current was much stronger than I'd expected, and the rocks more abrasive, and the footing more treacherous. Finding I'd fled from one deadly danger to embrace another.

For one second, I looked back.

Wexford had followed me a step or two into the sea, but only, it seemed, to reach one of the pages which had fallen shorter than the others. He was standing there with the frothy water swirling round his trouser legs, peering at the sodden paper.

Greene was beside the car, leaning in; by the front passenger seat.

Beetle-brows had his mouth open.

I reapplied myself to the problem of survival.

The shore shelved, as most shores do. Every forward step led into a stronger current, which sucked and pulled and shoved me around like a piece of flotsam. Hip-deep between waves, I found it difficult to stay on my feet, and every time I didn't I was in dire trouble because of the black needle-sharp rocks waiting in ranks above and below the surface to scratch and tear.

The rocks were not the kind I was used to: not the hard familiar lumpy rocks of Britain, polished by the sea. These were the raw stuff of volcanoes, as scratchy as pumice. One's groping hand didn't slide over them: one's skin stuck to them, and tore off. Clothes fared no better. Before I'd gone thirty yards I was running with blood from a dozen superficial grazes, and no blood vessels bleed more convincingly than the small surface capillaries.

My left arm was still tangled inside the sling, which had housed the Overseas Customers since Cup Day as an insurance against having my room robbed, as at Alice. Soaking wet, the bandages now clung like leeches, and my shirt also. Muscles weakened by a fracture and inactivity couldn't deal with them. I rolled around a lot from not having two hands free.

My foot stepped awkwardly on the side of a submerged rock and I felt it scrape my shin: lost my balance, fell forward, tried to save myself with my hand, failed, crashed chest first against a small jagged peak dead ahead, and jerked my head sharply sideways to avoid connecting with my nose.

The rock beside my cheek splintered suddenly as if exploding. Slivers of it prickled in my face. For a flicker of time I couldn't understand it: and then I struggled round and looked back to the shore with a flood of foreboding.

Greene was standing there, aiming the pistol, shooting to kill.

CHAPTER FIFTEEN

Thirty to thirty-five yards is a long way for a pistol; but Greene seemed so close.

I could see his drooping moustache and the lanky hair blowing in the wind. I could see his eyes and the concentration in his body. He was standing with his legs straddled and his arms out straight ahead, aiming the pistol with both hands.

I couldn't hear the shots above the crash of the waves on the rocks. I couldn't see him squeeze the trigger. But I did see the upward jerk of the arms at the recoil, and I reckoned it would be just plain silly to give him a stationary target.

I was, in all honesty, pretty frightened. I must have looked as close to him as he to me. He must have been quite certain he would hit me, even though his tenderness with the pistol in the car had made me think he was not an expert.

I turned and stumbled a yard or two onwards, though the going became even rougher, and the relentless fight against current and waves and rocks was draining me to dish-rags.

There would have to be an end to it.

Have to be.

I stumbled and fell on a jagged edge and gashed the inside of my forearm, and out poured more good red life. Christ, I thought, I must be scarlet all over, leaking from a hundred tiny nicks.

It gave me at least an idea.

I was waist-deep in dangerous green water, with most of the shore-line rocks now submerged beneath the surface. Close to one side a row of bigger rock-teeth ran out from the shore like a nightmarish breakwater, and I'd shied away from it, because of the even fiercer waves crashing against it. But it represented the only cover in sight. Three stumbling efforts took me nearer; and the current helped.

I looked back at Greene. He was reloading the gun. Wexford was practically dancing up and down beside him, urging him on; and Beetle-brows, from his disinclination to chase me, probably couldn't swim.

Greene slapped shut the gun and raised it again in my direction.

I took a frightful chance.

I held my fast-bleeding forearm close across my chest: and I stood up, swaying in the current, visible to him from the waist up.

I watched him aim, with both arms straight. It would take a marksman, I believed, to hit me with that pistol from that distance, in that wind. A marksman whose arms didn't jerk upwards when he fired.

The gun was pointing straight at me.

I saw the jerk as he squeezed the trigger.

For an absolutely petrifying second I was convinced he had shot accurately; but I didn't feel or see or even hear the passing of the flying death.

I flung my own right arm wide and high, and paused there facing him for a frozen second, letting him see that most of the front of my shirt was scarlet with blood.

Then I twisted artistically and fell flat, face downwards, into the water; and hoped to God he would think he had killed me.

The sea wasn't much better than bullets. Nothing less than extreme fear of the alternative would have kept me down in it, tumbling and crashing against the submerged razor edges like a piece of cheese in a grater.

The waves themselves swept me towards the taller breakwater teeth, and with a fair amount of desperation I tried to get a grip on them, to avoid being alternately sucked off and flung back, and losing a lot more skin.

There was also the problem of not struggling too visibly. If Wexford or Greene saw me threshing about, all my histrionics would have been in vain.

As much by luck as trying I found the sea shoving

me into a wedge-shaped crevice between the rocks, from where I was unable to see the shore. I clutched for a hand-hold, and then with bent knees found a good foothold, and clung there precariously while the sea tried to drag me out again. Every time the wave rolled in it tended to float my foot out of the niche it was lodged in, and every time it receded it tried to suck me with it, with a syphonic action. I clung, and see-sawed in the chest-high water, and clung, and see-sawed, and grew progressively more exhausted.

I could hear nothing except the waves on the rocks. I wondered forlornly how long Wexford and Greene would stay there, staring out to sea for signs of life. I didn't dare to look, in case they spotted my moving head.

The water was cold, and the grazes gradually stopped bleeding, including the useful gash on my forearm. Absolutely nothing, I thought, like having a young strong healthy body. Absolutely nothing like having a young strong healthy body on dry land with a paintbrush in one hand and a beer in the other, with the nice friendly airliners thundering overhead and no money to pay the gas.

Fatigue, in the end, made me look. It was either that or cling like a limpet until I literally fell off nervelessly, too weak to struggle back to life.

To look, I had to leave go. I tried to find other holds, but they weren't as good. The first out-going wave took me with it in no uncertain terms; and its incoming fellow threw me back.

In the tumbling interval I caught a glimpse of the shore.

The road, the cliffs, the quarry, as before. Also the car. Also people.

Bloody damn, I thought.

My hand scrambled for its former hold. My fingers were cramped, bleeding again, and cold. Oh Christ, I thought. How much longer.

It was a measure of my tiredness that it took the space of three in and out waves for me to realize that it wasn't Wexford's car, and it wasn't Wexford standing on the road.

If it wasn't Wexford, it didn't matter who it was.

I let go again of the hand-hold and tried to ride the wave as far out of the crevice as possible, and to swim away from the return force flinging me back. All the other rocks were still there under the surface. A few yards was a heck of a long way.

I stood up gingerly, feeling for my footing more carefully than on the outward flight, and took a longer look at the road.

A grey-white car. A couple beside it, standing close, the man with his arms round the girl.

A nice quiet spot for it, I thought sardonically. I hoped they would drive me somewhere dry.

They moved apart and stared out to sea.

I stared back.

For an instant it seemed impossible. Then they
tarted waving their arms furiously and ran towards
he water; and it was Sarah and Jik.

Throwing off his jacket, Jik ploughed into the waves
with enthusiasm, and came to a smart halt as the realit-
es of the situation scraped his legs. All the same, he
:ame on after a pause towards me, taking care.

I made my slow way back. Even without haste driv-
ng like a fury, any passage through those wave-swept
ocks was ruin to the epidermis. By the time we met
we were both streaked with red.

We looked at each other's blood. Jik said 'Jesus'
and I said 'Christ', and it occurred to me that maybe
he Almighty would think we had been calling for His
1elp a bit too often.

Jik put his arm round my waist and I held on to his
shoulders, and together we stumbled slowly to land.
We fell now and then. Got up gasping. Reclutched,
and went on.

He let go when we reached the road. I sat down
on the edge of it with my feet pointing out to sea, and
positively drooped.

'Todd,' Sarah said anxiously. She came nearer.
Todd.' Her voice was incredulous. 'Are you *laughing*?'

'Sure.' I looked up at her, grinning. 'Why ever not?'

ik's shirt was torn, and mine was in tatters. We took
hem off and used them to mop up the grazes which

were still persistently oozing. From the expression of Sarah's face, we must have looked crazy.

'What a damn silly place to bathe,' Jik said.

'Free back-scratchers,' I said.

He glanced round behind me. 'Your Alice Springs dressing has come off.'

'How're the stitches?'

'Intact.'

'Bully for them.'

'You'll both get pneumonia, sitting there,' Sarah said.

I took off the remnants of the sling. All in all, I thought, it had served me pretty well. The adhesive rib-supporting cummerbund was still more or less in place, but had mostly come unstuck through too much immersion. I pulled that off also. That only left the plasters on my leg, and they too, I found, had floated off in the mêlée. The trousers I'd worn over them had windows everywhere.

'Quite a dust-up,' Jik observed, pouring water out of his shoes and shivering.

'We need a telephone,' I said, doing the same.

'Give me strength,' Sarah said. 'What you need is hot baths, warm clothes, and half a dozen psychiatrists.'

'How did you get here?' I asked.

'How come you aren't dead?' Jik said.

'You first.'

'I came out of the shop where I'd bought the shampoo,' Sarah said, 'and I saw Greene drive past. I nearly

ied on the spot. I just stood still, hoping he wouldn't
ook my way, and he didn't ... The car turned to the
eft just past where I was ... and I could see there were
wo other people in the back ... and I went back to
ur car and told Jik.'

'We thought it damn lucky he hadn't spotted her,'
k said, dabbing at persistent scarlet trickles. 'We went
ack to the hotel, and you weren't there, so we asked
he girl at the desk if you'd left a message, and she
aid you'd gone off in a car with some friends ... With
man with a droopy moustache.'

'Friends!' Sarah said.

'Anyway,' Jik continued, 'choking down our rage,
orrow, indignation and what not, we thought we'd
etter look for your body.'

'Jik!' Sarah protested.

He grinned. 'And who was crying?'

'Shut up.'

'Sarah hadn't seen any sign of you in Greene's car
ut we thought you might be imitating a sack of
otatoes in the boot or something, so we got out the
oad map, applied our feet to the accelerator, and set
ff in pursuit. Turned left where Greene had gone, and
ound ourselves climbing a ruddy mountain.'

I surveyed our extensive grazes and scratches. 'I
hink we'd better get some disinfectant,' I said.

'We could bath in it.'

'Good idea.'

I could hear his teeth chattering even above the di
of my own.

'Let's get out of this wind,' I said. 'And bleed in th
car.'

We crawled stiffly into the seats. Sarah said it wa
lucky the upholstery was plastic. Jik automatically too
his place behind the wheel.

'We drove for miles,' he said. 'Growing, I may sa
a little frantic. Over the top of the mountain and dow
this side. At the bottom of the hill the road swing
round to the left and we could see from the map tha
it follows the coastline round a whole lot of bays an
eventually ends up right back in Wellington.'

He started the car, turned it, and rolled gentl
ahead. Naked to the waist, wet from there down, an
still with beads of blood forming and overflowing, h
looked an unorthodox chauffeur. The beard, abov
was undaunted.

'We went that way,' Sarah said. 'There was nothir
but miles of craggy rocks and sea.'

'I'll paint those rocks,' Jik said.

Sarah glanced at his face, and then at me. She
heard the fervour in that statement of intent. Th
golden time was almost over.

'After a bit we turned back,' Jik said. 'There wa
this bit of road saying "No through road", so we cam
down it. No you, of course. We stopped here on th
spot and Sarah got out of the car and started bawlir
her eyes out.'

'You weren't exactly cheering yourself,' she said.

'Huh,' he smiled. 'Anyway, I kicked a few stones about, wondering what to do next, and there were those cartridges.'

'Those what?'

'On the edge of the road. All close together. Maybe dropped out of one of those spider-ejection revolvers, or something like that.'

'When we saw them,' Sarah said, 'we thought . . .'

'It could have been anyone popping off at seabirds,' I said. 'And I think we might go back and pick them up.'

'Are you serious?' Jik said.

'Yeah.'

We stopped, turned again, and retraced our tyre treads.

'No one shoots seabirds with a revolver,' he said. 'But bloody awful painters of slow horses, that's different.'

The quarry came in sight again. Jik drew up and stopped, and Sarah, hopping out quickly, told us to stay where we were, she would fetch the bullet cases.

'They really did shoot at you?' Jik said.

'Greene. He missed.'

'Inefficient.' He shifted in his seat, wincing. 'They must have gone back over the hill while we were looking for you round the bays.' He glanced at Sarah as he searched along the side of the road. 'Did they take the list?'

267

'I threw it in the sea.' I smiled lopsidedly. 'It seeme[
too tame just to hand it over . . . and it made a hand
diversion. They salvaged enough to see that they'd g[
what they wanted.'

'It must all have been a bugger.'

'Hilarious.'

Sarah found the cases, picked them up, and cam[
running back. 'Here they are . . . I'll put them in n[
handbag.' She slid into the passenger seat. 'What now[

'Telephone,' I said.

'Like that?' She looked me over. 'Have you a[
idea . . .' She stopped. 'Well,' she said. 'I'll buy y[
each a shirt at the first shop we come to.' She swa[
lowed. 'And don't say what if it's a grocery.'

'What if it's a grocery?' Jik said.

We set off again, and at the intersection turned le[
to go back over the hill, because it was about a quart[
of the distance.

Near the top there was a large village with t[
sort of store which sold everything from hammers [
hairpins. Also groceries. Also, upon enquiry, shir[
Sarah made a face at Jik and vanished inside.

I pulled on the resulting navy tee-shirt and mad[
wobbly tracks for the telephone, clutching Sarah[
purse.

'Operator . . . which hotels have a telex?'

She told me three. One was the Townhouse. [
thanked her and rang off.

I called the Townhouse. Remembered, with an effort, that my name was Peel.

'But, Mr Peel . . .' said the girl, sounding bewildered. 'Your friend . . . the one with the moustache, not the one with the beard . . . He paid your account not half an hour ago and collected all your things . . . Yes, I suppose it is irregular, but he brought your note, asking us to let him have your room key . . . I'm sorry but I didn't know you hadn't written it . . . Yes, he took all your things, the room's being cleaned at this minute . . .'

'Look,' I said, 'can you send a telex for me? Put it on my friend Mr . . . er . . . Andrews' bill.'

She said she would. I dictated the message. She repeated it, and said she would send it at once.

'I'll call again soon for the reply,' I said.

Sarah had bought jeans for us, and dry socks. Jik drove out of the village to a more modest spot, and we put them on: hardly the world's best fit, but they did the damage.

'Where now?' he said. 'Intensive Care Unit?'

'Back to the telephone.'

'Jesus God Almighty.'

He drove back and I called the Townhouse. The girl said she'd received an answer, and read it out. 'Telephone at once, reverse charges,' she said, 'and here's a number . . .' She read it out, twice. I repeated it. 'That's right.'

I thanked her.

'No sweat,' she said. 'Sorry about your things.'

I called the international exchange and gave them the number. It had a priority rating, they said. The call would be through in ten minutes. They would ring back.

The telephone was on the wall of a booth inside the general store. There was nothing to sit on. I wished to God there was.

The ten minutes dragged slowly by. Nine and a half to be exact.

The bell rang, and I picked up the receiver.

'Your call to England . . .'

The modern miracle. Half-way round the world, and I was talking to Inspector Frost as if he were in the next room. Eleven-thirty in the morning at Wellington, eleven-thirty at night in Shropshire.

'Your letter arrived today, sir,' he said. 'And action has already been started.'

'Stop calling me sir. I'm used to Todd.'

'All right. Well, we telexed Melbourne to alert them and we've started checking on all the people on the England list. The results are already incredible. All the crossed-out names we've checked so far have been the victims of break-ins. We're alerting the police in all the other countries concerned. The only thing is we see the list you sent us is a photocopy. Do you have the original?'

'No . . . Most of it got destroyed. Does it matter?'

'Not really. Can you tell us how it came into your possession?'

'Er . . . I think we'd better say it just did.'

A dry laugh travelled twelve thousand miles.

'All right. Now what's so urgent that you're keeping me from my bed?'

'Are you at home?' I said contritely.

'On duty, as it happens. Fire away.'

'Two things . . . One is, I can save you time with the stock list numbers. But first . . .' I told him about Wexford and Greene being in Wellington, and about them stealing my things. 'They've got my passport and traveller's cheques, and also my suitcase which contains painting equipment.'

'I saw it at your cousin's,' he said.

'That's right. I think they may also have a page or two of the list . . .'

'Say that again.'

I said it again. 'Most of it got thrown into the sea, but I know Wexford regained at least one page. Well . . . I thought . . . they'd be going back to Melbourne, probably today, any minute really, and when they land there, there's a good chance they'll have at least some of those things with them . . .'

'I can fix a Customs search,' he said. 'But why should they risk stealing . . .?'

'They don't know I know,' I said. 'I think they think I'm dead.'

'Good God. Why?'

'They took a pot-shot at me. Would bullet cases be

271

of any use? Fortunately I didn't collect a bullet, bu I've got six shells.'

'They may be . . .' He sounded faint. 'What abou the stock list?'

'In the shorter list . . . Got it?'

'Yes, in front of me.'

'Right. The first letter is for the city the paintin was sold in; M for Melbourne, S for Sydney, W fc Wellington. The second letter identifies the painter; N for Munnings, H for Herring, and I think R for Raou Millais. The letter C stands for copy. All the paintin on that list are copies. All the ones on the longer li are originals. Got that?'

'Yes. Go on.'

'The numbers are just numbers. They'd sold 5 copies when I . . . er . . . when the list reached me. Th last letter R stands for Renbo. That's Harley Renb who was working at Alice Springs. If you remember, told you about him last time.'

'I remember,' he said.

'Wexford and Greene have spent the last couple days chasing around in New Zealand, so with a b of luck they will not have destroyed anything dodgy i the Melbourne gallery. If the Melbourne police ca arrange a search, there might be a harvest.'

'It's their belief that the disappearance of the li from the gallery will have already led to the immedia destruction of anything else incriminating.'

'They may be wrong. Wexford and Green don

272

now I photocopied the list and sent it to you. They
think the list is floating safely out to sea, and me
with it.'

'I'll pass your message to Melbourne.'

'There's also another gallery here in Wellington, and
an imitation Herring they sold to a man in
Auckland . . .'

'For heaven's sake . . .'

I gave him the Ruapehu address, and mentioned
Norman Updike.

'There's also a recurring B on the long stock list, so
there's probably another gallery. In Brisbane, maybe.
There may also be another one in Sydney. I shouldn't
think the suburban place I told you about had proved
central enough, so they shut it.'

'Stop,' he said.

'Sorry,' I said. 'But the organization is like a
mushroom . . . it burrows along underground and pops
up everywhere.'

'I only said stop so I could change the tape on the
recorder. You can carry right on now.'

'Oh.' I half laughed. 'Well . . . did you get any
answers from Donald to my questions?'

'Yes, we did.'

'Carefully?'

'Rest assured,' he said dryly. 'We carried out your
wishes to the letter. Mr Stuart's answers were "Yes, of
course" to the first question, and "No, why ever should
I" to the second, and "Yes" to the third.'

273

'Was he absolutely certain?'

'Absolutely.' He cleared his throat. 'He seems distant and withdrawn. Uninterested. But quite definite.'

'How is he?' I asked.

'He spends all his time looking at a picture of his wife. Every time we call at his house, we can see him through the front window, just sitting there.'

'He is still . . . sane?'

'I'm no judge.'

'You can at least let him know that he's no longer suspected of engineering the robbery and killing Regina.'

'That's a decision for my superiors,' he said.

'Well, kick them into it,' I said. 'Do the police positively yearn for bad publicity?'

'You were quick enough to ask our help,' he said tartly.

To do your job, I thought. I didn't say it aloud. The silence spoke for itself.

'Well . . .' his voice carried a mild apology. 'Our co-operation, then.' He paused. 'Where are you now? When I've telexed Melbourne, I may need to talk to you again.'

'I'm in a phone booth in a country store in a village on the hills above Wellington.'

'Where are you going next?'

'I'm staying right here. Wexford and Greene are still around in the city and I don't want to risk the outside chance of their seeing me.'

'Give me the number, then.'

I read it off the telephone.

'I want to come home as soon as possible,' I said.
'Can you do anything about my passport?'

'You'll have to find a consul.'

Oh ta, I though tiredly. I hung up the receiver and
wobbled back to the car.

'Tell you what,' I said, dragging into the back seat,
'I could do with a double hamburger and a bottle of
brandy.'

We sat in the car for two hours.

The store didn't sell liquor or hot food. Sarah
bought a packet of biscuits. We ate them.

'We can't stay here all day,' she said explosively,
after a lengthy glum silence.

I couldn't be sure that Wexford wasn't out searching
for her and Jik with murderous intent, and I didn't
think she'd be happy to know it.

'We're perfectly safe here,' I said.

'Just quietly dying of blood-poisoning,' Jik agreed.

'I left my pills in the Hilton,' Sarah said.

Jik stared. 'What's that got to do with it?'

'Nothing. I just thought you might like to know.'

'*The* pill?' I asked.

'Yes.'

'Jesus,' Jik said.

A delivery van struggled up the hill and stopped

outside the shop. A man in an overall opened the back
took out a large bakery tray, and carried it in.

'Food,' I said hopefully.

Sarah went in to investigate. Jik took the oppo
tunity to unstick his tee-shirt from his healing graze
but I didn't bother.

'You'll be glued to those clothes, if you don't,' Ji
said, grimacing over his task.

'I'll soak them off.'

'All those cuts and things didn't feel so bad whe
we were in the sea.'

'No.'

'Catches up with you a bit, doesn't it?'

'Mm.'

He glanced at me. 'Why don't you just scream c
something?'

'Can't be bothered. Why don't you?'

He grinned. 'I'll scream in paint.'

Sarah came back with fresh doughnuts and cans c
Coke. We made inroads, and I at least felt healthier.

After another half-hour, the storekeeper appeare
in the doorway, shouting and beckoning.

'A call for you . . .'

I went stiffly to the telephone. It was Frost, clear a
a bell.

'Wexford, Greene and Snell have booked a flight 1
Melbourne. They will be met at Melbourne airport . .

'Who's Snell?' I said.

'How do I know? He was travelling with the other wo.'

Beetle-brows, I thought.

'Now listen,' Frost said. 'The telex has been red-hot etween here and Melbourne, and the police there vant your co-operation, just to clinch things . . .' He vent on talking for a long time. At the end he said, Will you do that?'

I'm tired, I thought. I'm battered, and I hurt. I've lone just about enough.

'All right.'

Might as well finish it, I supposed.

'The Melbourne police want to know for sure that he three Munnings copies you . . . er . . . acquired rom the gallery are still where you told me.'

'Yes, they are.'

'Right. Well . . . good luck.'

CHAPTER SIXTEEN

We flew Air New Zealand back to Melbourne, tended
by angels in sea green. Sarah looked fresh, Jik defin
itely shop-worn, and I apparently like a mixture (Jik
said) of yellow ochre, Payne's grey, and white, which
didn't think was possible.

Our passage had been oiled by telexes from above
When we arrived at the airport after collecting Sarah'
belongings in their carrier bags from the Townhouse
we found ourselves whisked into a private room, plie
with strong drink, and subsequently taken by ca
straight out across the tarmac to the aeroplane.

A thousand miles across the Tasman Sea and a
afternoon tea later we were driven straight from the
aircraft's steps to another small airport room, whic
contained no strong drink but only a large hard Austra
lian plain-clothes policeman.

'Porter,' he said, introducing himself and squeezin
our bones in a blacksmith's grip. 'Which of you i
Charles Todd?'

'I am.'

'Right on, Mr Todd.' He looked at me without favour. 'Are you ill, or something?' He had a strong rough voice and a strong rough manner, natural aids to putting the fear of God into chummy and bringing on breakdowns in the nervous. To me, I gradually gathered, he was grudgingly offering the status of temporary inferior colleague.

'No,' I said, sighing slightly. Time and airline schedules waited for no man. If I'd spent time on first aid we'd have missed the only possible flight.

'His clothes are sticking to him,' Jik observed, giving the familiar phrase the usual meaning of being hot. It was cool in Melbourne. Porter looked at him uncertainly.

I grinned. 'Did you manage what you planned?' I asked him. He decided Jik was nuts and switched his gaze back to me.

'We decided not to go ahead until you had arrived,' he said, shrugging. 'There's a car waiting outside.' He wheeled out of the door without holding it for Sarah and marched briskly off.

The car had a chauffeur. Porter sat in front, talking on a radio, saying in stiltedly guarded sentences that the party had arrived and the proposals should be implemented.

'Where are we going?' Sarah said.

'To reunite you with your clothes,' I said.

Her face lit up. 'Are we really?'

'And what for?' Jik asked.

'To bring the mouse to the cheese.' And the bull to the sword, I thought: and the moment of truth to the conjuror.

'We got your things back, Todd,' Porter said with satisfaction. 'Wexford, Greene and Snell were turned over on entry, and they copped them with the lot. The locks on your suitcase were scratched and dented but they hadn't burst open. Everything inside should be O.K. You can collect everything in the morning.'

'That's great,' I said. 'Did they still have any of the lists of customers?'

'Yeah. Damp but readable. Names of guys in Canada.'

'Good.'

'We're turning over that Yarra gallery right this minute, and Wexford is there helping. We've let him overhear what we wanted him to, and as soon as I give the go-ahead we'll let him take action.'

'Do you think he will?' I said.

'Look, mister, wouldn't you?'

I thought I might be wary of gifts from the Greeks, but then I wasn't Wexford, and I didn't have a jail sentence breathing down my neck.

We pulled up at the side door of the Hilton. Porter raised himself agilely to the pavement and stood like a solid pillar, watching with half-concealed impatience while Jik, Sarah, and I eased ourselves slowly out. We all went across the familiar red-and-blue opulence of the great entrance hall, and from there through a gate

n the reception desk, and into the hotel manager's
ffice at the rear.

A tall dark-suited member of the hotel staff there
ffered us chairs, coffee, and sandwiches. Porter looked
t his watch and offered us an indeterminate wait.

It was six o'clock. After ten minutes a man in shirt
nd necktie brought a two-way personal radio for
orter, who slipped the ear-plug into place and began
istening to disembodied voices.

The office was a working room, lit by neon strips
nd furnished functionally, with a wall-papering of
harts and duty rosters. There were no outside win-
lows: nothing to show the fade of day to night.

We sat, and drank coffee, and waited. Porter ate
hree of the sandwiches simultaneously. Time passed.

Seven o'clock.

Sarah was looking pale in the artificial light, and
ired also. So was Jik, his beard on his chest. I sat
nd thought about life and death and polka dots.

At seven-eleven Porter clutched his ear and concen-
rated intently on the ceiling. When he relaxed, he
assed to us the galvanic message.

'Wexford did just what we reckoned he would, and
he engine's turning over.'

'What engine?' Sarah said.

Porter stared at her blankly. 'What we planned,' he
aid painstakingly, 'is happening.'

'Oh.'

Porter listened again to his private ear and spok directly to me. 'He's taken the bait.'

'He's a fool,' I said.

Porter came as near to a smile as he could. 'A crooks are fools, one way or another.'

Seven-thirty came and went. I raised my eyebrow at Porter. He shook his head.

'We can't say too much on the radio,' he said 'Because you get all sorts of ears listening in.'

Just like England, I thought. The Press could tur up at a crime before the police; and the mouse migh hear of the trap.

We waited. The time dragged. Jik yawned an Sarah's eyes were dark with fatigue. Outside, in th lobby, the busy rich life of the hotel chattered o unruffled, with guests' spirits rising towards the nex day's race meeting, the last of the carnival.

The Derby on Saturday, the Cup on Tuesday, th Oaks (which we'd missed) on Thursday, and the Inter national on Saturday. No serious racegoers went hom before the end of things, if they could help it.

Porter clutched his ear again, and stiffened.

'He's here,' he said.

My heart, for some unaccountable reason, bega beating overtime. We were in no danger that I coul see, yet there it was, thumping away like a steam organ

Porter disconnected himself from the radio, put on the Manager's desk, and went out into the foyer.

'What do we do?' Sarah said.

'Nothing much except listen.'

We all three went over to the door and held it six inches open. We listened to people asking for their room keys, asking for letters and messages, asking for Mr and Mrs So-and-So, and which way to Toorak, and how did you get to Fanny's.

Then suddenly, the familiar voice, sending electric fizzes to my fingertips. Confident: not expecting trouble. 'I've come to collect a package left here last Tuesday by a Mr Charles Todd. He says he checked it into the baggage-room. I have a letter here from him, authorizing you to release it to me.'

There was a crackle of paper as the letter was handed over. Sarah's eyes were round and startled.

'Did you write it?' she whispered.

I shook my head. 'No.'

The desk clerk outside said, 'Thank you, sir. If you'll just wait a moment I'll fetch the package.'

There was a long pause. My heart made a lot of noise, but nothing much else happened.

The desk clerk came back. 'Here you are, sir. Paintings, sir.'

'That's right.'

There were vague sounds of the bundle of paintings and the print-folder being carried along outside the door.

'I'll bring them round for you,' said the clerk, suddenly closer to us. 'Here we are, sir.' He went past the

283

office, through the door in the desk, and round to the front. 'Can you manage them, sir?'

'Yes. Yes. Thank you.' There was a haste in his voice now that he'd got his hands on the goods. 'Thank you. Goodbye.'

Sarah had begun to say 'Is that all?' in disappointment when Porter's loud voice chopped into the Hilton velvet like a hatchet.

'I guess we'll take care of those paintings, if you don't mind,' he said. 'Porter, Melbourne City Police.'

I opened the door a little, and looked out. Porter stood four-square in the lobby, large and rough, holding out a demanding hand.

At his elbows, two plain-clothes policemen. At the front door, two more, in uniform. There would be others, I supposed, at the other exits. They weren't taking any chances.

'Why . . . er . . . Inspector . . . I'm only on an errand . . . er . . . for my young friend, Charles Todd.'

'And these paintings?'

'I've no idea what they are. He asked me to fetch them for him.'

I walked quietly out of the office, through the gate and round to the front. I leaned a little wearily against the reception desk. He was only six feet away, in front of me to my right. I could have stretched forward and touched him. I hoped Porter would think it near enough, as requested.

A certain amount of unease had pervaded the

Hilton guests. They stood around in an uneven semi-
circle, eyeing the proceedings sideways.

'Mr Charles Todd asked you to fetch them?' Porter
said loudly.

'Yes, that's right.'

Porter's gaze switched abruptly to my face.

'Did you ask him?'

'No,' I said.

The explosive effect was all that the Melbourne
police could have asked, and a good deal more than
I expected. There was no polite quiet identification
followed by a polite quiet arrest. I should have remembered all my own theories about the basic brutality of
the directing mind.

I found myself staring straight into the eyes of the
bull. He realized that he'd been tricked. Had convicted
himself out of his own mouth and by his own presence
on such an errand. The fury rose in him like a geyser
and his hands reached out to grab my neck.

'You're dead,' he yelled. '*You're fucking dead.*'

His plunging weight took me off balance and down
on to one knee, smothering under his choking grip and
two hundred pounds of city suiting; trying to beat him
off with my fists and not succeeding. His anger poured
over me like lava. Heaven knows what he intended,
but Porter's men pulled him off before he did bloody
murder on the plushy carpet. As I got creakily to my
feet, I heard the handcuffs click.

He was standing there, close to me, quivering in the

restraining hands, breathing heavily, dishevelled and bitter-eyed. Civilized exterior all stripped away by one instant of ungovernable rage. The violent core plain to see.

'Hello, Hudson,' I said.

'Sorry,' Porter said perfunctorily. 'Didn't reckon he'd turn wild.'

'Revert,' I said.

'Uh?'

'He always was wild,' I said, 'underneath.'

'You'd know,' he said. 'I never saw the guy before.' He nodded to Jik and Sarah and finally to me, and hurried away after his departing prisoner.

We looked at each other a little blankly. The hotel guests stared at us curiously and began to drift away. We sat down weakly on the nearest blue velvet seat, Sarah in the middle.

Jik took her hand and squeezed it. She put her fingers over mine.

It had taken nine days.

It had been a long haul.

'Don't know about you,' Jik said. 'But I could do with a beer.'

'Todd,' said Sarah, 'start talking.'

We were upstairs in a bedroom (mine) with both of

286

hem in a relaxed mood, and me in Jik's dressing-
own, and he and I in a cloud of Dettol.

I yawned. 'About Hudson?'

'Who else? And don't go to sleep before you've told
s.'

'Well . . . I was looking for him, or someone like
im, before I ever met him.'

'But why?'

'Because of the wine,' I said. 'Because of the wine
vhich was stolen from Donald's cellar. Whoever stole
t not only knew it was there, down some stairs behind
n inconspicuous cupboard-like door . . . and I'd stayed
everal times in the house and never knew the cellar
xisted . . . but according to Donald they would have
ad to come prepared with proper cases to pack it in.
Wine is usually packed twelve bottles in a case . . . and
Donald had two thousand or more bottles stolen. In
ulk alone it would have taken a lot of shifting. A lot
f time, too, and time for housebreakers is risky. But
lso it was special wine. A small fortune, Donald said.
he sort of wine that's bought and sold as an asset and
nds up at a week's wage a bottle, if it's ever drunk at
ll. Anyway, it was the sort of wine that needed expert
andling and marketing if it was to be worth the diffi-
ulty of stealing it in the first place . . . and as Donald's
usiness is wine, and the reason for his journey to
Australia was wine, I started looking right away for
omeone who knew Donald, knew he'd bought a Mun-
ings, and knew about good wine and how to sell

it. And there, straightaway, was Hudson Taylor, who matched like a glove. But it seemed too easy . . . because he didn't *look* right.'

'Smooth and friendly,' said Sarah, nodding.

'And rich,' Jik added.

'Probably a moneyholic,' I said, pulling open the bed and looking longingly at the cool white sheets.

'A what?'

'Moneyholic. A word I've just made up to describe someone with an uncontrollable addiction to money.'

'The world's full of them,' Jik said, laughing.

I shook my head. 'The world is full of drinkers, but alcoholics are obsessive. Moneyholics are obsessive. They never have enough. They *cannot* have enough. However much they have, they want more. And I'm not talking about the average hard-up man, but about real screwballs. Money, money, money. Like a drug. Moneyholics will do anything to get it . . . Kidnap, murder, cook the computer, rob banks, sell their grandmothers . . . You name it.'

I sat on the bed with my feet up, feeling less than fit. Sore from too many bruises, on fire from too many cuts. Jik too, I guessed. They had been wicked rocks.

'Moneyholism,' Jik said, like a lecturer to a dimmish class, 'is a widespread disease easily understood by everyone who has ever felt a twinge of greed, which is everyone.'

'Go on about Hudson,' Sarah said.

'Hudson had the organizing ability . . . I didn't know

hen I came that the organization was so huge, but I
id know it was *organized*, if you see what I mean. It
as an overseas operation. It took some doing. Know-
ow.'

Jik tugged the ring off a can of beer and passed it
 me, wincing as he stretched.

'But he convinced me I was wrong about him,' I
aid, drinking through the triangular hole. 'Because he
as so careful. He pretended he had to look up the
ame of the gallery where Donald bought his picture.
Ie didn't think of me as a threat, of course, but just
s Donald's cousin. Not until he talked to Wexford
own on the lawn.'

'I remember,' Sarah said. 'When you said it had
ipped the whole works apart.'

'Mm . . . I thought it was only that he had told Wex-
)rd I was Donald's cousin, but of course Wexford also
old *him* that I'd met Greene in Maisie's ruins in Sussex
nd then turned up in the gallery looking at the original
f Maisie's burnt painting.'

'Jesus Almighty,' Jik said. 'No wonder we beat it to
lice Springs.'

'Yes, but by then I didn't think it could be Hudson
 was looking for. I was looking for someone brutal,
ho passed on his violence through his employees.
Iudson didn't look or act brutal.' I paused. 'The only
lightest crack was when his gamble went down the
rain at the races. He gripped his binoculars so hard
nat his knuckles showed white. But you can't think a

man is a big-time thug just because he gets upset ove
losing a bet.'

Jik grinned. 'I'd qualify.'

'In spades, redoubled,' Sarah said.

'I was thinking about it in the Alice Spring
hospital . . . There hadn't been time for the muscleme
to get to Alice from Melbourne between us buyin
Renbo's picture and me diving off the balcony, b
there had been time for them to come from *Adelaid*
and Hudson's base was at Adelaide . . . but it was muc
too flimsy.'

'They might have been in Alice to start with,' Ji
said reasonably.

'They might, but what for?' I yawned. 'Then on th
night of the Cup you said Hudson had made a poi
of asking you about me . . . and I wondered how h
knew you.'

'Do you know,' Sarah said, 'I did wonder too at th
time, but it didn't seem important. I mean, *we'd* see
him from the top of the stands, so it didn't seer
impossible that somewhere he'd seen you with us.'

'The boy knew you,' I said. 'And he was at the race
because he followed you, with Greene, to the Hilto
The boy must have pointed you out to Greene.'

'And Greene to Wexford, and Wexford to Hudson'
Jik asked.

'Quite likely.'

'And by then,' he said, 'they all knew they wante
to silence you pretty badly, and they'd had a chanc

and muffed it . . . I'd love to have heard what happened when they found we'd robbed the gallery.' He chuckled, tipping up his beer can to catch the last few drops.

'On the morning after,' I said, 'a letter from Hudson was delivered by hand to the Hilton. How did he know we were there?'

They stared. 'Greene must have told him,' Jik said. 'We certainly didn't. We didn't tell anybody. We were careful about it.'

'So was I,' I said. 'That letter offered to show me round a vineyard. Well . . . if I hadn't been so doubtful of him, I might have gone. He was a friend of Donald's . . . and a vineyard would be interesting. From his point of view, anyway, it was worth a try.'

'Jesus!'

'On the night of the Cup, when we were in that hotel near Box Hill, I telephoned the police in England and spoke to the man in charge of Donald's case, Inspector Frost. I asked him to ask Donald some questions . . . and this morning outside Wellington I got the answers.'

'This morning seems several light years away,' Sarah said.

'Mm . . .'

'What questions and what answers?' Jik said.

'The questions were, did Donald tell Hudson all about the wine in his cellar, and did Donald tell *Wexford* about the wine in the cellar, and was it Hudson

291

who had suggested to Donald that he and Regina
should go and look at the Munnings in the Art
Centre? And the answers were "Yes, of course", and
"No, why ever should I?", and "Yes".'

They thought about it in silence. Jik fiddled with
the dispenser in the room's in-built refrigerator and
liberated another can of Foster's.

'So what then?' Sarah said.

'So the Melbourne police said it was too insubstan-
tial, but if they could tie Hudson in definitely with the
gallery they might believe it. So they dangled in front
of Hudson the pictures and stuff we stole from the
gallery, and along he came to collect them.'

'How? How did they dangle them?'

'They let Wexford accidentally overhear snippets
from a fake report from several hotels about odd
deposits in their baggage rooms, including the painting
at the Hilton. Then after we got here they gave him
an opportunity to use the telephone when he thought
no one was listening, and he rang Hudson at the hous-
e's been staying in here for the races, and told him. So
Hudson wrote himself a letter to the Hilton from me
and zoomed along to remove the incriminating
evidence.'

'He must have been crazy.'

'Stupid. But he thought I was dead . . . and he'd no
idea anyone suspected him. He should have had the
sense to know that Wexford's call to him would be

ugged by the police ... but Frost told me that Wex-
ord would think he was using a public phone booth.'

'Sneaky,' Sarah said.

I yawned. 'It takes a sneak to catch a sneak.'

'You'd never have thought Hudson would blaze up
ke that,' she said. 'He looked so ... so dangerous.'
he shivered. 'You wouldn't think people could hide
uch really frightening violence under a friendly public
ace.'

'The nice Irish bloke next door,' Jik said, standing
p, 'can leave a bomb to blow the legs off children.'

He pulled Sarah to her feet. 'What do you think I
aint?' he said. 'Vases of flowers?' He looked down at
e. 'Horses?'

Ve parted the next morning at Melbourne airport,
here we seemed to have spent a good deal of our
ves.

'It seems strange, saying goodbye,' Sarah said.

'I'll be coming back,' I said.

They nodded.

'Well ...' We looked at watches.

It was like all partings. There wasn't much to say. I
aw in their eyes, as they must have seen in mine, that
e past ten days would quickly become a nostalgic
emory. Something we did in our crazy youth. Distant.

'Would you do it all again?' Jik said.

I thought inconsequentially of surviving wartime

pilots looking back from forty years on. Had their achievements been worth the blood and sweat and risk of death: did they regret?

I smiled. Forty years on didn't matter. What the future made of the past was its own tragedy. What we ourselves did on the day was all that counted.

'I guess I would.'

I leaned forward and kissed Sarah, my oldest friend's wife.

'Hey,' he said. 'Find one of your own.'

CHAPTER SEVENTEEN

Maisie saw me before I saw her, and came sweeping down like a great scarlet bird, wings outstretched.

Monday lunch-time at Wolverhampton races, misty and cold.

'Hello, dear, I'm so glad you've come. Did you have a good trip back, because of course it's such a long way, isn't it, with all that wretched jet lag?' She patted my arm and peered acutely at my face. 'You don't really look awfully well, dear, if you don't mind me saying so, and you don't seem to have collected any suntan, though I suppose as you haven't been away two weeks it isn't surprising, but those are nasty gashes on your hand, dear, aren't they, and you were walking very *carefully* just now.'

She stopped to watch a row of jockeys canter past on their way to the start. Bright shirts against the thin grey mist. A subject for Munnings.

'Have you backed anything, dear? And are you sure you're warm enough in that anorak? I never think jeans are good for people in the winter, they're only

cotton, dear, don't forget, and how did you get on i
Australia? I mean, dear, did you find out anythin
useful?'

'It's an awfully long story . . .'

'Best told in the bar, then, don't you think, dear?'

She bought us immense brandies with ginger al
and settled herself at a small table, her kind eye
alert and waiting.

I told her about Hudson's organization, about th
Melbourne gallery, and about the list of robbable cus
tomers.

'Was I on it?'

I nodded. 'Yes, you were.'

'And you gave it to the police?' she said anxiously

I grinned. 'Don't look so worried, Maisie. You
name was crossed out already. I just crossed it ou
more thoroughly. By the time I'd finished, no one coul
ever disentangle it, particularly on a photocopy.'

She smiled broadly. 'No one could call you a foo
dear.'

I wasn't so sure about that. 'I'm afraid, though,'
said, 'that you've lost your nine thousand quid.'

'Oh yes, dear,' she said cheerfully. 'Serves me right
doesn't it, for trying to cheat the Customs, thoug
frankly, dear, in the same circumstances I'd probabl
do it again, because that tax makes me so mad, dea
But I'm ever so glad, dear, that they won't come knock
ing on my door this time, or rather my sister Betty'
because of course I'm staying with her again up her

t the moment, as of course the Beach told you, until my house is ready.'

I blinked. 'What house?'

'Well, dear, I decided not to rebuild the house at Worthing because it wouldn't be the same without the things Archie and I bought together, so I'm selling that plot of seaside land for a fortune, dear, and I've chosen a nice place just down the road from Sandown Park Racecourse.'

'You're not going to live in Australia?'

'Oh no, dear, that would be too far away. From Archie, you see, dear.'

I saw. I liked Maisie very much.

'I'm afraid I spent all your money,' I said.

She smiled at me with her well-kept head on one side and absent-mindedly stroked her crocodile handbag.

'Never mind, dear. You can paint me *two* pictures. One of me, and one of my new house.'

left after the third race, took the train along the main line to Shrewsbury, and from there travelled by bus to Inspector Frost's official doorstep.

He was in an office, chin-deep in papers. Also present, the unblinking Superintendent Wall, who had so unnerved Donald, and whom I'd not previously met. Both men shook hands in a cool and businesslike manner, Wall's eyes traversing the anorak, jeans and desert boots, and remaining unimpressed. They offered me a chair, moulded plastic and armless.

Frost said, faintly smiling, 'You sure kicked open an ant-hill.'

Wall frowned, disliking such frivolity. 'It appears you stumbled on an organization of some size.'

The gaze of both men swept the mountain of paper.

'What about Donald?' I asked.

Frost kept his eyes down. His mouth twitched.

Wall said, 'We have informed Mr Stuart that we are satisfied the break-in at his house and the death of Mrs Stuart were the work of outside agencies, beyond his knowledge or control.'

Cold comfort words. 'Did he understand what he was hearing?'

The Wall eyebrows rose. 'I went to see him myself this morning. He appeared to understand perfectly.'

'And what about Regina?'

'The body of Mrs Stuart,' Wall said correctively.

'Donald wants her buried,' I said.

Frost looked up with an almost human look of compassion. 'The difficulty is,' he said, 'that in a murder case, one has to preserve the victim's body in case the defence wishes to call for its own post-mortem. In this case, we have not been able to accuse anyone of her murder, let alone get as far as them arranging a defence.' He cleared his throat. 'We'll release Mrs Stuart's body for burial as soon as official requirements have been met.'

I looked at my fingers, interlacing them.

Frost said, 'Your cousin already owes you a lot. You can't be expected to do more.'

I smiled twistedly and stood up. 'I'll go and see him,' I said.

Wall shook hands again, and Frost came with me through the hall and out into the street. The lights shone bright in the early winter evening.

'Unofficially,' he said, walking slowly with me along the pavement, 'I'll tell you that the Melbourne police found a list of names in the gallery which it turns out are of known housebreakers. Divided into countries, like the Overseas Customers. There were four names for England. I suppose I shouldn't guess and I certainly ought not to be saying this to you, but there's a good chance Mrs Stuart's killer may be one of them.'

'Really?'

'Yes. But don't quote me.' He looked worried.

'I won't,' I said. 'So the robberies were local labour?'

'It seems to have been their normal method.'

Greene, I thought. With an 'e'. Greene could have recruited them. And checked afterwards, in burnt houses, on work done.

I stopped walking. We were standing outside the flower shop where Regina had worked. Frost looked at the big bronze chrysanthemums in the brightly lit window, and then enquiringly at my face.

I put my hand in my pocket and pulled out the six revolver shell cases. Gave them to Frost.

'These came from the gun which the man called Greene fired at me,' I said. 'He dropped them when he was reloading. I told you about them on the telephone.'

He nodded.

'I don't imagine they're of much practical use,' I said. 'But they might persuade you that Greene is capable of murder.'

'Well . . . what of it?'

'It's only a feeling . . .'

'Get on with it.'

'Greene,' I said, 'was in England at about the time Regina died.'

He stared.

'Maybe Regina knew him,' I said. 'She had been in the gallery in Australia. Maybe she saw him helping to rob her house . . . supervising, perhaps . . . and maybe that's why she was killed, because it wouldn't have been enough just to tie her up and gag her . . . she could identify him for certain if she was alive.'

He looked as if he was trying to draw breath.

'That's all . . . guessing,' he said.

'I know for certain that Greene was in England two weeks after Regina's death. I know for certain he was up to his neck in selling paintings and stealing them back. I know for certain that he would kill someone who could get him convicted. The rest . . . well . . . it's over to you.'

'My God,' Frost said. 'My God.'

I started off again, towards the bus-stop. He came with me, looking glazed.

'What everyone wants to know,' he said, 'is what put you on to the organization in the first place.'

I smiled. 'A hot tip from an informer.'

'What informer?'

A smuggler in a scarlet coat, glossy hair-do and crocodile handbag. 'You can't grass on informers,' I said.

He sighed, shook his head, stopped walking, and pulled a piece of torn-off telex paper out of his jacket.

'Did you meet an Australian policeman called Porter?'

'I sure did.'

'He sent you a message.' He handed me the paper. I read the neatly typed words.

'*Tell that Pommie painter Thanks.*'

'Will you send a message back?'

He nodded. 'What is it?'

'No sweat,' I said.

I stood in the dark outside my cousin's house, look-ing in.

He sat in his lighted drawing-room, facing Regina, unframed on the mantelshelf. I sighed, and rang the bell.

Donald came slowly. Opened the door.

'Charles!' He was mildly surprised. 'I thought you were in Australia.'

'Got back yesterday.'

'Come in.'

We went into the kitchen, where at least it was warm, and sat one each side of the table. He looked gaunt and fifty, a shell of a man, retreating from life.

'How's business?' I said.

'Business?'

'The wine trade.'

'I haven't been to the office.'

'If you didn't have a critical cash flow problem before,' I said, 'you'll have one soon.'

'I don't really care.'

'You've got stuck,' I said. 'Like a needle in a record. Playing the same little bit of track over and over again.'

He looked blank.

'The police know you didn't fix the robbery,' I said.

He nodded slowly. 'That man Wall . . . came and told me so. This morning.'

'Well, then.'

'It doesn't seem to make much difference.'

'Because of Regina?'

He didn't answer.

'You've got to stop it, Donald,' I said. 'She's dead. She's been dead five weeks and three days. Do you want to see her?'

He looked absolutely horrified. 'No! Of course not.'

'Then stop thinking about her body.'

'Charles!' He stood up violently, knocking over his chair. He was somewhere between outrage and anger, and clearly shocked.

'She's in a cold drawer,' I said, 'and you want her in a box in the cold ground. So where's the difference?'

'Get out,' he said loudly. 'I don't want to hear you.'

'The bit of Regina you're obsessed about,' I said, not moving, 'is just a collection of minerals. That . . . that *shape* lying in storage isn't Regina. The real girl is in your head. In your memory. The only life you can give her is to remember her. That's her immortality, in your head. You're killing her all over again with your refusal to go on living.'

He turned on his heel and walked out. I heard him go across the hall, and guessed he was making for the sitting-room.

After a minute I followed him. The white-panelled door was shut.

I opened the door. Went in.

He was sitting in his chair, in the usual place.

'Go away,' he said.

What did it profit a man, I thought, if he got flung over balconies and shot at and mangled by rocks, and couldn't save his cousin's soul.

'I'm taking that picture with me to London,' I said.

He was alarmed. He stood up. 'You're *not*.'

'I am.'

'You can't. You gave it to me.'

'It needs a frame,' I said. 'Or it will warp.'

'You can't take it.'

'You can come as well.'

'I can't leave here,' he said.

'Why not?'

'Don't be stupid,' he said explosively. 'You know why not. Because of . . .' His voice died away.

I said, 'Regina will be with you wherever you are. Whenever you think of her, she'll be there.'

Nothing.

'She isn't in this room. She's in your head. You can go out of here and take her with you.'

Nothing.

'She was a great girl. It must be bloody without her. But she deserves the best you can do.'

Nothing.

I went over to the fireplace and picked up the picture. Regina's face smiled out, vitally alive. I hadn't done her left nostril too well, I thought.

Donald didn't try to stop me.

I put my hand on his arm.

'Let's get your car out,' I said, 'and drive down to my flat. Right this minute.'

A little silence.

'Come on,' I said.

He began, with difficulty, to cry.

I took a long breath and waited. 'O.K.,' I said. 'How are you off for petrol?'

'We can get some more . . .' he said, sniffing, '. . . on the motorway.'